LOUD SILENCE

To Lisa

RJesko

To Lisa

Ruesky

LOUD SILENCE

Rachael Jesko

Copyright © 2015 by Rachael Jesko.

Library of Congress Control Number:		2015902790
ISBN:	Hardcover	978-1-5035-4617-2
	Softcover	978-1-5035-4618-9
	eBook	978-1-5035-4619-6

All rights reserved. No part of this book may be reproduced or transmitted in any form or by any means, electronic or mechanical, including photocopying, recording, or by any information storage and retrieval system, without permission in writing from the copyright owner.

This is a work of fiction. Names, characters, places and incidents either are the product of the author's imagination or are used fictitiously, and any resemblance to any actual persons, living or dead, events, or locales is entirely coincidental.

Any people depicted in stock imagery provided by Thinkstock are models, and such images are being used for illustrative purposes only.
Certain stock imagery © Thinkstock.

Print information available on the last page.

Rev. date: 02/19/2015

To order additional copies of this book, contact:
Xlibris
1-888-795-4274
www.Xlibris.com
Orders@Xlibris.com
696430

MICAH

Chapter 1

I was finally able to sleep at night in my own bed without the sound of him coming home again. I didn't know what time it was, but I didn't want to wake up. I felt uncomfortable even with the relief that he's never coming back. I still have that feeling that he's going to fling the door open, slamming on the wall, and stmble around, knocking things over and shouting for no reason

I closed my eyes tightly with the reminder of that every morning or night. I wouldn't let him back in my life—back into our lives. I couldn't lie here alone anymore. No matter how hard I tried to forget, it kept popping up in my mind over and over as if I wanted to remember, but I didn't. How could you control something like that? I opened my eyes to see my window not yet lit by the sun, telling me that it's still night.

I couldn't just go back to sleep and wait for morning to arrive by myself. I haven't slept alone in over three years or longer. I didn't know. I was never able to fully stretch, so I thought that when I went to sleep alone, I would be happy. I didn't fully stretch my legs and arms out even though I can now. I stayed scrunched up just like I did before. It's too different. It seemed as if it were too much—too good.

I got the thin covers off and sat on the edge of my bed. I got up quickly but not without feeling the pain just under my arm my dad caused before he left. I winced at the slight pain it caused. I blocked out the memory quick enough to not fully picture it again as I walked out of my bedroom and peeked down the small hall. I stepped down the floor carefully as if someone would see me or wake up. I looked around worriedly as if he were here—he wasn't though. I got in front of my sister's bedroom door. It's closed. I looked down at the knob for a second before I gripped and turned it gently to not make any noise and wake her up.

I opened it and saw her with her blanket still over her. She's fast asleep as I entered cautiously. I approached her bed as I saw how peaceful she somehow looked. I swallowed the deep lump in my throat only to have her jolt awake all of the sudden. I stood frozen beside her as she looked up to see me only standing there.

"What's wrong?" she asked quietly as both our eyes made contact. I didn't answer. I just looked down at her. "Micah," she then whispered. She moved back in her bed and moved the covers back, gesturing for me to get in with her. I did as she intended and what I wanted, which was to climb on the mattress beside her. She pulled the blanket back up so I was encased in it with her.

I turned to her. "It's okay," she whispered. I can't find my voice to talk with her, so I just lay there in silence as she crawled closer to me and held on to one of my arms in reassurance, letting me stay in her room tonight.

I won't let anything happen to her ever again, I thought as I lay there, and she fell back asleep.

***

I was the first to wake up. I looked at Candice as she was still sleeping, still facing me as well. Everything went running through my mind. I looked away from her face as my breathing hitched. I reached my hand to my chest as it got harder to breath. *No! No!* I didn't want this to happen now. It's been a whole week since my last one. *No!* Why now? *No!* My heartbeat started feeling uneven under my trembling hands that I had set over it now. I felt my forehead get warm, and the trickling feeling of sweat began. I knew what's happening, but it still felt like a heart attack to me. My chest felt tight, and I felt sick. I felt like I'm becoming insane each time it happened. I felt dizzy. I started to freak out, causing my throat to get an awkward feeling at first until it started to feel as if I couldn't breathe. I started choking.

My breathing got louder and faster in an attempt to breathe better. In a short few seconds, Candice jolted out of her sleep as I was shaking and feeling really warm.

"Micah!" she said loudly in a state of fear from the sudden awakening. She knew what's going on too. She always does.

I tried to reply to her, but I couldn't speak. I was only able to open my mouth, as the feeling of being completely 100 percent uncomfortable wouldn't go away. Candice stared at me for a very quick second and then acted quickly, knowing how to help me. I felt her move closely to my body. She got behind me, wrapping her arms around my chest lightly, not pressing down.

"Okay, okay. Just relax, Micah. Come on," she said to me softly, trying to even and slow down my breathing. "Okay, okay," she repeated. "You're going to be okay," she whispered to my ear as her chin sat on my shoulder. She stitched her fingers together over the center of my chest, holding down and signaling for me to inhale. "One . . . two . . . three . . . four . . . five," she said softly. "Okay." She loosened her grip, allowing me to exhale. "One . . . two," she then said quietly for me to exhale. She repeated this twice.

My breathing slowed, but my heart rate still wasn't completely evened out. Then it started back up again. It's only done that a few times. Right when I feel it's all going to end, it comes back. I looked down at her hands set on my chest and the way I was breathing, making them move up and down quickly. Candice took her arms to my back with her legs stretched out with mine lying against them tightly as if they were hugging. She began rubbing my back. It made me feel more comfortable, and my heartbeat started to feel more even. With that, my breathing got slower until it seemed to be normal. Even after I went back to normal, she continued to rub and massage my back just in case it wasn't over as it may have seemed like. She continued for another minute. I didn't mind that.

I closed my eyes, setting my hands down on my legs. "You're okay. Just stay relaxed. You're all right," she whispered. I smiled a little at the relief I felt. "You good?" she asked sweetly.

I nodded in embarrassment. Candice patted my back lightly with one of her hands as she stood up off the bed. I looked at her, her hair wavy and a little messed up, wearing a plaid pair of pajama pants and an oversized gray shirt. I watched her as she walked over to her dresser, grabbing a ponytail band and pulling her hair up into a bun. She looked at me and grinned.

"I'll get you some water," she said.

I nodded a little, as my eyes felt glassy.

Candice left her room, as I heard her walking down the hallway. I looked at the doorway for a second. What if he came back? I got up quickly with that single question to motivate me to walk quickly into the kitchen. I walked in just in time to see her with a glass against the fridge as the cold water poured out. I stood back a few feet from her nervously. I felt embarrassed even though she's my sister and was always the one to help me when it happened.

She got the glass of water full and turned to see me and smiled politely. "You good?" she asked sweetly.

I nodded as I took the glass of cold water from her hand. I drank it till it was half empty.

"I'll see if Mom's up yet," she said, looking at me before she turned away and walked down the opposite hallway to our mother's bedroom. I looked around after I snuffled my nose and followed her quietly. What if something happened to them? To her? I couldn't take any chances. I felt like I always have to be right beside Candice. I couldn't afford to lose her.

I walked over to the opened door to see Candice standing in her room and my mother still asleep in bed with the blankets still thrown everywhere. It looked like she had a hard time going to sleep. I walked in. Candice turned quickly and grabbed my arm, taking me back out into the hallway, but not before I could see my mom's nightstand with a pill bottle and some other bottle with brown liquid that was just about empty.

I recognized the bottle. I didn't say anything. Instead, I just acted like I was clueless to why she forced me out of the room. "I'll make you something to eat. Just go watch TV or something, okay?" she said as we walked back into the kitchen.

"Okay," I responded quietly as I continued walking into the living room.

Chapter 2

I'm better now. I don't worry about the noise as much when I go to bed on my own. I'm finally able to stretch as much as my mind wishes me to do, but not everything is back to what I consider to be normal. My sister found a boyfriend eight months ago, and he couldn't be any worse than what my father was.

I'm sitting on the living room sofa, lying out fully, but its arm is stopping my longer legs from going any further. I clicked through the channels to hopefully find something good on. It's around eleven at night, so my mom is asleep, and I can barely hear my sister and Warren talking about something, more like arguing. That's how they always are, though, so I just ignored them and continued clicking the channel button.

I finally found a good movie to settle on, so I smiled, feeling accomplished somewhat. Then the sound of a door opening came. It was my sister's. She was pouting as I heard her go closer to the staircase that led down to the front door. I didn't get up though. I turned the television's volume down to hear what's going on first before I tried to step in again between them.

"Just fucking go say good-bye so we can leave," I heard Warren say harshly to her in a hushed voice as I turned the volume down a little more.

"I don't want to leave," she cried back, trying to be quiet. "I can't leave them, Warren," she added, trying to get him to let her stay. Where are they going?

I sat up in the couch to look over at them as they bickered. I got up only enough to see them both talking. My sister's body was against the wall, and he was right in front of her, pointing his finger as he

7

told her something more, but I couldn't fully hear what's being said between the two as they argued, and Candice cried softly.

His jawline tensed at something she said to him, and he took his right hand up and hit her across the face, the sound radiating throughout the house, as it was so loud. As I heard the aggressive move, my eyes widened as I witnessed her head go to the side, and her hands set over her cheek as she bent to the side a little with the pain that was created by her love.

I got off the couch rapidly as he grabbed her wrists and pinned her more to the wall. I rushed over to him, my mind set on only one thing. I said I wouldn't let anything bad happen to her, and I failed already. This is my fault. My anger took over my body, and I couldn't control myself.

"Get off her."

"Yeah, what the hell are you going to do, kid?" He laughed as my sister looked at me, and I saw the mark on her cheek.

It just made my anger boil more. It took over my body and mind even more. I can't control myself anymore. I looked back to him in full rage as I grabbed on to him and threw him down the two steps that led to the front door and quickly got to him.

"Micah! Micah, no!" Candice cried desperately for me to stop.

He got up and punched me in the face hard, but it's not my first time to get hit and the only pain I could feel was barely even there. I returned the favor almost immediately, hitting him with the same amount of force. It was the first punch that I ever threw, but I couldn't stop myself.

The front door was opened as I heard my sister run down the hall. I tossed him out of the house and on to the ground. I went to him and hit him again and again. "Micah!" my mother shouted.

"Micah, no! I love him. Stop it!" Candice cried loudly. I can't stop even if I wanted to. I wanted to kill him. I hit him again and again. "Micah, stop!" Candice cried again. I somehow got control of the darkness that was taking over me and slowed it down, stopping it from reaching any further inside me. I stopped hitting him, as I felt pain in my knuckles. I let go of his shirt. I was the only thing holding him up. I chucked him to the ground and saw what I did. His face was covered in blood, and his eye was puffy. I looked at my knuckles to see the pain coming from them. They're bleeding and busted. How did I do that? As Warren began to move a little, I just looked at him. I looked back and saw Candice and my mom standing in the doorway as she held my sister to her as she wept.

Their eyes are only on me and full of fear. No. This can't be happening. What have I done? No. They can't be afraid of me. Not now. Not even . . . No. I looked to them for some kind of comfort and love, but they held on to only fear of me. My mom was holding Candice tightly in a protective embrace as if I would go after them next. No.

"Mom," I said softly as I got closer to them. She and my sister backed up. I got closer, trying to hug them in some way to calm them and myself.

"Don't you touch us," my mother warned.

No. I would never hurt them. I can't do that. "Mom," I begged as I looked down at Candice next. They don't want me anymore. They looked at me in disgust. They don't love me. I can't have them both looking at me like that anymore. I've ruined it now. I can't stay here and look at them, as they only have fear running through their minds and bodies. Candice ran to Warren as my mother did too. I just walked back to my bedroom and locked the door and lay down in my bed. I held my knuckles to my chest, inspecting the redness on them both. How did I do that? How badly did I hurt him? No. I don't care what I did to him. I only care now what I did to them. I need them. What am I going to do now?

The next morning, I grabbed some of my things out of my room and then just paused. I didn't really sleep last night. I think my sister went into my mother's room to sleep. I couldn't though. The memory of how they looked at me just lingered in my thoughts. I put my head down in pain from the thought. I picked up my small bag that has some money in it, which was only $80, my toothbrush, drink, sweatpants, a picture, two shirts, and a pair of shorts and jeans. I'm leaving now.

I took a small piece of paper from the kitchen drawer as I wondered about what to write on it. I thought of writing something more on the lines of an apology, but I just wrote down three simple words that I really meant. I snuffled my nose as I set the pen down and grabbed my bag from the floor and went out the front door, not even looking back as I walked down the sidewalk.

I don't have any idea where I am going. I just want to get as far away from here as I can on foot. I don't want them ever looking at me like they did again. I love them both too much to ever have them afraid of me again. I have to leave. I have no other choice but to do so.

Where am I going to go? I am only eighteen now. I had my birthday two months ago. I don't feel as if I can live on my own. I have doubt running in my mind like crazy right now, but I have to ignore it. I can't go back now. I've walked too far away already. It's too late.

I have to find somewhere to go soon—to have some kind of plan on where I am going. I have no one, and I'm still only a teenager. I just continued walking with my backpack on my back and looking around everywhere that I am walking past. I don't know where I am anymore. That's a good thing in my situation. That's what I want. I don't want to see anything familiar. It would only set off a memory of some kind. No.

I got too tired to walk anymore. I don't know what time it is, but I'm guessing around ten in the morning. I'm not going to stop though. I have to get further than this. It's pathetic if I stop now. I grabbed some of the money from my bag as I sat at the bus stop, hoping for the bus to come by soon, as there are a few others sitting there. I felt one of them looking at me as I sorted out the money in my hands and only grabbed twenty out to put in my pocket. I ignored their stares. The bus then came and stopped, and I was the last to board.

I handed the man what was needed and went to the back and sat down all by myself. I feel so out of place here. I want to go home and just lie next to Candice and have her tell me that everything is okay and that she loves me but no. I've ruined all that by making them afraid of me. I should have savored that time with them better. I don't know what I am going to do anymore. I can't go back to school. What am I going to do with my life? What's a way to make money with no full education? What am I going to do? I have no idea whatsoever. I don't know where I am going or what to do. What am I doing?

I'm not crazy or stupid though. I'll find something. I set my head against the window as the bus made other stops, but I stayed on it. I don't want to get off until I am completely lost and somewhere I haven't been before. I can't get off yet.

I don't remember when I fell asleep. I only remember that when I woke up, it seemed to be much later. The bus driver must have just let me stay on for a long time, seeing that I looked young and tired. I woke up with a small headache and looked around to see an elderly woman sitting in the other seat by the opposite window. She looked at me, but I quickly looked away before she noticed I was staring at her. Who's ever going to like me? No one's going to want a dropout with no family or friends.

I looked out of the window, not recognizing at all where I was. I've been on the bus for hours—I think so anyway. When it stopped again, I decided to get off and get something to eat. I'm starved.

I got off my seat and walked up the path to exit. I stepped down the steps and looked to my left and right on the sidewalk to determine which way to go. I went left.

"Be careful, kid." I looked back at the bus driver as he said it and just looked at him. He then closed the doors and drove off.

I watched the bus go down the road. I don't know where the hell I am. I don't feel afraid though. I'm just a little worried about where I'm going to go from here. I just continued walking.

I looked at the boardwalk. It's nice here. Why haven't I been here before? I walked across the crosswalk to walk on the boardwalk instead to see the ocean. I live in South Carolina. It's nice. I looked out at the water once I was up, and I just grinned. I feel good where I am. I'll stay around here, I think. I want to live by the ocean—closer, that is. I started walking again.

I noticed a group of girls laughing as they sat on the wall that separated the boardwalk from the sand. They looked at me, and one smiled as I just looked at her and smirked normally as a hello. They then continued talking and laughing. What are they laughing at?

I have to find out where I am. I got the courage inside me to just walk over to them. As I walked to them, they seemed a little surprised. Why? I was too afraid to say anything at first. "Hi, um . . ." I started nervously.

One girl with short hair started to giggle a little with the one with longer dark hair and a pretty smile.

"Hi," the one with long dark hair greeted.

"Do you know where we are? Like what town?" I asked nervously.

She looked at me a little confused. She looked at her two friends and smiled in humor. What's so funny? I just looked to her for an answer. "Yes," she started. I looked to her for information, not for her to be a smartass. I got a little mad, and I felt the darkness creeping up, but she's a woman. I held it down and ignored her rudeness.

"What's your name?" she asked.

I looked at her friends and then back at her. "Micah," I answered her.

"I'm Lola," she said. "This is Bailey and Nora." She introduced her companions.

I smiled at them and awkwardly waved hello to them. They smiled back and giggled. Why are they finding it funny?

"How old are you, Micah?" Lola asked.

I looked at her, nervous to answer. "Eighteen," I said.

"You like girls?" she asked, keeping a straight face even as Bailey and Nora laughed.

"What?" I sort of laughed nervously at her question.

"Girls. Do you like girls?" she asked again.

I smiled. "Yeah." I sort of blushed at her.

"Okay." She laughed. "I just wanted to know."

"You should get your hair different," Nora butted in.

"What?"

"Dye your hair."

"Why?" I asked confused.

"Girls like blonds." She shrugged.

"Blond?"

"Yeah, they do."

I just sort of smiled at her. "So where are we?" I asked again, getting back on the subject I wanted to know, looking at Lola.

"Oh yeah, uh . . . well, right now we're in Pullers, and down that way is Westfield about not even a mile really."

"Okay, thank you," I thanked her politely and gave her a smile as I turned.

I want girls to like me now more than ever so that I can have someone. I want someone to love me like my sister and mom did. I need someone. I kept the thought up front in my mind as I continued walking.

Pullers. I don't really remember how far away that is from my house. Actually, I just remember how long I was on that bus, which was at least two hours. If I do dye my hair, maybe no one will really recognize me. I continued to walk down the wooden boardwalk as some people stared at me funny. Why? I don't know what else to do today. What can I do? I guess I should look for somewhere to stay, but where? A hotel?

As I was walking, I looked at the opposite side of the ocean to a few shops and restaurants. I should eat. I went up to one of them and just got a glass of water and cheeseburger. I spent $5 just on that. Before, it never seemed like a lot of money, but now that I only have sixty—well, fifty-five—it seemed like everything to me. How am I going to live on just $55? What am I going to do for money?

I went and sat on the wall that overlooked the ocean and just ate my food slowly as if I wouldn't be eating again for a long time. When I finished, I threw the cheeseburger wrapper into a trash can nearby.

They're probably looking for me by now. No, why would they look for me? What am I to them anymore? They don't want me.

I have to get people to like me if I am going to get a job. How am I going to do that? I thought back to what Nora said to me. I have to dye my hair, changing it. How much will that cost? I thought about it for a few minutes. I went down and began to look for somewhere to do it at. I can't do it on my own. I have to have someone else do it for me. I walked down the sidewalk in search of some kind of barbershop. I found one.

I'm not really sure what to think of it. It's a little shorter, and now it's blond. I look different—much different—but I kind of like it. It doesn't look bad. It was as if I were really a blond. What do I do now? I only have $40 left. I suck at handling money already.

When night came, it got a little colder and windier, so I got away from the beach. I'm hungry again. I can't spend any more of my money yet. I need it. I have to save it somehow.

I don't know what neighborhood I am in now. I just walked around the town for a little bit, trying to find out. I'm too nervous to ask anyone. I don't know what time it is at all. I have no idea. I'm just really tired and worn out. I went and sat on a bench that was by some of the trees. I just watched people walk by, some looking at me as I just watched others. One of the people who looked at me was a girl. I couldn't say anything to her though. I don't have a home. What would I talk to her about? I mean, I wouldn't be able to tell her anything about myself. I just watched her walk away after I sort of smiled at her when she looked over.

I didn't know how long it was until I fell asleep on the bench. I lay down for some time when I just didn't care anymore who may see me, and I lay on my backpack. I kept one leg bent and the other stretched out. I had my arms crossed on my chest, and my head on my bag. It was comfortable enough. I wasn't scared about the night. I don't mind the dark.

When I opened my eyes, they burned a little from the brightness. I sat up quickly and looked around. I had just spent the night on a bench. It took a while for it to sink in. I'm homeless, poor, and with nothing to me, and I'm just eighteen. It's not like I have anywhere to go though. What am I doing? What was I thinking? I can't just run away like this. I have nothing. I have no one anymore. I just left them behind all of the sudden. They're gone now. They're at home, and here I am waking up on a bench. They don't want me though. I can't look at them with that look of fear in their eyes—the look of fear of me in their eyes. I can't go back, and I won't.

I sat there for a few more minutes before I grabbed my bag and went walking around, looking for someplace to make more money to rent something and be more comfortable at night. I walked past a little shop, and my mouth started to water at the sight of food. I haven't eaten in what seemed like days, but it was only like eighteen hours. I stopped in front of the window and just stared at it. The way it looked made my mind go dark with only one picture floating around—the imagination of me biting into it and eating it slowly. I put my bottom lip between my teeth as I decided I have to eat. How am I going to work if I am hungry?

I spun my backpack around and opened it to grab my money. All I have is $40. I looked down at my money again and then back at the small café. I don't want to spend it. What if I really need it for something? I do need it. I'm hungry. No.

What am I going to do? I have no one to look after me. I looked down the street the way that I came. No. I can't go back, not now. It's too late. They don't want me there. I don't need them. I can do this by myself. I looked back down at my money slowly as I held it in both my hands sprawled out. I reached up and scratched my nose and looked over to my side and saw a man looking at me as a girl was talking to him. I just looked at him carefully. He has money, it looks like. He looked down at the girl he was with and just nodded and then back at me.

I don't know why he is staring at me. I looked away from him, and then I just went inside to eat. I have to eat. I hate being hungry. I went in and only got something small, but I'm not full. I went back outside, like ten minutes later, and then he's gone. I felt a little relieved. Where am I going to go now?

It's awkward not having anything to do. I would be in school if I didn't run away. I think I don't know what time it is right now. I only have $37 in my pocket, and it's only been barely two days. What am I going to do? How am I going to live on my own? How does anyone live on their own? Support. I don't have any support of any kind.

I left them.

I left the only people I really ever depended on: Candice, my mom. It's not like I can go back now. If I do go back, I can't think of how they'll react. Mad? Happy? Reject me? I can't stand those thoughts. What are they doing right now? Are they sad that I'm gone? Happy?

No.

I can't think of them if I'm going to do this on my own. I can't think of a backup to fall back on when things seem bad. If I'm doing this, I am going to do it by myself without them. I'll do this.

I just went and stood against a random building, just thinking of a way to get money quickly so I can have somewhere to sleep tonight. I have no idea what to do. I thought about it since I arrived here, and all that comes to mind is to rob somebody. I need to.

I watched everyone more carefully as they passed me, but I'm too scared, and I kept wimping out. I need to just suck it up and do it. I just can't. I can't bring myself to do something illegal. I have to though. When the next man passed me, I just went and grabbed his wallet off him from his back pocket as it hung out the top.

A second later, after I took it, I began to walk down the opposite way of the sidewalk. I kept calm and didn't draw attention to myself. I continued walking until I was away from everybody else. Once I was alone, I opened the wallet. I smiled as I looked inside it— $400. That was easy enough.

I took the money and brought my backpack around and unzipped it to put the money in there. I looked through the rest of the wallet and just looked at it. I just stole someone's wallet and everything in it. I just tossed it away in the trash can after. I don't know what to do now.

I do feel bad for doing something illegal, but I have no other choice.

When I turned around, there was a man standing there, watching me. I froze. Did he just see everything? I don't know what to do, so I just weakly smiled at him nervously.

"I've seen you before."

I just looked at him. It's him, the guy who was looking at me in front of the café. I just weakly smiled at him again and then began to walk past him.

"How old are you?" he asked, looking back at me. I just looked at him. I didn't answer. I just looked at him and then away, not wanting to answer him.

"Eighteen," I answered after a long moment.

"Where you staying tonight?" he asked after.

"What?" I asked. I don't know where I am staying tonight. I don't feel comfortable answering, so I just decided to stall him from asking it again, and maybe he will forget. I feel pathetic right now and a little proud for just making $400 in just a matter of minutes really.

"Do you have somewhere to stay tonight?" he asked, being nice to me. It's weird to have an elderly man being nice to me. I just looked at what he was wearing, a pair of blue gym shorts and a plain black T-shirt. "What's your name?" he asked after he knew I wasn't going to answer him.

I didn't answer for a second. "Micah . . . Harlan," I told him. He reached his hand out.

"Josh Slater." I shook his hand. His hand was firm and large; it made mine feel like a boy's.

"I'll be fine."

He raised his eyebrows a little, knowing that I was lying. "I was just asking because I've never seen you around, and you don't . . . don't seem to know where you are," he told me honestly, and he's right. I have no fucking idea where I am.

"Why do you care?"

"I just . . . You seem young."

I just looked at him again before I turned and continued walking down the street. Why does he care about what happens to me? I never really had another man care about me. I felt confused as I continued to walk. I glanced back at him and saw him watching me to see where I was going. I looked back in front of me. He's strange. I don't know if I like him.

I turned at the corner so that I was out of his sight.

That night, I was able to rent a motel room just a few blocks away from the beach. As I got the key from the receptionist I walked back outside to go to my room. He didn't seem suspicious of me at all. It's not a nice motel. It's grubby, but I don't care. It's not like I've grown up in much better conditions. It feels more like home to me. I like it here.

I held the single key in my hand, flipping it around as I whistled quietly, going to my room on the bottom floor. I saw a man with a few other men with their backs turned to me but one who's leaned up against one of the poles supporting the deck above. One of the men just handed him a large stack of cash as I reached my room. I looked at them both. How did he just make that much money? What did he do for it? How can I do that?

He looked over at me as he then patted one guy on the shoulder and handed him a bag, and they left quickly, laughing happily as they got into their car and drove off fast out of the lot. I watched their car leave.

"What are you looking at?" the man asked seriously as he saw me looking at him. I froze as fear overcame me.

"I . . ." He just stood there and examined me. "That's just a lot of money," I told him, lifting my arm a little.

"Yeah," he said as he put it away in his dark wallet and then in his pocket.

"How'd you do it?"

He just stared at me for a second and saw what I was wearing and what I had with me and then looked over me to see if anyone was around. I looked over my shoulder and saw no one.

He lifted his arm and signaled for me to "come here."

I don't know if I trust him, but I went anyway, noticing a few tattoos covering his arms. "Yeah?" I asked as I got closer.

"You with anyone?" I shook my head. He shook his head in doubt. "No one?"

"No one."

"What's your name?"

"Micah."

"I'm Walter." He didn't reach out to shake my hand though.

"Hi."

"So uh, Micah, you wanna know how to make that kind of money?" he asked, raising his brows.

I nodded and smiled a little. "Yeah, I do."

He nodded and grinned at me, examining me once again. "You meet me here tomorrow, and we'll talk," he said, handing me a slip of paper with an address on it.

I nodded, taking it from his rough and dirty hand. He smells awkward, but I know I've smelled it before. "Okay," I said, now holding the paper in my hand.

"No one else either," he warned.

I shook my head. "No."

"I mean it, kid," he said. I nodded quickly.

He nodded as he licked his bottom lip. He then patted my shoulder and walked off and got in a black car and drove off. I looked back down at the paper, and then I looked up to see him leaving. I smiled when he was gone. I may have just found the best job ever.

I went to my room and got situated, changing into my sweatpants. Once I had them on, though, I just looked down and thought to myself, *Screw it*, and then took them off, now being only in my underwear. I went to sleep wearing only them. I can do what I want now and not worry about my sister or mom seeing me like this, them never letting me before. I can do what I want now. I don't have anyone, but the good part is that I don't have to listen to anyone ever again as long as I stay on my own. I like it like this. I lay down in the bed, turning on the small television set and getting under the blanket. I fell asleep late with the TV on.

I woke up suddenly from a dream, a nightmare. I opened my eyes quickly, as I was breathing heavily from the nightmare. I sat up in bed and threw the covers off me to the side of the bed and just licked my lips, then taking my hand up and wiped my face slowly. I don't like it anymore. I want Candice. I want my mom. I don't want to live on my own. I can't take it. I need someone to go to in the middle of the night or morning when I have a bad dream. I took another deep breath. "I can't do this," I whispered to myself with my head down. I'm still too young to live on my own and depend only on myself. I got to the front of the bed with the thought of having another attack, so I started doing push-ups. I remembered Candice saying something to me a long time ago when the attacks first started occurring that exercising helps prevent them.

I looked at the door and then down at my bag. Are they looking for me at all? I don't know anymore. I want to go home and lay with Candice and have her hug me safely. She won't hug me ever again though. She hates me now. I love her so much. I want her here with me to eat breakfast with her and watch TV with her. I got out of bed and stretched.

"Okay," I told myself softly as I wiped my eyes again, preventing myself from weeping. I don't want to cry. I went over to my bag and grabbed my toothbrush. I haven't brushed my teeth since I've been away, so I went into the bathroom and brushed them carefully. Afterward, I went and taught myself how to use the small shower and got completely bare and stepped in.

Then Walter came to my mind. What is his job? I have to go to meet him. It may be the only offer I get for a while, and I need the money. I finished up in the shower and turned off the water and stepped out. I wrapped the towel around my waist after rubbing it through my hair and drying my arms and legs. I looked in the mirror. This isn't me. My hair isn't completely dyed blond, just like a dirty blond. I still don't think that it looks bad, just much different.

I went out after grabbing my underwear from the floor. That's what I forgot, to bring more. I got mad at myself. "Fuck," I said to myself. I've never really cussed before. It's strange. I felt too different. I smiled. I can do whatever I want now, and I like that.

I got dressed in my other shorts and T-shirt and combed through my hair with my hands, fixing it properly like I always do. I don't know what time Walter wants me to meet him, and it's bugging me. What if I show up too late? What if I show up too early? I can't ruin this for me. I need this job, whatever it is, if I want to do well on my own. I need the money.

I just decided that I should be there early enough and just wait, not wanting to take any chances with it. I grabbed $50 and tucked them into the very bottom of my pocket, not wanting to lose them. I need them all. I then walked outside. It's very hot. I squinted up as I looked at the sun. I then closed my door and slid the key down in my pocket with the money I have.

I looked down at the piece of paper again. How am I going to find it? I've never been good with directions really, but I have to find this place. I depend on it. I walked around, trying to find the street. I finally found it. I looked up at the building that the address indicated. Is this it? Do I just knock on the door?

"Micah!" I heard a voice shout.

I looked over to my side. It's Walter. I grinned at him. "Hey, I didn't . . . didn't know what time," I explained to him nicely but a little nervous.

"Just come this way." He walked away. I looked around and then followed him nervously. Where is he taking me? Where am I going? I still continued to follow him, though still not trusting him, but I don't care. I have to.

"Where we going?" I asked, walking behind him. He just looked back at me and then continued walking toward a shed-looking place. "Walter?" I asked again, trying to get an answer as we got to the door.

"Okay, just come in here," he said as he opened the door. It's sort of dark inside with the exception of a few lights. My heart felt as if it stopped when I saw the two men standing inside. I examined them with my eyes carefully, not letting them know as I did it.

"This him?" one asked.

"Yeah, this is Micah," Walter replied to them.

I looked down at the waist of one of them and saw a handle of a gun sticking out the top. A gun—why does he have a gun? I froze with my eyes wide and just weakly smirked at the man as the other came over to me. I looked over at Walter. I'm scared now.

"Against the wall," he instructed me to do so.

"What?" I asked confused. Against the wall—why?

"Micah," Walter warned.

I looked back at the two men as I slowly went to the wall closest to me. The large man then slammed me to it, as I was still a few inches away from it.

"What are you doing?" I asked, shaking.

What have I gotten myself into? Who are these men? What is going on? What is going to happen to me? He patted all over me, searching. I looked over my shoulder to Walter in worry. What's going on? He just looked at me and at the man with the gun.

"He's good, Walt," he told him as he let go of me.

I turned around quickly, not wanting to let my guard down and possibly get hurt. The man then reached his hand out. "Kevin," he said as I warily shook his hand and weakly smiled at him.

"Okay." Walter smiled. "And that's Shaun," he said, pointing to a large man, all muscle too.

"Now you want in this?" Kevin asked.

I nodded. "Yeah." Whatever the hell it is, I need the money.

"Okay, all you have to do is deliver this for us," Walter said to me as he turned to Shaun. Shaun handed him a bag, and then Walter turned to me and handed it over. I took it awkwardly, looking at Kevin and holding it in my hands. I looked at Walter in confusion.

"What . . . Just . . . just hand it off?" I asked, kind of smiling. It seems easy enough.

"Yeah, they give you the money, you bring it back to us, and we give you your cut. That's all you have to do for it."

I looked at them curiously. "Well, what is it?" I asked as I opened the bag, wanting to know what I was going to give off. Inside was another bag, and I looked at it in surprise. I looked back at Walter. I don't want to be involved in drugs. I have to though. This is how I would make money fast, and I need that if I'm going to be on my own. I just have to hand it off and get the money. That's it. I can do this.

I looked back down at the green substance in the bag and took a deep breath. "You in?" Walter asked.

I looked at Walter and then to Shaun and nodded. "Where to?" I asked softly.

Walter smiled.

***

I went back to my motel room, still with the bag from Walter. Are they testing me in some way? Are they really what they seem to be? I don't want to get in trouble with the police, but I have to take a chance. This is how I am going to live. I set it down on the dresser as I just sat on the edge of the bed and stared at it. I never imagined my life going in this direction. I promised myself, though, that I won't let it get out of control.

I took a deep breath with my back bent so I was leaning from the bed with my hands fisted under my chin. I have to do it. Yes, I have to. It's my only choice. It's easy, and I can do it. I got up off the squeaky bed and grabbed the bag as I went out the door. Should I have some sort of protection? I don't know what I am really doing. I've never done anything like this before.

I walked to the address he told me to deliver it to. It's already a little dark out around eight thirty. I walked quickly to the location, wanting to get this over as soon as possible. When I got to the dark area, there was no one around. Oh no. What am I doing? What's going on? What's going to happen to me? What would Candice think? What would my mother think of this? I don't have to think about the question twice.

I waited there for five minutes until I finally saw a car pulling up a little away. Two men came walking up to me. I just stared at them as they came closer. They looked young, like only a year younger than me, their hair black, and the other was brown, tanned skin from the sun. I don't think that they live around here.

The one with the darker hair raised his eyebrows at me. "You Kyle?" I asked, thinking back to what Walter told me the man's name was that I was giving this to.

"Uh yeah," he said kind of nervously, taking the cigarette from his mouth, dropping it, and stomping on it on the ground.

I acted serious and didn't act scared at all. I don't know how I pulled that off. I feel kind of tough and in charge in the position I am in right now.

"Money," I told him as I held the bag out to show him. Their faces somewhat lit up with seeing what I brought, their order, I guess.

One of them pulled out a stack of cash for the large amount I gave him. After, I just looked at them to leave, and they walked off quickly back to their car, but they didn't drive off. I just set the stack in my deep pocket to the very bottom and walked back to my home. I pulled out my key and unlocked the door. I went and took the money stack out of my pocket and just set it down.

It took me a moment to fully think about what I had just done. I don't know what to think of myself. I feel different—matured. I kind of feel like somebody for seeing them smile but, at the same time, a nobody for leading myself to do something illegal, but it's so easy. I like it.

Chapter 3

I've done more and more of the selling now. I don't mind just handing the goods off. I just deliver them and collect the money. Walter and Shaun seem to trust me now, as I always give them the money in the morning, all of it. I don't feel safe if I were to take any of it and cheat them even though I am tempted every time.

I'm living in an apartment now, and it's so much better than just a small motel room. I don't feel bad for abandoning my mom and sister. Every time I try to think about the both of them, the memory of how they last looked at me comes to my thoughts, and then I stop thinking about them. I make sure to exercise for at least thirty minutes every day. What would I do if I had an attack right now? Yes, I do wish that I still have them both in my life for a family because I am all alone, but I have Walter though.

My place is always a mess. I don't really know how to clean. I mean, the only ones that ever come over are Walter and Shaun, and another guy Corey just started to come with them a few times. Corey has blond hair and brown eyes, and he's like twenty-three. We don't stay here for long though. They usually just pick me up because I can't drive, walk, or take the bus everywhere I have to go to.

I notice now that in some places I go to, I get weird looks from people, who maybe know what I do. Every time I leave my apartment, I seem to get at least one scared gaze but only for a short second. They know something or know the men I hang out with. They don't like me. I've grown used to all of them though. I don't care how everyone looks at me anymore. Their opinion of me doesn't define who I am. They don't know me. As for Shaun, Corey, and Walter, they don't care at all. It was as if they don't have a care in the world. The only times that I ever hang out with them, though, is usually to give them the money I got or to get what I have to deliver. I haven't done any of it, and I don't plan to.

I got out of my bed, and then I got dressed after brushing my teeth and running my hands through my hair to fix it a little. I then went out the front door. When I was walking down the stairs, I noticed a woman sitting on the stairs next to one of the apartment doors. I looked back at her. She's pretty with thick dark brown hair and a nice figure.

"Hey." She awkwardly waved to me as I walked down the steps.

I looked back at her as I held my sunglasses in one of my hands and the other in my hair, trying to prevent the breeze from messing it up. I grinned at her, a little confused. She's talking to me first.

"Hi," I said back to her. It was awkward for a few seconds, and then I broke the ice "You live around here?" I asked, being friendly to her since she looks very bored.

She smiled up at me. "Yeah, I just moved here, but I locked myself out."

"Micah." I told her my name since she is my new neighbor. I reached down to her and shook her hand lightly, my hand being much larger compared to her smoother and cleaner and smaller one. I grinned at her as I fully stood back up.

"Shailene," she told me.

I nodded to her. "Well uh, do you need help getting back inside?" I asked, trying to be helpful.

"Oh, I have my . . . my boyfriend coming over to help me. Thank you though." She smiled.

I just grinned at her and nodded to her, still being nice even though I have no chance with her due to the fact that she already has a boyfriend. Why would she like me anyway?

"Okay, well, nice meeting you," I said to her as I then walked off.

"Bye," I heard her say as I walked off. I don't care that I don't have any girls in my life who mean anything. The only women that I want in my life are my mom and sister. I don't need any others, although it would be nice. I walked to a small restaurant to get something small to eat for my breakfast, although it's already like twelve forty. I got in line and ordered a sandwich and handed the man the money he asked for.

"Micah, right?" I heard a voice ask from my side.

I turned my head to see Josh standing by me as he was getting his food.

"Yeah," I answered.

He just sort of smiled at me as I just looked at him like he was a freak. "You look good now," he said to me.

I just grinned at him awkwardly and then looked down at my watch. I have to go in a little while because Walter wanted me at his house at one. Right when the man handed me my order, I said bye to Josh, and he just looked at me as I left the place.

I got my sandwich and began to walk over to Walter's home to meet him for something that I assume is just another delivery. I ate my food on the walk over, ignoring everyone that seemed to "know" me. I arrived at Walter's house after a few minutes.

I went up to his door and knocked only twice before it was opened. All the time I have known Walter for almost three weeks, he has had about five women over his house. When I got there, I never said anything to him about them. I don't care. It's not me, although it does make him look like a pig, and that's the way he acts. He doesn't care what anyone else thinks of him anymore, so it doesn't bother him when he sees his neighbors look at him in disgust each time one leaves when I get there in the "morning."

"Can I help you?" she asked, smiling to me.

I just grinned at her. "Micah. I'm here to see Walter," I told her.

She smiled. "Okay," she said softly. I noticed that she was wearing one of his shirts and that's about it, but I can see her underwear. I just took a deep breath silently as she walked away, and I walked in. She went into his bedroom, and I just went and waited for him in his living room.

A minute or two later, Walter came walking out in just a pair of sweatpants and grinned at me as he sat down on the chair in his living room. I sat on the couch. The woman then came out of his room still with his shirt on and a pair of jean shorts that I guess are hers. She walked over to us and just went straight to Walter and sat on his lap sideways. He didn't even really acknowledge her, as he just set his arms over her long tanned legs.

"So uh . . . what was it you . . . you wanted me to be here . . . here for?" I stuttered, not being able to fully concentrate because of the woman's presence. Walter just looked up at the woman.

"I'll leave you guys be," she said sweetly to him and then looked over at me and grinned. What's she doing? She got off his lap after kissing him a few times. "I'll see you another time," she told him as she then left after grabbing her purse by the door.

"She just stole your shirt," I told him, kind of laughing.

He just looked at me and grinned and then laughed. "I don't want that back," he commented—why?

"You just don't care?" I asked curiously. She stole his shirt—why doesn't he care?

He looked at me a little confused. "Micah?" he asked, kind of smiling.

I directed my attention back over to him after looking around his house. I raised my brows to him, wanting to know what he is asking. He raised his eyebrows to me. "How old are you again?" he asked humorously.

"Eighteen," I told him, awkwardly smiling. What's he talking about? He looked at me again more surprisingly. "What?" I asked curiously, wanting to know what he is thinking. After I thought about it for a minute, I understood what he is talking about. I weakly smiled at him. "Oh." I laughed. "No," I added. It never bothered me before. I never really thought about women like that due to my close relationship with Candice and my mother. I have too much respect.

"Are you serious?" he asked, sort of not believing me.

I nodded warily back to him. I feel kind of uncomfortable telling him about this. I never said anything like that to anyone before.

Walter stood up and walked off. Where's he going? I didn't ask him. I just sat still in my spot on the couch, waiting for him to return. He came back a minute or two later with something in his hand. I just watched him as he sat down and took it to his mouth and then lit it. I looked away awkwardly. Is he serious? I wasn't sure if he was like me and only sold the drugs, but now I know he wasn't. He just did it right in front of me as I sat there, feeling quite uncomfortable with him doing so. I glanced over to him as he took it to his mouth again. He looked at me as he did it. He then held it out for me.

"Oh no. No thanks." I waved it off. I don't want to do it.

He tried again, urging me to do it. I just looked up at him and gave him a fake smirk as I reached my hand out and took it from his fingers that were holding it out. What do I do? I felt awkward, as I knew he was staring at me, waiting for me to do it. I took it to my mouth and tried to mimic what I witnessed him do. It was weird but exhilarating. My heart was thumping fast as I drew it out after breathing it in and coughed, taking my hand to my mouth in a fist. I heard Walter chuckle at me. I just looked at him. I didn't like him laughing at me, making me feel pathetic. I took it back up to my lips and did it again, this time fully ignoring what my mind was thinking and just did it freely and successfully without an awkward reaction like the first time.

I got more used to it the more I did it that day. I stayed at Walter's house for a few hours. Actually, until I just wanted to go home. When I left his house, I just went straight to get something to eat. I can't cook. I just felt so hungry when I walked in the small grocery store that I ended up getting $20 worth of food. After I ate, I just started walking home. I walked back to my apartment and up the few steps to my door. When I got to my door, I just stood there for a second and then dug my hands down into my pocket and began looking for my key to get inside. I turned as I heard my neighbor's door open. I felt so tired, so I just watched as a man exited, and then Shailene stepped out.

I watched as Shailene held the man's hands with his back to me, and they kissed happily. I just feel so tired that I stumbled a little into my own door, still with my hand in my pocket, looking for my key.

"You okay?" I heard the man ask.

I turned back around to face him a little, turning my head. Shailene and he were both looking at me. I just smiled and then nodded sleepily. "Hi," I just said, looking down at Shailene.

"Greg, this is Micah," Shailene told him.

I watched Greg as he nodded to me and then kissed her again and walked away to his car. I looked back at Shailene, as she just stood in her doorway, looking at me. "You okay?" she asked, sounding a little worried.

I decided to check my other pocket for my key after spending a minute searching in the same one. I took it out and unlocked my door. I just walked in, forgetting that she was there until I closed my door. I don't feel like talking right now. I just want to go to sleep. I walked to my bed and just went right to sleep.

When I woke up, I still felt so tired. I was like sideways on the bed when I opened my eyes. The sun is beaming through the curtainless window right in my face. I got up, trying to avoid it, not wanting to wake up yet. I'm still too tired. Then there was a loud knocking on my door. I got up to the side of my bed. I didn't even remember stripping down last night to only my underwear, but I just sat up on the edge of my bed and then with another heavy knock, I got up. Who is it?

I walked over to the door and opened it after a few more knocks. "Shaun?" I asked, wiping my face with my hands as he stood there.

"Well, good morning, sleepy head." He smiled as he joked with me.

"What time is it?" I asked sleepily.

"It's two o'clock. Thought you were dead." He laughed.

"What?" I asked, waking almost right up. How did I sleep that long! "Are you serious?" I asked. Maybe he's just messing with me.

"Yeah, honest. Well, anyway . . .," he started, but we both looked back at the door across the hall as it was opened quickly, and Shailene came out, locking it up. Shaun turned to her as she looked at him and then awkwardly to me and looked a little embarrassed.

We both just stared at her. Well, Shaun stared at her. I just looked at her. I know why he won't say anything more while she is standing there, looking at us looking at her. It has to be about a delivery. I grinned to Shailene. I got why Shaun is here, as I remembered about the money in my drawer in my bedroom.

"I'll go get it," I told him as I walked back into my home and into my room and opened the drawer dresser and grabbed his share that Walter told me to give him. I walked back out after putting on some more appropriate clothes and went to my doorway and saw them immediately. My eyes stayed the same, just in a little shock, and my mouth opened a little at the sight. She has a boyfriend. What the hell? Shaun is by Shailene, making out with her. What—how did that happen in five minutes?

"Shaun?"

He turned around after he kissed her a few more times, and they both looked at me, and I felt completely unwelcome now. He came back over to me, leaving Shailene against the wall by herself. He reached down for my hand, and I gave him the money, which he quickly tucked away safely. "Sorry about that." He smiled as he then left, not saying anymore to Shailene or me, just glancing at her as he left. Wait, what just happened?

I looked over at her as she stood, now getting off the wall. She looked back at me as I just gave her a fake and weak smile. What made her want to cheat on Greg with Shaun and not me? What did he do to do that with her? She just looked at me and then sort of tried to smile at me before she just turned and left. I watched her walk off and then just went back inside. I went and got a shower and then got dressed in a new pair of shorts I got and a blue plain T-shirt. I decided that I'm going to keep my hair blond, so I kept dying it when it's almost gone. Shaun and all of them have asked me why I dye it, but I never told them. I always just shrugged my shoulders when, really, I think of what Nora said to me.

Walter gave me a bag to deliver to someone later today around four thirty, and now it's three. I went and grabbed it where I set it down and left to start the walk to where he told me to meet him. As I was walking, I walked past the gym that I almost always have to pass to get to Walter's. I never think about working out really. I do sometimes when I get home, that's all though, and only for like a half an hour just to stay in shape, plus I walk everywhere. I got to where I was meant to meet this guy and just sat and waited for him to arrive.

"You Micah?" I heard a voice ask as I was just fiddling around with my hands. I looked up to see a man with a woman.

I nodded. "Yeah."

He reached into his pocket as I glanced at the woman. She looked so much younger compared to him and shaky and nervous. "Okay," he said as he sorted the cash.

I took out the bag and handed it to him as he gave me the money first though. He took it in his hands, and then they left. I watched them leaving, and I only thought back to when I was last at Walter's. I feel as if I am craving it again, the way it felt. I took a deep breath and just ran my hand through my hair. What have I done? I don't regret it, although I never planned on getting involved in that.

After they were gone, I turned and saw Corey behind me. "Oh god." I gasped.

He laughed. "Sorry."

I just took a deep breath. "I wasn't expecting you to be there."

"Were you expecting someone else?" He smiled. I shook my head, trying to get my normal heart rate back. "Maybe a cop?" He laughed.

I just looked up at him. "I never even really thought of that." I sort of smiled. Getting caught seriously never crossed my mind. He just gave me a confused look. "Did you need something?" I asked curiously as to why he is here.

"Oh yeah." He smiled. "Come by Walter's tonight," he added, still smiling as if he were going to laugh.

I peered up at him in confusion. "What? Why? What's going on?" I sort of smiled in confusion as I asked him.

"Just be there around seven or eight," he told me.

"Okay." I smiled, not laughing.

He just nodded. "I would have never guessed," he said, looking at me with a smile on his face.

"What do you mean?" I asked, as I was so flustered by what he was talking about. "Corey?"

He just shook his head. "I'll drive you home," he said as he directed me to his vehicle. I tried to tell him that I can just walk, but he insisted to drive me. I got in as he did almost at the same time and drove me back to my apartment. He started to walk me up to my door. When we reached the top of the steps, there was yelling and shouting coming from Shailene's apartment. We both just stood by my door as I was unlocking it. Then her door abruptly opened with force. Corey and I both turned to be nosy to what's going on as Greg was coming out with Shailene with tears in her eyes, and he's still shouting at her.

I raised my brows when he called her a whore and a bitch. I heard Corey laugh. I looked up at him. What's so funny? Shailene grabbed on to Greg's arm, trying to talk to him about something and take him back inside, but he turned quickly and hit her and shoved her down to her floor back inside. My eyes widened from seeing her fall harshly, which looked painful.

The sight brought the image of my mother being shoved by my father back into my mind and the way my sister's "love" hit her. I felt the anger take over quickly inside me as I lashed out uncontrollably at Greg, attacking him. I hit him against the wall after punching him in the face again and again, harder and harder.

"Whoa, Micah!" Corey cheered on

"Micah!" Shailene shouted.

I heard Shailene yelling something else, but I just blocked her out. Greg hit me back a few times, but with this, I couldn't even feel the pain.

"Micah, man, stop it! Calm down!" Corey said louder as I felt his hands on my shoulders, pulling me away.

Corey shoved me off, taking me to my feet. I looked down at Greg. He has a bleeding nose, a busted lip, and a small bruise on the side of his face. He put his hands over his nose. Corey picked him up and told him to get out of here, and he obeyed him. I watched him leave as the rage lowered inside me. It got what it wanted. I looked over at Shailene as she stood in her doorway with her eyes wide.

"Well, damn," Corey commented. "I didn't know you could do that," he added with a smile on his face.

I looked up at him with my mouth opened slightly as I clenched my knuckles together, then looking down at them, as they were a little red.

She looked at me in fear. No. I don't want her afraid of me like my mom and sister are. "I'm sorry," I said softly, looking over at her.

She grinned at me with her eyes glassy only now but only a little. She shook her head as if I don't owe her an apology. I just looked at her. "You okay?" Corey asked her as he went up to her to check. She has a darkened spot where Greg hit her on the side of her face.

She smiled at him as she wiped her eyes. "Yeah, thanks," she said to him. I just watched him as he rubbed his hand on her back, standing by myself in the heat. Shailene came over and snaked her arms around me. It caught me by surprise. I wasn't expecting her to be thankful like this. I looked over at Corey, who looked a little surprised as well. He smirked at me as I slowly put my arms gently on her back but not fully hugging her.

She released me from her arms and backed up a little, feeling awkward. I just looked down at her. "Micah," Corey said as I jolted my eyesight up to him from looking down at Shailene.

"Yeah?" I asked him to know what he was thinking.

"Just be there tonight." He reminded.

I nodded to him. Corey then said bye and left us alone. Shailene turned to watch him leave, still standing in front of me. When she turned back around, she looked up at me. "Where you going tonight?" she asked in a friendly manner.

I shook my head lightly. I really don't know. "Just with my friends for some reason," I told her honestly.

"You don't know?"

"He wouldn't tell me." I smiled.

She grinned up at me. "What time?" she asked.

I looked down at her with my brows creased to the middle. "Around seven."

She grinned again up at me. "Want to go somewhere?" she asked sweetly. What? "Just as friends," she added quickly and then smiled.

I smirked at her. "Yeah." I don't know if I can ever think of Shailene as more than a friend. She reminds me too much of my sister. I respect her too much already.

"Okay, well, just give me a few minutes. You can come in," she said, turning and going back into her apartment. I felt awkward as I followed her in after looking to see if anyone was around. Her place was neat and clean. "I just have to get dressed and cover this up." She informed me as she left me in her living room.

"Okay," I said back to her softly as I looked around her house. I decided to just sit down after a few seconds. I sat on the edge of her small couch and just waited for her return. She was ready quick, coming back to me in just three minutes.

"Okay," she said from behind me. I got up and turned to her. She was wearing a pair of jean shorts and a gray V-neck with yellow polka dots covering it. I grinned at her and nodded as we both went to her door.

***

Shailene and I walked to the boardwalk together, and she talked mostly. She walked close to my side, continually just bumping into me from time to me but not on purpose. We stopped and got some fries and cheese, and I paid. After we got them, we went and sat on the wall that separated the walk from the sandy beach as many people passed by us.

"How old are you?" she asked after she ate a fry.

I looked at her for a second and then answered, "Does it matter?"

She shrugged. "I guess not." She glanced over. "You seem young though."

I didn't know how to answer or respond to her. I don't want to look like a kid in front of her. I don't want to be some adolescent to her who's run away.

She just stared up at me as she had her legs swinging around from the wall, and mine planted on the ground due to mine being longer than hers. "I'm sorry about earlier," she said suddenly. I looked down at her. Why's she apologizing to me? "With Shaun." I shook my head. "I told Greg, and he just got really mad at me."

It was quiet for a second, but only between us though. Laughter and loud voices and the sounds from the ocean water were surrounding us. "Why'd you do it?"

She looked away at everyone else and then back to me. "I don't know." She sort of laughed.

I just watched her as she fiddled around with her hands. "Do you like him?"

She peered up into my eyes. "No, just at the time." I don't understand what that means. At the time? What does that even mean? She sounds like my sister. How can you only like someone for a short time and then not really like them after all? "It just happened," she added, seeing that I was confused in my expression. "It's exciting, I suppose. So I just do it."

I took her garbage in my hands to throw it away for her and myself. When I came back to her, she hopped off the wall, and we began to walk together, just talking about random things. Shailene stopped us and went inside one of the shops, as she saw something that she liked and went to buy it. I stood waiting for her outside because of the crowded area inside. She told me she'd be quick and to just wait for her.

Shailene came out about five minutes later. She smiled over to me. "Sorry." She blushed.

I shook my head to her. "No, it's fine." This is too much. She's reminding me too much of before. I know that my sister was a whore somewhat, and now, when I look at Shailene, I see her. I need to calm down before I have another panic attack. I don't want to have one out in the open and look pathetic as I freak out. Breathe slowly now. Relax. I slid my hands in my pockets as we began to walk more down the boardwalk. She's not her. She's not her. Calm down.

"You okay?" She looked at me. I looked right into her eyes, and it helped.

I pretended to cough it out. "Yeah, fine." I tried to smile.

Eventually, we made our way back to her car, and she drove us back at around six forty. We walked up the stairs with her going first in front. The whole time, I just stared at the back of her head as she went to her door, and I just went slowly behind her frame. When she got her door open, I just stood by mine after it was opened as well.

"Well, good luck tonight." She smiled. I just grinned back to her. "Bye," she added, going inside and closing the door behind her. I just watched the door as if it were interesting, trying to force myself to go and knock on it. I can't though. I just went inside and brushed my teeth and left to go to Walter's for whatever reason he wanted me to be there tonight.

***

I was late getting to Walter's at seven ten. I feel sort of nervous seeing a couple of cars outside of his house as I knocked on the door once, and then it was opened by Kevin. He smiled at me as I stepped in as he backed to the side for me to enter. When I got inside, I saw Corey, Shaun, Walter, and another guy, whom Shaun introduced to me as Brian.

I smiled at Shaun and Corey as they sat on the same couch together with Brian sitting on one of the chairs. Kevin was drinking something, and Walter was going into his bedroom for something and was out a minute later. I went and sat on the other couch. I looked over to Shaun as he took a glass of clear liquid to his mouth and finished it all. I know that it's alcohol though. I know the smell automatically. I've become accustomed to it after so many years but not yet so to taste any sort of it. Brian began smoking a cigarette a minute later, setting off the powerful smell of smoke in the air.

We all sat while Brian and Corey smoked. Walter drank and Kevin joined in, smoking a while later, until there was a knock at the door. They all looked at one another and grinned or laughed about whoever is there, I guess. I just sat there in confusion.

"Who's here?" I asked. Walter chuckled as he sat up and went to the door.

He opened the door and smiled to whoever is there until I heard a woman's voice say hi back and a few others. I tried to look over and wonder why girls are here when it seems to be just a guy's night. I looked over at Shaun for some kind of explanation. He just smiled at me as Kevin and Brian laughed.

I just sat back in the couch as Walter was busy with the woman at the door, doing I don't even know. A minute later, Walter came walking back into the living room, not alone.

Behind him were four women. I looked around nervously as they looked at all of us, and Shaun whistled. I kind of laughed at him. They wore something like long coats with their hair long and wavy and long lashes. They're pretty, and I can't seem to take my eyes off them. I don't know how to act with them standing there and looking at all of us. What's going on?

I took a deep breath. "Well, I'm gonna go." Kevin smiled at me as he got up and left.

"He's whipped." Shaun snickered as he took another swig of his beer and approached one of the women. I looked at him with a confused and uncomfortable expression, which caused him to grin and take another swig of his beer. "He has a girlfriend." He clarified for me.

Walter already had his arm wrapped around one of the women's waist who had long curly dark hair and dark eye makeup. "This is Shaun, Brian, Micah, and Corey." He introduced.

I awkwardly waved and felt even more uncomfortable and like an idiot.

I was the only one who wasn't drinking at this point, and two of the women of the four women were dancing against each other in front of Corey and Brian. I felt more uncomfortable when one of them sat on the couch beside me, and every now and then, we'd make eye contact, and I'd awkwardly smile at her. Walter had one of the girls on his lap, kissing. They had taken off their coats and were now dressed in what looks to be some sort of bikinis and lingerie. It got stuffy in the room, and the temperature seemed to rise. "So . . .," the girl beside me spoke.

"Yeah?" I looked over at her, my eyebrows knitted together.

"You're Micah?"

I nodded. "Yeah,"

"You don't talk too much, huh?"

I shook my head. "No." She smiled and even giggled a little bit. "Your name?"

She shrugged. "Does it matter, Micah?" I didn't know what to think about that. I guess I won't get to know her name.

"You're really not gonna tell me?" She shook her head, grinning to herself as if she was trying not to laugh. "But you know mine?"

She shrugged again. "It's just a name. People call people lots of names. It can hurt . . ." She looked back over to me again before continuing. "So if you don't have one specific name, it doesn't hurt all that bad." She awkwardly finished with a squeaky laugh.

"That's a way to put it, I guess." She took another drink, and I couldn't help but look down at her chest every time she looked away from me.

But at that time, as she skimmed her eyes on me, I thought back to Shailene. She isn't Shailene. I didn't realize how much I am attracted to her until this girl came along. I just grinned at her as some kind of response as she walked up to me and then instantly sat against me. I looked around in confusion.

"Hi." I laughed to her as she set her hands on my chest. I want her to stop, but I can't get the words out to tell her. There's something stopping me as she took her glossed lips to my cheek and began kissing it. I don't want this to happen like this. I'm uncomfortable, and I can hear my own heartbeat getting louder with each passing moment. Not now, not in front of everyone. I don't want them to think I'm some freak that has panic attacks just because some girl is sitting beside me. I sat up a little too quickly and got dizzy. "I have to go actually." I adjusted my pants and looked over at Walter to see him look over at Brian with a grin on his face before looking over to me. This isn't my life. I don't do these kinds of things, and I don't want to. I'll accept being the middleman for Walter because I need money. This just isn't what I had in mind.

"What?" Walter finally said. I feel like I'm sweating, and I'm breathing faster. I need to get some air.

"I need to leave." I said quickly and heard Brian laugh at me. Everyone is amused with me. Finally, Walter stands from his spot and waves for me to follow him to another room. He gives me a bag and tells me where and whom to deliver it to. I left with everyone's eyes still on me.

***

I looked over at the bag that I set on the small counter and just stared at it for a minute. I clenched my jaw at the remembrance of the time I tried it. The relief it caused. I just decided that I don't care anymore that I've ruined everything. I have no one really. I still don't fully think that I can trust Walter and them. All I have is myself, and I don't think any less of me anymore, so I don't care about others. They are just other people to me now. I took some of the stuff out of the bag and still just looked at it.

Will they find out? Will they know I took some? What would they do to me if they knew I practically stole from them? I ignored the trembling questions and just decided to go and do this much. What do I have to lose?

The buyer didn't seem to recognize the lack of stuff that he got just as long as he got it. It made me nervous, but I did my best to not make it obvious what I did. I don't care what others think anyway, which helped me out. I haven't talked to Shailene since the last time I hung out with her. I don't want to anyway. I'm too different for her that I don't even want to try and see or talk to her. I don't like her anymore.

The only thing I waited for was when I got another bag to deliver and get some for myself and store some away for another time. I don't seem to care about anything anymore. Nothing seems to register anymore to me.

Yesterday, Walter, Shaun, and Corey all invited me to go with them to club tonight. I turned the knob to turn the shower off and stepped out, grabbing the towel and wrapping it around myself and pausing in my spot with my eyes closed. I thought of how I have no one. Candice and my mother coming back into play. I kept my eyes shut, knowing what will happen if I open them. I held the towel tighter in my fingers as I bit down on my lips. I'm alone.

I stopped from letting myself cry out pathetically and making myself feel weak. I don't need them. I don't need them. I only need myself. I only have myself. I don't need them in my life. They don't want me in their lives. I don't want them in mine.

"No," I whispered to myself. I shook my head as I took the towel down to my waist and slugged it over so it wouldn't fall. I walked over to the small mirror and dealt with my hair. The blond helping me believe that I'm not Micah, the one that needs them, because I don't.

I stared at the mirror for a minute. I'm fine. I can do this on my own. I don't need anyone to help me. I'm doing better than I would be without them.

I walked out of the bathroom at my own pace to my small amount of clothing and slid up a pair of blue plaid boxers and a pair of khaki shorts and a navy T-shirt. It's seven thirty now. I can't leave though. I went over to where I put the substance and grabbed the lighter and finished it all off. I didn't regret it after that time. I feel that I can't be around Walter without having it in me. My anger might go out on him. I can't let that happen. I need him—them. Without them, I have absolutely no one, nobody, and I'll be homeless again.

As I walked to my door, though, I thought back to the friendly guy that was awkwardly acting like he cared about me. I stopped my feet from going closer to the door as I just stood there and stared. Why was he nice? I left for Walter's a few minutes later. I only glanced at Shailene's door as I walked out of mine. I felt grateful that she didn't walk out at the same time as me. I still don't know what I'm going to say to her. What will I say? Will I say anything? Is she still with Greg?

When I got to Walter's, Corey was already there. Do they know I stole from them? I don't want them angry with me. I got nervous when I got to his door. I only knocked once until it was opened a little, and I saw Corey, and he grinned and let me in. "Hey, killer." He laughed a little.

"What?" I asked back confused—killer?

"Corey said that you beat the hell out of that guy." He smiled.

"He hit her."

"Still wasn't your problem."

I didn't answer back to him. I have my reasons and don't have to explain myself to anyone. I like keeping my thoughts to myself because they're my thoughts for a reason. "Where are we going again?"

"Just a little way out of town to a club."

"I'm not old enough for that." I laughed lightly as I spoke, a little embarrassed.

"You're with us. You'll get in."

"Okay."

Walter came walking to the front door to us before an awkward silence started, and of course, he had a small bag hanging out of the front pocket of his jeans. I pointed down, indicating that it was showing. He looked down and laughed before shoving it further down and pulling the hem of his shirt down a little more to completely cover the top of the pocket up.

We all got into Walter's truck as he drove, and I sat in the back behind Corey, just looking out of the window. Why did they invite me to hang out with them? Are they really my friends? Do they trust me that much? "Micah?" Walter shouted back to me.

"Yeah?" I asked back louder as he had the music turned up very loudly.

"Do you just walk everywhere?" he asked, turning the music's volume down.

"Yeah."

"Really? Don't you get worn out?" he asked, glancing back to me quickly as I held my elbow propped up on the door and the other on my leg.

"Not really, I don't mind it."

"You should get a car. Don't you think?"

"I don't have a license." Why does he care how I get around?

"You can get one."

"Yeah, I don't really have enough money to get one anyway though."

He went silent for the rest of the ride there. Walter stopped his vehicle about twelve minutes later. I waited for one of them to open their door first, but they didn't. After a few moments of just sitting there, I noticed Corey looking around the place. I looked out the windshield to see the lights of the club and a long line halfway down the sidewalk.

"Micah," Walter turned back in his seat to face me and leaned to give me the joint. I looked at him for a second before I looked down at it as he held it out for me to take. I smelled already that Corey already lit his, and I felt more pressured. "Come on." He laughed a little at my stubbornness. I want it. I mean, I really want it. I took it from him as I held it to my mouth, and he handed me a small orange lighter. I lit it. Finally, I got used to it by now and didn't cough at all anymore. I still don't fully know how to use it, though, but I just watch them for tips. I looked up at Walter as he was doing the same, and I did my best to do it like him. He seems to know what he's doing.

Nobody was around us, but I had to keep looking out of the tinted windows for someone. I can't shake that feeling that someone's going to see us. I heard Walter say something, but I wasn't fully tuned into him to hear the whole thing, and then Corey laughed for a minute at him. I kind of smiled. I feel like I finally fit in with them both after this long.

"Okay," I looked up at Walter as he said it quietly and then opened his door. All of the worry and awkward feelings about what is or could happen tonight was gone out of my mind. I feel relaxed now. I just don't care anymore. I got out of the back as I saw Walter get out followed by Corey. We walked over together across the dark street after Walter locked his doors. When we got to the line, I immediately saw a group of girls that were dressed up in skimpy dresses. One of them caught my eye more than the other three. She had long and black hair and thin long legs. I looked away from her as she looked up at me and smirked—what?

"Hey, Warren," I heard Walter's voice. I quickly turned my head to not see the same Warren, but a different one—thank God— the guard at the door. Warren's a large man and smiled at Corey and Walter. I looked back at the group of girls as they were giggling.

"You with them?" I heard the one with the black hair ask.

I raised my eyebrows a little in shock. She's talking to me. I nodded, too shy to speak. She gave me a small smile. "They're with us too." I looked back up at Walter as he was looking at the girls. I was confused. No they're not? The girls all smiled brightly as they made their way up to us three. Why did he lie to Warren? I wouldn't lie to him. It's not bothering me though. I watched as one of the girls made their way to Corey's side as he set his arm around her lower back. What just happened? He doesn't even know her. The worry only lasted for a short second. I shook my head a little, feeling slightly dizzy all of the sudden.

"You okay?" the girl with the black hair asked, walking beside me.

I looked over at her as I reached one of my hands to the back of my neck to get rid of the slight itching sensation and discomfort. "Huh? Yeah," I answered her. "Why?"

She smiled at me for some reason. "I don't know you seem . . . a little awkward." She laughed. Awkward? How do I seem awkward?

I laughed, knowing she was only being nice to me. "Sorry." I smiled down at her. With that, we got inside to the ear-piercing music. I opened my eyes a little wider in the darkness to look over at the bar and the drunk people messing around.

Two of the girls walked over to the bar with Walter. Corey and I with the other two girls walked over to a booth and sat down together. It didn't take long for Corey and the one tall blond to start talking and then get up, leaving me with the stranger. "How do you know Walter?" I asked to try and not let an awkward silence start.

"Who the hell's Walter?" She was confused. I just smiled to myself and looked down awkwardly. I pointed over to Walter as he stood at the bar with the two girls. "I don't know him." She smiled. She laughed a little at me, getting why I was asking. "You're funny," she said after she stopped giggling at me.

"How?" I smiled. I never thought of myself to be funny at all.

She just shrugged her shoulders, leaning up against my side closely. I looked over at Walter who was still at the bar with the two girls I guessed were waiting for something. I wasn't prepared when her small tanned hand was set on my leg, and she was leaning even closer to me and was now making her lips make contact with the sides of mine. I was taken off guard. What's she doing? Does she actually like me?

I turned a little to face her better. I reached with one of my hands up and set the tips of my fingers under her chin, holding it gently. I looked up at her eyes as she just smiled a little at me, and then I looked down at her lips and leaned in slowly and kissed her. I don't really know how to kiss though. I did what I remembered from the one night. I don't want to seem rude or retarded in this situation. She seemed to get more into it as I smiled. It made me feel more confident, like I'm doing it all right so far. I moved my hand from her smooth chin down her sides as she held my hip, keeping mine on her hip when I reached it. I didn't keep it still though. I massaged her hip while I made sure to keep focused on kissing her at the same time.

My breathing was getting heavier as I pulled back a little. She squeezed my hip and stared up at my eyes. I laughed lightly and tiredly at her. She smirked at me. Really? Does she actually like me? I grinned at her. I know what she's doing.

After a minute or so, Walter returned with a tray of small drinks. Shots, I think? The dark-haired girl started on her first one right away, and the other two cheered. I tried and sipped mine awkwardly and hesitantly. "Just tip it back." She set her hand on the bottom and tipped it further back, so more of the burning-like liquid slid down my throat. When I removed the cool glass from my burning mouth, I scrunched my nose.

"That was terrible."

"Then have another." She slid another down to me, giggling.

Four shots later, I was dancing for my first time with no idea what I was doing or how to move at all. It definitely isn't her first though.

She held herself right up against me, and I couldn't care less of what was going on at that moment or whatever was coming next.

***

She sat against me in the backseat in Walter's car with Corey in the passenger's seat in front with him. We didn't say anything to each other. She kept her thin and perfectly tanned legs crossed as my large hand sat on top of them. She didn't seem to mind anyway, which helped my mind feel a lot easier in this situation.

When Walter stopped his vehicle, she didn't seem too nervous. "Seeeee ya, Walter, Corey," I slurred a good-bye as I opened my door and helped her out as much as I could manage, taking her hand, which she seemed really grateful for. She smiled up at me, her teeth white and straight.

"Good night, Micah," I heard Corey say in a different voice before I closed his door, and they drove off. I took her small and well-manicured hand in mine and held on to it.

"Soooo, what your name?"

She grinned and giggled. "Holly."

"That's a pretty name."

"Thanks. I like Micah too."

I looked down at her and smiled. Dammit. I stubbed my toe. Walking is hard. She giggled again. I stopped us both when I got to my door. I had to let go of her hand to dig in my pockets for my key to unlock the door. I finally found it and slid it into the lock with some trouble and turned it, hearing it click and open my door. I looked back at Holly and grabbed her hand to get her attention back to me. She was looking around down the hallway. Her head snapped back at me, and she blushed before she set both of her hands on my chest and started kissing me again. She moved down to my neck with her lips harshly. I wasn't completely taken off guard, but I wasn't expecting for her to make the first move like that. I set my hands on her hips, moving one of them to her lower back. She didn't stop me as I then moved it down to be over her bum. Her hands weren't staying stationary either as they went from my chest to my chin to my back and up my sides, easing my top around.

"Holly," I whispered after her lips kissed mine again before going back to my neck.

"What?" she mumbled back as she continued on her tiptoes.

"We . . . we don't have to," I whispered.

"Shut up," she mumbled again as her hands slipped down into the top hem of my bottoms.

I took a deep breath before I opened my eyes and looked over at Shailene's door. I rubbed it out of my mind as one of her hands stretched up into my hair, fisting it roughly through her fingers. I closed my eyes tighter to get Shailene's face out of my mind as I hoisted her up in my arms, and her legs instantly wrapped around my waist tightly, and I backed up and turned around to kick the door shut and turn the lock.

***

During the middle of the night, I had the urge to get closer to her sleeping and bare body and just hold her against me and then go to sleep. I was too afraid, though, that it would freak her out, or she would reject me and get up and leave, and I would be alone.

***

When morning came, the first thing I did was yawn and then I remembered about Holly. I flipped my body around slowly to try and not wake her up. I creased my eyebrows when I opened my eyes completely after blinking a few times. "Holly?" I asked, my voice hoarse and deep from just waking up. What's she doing? And why does my head hurt so damn bad? I groaned.

She turned around quickly in surprise and blushed. "Oh, good morning," she responded, still tiredly. Heat rushed to my cheeks as she was only dressed in the sparkly black shorts that she was wearing last night and her lace bra that held her breasts perfectly, it seemed, and I seemed to not be able to move my line of vision.

"Why don't you just go back to sleep?" I asked, wiping my eyes and sitting up a little. I rushed my hand down to the sheet when I realized that I don't have anything on and tugged it up better. I really have no memory of what actually happened between us last night. I mean, I know we had sex . . . but . . . I don't remember any of it.

She laughed a little at my actions. "Micah, I've seen you naked. You don't have to be ashamed," she said, leaning over on my bed and getting closer to me.

I blushed and smiled at her. Really? I felt even more confident about myself thanks to her. "Well, are you hungry?" I know that she's practically saying that she is leaving, and it hurts me a little that she was trying to leave while I was still sleeping.

She smiled down at me as she sat on her knees, leaning over me. "You're so sweet," she said softly. Holly leaned down and pressed her lips gently on mine as her hands went around my neck and then one of them into my hair, fisting it tightly. I groaned at the feeling she gave me and the sudden friction. I liked it, and she knew that. I groaned when she pulled back. "But I have to go."

I sighed. "Are you sure?"

She giggled as she got off the bed and slipped her shirt over her head. "Yes, I can stop somewhere and get something later to eat," she said, waving good-bye as she began to walk out of my bedroom.

"I'll walk you out." I threw the blanket off me and slid on a pair of underwear. When I reached her, she stood in the middle of the kitchen and living area, clutching her purse all innocently. Okay, sure, Ms. Innocent. Screw this headache.

"You're house is a mess." She laughed as she observed it better.

"I live alone so . . ." I trailed off and then walked over to the door. I went first and opened it for her as she stepped out after picking up her shiny black heels in her hands and pulled a pair of flip-flops out of her bag. I was a little confused.

She planned this.

"Bye," she said, leaning close and kissing me again.

"Bye."

She let go of my hand as she turned around and walked away, only glancing back one time as I weakly grinned at her. I gripped my door frame tightly as one of my hands rested on it. I clenched my jaw firmly. All she wanted was a one-night stand, not anything more than that with me. I took a deep breath as I stood there all alone. Holly was still in my sight as she held her phone up to her ear, calling somebody to pick her up, I guess. I watched her, trying to remember anything about what we did last night.

My attention was taken away from her as Shailene's door creaked open, and she came outside with her hair waved and a pair of orange shorts and white top. I looked at her nervously. She smiled, looking up at my face sweetly. Her eyes drifted over my body, and I remembered that I was completely bare besides my light blue plain underwear hugging my lower hips. My eyes got wider out of nervousness that took over my mind and body.

Her eyebrows rose. "You planning on going out like that?"

I couldn't help but laugh lightly. "No, I-I just woke up." I leaned one elbow on the door frame and scratched the back of my neck with that hand, the other arm hanging down my side.

She nodded, but her eyes were skeptical. "So what are you doing over there in your underwear . . . just standing in the door?" She laughed.

"Um . . ." I shrugged. "I-I was checking the weather . . ." I looked down the sidewalk and squinted.

"Oh . . . okay then." She chuckled again awkwardly. "See you later."

***

After I got a shower, I wrapped the plush towel around my waist after wiping it through my hair a few times to dry it and walked over to my mirror. I tilted my head around when I lifted my hand to go through my hair to fix it. I noticed a small reddened spot on my neck. I brushed my fingers over it lightly and noticed the small bruising. I winced at the pain it caused me. I looked down at my chest and noticed other little ones that covered it. It made me mad to look at them. I don't want any reminders from her now. I hated her for using me.

***

After four days passed, I was just sitting on my couch doing nothing when I started to look around my place blankly with my legs planted on the floor and my hands stitched together with my elbows lying on my knees. I got up and started to clean my apartment up. If Holly thought of it as dirty and messy like she said it was, it should be neat and clean. I mean, if I ever do want Shailene to like me, I should tidy up a bit so that I do not look like a slob if she ever came inside for something. It went through my mind that if a trashy girl like Holly thought it was dirty, then what would a classy and nice girl like Shailene think of it? I have to clean it. I scrambled around my house, quickly cleaning every inch of it until it was very clean. I stood in my living room, still in my underwear with my hands on my hips, looking at what I did. I felt good until I got a craving. I walked back into my bedroom and rolled some marijuana up and took it to my lips and lit it with my blue lighter.

Chapter 4

I sat at the table with Shaun and Corey eating fries as they were talking about something, and I was just sitting low in my chair, looking over at the ocean as we sat at a small round table in front of the restaurant on the boardwalk. I took another cheese fry into my mouth when I looked at a group of girls talking. Their legs tanned and their hairs long, cascading down their backs. One of them looked back at me from their conversation while laughing. Her vision stayed on me for a long moment before her other friends looked back at me. I smirked at her when her friends turned back around. She blushed and half smiled back at me. She is very pretty. Does she actually like me though?

"Micah?" Corey spoke.

"Yeah?" I glanced.

"Did you bring the money?"

"Yeah, in my pocket."

This time, when I looked at the brunette, she had a man next to her with his arm around her waist. He looked over at me. He had black hair and a muscular body. I grinned at her as her cheeks flushed again, and she looked down. I saw him saying something to her and then looked over at me, and her friends turned around again, all brunettes. He let go of her waist and in my direction. I just sighed and watched him as he came closer. Why should I be afraid of him?

"Hey, keep your eyes off my girlfriend," he pointed his finger at me and spoke sternly.

I looked away from her and then to the man and just stared. I stood up from my chair right in front of him. "Or what?" I stayed calm and said it normally to him. This only seemed to provoke him.

I raised my brow, just staring at him. He's taller and looks stronger, but he is not intimidating to me.

"Just stay the hell away." He shoved me away, causing me to hit the table.

I looked back at Shaun and then clenched my jaw, turning my back around.

"Micah, don't start something here." He laughed a little. The man looked at him.

"You two shut you mouths, you bunch of druggies."

I took a deep breath and looked back at Corey, and he nodded, smirking. "Watch him," I heard him say to Shaun. I couldn't control the anger boiling inside me. I shoved the man back away from me, catching many pairs of eyes to look this way and some to pull out their phones to record, I guess. I kicked him in the crotch and then, when he got back up, grabbed a hold of his shirt and punched the side of his face. He got back in control and punched me in my stomach. The pain only lasted a second, and I was back in control of the situation. I took him to the ground by tackling him.

"Drew, no! Stop it! No!" the girl was screaming.

I heard the laughter faintly coming from Corey and Shaun as they both watched on around the crowd that surrounded us both as I had him pinned, punching his face over and over again, not stopping. I can't stop, though, even if I wanted to. I have no control when I'm like this.

I struggled when someone lifted me, desperate to have my fist have more contact with the man's face. Before I knew it, I was shoved against a wall with my hands behind my back, having cold metal clamped around my wrists. I wasn't even listening as the officer was speaking to me. I only looked over at the girl I have been staring at. She looked scared. There was an ambulance's siren coming closer. Wow, how badly did I get him?

I was shoved into a car with the siren's lights on—blue, red, blue, red—over and over so many times that it gave me a headache. I lost sight of Corey and Shaun, though, when I was handcuffed. The police man got in his car and drove off with me in the backseat. I blinked a few times as the sun was going down. I watched it go down from across the ocean as the man backed up when the other officer got into the car as well. I know what's going on. I'm being arrested. I feel ashamed and awkward, but I couldn't care less.

I looked around as he drove, and they laughed at something the driver said. I peeked up at them from glancing down my legs, shaking.

The one cop looked back at me but quickly looked back up front. What's his deal? About ten minutes later, the cruiser stopped, and I looked out the window to see the station. What's going to happen to me?

I was shoved inside, and one officer held on to my wrists while the other led the way down the hall. It wasn't long before he took the cuffs off me by a pay phone and handed me the change needed.

"You can call someone." I stood there and stared at him for a moment. I looked at the phone. Whom do I call? There isn't anyone I can call. He walked away and went and sat down at a desk. I watched him plop down, and then I inserted the coin. I called the only number I do know.

The phone rang and rang twice, four times, and finally, it was answered. A weak and tired-seeming voice answered, "Hello?" It was my mother. I already knew who sounded like she was crying.

"What's wrong?" I asked softly. I can't stand to see her or Candice crying. I love them too much. A tear ran down my cheek, but I quickly wiped it away so nobody could see. It was her voice. Not in the best tone, but her voice. I didn't realize how much I missed it until now. I want to hear Candice now.

"What? Who is this?"

I breathed through my nose heavier as if I were laughing or about to cry. "I love you so much." I sounded as if I were crying into the phone. I leaned against the wall with one of my arms across my forehead with my eyes closed and the other holding the black phone right up to my ear as if I'd miss something if she spoke.

"Candice!" she shouted. I grinned, still with my eyes closed.

"Only a few minutes, man." I turned to the officer and then back around.

"Candice, come here! Hurry!"

She was crying already. "Don't cry, Mom. Don't cry. I'm all right. I'm all right."

"Where are you?"

"Mom, what is it? What's going on?" I heard her voice faintly in the back, my Candice.

"Candice," I whispered.

"It's your brother," she spoke quickly.

I heard the phone quickly get taken away from my mother. "Micah!"

"Hi." I smiled.

"Hey, I said only a few minutes over there!" he shouted again.

"I love you, Candice. I don't have much time though." I don't want to tell them I've been arrested. I don't want them to know where I am. I don't want them to come get me. I don't need them in my life anymore. I don't want them in my life.

"Why? What's going on? Why did you leave? Micah? Micah, come home. Where are you?" She was frantic and sounded stressed.

"Just breathe." I laughed. "I'm not coming home. Don't look for me. I have to go now."

"Micah!" she shouted, trying to talk to me more. I ignored it though. With that, I hung the phone up, setting it back on its place on the wall in the case. I closed my eyes and then looked at the officer as he approached and turned me around and dragged me down a short corridor and by a desk with another man who sat at it. He looked up at me shortly before taking his mug back up to his pouted mouth, surrounded with dark stubby facial hair. I was so nervous. What's going on?

***

I looked down at my ink-covered digits, and then I was told to stand in front of a white wall with some lines on it. I did it without hesitation, my nerves surely showing. I held up a board with my name and some other things on it, and then the camera took a shot of me. I was instructed to turn right then left, and I did it as the camera caught me at each angle. I was soon shoved into a cell, and the door clamped shut and locked me up.

Minutes passed until it became a half an hour later. I sat down on the long bench that lined the wall with my elbows on my knees, and my head resting on my hands stitched together.

"He's innocent!" I heard a voice shout.

"Well, I saw him beat the heck out of that guy."

"Look, we saw everything. The other guy started it, and you should arrest him!"

There was a pause.

"Just give me the man's name," he spoke finally. There was a girly squeal, and I looked up to see the three brunettes standing there, staring down at me as I sat down. I was confused. Why are they here? The man came back and unlocked the small holding cell, and I walked out more confused than ever. I looked at the brunettes but more frequently to the one I was eyeing up earlier.

***

When we got out of the station, it was awkward. "I'm Nina," the one whom I was staring at said. I smirked at her. "This is Ally and Devan." She gestured her small hands to her friends.

"Micah," I spoke softly.

"Well, Micah, how are you?"

"What do you mean?"

"You were just arrested and crap."

"I'm not the one that got beat the shit out of." I joked. Wait, I just cursed. Since when do I do that? No. I couldn't have. But it felt good.

We reached a jeep, and then Devan and Ally got into the backseats. "Well, get in." She laughed. I smiled at her and got into the passenger's seat. "Where to?" she asked happily.

"Why'd you get me out?"

She looked back at her friends.

"He was an ass. He's the one that should be in jail, but now, he's in the hospital with a concussion."

"Are you serious?" I smiled. I knocked him out that badly. Dang. I must say I feel a little accomplished and pleased with myself. I told Nina which way to go to get to my apartment. When she pulled up, I didn't see Shailene's vehicle parked anywhere. Thank God for that. I don't need to deal with her nagging about bringing any women here.

"Okay." She parked.

"You're just dropping me off?" My voice deep and holding only some question but mostly invitation.

She stared at my eyes with her light hazel ones and dark eye makeup. "Could've just left you in that cell." She looked over.

I smirked at her. She knew what I was asking her. I didn't believe that she was really turning me down though. She had her friends with her. I just nodded to her and then said good-bye to her friends and her. When I got out of the car, I was a little surprised when she did as well, telling her friends to wait a minute.

Nina walked beside me with her hands nervously at her sides. "Right here." I stopped and got my key out of my pocket and slid them into my lock.

"You live alone?"

I looked back at her. "Yep."

"Really? You seem kind of young to be living on your own."

"I've heard that." I smiled, turning around to face her.

"Well, see you around." But she didn't move away from me. She got closer instead. I stepped closer to her and looked down at her for only a second before wrapping my arms around her waist and pulling her to me. I didn't kiss her though. Well, not where she was expecting. I only placed my lips delicately on the corner of her mouth. I pulled away and smiled down at her when she opened her eyes.

"Thanks for tonight," I told her as I stepped back.

She just smiled as she looked up at me and blushed looking down. Nina then turned and started walking back down the cement hall to her car. I watched her walk off with a small smirk on my face.

***

I passed out for some time after I finished washing my face and cleaning out the cuts on my knuckles. The sudden pounding on my door made me jolt awake. I know who it was already. That's how he always knocks on my door. I got up slowly as I groaned, still with my eyes closed. I walked lazily to my door in my boxers only.

"All right already," I said, still half asleep as I opened my door to see Corey and Shaun standing there.

"Well, good morning to you too." Shaun laughed.

I just took a second to open my eyes fully, as it was quite hot out already. I stepped back as they both stepped in, walking past me. Then I looked up wide awake as the door across from mine opened, and Shailene came walking out. I couldn't help but stare at her. She's so beautiful. She looked up at me from locking her door and I just looked back and grinned at her.

"Micah, get your lazy ass in here!" Corey shouted from inside.

I smiled at her then as she lightly laughed and blushed a little. I backed up, giving her a side nod like saying "I got to go." She just grinned in return as I closed my door and locked it and turned to see Shaun and Corey in the living room part with only one couch. I walked into the room only to have them both saying something and their attention on me.

"You're a hell of a fighter," Shaun spoke up.

I sat down. "You both left me."

There was a moment of silence as I looked down. "We couldn't stay where the cops were. You understand that, Micah," Shaun said, sounding honest. I thought over it for a minute or two.

"You really cleaned up here." Corey spoke while looking around.

"Was there something you guys wanted?" I asked, being polite.

They both exchanged glances. "You want to make more money, right?" Shaun asked. I just stared at him for a second and then looked over at Corey. I nodded, looking back at Shaun. "We have a different kind of job for you then."

"Wha-what kind of job do you mean?"

"Where'd you learn to fight like that?" Corey asked, rather amused by the tone he used. It was almost as if he were excited.

I just shook my head. My mouth slightly hung open in question to myself as well. I never learned how to fight from anyone. "We . . . well . . . we need money from some people, and we think you could help for that job."

I looked at both of them, feeling very confused. "Excuse me?"

They both just stared as Corey came by, settling in the living room with us now.

"As nonbuilt as you look, you're a hell of a fighter. You knocked that guy out with a few blows. You're kind of scary. You go crazy when worked up, Micah. You would get a share of the money for your help, of course. You can still have your other job and this one. You said you could use more money," Corey explained to me as I listened closely.

"So you want me to beat people up. I . . . I don't like fighting really. It just happens . . . like I can't control it," I admitted sort of quietly out of embarrassment. That's a lie. I love to beat up people.

"Not just walk up to them and start something that physical exactly. Just if they don't cooperate, you take control," Corey answered again.

I pondered over the thought of making more money than I do now, which is sort of a lot for someone at my age and living on my own. "I . . ." I looked down.

"I'll be there," Shaun said surprisingly. It sounded like he was trying to comfort me, persuade me in a manner like he really needs me.

I looked up at him. In that moment, it was like we were brothers related in some way. I grinned a little bit shyly. "Only if they don't cooperate?" I looked at Corey and Shaun, thinking about it.

"Yep," Corey answered as I saw Shaun nodding in the corner of my eye.

I started thinking of it more. "You don't have to make the decision right now," Shaun said calmly to me. I looked over at him.

"Okay," I whispered, "I'll think about it. Thanks." I looked at Corey.

He just nodded. "All right, we'll see you later then," Corey said, patting my back and then walking out. Shaun got up, saying bye, and left with Corey. I sat there and just looked around for a minute.

Chapter 5

I went outside and got my mail and started picking through it as I walked back to my apartment. Each one seemed to be a bill for everything. On my way back, I glanced up and saw Shailene as she was leaving. I just stared at her. It was like I just couldn't look away from her. When she stared walking past me, I couldn't help my face from splitting a smile.

"Hi."

She made a laughing-like noise. "Hello," she said, a little confused as she looked over at me, continuing to walk by.

I looked back at her as she went to her jeep and then looked back and went to my apartment. I set the mail down on the counter and grabbed the bag of chips and opened it up. I grabbed a handful and shoved it in my mouth as I opened the envelope about electricity—$150. I stopped chewing and read it again. I finished the chips in my mouth and then went to the next bill. All together with the electricity, cable, gas, plumbing, and a few others, it was a lot of money.

I went to my room and got dressed quickly. After that was done with, I brushed my teeth and ran my fingers through my hair until I was satisfied enough with it. I went out my door. I walked over to Corey's house.

He doesn't live far away from me—thank God. Only a few blocks actually. His house isn't big, but it's not small. I've been inside only once to get a bag of pot to deliver, that's all. I went up and knocked on his door. I knocked again. Again. Then he finally came.

"Micah? Hey, what're you doing here this early?" he asked as he looked at me in confusion.

"Um ah . . . sorry. I wasn't thinking about the time man. I just . . . I was thinking—"

"Okay, okay, just calm the hell down, blondie. What is it?"

"The job you offered? You said that I only have to really step in if they don't cooperate?"

He nodded. "Are you in then?"

"Who else is?"

He took a step outside and looked around his house like someone was watching us. "Why don't you come inside?" he said, stepping aside. I just complied and stepped into his house. He closed and locked his door behind him. "Come on." He waved his hand for me to follow him. I did. He led me into his living area. The TV was off, and his curtains shut. I sat down as he did as well on the opposite couch as me. "You're eighteen, yeah?"

"Yeah."

His eyebrows rose. "Why are you on your own then?" I just looked at him plainly. I never spoke of it before. I never said anything to anyone about my family.

"I just . . . I-I left." That's all I could say. Nothing else was leaving my lips.

He just nodded slightly. "All right, fair enough. I was just curious." He paused. "This is what you want?"

I thought for a second—only a second. That's all I needed. "I can't think of anything else."

He smirked. "It's only Shaun and Anthony."

"Who's Anthony?"

"You haven't met him?" I shook my head, sort of smiling at the same time. "Well, he met Shaun somewhere." He made a movement with his hand, letting me know that he couldn't remember where. "And then offered him the same offer I'm giving you. People don't always deliver the money they owe us." I nodded. "So what happens is, they go to their home, and they get it."

It seemed simple enough.

"Okay, I do need the job. I'll do it, Corey."

"Well, okay then."

***

The next day, I went back to Corey's house. It's weird how he works with Walter and them, and then he sort of is my boss for another job as well. I can't explain it, but it's some kind of excitement in the work I do. It's wrong. It gets to me in weird ways that I like. Strangers don't bother me. They don't stare and give me odd looks. They glance and quickly look away. I like that.

When I got there, I was told yesterday when I left to come in the back way, so I did. I knocked a few times again, and Corey answered. We went to his kitchen where Shaun was smoking a cigarette and there was another man there as well.

"Micah, this is Anthony," Corey said, walking over to his fridge.

I grinned nervously as I walked inside. "Hi."

He reached over and shook my hand. Shaun looked up at me from looking at his cell phone. "Hey, Micah."

"So what's going on?"

Shaun and Anthony exchanged glances after I asked. Corey closed the fridge after taking out four beer bottles. He turned and handed one to Anthony and to Shaun and then walked over to where I stood.

"Oh no, I don't drink." I waved my hand.

"Oh, come on, you smoke pot, but you won't drink?" He laughed as the other chuckled a little behind him. I glanced back at them before I took the drink in my hand. I undid the cap and took it to my trembling lips and chugged some of it down. The look on his face was arrogant, and as if he were sort of proud of me.

My throat felt odd and just different after I swallowed. It didn't taste good, but it somehow felt good in a weird way. I liked the feeling. I stood in front of Shaun on the other side of the counter. He only sipped on the drink every now and then. I did what he did—drank mine how he drank his.

***

Anthony's funny. I like him. I sat in the backseat again, and he sat in the passenger's side, and Shaun drove. We had to go and get some money from somebody. I feel a little nervous. I need the money. I have to do this. There's no way I'm going back to my mom and Candice now. After how long I've been gone, I can't go back.

"Where is it we're going?" I looked up over at Shaun from the window.

"We're almost there."

I just looked at him and then back out the window. Shaun stopped the car a few minutes later. I watched as Shaun opened his glove compartment and pulled out a small handgun. "Shaun, what the hell?" I asked quickly.

He looked back at me and laughed a little. "Relax, Micah." He smiled.

"Why do you have a gun?"

"You never know who these people are." He snickered back.

I swallowed the awkward lump in my throat as he got out of the car, as well as Anthony, and stuffed the gun in the back of his shorts. I got out on his side. We walked up the steps to an apartment sort of away from the beach area, where we all live. Anthony started pounding on the door.

"Just relax, Micah," Shaun said, patting my shoulder.

I took another deep breath. When the door was opened, it was an elderly man. He looked at Anthony and then to Shaun and me, wide eyed. "Look, I told your friend I don't have the money," he spoke quickly while going to close the door. Shaun looked at Anthony before the man closed it and then shoved the door back open. The man fell to the wall.

Anthony had him by his shirt collar on the wall. "This would go a lot easier if you wouldn't lie." He spat in his face.

"I don't—"

"Where the hell is it?"

"Just calm down."

"Give us the damn money." He shoved him into the wall again, harder.

"Okay, okay." Anthony let go of him. The man looked at me then, shaking. I held my stare as he was frightened. I like this position.

"Micah, you stay right here," Shaun told me to wait by the front door. They followed him into another room.

"Now, I don't have it all," the man said as I heard something open and then there was a loud thud. I bit the inside of my lip. What's going on? Whatever was going on was loud, and I just stared down where they vanished. My ears just weren't processing all of the noise. Then Shaun and Anthony came walking quickly back to the door where I stood.

"Wha-what happened?" I asked quickly, as I could only stare.

Shaun grabbed on to my shoulder, dragging me out of the home and back outside.

I was shoved back to the car and ordered to get inside. Although I kept asking my question over and over to what's happening, I was ignored by both of them. I sat in the back. I looked out the window to the car beside us to see a woman getting out of the vehicle and then going to the back and lifting a young child out. A girl. What if she knows the man? Is he the baby's father? What's going to happen to them? She looked over at me and then just walked away with the child. What have I done?

The bills were paid. Every week went by fine as long as I had something to calm me down when I got home from a job to collect money. Each job I did for Walter, I'd steal a little from the bag and then sell it to the buyer. I haven't brought myself to take on a full conversation with Shailene, although I've been dying to hear her voice. Even though I don't always talk to Shailene like I always want to, it does not mean I don't think about her.

A year ago was so different, and I would have never pictured my life going the way that it is now. Every man I beat up on the job with Shaun and Anthony, my father's face is there. The other week, Shaun gave me a gun, and I learned how to use it pretty well, I'd say. It's just like a pistol really. It's not very big. I think it's a small revolver. I don't remember what he said it was really.

I've lived on my own for a year now. I'm eighteen. Yesterday, I ran into Josh at a bar when I was with Shaun. He was still nice to me and stuff. Shaun didn't seem to care for him though. I started talking to him more for the next few days that passed since I now have a cell phone. Every time I go out with Shaun, Corey, Anthony, and Walter, I always just end up going home with another whore. Their place or mine, it never matters because she or I always leave each other right after. Although when they come back to my place, I'm nice about it, and I don't just leave while she is still sleeping without any words like they do to me.

I'm nineteen now. I started working with Josh at the gym that he works at. I love it there. It was hard at first. I started working out now more and more. I haven't had any panic attacks since I left my home and my mom and sister. The photograph of my sister and I from a while back sits on the table beside my bed. It took me a year to finally take it out of the old backpack I left with. I didn't trust myself to look at it. I always thought I'd start hyperventilating with the memories of how it was back home and how I just left them that early morning. They're alone now, aren't they? I don't even really think of them anymore.

I tried out boxing at the gym, but I'm not allowed to become one. They said I hit out of my weight class or something. It made me mad. I actually thought that I could become like a famous boxer at one point. I lived on that for weeks. Now, that's ruined. The thought of me becoming famous and then seeing my mom and Candice and moving into a nice home all together just intrigued me so much that it gave me hope. I became a boxing trainer though. I wanted to be a boxer so bad, though, some sort of fighter. I thought that if I can take my anger out enough, I won't have those sudden rage reactions and attack someone who makes me angry over just about anything. I got into a fight club. The place was left empty and out where no other building is even near it in the woods. People constantly fight out in the crowd even when they aren't a part of the match up in the ring.

Shaun introduced me to it. He took me to a fight that his cousin Gavin was in. He won, knocking his opponent unconscious. It was brutal with no rules really. I loved it. After a week, I got a fight there. The constant shouting from the crowd just enraged me more and more until my opponent was down and out for the count, and I'd won. I've won eight matches now. I got known by people—feared by people. That's the way I like it now. I have respect from people I don't even know. Nobody stares but women that I take home with me.

Every girl was just a one-night stand. Well, not even that really. Usually, we would just lie down for a moment before dressing and leaving each other. There was nothing even intimate about being in bed with them. We would barely make eye contact. There was no passionate kissing or anything romantic the whole time. They were just for sex. It's always rough too, nothing gentle about it. They wanted it that way, and I never had the heart to deny them. I couldn't do that. They encouraged me to be rough with them. They found it more arousing. I don't even recall anything that happens during my time with them really. They made me mad during it, thinking about Shailene and what she'd think of me for being like a man whore. Her judgment about me always crosses my mind. So I lose it, and my rage takes over, and I sort of black out the entire time. Afterward, there is no such thing as cuddling or talking, just an awkward minute of lying there a foot away from each other, and then the other leaves you. I use each woman. I don't even try to really talk to them anymore very much. I started using physical moments to replace my emotions.

I munched on the bag of chips as the TV was on some movie about something. I'm not paying attention at all, just staring at it really. A knock at the door disturbed me though. I picked up my phone after shoving the handful of chips into my mouth to check if Corey or Walter had texted me if they were stopping by. No. Not one text. I got confused as I got up and dusted the chips off me. I walked over to the door and unlocked and opened it.

"Shailene?"

There she stood, her hair straight and with a pair of shorts and a loose pink T-shirt adoring her body. "Hi, Micah." She smiled.

I grinned back at her, still with a confused look on my face. "Hi, can I . . . can I help you with something?"

She looked nervous. "I don't know. I just wanted to tell you happy birthday and all. I didn't really get to last time."

"Oh well, that's fine. And thank you." I sort of laughed at her.

"Can I come in?" She gestured toward my door.

I looked behind me into my home and then back at her. "Yeah, sure." I moved out of the way to let her in. I followed after her into my living room after locking my door up. "So how'd you know about my birthday?"

"Shaun told me," she answered while she turned around to face me.

"Oh?" I paused as I just stared at her face. "So uh, you want a drink or something? Is there something you wanted to talk about?"

"Um . . . sure. I don't know. I just felt like talking to you really."

I looked back at her and awkwardly laughed and smiled as I got two drinks out of the fridge for both her and me. "You just wanted to talk to me?" I turned to her as she walked closer to me.

I set my hands on the counter by the fridge as she walked over closer toward me until she was directly in front of me. I looked down at her eyes as she looked back up at me. She looked down my body and placed her hand on my hip and slowly slid it over to my stomach and then up to my chest until it was lying gently on my shoulder. "Not really." I closed my eyes as I leaned down to her face. I gently placed my lips on hers. They were soft against mine. I lifted one of my hands to rest it on her face as we kissed.

After I pulled away slowly and opened my eyes to look down at her, she just looked sort of peaceful. "Shailene?" I asked in confusion to why she is really here.

"I want more from you," she whispered.

"But . . . you're screwing Shaun." Her eyes got wide as she stared up at me angrily. "I like you a lot," I admitted to her as I nervously laughed and smiled. I just want a girl to hold hands with, then she can kiss me, and we can fall in love. But I'm not so sure that I can have that with Shailene anymore. I know she and Shaun are benefiting from each other, and it's really nothing to either of them, but I just don't know if I'll be able to look at her every day anymore with the thought of his hands roaming her body. "Every time you look at me, I look away, but every time you look away, I look at you. I just don't want to see him when I look at you," I continued, caressing her face with one of my hands while the other stayed on her side.

"Don't think about it. I like you." She leaned up and kissed me. I didn't kiss her back at first. After she pulled away, I stared down at her for a few seconds and then rubbed my thumb across her cheek and leaned down to kiss her again. After a few more, I took my hands under her thighs and walked her over to the counter and set her down on it. I reached my hands up under her shirt but stopped when I reached the lining of her bra.

"Are you sure?" I asked as I stared at her eyes as she stared at me. I don't want to ruin it with her. I actually do like her. But I think she already ruined our chances together when she decided to sleep with Shaun for fun.

She nodded, smiling while biting her bottom lip at the same time. I didn't smile back at her. I know that she's not looking for a relationship or anything special other than a friendship with me. But my desire to have her undressed in front of me got the better of me. Plus if I can't have a relationship with her, I don't want to lose her as a friend; and if this is what it takes to keep her as a friend, I'll do it.

I leaned in and started kissing her again with my tongue now working with hers. My hands lifted her shirt off, and then she reached down to take mine over my head while I placed light kisses on her forehead. I don't want her right here though. I couldn't do that, although it is crossing my mind. I want her in bed. It'd be better that way and more comfortable for both of us. She sat on my counter now with only her undergarments on her body while my boxers were the only thing hugging my hips. I lifted her as her legs instantly wrapped around my waist as she continued to kiss me.

Everything went by so fast. The next morning, I woke up alone, but when I looked over more carefully, I noticed the small piece of torn paper.

    Micah, I had to go to work, sorry. See you later.

                                          -Shailene

I smiled, knowing that she didn't just leave me to get away but to actually do something important and tell me the truth.

***

Shailene and I would only wave and say hi to the other when we passed each other the next few days. I went to my normal job every day at the gym with Josh. He helped me get my license the next few months, and I saved up enough money to buy my own vehicle.

I parked my car and started walking back to my apartment. As I was unlocking my door, I heard some loud smashes and a scream come from behind Shailene's door. I kept my eyes on the door, too unsure of what to do. Then the door opened. Shaun came out, buttoning up his shirt. He looked over at me.

"Oh hey, Micah." He smiled.

I didn't say anything back to him. I just stared. Once he was gone, I hurried over to Shailene's door, which he left cracked. I rushed inside, closing the door behind me.

"Shailene!" I shouted.

I heard crying. I looked in her kitchen and saw her curled up in a ball on the floor, crying.

"Shailene!" I yelled as I ran over to her and crouched down beside her. I lifted her as she had her hands covering her face as she cried uncontrollably.

"Oh my god, what happened?" Then I saw it, the blood.

"Micah," she cried.

I looked at her hand more carefully as she had it placed over the area just above her ear, blood starting to cover her fingers from underneath. I lifted it slowly and took the hand into mine. There was like a long gash. I quickly grabbed the small rag that was on her counter and put it over it to try and help the bleeding.

"What the hell happened?" I asked quickly as she continued crying.

"He . . . he . . . he hit me. I hit my . . . my head." She paused, still crying. "Shaun. He hit me hard. He called me a whore for getting with you and trash and then he hit me." She paused again. I took her in my arms quickly.

"We're gonna get ya some help," I reassured her as she set one arm around my neck and held the rag in her hand against the gash with the other.

"It hurts so badly," she cried against me.

"Shhh. Just relax. We'll get it fixed." I hurried out of her apartment and locked her door with her still in my arms. I walked quickly back to my car and set her in the front passenger seat, and then I drove her to the hospital.

    Shailene ended up getting twenty stitches on the cut. On the ride back home, Shailene fell asleep in the car. Every red light, I turned and looked at her. Shaun. He did this to her. He physically hurt her like my father hurt my family and me. I'll kill him.

Chapter 6

As I was walking to work and was talking with Dane, the door opened and I turned around to see who it was as did he. "Micah." He smiled.

I just glared at him. How can he come up to me so happy and smiling like this? Who does he think he is? "What the hell are you doing here?" I spat. Lucky I just didn't kill him right then.

"What's your problem? I came to tell you some good news," Shaun retorted.

"You're lucky I haven't killed you yet." I turned fully around to face him.

He snorted, trying to hold back his laughter. "Why?" He laughed. "Why would want to kill me?"

"Didn't you see what you did to her? You fucking hit her! Now, she's in bed with twenty damn stitches in her head, Shaun!" I shouted back at him. My face inches from his face.

He just stared. "Why would you care? She's a damn whore. I hit them all." He snickered back with no care. "She went and slept with you after she screwed the hell out of me and then came right back to me Micah. She's nothing but a whore."

I didn't want to listen anymore to his words about her being a whore. I don't think of her that way, and I never will. She's not my sister. She's nothing like her. I don't even want to look at him anymore. I tackled him to the ground and then punched him in the face as hard as I could. I did it again and again. My anger only boiling hotter with each hit to his face. His nose was now bleeding. I heard numerous words being yelled at us to stop, and then a firm grip held on my waist as I was pulled off the man I so desperately intended to kill then and there.

"Micah, calm the hell down!" I heard Josh yell at me as he held me tightly so that I couldn't break free.

I stared at Shaun as Josh held my arms back from swinging at him again. He reached his arm up and wiped off some of the blood from his nose and then just stared at me. "You're no better." He spat through his teeth, and some were covered in his own blood.

"Get out of here before I call the damn cops!" Josh yelled.

Shaun smiled crookedly at me before turning and walking away. I watched his every move as he left down the sidewalk back to his parked vehicle and left, but I couldn't help but think what the good news was about.

Josh turned me around quickly. "What the heck was that about?" I looked over at Dane and Zach as they stared as well as some of the other workers like Frank, who sits at the front desk, and some of the customers. "Get back to work!" Josh shouted.

I shook out of Josh's grip. "You'd understand if you saw her face," I said angrily back to Josh who stared at me, waiting for an explanation for making such a scene this early.

The next day of work was somewhat quieter than normal. No extra talking being held from the people who saw my outburst yesterday morning. Nobody gave me mean looks, only a few cautious glances were shot over in my direction as a new client of mine came walking over toward me.

After I got cleaned up in the locker room at the end of the day, Josh stopped me as I was walking home. "What'd he do to her face?"

I just shook my head. "He hit her hard, and she hit her head. I found her on the floor crying with blood coming out. She had to get stitches," I told him softly.

"Shailene?" I've told him all about her, and they've even met on one of our trips to the bar.

I nodded.

"Well, um . . ." He scratched the back of his head, a gesture he does whenever he's nervous. "I've heard some rumors about you, Micah."

I looked at him confused and then just laughed a little. "Like what?" I smiled, still trying to contain my laughter.

"You're a drug dealer—money collector."

"What's it to you?"

"I can't have you ruining the gym's reputation."

"I'm done working for Shaun if that's what you're asking."

"You may be done working for me too if you don't pull your shit together." He walked away after. I furrowed my eyebrows together.

***

Things were a little harder to manage working for Walter. I don't collect money anymore. And after twenty jobs of doing that and having to shoot somebody in the arm once and another in the leg was enough for me. I never thought I would ever fire a gun and especially at another person. They ran though. They were going to the cops. I had to do it. The week went by awkwardly. Work with Josh was a little weird. We avoided my other job in our conversations.

Everything was going back to normal after two months passed. Shailene's stitches were taken out, but now, she has a nasty scar there. But lucky for her, it's in a spot where her hair can cover it up pretty good that you can't even see it unless you know it's there. She always has one of her friends over, Call. I don't make any sort of moves on her or flirt at all since they're friends. We never talked about our night spent in my bedroom yet, although I want to. I don't know what to say anyway. Maybe she just doesn't either. I told her I like her a lot. Maybe I sort of scared her?

No matter what was going on in my life with Shailene, I just didn't feel like it was enough yet. I want more. I don't understand what I really feel. With working for Walter and Josh, I just feel like I'm leaving my family out on everything. I took a box full of money and buried it in the backyard of my mother's house. I went at like four in the morning so I wouldn't risk them seeing me or me seeing them.

After working with Walter, being my boss really, he said that he completely trusted me now and took me to meet Keegan and Lucas. Apparently, they're the ones that run the whole business. He took me out to the warehouse, where everything is grown and made, blindfolded the first few times, but after like the sixth, he didn't feel the need to do so. They're both complete dicks, not like I would ever say that to their faces from the things I've heard about them.

I started a small business of my own with a guy named Newton. He's like twelve years older than me. We got drunk together at the piers and just started talking about it. Why the hell not? Then I really started bringing home money after that. But it seemed to go straight back into the business of how much weed I get. Newton owns a small bar in New Bucking, Blazer's Bar. He's nice and cool to me but with everyone else. They wouldn't dare give him the wrong impression.

I never felt safe with my money. I always had the dream where Shaun came and killed me for it. He's going to get revenge on me someday. That's what really scares me, not knowing when. Shailene and I decided we'd just be friends.

Newton holds all the money that we both make in a few safes at the bar as well as some of the money I get from the fight club every match that I win, and I haven't lost for two years really. I went back and got enough of it to buy a house and get that all set up. I didn't want to be so close to Shailene like that and see her every day because it just doesn't feel right. She came over the week that I turned twenty, and she did end up staying the night.

For my twenty-first birthday, Walter, Shailene, Josh, Brian, Johnathan, Corey, Anthony, and Brian's cousin Tyler took me barhopping all around. I was surprised that Josh was actually getting along with them all tonight. I hung out with them mostly at each bar we went to, but there was a different girl partying with me too each time we changed our location. I got my first lap dance as well and . . . I can't even remember her name and she sucked me off. Josh left the party when Anthony, Walter, and Corey pulled out a joint. He doesn't do drugs. He knows I do, though, but I'm not dumb enough to do it in front of him when he said he would fire me if I continued to ruin the gym's reputation. I slowed down a lot actually to keep that job. I haven't been doing anything for a while, only drinking sometimes. When I got home on some days, though, I would smoke cigarettes. At the last bar we were at, I met Carla. She's not the prettiest girl, but she knows how to hook a guy, which I didn't fight against at all even with Shailene there. We weren't anything and we never will be, and we're both fine with that.

Every once in a while, Carla would come by my house, and we'd sleep together. She was like my regular. I don't like thinking of her that way, but what other way is there to think of her? That's what she is.

A few weeks later, Corey, Walter, Brian, and Johnathan took me to someone's graduation party to sell some things to some of the people. We were drinking, but Walter was acting a little weird and a little bit shy because his sister had been diagnosed with cancer last week. We tried cheering him up every way we thought of, and this party was a part of one of those ideas.

I was walking back to the kitchen to grab another beer when I saw a guy pretty much dragging a girl into the closest bedroom as she called out for help and was crying a little in fright of the man holding on to her. If I help her, maybe she'll go home with me tonight. I took a gulp of my beer before I headed over to where they were struggling.

KENDALL

Chapter 7

Ten minutes earlier

The music is loud and annoying, and I have already lost sight of my friends. I came to the party with Savanna and Emily. Emily drove us though. I'm eighteen, and I had just finished my senior year in high school in South Carolina. I live with my mom in a cozy home not too far from the beach. But I'm not really sure where I am right now. I am just walking around this person's house party of which I don't know anyone, and the people I do know, I didn't know that they could drink that much.

I just keep walking around, looking for them, either of them while Lucas Fischer's voice blares from some speakers. I just feel desperate right now. I don't even know how I became separated from them both. I should have never agreed to come in the first place. I stop as I reach the person's kitchen, which was still filled with people. Well, the whole home is along with the strong scent of alcohol. I glance around when I see a tall man standing in the opposite doorway at the other end of the kitchen. He grins at me. I like him.

I want to walk over and start to talk to him so that I don't look so awkward or weird just standing there by myself. He keeps looking over at me, so I start to move my legs forward when I suddenly realize he wasn't looking at me anymore. Of course.

As I tried to see where he was looking, I could tell that he was looking behind me now. His dark blue eyes widened and quickly looked anywhere else but in my direction. He then took his drink to his mouth and began to drink it down as he turned away and left the doorway, going back to whatever room he was in previously.

It made me feel weirder, having no one with me and being suddenly kind of rejected.

I felt uneasy and sort of scared at the same time. I don't know why. I feel more freaked out now. That's the perfect way to describe it. I felt uncomfortable and freaked out. I felt the urge to look back, but something kept catching me from doing so. I don't know what. There were people everywhere though.

I thought, *The hell with it then,* as I began to reach into my back pocket and pull out my tightly nudged cell phone inside.

I brought it in front of me and unlocked it. I wanted to just try and text or call my friends to find them, being lazy instead of just continuing looking for them both in this large crowd that seemed to be just everywhere that I turned probably because there are like over a hundred people here.

But it felt awkward after I had pressed my thumbs on the screen, punching in the code of numbers. I moved my eyes around from where their sights could wander, not moving my head at all the whole time as I kept it tilted down at my phone, trying to make others think that I was just staring at my screen.

But then I really got the feeling of someone standing behind me. Someone of bigger height. I became irritated and turned around to find a tall black-haired man standing close enough to be looking over my shoulders. I looked up at him in annoyance. A look that I intended for him to just walk away that I didn't feel like talking to anyone anymore besides my friends. I want to just go home and go to sleep for the night.

"Can I help you?" I asked angrily at the elderly guy.

"You can come with me . . .," he said softly as he became instantly closer to me. I realized that it wasn't a question but a statement for me to go with him, away from everyone else around us.

"No, I was just leaving," I said seriously back to him, trying to ignore my knowledge of already knowing what he was saying and how he was saying it to me.

"It wasn't a question" he said back to me, getting even closer. Right when he got in my face even more, I smelled it. He, whoever he is, is drunk. His breath sharply smells of alcohol. It made me gag a little. I've smelled the smell many times, but with it being right in my face made me feel harshly sick, and my eyes stung as they felt glassy.

I just looked up at him, though, in disgust and shoved him out of my way, holding on to my cell phone tightly as it locked by itself.

Once I exited the kitchen, I walked past a crowd of people, then turning to walk down a hall of which I haven't checked yet for Savanna or Emily. I started walking, but as I did, a hand constricted around my wrist, pulling me to the side. From the strength and size, I knew that the grip and harsh pull did not come from a girl.

The feeling of being shoved up against a near wall hurt, and I winced at the contact as I became pinned there, but before I was, I quickly slid my phone back into its recent spot in my back pocket. It wasn't to my surprise that it was the same man. Not even five seconds passed until he tried and forced himself on me against the hard wall. "Get off me!" I shouted, pushing him away with all of my strength, but it wasn't enough. He came right back with even more strength. He looked into my eyes only once as I was terrified. Even though we were in a crowded place, no one tried to stop him or pull him off me. Although I screamed for help and yelled at him to get off, nothing helped.

He started to slide his hands down my sides as his body held me against the wall. He forced his hips against mine hard and made me whimper. I tried pushing him away the entire time too, but I'm not strong enough.

"Get off me!" I shouted again, trying to break free of him as I screamed it loudly. "Somebody help me!" I screamed even louder. No one seemed to hear me, though, as the music was blaring.

"Nobody can hear you," he whispered down to my ear as he continued to press hard on my neck with his lips. He began to move me to the nearby door as he opened it quickly, but as he began to move me in first as he stayed in front of me, I noticed a hand grab on to his shoulder.

"Get off her," a deep voice demanded.

"We're just having a little fun, man. Chill out, would ya?" The man said back, replying back to the other behind him.

"Well, it doesn't look like she is having too much fun," he said now, more demanding than before.

"Hey, get your damn hand off me," the man told him seriously. The stranger yanked him off me immediately.

As the large man was yanked off my body, I saw the man who had done it to him. He was now throwing a powerful punch right in the side of his face, causing the man to flop to the side as my rescuer still held on to his shoulder, his tight grip on him being the only thing now holding him up.

He threw the man to the ground. The man who did this didn't say anything to the one on the ground, only staring at him. The drunk man looked up into the man's eyes as if he knew him and then quickly got back to his feet but stumbled along as he bumped into just about everyone around him, still being intoxicated by the alcohol. He took his eyes off the man who hit him and went as quickly as he could through the crowd, trying to get as much distance from him as he could, being drunk at the same time, finding it hard, but before he did turn, he looked over at me. When he did that, my rescuer took a step toward him, and it scared him, causing him to look away and leave me—us.

The man turned to me. He's tall and well built, muscular. His hair is thick and not long but not short. It's dirty blond, not naturally, though, I can tell. He is tanned. He looks into my eyes. His are green. Even though he had just saved me from being possibly raped, I felt scared of him, knowing his strength already was stronger than the man before and most definitely much stronger than me. It made me shiver with fear. He could see that I was frightened as he walked closer to me swiftly.

"It's all right," he said to me. "You're safe now," he added. His voice is deep and well matured. It made me feel even more frightened, though, knowing his tone was already deep.

"Thank you . . .," I said, not knowing how else to respond to him. He nodded back to me.

"Yeah," he said quietly back to me. "You okay?" he asked, taking his tone down from the anger that for some reason filled his body and voice, knowing it scared me.

"Yeah." I took a deep breath.

He grinned at me, revealing his deep dimples. He then came even closer to me. I didn't want to be on this wall anymore. It's very uncomfortable. "Thanks again." I start to walk away.

"Where are you going?"

"I was leaving anyway before he grabbed me," I answered his question even though it was none of his business to know.

"You need a ride?"

"Uh no, I came with my friends. One of them drove me, so I'm good. Thanks though," I said, trying to be nice to him.

"Oh, come on, at least dance with me. I just saved you from being raped," he said back as he turned around to face me as I was now closer to the other room.

"Yeah, and you could be a murderer, and I'm leaving," I said after I turned to look at everyone dancing. It wasn't normal dancing either. They were close to their partners—very close—as they moved to the music. I knew that he knew what kind of dancing style it was too, which made me not want to even more and become somewhat disgusted with the man.

"I don't dance anyway," I added to my answer.

"You owe me something," he said back to me, looking right into my eyes.

"It was your choice to help me," I snapped.

He just stared at me. "So where are your friends?" he asked as if he didn't believe me, looking around the room as if he were an explorer.

"I'm gonna call them," I replied back after.

"They won't hear their phones." He shrugged.

"You don't know that," I said back to him as I pulled out my phone. He just looked at me, knowing that I knew that I was lying to him. He began to walk closer to me once again. "My friends are here if you don't believe me." He just stared at me though. I unlocked my iPhone once again and went to my contacts, clicking on Emily and calling her phone. It went straight to voice mail. He cocked his brows at me. I became embarrassed for some odd reason. I then just texted her and Savanna, telling them that I was leaving so that they wouldn't look for me.

"Want that ride?" he asked, smirking at me. He's only flirting so he can get me alone.

I looked at him in disgust as I just replied, "I don't even know you." I didn't say it in a mean way though. I was polite with my words to him. He saved me not so long ago, only a few minutes.

"We can talk in the car back to my place . . . or yours," he suggested.

"Excuse me?" I had to try and not laugh at his arrogance.

"Or we can have some fun here."

"You can't be serious? You think I'm going to sleep with you?"

He shrugged. "It would make this situation a hell of a lot more interesting. We can talk for a few seconds, and you can take off your shirt. Maybe you can keep your bra on. We can figure that out once your shirt is off."

I stared at him, eyes wide, and my mouth clenched shut. "What did I do to make you think any of this?"

"Nothing."

"Then . . . wait . . . what?" I'm confused. Who the hell am I talking to even? This guy doesn't even know my name. "You don't even know my name."

"I can guess." He smiled and made a pose as if he were thinking really hard. "Stacy. Your name is Stacy." I shook my head.

"Not even close."

He looked around the rooms and then sighed and took a deep breath and looked back down at me. "Is it . . . Karen?"

"No."

"Okay, damn. How about . . . what the hell's your name?"

"What? You can't guess it?"

"I can do a lot of things with girls, but I don't guess names—no."

"Kendall. My name's Kendall."

"I knew that."

"Shut up." He smiled again, and his cheeks indented with dimples, and I had to hold back my smile. Oh my. I had to start laughing at him now, and I can't stop even when the sound of the front door slamming open and yelling erupted.

"Fuck," the man whose name I still don't know started cursing and grabbed on to my arm, dragging me through the house.

I didn't start to fight him. I don't want to be caught by the cops either. He ran through the house, tugging me behind him and out the backdoor. My friends. "No! Wait. My friends. No! I have to go back!" I shouted to him as he ran to the street.

"They'll be fine."

"No!" He stopped once we couldn't see the house any longer and started to control his breathing. "I wasn't going to get arrested anyway."

"I didn't say you would."

"Then what the heck?"

"Who's this?" one of the men that followed us asked, gesturing to my direction.

"Kendall." He breathed.

"You joining us?"

"What? No."

One of the men grabbed a cigarette pack out of his pocket and handed one to one of the others and lit it up. Then he held the pack out to me. I shook my head. "I need to go back," I insisted again. I don't want to be here.

"You need to relax," one of them spoke while smiling at me, and two others laughed.

"Don't talk to me like that!" I yelled at him.

"You picked a feisty one for tonight. Have fun."

"Johnathan went to get the car. He'll be here in a minute." A few seconds later a dark car pulled up, and my heart stopped.

"I'm not going anywhere with you guys." I turned.

"We know he doesn't share." I started walking away at a fast pace, and seconds later, the car left, and the sound of feet were running after me.

"Okay, okay. Wait up!" he shouted and caught up to me.

"Why should I? You're rude and arrogant and everything I don't like, and I haven't even met you yet."

His brows rose. "Well, maybe I've been lying this entire time."

"What does that even mean?"

"You don't know me," he answered simply. "You know me around them and at parties, but not me." I looked over at him as we walked. "At least give me the chance to walk you home, Kendall."

"I'd rather you didn't."

"Why not?"

"Because I don't want you to know where I live." I stopped walking and looked over at him to yell directly at him. The look on his face made me relax and calm down and make me not want to yell at him anymore. He looked lost, and the only thing reminding me that he's a grown man is the cigarette hanging between his lips. "I don't know you, and you've made your intentions very clear before the party got busted." I turned back around and continued my walk home.

"Then ask me something. Anything."

I glanced over at him again. "What's your name then?"

"Micah."

"What's your mother's name?" I waited for his answer for twenty steps, but nothing came out. When I looked over, his eyes were fixated on the sidewalk, and he looked worried. "Micah?" He looked up suddenly.

"I don't know."

"You don't know your mom's name?" I laughed but stopped once I saw his expression. "Okay, ignore it. Are you an only child?"

"I don't like this game anymore." He sounded mad.

"You told me to ask you questions."

"Not personal questions."

"Every question is pretty much personal."

"No more questions."

What is wrong with him? "Then it's gonna be really awkward all the way to my house."

"I have an older sister named Candice. Happy?"

"Micah, I didn't mean to . . . make you upset, I guess?"

"I'm not upset," he snapped again. I just want to walk home, and now I have to deal with a psychopath. I rolled my eyes and then looked back over at him. "You just graduated then?"

"Yeah, you?"

"No." He laughed, his hands in his pockets.

"So are you still in school?"

"Nope. No school."

"You dropped out?"

"Yep." He nodded, looking over at me. "It was a long time ago."

My phone started vibrating in my back pocket, causing me to jump at first, but I quickly pulled it out of my skinnies and answered Savanna's call. "Where are you?"

"On my way home."

"What!" she shouted. "You're walking?"

"I'm fine. I'm not alone . . . Look, I'll let you know when I get home." I pulled the phone away from my ear when she started to attack me with more questions.

"Your friend, I'm guessing?" Micah smiled. So he goes from being all arrogant to bossy to mad and irritated to amused with me? Who the hell is this guy?

"Now, you believe me?"

He shrugged. "Sure." We walked across the street to my house, and I stopped once I got to the top step in front of my door. He stepped back to examine my home and then looked back down at me and smirked. "Do you live alone?"

"No, my mom. I only just graduated." My palms started to sweat, my voice starting to shake.

"She here?" he asked as I slid my key into the lock.

"Yes," I spoke quickly, not wanting him to know that she actually wasn't. "Thanks for walking me." I walked inside and expected him to just walk away, but he stays in his spot.

"Aren't you going to invite me in?" he asked, his voice naturally deep. It makes him sound older; therefore, making me feel even more frightened by him, making me feel smaller.

"I-I don't know you . . . so no," I said, stuttering at first.

"We've been talking. You can keep the lights off," he spoke like he's irritated. What the hell? Is he going to keep saying things like this?

I knew what he was doing as I quickly turned my head to the side, leaving him to only be able to kiss me lightly on my cheek. He grunted as if he were upset once again. He grabbed on to my hips tightly with his large hands. Then he traveled one up the side, grabbing on to my neck and tilting my head to the side as he leaned in and his lips pressed to my skin. I felt shocked and couldn't move at first.

I tried to free myself from his tight grip, although I knew that it was no use. I was much smaller than him. He had to bend down because of his height.

I brought my hands up quickly as I gained my mind back to myself and set them on his firm chest, pushing him off, my neck hurting now more than it did when he started.

He let me go once I shoved him away.

"It's all right," he tried to reassure me, knowing that I was afraid of him, making him feel even more in charge probably. "Don't be afraid of me," he spoke quietly, calmly.

"No," I said firmly to him as I took my hand up and slapped him in the face as hard as I could. His face went to the side with my action but quickly regained himself again.

"Good night then, Kendall."

A quick shiver ran through my body. I felt helpless then. This man had just tried to take advantage of me, but I won. Maybe he does have respect? Maybe he won't come back and finish what he had tried to start. Nothing will happen between us that I will like or want. I don't want him, do I? Sure, he is attractive, but he's rude and ignorant to everything so far since I've known him and arrogant.

I watched him make his way to the street as I closed my door, locking it immediately after. I don't know what to think about now. I walked straight into the kitchen, grabbing a water bottle out of the fridge and walking over to the staircase that lead right up into my room. My dog, Oscar, came and followed me.

I went into my bedroom and took my cell phone out of my back pocket, checking to see if I had any messages. Thankfully, I actually did from Emily.

Strangely, though, I do feel sort of attracted to him. I have the feeling that I have my chance with a bad boy type. But that's the only thing attracting me to him, right? It has to be. I'm reading too much into this. I can't like him. But I don't want it. He makes me feel useless and scared. I don't even see myself with him because of his lack of manners and respect.

I quickly glided my thumbs around the touch screen to respond to her text, which was sent about ten minutes ago, only telling her that he had taken me home. I tossed my phone on to my bed, and it bounced. I walked over to my dresser, pulling out a pair of sweatpants and a T-shirt as Oscar went and lay on my bed. I stripped down to my bra and underwear, putting on more comfortable clothing.

Once I was all fully clothed again, I went to my bathroom that connected to my bedroom on the side across from my large window that was covered up with dark purple curtains. I snatched up my toothbrush and cleaned my teeth. When I had done that, I put the brush down and looked into the mirror above my single sink. After a second, though, of looking in it, I noticed a dark spot on the side of my neck. I swiped my hair away from it, whimpering at the sight of it.

I looked at it confused. It really didn't cross my mind that he was leaving his mark on my neck. Holy hell, it sort of hurt when I rubbed my fingers across it lightly and smoothly. "Ow . . ." A hickey! He gave me a hickey!

Then it came to my mind that not fighting even harder to stop him from doing this most likely led him on. Now that he knows where I live made me think that I should have fought even harder against his words about taking me back home.

"Oh god . . .," I said to myself in a whisper, realizing that I will now have to hide it from my mother to save myself from her annoying questioning and my own embarrassment.

Then I heard my phone vibrating on my bed. I rushed out of my bathroom, flipping my hair back to cover the bruised area. I walked over to my bed quickly and picked up my phone and realized that my mom was calling me as her name popped up. I answered the call. She started with a simple hello and asked where I was, and once I answered her simple and caring question, she told me that she was on her way home. I just answered back with a simple okay and see you soon.

We said our good-byes to each other, and I set my phone back down and lay down as well and turned off my lights.

I didn't want to open my eyes as I felt the sunlight barely beam through my window and glare on my bed. I rolled over and began to open them even though I didn't want to at all. I opened them to just look up at my white plain ceiling. I then sat up hesitantly and then forced myself to get up out of bed as I smelled my mother cooking breakfast for me.

I rushed over to the staircase and trotted down them, careful not to fall. I was hungry but still quite tired. I walked as fast as I could down the steps, still being tired.

"Kendall!" she shouted as I neared the bottom of the stairs.

"I'm com—" but I was cut short of my answer by the sight that was in front of me. How . . . why?

He sat there as if he were completely comfortable.

"Hi, Kendall," he greeted me as I just looked at him and then at my mother again.

"H-hello . . ." I couldn't help the lump in my throat at the sight of him. I wiped my already sweaty hands on my bottoms quickly and swallowed back my anxiety.

"Did you sleep okay?" my mother asked me, trying to break the awkwardness, I think. Oscar ran down the steps after me.

"Uh yeah, what . . . what are you doing here?" I asked, looking over at Micah.

He laughed at my remark and reaction to him being there. I would find it funny too, though, if I were to see my face rather than just picture what it looked like.

"Kendall, he was outside and said that he was a friend of yours, so I invited him in," she said, smiling at me as he smiled at her.

"Oh well, okay?" I said questionably.

I just walked over to the stool on the island table in the middle to where Micah sat on the other seat. I didn't know what to expect now. He looked over at me and smiled. I just looked back at him plainly though.

What is he doing here? What does he want?

I made sure that my rather large bruising from him was well covered from my mother's sight once she turned around again.

He chuckled, noticing it on my skin. I just looked at him in annoyance still. Then I felt his hand touch my leg as he slid it around as if to calm me and then gripped it with his fingers. I felt myself jump at his movements, and he acted as if I was his girlfriend and that we had known each other for a long amount of time. I put my hand on his wrist and pried his hand off my leg. He smiled, not showing his teeth, as his dimples only showed, trying not to laugh at me obviously.

"So, Micah, where do you live?" my mother asked him.

"Oh, just a few blocks down," he answered her politely. I just looked at my mom.

"Kendall." He started to say my name to get my attention.

"What?" I asked normally, playing along.

He grinned.

"I was thinking about taking you out tonight," he said, more of a statement than a question.

"Oh, she would love that!" my mom said in excitement as she turned around, answering his "question" for me. Oscar made his way to Micah happily and sat on the floor by him. He seems to like him, but how? Why? I think I hate him.

"What?" I asked quietly.

"Okay, well, I'll come by and pick you up around seven," he stated.

"Okay, she'll be ready," my mom said to him, once again answering for me.

Micah smiled at her. "Well, okay then. See you tonight, Kendall," he said, looking over at me, smirking as he stood up and spoke again, kissing my cheek lightly as I just stood. "Well, I have to go now. Thanks for the breakfast, Linda." He smiled at my mother, and she smiled right back, obviously charmed by him.

I got up with him. My mother was still shocked with excitement about what had just happened as if she were the one going out with him. We reached the short hallway that led to the front door. Once we reached it, he opened it and stepped out. I did as well. I shut the door behind me firmly.

"What are you doing here?" I said to him in a loud whisper.

"I wanted to ask you out," he answered obviously. I looked at him in a way like I don't like him, but he didn't accept it. He then put his hand on the side of my hair and moved it all to the back, uncovering the bruise that he imprinted on my neck. He smirked at it, looking into my eyes. "You're actually really pretty."

"Get off."

"Okay, calm down, babe."

"Don't call me that," I snapped, which caused another smile to erupt on his face. "What is wrong with you?" He shrugged.

There was a pause, and we both just stood there awkwardly. I looked down and all around to try and avoid the tension while he just stared at me. Why won't he just leave me alone already? "Your mom has my number. I didn't think she would actually make you come downstairs like that though." He chuckled, his dimples coming into my view. "See you tonight, beautiful," he said as he turned to go back to his car, which was parked right across the street.

***

I sat up on my bed, just thinking about what I have gotten myself into. I should have just told my mom how I know him and how he is. I should have spoken for myself instead of letting my mom do it all for me. I probably looked pathetic. My mom shouted something up the stairs, causing me to lose whatever I was thinking about.

"What!" I shouted back down to her, not knowing what she had just yelled.

"Savanna's here!" she yelled back again as I saw her appear in my doorway.

"Hi, Kendall," she said, smiling to me as she walked over and sat on my bed with me. "It was pretty crazy last night. I had a heart attack almost when I couldn't find you. Jeremy got arrested last night. It was weird since we've grown up with him."

"What? Why'd he get arrested though?"

"They found a ton of pot on him."

My eyes widened even more. I hadn't known anything of him ever doing drugs before. He was always so nice in high school. "Seriously? That's terrible but pathetic of him." She shrugged.

"Oh sorry, I didn't text you," she said in realization. "I was just on my way home from work and thought that I'd stop by to ask what happened last night," she added in sort of a tint of humor.

"Oh yeah, ha-ha."

"So what did happen? We looked for you, but Em said she saw you get out the back."

"Nothing happened that you may be thinking . . ."

"Oh yeah?" she asked. "Then who gave you that?" she said, laughing and peering over my neck.

I rushed my hand up to my neck over the bruise and remembered. I just looked at her in sadness.

"Oh my god, Kendall, what's wrong?" she asked as a tear slipped from the corner of my one eye. I shook my head as she got closer in and hugged me gently and then held me tightly. "What happened to you Ken?" she asked, now demanding an answer. I began to cry even more now. "Kendall?" she asked again.

I calmed myself down now, leaning out of her hug and ready to talk. "Well, at the party I got separated from you and Em, so when I was looking, I was attack—" she interrupted.

"Oh my god . . .," she said silently.

"No, no, nothing happened to me then," I reassured her. "The man tried to . . . but . . . he saved me. He took the guy away from me," I told her as tears started to run down my check once again.

She looked at me as if she were going to start crying as well. "I'm confused—the one who walked you home?" she asked with a shaky voice to me. I knew, though, that she wasn't being pushy, only concerned about me.

"Yeah, he saved me, so I felt that I could trust him from that. But he offered to take me home. I hate him though. He's so rude and . . . obnoxious." Then I realized at my own words why he really offered to take me home. He was worried about me and just wanted to take me home to safety away from other men like that. I opened my eyes widely.

A single tear droplet rolled down from Savanna's eye.

"He brought me home and then forced himself on me, only doing this though. And then this morning, when I went downstairs to eat . . . he . . . he was just sitting down there with my mom and talking all normally, and then he asked me out right in front of her on purpose, I know. My mom answered yes to him, and he's picking me up tonight," I told her calmer and no longer whimpering or crying now, my voice steadier.

Her eyes widened.

"Why didn't you just say something?" she said loudly to me in a question form.

"I don't know. I should have. I was scared though, still in shock. He knows where I live though. I can't stop him from coming over Savanna."

"You shouldn't go if you're that uncomfortable."

"My mom leaves in a half hour for her shift," I told her. "He'll be here at seven. It's four now."

She seemed to relax for some reason to my words. "He probably just wanted you to trust him, Kendall. What's his name?"

"Micah," I told her.

"Micah? Micah what?"

"I don't know yet." I sighed.

"Well, at least you can have something to talk about. Make a list of questions to ask." She shrugged. That's the thing, though, I don't want to ask him questions. I don't want to get to know him. "I'm sorry. But he is hot, so . . . it sort of helps?" she said, trying to comfort me.

"I really haven't noticed." I wiped my eyes with the backs of my hands.

She just looked at me, though, as if I were lying to her.

"Well, I have to go. Just let me know what happens," she said as she got up and gave me another short and light hug and walked toward the door.

"Bye," I said quietly to her.

A few minutes after she had left, I just lay down for like a half an hour, then my mom shouted up the stairs that she was leaving for work. I let out a sigh in stress.

Then I started to think about Micah.

Then I just passed out, falling into a deep sleep.

I began to open my eyes slowly. I don't know why I fell asleep when I wasn't even tired. When I did open my eyes fully, I began to panic, wondering what time it was. I then heard my phone vibrate on the nightstand. I picked it up quickly, but before I unlocked it, I saw who was texting me—a random number.

Be there in 20mins
Micah.

I looked up at the clock on my phone quickly and noticed that it was already 6:40 p.m. I gasped and shot out of bed and got ready quickly. But after about five minutes, I realized again that I was going out with the rude and arrogant man that I don't even know or care about. I slowed myself down and caught my breath and slowly got ready, not happily at all. I felt as though that if I don't go out with him tonight, I would have to eventually understand that he wouldn't leave me alone until I did. Maybe after tonight, he will fully understand that I am not interested in him and leave me alone for good.

Once I was ready, I received another text from him saying that he is here. After I read it, I just paused, trying not to think of what he may try to do tonight. I heard a knock at my door then. I grabbed my jacket and walked quickly down my stairs and to the front door.

I opened the door and saw him standing there. I looked up into his eyes. I never really realized them before, but they look perfect—they sparkle. I paused, just looking up at his tall figure.

"Hi." He grinned.

"Hi," I said back, my voice shaking. I don't know if I should be scared or horrified.

He gripped my waist and pulled me a little closer to him. "Are you ready?" he asked smoothly, his voice deep, which caused a random shiver to run down my body and instantly made me wish I was more dressed up for some reason. How does he make me feel like that?

"Yeah."

"Well, come on then," he said, smiling down at me. I held my phone tightly and slid it into my back pocket of my dark skinny jeans. I stepped out of my doorway. He let go of my waist lightly to grab hold of my hand. I took another deep breath.

We walked across the street to his car. He walked with me to the passenger's side and opened the door as I hopped in quickly. I tightened up at his smirk. I didn't know why he was doing it. It made me feel more nervous at the time. "Try not to look so nervous, Kendall," he said, laughing while he spoke.

"Where are we going?" I asked, still shaking.

"The middle of the woods." I looked over at him, and he grinned. "Just kidding. Calm down." He glanced over. "You really believed me? We're just going to get something to eat. You eat, don't you?"

"Yeah," I whispered for some reason. *Get it together, Kendall.* "That's fine."

I felt a sudden rush of relief run through my body. I was hoping that he wouldn't just say somewhere else where we would be alone. I don't even know what to think of what he might have done to me then. I'm not that strong, and compared to him, I'm not strong at all.

"How old are you?" I asked, trying to calm myself down. I still don't know his age, so maybe it will help. Maybe learning more about him will calm me down.

He grinned before answering me. "Twenty-one," he answered me.

"What? I wouldn't have guessed that. You look older."

"Wow, thanks. Well, how old are you?"

"Eighteen," I answered back after a few seconds.

"What? I didn't know that?" he said back to me sarcastically.

I laughed at him for a minute. I don't know what it was about his answer to my age that made me find him charming.

"Didn't know I was so funny before." I giggled again.

The rest of the ride was an awkward silence. I mostly just looked out the window, which may have seemed weird to him. I'm sure that all of the other girls that he ever went out with weren't nervous or scared to reach out to put their hands on his lap. I bet that they were more than willing to go out with him, sitting up against his side, prepared for their night with him.

But the more that I thought about it, I don't even think that he has ever gone out with many girls. I can see that just by looking at him and the way that he looks at other women—the way that he looks at me.

The vehicle then came to a steady stop. "We're here." He isn't nervous at all.

I felt my heart rate slow down as I relaxed a little more. I saw the building, which sat by the beach.

He took his keys out of the ignition and opened his door and walked over to my side and opened it for me, surprising me. I hopped out carefully, not letting my nerves get the best of me and making me trip and fall to embarrass myself in front of him. Even though I do already feel embarrassed for the way that I am feeling, knowing that he knows the way that I am feeling. I need to stop thinking altogether, I think.

Once we were out, we both walked together toward the restaurant. He went in first, opening the door for me. We went up to the podium where a woman with blond hair pulled up in a ponytail stood.

"Can I help you two?" she asked, not even looking over at me but looking right at Micah. I can tell that she likes him. It made me feel pathetic. I think that he knew that too. He reassured me by putting his arm around my back, tugging me slowly closer up against himself. Oh my . . .

It made me feel better—more proud. Just to kind of show off to the lady that I was with him. She didn't seem completely convinced as she held that smug look and stared at Micah up and down.

"Yeah, I called earlier. Micah Harlan," he told the lady as she checked him out.

She looked at him a quick second and then glanced down at me and smiled. "Right this way." Micah only looked at her with a plain smile.

She led us toward the back of the restaurant.

"Okay," she said as we sat down. "Your waitress will be over in a minute," she added as she handed us the menus.

I looked over at Micah, who flashed her just a quick grin.

I feel so useless and pathetic. "You okay?" he asked me.

I looked back at him. "Yeah," I answered back to him, looking into his eyes.

"Well, why are you so nervous?" he asked humorously.

"I-I don't know. I'll be right back," I said to him as I stood up and walked away to the bathroom quickly.

"Okay," he said as I walked off. I think that he already knew where I was going anyway.

I went into the bathroom, although I don't have to go. Then, when I got in there, I just looked into the mirror at myself.

What am I doing? I shouldn't be here! I shouldn't be with him at all. What is going on? I shouldn't be here! This isn't me.

My mind is going crazy. I don't know what to do to control my thoughts. I can't do anything to do so. That's what's making me so nervous. I took a deep breath and put my head down. I then lifted my head back and looked to my left. There was a window. It's not a large window, but it's big enough for me to slip out of and just leave. No. That's crazy.

I can't—I just can't. I'm not that crazy, am I? No. I walked to the window, thinking more and more of just leaving, just running out on him. Then I realized why I can't just do that. He knows where I live. He will just come there. I am too confused to even hoist myself up to the window. It was already opened. I looked out of it. It led to the boardwalk. But even if I did make it there, what if he saw me?

Would he run after me?

I walked out of the bathroom and slowly back to our table where I saw him, still sitting down, waiting for my return.

I sat back down in my chair. He looked up at me. I stared into his dark green eyes for a moment. "What?" he asked, laughing. I just shook my head to him. "Is something wrong, Kendall?"

"No," I said back softly to him.

"You're lying."

"Well, it's just . . . it's just that I don't know you . . . like at all," I told him nervously.

He just smirked at me, his deep dimples showing. That's not calming me down. "Well then, let's get to know each other," he said, trying to relax me, I think. No, probably not. "So uh, what's your last name?" he asked, smirking at me.

I laughed for a second, trying not to let my nerves show. "Starla," I answered back to him. "What's your middle name?" I asked him next.

"It's Mathew," he answered back. "What's yours?"

"Eileen."

"Do you have any brothers or sisters?" he asked, smiling down at me.

I shook my head. "No, do you?" I asked him, and when I did, his smile was wiped off his face. I looked at him a bit puzzled at his reaction. He then looked down and back up at me and grinned.

"I have a sister. I told you last night," he answered after a good minute that seemed to take forever. Crap. Why didn't I remember that? No personal questions either. *Keep on track, Kendall.*

"Where's she?" I asked curiously. "I'm sorry." I rushed. "No personal questions. I forgot." I looked back down at my menu.

He shrugged. "We need something to talk about. I'm just not used to this is all. We're not in touch," he answered in a normal tone to me.

I just looked at him, still trying to understand a little more about him. I do want to know about him, but I still don't trust him. "Why not?" I asked.

"Kendall," he said sharply to me. I got what he was doing. He didn't want to talk about it, and I felt like I understood. I don't know if it's being nice to him, though, that's keeping me from asking why again or the fact that I am terrified of him. Either way, it's not my business anyway. I just looked at him in understanding a little. I never imagined this would happen. I made him speechless. I didn't imagine that I could ever have that power over him, but I did. I made him nervous and not wanting to answer me. He brushed it off, not wanting to create anything weird that I had already created though.

"Okay. How many guys have you slept with?" he asked, grinning at me. He can't be serious.

My heart began to race again. "What?" Maybe I didn't hear that correctly. I want to just walk away, but I can't. I'm frozen. I can't believe he just asked me that. He just looked at me while I made sure nobody was paying any attention to us. "That's none of your business," I said. My hands began to get sweaty. Now, I was more nervous than before. My legs started to shake.

"Okay."

"How many girls have you been with?" I asked back, regaining my nerves under control.

"Well, I'm not a virgin, if that's what you mean," he said back. I really wasn't expecting him to say it like that. I was really sort of disgusted. I knew when I saw him that he wasn't. One thing that made it really stand out was his ego.

He came over and sat on the same side of the booth as me.

I just looked at him like "okay then." Now, this is just even more awkward. He then set his large hand, compared to mine but normal for him, on my leg.

"What are you doing?" I asked him nervously, looking down at his hand as it rested on me.

He just smiled. He then realized that I was uncomfortable with his actions and took it off me.

"Do you have a job?"

"I . . . Yeah . . . I-I work in a bookstore by my house," I told him, stuttering. He smiled down at me. "Do you?" I asked him back, trying to carry on the conversation to not let an awkward silence come in.

"I work in a gym," he answered back, looking over at me.

"Oh," I said back a little quieter, not in my usual tone. But it's usual when I am with him. Those words made me feel awkward and scared a little more. That just means that he is stronger than I think. It makes me feel more powerless. It's insulting, really. "I'm not that hungry, actually," I said suddenly.

He looked at me with a confused face and then smiled. "Well, what do you want to do then?" he asked.

"I don't know . . .," I said quietly.

He smirked.

"Well, okay," he said, standing up. "Then let's go somewhere else," he then said as I stood up.

The girl with the ponytail then came over. "I'm sorry about the wait. She'll be over in a minute."

"Oh well, you know what, we're just gonna leave. We forgot about something."

She looked upset. The only reason that I could think of, though, is because she wouldn't be able to just stare at him or try to take him away from me. Little did she know that I wasn't interested in him and wasn't his.

"Oh well, okay. Come back soon," she responded back to him. I looked up at her—just looked. I didn't really have an expression on my face. Micah then reached his hand down and cupped mine into his. I knew that the lady was watching us walk away too. For the first time, I actually held his hand back. I looked up to see his face, and he was looking straight ahead normally.

He ran his fingers through his blond hair and opened the door afterward to leave the restaurant. The cool ocean breeze brushed my face as we walked out. I still held on to his right hand though. I tucked my hair behind my ear with my free one, trying to keep it under control from the beach wind.

Then, when we were out and on the cement outside, he spoke. "Want to just take a walk?" he asked me.

"Sure," I said, still a little shaky.

He then gripped my hand a little tighter. I don't think that he knew, though, how tight he was holding on to me. "You grow up here?"

"No, Kendall, I didn't."

"Where you from then?"

"Nothing personal remember?"

"Yeah," I whispered, embarrassed once more. "Have any pets?" He gave a weak laugh and shook his head. "I only have the one." He still said nothing. Now, what's wrong with him? Oh god, now, he's not even talking to me. "Do you have a favorite color?"

By the time we walked half the length of the boardwalk and got a cup of Polish Water Ice, I have learned that his favorite color is black. He's never had any pets except a stray dog he used to feed when he was twelve, but his mom took the mutt to the pound and said that they can't have any pets after he had snuck him inside one night during a vicious storm. He used to sleep with an old stuffed bear. He hated school, so he dropped out, and he's never had a girlfriend.

We went to his car, and he opened the door for me. I looked down at my phone quickly and saw the time. It's already eight thirty. It doesn't even feel like an hour has passed, let alone an hour and a half.

He started the ignition quickly and pulled out in the same manor after lighting a cigarette. "When did you start that?"

He took it from in between his lips and glanced over at me. "Start what?"

"That. Smoking." I clarified.

"Oh, I don't know. Almost a year ago, I think. I usually don't." He took another puff.

The entire ride home, I was shaken up, thinking that he might wreck due to his anger. Why did he suddenly get so angry? I still don't really understand what had sparked it, though, but then again, I'm not really sure if I fully want to understand everything about Micah Harlan.

We arrived back at my house, and he parked on the opposite side of the road again for some reason.

"Do I frighten you?" he asked after taking the keys out and not making eye contact with me.

I just stared at him though. He seems different from before. I am seeing a different side of him. He seems almost . . . vulnerable. I didn't answer him. I just stared at him. His eyes looking right back into mine. I wanted to say yes, but I was frightened. But at the same time, my answer was a no. I think that I do like him. Then my phone buzzed. I smiled at him, but not because I was happy with him, but happy that my phone interrupted. He didn't smile though. He was unhappy and annoyed.

"I have to go," I told him as I looked down at my phone and realized that Savanna was texting me, seeing what was going on with Micah. He just still stared at me.

"I'll be back tomorrow."

I nodded to him in approval, although I'm still not sure about him. I can't trust him still. I didn't reject it due to the fact that I know it won't help anyway.

"Good night. Thanks for . . . almost dinner, I guess?"

"Good night, beautiful."

I don't know how else to respond to his actions when he calls me a name like that. No man has ever called me "beautiful" or "babe" or anything else but Micah.

I turned to open the door until I felt his strong hands grip around me and pull me back to my previous position, but even closer and closer to his face as he anxiously pressed his lips to mine. It wasn't my first kiss, but none of them compared to Micah's. My eyes were open for a second, but then they slowly closed at their own will. This one was so much different from my previous ones. But this was our first kiss, and I couldn't help but feel like just the next girl on his list, remembering how experienced he obviously seems to be and confident he is.

When I took my hands and pushed him off, he looked at me confused, showing his dimples. "It wasn't that bad, was it?" He joked.

I pulled back from his hands on me. "Good night," I whispered to him.

He smiled largely. "It was," he said back to me as I turned back around and opened the passenger's door looking back at him one last time before I stepped off his vehicle. He just watched me walk around his car before he got out as well and walked with me across the street to my front door, slamming his door. What now?

"Okay, see you tomorrow," he said, leaning in to kiss me again. I didn't let him though. Instead, I turned my head to the side so he could only place his lips to my cheek. He released his touch and looked at me a little confused as I left him unsatisfied at my doorstep.

He backed up and finally turned around and walked back to his car, unlocking it from his key's button and getting in. My mother still wasn't home yet as I looked over at the driveway. He got into his vehicle as I closed my front door and went straight up to my bedroom.

When I got there, I texted Savanna, telling her that I was home now. I went over to my drawers and pulled out a pair of more comfortable shorts and an oversized T-shirt. I then stripped down to my bra and underwear, changing into the outfit that I poorly picked out, just wanting to be more comfortable.

Then I heard my phone buzz once on my bed.

I walked over to it while pulling my hair out from being tucked in the shirt. I picked up my phone quickly from my bed to see whom the sudden text was from.

> From Micah:
> Not complaining, but it would be a good idea of you to close the blinds before stripping down into your pink bra and black underwear. Again not complaining. Thanks for the show, babe.

I felt my heart sink inside me, and my mind went black.
What!

Then I heard a car pull away. I looked over at my large window and saw that my curtains were pulled back all the way. I hurried up and closed them quickly. I feel so uncomfortable, so ruined, embarrassed, and violated. Oh no. And now, knowing that Micah has seen me in just my undergarments makes me even more nervous about tomorrow night. And the fact that he had to add the word "babe" at the end of the message made my hands tremble. I quickly grabbed ahold of the fabric and pulled it over the windows. I don't want to ever see him again. I'm too embarrassed. I went to pull my hair up to keep it out of my face because I just felt so irritated, then I remembered how he had left his mark on me, and I just covered my face and plunged on to my bed. I lay down for like ten minutes before my phone buzzed again.

> From Micah:
> Have a lovely night.
>
> xx

It came to my attention then that I was just the next girl to him. Was I? Yes, I have to be. Guys like Micah just don't change over one girl's actions toward him, not giving him enough. I sighed before I just set my phone down beside me and went to sleep.

The next day, I went to work normally, and when I got outside, I saw Micah's car parked. I walked over to it, seeing him smiling over at me. I got in with him. "Hi," I greeted.

"Hello." He smiled. Micah drove me home, stopping across my street, parking. "I told my friend Brian and them that we'd go out with them all tonight," he told me.

"What? When?" I asked, a little stunned. Who the hell is Brian? How's he making plans with me without me even knowing?

"Tonight at around nine."

"Where?"

"Just a club not too far from here."

A club? But I'm not old enough to get into a club? "Okay," I said softly. What else am I supposed to say? I think that if I say no, he won't accept it. He looked at me with guilt into my eyes, his green orbs peering down at me.

He looked at me in awe and leaned in again as he walked me to my door and kissed me good-bye for a while. My mom was home now, finally. I felt relieved by it. I went in and greeted her, and we talked for a good hour. She made me some food, and we ate together, and then she told me that one of her cousins in Georgia is very sick and that she has to leave tomorrow and that she won't be back for a few days. I don't really know him, though, so I don't have to go, and I am considered an adult now, so I can stay home alone.

I went upstairs and got a few minutes to rest a little better and then began texting Emily about what has happened to me the last few days. By nine o'clock, I was ready, only putting on a pair of mid-thigh shorts with some sequence in them and a loose shirt that I tucked halfway in.

Micah came to my door. We then left to go and meet up with his friends, whom I still don't really know anything about but their names. I got back into his car, and he looked over at me.

Micah pulled in on the side of the road by a building with a large line of people going all the way to the curb. "We're here," he said, looking over at me. The place didn't look all that great. The bricks were obviously old and not too clean. The people in line looked trashy and scary to someone like me.

"You sure that we're going to get in?"

He laughed. "Don't worry," he answered as he threw his cigarette on to the ground out the window.

He got out as I sat there a little confused as he came and opened my door for me. We walked across the street to the front entrance.

As soon as we walked up by the bouncer he looked over at Micah as he held my hand tightly as we stood beside all of the people. Micah looked back at the man. The big man quickly opened the rope for Micah and me. I had a feeling that he knew him well enough—or of him.

We walked through the doorway and walked down the hallway as we reached the short corridor. He opened the swinging door, and we entered the place. As weird as it sounds, I have to say that I feel like Karen from *Good Fellas* right now. The smell of liquor and other smells that I'm not completely sure about filled my senses. The loud music that thumped throughout the building made me forget for a moment about whom I'm actually with, then he squeezed my hand, and I realized that I had become right up against his side and was now holding on to his arm as well with my other hand. "You're safe with me." He leaned down to my ear. I looked up at him, and he nodded in reassurance. I actually feel safer with his word and released my grip somewhat a little. I flinched at the smell and the sight of some of the drunk people, which caused him to rub his thumb along my hand.

We walked over to where I noticed his friends whom I met once before. They looked up at us happily, two of them with bloodshot eyes. We sat down next to them at the round booth. I felt uncomfortable. "This is Brian, Corey, Walter, and Johnathan." Micah spoke. "And Shailene and Cally."

"Hey," Brian greeted.

I smiled politely.

I smiled shyly at them. "Oh, Kendall," Corey said, looking over at me.

"Hi," I said quietly. I know that he couldn't fully hear me because of the blasting music, but he knew what I was saying to him.

Shailene has thick brown hair that is curled and brown eyes. Call has light blond hair and brown eyes. They look to be as old as Micah, but I'm not sure. I feel a little intimidated by them both. They all talked for a few minutes when Walter stood up and began to walk to another man at the bar. I looked over in curiosity to see him then look over at Micah and the others and then leave with the man.

Where are they going? Who was that man?

The others did realize his disappearance but thought nothing of it as if it always happens. Micah kept his arm around me until he finally removed it. The restriction made me feel alone and out of place. He stood up and then bent down to my ear. "I'm going to get us a drink. I'll just get you something clean though." I smiled up at him but was silently begging him not to leave me here. I nodded, knowing that if I have said okay, he wouldn't have been able to hear me. "Just one minute," he added down in my ear. I smiled nervously again as I watched him walk away, leaving me with his friends. He glanced back as he was walking to the bar area. Once he arrived, he continued to look over his shoulder at me as if to check if I was still here.

After a few seconds of him leaving my side, Shailene came scooting over beside me as Call and Brian and Johnathan went to dance. "So what do you think of Micah?" she shouted to my ear so that I could hear her.

I didn't know what to say yet. I don't know how to explain him to someone. "Well, he has an anger issue," I told her as I looked up to her, sitting right by my side with Corey on the other side of her.

She already knew that, though, and I knew that, but I didn't know what else to say. It's the first thing that came to my mind. She laughed at my answer to her. "He really likes you, Kendall!" she then shouted to me.

I was a bit stunned at what she had just said to me. I just looked up at her and smiled shyly and then glanced over at Micah, still in the same spot at the bar as I saw a girl looking at him, but he completely ignored her. It made me feel good about myself in a way.

"Well, we're going to go dance!" She and Corey got up and went over to the dance floor. I looked over to see Micah still at the bar.

I just looked around at everyone around me. I didn't know how to act as I sat alone for a few long moments. Then a man abruptly came over and sat next to me. I don't know him. "You must be, Kendall!" he said loudly to get my attention more. I looked over at him in a bit of a shock.

"How would you know that?" I shouted to him.

He laughed at my comment. "I'm a friend of Micah's. I've heard about you, and then I saw you with him!" he shouted back to me.

"Oh."

"Anthony," he said to me, saying his name. "You want to dance?" he asked. I knew that if I danced with him, Micah would be angry. He has to know that, being his friend and all. But besides Micah, I didn't want to dance at all. It would be embarrassing. I'm not one to dance much, especially with guys and especially here.

I shook my head. "I'm waiting for Micah!"

I noticed his eyes skimming up and down me as I sat down by him. He then got up and pulled me to my feet suddenly. I had no time to react or fight back as he did it. "I said I don't dance anyway!" I yelled to him.

He looked back at me. "Relax. I'm taking you to Micah." He turned and pulled me further from the table. I was a little shocked by Anthony's actions for me to get up. Instead, he slipped me past Micah as I tried to break free from his grip.

"Anthony! No get off me!" I shouted, but he ignored.

He took me to a door as I still tried to get free from his tight grip. He took me past the door quickly. I begin to hear the music fading away in my ears. I don't know what to do. I don't know how to act. I am panicking with what Anthony might have going through his mind.

He then shoved me against the wall. He held me tightly down as he started to remove my hair to one side only. "Get off!" I screamed at him. This reminded me of something. I don't know what else to scream but "no" or "get off." I have to yell for him. He's probably the only one who can help me now. "Micah!" I screamed. "Someone help me!" I screamed again. I know what Anthony is thinking now as he sets his one hand tightly on my leg.

"Shhh, no one can hear you," he said in my ear as he began to kiss down my neck.

"Get off!" I screamed again. "Anthony, no! Get off! Micah!" I screamed and shouted as loud as I could as he kept harshly on me. He kissed my neck roughly, sucking hard on the skin and biting at it as he kept going lower. I closed my eyes as I kept sobbing even more so when his hips grinded into mine.

"Shut up!" he shouted. "Micah isn't here."

He gripped me tighter with one hand on my hips, his fingers inching their way into the top hem of the shorts. "No." I pouted to him as I had lost my voice as tears started down my cheeks. I lost my strength as he was pinning me down with his strength. I repeated the small word over and over as I sobbed.

"What the hell are you doing?" Relief washed over me entirely.

Anthony's attention then went directly down the hall, as Micah was coming. I was crying now, sobbing badly. "Relax, man. We're just having a little fun."

"Get the hell off her!" he shouted as he turned him around, and I was quickly grabbed by my wrist into Micah, and I hung tightly to Micah's arm and slumped into his back as I stood halfway behind him. "What were you thinking?" he asked him loudly with anger in his voice.

"Calm down, Micah. Kendall and I were just having fun. Right?" he said calmly as he stood in front of us both and then peering around Micah's body as he didn't move to reveal me fully to Anthony's eyes as he asked and called me "babe." I don't want him calling me that. "You can't have her all to yourself man," he added with his voice still in a calm manner as he stood closer as if he were going to get me from Micah.

I found myself praying over and over that Micah will keep me with him and not hand me off like I were a whore. I don't want to go with Anthony anywhere. Please. Please. Please. I held Micah tighter with my eyes wide as tears rolled down my cheeks, and worry filling my mind as my body trembled right up against Micah's back. I don't want to be without him. My only hope is to stay right where I am and hold my ground behind him. I gripped Micah's arms tighter in hopes of protection from the man. I felt Micah's muscles in his arms tense. My breath was uneven as well as Micah's.

I tried to hold on to Micah's arm as I felt him move a little closer to Anthony's frame as he was grinning largely to Micah. What? No! What's going on? Micah! No! I stood there with my arms at my sides, praying what I am thinking isn't true. Micah won't do this to me. No. No. No. Before I knew it, Micah's fist landed a heavy punch to the side of Anthony's face, forcing it to jerk to the side. A monstrous flood of relief flowed through my mind and body. He had his vast palm on his shoulder, holding him up as he landed another on his face and another and another to the chest area, then the stomach, and before I knew it, he had Anthony on the ground as he stood over him, holding his shirt tightly in his fists as he continued punching him continually with what I'm guessing is in full force.

I got my emotions under control. Then I realized that Micah was going to kill him. That's how strong he is. "Micah, no!" I shouted. "Micah!" I tried again. I was scared to put my hand on him. I did, though, as I tried pulling him away. "Micah, you're going to kill him!" I shouted.

The door was shoved open.

Brian and Corey started running to Micah. Corey went to Micah, trying to calm him down and pull him off Anthony. Brian came to me, helping me calm down a little more.

"Micah, calm the hell down!" Corey shouted as he gripped Micah and pulled him away from Anthony. Micah got to his feet, looking down at Anthony and kicking him in the side before he walked a few steps away to where I was standing with Brian.

"You okay?" he asked as he came right into my vision. I nodded, grabbing hold of his waist as he pulled me in for a hug. "It's all right now," he whispered.

I looked back at Anthony, who was covered in his own blood. He looked up at me and grinned. It sent chills down my spine and gave me goose bumps. I don't want Anthony looking at me like that. I don't want him ever looking at me ever again. His arms are large with muscles, and he is very strong, but he scares me. But Micah is the same way, built.

Micah looked over at Brian who had helped me up to my feet and relaxed and nodded to him. Micah took me close to his side as he wrapped his arm around me and began walking me out of the backdoor. Corey and Brian just left Anthony in the hall though. Nobody cared.

I thought back to the image of Micah beating him almost to death, and I was happy that I sucked up my fear and pulled him to stop a little until Corey helped out. Anthony would have died that night. Although I wish he did, I still don't at the same time.

"I'll take you home, baby," he whispered in my ear as he opened the door, and the wind cascaded across my face coldly. He took me to his car, setting me inside and getting in himself and then driving me back to my house. I still sobbed a little but kept it under control and just kept wiping my cheeks.

I fell asleep in the car at some time that I don't remember. "Kendall," I heard his voice say softly as his hand nudged for me to awake. "Kendall, time to get up." He weakly laughed. I moaned and then opened my eyes gently, tiredly. I don't know why I am so tired. I wasn't when I got in the car first. I don't know. I heard his door open as he stepped out, and not four seconds later, my door was opened with a pair of large, warm arms and busted knuckles, wrapping around me and pulling me out of the seat and into the air in his arms, cradling me. He walked me to my door and knocked. I heard a faint whisper through my tiredness. "She fell asleep." Even though it was a whisper, I knew it was his deep voice.

"Oh, well, just take her upstairs or just on the couch." I recognized my mother's voice.

I felt him walking up the stairs as I clung to his firm chest. I then felt the comfort and coldness of my bed as the blanket was covered on top of my body as I curled up. I felt Micah staring at me. "Good night, beautiful," I heard him whisper as he bent down in my face, placing a gentle kiss on my forehead.

"Good night," I said quietly to him as he stood up. I knew that he had to be smiling, realizing that I was listening to him.

"See you tomorrow," he added. I smiled, but I didn't open my eyes to look until I knew that he was at the stairs, heading down. I closed my eyes at the last sight of him walking down them and went to sleep.

***

I got up a little later than I usually do that morning. I got up and walked downstairs, not hearing my mother in the kitchen though. But before I went fully down the stairs and into the kitchen, I stopped on the bottom step, trying my best not to make any noise and peeked around the corner, just making sure.

Once I saw that the path was clear of anyone, my mom or anyone else that I wouldn't be aware of, I stepped off the last step and on to the wooden floor. I walked over to the fridge and grabbed a water bottle out and walked over into the living room to look for my mom and saw her asleep on the big couch. I then just went back up to my room.

Once I was there, I just turned on my television and watched for a while. After about two hours of that, it was around one o'clock almost.

I got up off my bed after there seemed to be nothing on the television anymore and went through my movies, picking out one of my favorites and popping it into the DVD player, skipping all of the previews and clicking Play right away when it showed.

I haven't done anything today. I had pretty much just stayed up in my room the entire day besides going down to get a drink or snack. I watched movies mostly. Then it was almost 5:00 p.m. when I looked at the time on my phone, and I immediately thought of Micah. He hasn't texted me. Isn't that a good thing though? Something inside me says it isn't. Why do I feel so disappointed? Maybe he realized he actually doesn't like me.

I don't know what it is about him that I am sort of attracted to. It's just him. He seems protective and bossy. I'm glad he's protective in a sense, but that wouldn't have happened if it weren't for him. What about the night of the graduation party? He saved me then . . . That's what frightens me most about him. His dark side is bigger than his light side, and I don't know how much he can control himself after how he acted last night to whom I think to be his best friends.

He makes me nervous and my heart race. Isn't that a good thing? I tremble when his hand touches mine. I feel safe with him, but at the same time, I don't, but only because I don't truly know who he is. Right? He won't hurt me?

I don't want to go back to work. I don't work anywhere that is always busy. I don't feel like I am ready for that kind of job. I have only been working there for like five months.

Then I heard my phone vibrate, making my mind get lost from the topic of my job. It was Savanna. She asked if I wanted to come over and stay with her, Sadie, and Emily. Sadie is gorgeous. She always looks perfect. Her hair is a thick dark blond, her eyes are a light sparkly blue, and she has long legs. She has a nice figure. But she isn't really one of my "friend friends." She is friends with Savanna, really. That's the only reason that I ever do talk to Sadie, just to be friendly. I texted her back and asked what time. After a few seconds, she texted back, and told me whenever I was ready.

I got a small bag and packed what I would need into it to go over to her house. I then went downstairs and told my mother that I was leaving and going over to Savanna's. She didn't mind. She took me over and dropped me off at her house.

"Hi," Savanna greeted me at her door as she opened it.

I smiled back at her. "Hello."

We went up to her bedroom where everyone else was sitting around. "Kendall, hey," Sadie greeted me. Emily was there and said hi to me as well. I went and sat around them and talked and talked about nothing, really, but at the same time, everything.

"So, Kendall, what about Micah?" Savanna asked, trying to get something out of me about him.

"Who's Micah?" Sadie asked, looking over at Savanna and then me anxiously. Oh god.

"Some guy that's she's been hanging out with," Savanna told her.

"No, no, no. It's not anything like that. We went on two dates, and that's it," I told her.

"Oh yeah? His name's Micah?" Sadie asked me.

"Yes, Micah," I told her again.

"Micah what?" she asked again.

"Micah Harlan," I told her.

"Harlan? Why does that sound so familiar?"

I just smiled at her. I don't know how to respond to her. I don't feel right around her. I don't feel comfortable.

The questioning made me feel uneasy, especially since it was all coming from Sadie. The Sadie that every guy instantly liked, but I think only for her looks. The Sadie that I feel Micah would forget about me for her and for her large chest and long legs. But even if I don't want him, why should she have him? I'd rather keep him instead of letting her have him, which I won't do.

"How old is he?" she finally asked. I felt the question coming before she asked it. And when she did, I was still unprepared. I paused, looking over at her face as I felt everyone else staring at me, dying for the answer.

"Twenty-one," I finally answered after a few seconds that seemed to drag on as minutes.

"Oh my, Kendall," she said back in a smiley face to me. I kind of blushed but was embarrassed to tell her anything—to tell anyone. I thought that I wanted to talk about him, but when I did, I realized that I didn't more and more.

My phone then buzzed.

> From Micah:
> Hey gorgeous.

I stared down at the screen in sort of a shock. I didn't think that he would text me. I was unprepared for this as well.

"Who is it?" Emily asked curiously.

I looked up at her. "Micah," I told her, only looking at her.

"Well, what'd he say?" Sadie asked me.

I just shook my head at her. "You guys just want to play a game?" Savanna asked, trying to change the subject.

I texted him back for the first time with just a simple hello.

> From Micah:
> Where r u?

He then asked. It wasn't what are you doing or how are you, but where are you.

Savanna went and grabbed a board game from her closet, and we all began playing. We kept on texting and texting each other, just asking questions about the other as I multitasked playing along with my friends as well.

From Micah:
What r u wearing?

To Micah:
Why?

From Micah:
Because im board. Send me pics of u in your underwear

I felt uncomfortable, and my heart changed its pace. I stared down at my phone, my friends knowing what I was doing, and they laughed a little.

"What?" Savanna asked me.

I shook my head again at them. "Nothing." Would I want to do that? I've never sent a guy even a picture of myself, and now, he wants one of just me in my panties? I don't know what to do.

"Oh, come on," she insisted of me to share what it was.

"It's nothing," I told them once more. "I have to use the restroom." I stood with my phone in my hand.

"Okay, okay," she answered back, just dropping it at the same time as Sadie spoke, "Uh-huh sure."

When I got into the bathroom, my heart was racing a million miles a second, and I felt like I was starting to sweat. It's just a picture. It's just a picture. Calm down. I took a deep breath after locking the door and going in front of the big mirror to look at my body, fully clothed. I unbuttoned my bottoms and slid them down my legs. My panties aren't anything special, and no guy would ever be turned on by them. I need different underwear. Sure, they got some lace at the top, but the rest is plain. Does he just want a picture of my underwear or me naked with only them on? I'm not sending a nude, that's for sure. This guy is a few years older than me, and I've only went on a couple of dates with the guy, and the one . . . One of his friends was trying to practically rape me in the hallway. I feel like a whore.

Sadie would do this.

I took my shirt over my head. This guy has already seen me in my underwear, but that was by accident. I looked at myself again in my bra and underwear. They don't match. I pulled out my phone and went to the camera. I tried sucking in a little and posed somewhat after unclasping my bra and covered my breast with my other arm. I snapped the photo and stared at it. He'll definitely stop seeing me after this. Even if it makes me look easy, I don't have a body that he would want. He's a man and would want a bigger ass and boobs like Sadie's. I deleted the photo and got dressed and went out of the bathroom.

"Did you send 'em?" Sadie spoke first as soon as I came out.

"What?"

"The pictures. You sent them then?"

"What pictures?" Oh no.

"Oh, come on. I know what you were doing in there, Kendall. He asked you for nudes, didn't he? I'm right, aren't I?" I only stared at her and then looked down. "So'd you do it then?" I shook my head.

"How did you ever do it?"

"Send nudes?" I nodded. She shrugged as Savanna and Emily watched us carefully. "I don't know. I didn't care. It's just skin."

"Yeah, but still . . . he wanted one of me in my underwear," I quietly told my friends.

My friends' eyes widened, and Savanna held in her laugh when I looked at her. "He's confident. I'll give him that," Sadie spoke. I couldn't help but laugh.

"You have no idea." She smiled back at me.

I left Savanna's house at ten in the morning. She'd already known that I'd be leaving probably before any of them were awake.

I walked home and got ready quickly by taking a shower and getting dressed, leading to fixing my hair a little and doing my makeup. I then went out of the front door and left for work. I was on time when I got there at eleven o'clock in the morning. I work until seven.

I walked in as if I were in a rush. I went straight to the back and pinned on my little name tag. "Morning, Kendall," a familiar voice called out to me.

"Good morning, Ashton," I said back to him. I turned to see him smiling at me as I set my bag into my small locker in the back.

"What's so good about it?" he asked me, still smiling.

"I don't know?" I asked, laughing at his question.

He walked out to the store. I walked out a minute after. I work with Ashton and a girl named Brandy. Brandy has short brown hair and brown eyes. She's nice, but we don't usually talk all that much. Ashton has dark brown hair that's short and dark blue eyes. He's always nice to me, and we always talk.

We both went and sorted out the new merchandise to where it belonged. Once Ashton finished his stack, he went behind the counter to check a woman and a man out. He kept looking over at me.

"So what'd you do this weekend?" he asked as he began doing something over at the register.

"Oh, nothing much, really. You?" I asked back just to ask.

"Just about the same. Stayed at home. You really didn't do anything at all?" he asked again as if he didn't believe me the first time.

I smiled at him, and then I heard the bell ring as the glass door opened.

I looked over casually to greet the customer, but I stood there confused when I saw who it was.

Chapter 8

My eyes felt as if they had popped out of my head. My heart literally felt like it had stopped and fell out of my chest. I looked right at him, but he didn't see me. Thank God. Ashton looked at me in pure confusion. He has no idea what is going on. I had just finished putting my share of the shipment away on the shelves, so I just fell to the floor as quickly as I could, trying my best to hide from him. I don't want him to find me.

I heard him then walking around. I can't imagine what Ashton must be thinking. I guess that I will have to explain to him later. I started to crawl away to try and make it back into the backroom.

"Can I help you, sir?" I heard Ashton ask.

I heard Micah's footsteps suddenly stop. "Where's Kendall?"

I think that Ashton got the message that I was hiding from this man.

"Sorry, she isn't here."

Thank God.

I felt a sudden rush of relief run through my body as I began crawling to the door to the backroom. "Are you sure? She told me that she worked here." Micah asked again, sort of being more persistent this time.

"I'm sorry. Who did you say you were?"

Then his footsteps continued and stopped. I looked in front of me to see his feet at the start of the aisle in which I was at the same point.

"Kendall?" he asked. I looked up at him. "What the hell are you doing on the floor?" he added, his voice sounding concerned. I didn't know what to say to him as my heart raced.

"Uh . . . I-I . . . I dropped something . . .," I said, stuttering to him. I didn't know what else to say. I couldn't think of anything. Whenever I see him, my mind becomes a jumbled mess.

He reached his hand down and picked me up from the floor quickly. I looked over at Ashton. "Kendall, there you are!" he said, looking at me. Micah gave him a look then. Not just a look over at him, but it was a scary look—a shut-the-hell-up kind of look. I don't know how else to describe it. I don't even know how to describe him. He is too unpredictable.

"What are you doing here?" I asked him, shaky.

"You wouldn't text me back."

I looked at Ashton in embarrassment as Micah grabbed hold of my wrist, bringing me closer to him. I had to answer him in front of Ashton. I have no other choice but to. Micah is holding me there against my will and won't let me go. I'm shaking.

I gained enough breath to answer his question. "I wasn't sending you a picture . . .," I said quietly back to him so that Ashton wouldn't hear us, not making any eye contact with either of the men, finding the tile covering the floor very interesting.

"Would it have helped if I sent you one? I assumed that you were naked," he said back loudly so that Ashton could hear with the same smirk plastered on his face.

He lifted one of his hands to the point of my neck and moved my hair out of the way. He then looked at Ashton, who I knew could see the bruise that he left on me.

"Sir, I think that you should leave," Ashton interrupted.

"Why is that?"

"You're kind of making a scene." They stared at each other, and I started to feel like I was in the middle of a pissing contest between the two. "I think that you should go," he said more sternly.

He let go of my wrist. "I'll see you tonight then," he said as he looked over at Ashton one last time, then leaning in and kissing me politely, actually. I jumped at the touch of his cold lips against mine. I wasn't expecting that. When he released, I just looked up at him. He smiled down at me. That felt wrong. Why didn't I pull away? What the hell is going on in my life?

"Okay," I whispered. I don't know what else to say to him. I can only agree. He wouldn't allow me to say no to him anyway. And although I haven't ever really said no to him, I just know that he wouldn't listen to me. He walked out of the store, the bell ringing above his head.

I took a deep breath, just standing where he left me. "Kendall?" Ashton asked, rushing over to me. I looked up at him with my glassy blue eyes. "Are you okay?"

"Uh yeah . . . yeah, I'm fine. Thanks for that," I said to Ashton. He looked over at my bruise.

"So is that your boyfriend then?"

"He's not my boyfriend." I just pulled my hair back to its previous position around my neck. "I'm fine."

"Kendall," he said again as I went to walk away.

"I said that I was fine. Really!"

"You can't go out with someone like that Kendall. He doesn't even respect you," he continued while we walked into the backroom.

"It's not for you to say, and we're not even dating. It's not like that," I said quietly back to him as my eyes filled up again.

"I know, but you can't. He'll hurt you, Ken," he told me, trying to convince me more. I already am though. I think . . .

I just looked at him, and a tear ran down my cheek. I could feel it. "What makes you think that?" I asked irritated.

He looked at me in concern and walked closer to where I was standing. "I'm sorry. I know I shouldn't have said anything more."

"Just forget about it."

"You guys need to get back to work," Brandy told us both as she opened the door and then closed it, going back out to the front.

The day was slow, but we were still getting customers every ten minutes or so. At the end of the day, I went back and grabbed my bag, putting my new novel, *French Silk* by Sandra Brown, in the front pocket, and removed my name tag. Ashton said nothing more concerning Micah the entire day that we worked. But that didn't last.

As I was walking out, Ashton spoke, causing me to stop. "What's his name?" he asked, wanting to know, but being nice and kind about it. The way he asks it sounds like he's been wanting to ask me all day.

"Micah," I answered.

"Micah who?" He asked as we walked out together.

"Harlan," I told him as he opened the front door for me, and we walked out of the building, locking the doors as we did.

"Harlan. I've heard that before," he said back after a second.

"Yeah, well, he—" I was cut off by the sight of Micah's car on the other side of the road.

"What?" Ashton asked, laughing to what I may be staring at. "Oh," he said back. "You want me to take you home?" he asked. I shook my head. "Really?" he asked again.

If I say yes, there isn't a doubt in my mind that Micah will do something to him. The door of Micah's car then opened as he got out and walked over to me. "Kendall."

"Hi."

Ashton just stood there as Micah took hold of my hand. "You ready?" he asked.

"Yeah."

Micah gripped my hand tighter in his when I looked up to see his jaw clenched and his eyes set ahead of him. He opened the passenger door for me. He then walked over to his side and got in.

"You really have to work with that prick?" he asked, chuckling.

This is how he's going to act? Like a five-year-old? "Yeah. What is our problem? How dare you think you can just show up and embarrass me in front of people," I snapped. "You can't do that, especially if this is going to continue, or you can just leave me the hell alone like I want." I'm fuming.

"You're embarrassed of me?"

"You're acting like a child. That was a pissing contest. Yes, I'm going to be embarrassed of you when you show up and talk like that when people can hear you."

"I was just upset, I guess," he spoke quietly, eyes on the road as he drove.

"Upset over what?" I looked over at him. He didn't answer. "What are you upset about?"

"You ignored me," he admitted.

"You're upset because I wouldn't text you back? Grow up, Micah. You were being inappropriate, and I was busy. I was uncomfortable."

"You're not comfortable with me?" He glanced over.

"We only just met."

"So I'm comfortable with you. What's the big deal?"

"I've seen you almost beat somebody to death!" I shouted in an obvious tone. How doesn't he get this?

"He deserved it, and I should have killed the prick for what he was doing to you."

I shook my head with my eyes closed, and then I looked down at my lap. "Okay, okay, I don't want to talk about that. Just don't ever do that to me, at work especially." I calmed down. "Where are we going?"

"I'll just take you home if you're not comfortable with me." I sighed.

"Micah, it's not like I don't like you at all. I just . . . I'm not like you and don't have as much as experience as you. That's what I'm uncomfortable with."

"Me being with a lot of women?"

I stared out the window for a moment, then looked back over at him. "Not that entirely. Just the fact that I know you expect more. I was uncomfortable with sending you a photo of me . . . practically . . . naked . . .," I spoke quietly. "Because I've never done anything like that before." I'm so uncomfortable right now, but I need to say this.

"You've never done anything?" I shook my head. I knew that his eyes were on me without even having to look over at him. "I like that." He spoke so quietly that I don't even think that I was meant to hear him, so I don't take on it. "The fair," he spoke softly.

"The fair? What?"

"Don't laugh. We are going to the boardwalk to the fair," he spoke seriously. "Girls like that sort of thing . . . right?" I shrugged when I felt him glance over at me again. "Or not. We can go—"

"I'll go to the fair with you." This'll be fun . . . interesting mostly. Is he nervous?

The drive was silent, which confirmed my suspicions. For some reason, I didn't even check my phone at all for any messages for the whole day. The sun was already down.

It was around eight thirty when we got there, and there were many people around. "I'm sorry about earlier," he told me quietly. "I just . . . I didn't know what to think when you didn't answer me."

"I told you already, I was with my friends. It was inappropriate of you."

He got out and waited for me in front of the vehicle. The park is set up on the large opening on the boardwalk. He grabbed hold of my hand as we walked inside. He paid for both of us to enter. He was different now.

We walked around the crowd of people there from ride to ride. We were actually having fun. I wasn't scared or nervous around him the entire time that we were spending together. It just kept reminding me again that I know nothing about him; therefore, I cannot judge him on how he acts sometimes . . . or all the time. As we were walking around, we were talking and laughing with each other when his phone started ringing in his pocket.

"Oh, I'm sorry," he said, looking at his phone screen. "I have to take this. Just stay right here. Don't move," he told me as he walked away.

I went just a few feet back to sit on a bench. I waited for a few minutes as I kept looking over to see him looking in on me just to check on me. I always smiled at him when he did. Then a group of teenagers came over and sat, taking up the rest of the bench. I heard a few remarks, but I ignored them completely and waited for Micah to be done with his phone call.

"Hey," one of them said. I knew that he was staring at me.

I looked back and grinned at him, then turned back around, hoping he'd get the message.

"You here alone?"

"Um no, I am waiting for my friend," I said back, looking at all of them. I can guess that they are still in high school.

"Your boyfriend?" He paused. "Why don't you just come with us?" one of them asked after.

"No."

"Oh, come on," one of them said to me, getting closer as I stood up to walk over to Micah and just to let them have the bench. He then grabbed hold of my wrist, but I quickly tried to squirm away from him. Next thing I knew, Micah was in front of me and shoved the kid that held on to me. He didn't hit him too hard, just hard enough to get him off me and fall back, attracting pairs of eyes to stare in our direction.

"Get the hell off her, you little prick," he said as he grabbed hold of my hand tightly, moving me to his side.

"Whatever, bitch," one of the boys commented as our backs were turned and walking away from them. I felt Micah's grip on me loosen as we turned around, letting go of my hand. No. I don't want him getting in a fight.

"You better shut the hell up right now, or I'll just kick all of your little asses," he told them as if it were a promise. I just stood behind him. "Stupid fucks. Get the fuck out of here."

"Micah," I pleaded, trying to get him to calm down as I latched on to his arm.

"Micah, huh?"

"Come on," I said, tugging on his arm to just walk away instead of getting us kicked out and left with nothing to do or even getting him arrested. I tugged on his arm a little harder as he finally just turned around.

"You okay?" He looked down at me.

"Yes, thank you. I don't fancy visiting you in prison." I laughed, smiling at him. Then I stopped my mind for a moment and thought about his anger problems. Have they ever gotten him arrested before?

"Every time I leave you alone, some assholes seem to find you," he said in humor, even though I know he's still mad. He noticed that I wasn't responding as I thought about his anger. "And no, Kendall, I haven't been to prison before, but I've been arrested a few times," he said as I was still moving, but inside, I was frozen in shock. What got him arrested? What did he do? "No, I didn't kill anyone," he said, chuckling down at me. I smiled up at him. "Now, what do you want to do?" he asked, breaking the awkwardness that was formed.

"Um, let's play a game."

"What?" He was confused at what I was talking about.

"Come on," I said, leading him over to a few games.

"Oh." He laughed. "One of these ones?" he asked as if they were for babies. "Oh, come on," he whined, leading us over to one with bottles far away that you have to knock off a table.

"Okay," I said to him, inspecting the game out.

"Just one," he said, handing the man a few dollars for three soft balls.

"Okay," I said as I picked one up, trying to concentrate and then throwing it and missing by like a whole foot from the bottles. I heard him laugh. "What?" I asked him, laughing. "You try," I told him, handing him one of the balls left.

"Okay," he said, looking down at me, uncrossing his arms and gripping the ball tightly and then throwing it fast to the table, knocking down all of the bottles in one throw.

"Dang."

"It's not hard."

"Yay." the man said sarcastically, just doing his job and handing me a prize.

I smiled up at Micah as I held my prize in my hand—a stuffed dog. I grabbed hold of Micah's side and kissed him on the cheek.

"Thank you," I said, still latched on to his side. He feels so much different from any other guy that I have ever stood beside and held on to. Not that I've held on to many others, only like two, considering that I've only had two boyfriends in my whole life. He didn't say, "You're welcome." He just looked down at me and smiled before kissing me back. It feels different with Micah, I guess, because he is older. It feels more promising with him though. I feel okay around him. It makes me long for him to be by my side whenever he isn't.

"Let's go on the roller coaster," I told him as we were walking by it.
"Why?"

"Micah," I pleaded, messing with him.

He looked up at it. It isn't that big with only like four tall hills. "You're crazy," he said, smiling down at me as I held his hand.

"Maybe . . .," I said back to his comment to me. "But come on, you're not scared are you?" I said, playing around with him. "I'll hold your hand," I stated to him as I gripped his tighter in mine.

"Okay," he said as if he were taking a deep breath like he was actually afraid, which made me smile. We got in line, and then it was our time in a few minutes.

"Smaller person on the right," I let go of his hand as the man spoke and slid into the red seat. Micah slowly got in beside me. Yep, he's scared. This is fun. He's staring straight ahead to where the hill starts. He's shaking.

"Micah." I caught his attention. He looked over. "It's okay." I laughed.

"Uh-huh." I looked down as the bar closed, and he gripped it immediately. I set one of my hands over his thigh. He looked down at it and grinned, his dimples surfacing. "This is what I had to do for you to touch me?" he said, trying to play it cool. I nodded, still smiling.

When we jolted forward, his face snapped forward. I laughed. "You're scared."

He looked back over at me. One of his hands set over mine that lies on his thigh. He slid it up so that my fingers brushed over his crotch. "You're scared," he spoke back. I took my hand back. What the hell have I started now? Oh god.

"I'm not holding your hand now."

"Don't be like that." I grabbed my hand back, grinning. Then, as we reached the top of the hill, he became aware of it all, and he squeezed my hand tightly. He is a child. A child that is afraid of heights definitely.

Micah is now shaking like it's below zero and biting his lip. I scooted over so that our legs are touching. He seems sort of relieved. Then we went down the first hill. At least he's not screaming. He's just stiff as a board. "Micah!" I shouted to try and get him to smile and at least pretend that he was having fun.

His hand is holding mine so tight, and he has the same arm over my knee so that I'm like squished against him. After the biggest hill comes a sharp turn, then another hill and another and another.

When we came to a stop, I could see his shoulders fall. "And it's over." I laughed while looking over at him. He finally smiled.

When we moved forward to get off, his hand squeezed my knee, then moved up my leg smoothly, making shivers shoot through my body instantly. I took a deep breath. What's he doing now? I set my hand on top of his and slowly slid it back down to my knee. A part of me, though, was against the whole movement. I couldn't help but stare at his jawline up to his partially parted soft pinkish lips.

He started smiling, and then I knew that I was caught. "Kendall," he said, laughing.

"What?"

"You're staring," he said, smiling at me.

"Sorry."

"It's okay," he said back down to me. He turned to face me better. "Why are you so different?" he barely spoke. I shook my head, confused on how to answer such a question. He leaned closer and closer slowly and set his hand on my thigh, the other on my face as his chapped lips barely touched mine, and his tongue pushed its way in without me agreeing. I could feel his hand move further and further up my body, and when the ride came to a complete stop and all of the bars lifted, his lips disconnected from mine, and his hand was just below my breast. Did anyone see anything? Nobody seems to be paying any attention to us. We're good. Well, Micah wouldn't have minded, I'm sure. I'm good.

When we were off, we started walking around again together, holding on to the other. Micah is afraid of heights. I know, even though he never said it. He had his eyes closed for most of it, not wanting to look how far off the ground he was when we would go up the hills. He held my hand tightly, and just about the whole time, the others he was trying not to hold on so tight. I don't think any less of him.

"You wanna go?" he asked as we neared the entrance.

"Uh . . . sure."

We walked out of the fair, and as he held me to the side of his body, I knew that he would always protect me from anyone. He cared about me. I guess that I sort of care about him too. I looked up at him as he led the way to the long boardwalk as we walked down it past all of the shops and yogurt places. He then took us through an opening.

"What are we doing?" I asked, smiling up at him.

"Just walking down here."

I took a deep breath as we went and walked down to the beach on the cool sand. We just walked and walked around down on the sand as the waves rolled in and out, roaring and collapsing back into each other. A commotion started down the beach but Micah didn't seem to care much so I said nothing. There aren't many people down in the sand.

After about an hour or so, I really don't know how I lost track of time. We began walking back up to the boardwalk. We just walked back to his car, and he opened the door for me as I got in after and drove me back home.

Before I got out of his car, though, I just looked over at him, and he looked back at me. I leaned over the middle console and kissed him gently on the cheek. He was expecting something more.

"Good night," I said as I got out.

"Good night, Kendall," he spoke in a way that made me feel out of breath, and a shiver flowed through my body.

I got out and walked over to my front door and opened it. I stood in the doorway and just looked back at him before closing it.

I went up to my room after saying hello and good night to my mother, taking my dinner upstairs. I went up and just sat on my bed and sat the stuffed dog down on my side of the bed against the light wall. I just looked at it and remembered his strength.

About twenty minutes later, my phone buzzed beside me as I lay down on top of my blankets on my bed. I finished eating a while ago. I looked over to it, opening my eyes from being tired, and picked it up tiredly.

> From Micah:
> thanks for the fun night. Good night princess. Xx

I texted him back and said that I had a good time and good night. I went to sleep after texting him.

Chapter 9

I walked through the door for work and went straight into the back like I always do and got suited up for my job. Well, just pinned my nametag on and put my stuff away. I kept my phone with me though. I texted Micah only like once or twice due to how surprisingly busy today was. That is up until like six when there hadn't been anyone around for a good hour.

Ashton walked up to me. I looked back at him. "Hey," I greeted him. We weren't really able to talk at all that day until now.

"Hey," he mumbled. "Everything go all right yesterday?" he asked me after a minute.

I looked at him in confusion before remembering what happened yesterday at work. "Oh yeah, yeah, everything was fine."

He looked at me as if he didn't believe me then. "You can tell me, Kendall."

"Everything was fine. Honest."

We went outside and Brandy left. "Do you need a ride home?" Ashton asked me after we had closed up.

"No, I'll just walk," I told him as I began to walk down the sidewalk.

"No, come on, just come on. I'll take you home." He smiled.

"No," I said back to him. "I'm fine."

"Come on," he said again as he grabbed on to my wrist, pulling me with him to his car.

"Ashton, really, I'd rather walk," I told him again.

Just then, I heard a car pull up on the other side of the road and heard a door open and slam shut. Then, not a few seconds later, Micah was at my side. Ashton let go of me finally.

Micah took me over to his car and opened the passenger door for me. "Thanks," I mumbled. He didn't say anything, though, and his jaw was clenched, and I could tell just by that simple action from him that I won't like what's about to happen. "Micah, no." He closed the door and began walking back over to where Ashton stood. "Micah," I spoke desperately again as he locked the doors with me inside. "Micah! No!" I screamed out, but all of the windows were rolled up. I don't know if he heard me. Then I knew that he did when he looked back, a protective and angry look on his face.

He walked right up into Ashton's face and was saying something to him. I noticed his fists at his sides that he held tightly together, but he seemed to keep them under control. About a minute or two later, after watching them both closely, Micah turned around, coming back to his car.

He opened the door and hopped in quickly. He looked up and smiled at me weakly. "What was that!"

"It was nothing."

"What did you say to him?"

"What he needed to hear."

"I work with him, and he was offering me a ride home so that I didn't have to walk alone in the dark."

"Yeah, I'm sure that's all that he wanted to do with you, Kendall," he said to himself as he started the car and gripped the wheel tightly and drove off. "You're so fucking naïve."

"Excuse me? Micah, I'm sure a lot of people would say the same to me about you." I felt guilty as soon as I said it, but I couldn't help it. This is what he needs to hear. He can't think that he can control me like this.

He didn't speak back to me for what seemed like hours, but I'm sure only a minute or two passed by. "Sorry. I know I'm a jackass."

I'm not sure why my heart constricted at his words. Maybe it was how broken his voice sounded or how lost he seems with himself as if he has no idea what he is truly doing all of the time. It reminded me why I'm here, sitting next to him and trying to make things work between us, even though I don't even know what this is between us.

We pulled up right in front of my house this time. Micah leaned over the middle and kissed me twice. "Kendall, I'll come and pick you up every day and take you home," he stated.

"Okay, see you tomorrow." I went inside my house and saw that my mom wasn't home yet. I still had the door opened as I was only standing there in the doorway before noticing. I turned around and looked over at Micah who was looking back at me. He smiled at me. I smiled to him and then closed my door.

The next day, I went to work on time. I went in the back and then went back out to the floor where I helped a few customers and straightened up the shop a little. Ashton came in like three hours late. I was behind the counter, checking out a customer when he came in. He didn't even look over at me. After I was done with the customer, Ashton came out. He started doing his job, organizing papers behind the counter as well. He wasn't saying anything to me, and it was weird. He always says hi to me when he comes in, and when he does come in, he is never late. I just stood there as I helped another customer check out. Then, a few minutes later, I decided to break the silence between Ashton and me.

"Hey," I said, looking back at him.

"Hi," he said softly.

"Why'd you come in late?"

"I-I slept in," he told me, looking away. He wouldn't look over to my face. He only glanced over while I was talking to him.

I looked at him, a bit more puzzled. I don't think that he slept in at all. "Really? That's a first," I said, smiling back at him.

"Yeah." He smiled shyly. I looked back at him, turning around and leaning on the desk.

"What's wrong?" I know that something is wrong with him.

"Nothing," he said, still looking down as he organized some of the papers.

"Then why are you hiding from me?" I asked, looking down at him as he worked.

He stopped for a second before lifting and facing me. "I shouldn't even be talking to you," he said, looking into my eyes.

"Ashton!" I shouted. "What's happened?" I asked, surprised. He had bruises all over him and a small black eye.

"Why don't you ask your boyfriend?"

"What are you talking about?"

"Who else would do this?"

"Micah? But why . . . When? He couldn't have done this," I said back sort of harshly to him. "He's not my boyfriend."

"This morning, okay? That's why I came in late."

I don't know how to respond to him. Sorry? But sorry for what? I didn't do anything to him. But apparently, Micah did.

"I shouldn't even be talking to you."

"Why's that?"

"Because he said that he'd fucking kill me if he ever saw me with my hand on you again or talking to you," he told me. I just looked at him. "Kendall, you shouldn't be hanging out with him. He's dangerous. He's older and more powerful than you. You shouldn't trust him."

"I don't know what to say," I said quietly to him. We would be closing soon.

"Kendall, just stay away from him," he told me as if he were begging.

"Ashton, I can't just ignore him," I said back. I like Micah, but I know that I can't trust him. I don't know him at all.

Then I heard the door open and looked over quickly and saw Micah. He noticed me right away and flashed a smile, walking over to me. "Hey, beautiful," he said as he stood in front of me. I looked at him for a moment. "What is it?" he finally asked after I said nothing.

I shook my head as if I didn't know what he was talking about. I didn't even notice that Ashton has gone to the backroom when the door opened and Micah entered. "Nothing," I said as I walked around the counter.

I began kissing him. I don't want him to think that I know yet for some reason. I pulled away from Micah. "You ready?" he asked me as he held on to me still as he caught his breathe.

"Yeah, just give me a minute," I said back to him as he let go of me, and I went into the back.

"See you tomorrow, Ashton," I said as I turned and smiled at him and went back out. "Okay," I said to Micah as we walked out together.

Once we were in the car, he started it and then put his hands on the wheel, ready to drive away. I then noticed his knuckles better, all red and black and busted. I didn't say anything though. I'm afraid. I feel protected though. He was only protecting me, and he cares about me. I know that he meant nothing by it than to protect me.

He drove me home to know I would arrive safely. When he stopped his car in front of my house, he paused and looked over at me. "You wanna go somewhere tonight?" he asked.

I looked over at him. "Where?"

"My friend, Tyler. He's having a party."

I still kept my eyes locked on him—his features. "What time?" He smiled, knowing I was meaning yes by that question.

"Starts at nine thirty," he told me, grinning.

"Okay." I nodded.

"Okay, I'll pick you up in a little bit."

I went up to my room, and about a half hour later and an hour before the event started, Micah texted me to wear a dress. I texted him back, saying, "No, I know what you're doing." He texted me back, saying, "You know me so well." I stopped texting him after that and got ready. I put on a lightweight knit sweater with my hair fixed in loose curls and a sparkly skirt, but I put on a pair of spandex under my skirt. I don't trust Micah with me wearing a skirt. I know not to.

I walked downstairs before my mom was leaving and told her that I was leaving anyway. Then I heard a knock at the door as I was downstairs with my mom. My mom went and answered the door. Before I realized it, I left my phone upstairs in my room. It was Micah. I was standing in the kitchen with my arms on the counter as my mom yelled out that Micah was here. I went upstairs quickly and grabbed my phone and came back down and found my mom talking to him down there. I rushed over to him and started shoving him out of the door with me.

We went to his car where he opened the door for me, and I got in. "You look fucking hot," he said as he lit a cigarette and skimmed his eyes up and down me.

I glanced at him shyly. He looked down at my skirt and then looked away as if he were proud of me. I just looked up at him, not knowing what he may be thinking of. Yes, I do.

When he stopped his car like thirty minutes later, we were parked by a lot of other cars. The house was huge in my opinion. The music thumping was so loud. If the house wasn't out in the middle of nowhere, the cops would have already shut it down. I'm scared. Micah's most likely going to be the only one here that I know. He looked over at me and flashed his dimples. I don't know what he is trying to do. I really don't. My mind is blank, and I am extremely nervous. "Micah?" I asked.

He took his keys out and opened his door, coming over to my side after stepping on his cigarette. I felt thankful that he didn't try anything, although I feel that he wanted to but resisted. I know what he was thinking completely now. He opened my door as I turned and got out.

Micah instantly noticed my discomfort once we were both standing beside his car, my door now closed. "You all right?" He set his hand softly on me.

I looked over at the house and then back at Micah with my eyebrows slightly raised. "I just . . . I'm not going to know anybody."

He grinned. He tilted his head, thinking about it. "You came with me. Just hang out with me the whole time. You're safe, Kendall. You don't have to be scared. No one will hurt you," He reassured me, as I kept looking over at the mansion, seeing through some of the opened windows as people danced like crazy. I don't want to be out here. I don't fully trust Micah. Will he really protect me?

"Just don't leave me by myself please." I looked up at him, shaking a little as my heart was pounding quickly in my chest.

He shook his head. "Kendall, just relax. Why are you so nervous? I won't leave you." I'm not going to straight out tell him why I am. How would he react? Would he drag me into the woods? The whole home was surrounded with them. "You all right now?" he asked after a minute of just standing there.

I nodded silently as I looked back up at him. We started walking toward the back of the house where it was all surrounded by a tall wooden fence. We approached the gate. I stared right up against Micah's side the whole walk.

"So Tyler, how—I mean—is he like your age?" I asked, messing with my fingers.

"He's twenty-three."

"He lives alone?"

"Well, his parents left him the house a few years ago when they passed." I looked up at Micah sadly. "It's okay, Ken." He draped his arm over my shoulder as I leaned in closer to his side. Micah opened the latch and the gate was opened. My eyes widened as I took Micah's hand into mine quickly. There was an inground pool that people were leaping into. Beer and other alcoholic drinks were being passed around and chugged. There were people making out against the fence, in the pool, and even on the lawn chairs. I wouldn't be surprised if they didn't even know each other. They looked so wasted. Micah was instantly greeted by a man, slapping hands with him, smiling to one another.

"Tyler," Micah greeted back, smiling at him.

"I wasn't sure if you were coming," he said curiously to Micah, looking only at him. He didn't even look at me at all yet. This was very uncomfortable now. "Brian was saying something—" then he broke himself off and looked down at me. "I'm sorry. I'm Tyler. You must be Kendall?" he asked.

"Yeah, hi," I said to him, smiling.

"It's very nice to finally meet you," he said back. I just smiled. He acted like I was hanging out with Micah for over a few months the way that he was saying it. "I've heard a few things about you." He looked up at Micah as he was already glaring at him. I couldn't help but smile back at Tyler though.

I just smiled up at him shyly. I don't know how to act around so many older people than me in their twenties, probably. Not everyone looks that old though. Some are teenagers. I am only eighteen and just graduated. It feels strange. I feel so much younger, too young to be here, as everyone just walked around, talking to others and meeting new ones as they drank from their red plastic cups.

Micah and Tyler talked for a little bit, laughing and then getting a little serious about a topic, which I found funny and laughed at them both. It made Micah blush, and his dimples indented his cheeks, and then he would just squeeze me closer to his body.

"Okay, well, I'm gonna find someone for the night," Tyler said, bringing his cup to his lips as he sipped from it, checking everyone around him out closely and patted Micah's shoulder. "Nice meeting you, Kendall." He smiled before walking away.

"You wanna get a drink?" He looked down at me as we walked around.

"Okay."

Micah held my hand tightly as we slid past the intoxicated people. The house was just the same as outside minus the pool. People were everywhere. They were all just the same though—dancing, drinking, kissing, a few falling over, and arguing. I looked over at the living area where people were all sitting together. Once I got the chance to actually study them, I realized what they were smoking, as the smell of marijuana came to me. I looked away quickly. I noticed Micah glancing over at them a few times, but when he noticed I was avoiding the whole area, he quickly looked away.

"Is these the kind of parties you always come to?" I peered up at Micah as he walked us into the kitchen.

He shrugged as we got there. "Sometimes. It's been a while though." He smiled.

I bit the inside of my cheek as I looked at who was in the kitchen area: a girl against the counter while a guy groped her thighs and stuck his tongue down her throat. It disgusted me. This entire environment sickened me. It's a complete contrast to our last date at the fair.

"Micah!" We both looked over to see Shailene, rushing over with opened arms, taking him into a quick hug and then me. "It's nice to see you again." She smiled down at me.

"You too."

I looked back over at Micah as he got himself a drink. "Do you drink, Kendall?" Shailene caught my attention back to her.

"Oh um, I have. Never a lot though," I admitted shyly.

"You've never been drunk?" She smiled down at me. I shook my head.

"I don't plan to tonight either." I clarified to her. I watched her as she got me a red cup and poured some liquid into it until it was almost full but not too much.

"Here, try this." She smiled while handing it to me.

When I looked back over at Micah, I saw that he was talking to a few guys. Micah soon waved them off once he noticed my thumb rubbing over the back of his hand as our fingers were laced tightly together. "You drink?" He looked at my cup as I sipped it, and it rushed down my throat, burning a little as I completely swallowed without spitting it back out everywhere like the first time I've ever drank—this is only the second.

I shrugged a shoulder as I still had the cup lifted to my mouth. "A couple of times," I answered after swallowing the drink.

A few girls came over and took Shailene away to talk to some guy who was asking about her, and they were all excited. Micah wished her luck, and she laughed back while saying her good-byes to us both.

Micah and I were just walking around a while until he grabbed a hold of my hips while crossing through where everyone was dancing. "Do you dance?" He smirked.

I laughed awkwardly as I looked away shyly. "I don't do much of it." I laughed uncomfortably as I took another drink from my cup. The night was going surprisingly well. I ignored myself every time. I was about to bring up that I want to go home and not be around everyone smoking pot and getting wasted and probably laid upstairs. It's not my kind of party to go to. Apparently, this is the guy Micah is.

We both started walking back outside after we only danced for a few minutes. It was actually nice. I wasn't scared to dance with him after a good minute, and we had some fun with it, keeping close to one another while a few songs from Lucas Fischer played from the speakers. "We'll leave in a little bit," he said in my ear. That trust dropped a little when we passed more people doing weed, and I kept my attention on Micah as he looked over at them as if he were dying to go over there like I was holding him back, which, strangely enough, it felt like I actually was. I am.

I nodded. "I don't care when we leave. I'm fine," I reassured him as he took another drink from his beer bottle. I was worried that he'd get drunk, and we'd be stuck here, and he must have known by the look I gave him when he started drinking his beer. The cup he got earlier was only barely filled with some vodka. I guess he has a strong tolerance or whatever because he doesn't seem fazed at all by what he's had to drink so far.

"I won't drink anymore. I know you wouldn't want to stay here, Kendall." I smiled up at him and rolled my eyes playfully back, which caused him to chuckle a little.

Just when Micah and I got outside, a loud voice caught both of our attention. "Micah!" We both spotted a woman with long legs with a pair of jean shorts and a shirt showing lots of cleavage, rushing over to him. Her hair shoulder length and brown. Her makeup a little too heavy, I'd say.

"Oh no," I heard him say under his breath. I don't think that he knows that I heard him though.

"Oh my god, I just can't believe that you're here. I haven't seen you in a while, Micah," she said to him as she came intensely close on him, setting her hand on his shoulder tightly.

"Hi, Carla," he spoke as if he didn't even care, but his eyes were in surprise as they were slightly widened by her appearance. He looked nervous, uncomfortable even.

But why? Who is she?

"Where have you been hiding?" She smiled largely, still holding on to his shoulder as she flirted with him. "Oh, who's this?" she asked, looking down at me.

"This is Kendall," he told her. She let go of his shoulder and went to an original standing position. She didn't like to take her eyes off him. I can tell that they've been together. He then put his right hand on my back smoothly. It relaxed me a little.

"Oh . . . are you two together?" she asked, wondering, trying to understand what exactly was going on with us.

Then Tyler's voice came by, and Micah immediately caught it as he called him over to meet some of his friends. "I . . . um—"

"Oh go. I'll look after her," she told him, not taking her eyes off him. Micah hesitated, not wanting to leave me alone with her. I didn't want to be left with her any more than he wanted me to. "Go," she insisted once more.

"I'll be just one minute," he said, looking at me, not making eye contact with her until he was almost completely turned around. She flashed her bright smile at him. He didn't smile at her at all, just gave her a plain expression as he walked away, leaving me with her. After he said he wouldn't leave me alone, he just did.

It seemed that as soon as Micah left us together, Carla dropped her act on being nice. "You know," she started, looking down at me. "You really shouldn't waste your time on someone like that. You're not his type," she said, looking at me in disgust.

I had nothing to say. My mind was blank. Then it just came out. "Excuse me?" I said to her as if she were crazy, which she is. She has no right to be talking to me like that, really. I don't care how much she and Micah are or were good "friends" in the past. He's with me because he wouldn't leave me alone. I really had no choice but to start going out with him.

"Well then, you obviously don't know him as well as I do. You must have never seen him hit someone," she said mockingly to me, fake smiling.

"Yes, I have."

"And you're still here?" she asked meanly to me. "Thought that would have scared someone like you off . . .," she stated. "Despite his anger issues, though, Micah's the best that I've ever had in bed. He likes it rough." She stopped for a second, and I glanced up at her. "The things he can do with that tongue," she spoke low. "Have fun with him because once he gets into your pants, he's gone. But that's just Micah. Don't take it personal, kid."

I looked over at her as I noticed Micah glancing over at me to see what was going on with us as I looked at her. Is that really how he used women? Did he create this bitch in front of me, or was she just always like this naturally? I knew that he knew her like that, but I didn't want to hear about it. I don't want to hear it from her, trying to rub it in my face. She continued to talk about him like that as I was sort of forced to listen. I shook my head in disgust toward her. It was quite clear that she only knew him on that level. She doesn't know him.

She just looked down at me one more time, realizing that I was listening but pretending not to, and she just walked away. After about a minute, I started to walk around the house, looking for Micah as he disappeared, meeting everyone that Tyler took him to. My ears were then filled with a familiar voice, echoing in a giggle now. It was her. I knew it was her by her tone in her voice, leading to a giggle. I saw Micah's back as he faced her. Then, when she knew that I was watching, she leaned in very close right up against him as she kissed him, holding his body tightly to hers. My eyes filled up. I wanted to just scream then and there. This is what she wanted though. But Micah isn't even mine. He isn't mine to be jealous about. So why do I feel like this?

I just stood there for a second as I turned around angrily and confusedly and began to walk back, shoving past everyone that surrounded the place. I want to go home now. Right now. I walked down the stairs and out of the door, wiping my eyes as tears began to fall out, but I kept them under control as I stopped. I should have expected this. I should have never even thought of ever going anywhere with Micah.

As I was walking, I heard someone running from up behind me. I began to walk faster through the crowd. "Kendall!" the voice yelled out to me. I began to walk even faster and faster. Soon, I was running away from him, away from Micah. I don't want to see him, let alone have to talk to him as he made something up. "Kendall, stop!" he shouted again, running after me quickly. I ran away from him though. I mean, would you stop if you were in my position?

I opened the gate quickly and just ran. I feel sort of broken, actually. I was going to give him a chance, and he goes and kisses someone, who is, in my opinion, a complete slut and bitch. I care about Micah. I do. I started trusting him a little while we were dancing. He shoved a drunk guy off me that grabbed my body, trying to dance behind me. He protected me. It was nice then; it hurts now. He was just acting.

I didn't even care that I was running into the woods. My shoes getting a little muddy as well as my feet. I just kept going. I want to get away from him, from all of them. I'm so mad and furious at him and myself. I set myself up for this. You can't trust someone like Micah. I was suddenly pulled to a halt as my heart felt like it stopped in my chest as a pair of strong arms held me to a tree.

"Are you fucking crazy?!" Micah yelled at me as he held me against the bark. "You could have gotten yourself killed!" he added loudly to me.

"Get off me!" I yelled back at him, trying to break free of his grip. Micah didn't care what I said to him or how I said it then. He was angry at me. He didn't loosen his grip at all on my arms. "Stop it!" I tried to yell it loudly to get him off me, but that didn't happen. I began sobbing as I said it loudly. It was quiet now. I looked down between us as tears fell from my eyes. He looked upset, but with me.

"Kendall," he said softly to me. He let go of one of my arms, then grabbing on to my face lightly and pulling it up so that I was forced to look into his eyes as he looked into mine. "She kissed me," he said to me as I looked at him. But I didn't believe him. "Kendall," he pleaded, sounding sad. "Kendall, you have to believe me," he whispered vulnerably.

I nodded. "I do," I said quietly to him as he let go of me a little but still holding me there in place. Why did I just say that? And why do I actually feel like I do believe him? I don't want to. I don't want to get myself set up again for something that is sure to backfire. He isn't my type of crowd to hang out with, to even date. But I'm selfish enough to try and pull him away from it all. I want him.

He then leaned in and kissed me lightly on my lips, pausing centimeters away from mine as if to ask for permission.

"I'm yours," he said, looking in my eyes. "If you'll have me, I'm yours," he said it again more sincerely.

I like him, and I want him to be mine and only mine officially.

"I know I'm a jerk. But there's something about you that I always need."

I stared at the ground, and he brought his hand under my chin and tilted my head upward so I was now looking right at him.

"Be my girlfriend," he said looking right at me.

I wasn't expecting that. I didn't answer. I was speechless.

"Come on," he said in the silence. "I want you."

He's acting like a different person right now. Completely. He's being honest, I think, and I can't help but be reminded how much I actually like this man and how much I actually care for him.

I stared up into his eyes. Do I want this? Really? His green eyes stared into mine as if he was searching, and his patience was killing him. What's he looking at me with? Pain? Fear? What's he scared of? I can't just say no. I like him. I want him. "Yes," I whispered. He smiled at me, showing his dimples and then letting go of me. I felt off. I feel like I am his first girlfriend. I know that's not true, maybe the first one in a long time.

He leaned in and kissed me again and again. It was heated and full of need. He took my hand as we walked back to his car, and we got inside. "Just to let you know, I have no idea how this works," he admitted shyly as he started the engine. I glanced at him, wanting to see his face of him being shy for once. While he was driving, my phone buzzed from my bag, so I took it out.

"What is it?" he asked as he glanced over at me as I stared at my phone screen.

"Oh, just my mom," I told him, looking up at him.

"Everything good?"

"Yeah, she just . . . She's in Georgia and won't be home for a few days."

When we got to where I started to recognize things better outside, I noticed that he wasn't going the original way to my house. I didn't recognize anything anymore after a minute.

Where are we going? Where is he taking me?

I didn't say anything. Although I was now considered as Micah's girlfriend and he my boyfriend, I was still nervous around him and scared to ask questions to him about where we are going. After about two more minutes, he pulled his car into a driveway that seemed just random. He then got out of his vehicle and came over to my side and opened my door calmly. "Where are we?" I asked curiously, looking up at him. It was a house, nice looking and clean from the outside. It was surrounded by other houses but not really close together. It's night, so I can't really see everything around.

"My house," he answered to me as I got out of the car and looked at it.

This is his house?

"Why are we at your house?" I asked, looking up at him as we walked up his sidewalk from the driveway to the front door.

"I don't want you to be alone tonight," he told me as he put his hand in his pocket and pulled out a little silver key and slid it into the lock as it clicked open, and he opened the door. The lights were all off. I'm not comfortable being here. I don't want to be here. I know that he knows that I'm nervous too by my actions. I stood in the doorway as he walked in and then realized I wasn't behind him and looked back, finding me still standing where he entered. "You can come in, you know." He laughed. I looked around until I finally entered. I don't trust him yet. I don't want to walk into the darkness with Micah.

I stepped in as he looked back at me still. I could see his body and face well enough, but it's very dark inside his house without any of the lights on. He was smiling back at me and laughing a little bit.

"Just one second," he said to me as he turned and lifted his hand on the wall, flicking the switch up as a light turned on and lit up the hallway. The kitchen was straight ahead, and I saw a door a little further down, but it was closed, and another opening with no door, only a few feet away on the opposite side of the closed door.

"Come on," he said as he turned to face me again. I began to walk closer to him as he walked over to the closed door, opening it and entering. I peeked in before I stepped in carefully and quietly as if I would wake someone. He turned on the light in there then.

It was his bedroom, as the first thing I saw was a large bed in the middle of the room and a door off to the side of which was closed and a dresser on the side where there was a window. He walked over to it, opening one of the drawers and pulling out two T-shirts and then going to another and grabbing a pair of sweatpants and a pair of boxers. He walked over to me as I stood in his doorway.

"Do you live alone?" I asked, wanting to know if anyone was around.

He smiled at me. "Yeah, it's just me," he answered as he walked closer to me. "Here, you can change in here," he said as he handed me one of the T-shirts and the pair of boxers. I grinned up at him shyly.

He walked out, closing the door behind him. I quickly stripped down out of my clothing and set them down in a pile and slid up the boxers and put on his shirt. It was long on me and hung down to the end of the dark boxers that I had to roll over more than once. Then a minute later, the door opened. He looked at me and smiled as he wore the clothes that he picked out for himself.

I smiled at him shyly. He then leaned in to me, kissing me softly as I did it back to him, although I was unprepared for it. He held his hands on my face as I kept my palms down on his chest, keeping him from being pressed against my body. He sighed in defeat as I came to the realization that this is now my boyfriend, but that doesn't mean that I'm going to jump into bed with him after we had just said we are together.

"You can sleep in here," he whispered in my ear.

I looked up at him nervously before I spoke back to him. "No, I-I can sleep on your couch," I told him. I don't want to sleep in his bed whether he was there with me or not.

"No."

"Micah, really, it's fine. I can sleep on the couch. I don't mind."

"Kendall," he said as he began to walk me to his bed behind me.

"Micah, please," I said to him, laughing as I fought against him to get out of his bedroom to the living room. He seems mad.

I got free from him, knowing that he wasn't using all of his strength against me though. "Kendall, it's okay. I'd never hurt you," he said softly to me as I looked up at him.

"I can sleep on the couch."

"Okay, okay," he groaned. "Fine, whatever."

We walked out of his room and out into the hallway as he grabbed an extra blanket for me and one of his pillows on his bed, and we walked into the room with no door that I noticed to now be his living room. "Kendall," he pleaded for me to just sleep in the bed.

"Micah, it's fine. I wouldn't be comfortable," I reassured him. Just because I am now his girlfriend doesn't mean that I am willing to sleep in his bed with him. It's too uncomfortable for me now.

"Okay," he said as he set up the blanket and pillow, making a bed on his couch for me to sleep on. I sat down on his comfy couch on to the blanket as it flowed to the side, to the top, and down over the couch. "You sure?" He was confused at my insistence.

"Yeah, Micah, really."

"Okay," he said as he sauntered out of the room and back into his bedroom, making sure to leave the door wide open and look back at me, still smiling in my direction. I smiled at his willingness to not let me sleep on the couch. I love how he acts, really. I saw a picture on the table beside the couch. I hoisted myself up to get a better look at it. It was of Micah and a lady. They both sort of resembled each other, but I'm not sure. But Micah looked so much younger and different. His hair is different. It was a different color, and it wasn't blond but brown. And he wasn't as built as he is now. It's weird to look back at him.

Why did he dye his hair though? Who is she?

I lay down on his couch and got comfortable, pulling the blanket down on top of my body. I then set my head down lightly and closed my eyes and eventually fell asleep.

***

I woke up but didn't yet open my eyes. I don't want to. I felt different as I noticed how much larger his couch seemed from last night. My sensations then came back to me as I didn't notice before an arm on top of me. My eyes then shot open widely and quickly. I saw the familiar sight of the dresser in front of me and the window. I was in Micah's bedroom—in Micah's bed. My nerves took control of my mind as I lie frozen in the same spot as I felt a strong arm and a body up against me, Micah's.

How did I get in his room?

I then closed my eyes quickly as I felt Micah stir behind me. It was uncomfortable to have him behind me against my body. I felt, though, that I still had clothes on, so I was relieved by that much, but still, what is going on? How have I gotten in his bed?

He then lifted his arm and scooted back as I felt him get off the bed. I still lay frozen though. I'm scared to move. I then heard his laugh ring through my ears suddenly.

"I know that you're up, Kendall." He laughed at me.

How does he know that? He can't? How would he?

"Kendall?" he asked curiously. I began to move, realizing that he did already know that I was awake. But I have it in my mind that the only reason that he could have known that is by being awake already for a while.

"What?" I asked him tiredly as I still lay in the same position.

"What are you doing?" he asked curiously, knowing that I have been awake the entire time, a bit of laughter in his voice.

"How did I get in here?" I asked suddenly.

"I carried you in last night while you were asleep."

"But why?"

"Kendall, you're mine. It's all right to sleep in my bed."

I didn't know how to respond to him as I sat up and looked over to where his voice was coming from. The door was now opening as I looked over to see him standing in the bathroom, brushing his teeth. Then I realized that he was wearing nothing but his boxers. I sat up on his bed as the duvet cover was still on me. I looked around his room as he entered again, seeing me fully awake now.

"Good morning, beautiful." He smiled at me as he walked by.

I smiled at his comment. "Morning," I said, still a little tired. "Oh my god, what time is it?"

"Whoa, calm down," he said, laughing at my reaction. He grabbed his phone off the nightstand to check for me. "It's ten thirty."

"What!"

His face was twisted with amusement as he smirked and bit his lip, trying to hide it.

"What is it?" he asked, sitting down on the end of his bed in front of me.

"I have to be at work at eleven."

"Okay, I'll take you home then. Just relax."

He then went over to his drawers, pulling out a pair of jeans and a shirt for himself as he got dressed right there, not caring if I was around or not. He was muscular. The size of his body kept my eyes in shock as I watched him. I took my gaze off him as he glanced back at me and smirked. I got up off the bed and walked over to my clothes.

I took them in my hand and went into his bathroom quickly to get dressed.

"You know I don't mind if you change in here!" Micah shouted over through the door so that I could hear him.

I have to admit that I blushed at his words to me. Of course he didn't. I have a feeling that Micah isn't shy about anything. I came out dressed in my previous outfit from last night.

"Where do I put these?" I asked, holding his clothes that he let me sleep in comfortably.

"You can just set them on the bed. I don't care," he answered, looking over at me, smiling. I set them carefully down on his side of the bed that he slept on. "Okay," he said as he was fully dressed now with me. "You good?" he asked me then.

"Yeah," I said, smiling up at him as he came over and stood, towering over me. He leaned down and kissed me lightly then. I didn't even get to brush my teeth, but he didn't say anything. He knows that I didn't have anything to brush my teeth with anyway that morning.

"Where's my phone?" I asked as we were ready to leave, remembering about it.

"Oh, it was still in the living room," he answered as he rushed away from me at the front door to grab it for me.

He came back in a second, handing it to me. He opened the door for me as he grabbed on to my hand and led me to the passenger's door and opened it as I stepped up inside. He then rushed over to his side and got in; thus, starting it. He then backed out of his driveway and onto the road. As he drove, I didn't say much. "Thanks for letting me stay," I thanked him, although I don't mind staying at home by myself.

He glanced over at me, his hair still in a bit of a mess, but he didn't look bad at all. I can't see him looking bad. He doesn't even have to try to look good. I don't even think that he can look bad. He's too perfect looking. He grinned at my words to him. "You don't have to thank me, Kendall." He chuckled. "You're my girlfriend. You can stay anytime," he added.

I smiled at his word to me: girlfriend. He is mine, and I am his. "Micah?" I asked then.

"What is it?" he asked back at me, curious to what I may ask.

"Who is it in the photo with you in your living room?" I asked, wondering.

He looked over at me for a long second before setting his eyes back on the road. He didn't answer for at least a minute and then his jaw tensed up. "My . . . my sister," he answered slowly to me.

I just looked at him.

"She's beautiful," I commented on her. He smiled, not showing his teeth, only dimples.

"Why aren't you in touch with her?" I asked curiously.

He didn't answer for a few seconds, just looked a bit nervous to answer me. "Uh well, I left home when I was eighteen, Kendall. I never went back to them," he said softly to me.

"Can I ask why?" I asked him cautiously. He smiled gently at me.

He sort of laughed out of his nerves. "Let's just say my father was an alcoholic, and when he left, she got a boyfriend just like him, and I saw him hit her, so I almost killed him. That night, I left and haven't seen or talked to them in about five or so years," he told me.

I didn't know what to say. I stayed quiet for a moment, thinking about Micah's past. He wasn't always like this. He was made into this. "I didn't . . . Micah, I'm sorry . . .," I whispered as I got a little closer to him.

"No, it's okay, Kendall. I just didn't understand why she would pick a guy that was the same as my dad." He shrugged and clenched his jaw and took a few deep breaths. What have I done? I probably just ruined his entire day by bringing up something so personal that I really shouldn't have just asked him. "I just don't see how a man can hit a woman and continue living his life." His voice was barely audible. "I'd never hurt you, Kendall," he added softly. I grinned at him, my eyes glossing over. I didn't fear his aggression anymore like I used to. I understand it now. He is only trying to protect me. "Don't pity me," he snapped.

"I'm . . . I just . . . Nobody should have to go through that." We both stayed silent as I leaned my head against his shoulder.

We then arrived in front of my house. I realized now in the light of the morning that his house really isn't far away from mine, just about walkable, making it closer to my work. He got out and opened the door for me as I got out, holding on to my phone and walking up to my door with him behind me as I got the hidden key and unlocked it. I walked in as he followed me.

"I'll be ready in fifteen minutes," I told him as I rushed upstairs to my bathroom to get a quick shower and get ready for work. It was ten forty now. I got my shower and then walked into my bedroom and grabbed my outfit that was laid out. I realized that Micah was standing in front of my drawer dresser opened in front of him as he picked up a pair of my underwear.

"Is this like what you always have on?" He looked down to what he was holding and examined them closely. Oh god. I want . . . I don't know what I want right now. This is all so weird right now. "'Cause damn."

"Micah!" I squeaked.

I felt embarrassed as I went back into my bathroom to get dressed quickly. I came back out after blow drying my hair and applying some light makeup and feeling uncomfortable at what I had just caught him doing. "Okay," I said to him as he turned to look at me from my bed.

"You ready?" he asked. I nodded. "That was fast," he added, getting up off my bed and walking over to me as we went back downstairs and out of my front door.

We went back to his car as we both got inside, strapping in. I began to trust Micah a little. He drove me to work quickly but safely. I was five minutes late. He got out and opened my door for me in front of the shop. He leaned in and began kissing me sort of roughly, but I didn't resist him at all. He then pulled away as I was holding on to his waist as he held on to mine. "I gotta go to work too. I'll pick you up, okay," he told me as he smiled, and then he leaned in and kissed me once more before he got back in his car, and I walked inside, and he drove away.

I went and got my stuff from the back and came back out. Ashton wasn't there today. I still hadn't said anything to Micah about him either. Brandy then came into sight. "Where's Ashton?" I asked her.

"Oh, he quit this morning," she told me.

"What? But why?" I asked back.

"I don't know. He didn't say," she responded back.

I looked at her, confused about Ashton's sudden quitting his job. Was it because of Micah? Did Micah scare him that much? Micah has that effect of scaring people with his actions like he did to me before. I can't imagine how hard he must punch, and I assume the way that he hit Ashton was taking it easy.

"We have somebody starting today though. His name's Ben," she then said as she walked away, getting back to work as I did the same.

About an hour later, the door opened, and a man with dark hair and light skin walked in. He came straight to where I was. "Hey, I'm Ben. I'm supposed to be starting today."

"What makes you think that I work here?" I asked, messing with him as he stared at me.

"You have a name tag, and it says that you do." He laughed. I smiled back at him.

I showed Ben what to do until the day was done with, and we were closing up, and we walked out together, talking. I stumbled out of the door, and he brought me back to my balance. "Why don't you show me around sometime? I mean, since I'm new here and all?" he asked, smiling at me.

"Uh yeah, sure, why not," I answered, not knowing what else to say. Ben then handed me his phone as I put my number in.

He smiled back at me.

I began to walk to where I saw Micah parked across the street. I got into his vehicle. "Who's that?" he asked.

"Well, hello to you too," I greeted, playing around with him as I leaned in and kissed him on the cheek with my one hand on his neck and the other running through his thick dyed hair.

"Who is that?" he asked more angrily to me, being completely serious and not playing around. I then looked across the street to see Ben still standing there like he was waiting for someone to pick him up, I think.

"Oh, that's Ben. He just started today," I answered him, trying to cheer him up.

"Why the hell did he hand you his phone?" he asked, staring Ben down from his window, not even looking over at me.

"He wants me to show him around. He just moved here. I gave him my number, Micah," I told him, defending myself once more.

He paused for a moment and then turned to me. "You're not showing him around, and I'm sure that's all that he wants to do with you," he sarcastically responds back to me.

"Micah!"

"Well, did you tell him that you have a boyfriend?" he asked, still filled with anger. "Did you?"

"No, it didn't come up. But it's not like I would ever . . ." I stopped. "I shouldn't even have to say that to you."

I wouldn't ever dream of cheating on Micah. I've never been in a relationship as good as this one, really, and I wouldn't do anything to mess it up.

"Well, I'll be back in a minute," he said as he took his keys out.

"Where are you going?" I asked worriedly.

"To have a talk with this Ben," he answered as he got out and locked me inside.

"Micah!" I shouted to him. He looked back at me just to check and then looked back to Ben as he approached him. I could only watch, not knowing what Micah might do to him. He was only gone for a minute, leaving Ben to look a little confused and frightened at the same time as he stayed where he was before.

Micah came back, unlocking the door. I just sat there, though, as he climbed back in as if nothing had just happened. "What did you say to him?" I asked in a scared and shaky tone.

"I told him to not fucking ever touch you, and that you aren't going to be able to show him around," he answered me. He then turned and leaned in and began kissing me. He started at my mouth, moving down to where my neck met my head. I whimpered at his harsh movements on me. I know what he is doing too. I don't like it, but I'm not fighting back at him.

"Micah . . .," I said softly, catching my breath, begging him to stop.

He calmed down a bit and then eventually pulled away. He went back to his chair. I lifted my hand lightly over to where he was kissing hardly to only feel a harsh sensation there.

I felt disgusted with his intense actions on me as I noticed Ben was no longer watching us, and it helped relieve me, only a little.

Chapter 10

I helped Ben around the shop so that he could get the hang of it all. It's not hard at all though. He is sweet and nice to me, but I stay clear from flirting at all with him. We talked all day even with my restrictions with him. "Hey, Kendall, we can close up early today," Brandy said, walking past me to the back.

"Oh okay," I responded back to her. We only had a few customers today, so it's understandable. I went to the back and grabbed my bag. Ben then came back.

"So your boyfriend's really assertive," he said, smiling at me.

I didn't know what to say to him for him to fully understand why he is like that. "No, he . . . he's just a little protective."

He widened his eyes a little to my response. "A little protective? You can't believe that?" he said, trying to convince me of Micah.

"You don't know him, Ben."

"Okay, okay, fair enough. He doesn't hurt you though?"

I looked at him in disbelief for him to ever think of that about Micah. "No!" I said loudly to him. "He would never hurt me like that, Ben. He has his reasons for his protectiveness with me," I spat back to him.

He nodded to me. "Okay," he softly said in response. "Is he picking you up then?"

"Uh no. I'm just going to walk. I think he's at work, and I don't want to make him worry. I'll be fine."

"Okay, see you later," he said as I walked out of the front door. I turned and waved back at him, but I felt his eyes still on me as I left. I pulled my phone out of my bag, just in case of anything, I would have it handy.

I walked and walked down the sidewalks until I came upon a familiar sight. I looked at it really confused. It has to be Micah's car. It's identical, and I recognize half of the license plate as well. I stopped and just looked at it for a second.

Is it his car?

I then looked up to see where it was parked at. A gym of some sort. I do remember him saying that he works at a gym. I then began walking across the street to the gym. I looked inside, pausing at the window and then opening the heavy glass door, struggling but opening it. I stepped inside and looked around for a few seconds.

"Can I help you, miss?" a man's voice asked as he neared me.

I looked up at a tall man who was well built, standing beside me, looking down. I fixed my bag on my shoulder before answering him. "Uh yeah, i-is Micah here?" I asked him.

He looked at me a little confused. "Harlan?" he asked, a little confusion coming on his face. I nodded to his question. "Uh yeah, he is actually. He's right—he's back this way," he told me as he looked very confused at my questions about Micah. He then began to lead me to the very back and down a little hallway to the right of the building. The smell was awkward but bearable. I understand, though, because it's a gym. Many of their eyes came to me, making me feel awkward for being here. "He's right back there," he said, pointing in the back corner of the room.

"Okay, thank you." I smiled, expecting him to walk away, but he didn't. I guess he is still flustered about my interest in him. I saw Micah in the corner on a large mat with another man. Micah's hands were covered with a pair of boxing punch mitts.

"Again!" Micah yelled to the other man as he punched it, not even affecting Micah's stance. I walked over, still keeping my eyes on them as I swept my straightened hair back behind my ears. I walked over to a table and sat down on it as I continued watching them. The man then stopped with his attention on Micah and turned to me. I laughed as Micah hit him, getting his attention back at him. "Don't take your eyes off your opponent," he told him firmly.

"Even not to look at her?" I heard him as he asked Micah, laughing.

Micah turned around confused, not seeing what he was talking about, and then he looked over at me, staring at him smiling. He smiled over at me. Micah turned back to the guy and hit him lightly, messing around. "Let's take a break," I heard him tell his partner. The man laughed for a second before looking over at me and then walking away from Micah. Micah then looked at him, leaving, and began walking over to me.

When he reached, I smiled bigger at him, feeling the butterflies in my stomach. "Hi," I said.

"Hey," he said, worn out, as he took off the mitts and grabbed a water bottle that was on the floor and began to drink out of it. I kept my eyes on his face, which was glistening with sweat. He doesn't smell though. He then took the water bottle from his mouth and looked down at me. "How'd you know I was here?" he asked as he lifted the bottom of his shirt to wipe his forehead off. I felt, though, that he was making it more for my benefit rather than for him, as he glanced down at me looking at his toned abs and muscles and smirked. I looked up at his face as he dropped it back down.

"I was walking home, and I saw your car," I told him, focusing back on the topic as he smirked at me.

"Why were you walking home?" he asked, beginning to be more serious with me.

"I got off early," I said back to him offensively.

"Why wouldn't you just call me? I would have come and got you, Kendall." he asked, calming down a little.

"Okay, I'm sorry. I just figured you were at work and . . ." I stopped.

He then just looked into my eyes intently and stood directly in front of me as he set each of his large palms on both of my knees, spreading them as he stepped in between them. I looked around nervously and saw a few pairs of eyes watching.

Why are they staring at us?

He leaned in more and more until he was directly in between my legs, and his face right in my own until his forehead lightly touched mine. He then pushed me a little back, but I set my one hand back to help resist his movement while my other hand was lightly on his waist. He smiled at my actions to stay sitting up. He then chuckled before leaning his face in more as he placed a gentle kiss on my lips for few seconds. I smiled as he released me.

He had his hands on my hips now tightly as I held on to him. He then stepped back from me as he let go and walked back to his water bottle and picked it up, taking a few drinks. He was still sweaty. I watched him closely as he made every move beside me.

"So you're a personal trainer?" I asked.

"No," he answered.

"No?" I asked confused. Then what is he?

"I'm a boxing trainer." He corrected me. "Big difference." He tried to be serious.

"Uh-huh."

"Yeah, it helps me with my anger issues. Well, it's supposed to anyway." He smiled.

I smiled at him, holding in my laughter. "Why don't you just box?" I asked curiously.

"Well, apparently I hit above my weight class, and it would be dangerous for my opponent," he told me. I understood him too. I couldn't imagine how his opponent would look like after Micah was done with him.

I smiled weakly at him. "You wanna try?" he asked.

I was caught off guard by his question. "Oh, I-"

He interrupted me. "Come on," he said, picking me off the table without any trouble. I smiled at him doing so. He then quickly grabbed on to my hand before grabbing a pair of gloves for me. They were light blue and small enough for my hands. He then dragged me over to the boxing ring that sat in the middle of the floor.

"Micah . . .," I pleaded. He just looked back and smiled at me, trying to break free of his grip as he got up to the ring and helped me up, lifting the ropes for me to go under and meet him up in the center. "I can't do this." I looked around at everyone around us.

"It's okay." He smiled as he picked up my left hand and began to lace the glove on it as he continued his actions to my right hand. "They can go fuck themselves. Don't worry about 'em." He glanced up at me, then continued lacing the gloves. "Okay," he said under his breath as he finished lacing both of them. "You ever did anything like this before?" he asked, looking into my eyes.

I shook my head. "Nope," I sort of said shyly back to him.

"Okay," he reassured me.

He began to show me different defense movements as he pretended like he would hit me but barely touched me with his fists. I then playfully hit his right side as he began to pretend that it hurt, holding his hand on the spot. Micah took me a little off guard as he leaned his head down to the side toward my ear, bending to my height with his knees. "You look incredibly sexy up here." I smiled and giggled at him and lightly hit him on the shoulder, having to lean up to reach. I jumped onto him, causing him to fall back. I fell with him, landing on top of him. He smiled.

"I'm sorry." I laughed. I began to get up, but he pulled me back down to him.

"Wait a minute," he said as he grabbed on to my wrists and began to unlace the gloves I had on. I bent down and kissed him. It was then that I remembered that we were in the middle of a gym, attracting many sets of eyes as I sat on top of Micah in the ring.

He got the gloves off me as he sprang up from his previous position. He took me up with him, taking me to my feet. He leaned down and kissed me one last time before we got out of the ring. I went and sat back down on the table as Micah grabbed his bag that was on the other side and approached me.

MICAH

Chapter 11

"I just gotta shower and change, Kendall," I told her as she sat back down on the table. I hoisted my duffel on my shoulder and began walking into the locker room, but then walking back over to her and leaning down slightly. "Unless you'd like to join me," I spoke softly. She found it amusing and started giggling and pushed me away toward the locker room. "All right, all right. Just a few minutes then." I looked back at her to see her watching me walking away and blushing.

I got a quick shower in the back and got dressed into my other pair of shorts and T-shirt. I grabbed my duffel and walked out, waiting to see her waiting for me. I walked out to the entrance of the room to see her facing away from the locker room. She was conversing with Josh, not looking my way like I'd been working myself up to seeing once I walked out.

My attention was taken back to Kendall as she brought her hand up to her mouth as she laughed. He didn't laugh, which told me that he was the one that said something that she found funny as he just smiled, watching her laugh. I broke their fun together as I dropped my bag down when I neared them, being an asshole.

"Micah," Kendall said in astonishment to my appearance. "I didn't even know you were there," she said, smiling up at me. Okay?

I looked down at her as her eyes sparkled at my sight. "Josh," I greeted him. He set his water down from getting a drink.

"Micah," he replied. She glanced back at him when he said my name.

"You ready?" she asked, directing her attention right to me only.

"Yeah, you?" I asked, being rude to Josh. He got what I was saying as he dropped his gaze away from Kendall and back to me.

She looked confused from my question. "I've been waiting for you?" she asked bewildered from my question.

I just looked at her, though, and then at Josh. She stepped off the table as Josh did the same. She stumbled as he quickly helped her to her feet immediately. I know that he was only being nice and wouldn't think about taking her away from me, but I can't stand to see any other guy with their hands on her. I grabbed on to her other arm. I saw in her facial expression that she was feeling weird with us both holding on to her arms.

"I've got her," I told him, tugging her close to me.

"Micah?" she asked, trying to figure out what I was doing. I ignored her.

Josh smiled. "See you later, Micah." He paused. "Kendall," he said as he turned and went into the locker room.

"You okay?" she asked as I held her to my side, and we walked out of the room as other workers began to clean up.

I looked down at her, pulling her a little closer. "Yeah." I lied. No, I'm not okay. I'm gonna freak out.

"You sure?" she asked, gripping my side as we walked down the hall. I wasn't being believable.

I didn't answer her as we walked outside. I held her close as I heard the door open behind us to see Josh exiting the building as well, his hair damp. He smiled at me and glanced at Kendall.

"See you tomorrow, man," he said loud enough for me to hear. I didn't say good-bye to him, and he got why I didn't. He turned and continued walking to his car and got in and drove away.

Kendall and I got to my car, but I stopped her from getting in the passenger's side, holding her to me closely and kissing her roughly. She whimpered under my touch to her hips. "Micah," she whispered, trying to get me to calm down.

"Do you like him?" I asked, keeping my eyes closed against her face.

"What? Like who?" she asked confused.

"Josh. Do you like him? Do you want him?" I began asking more about him in a whispered tone. "You want to screw him, don't you? Suck him off?" What the hell am I saying? I can't help it though. I can't think straight, only seeing her actions to him, smiling at him as she talked back to him, his hands on her.

"What? Micah, what are you talking about? You seriously think of me that way?" She stared at me, her gaze hard and disbelieving. "I'm not like the whores you've been with, if you haven't noticed," she spat. What's she talking about? What does she know about me? She has no idea what she's talking about.

"You have no idea what you're talking about. Don't call them that." I raised my voice. "When they're with me, they're with *me*." I stared down at her. I feel as if I'm scolding a child. I feel pathetic.

"Listen to yourself." *I am*, I thought. Then I remembered she can't read my mind. People don't speak the way they think though. That's what books are for. Writers are the brave ones that aren't scared to share their thoughts. I'm not going to be the one to say what I'm thinking. I never have been and can't imagine myself doing so.

"Listen to myself?" Think of something. Think of something to say. Where am I going to take this? "You're in there embarrassing me by hanging on one of my friends. You're mocking me in front of everyone in there. Those are people I have to see every day, Kendall. You can't be flaunting around here."

"Flaunting?" She scoffed. "Micah, we were talking." She paused. "Talking. We weren't flirting at all. I'm not like that. I'm your girlfriend. I wouldn't behave like that even if you weren't my boyfriend. I like you. You should know that. You should trust me." She stared up at me, her hand now on my chest.

"I only want you. It's only you, Micah," she told me sincerely. Her words took my eyes right back up to hers from her body. No one has ever said that I was their only one, never. I just stared into her blue eyes and grinned shyly. She gave me a chance, and I got her to like me more than any other girl I've ever been with. At first I thought of Kendall as just every other girl and was only hoping for a one-night stand after I got the one guy off her. "We were talking about you anyways. I asked him about you, Micah," she added sweetly, holding my hand in hers with her fingers curled around my fist.

I grinned at her with my breath fanning out. "Want to get ice cream?" I asked, trying to think of something more for us to do. What the hell is wrong with us? What the hell is wrong with me?

She smiled over at me as I started the vehicle. "Ice cream?" She smiled. We're too crazy to be together.

I nodded, grinning over at her. "Yeah." She smiled. I drove over to the place where I went before with Josh and Shailene. I drove to the boardwalk and parked. It's kind of dark but not really dark. The streets are lit up as well as the boardwalk by lights.

We both got out of the car and met in the front of it as I grabbed on to her hand. I held on to her hand as we walked up the steps onto the boardwalk. It's crowded tonight with people all around, but not so packed that there isn't much room. I could tell by the way that Kendall stayed up against my side and held on to my arm and hand that she was sort of proud to be with me, showing me off. It made me grin down at her in my head.

I led us over to a small shop with the counter opened and only a few people in line. I tugged us both over to wait in the line together. After we both got ours, we went and sat on the wall. As we both sat together in which Kendall sat right up against me, I looked around. I have a feeling that I was in this exact spot before. I grinned to myself, remembering what it was. This is the same spot that I met Bailey, Nora, and Lola. They sort of helped me out the first day. They're the reason I dyed my hair. I never told anyone that before though.

After we both finished, I took her small cup of finished ice cream to throw away for her, the trash can only being right in the middle of the walk. "I'll be right back," I informed her as I took it out of her hands. "Just stay right here."

"Okay." She smiled up at me, letting go of my other hand.

I went over and threw them away and just remembered my first time here and then looked back over at Kendall. She's talking to another guy like she knows who he is. I don't. I looked at them with my eyebrows creased and walked back over to her and picked her up to wrap my arms around her as she barely sat on the cement walling.

"Hi," the man said to me politely. He's a little weird though. He seems like it, that is.

I just nodded to him, not saying anything.

"This is Tate," Kendall informed me. "I went to school with him. Well, he's a senior this year."

"Oh hi," I told him, still holding on to Kendall to show him she's mine.

"You're Micah?"

"Yeah," I said to him nicely as Kendall seems only to be friends with him. I need to trust her. I need to try.

"Well, I-I gotta go. It was nice seeing you, Kendall, and meeting you, Micah," he said as he then nodded to us both.

"Oh okay, bye, Tate," Kendall said her good-bye as I just grinned at him, and he walked off and went down to the beach and walked toward the pier part.

I laughed silently to myself. "What?" Kendall smiled, looking up at me.

"Nothing." I laughed, holding on to her hand.

"Oh, come on."

"He's just a little . . . weird," I admitted, still sort of laughing.

She lightly shrugged one shoulder. "I don't remember him being like that," she said, glancing up to me.

"I'm sure," I joked with her.

She just looked up at me and then kissed me and smiled afterward.

"Come on," I said to her as I stood up, still holding on to her hand, helping her get up with me. She wrapped her hands around one of mine.

We got into my car as I drove back to my house. She didn't reject when I pulled up to my home. She just looked over at me a little surprised. She got out before I could help with the door, and we walked up to my front door, as it was already night time. I went in first, turning the light switch on in the hallway and looking back at her again who was still hesitantly standing in the doorway as if she felt unwelcome.

"Kendall." I smiled as I went back to her. She took a few steps until she bumped into my chest, hugging me. I didn't know why she was doing it so intensely. "What?" I asked, laughing in my voice.

"Nothing," she said as she dug her face into my chest. I hugged her back as she hummed in appreciation. I don't get what she's doing. Then it hit me. She is just happy, but why?

I guess to be with me, but I'm not sure. I don't really understand her. Why would she be happy to be with me? "Okay," I said, releasing her warmth from me. "Are you tired?" I asked, looking down into her blue eyes as they peered up at me.

"Kind of," she said softly in response.

I smiled at her. "Okay. Well, what do you want to do?" I asked. I can't imagine forcing myself on her like I would have already done with any other woman. But I can't do that with her. I can't see it. Not like I don't want to. She's too sweet and innocent. I can't even think about it, although I really like her. Why is this so different? Why does this feel so strange?

She looked nervous at my question and shy. She smiled as she looked down at my flooring. I laughed at the expression she expressed to my question. I know that we were both thinking the same thing. But I can't. I won't ruin her. It doesn't feel right. I held her in my arms again tightly. She hugged only lightly, and I found myself feeling disappointed.

"Come on," I said, releasing her and taking her hand instead and leading her to my bedroom. I felt her palm get a little sweaty and very warm. I'm not going to do what she is thinking though.

"Micah," she said quietly to me as she followed behind me.

I looked back at her, but I didn't answer. I let go of her hand.

"Do you want to change?" I asked her. Her eyes became filled with embarrassment and nervousness. I laughed. "That's not what I mean." Her face became just a little confused. I opened my drawer and pulled out a shirt and then the other drawer and grabbed a pair of boxers and held them up.

She smiled. "Yes, please," she said, walking over to me. I never did let any other woman wear my clothes except for Kendall. The other girls had no meaning to me but one, and it never lasted long, and they weren't always the cleanest, but I couldn't care less. They didn't seem to care to just walk around naked anyway, well, neither did I. They didn't want a relationship, and neither did I, and that was it. That was the way I liked and wanted it.

She took them gently out of my hand as I watched her walk over to my bathroom and closed the door behind her. I guess I get how she is uncomfortable to change in front of me, but I don't at the same time. Most girls were willing to do it in front of me. Kendall is different. I like her more than any other.

I took off my shirt and got into only my underwear. She came out with her hair in loose waves, looser than before from changing. She looked over at me after setting her clothes down on the floor in a neat, folded pile. She's too good for me. I can tell how nervous she always acts with me, not knowing how to act, and how badly she wants this to work. Why does she want this to work? Maybe it's me that wants this to work so badly . . . I don't always know how to act around her either, but I ignore it, whereas she just lets it all take over. I've been through enough where it's easy to ignore something and get comfortable faster than others.

I couldn't help but stare at her. Her innocence and purity dressed in my clothes partially already. I shouldn't be with her, this close to her with her right in front of me. I should stay away from her. I should kick her out. I can't stay away, though, now that I've had so much time to actually think about how beautiful she is standing there in my clothes.

Her eyes were on my chest. I just stared at her from across the room. "You just wanna go watch TV?" I broke the ice.

Her eyes peered around my bedroom. "You don't have one in here?" she asked curiously, her hands intertwined below where I'd imagine her belly button is, and she awkwardly looked about my bedroom.

I shook my head. "No." I laughed.

"But how can't you?" She laughed. "How do you fall asleep at night?" She giggled. "That's crazy." She looked at me and then down at her feet, obviously feeling out of place and drawing a blank for words.

"Uh . . ." I didn't know what to say, knowing that my answer would only make her more uncomfortable. I smiled at her. I then pulled out another drawer and grabbed a pair of gray sweatpants and took them up my legs. She looked a little relieved, as I now had pants on, letting out a quiet breath that I wasn't supposed to hear.

"Just relax." I grinned, which made her eyes meet mine, and her lips to be taken between her teeth. Dammit, how didn't I notice her lips before? "We're not doing anything you don't want to." With this, I earned a nervous smile that only tempted me to want to kiss her again. Looking over at her smile and her sweet, alluring, perfect-sized lips form that smile made me forget everything else that was happening, and I could only stare even more at her. I walked over to her and looked straight down at her as she tilted her head up.

"What are you doing?" She barely had the voice to speak. I shook my head, as I was lost for words or in thoughts of her.

"I could ask the same thing."

My hands pressed against her hips. The small curves she had felt so different from the other women I've laid my hands on. She's so small and virginal to everything as if this is all a first to her. I blinked to her as I leaned down closer to her face and very lightly pressed my lips to hers and was caught off guard when her hands touched my hips. Her lips molded against mine in a soft but then more serious kiss. I couldn't help myself when I took control of her and didn't wait for permission as I pushed my tongue between her soft lips and met hers. I barely opened my eyes to see hers squeezed closed. I can't do this with her. I don't just want sex from her. I don't even wish to see her naked right now because I feel like if I do see her that way, it will be like I would have tainted her completely and ruined her like all the other women I've seen naked. She doesn't deserve to be seen that way.

I pulled away from her as soon as she pushed against my chest for me to stop. Our breathing was heavy and loud as she stared at my chest, and I down at her. "Sorry." I kissed her forehead.

"Don't apologize. I wasn't ready is all . . ."

I nodded. It was quiet as she caught her breath and relaxed under my touch.

We sat on my couch, her lips molding mine still. My hands lightly touched her sides as she stayed still, only leaning up against my side to kiss me. "Kendall," I said softly to her, trying to figure out what she is thinking. She didn't stop, though, as she gripped me tighter. She began to readjust her hands as one of them went down on my cock a little roughly, and I moaned a little taken off guard but not unhappy with the motion. I was insistently hard under her touch. I stopped for a second as she did too, although the action just made me want more when she stopped. I felt if I tried anything, she would reject me.

She looked immediately embarrassed by her action. Obviously she didn't do it on purpose. She immediately moved her hand off me from there and looked up at me after saying sorry for her clumsiness. "It's fine." I laughed.

She kissed me again as I could tell that she wasn't really into watching TV anymore. I laughed again. My hands have been now wrapped around her waist as she sat on my side, too nervous to get any closer, I think. I'm leaning too because I am a few years older than her, and she knows that I am more experienced. I felt her stop as she felt my laughter. "What?" She smiled.

"Most girls wouldn't have apologized." I laughed back at her before grabbing her and setting her down. She was unprepared, for I didn't make any moves as she did until now. I don't think that she has ever done anything like this before, and it's noticeable. She doesn't know what to do with her legs or arms. So she just kept still underneath me and lifted her hands, one going around my neck, holding me closer, and the other going through my hair and and tugging at the roots. I smiled for a second down at her. I'm not taking it any further than this. I knew that she started to feel a little more uncomfortable feeling me.

"It's okay," I whispered down to her, trying to relax her. She stopped and smiled up at me and laughed a little for some reason.

"What's so funny?" I asked, laughing with her.

She stopped her laughter, trying to be serious with the situation, but she couldn't help but keep smiling with every kiss I gave her. She then stopped as she breathed sort of heavily under me. I didn't force her to keep going as she acted exhausted. She stared up into my eyes. No one has ever been this gentle with me whether it was doing this or something a little more.

I can't lose, Kendall. I got up off the couch and just picked her up bridal style in my arms as she held on to me, wrapping her arms around my neck carefully.

I carried her into my room. "You're sleeping in here," I stated. She smiled, looking over at my large bed. I shook my head, knowing what she was thinking. I went to the opposite side from where I sleep and set her down. She was more tired now. I can tell, as she yawned twice already.

I then climbed in on the other side. She turned, facing me. She set her hand on my cheek as she got closer to me. She came right up against me, but she backed up, as she felt me again. I laughed under my breath at her reaction. I don't doubt that she hasn't seen a guy before, making it worse on her half. She doesn't know what to do.

I set my hand on her side as she was turned on the other. She leaned in and began kissing me again. I took my chance when she pulled away a little to breathe to speak. "Just go to sleep, Kendall. It's late," I told her. "Sleep." She looked a little disappointed.

I just looked down between us and grinned, looking back up at her. I wrapped her up in my arms. She obviously took a lot to try and get this far, but I can't. Eventually, she fell asleep in my arms, and I could think of no other better night in my life.

KENDALL

Chapter 12

I don't want to wake up. It feels like if I wake up, last night will be completely over, and I don't want it to end. I don't want it to be morning yet. I clenched my eyes together tightly before I felt his arm on me, not around me. I just felt his arm touching me. Then I knew that he is still fully asleep. I opened my eyes. I flipped around carefully to not wake him up. I lay on my side, looking over at him, laying his face against the pillow, lying on his chest as he's lightly snoring.

I just stared at him though. I don't know what to do. I moved a little closer quietly. I can't help but smile at him, sleeping still. I can't believe how captivating he looks, even though he's unconscious. I feel lucky. But I'm confused. I don't fully trust him, although I understand more of his past from what he told me last time I stayed here. I don't understand what held him back last night. It seemed fine for me.

I gained up enough courage to set my hand on his bare side. The blankets are up, covering his waist down as well as mine. I just set my hand on him lightly as he still snores lightly against the pillow, facing me. I don't want him to wake up so I can just continue. I set my hand down better, relaxing it against him. I move a little closer. I want to hug him again. I move even closer, gaining more courage.

I start to slide my hand down to the middle of his toned back, laying my arm on him now. I then heard him moan in his sleep. I moved even closer so my body was against his. I feel better now, happier, as I am right by his side. I can't help but think of the story he told me before, though, about his father and his sister's boyfriend. Although I don't think that he lied to me, I think that there is more to the story. I want to know. I want to know more about him. I want to become a part of his life even more now.

He took a deep breath before I felt his hand slide up to me. "Good morning, beautiful," he said quietly, knowing that I've been awake.

I smiled calmly and relaxed. I don't answer him. I just move my face closer to his so I am right in his. I then kiss his cheek. He smiled at me with his eyes still closed. He doesn't want to wake up. "You getting up?" I whispered to him.

He moaned. His eyes opened to see me right up against him. He kept his green eyes on mine as he brought his arm up and set it across my back. "Do you have to go to work?" he asked.

"Yeah," I answered quietly to him. "Not for a while though," I added quietly to him. He smiled, his eyes closing again. He opened them as he opened them as he appeared visibly awake now. "Micah?" I asked, getting his attention more.

He looked up at me more intently now. "You need something?"

"No, uh, I-I just . . . How did you manage without . . . on your own at eighteen?"

He paused, looking up at me. "You don't want to know about that, Kendall," he said back, releasing his arm off me.

What did he do?

He got up out of bed and walked out of his bedroom, not saying anything more to me. I sat up on his bed, wondering why he left me like that. I got up and walked out of his room and peeked in the living room down the hall, but he wasn't there. I then heard the breaking of glass as I jumped a little at it when it hit the hard flooring. "Micah?" I asked out, following the sound to his kitchen. "Micah?" I asked again as I stepped on to the cold tile barefoot.

I looked and saw him in front of the sink. I then saw about two plates that had shattered on the floor.

He turned to see me in the doorway, coming closer. "Kendall, just stay over there. You'll get hurt," he said, walking over to me. He's irritated.

"Micah, what's wrong?" I asked. I didn't want to hurt his feelings. I was just curious. But curiosity killed the cat.

"It's fine, Kendall. I'll clean it up," he said as he sat me down on his counter.

I set my hand on his shoulder. "I'm sorry," I whispered to him, looking into his green orbs. He shook his head as he leaned in and kissed me as he set his one hand on my one leg, and I began to lean back.

"I should clean this up," he said as he bent down and started to pick up the glass off the tile floor.

I got up, standing beside him and then stepping over a few pieces and bending down to pick up some of the bigger pieces.

"Kendall, don't. You'll get hurt." He's mad.

"Micah, it's fine," I told him as I grabbed a few more pieces into my hand.

One of the pieces then slipped and cut my hand. I whimpered at it as blood already started to ooze out of it as I dropped the other pieces of glass I had in the hand.

"I told you," he said, grabbing on to me and taking me over to his sink and setting me on the countertop beside it. He grabbed a rag and wet it, dabbing it over the cut.

"It's fine, Micah."

"Kendall," he just responded. "One moment," he added as he left me alone in his kitchen, walking down the hall as I saw him go into his bedroom. He returned a minute or two later with a little kit. "Okay," he said, taking a deep breath.

I can tell that I brought up bad memories to his mind. Making them surface after I don't know how long. He probably just forgot about them and buried them deep inside. I don't want to see him hurt like this.

"Micah," I whispered to him.

He just hushed me as he wrapped a little bandage around the long cut. It burned. I pulled away at the touch of it on me. "It's okay," he said quietly.

I didn't know what to do after my hand was gently wrapped. "Thank you," I said quietly to him. He lifted his head to look at me.

"You want a shower?"

I nodded. "Yeah, but I don't have any clothes here."

"We can get you some before you go to work."

"Okay," I responded, still quiet with him.

He picked me up like a child as I put my arms around him. I can tell that I am no trouble to him as he carried me into his room. He started his shower for me. "Okay," he said as he came over to me and kissed me on the corner of my mouth.

I smiled as I went into his bathroom and closed the door. I got in. The water was very warm but not too hot. I then heard the door open, and I knew it was Micah walking in and sitting down on the closed lid.

"I want to tell you, Kendall," he started. I listened closely.

"Micah, it's fine really. You . . . you don't have to. I'm just wondering b-because you were so young," I stuttered out to him on the other side of the dark curtain. It was silent for a moment. "So why haven't you contacted your family though?" I asked suddenly. I know that I caught him off guard too.

It's been seven minutes since I got into the shower. "You done?"

"Uh . . . yeah."

I turned off the water as he handed me a fluffy and soft towel. I wrapped it around me as he took the curtain back. I just looked at him awkwardly. It's weird. He then helped me step out of the tub and into his arms as he started rubbing his hands on me as if to dry me faster. He looked down at me and smiled.

I then gained enough courage to speak to him again. "I think that you should contact them, Micah," I said to him calmly, surprising myself.

"I don't want to talk about that, Kendall. That part of my life is done with." How could he say that? Of course, it isn't just done with. Things are still bothering him, I can tell.

"It isn't done with. It still bothers you. You should talk about it."

"I don't want to."

"Micah, please try." I want him to be happy and to have his family in his life. He has none that I know of at this time.

A long pause was made. "I'm not promising anything," he whispered.

***

I spent a whole two minutes looking for the *R* section to set the merchandise back. I don't understand why it takes me so long though. I always forget where everything is though. "Hey," I heard Ben say as he came from behind me, working on the other shelf.

I turned my head a little to look back, just to make sure it was him. He was putting some things away as well. "Hi," I said back.

"So what did all of you do yesterday?" he asked, just to start a conversation. I laughed, thinking back to last night.

"Uh . . . I was with Micah," I answered with laughter in my voice.

"Oh okay, you can stop right there."

"No," I said, shaking my head. "That . . . No," I tried to say to him. He laughed.

"Okay, it's none of my business anyway," he added, still smiling. I could tell by his tone.

"Ben, really," I reassured him as I turned around smiling.

"Okay."

"So what about yourself?" I asked to keep it going.

"Well, I . . . I went home, and I sat down and . . . Well, nothing, really." He laughed. I laughed a little at him.

"Really? Nothing?"

He shook his head. "No, nothing, really." He had a smile plastered on his face.

"I'll close up today," Brandy spoke from behind the register.

I looked over in her direction and then back at Ben. "Yay . . .," he said quietly. I laughed under my breath at his response.

"Is he picking you up?" Ben asked as we walked outside.

"Uh, he's at work still."

"Oh yeah, well, do you need a ride?"

"Ben." I just stared at him.

"It's not like I would do anything like he may think, just taking you back home safely," he said, trying to get me to agree.

"No, really, it's okay. I want to walk. It's only a few blocks from here," I told him.

"A few blocks? Kendall, it's like a mile to your house."

I looked at him in confusion.

"No, I-I go to the gym after now."

"The gym?" he asked, smirking down at me.

"It's where he works."

"Oh wow. Well, that's understandable." He puffed.

I smiled at him. "Yeah, well, see you later," I told him as I turned and began walking down the sidewalk to the other side of the road from the place I work since his work is on that side anyway.

I felt his eyes still on me, though, like he doesn't believe where I am going. I think that he thinks that Micah is abusive. But he isn't. He wouldn't ever hit or hurt me. He can't hit a girl. The reason that he is so protective of a girl is because he saw his mom and sister both get beat by men. He grew up too fast, only at eighteen.

What else don't I know about him?

A lot.

He is mature and responsible, owning his own home and getting his life mostly stable for living completely on his own.

How did he do that though? How did he get so far like that on his own?

I neared the building, seeing his car outside again. I walked in as the one man from yesterday nodded to me. I walked to the backroom again. I looked around for Micah back there, but I didn't see him. I then looked over at the other corners, but I still didn't see him. I just decided to walk in further. I'm nervous.

I began to walk around the gym's floor, passing different men and women working out and training for stuff.

"You Kendall?" a voice asked, coming up behind me. I looked back to see a shirtless and muscular man with dark brown hair and blue eyes. He was very sweaty.

"Uh . . . yeah."

"Hi, I'm Dane," he introduced himself. I smiled. "You looking for Micah?" he asked, looking right at my eyes.

I looked at him a little nervous. He laughed because I was shaking a little bit. "Yeah," I responded with my voice a little shaky.

He smiled, and it relaxed me a little. "It's okay." He laughed. "He's right over here," he said, turning around. I followed as he led me to a different room. I walked in as he did before me and looked around instantly. "Uh, he's . . . He should be . . .," he began saying, trying to let me know where he is, but he couldn't seem to see him himself. "Where the heck did he go?" he said softly, looking around.

Then a man was walking past us both, standing in the doorway to the room when Dane stopped him. "Hey, Kyle, where's Micah?" he asked the man.

"Uh, he had to take a call again. He's in the locker room, I think," Kyle told him.

His light eyes then looked down at me behind Dane. "Who's this?" he asked, smiling at me.

"This is Kendall," he said to him. As soon as he spoke my name, Kyle's eyes left my body and went back up to Dane's face.

"Oh finally, we get to see you." He laughed.

I looked at him confused before I realized that Micah must have said something to him about me. I don't feel that Micah goes around talking about me though because of his protective nature to keep me safe. "Okay," Dane then said. "He's back this way then." He smiled as he turned around, and I turned with him, following his direction. We went back to the direction that we had come from to the boxing room.

"Just sit right here. I'll tell him you're here," he said as I stood beside the one table I did before as Dane went into the men's locker room for me.

"Thank you," I said as he disappeared into the room.

He went in, and I just stayed on the table and looked around. I heard curse words and screams in the locker room then and looked back to see what all the commotion was about. "Kendall's here," I heard Dane's voice.

"What?" I heard Micah ask as he was laughing at something, not hearing Dane.

"Kendall. She's waiting out there for you."

"Oh, she's here? Right now, you mean?"

"Yeah, she's right out there."

I heard Josh's voice then, but I can't tell what he's saying. I turned, looking around again at everyone around me and what they were doing. I was a little bit surprised when I felt a pair of strong arms wrap around me as I stood by the table.

I smiled at his greeting. "Hey, beautiful."

I turned around to face him. "Hello," I said, standing on my toes to reach up and kiss him as he set his hands on my sides lightly, leaning down a little from his height to kiss me back. His hair is sweaty, and he is only wearing a pair of navy athletic shorts just above his knees. Even though he is sweaty, it doesn't drive me away even a little. I drew back, going back down to my feet, smiling.

"What are you doing here?"

"I got off early again, so . . ."

"Okay, well, I'm still working, so you just have to wait though."

"Okay, that's fine." I smiled up at him, holding my arms around him.

"Micah!" a voice shouted from across the floor. His vision left mine to look to where the voice came from.

"I gotta go," he said to me as he let go of me and left me by the table again to get back to work.

I sat and watched Micah for a while before I started to read on my phone and play games. Josh walked past me and nodded in a hello form. I just grinned up at him as he went to the locker room.

The sound of a phone ringing then came to my hearing. I looked to see that it was coming from the locker room. Josh came out a few seconds, as it continued ringing. "Micah, your phone again!" Josh shouted over to him.

Micah said something to his client as he jogged past me into the room. He was in there for only a quick minute before coming back out, sliding his hand across my leg as he jogged back over to the man he was training.

I stayed the whole three more hours to wait for Micah to finish up. I knew that the place was closing, as stuff was being put away, and

Micah came over to me. "Okay, all done, babe," he said as he leaned down and kissed me like it had been weeks on my cheek.

I smiled as he drew back after a few seconds. He helped me down off the table and grabbed on to my hand, and with his other hand, he picked up his black bag from the floor. We walked out together as he said good-bye to Josh and Dane and a few other guys whose names I don't know. We walked out into the cool breeze. He guided me over to his car, and I got in on my side.

"Uh . . ." He sighed in annoyance, as his phone started ringing again. I sat facing out of the car as he stood closely in front of me. After kissing me again, he reached into his bag pocket on the side and pulled out his phone.

"Who is it?" I asked curiously. He just glanced up at me as if he didn't feel comfortable, answering my question. "It's okay. You don't have to tell me. I was just curious," I told him, even though I really wanted to know.

"Just give me a minute," he said as he turned and walked a few steps away. I watched him closely, maybe being able to hear a few words of the conversation.

"Hey, I'm busy right now," he told the person on the other end, reaching with his free hand up through his hair as he spoke. He spoke again after a few seconds. "Okay, I gotta go talk to you later. Okay, bye." He ended the call. He turned back around, facing me as he ran back over from the short distance and taking my legs into his hands and kissing me happily and then swiftly turning me around so my legs were in the car and then he closed my door, going over to his side and getting in.

"Did your mom tell you when she's coming back yet?" he asked, keeping his eyes on the road as he drove down the street.

"No, she didn't. She said that she'd be gone just a few days though."

"You'll stay with me so that you're not alone," he told me, glancing over to maybe catch a glimpse of my reaction to his offer. I stared at him. Is he telling me what to do?

"I have to feed my dog first, even if I do stay at your house. I'm fine alone."

"No, you're not."

"Micah, its fine."

"Stop making such a big damn deal. You're staying with me, Ken."

"You can't just tell me what to do, Micah."

He gave me a dirty look, and I felt out of place, and I wanted to get away from him now.

"I don't want you to be alone."

"Micah, its fine. I don't mind it. Seriously." He refused to listen to me and instead continued driving.

He pulled into his driveway, and we were both quiet for a moment before he took the keys out and got out of the vehicle. At first, I thought he'd come to my door, but he didn't. Instead, he went straight to his front door as I got out and met him as he was going inside.

I walked backward down his hallway as he continued to follow with me, continuing to kiss me. I ran my hands up his firm sides and up to his face, stopping for a second and then continuing up, taking his thick blond hair into my hands. He moaned at my actions.

"You hungry?" he asked me, looking down at my face as his hands still stayed on my hips. I nodded. "Do you want to go out?" he asked after.

"I don't know. Do you have anything here?" I asked as I took my hands against his chest as he smiled down at me. I realized then just how beautiful and perfect he looks and is. I now feel strongly attracted to him, not wanting to retract my hands from his body, feeling that I might lose him, and he will just simply slip away from me or I might wake up.

"Uh . . ." He paused. "I'm not sure?" he questioned himself. He then scooted me over to the side, but I didn't let go. I just followed behind him as I wrapped my arms around him as he walked into his kitchen. He laughed as he realized that I wasn't going to let go of him. He set his much larger hands on top of mine as they locked on his stomach with each other.

He stepped up by his upper cabinets and opened them. It still surprises me how clean and neat his place is. If I were to just walk in not knowing him, I would think that a woman or a neat freak lived here. I never could have imagined that his house would have looked like this from just looking at him. He shuffled through the shelves before speaking to me. "We can make cupcakes?" he asked, trying to look back at me, as I was still latched on behind him, holding on. "Kendall?" He laughed as he spoke.

He turned, setting the box of mix on his countertop, looking down at me. He was able to turn fully around to look down at me as I loosened my grip around him, and he twirled within them. "Cupcakes?" I smiled. "Why do you not have any food but cupcake batter?"

He shrugged. "I like cupcakes." He paused. "And plus I can eat as much batter as I want when I'm alone."

"You're such a child." I giggled. "I'll make some cupcakes with you," I said softly to him, leaning up to kiss him on the cheek.

"Okay then," he said, turning around.

We got the ingredients that it called for all out on the top and began to mix it all together after he turned on the oven. As I was stirring and he was holding on to me, his phone interrupted us once again, ringing loudly. He sighed at the sound. "I'm sorry. Just give me one minute," he said, letting go and walking over to where he set his phone down.

He walked back into the kitchen as he got a drink. "I'm busy right now. Can't I just call you back?" he asked, looking over at me. I then heard the voice on the other end, a girl's voice. My expression dropped as soon as it rang in my ears.

"Is that her? Is it Kendall?" she asked. Micah coughed awkwardly as she spoke louder, asking the questions containing my name. I know that it was an attempt to cover up the voice on the other end.

"Look, I gotta go, really," he said to her.

"Okay, bye, Micah. Love you," she said loudly.

Her words ran through my mind, throwing all of the thoughts for Micah to the side. "Love you." I paused at the words.

Who is she? Why does she keep calling him? Why didn't he tell me who it was?

He hung up the phone after just saying a plain good-bye. He smiled as he set his phone down on the table and walked back over to me.

I weakly smiled at him. I was already turned around, facing him as he neared even closer to me. "You okay?" he asked me softly, looking down at me. I nodded. "You sure? You seem different?" he questioned me.

I didn't want to say anything because I would just end up crying, and he would see how jealous I became in just a minute from hearing another girl talk to him. "I'm fine, Micah," I said back up to him as I leaned up, trying to convince him that I was but really wasn't, and then I kissed him gently. I can tell that he didn't believe me, though, by his expression.

"Okay," he just said in disbelief to me. "These good?" he asked as his one hand was set firmly on my side and the other reached for the chocolate-filled bowl of cupcake mix.

"Yeah," I said quietly to him.

"You sure you're okay?" he asked again, trying to get me to spill. I nodded. "Please, don't lie to me, Kendall," he said firmly to me, looking directly into my eyes intently.

I didn't want to say anything. I would just end up crying if I spoke. The thought of him cheating on me flooded through my thoughts, his arms around another girl's waist and kissing her and talking nicely to her and protecting her. I can't say anything to him.

I just looked up at him closely. "Micah," I whispered as I kissed him firmly on his lips. He was caught off guard as I did so. I never did it like that to him, but I did it because he's mine. I don't want to share him. I don't want to think about sharing him either. He's mine. I don't know what I'd do if he is cheating on me.

He raised his eyebrows and then took the bowl from behind me, setting the right amount into the foils for them and sliding the pan into the oven gently and closing the hatch.

"I don't want you upset, Kendall," he said, looking down at me. After I didn't answer for a moment, I figured I would just tell him. "Are you on your—"

I quickly cut him off, not wanting to finish his question, as I already knew what it was. I blushed at him. "No," I responded quickly.

"Well, okay, I'm just trying to figure it out. You don't have to be embarrassed, Ken." He laughed, smiling down at me sweetly but being serious.

"Micah, just forget about it. It's nothing. Honest." I lied.

He then lifted me quickly into his arms bridal style after a few seconds of just looking down at me and carried me into his living room as I laughed. He set me down on his longer couch and handed me the remote. "Just find something," he said as he kissed me playfully and walked off.

I watched him as he walked into his bedroom with his phone in his hand. I flickered through the channels until I stumbled upon a movie that I like, *The Breakfast Club*. I lay down on his couch for about five minutes before his bedroom door opened again, and he emerged. He came out in a plain white shirt and black boxers on. I looked away back to the television as he looked over at me.

He came over to the couch where I lay full out on comfortably and grabbed my legs and picked them up as he sat where they once were and set them back down on to his lap. "What'd you put on?" he asked, looking at the screen.

"*The Breakfast Club*," I answered, smiling up at him. It had just started when I found it, so it was only like eight minutes into it now. "It just started," I told him.

"I've seen it," he said.

"You don't care if we watch it?"

"No, I like it," he responded, setting his hands on my feet that lay on his lap.

We sat and watched the movie together until the timer went off in his kitchen, and he lifted my legs back and went in. I followed. I still couldn't get the girl's voice out of my mind though. Her words tortured my thoughts with different possibilities. I tried my best to just block her out. I have to force myself to try even more with Micah to choose me. I want him more than anything else that I have ever wanted before. I feel that without him in my life, I will just fall apart. I can't see myself without Micah, and I don't know if that's a good or bad thing though. I walked to him, taking the cupcakes out of the oven and setting them on the counter. I don't even know how to explain my feelings for him that have grown with every step taken with him. But I still know that he is keeping secrets from me. I don't know what to think they are though. I'm confused. My mind is just a fuzz ball now.

"Micah?" I asked as I stood behind him.

He turned around, his cheeks showing me his dimples. "What's wrong?" he asked, staring back at me.

"Oh nothing, I was just wondering if I can borrow something to wear to bed," I told him sort of nervous.

He smiled at me. "Yeah, of course," he answered, walking a little closer to me. He walked past me as I followed him into his bedroom. He handed me a shirt and a pair of boxers. I went and closed the door to the bathroom once I was inside. I put his longer shirt on me, not taking the boxers with me to change into. I walked out of his bathroom, only wearing his shirt and my undergarments. The shirt was longer than the others that I have worn before and came down just below my bum.

He wasn't there when I came out. I set my clothes down in a pile, folded. I walked back out to find him in the kitchen. "Sorry. I don't have anything to put on them," he told me, looking back to see me.

I shook my head. "It's fine," I told him. I smiled up at him to find him skimming me. He took his eyes up to my own, his green eyes sparkling as they looked into my brown ones.

He then handed me one of the cakes as he leaned back on the counter to look at me as he held one too. I peeled back the foil part, cupping it, and took a bite. We both ate the one cupcake as he wrapped up the rest and then went to sleep.

I was still a little nervous sleeping in the same bed as him, but I forced myself to just suck it up and not wimp out on anything with him.

"Good night, Kendall," he said as he lay down beside me and pulled the covers up over himself and me.

I flopped around to face him. But he wasn't lying on his side, rather on his back with his eyes already closed. He was really tired, I guess. I'm not tired though. I just stared at his face, adoring every feature on it. I saw him grin, as he knew that I was looking at him, and I was caught.

"Kendall," he whispered.

I smiled at him saying my name. I got closer to him as he picked up his right arm closest to me and set it behind my head as I got up against his side. I leaned up and kissed his cheek. "Good night," I whispered. He then opened his eyes one last time and kissed me back. He closed his eyes again after smiling down at me as I set my arms on his chest and wrapped my legs around his as he held on to me, and we went to sleep.

I forgot where I was for a minute. I'm at Micah's. I don't know how I forgot though. I roll back over, but he isn't there. I open my eyes, for my arm just stretched out to where he fell asleep at. I hear him though. I sit up on his bed. I look around his room and peek into the bathroom. The door's open. I look around more anxious to where he has disappeared. I decide to just get up.

I get up quietly. I feel weird to make any noise. I take one step and then another silently to his open bedroom door. I grab on to the frame and peek around, looking in the kitchen's direction first and then down the other way to his front door. He's there. The door is open, and he is talking to a few men. The men don't look good either. I get a chill up my back from just looking at them. I look a little closer. Micah doesn't know that I am watching. I can't fully hear what they are talking about.

Micah is wearing a pair of sweatpants and a white plain T-shirt. I had to force myself to try and pay more attention to the conversation going on and not Micah's back. I begin to listen a little more carefully.

"Micah, come on," one of the men said to him, trying to convince him, I guess, to do something I don't know. I'm confused at his words.

"I said no. I don't want to do that anymore," Micah said back to him.

"Don't be a baby, Harlan," the other man said.

"Listen, I told you I've been done with all that. I just needed it for a while," Micah snapped back.

"You can't say that you don't do anymore completely because that's the biggest lie you've told." The one man began to talk again. "That's not the Micah I know."

The tall and dark male's eyes then saw me. I froze, too scared to slip back into Micah's bedroom. I got the chills quickly and felt sick. What do I do? He smiles at me. I can tell that Micah is confused by the way that he tensed as they both stared at me from the doorway.

"Well, hello there," the dark one said, looking at me.

"Dang, Micah," the other said.

Micah turned quickly as I looked directly at him, frightened. I then remembered when he looked from my eyes down that I was only wearing his black shirt and my pink lace underwear. I felt embarrassed. He rushed over to me and grabbed me, turning me back into his bedroom. "Just one minute, babe," he said, setting me down on the edge of his bed and kissing my cheek before exiting again.

I heard his feet pat down the hallway back to the front door, back to the two men waiting for him. I heard him then continue talking. "Look, I said that I'm done. My life is fine now. I don't need it anymore," I heard faintly. I can't hear if he said anything else though. It's too distant.

"Who the hell was that?" one of the men asked.

"She's none of your concern," Micah spat back loudly, so I completely heard.

"Oh, I don't know. I think I want her to be," the other spoke up.

"You should leave now," I heard him say. I think that he said something else too, but I'm not sure. He was too quiet, knowing I was most likely listening which I really am. I imagined him freaking out then and punching the man, but he didn't.

"Don't come back here either," I heard Micah say as they began to walk away, I think.

I heard a laugh, knowing it wasn't Micah's though. "Okay, see you in a few days then, Micah," one said loudly, but I knew that they were leaving, as the door closed loudly, Micah slamming it a little.

I heard him then approaching his bedroom again. I tensed up, pretending that I didn't hear anything that he was talking about.

What was he talking about with the two men? Who were they? Why were they here? What's going on?

He came back into the room and looked down at me from his height, walking over as he flashed his dimples. I smiled at his perfection. "Good morning, beautiful," he said, leaning down to my eyesight and kissing me lightly on the mouth. I glanced to his side and noticed that his right pocket had something inside it, it being kind of lumpy. I looked over at it confused, but I didn't let him notice my confusion plastered on my face. What's in his pocket? Did they give him something? What?

I was too distracted, and I think he could tell. "What's going on?" I asked quietly, looking into his green eyes.

He looked at me like I was crazy for a second and then shook his head. "Nothing," he responded, leaning in to kiss me again.

"Micah," I said, trying to get something out of him.

"It's nothing you need to worry 'bout." He tried again to just get me to forget about the men.

"Who were they at least?" I asked, trying once more.

He paused, setting his hand on my leg and rubbing it and then looking up at me. "Old friends is all," he told me.

I looked down right into his eyes as he looked into mine. "Everything okay?"

He nodded in a little confusion, and he was taken off guard as well, and I know that he isn't telling me the whole story at all, only one corner of it all. "Yeah, yeah, it's all okay, Kendall," he tried to reassure me. I smiled weakly at him before I decided to kiss him back when he tried again. He leaned back and smiled at me, still at eye level. "You hungry or anything?" he then asked, standing up to his full towering height.

"No, I'm fine," I told him, standing up in front of him.

"Are you sure?" he asked again.

"Yeah, I'm good, Micah," I told him again, smiling up at his face as he stared down at me.

"Okay." He sighed, kissing me again. "Your lips are so soft," he murmured as he cupped my face.

His phone began ringing, and I knew what was going to happen as he left for one minute, leaving me by myself again and then returning and not telling me anything as he talked to the girl on the other end. And that's what happened—that's what exactly happened.

When he came back, I weakly smiled at him again, trying to make him think that I was all right. "I know you're fine."

"Do you know what time it is?" I asked him.

"Uh, like nine forty, I think. You have to work again?" he asked, holding on to me.

"Yeah."

"Okay, I'll get a quick shower, then I'll take you home so that you can get ready." Micah turned to walk away from me to shower but turned around to me again. I giggled at him. I know what he's doing. I just had to laugh and shake my head a little for him to know the answer as he just flashed his dimples to me, taking off his shirt right there as if teasing me and then walking toward his bedroom and then to the bathroom. "Okay, okay." He laughed before leaving. He left me standing as he went to get all washed up. He didn't even close the door, but I didn't stay to watch, knowing that he wasn't just showing off—that he just didn't care if I saw him. I went into the living room to wait for him as I messed around on my phone and watched TV as I ate two of the cupcakes from last night.

He came and found me sitting on his couch ten minutes later. "Okay," he said. He wore a beanie over his hair, some of his dirty blond hair sweeping out the front. I stared at him for a moment, taken away from it all, standing in front of me. I just can't believe that I get to call him mine. I feel complete for now.

I smiled up at him as I stood up and went into his room and got dressed into my outfit from the previous day. Micah took me home, and I got a quick shower and got ready. He then dropped me off at work. He got out of his car with me, walking me across the street to the building. He kissed me good-bye passionately. But when I turned to leave him, he wouldn't let go of my hand, pulling me back in for another, this time longer. I giggled as he then let me go inside.

"Just call me if you get off early again, okay? I don't want you walking anymore. I'll come get you, Kendall," he demanded of me.

I turned and smiled. "Okay, yes, sir." I joked.

He didn't look like he was going to laugh, and he didn't. He just watched me get inside safely before leaving for himself to arrive at work most likely late, but he didn't care.

Work was boring again today. It hasn't been busy in a long time. It's slow. "Kendall," Ben said from behind me at the counter.

"Ben," I said back plainly.

There was a pause. "Something wrong?" he asked curiously, still standing behind me. I didn't answer for a second, thinking about Micah the whole time and whom he might always interrupt our time together to answer the phone for and who the men were this morning. "Kendall?" he asked.

"Huh?" I asked, forgetting that he ever asked me as I turned to face him for a moment.

"I asked if something was wrong," he repeated.

"Oh yeah, yeah, I'm fine. I just zoned out," I said, trying to just keep him out of my business.

"Okay."

After work, I grabbed my bag and stuff and walked outside. I waited by the door for about ten minutes. Micah was running late for some reason. He is always here on time. I looked around, looking down both ways of the street. I pulled out my phone and checked for any messages or calls from him. There was none. I'm confused.

Where is he?

Then the door opened beside me as I was looking down the street again, hoping to see his car coming. I glanced back to see Ben standing there by the door.

"He late?" he asked.

"Just like ten minutes," I said softly as I turned to face him. He smiled with a little laughter. "What?" I asked confused from him.

"Nothing. Just . . . I didn't think that he would ever do that," he said, smiling.

I just looked at him plainly and with some anger. It's none of his business to talk about Micah like that. He doesn't know him. "Ben," I said, meaning for him to just shut up.

His smile went away slowly due to my anger. My phone then started buzzing from a call coming through. I hurriedly got it out of my bag. He watched me pull it out. "That him?" he asked.

I didn't answer or look up at him as I answered the call. It's Micah. "Hey, sorry. I'm not able to pick you up. Josh is on his way to get you now. I have to stay a little later. He'll just bring you back here," he told me.

"Oh okay, I was just waiting on you."

"Where are you?" he suddenly asked.

"I . . . I'm just waiting outside by the door."

"Well, just wait inside. Are you alone?"

"No, Ben's with me," I answered. Ben's eyes quickly looked up at me upon saying his name to Micah. He looked at me funnily. I laughed.

"What is he doing with you?" he snapped. Here we go.

"Micah, calm down." I looked over at Ben, who was watching closely as he looked worried. I turned around so I wouldn't be facing him and took a few steps away from him to talk to Micah more privately. I heard his breathing pick up a little. I need to calm him down now. "You look so cute when you're angry," I whispered, trying to succeed with my plan.

I heard him chuckle with my comment. "Kendall," he said, trying to stick to the subject with Ben in it. "Don't change the subject." He paused. "How else do I look when I'm angry?" he talked lowly.

"That's a conversation for another day." I couldn't help but smile. "Micah, it's fine. He's just waiting with me. It's okay. You're the only one," I said quietly so that Ben couldn't hear, but I knew that he was watching me as I spoke. I can tell that he was relaxed now. Then a car pulled up, and I saw Josh in the driver's seat, knowing that he was here to pick me up. I smiled. "Okay, Josh is here," I reassured him as I saw Josh get out of his car. He parked right in front of the shop.

He got out and walked over to me. "Okay, see you in a few minutes, beautiful," Micah said to me.

"Okay, bye." I smiled as I hung up the phone, tucking it back into my bag. Ben walked up to me, only a few feet away.

"You ready?" Josh asked.

"Yeah, yeah, I am," I said, smiling up at his height. He's just like barely an inch taller than Micah. I looked back at Ben as Josh noticed me looking at him and looked back as well.

"Oh hey," Josh said, turning around to greet him. Ben froze. "I'm Josh," he added.

"Ben," he said, shaking his hand firmly. Ben was obviously very nervous. I saw Josh's eyebrows rise at learning his name.

"Ben, huh?" He laughed. "I'm Micah's friend. Just picking her up for him," he told him, knowing that Ben was confused with another man picking me up from work besides Micah himself.

"Oh okay." Ben weakly smiled.

"Okay, see you later," Josh said to Ben as he turned back to me and walked over to his car and got in.

I got in as well, a little surprised that he didn't open the door for me. He looked over at me as I sat in and shut the door and buckled up. "Oh, I'm sorry. I'm just not used to opening doors for people. You can get out, and we can retry?" He joked.

I laughed at his humor, making me blush. "No, it's fine," I said, laughing at him.

He just smiled as he drove off back to the gym.

When we got back, he opened the door for me, entering the gym. I laughed. We went to the boxing room in the back. I immediately saw Micah who was in the corner mat with another man training. "You want a drink?" Josh asked as I sat on the table in the back by the locker rooms.

"Uh no, thanks, I'm good," I told him as he just looked at me and then looked away as he walked off. I stared over at Micah, watching him train the other man.

My phone then buzzed, and it was my mom saying that she'd be home in two days. I smiled at her text, knowing that she would finally be coming home. I would finally be in my own bed. Not that I don't like sleeping at Micah's, but it's just not home. It doesn't feel as comfortable as being at home. I haven't spent any time over there since she's been gone either, so I can't wait.

Then I looked up to see Micah walking toward me and smiling. As soon as he got close enough, he caught me in his arms and began kissing my cheek playfully, and I complied, throwing my arms over his neck, and laughed as his kisses went down to my neck and then back up and eventually going to my lips. "Hello," he said softly as his eyes were directly in front of my own.

"Hi." I smiled back, kissing him after.

"We can leave in just half an hour," he told me. It's around seven thirty now.

"Okay." I smiled back up at him.

He left me at the table as I began waiting for the half hour to pass. After the thirty minutes was over, Micah didn't come right over to me. He just acknowledged me by grinning over to where I sat. Instead, he went right over to Josh. They both stood beside the table where I sat, talking. I don't know what about though. I can't fully hear them, as everyone else started to pack everything away for tomorrow. I glanced over at them a few times, curious to what they may be talking about. Then I heard something about a fight with Micah's name in it.

"A fight?" I asked, breaking into their conversation.

They both looked back at me. "Yeah," Micah said, answering my curiosity.

"But you said that you don't fight."

"Yeah, I know. But something's worked out for Friday night."

I looked at him with confusion.

What?

"Micah," I said, getting his attention back to me. "What do you mean?" I asked. I am so confused. How can they suddenly just let him fight in his weight class?

"Kendall, it's okay."

"Is he in your weight class then?" I asked again. Josh watched me as I was talking to Micah without any fear as I spoke questioning him.

He paused, knowing that I was upset. "He's in the next class up," he finally answered.

"Isn't that dangerous?"

"Don't worry, Kendall. Micah will take him out easily," Josh tried to calm me down as he laughed a bit as he spoke to me.

I got up off the table as I went over to stand closer to them both. Then a sudden thought rushed into my mind. Where would it be held? I don't think here because I know that he isn't allowed to fight in his class. So is it illegal?

"Micah, is it legal?" I asked quietly so that only he and Josh could hear me.

He smiled down at me. I knew that Josh was watching me closely as I spoke, but right now, I couldn't care less. He also let out a little laugh at my worried question. "Not exactly," he said back down to me.

"Micah, then . . . then you shouldn't do it. It's even more dangerous," I said louder to him angrily.

Josh's eyebrows rose as I raised my voice to Micah. He was surprised how comfortable I have become with him. Micah looked up at Josh as I kept my eyes locked on his face, not letting him change the subject. "Will you give us a minute?" He laughed to Josh.

"Good luck." He joked as he patted Micah on the shoulder with his free hand, the other holding a bottle of water, and then he trailed off.

"Look, Kendall, you shouldn't worry about it. It's fine." He tried to calm me. I grew angry with him. He can't fight, and especially can't illegally. He will get in trouble with the cops most likely. And I've said it before, I don't fancy visiting him in prison.

"Micah, don't," I pleaded. I don't want anything to happen to him. I feel like I wouldn't be able to function right without him. He has become a part of my life, and I don't wish for the old one back. I can't lose this. It's hard to explain how this all began and how much it has grown into. I trust Micah. I don't want that to change. I don't think that he will ever do anything to hurt me.

"Kendall, I'm going to do this fight. It's my decision," he snapped back seriously.

I gave him an annoyed look and a frustrated one at the same time. I know that I cannot control him, nobody can, but he should know that he shouldn't be doing this. I just looked up at his face for a long second. "Micah, it's illegal." I bit back harshly. Then the sound of a phone ringing came from the men's locker room and there was no doubt in my mind whose it is—Micah's. I knew the routine. And it all happened with him, just leaving me as he went to answer it, not saying anything as he did so.

He had embarrassed me in front of like ten guys that I know were watching our little discussion. I stood for a second, knowing that Josh's eyes were on me. Then my mind got together, and I busted. I can't take it anymore. I began walking to follow where Micah had walked into the locker room to go after him. I walked quickly inside as I saw the other men's faces become shocked with a woman's sudden presence.

"Look, I'm already having some trouble with Kendall over this. I can do as I want," Micah said loudly to the person on the other end of the phone. "You're not my fucking boss."

I got in front of him as the other men exited the room quickly, knowing that I was angry and about to flip. "Get off the phone, Micah!" I shouted to him. I can't take him constantly talking on the phone anymore. And the fact that I knew it was a girl made me furious with him, although I never showed it—well, sort of, once. His eyes grew wide as I took the phone from him, ending the call and tossing it into his bag.

His sparkling light green eyes seemed to change a little, becoming filled with anger I could see. I immediately backed up a step, knowing I've set off his darkness. Before I could try to calm myself from the frightening image, large hands tightly gripped my wrists, holding me hostage. I whimpered from the grip, trying to pull back, but it was useless. Micah lost control. I screamed a little when my back was shoved into the lockers behind him hard. It hurt badly. His breathing increased. I could feel it down on me as he took my arms over my head, holding them down against the lockers. He's furious. I struggled in his grip as he held me down. I didn't make eye contact with him. I was scared to. I tried to keep my head down, but I couldn't. I looked up at his face only to see the darkness taking over him in his eyes, where it was the most noticeable. I tried to break free. I tried pushing him away with my legs, but he's too strong for me. I can't win against him ever. His grip tightened on my wrists as I struggled against him, my hands in fists as he held them down as they trembled along with my legs. Fear took over my mind. But I gained myself back, pushing all of the fear to the back of my mind, thinking about how sweet Micah can be and that this isn't him. I lashed out then.

"Was that someone else telling you how stupid this is!" I shouted in his face as a tear ran down my cheek. "You should listen to them, Micah. It's just stupid."

He looked down into my eyes as they calmed with no tears and anger no longer lingering in them. "That's what they said about you," he said, not yelling but quietly and calmly. My wrists were then released harshly as I took them quickly down to my stomach, holding the other in one of my hands, rubbing over the soreness he caused so quickly with his strength. But it wasn't long before my body was suddenly pressed back up against the wall of lockers by Micah, trapping me. I was confused.

I was left no time to think about what he had told me, what the other person told him about me—the other girl, that is. His gaze came into my eyes as I made eye contact with the fury inside him as he calmed just a little and shook his head with the thought. "What the hell is it with you women? I can do what I want! I don't care if you don't like it!" he snapped again, yelling in my face. I'm not completely sure that he was aware that he was once again pinning my arms down, holding me in place so that I couldn't escape him. I pouted slightly at his words to me, cruel and immature and hurtful words that I never imagined him ever saying to me. I cowered back from his strong hold. I need to break free. The pain is too much for me physically. My body began to tremble even more as the pain kept shooting through my body from his grip on me. I began breathing quicker as I panicked at his actions on me.

I have to say something now. I can't take it anymore. "You're hurting me," I whimpered, looking up at him slightly.

His eyes came back to me, the fury burning away back down inside him deeply. His face became shocked. His jaw tensed a bit as he let go of me slowly and backed away from my body. I looked at him sadly in relief with his grip finally off me. Another small tear ran down my cheek. I took my injured arms against my chest, holding them loosely, not touching the bruises that he caused, only smoothly rubbing over them lightly. I then felt the burn from the bruises erupt in me. It hurts even more than when he was causing them. I took my bottom lip back a little and then released it as I watched him look so innocent and guilty, just standing a few feet away from me, watching me like a scared child.

He looked so guilty from his previous actions on me. "Kendall," he whispered, looking at me. I looked up at his face as he took steps closer to me. I was terrified that he may be walking back to hurt me further, but there was nowhere I could run from him. I can't run away from him anyway. I can't win with Micah, and I know that. That's what scares me most of all.

"Oh god, no . . . Not again . . . Please, no." He pouted as I tried to get closer to the wall, frightened of him now. "No, please."

The pain displayed in his eyes alerted me that my Micah was back to me. He came back from my words that I'm sure he has heard before from his family. I thought of his sister being beaten by her boyfriend.

The look in his eyes is heartbreaking, but I'm too afraid to do anything about it. I can't just walk up and hug him with my head buried in his chest to comfort him. I can't, and I won't. He dropped to his knees in front of my frame, his face by my stomach. I gasped, shaking as his hands slid up my legs smoothly until they reached my hips, staying stationary there as he made eye contact with my glassy eyes. He felt my trembling from his touch as his hands moved up closer on me to my face. He looked as if he were about to explode with tears and anger with himself and me from starting this all.

"Kendall, please, no. Don't. I-I didn't. No, it wasn't on purpose I would never hurt you. Kendall, please, I didn't mean to. That's the last thing I would ever want to do to you. I'm sorry, baby. Just don't be afraid of me," he said sweetly, locking his green now sparkling eyes on mine with the tears lingering in his eyes.

I closed my eyes tightly as I felt another tear run down my cheek. I don't want to start crying in front of him to hurt him even more. His warm body rose as I still kept my eyes sealed shut, not wanting to look into his. I want to comfort him, but I need it too much for myself to offer it out. I stood frozen on the spot as I felt his hand brush through my hair, pushing the strands from my burning-with-fear face.

Chapter 13

"Please, look at me." He winced desperately. I opened my eyes to accompany his request. He looked like a lost child searching for any sort of love to hold on to. "Please," he whispered as he held my face in his large hands. My one knee bent, making me fall a little shorter from him as it stayed against his knee gently. I brought my hands up to hold on to his arms as I kept my eye contact with him as tears still ran down my face slowly. He began to calm down a little, knowing that I was trying to comfort and soothe him from his sadness.

His eyes glanced to my arms as I gripped him a little tighter as I sobbed silently from the pain, not from my emotions. He saw them then, the bruises he had inflicted to my skin. His eyebrows creased at the sight. His eyes came back into my sight as he looked back up, hurt. His fingers perfectly purpled on my wrists and a little on my arm part. "I'm so sorry, baby." I looked down from his gaze. He took his face against my left cheek, lightly brushing his lips against the skin.

I let go of my stubbornness. "It's okay, Micah." I moved my still shaking hands up to one of his shoulders and the other on his right cheek. He smiled weakly at my movements, knowing that I forgave him. He shook his head at my words, though, not believing me. I took both of my hands onto his face as he loosened his hands from me down to my hips. The situation had calmed now. I could feel it in his breathing against my skin. I then leaned in closer to him. I set my one hand in his thick blond hair, rubbing it through.

"I didn't mean to," he whispered again, obviously feeling really bad for it.

I shook my head a little at his words, looking down and stopping my hands from moving on him. "Please don't fight," I said quietly to him, trying to win this.

His jaw tensed again. "Kendall, I'm going to fight," he said sternly back. I stopped, not wanting to let out his darkness again.

"I don't want you to get hurt," I whispered, looking at all of his perfect features laid upon his smooth and clear face. I don't want them harmed. I don't want him hurt or scared any further.

"I'm not backing down, Kendall," he whispered. I felt a pain in my stomach from his words back to me. I definitely lost the fight. I don't want things to escalate again, so I stopped my pleading. "Please don't leave me," he quietly said, holding me to him now, a little tight. But I know it's not to hurt me. It's out of passion. He doesn't want to lose me, and I don't want to lose him.

I shook my head immediately. "I won't," I whispered to him in response. I can't imagine my life without him anymore. I know that I would fall apart without him in it.

***

It's strange watching Micah train instead of him training someone else. I sat and watched him, observing him move around the mat as he seemed to dominate his trainer. I laughed when the man fell back a little from one of his hard and powerful blows. Josh came over and stood beside me.

"He'll be fine," he said as we both watched Micah.

I looked up at him, still looking at Micah punching. "How do you know?"

"I know him. He'll be just fine. I know what he's capable of, Kendall," he said, glancing down at me.

"That long? How'd you meet him?" I asked curiously, peering up at his face.

He didn't answer, though, as Micah started to approach us. He just shook his head a little. It's not that he wasn't able to answer with Micah's presence coming up, but it was because he didn't want to say it to me.

I sat confused as Josh left my side, nodding to Micah as they passed paths. I smiled as he came in front of me, taking a drink of water. "You're really good," I commented, setting my hands on the sides of his abs smoothly. He smiled.

"Yeah?" he asked as he came closer, setting the water on the table. I nodded shyly.

"You okay?" he asked, still smiling.

I nodded as I spoke the words, "I'm fine."

"I know that's not true."

"Micah!" a voice shouted as he quickly turned to see his trainer.

"Go," I whispered, pushing him a little away.

He grinned at me. He kissed my forehead before he went back over. My phone buzzed from inside my bag, and I picked it out and unlocked it, seeing the text from Emily, wanting me to come over for a while and catch up. I looked over at Micah. I then texted her back, saying that she would have to pick me up at the gym I'm currently at since she has her driver's license. I walked over to Micah slowly.

"Micah?" I said to get his attention as I stood behind him. He turned, hearing my sudden interruption.

He peered at me curiously. "Uh well, Emily's coming to pick me up. I'm going over there for a while," I said to him.

"You don't want me to just take you over?" He panted.

"No, she's already on her way, I mean."

"You sure?" He ignored his trainer.

"Yeah, it's fine."

I smiled to relax him. "It's just Emily," I reassured him, trying to spark a laugh from him to cheer him up.

"Okay, have fun."

"Okay, bye." I leaned up and pecked his cheek.

He smiled as I took back my hand from his chest. I then walked off, walking outside the gym. Its five o'clock now, and she arrived at five ten and picked me up.

"Hi." I smiled at her.

"Hey, haven't seen you in a while." She smiled back to me.

We then went back to her house, and I stayed for a few long hours there. I decided, though, that I wanted to walk home to just get some air. The wind blew my hair back behind me, and I just decided to let it after it happened four times before. I then fixed my bag onto my shoulder. I heard some noises, though, as I continued to walk down the sidewalk. I looked around, trying to figure out what it was, but it sounds too far away, so I just ignored it. I walked for about another minute, my house still a few streets away. Then my attention was taken by seeing a group of men.

I looked at them confused at what they may be up to, just standing by an old brick building that sat alone on that side. Then I noticed another man and two men holding on to his arms as one just stood there, looking around for others, and the last one was punching and kicking the man being held down. I grew filled with fear as I wanted to run, but I was too afraid.

My mouth opened slightly as my eyes widened, seeing the man being held down and punched in the face and stomach roughly and very strongly as he looked in pain from each blow. Then the man hitting him moved over a little as he laughed. I then saw the man being attacked, his hair blond and tall in height, Micah. My heart sank. It's Micah. I know it's Micah. It looks just like him.

"Oh my god," I whispered to myself. "Micah!" I shouted as I began to run over, not even caring about my safety. The men all looked over at me as I ran to them. They acted in a panic, hitting him one more time before they let go of his arms, and he dropped to the ground, and then they kicked him again before they left down the alleyway.

I ran to his side as fast as I could. When I got to him, I immediately started to think that he was unconscious, but, thank God, he wasn't. "Micah!" I said again as I got down to him as he lay on the ground. He smelled of liquor and something else, but I don't know. I crinkled my nose at the odor coming from him. It was horrid. "Oh my god, are you okay?" I asked frantically down to him as I picked him up a little. "Micah!" I repeated, still panicking.

He grinned up at me. His face covered in blood, dripping from his mouth and nose. I looked at him with confusion as he smiled at me. "What happened!" I asked, still freaking out about the situation.

"I-I was, uh . . . I don't remember, but I know that Anthony was hitting me," he said tiredly.

I know Anthony. He's the one from the club that tried to attack me when Micah attacked him, beating him badly. This was payback. "Anthony?" I asked to make sure. He nodded.

He was so beaten up, but he showed no more signs of pain due to being drunk, obviously. "Come on," I said to him as I tried picking him up, but he was too heavy for me. He laughed a little as he helped me out by stumbling up to his wobbly feet.

"Where we goin', babe?" he asked with his eyes half closed and his voice slurred. I put his arm around my neck for some sort of support to hold him up to walk back to my house.

"My place," I told him as I struggled to hold him up completely.

He smiled at my answer and hummed. "Now we're getting somewhere."

"Micah." I scolded him. "Help me out here," I demanded as he laughed a little.

"I missed you," he said quietly as he began to fall back down.

"No, no, no," I said as he began to fall. "Don't do that," I said, holding him back up as I got it under control now how to hold him so that he wouldn't fall back over. He's so freaking heavy. "Come on." I tried again to get him away from the building and over to the sidewalk. It worked finally.

We stumbled around all the way to my doorstep after a good ten minutes at least. He was falling asleep, though, as he sat on my doorstep. I scrambled around in my bag for the key to unlock the door. He set his hand on my leg, messing around. "Micah," I said as I laughed a little. It's funny actually. He looked up at me, his green in his eyes, just staring through me. They were bloodshot and tired looking like he would pass out at any second. I looked down at him as he began to fall asleep again. "You're almost there," I said as I helped him back up after unlocking and swinging the door open. "You okay?" I asked as I took him inside the door.

He moaned, "I don't feeeeeel good . . ." He spoke slowly as he put his head down as I carried him by his arm over my shoulder. I thought in my mind at his statement. He got drunk and then was beaten. I was expecting that he didn't feel good.

I somehow made it up my stairs and up to my bedroom with him still holding on to me. Every few seconds, he would pretend that he had no control over where his hands went, and they would brush over my bum. He was much heavier, being that he's drunk, it adds weight on. I let go of him once he was standing at the foot of my bed, and he fell down on his back and groaned.

"I'll be right back," I said to him as I turned around and went back downstairs to get a first aid kit to fix up his face a little better. I went down to the kitchen and opened the cupboard underneath the sink and looked around for it, but it wasn't there like usual. I went into the bathroom down there next and started looking through a cabinet and finally found it. I picked it up and rushed back upstairs before he fully fell asleep.

When I got back up into my bedroom, I saw Micah. He had moved himself to the top of the bed and under the covers with his head on the pillow, asleep. I gazed at him as he lazily opened his eyes, looking over at me. He looked so tired, though, as if he couldn't keep them open. I noticed that his shirt lay on my floor, and I prayed to God that he was still dressed under those covers. I walked over and sat on the bed beside him and pulled out stuff that I knew I would need to clean out the cuts on his skin from the punches and kicks. I dabbed the alcohol over each of them gently, not wanting to hurt him. His eyes were half shut, barely watching me as I did it.

He closed his eyes tightly as I swiped the dissenfectant over a larger cut. "Sorry," I whispered as I continued. He smiled a little with his eyes still closed, now only lightly.

"It's okay," he whispered back lowly. I stopped for a second, noticing his bruises on his chest. I couldn't stand the fact of him getting beat up in my mind. The fact that I saw some of them makes me want to just beat the hell out of Anthony myself. I think it hurts me more than it hurts Micah.

Once the bleeding all stopped on his face, I packed everything back away and left the bed. I went into my bathroom and put them in the cabinet in there, not wanting to go back downstairs.

I walked back out to see Micah fully passed out and snoring quietly with his face smashed into the pillow. I paused as I stood there and just looked at him. He's mine. I can't get over the fact that he would ever like me like I like him. It's strange. I never would have pictured myself with him when I first saw or met him. I don't know how it happened. I feel as though I have a stronger connection with him than he does with me. That scares me. I don't want to lose him.

I grabbed something to sleep in and went back into my bathroom and got dressed. I came back out and tiptoed over to the bed, not wanting to wake him up from his already deep sleep. I lay down cautiously and pulled the duvet and sheet up over me as I lay back and turned to my side to face the opposite way of him.

I felt him move a little closer to me, and his hand moved behind me. I felt a little weird with what's going on. I was smiling inside, though, at the thought and reality of him sleeping behind me in my bed.

I eventually fell asleep after finally getting the bad memories out of my mind.

***

I felt the sunlight coming through the window, but I didn't want to wake up yet, so I just lay still there. I then felt a kiss on my forehead. But I still didn't wake up. I didn't even think about Micah until I heard a car pulling in and out of my driveway.

Who picked him up?

I finally decided to get up as I heard my phone and Micah texted me saying good morning and that he had to go and that he was sorry about last night and that he'd see me tonight after work.

Why was he sorry?

I got out of bed and got a shower and curled my hair when it was dry. I stayed home all day, not having to work today. I then remembered that my mom is coming home tomorrow. But that happy remembrance was cut short when I remembered that tomorrow was Friday.

I don't want Friday to come. I can't stand the thought of him up in the ring illegally. That just makes it worse. He was just jumped too. I don't know if that will affect him though. I tried to tell myself that he'll be fine. I can't say it though. I can only picture Josh saying it over and over again. I waited for him to get off work all day, longing for more time with my blond protector. I never thought that I could feel so strongly for a guy. It's weird, but it makes me feel more complete with him in my life. I never want him to disappear.

Then my phone rang at about seven thirty. I answered to hear the usual greeting by Micah, although he always says it to me, I can't help but feel butterflies in my stomach and erupt a smile.

"Do you want me to pick you up?" he asked after both of us said hello.

"You don't have to," I replied.

"Well, how the hell would you get over here then?" He laughed.

I paused. I felt stupid. What was I doing saying that back to him? Who else would give me a ride?

I laughed as I stood in my kitchen after eating a plate of waffles. I held my phone to my ear with one hand and the other covering my face as I smiled at myself, feeling embarrassed. "So am I going to have to pick you up?" He laughed again.

I paused for a second. "I don't know. I guess so," I said, still with laughter in my voice.

"Okay, I'll see you in ten minutes then, babe," he said, still laughing at me.

"Okay, bye," I said back as I hung up my phone. I ran upstairs and packed a small bag, knowing that I would most likely be staying the night again. I was flustered on what to exactly pack though. I just grabbed some pajamas, my toothbrush, phone charger, and straightener for my hair plus an outfit for the next day. I didn't know what else, so that was all that I packed into my small duffel.

In about twelve minutes, when I was up in my room, I heard a couple of loud knocks at the door. I pushed my hair from my face and grabbed my bag off the floor after zipping it together. I then ran down my steps and set the bag down there, trying not to make it look like I was in a hurry for some reason. I walked over to the door, but I fell. I hit my side off the side of the staircase. I moaned as I put my hands on it. "Ow!" I said loudly.

"Kendall!" Micah shouted from outside. I fell on the floor due to the sudden horrific pain in my side. I lay on the ground when the front door was opened as he rushed over to me, lying down on my wooden flooring. "What the hell happened to you?" he asked as he set his hands on my side.

"I hit into my staircase," I said, smiling as I kept my hands on the area.

He chuckled at what happened to me.

"You okay?" He laughed but tried not to.

"No," I moaned.

"Oh god," he said, laughing at my clumsiness. "Well, you know you should lock your door. Anyone could have just walked in."

"I can see that." I laughed.

He then picked me up off the floor without any sort of trouble and took me over his shoulder. "I need my bag," I told him as he held me.

"Your bag?" he asked, a little confused.

"Yeah, if I'm staying," I said as I leaned in his arms toward the direction I left it sitting.

"Okay, yeah," he said, smiling as he bent down and picked it up from the floor. "That it?"

"Yep." I smiled.

"Okay then."

He set me down in his car and got in as well, putting my bag in the back on my side. The thought of the fight then came back to me. I don't want tomorrow to come. I broke the silence in the car with the subject.

"You still are fighting tomorrow?" I asked abruptly.

He looked over quickly right into my eyes as I stared at him.

"Yeah," he said a little awkwardly. I didn't say anything after that. "Ken, it's only boxing." He tried.

"It's dangerous," I said, trying to win.

"Well, so is you coming down the steps," he said, back trying to get me to relax off the subject.

I smiled, but then I got serious again.

"It's not the same," I pleaded.

"Kendall, don't," he warned for me to just stop right there.

I sat in defeat.

We went back to his house and just talked for a while when he left to go change into a pair of more comfortable shorts. He came back to sit on the couch with me. "I like your shorts," I said, going up against his side.

"I like your backside," he commented back.

I blushed at his comment. I didn't know what to do. I was caught off guard. I laughed then. There was an awkward silence for a minute as we just sat on his couch with the television on. "I know that you hit Ashton," I randomly said.

"That douchebag you work with?" he asked as I stayed by his side with my one hand on his chest.

I didn't respond to him. I just looked up at him. "He quit," I stated, still looking up at him. He laughed a little. "Micah," I said.

"I just didn't like him touching you."

"So you attacked him?" I said, sitting up, being upset with him.

"No one's allowed to touch you," he said back seriously as he looked down at me.

I just stared up at him. "I'll be right back," he said, kissing my forehead and getting up off the couch, and then he walked to his bedroom to use the restroom. I sat there just for a few seconds, as I was frustrated with him, then there was a knock at the door.

I waited a second to see if Micah was going to answer it and then came another knock. I decided to just go and answer it myself. I walked over to his front door. I opened it to immediately see an intimidating tall and large man with tattoos on his arms. I looked up at him as he noticed me standing there. "Dang," he said as he stared down at me.

I was quickly uncomfortable with him, not knowing who he is. "Micah!" I shouted, looking behind me for him to take over the conversation as I crossed my arms over my chest, feeling uncomfortable with his gaze.

The large man took a step inside as I stepped back a little at his movements. He set his hand on me as I stood in front of him. "Please don't touch me," I said as I went back another step so that his hand was off my shoulder.

"It's all right. He can't have you all to himself," he said, coming closer to me.

I stayed in shock as I prayed for Micah to hurry up. "Micah!" I shouted louder for him to hurry up for the man to go away. I was shaking as my palms got sweaty as they stayed stationary at my sides. "Micah!" I tried again.

I heard the sound of his footsteps coming quickly. I didn't look back though. I was too scared to. It would make me more vulnerable to the stranger in the doorway. The man's eyes stayed on me as I felt Micah's large hand on my shoulder, gently pushing me off to the side and behind him. "What are you doing here?" he asked sharply to the man as he kept his eyes on me.

"I need to talk to you," he said, still with his eyes on me as I looked at both of them as they interacted.

"Go wait in the living room," he said as he pushed me gently, still facing the man, as I was behind him with my hands smoothly on his back. He looked back at me for a very quick second as I stared at him.

He looked back to see if I was fully gone and then began to talk. I couldn't fully hear, so I went to the doorway. "I'm just here to make sure that you don't chicken out of tomorrow night," he said meanly to Micah.

"I'm going to be there," he said back harshly.

He saw me standing in the doorway to the living room. "You should bring her too," he said as he stared me down. Micah glanced back at me.

"Screw you," Micah said, taking his attention back to the man.

"No, man, I'd rather bed her," he said back as he took a step inside further. But I still felt safe. I know that Micah won't let him near me as long as he was around. He wouldn't let him touch me. He would always protect me.

Micah then seemed to lose it. He pushed the man out of his house quickly as he fell back. He then closed the door behind him as he took the man outside. I didn't hear anything outside as I took a few steps to the door. I didn't get close enough to hear anything being said out there before the door opened back up, and Micah came walking back inside, locking the door behind him immediately.

He looked back at me. I was scared. "You all right?" he asked, staring back at me with his eyebrows lifted at the question.

"Yeah," I said quietly, as I was nervous.

"He didn't touch you?"

I shook my head. I don't want to tell him, knowing that he would flip. Then I just decided to tell him after a second. "He just set his hand on my shoulder," I admitted, still speaking quietly.

"But you're okay? That's all he did?" he asked again, thinking maybe that there was more.

"Yeah," I said as he started walking to me.

He smiled in relief, running his hands through his hair. "I didn't know what to think when I heard you yelling my name," he said as he came over, embracing me in his arms. I hugged him back with my cheek pressed into his firm torso.

"He just scared me is all," I said, calming him down. "Who was he?" I wanted to know.

"Just the brother of the guy that I'm fighting tomorrow," he said, still holding me in his embrace. I held on to him tighter at the words of him fighting tomorrow. He laughed lightly as I tightly held on to his body with my eyes now glassy. "It's okay," he said lightly to me, knowing that I was upset.

"I don't want you to get hurt," I said as I lightly started sobbing. I didn't want to, but I couldn't control it from happening.

"Kendall, it's fine." He laughed. I held his sides with my hands tightly though. He held me out from him with his hands on my arms to look at my face. "You don't have to worry about me," he said, looking down into my eyes. I can't help but worry about him though. I can't deal with the thought of him getting hurt again. I looked up at his face, noticing one of the scratches still there from him being jumped by Anthony and his friends. I lifted my hand and set it lightly over the mark. He smiled at my gentle gesture.

"You don't have to do this," I pleaded.

He smiled as he took his eyes off me, looking around. "Kendall, I'm not going to change my mind," he said, looking back down at me. I knew then that he wouldn't back down from it.

Then his phone rang. He looked at me for a moment before he left me to go and answer it. I stood there, upset still. I wiped my eyes quickly as I looked to see where he went. I found him in his bedroom, sitting on the bed with his cell phone to his ear and talking to the other girl. I walked in the doorway as he quickly saw me standing there. I sat on his bed on the other side. "Okay, I gotta go," he said suddenly.

I heard the loud voice. "Oh, I'm sorry. I didn't know that she was there with you," she said as she really felt sorry I heard it in her loud tone.

He chuckled at it. "Yeah," he said back happily, looking down at the floor as I crawled into bed. I watched him as he still held the phone to his ear.

"When can I finally meet her?" she asked then, still loud and happy.

"I don't know." He laughed.

"Come on," she pleaded on the other end.

Meet me?

I lay down and thought about why she would ever want to meet me, whoever she is. And obviously she knows about me.

Why would he tell her about me?

He must trust her then.

"I have to go. Just call back tomorrow," he said back. I heard her say good-bye to him as he hung up after quickly setting the phone down on his bedside table and pausing for a moment.

He glanced back at me as I kept my eyes on him. He smiled back at me with his dimples.

"You tired?" he asked, falling backward on to the bed.

I hummed to him instead of answering. He smiled. I set my fingers in his hair as I played with it. He just stared up at me the entire time.

"Who is it that you talk to all the time?" I asked. I need to know. It's killing me.

I could tell then that he was thinking about it but still didn't want to tell me. I loosened my hands from his thick hair, taking them back. I could tell that the restriction made him upset, but I was angry and jealous with the person on the other line. He sat up and came closer to me and laid me under him.

"You don't need to worry, Kendall," he said quietly as he leaned down and kissed me on the cheek.

"Micah," I said softly, looking up at him.

I can tell that he's now annoyed by my questioning, as he inhaled and puffed out deeply. I lift my hands and place them on his head and entwine my fingers back into his thick blond hair. "Tell me," I whispered as I began to play with it and position myself better under him.

He just stared down at me. And then he just put his head down and looked back up at me. He leaned down and kissed me again only on the cheek. "Just go to sleep," he said as he rolled off me.

I couldn't fall asleep with the thought still scrambling around in my mind about the other girl and, on top of that, about the fight tomorrow. I looked over at him to see him facing the other way on his side, and then I rolled to my side to face the other way instead. About five minutes later, I felt him roll over and get close up against my backside. He set his hand over my arm, looking down at me. He paused for a second and then just cuddled up against me gently. I reached up and grabbed on to his hand. I feel pressured when I am this close to him and in his house. It's uneasy. I know because he is older and has been with plenty of other women. He expects something. But the fact that he doesn't try anything on me makes it worse. I feel like I am in a competition.

My thoughts were broken when he suddenly began to speak quietly behind me. "It's my mom and sister," he whispered. "Well, mostly my sister."

Wait, what?

I was stunned for a second. "What?" I asked back as I turned over to look at him.

"You want to know who I'm always talking to." He reminded me.

I stared into his eyes for a second, amazed from what he just told me, a smiled spread on my face. "But I-I thought that you . . . you said that . . . that you don't?" I was still in a surprise, not able to talk right and finish my question.

He said that he doesn't keep in touch with them?

He smiled, propping up on his elbow and leaning over me. "I got their number and called them," he told me, smiling down at me.

I leaned up and kissed him suddenly. I felt so happy for some reason. "What? When?" I asked, wanting to know more.

He didn't answer. He just kept his eyes on my face as I smiled. He leaned down and kissed me. "Thank you," he said as he kept kissing me down my neck lightly and playfully as I giggled.

I was confused by his thanking me. "For what?" I asked as I controlled my laughter.

He stopped and looked at me. "I called them because of you."

"Have you seen them at all?" I asked, smiling up at him as he set his arms around my body.

He nodded. "Only once, and it was brief," he said.

"Aw," I said sweetly to him. I got up and kissed him again as he laughed. "How was it?" I asked as I moved closer to him. I had my one hand around his neck and the other around his back.

"It was weird at first and strange after so many years. But it was nice to see them." He shook his head as if something had happened, but I didn't ask any further. "I can't thank you enough, Kendall," he said happily as he stared down at me.

I didn't know what to say. I never thought that I could have this kind of relationship with Micah. I would have never thought of it when I first saw him that night a few weeks ago. As I rubbed my one hand on his back, he winced at one of the areas I came across. "What is it?" I asked, cautiously moving my hand away.

"I'm bruised back there still," he admitted as his eyes squinted from the slight pain.

"I'm sorry. I wasn't—"

He interrupted. "It's fine," he said, leaning down and kissing me again.

He moved my one hand from his back. When he grabbed it, though, he saw the bruises he had put on me on my wrists. He paused and looked up at me. "It's okay," I said quietly to him as he stared at the marks of his hands on me. He looked down at me, and then I moved my hand out of his and up into his hair, joining the other. "I know you didn't mean it," I said as he moved more comfortably on top of me and began to kiss me over and over. I don't think that I've ever been feeling more pressured than now to do something with him. I don't know what to do now. I've never been this close with a guy. I moved my one hand down his back and slid it up inside his white T-shirt gently, not wanting to hit any of his bruises again and hurt him. He quickly moved his arms back and grabbed his shirt and pulled it over his head and chucked it on to the floor. I smiled, trying to hide my nervousness.

I moved my hand back and forth on his back, not knowing what else to do before. I just wasn't even thinking, and my hand moved from his back to his bum. He laughed at the sudden movement. I felt embarrassed. "It's okay." He giggled.

I didn't laugh at all though. I felt so embarrassed lying under him. But then I decided to just push it all to the back of my head. I slid my fingers into his shorts and nudged them down a little from his hips. I felt his underwear then as his shorts moved down. "Kendall?" he whispered my name in our kiss in confusion to what I was doing as I continued to remove his shorts from him.

I didn't know what to do. I don't want to wimp out from my actions. I don't want to ruin this moment. I didn't stop my hand movement as it gently squeezed the top of one side of his butt. He laughed at it.

Why did he laugh? Why is he laughing?

"Micah," I whispered in the kiss.

I felt his member against me now. It made me stop from it. I didn't know how to react to it. I didn't move my hand from his butt, but I seized the movement, keeping it in the same spot there. "What's wrong?" he whispered during one of the kisses.

"I just . . . I-I never . . ." I stopped myself from the embarrassment.

He stopped and just looked down at my face. He smiled as he leaned up against my stomach. His hand, I didn't even realize, was on my stomach, as my shirt was only lifted a little bit. He moved his hand, rubbing it in the spot of my skin, trying to relax me.

"It's okay," he said, looking down at me. "We don't have to," he added nicely.

Why though? Why does he hold back with me?

I moved my hand from his ass back up his back. He leaned down and kissed my nose after it reached the middle of his back.

I could tell that he knew I was confused with him holding back all the time with me. "I don't want to force you. I know you're not ready," he admitted.

I felt embarrassed as I tried to smile but failed, pulling it away off my face. "It's that noticeable?" I asked, being embarrassed. He smiled and looked down between us. He moved his hips off me, knowing it was making me tremble. He looked down between us as he did so.

He nodded. "Yeah." He smiled down at me. He saw my nervousness and embarrassment as I tried not to make eye contact with him. "It's okay," he said, removing his hand from my hip and taking my shirt back to cover the area where he lifted it from. I smiled weakly at him.

My eyes got glassy. I felt too embarrassed to talk to him for some reason. I couldn't reply to him. I knew he saw my eyes as his eyebrows creased to the middle. "Kendall, it's all right." He tried to comfort me. He knew it didn't work though. "Really," he added, trying again.

"No, it's not," I said as a tear ran down my cheek, tickling it as it washed down slowly. He looked down at me confused with me crying.

"Kendall?"

"You expect more," I admitted through the tears, making sure no more came out. I ruined the moment. That's why I was crying.

"What do you mean?" he asked, as he was really confused.

"You're older, and I know that you want more from girls," I said as another tear came out.

He sort of smiled at my words. "Kendall." He blushed. "That's different. I like you." He smiled down at me. I looked away from him.

He leaned up off me, taking his hands behind him and pulling his shorts back up his thighs. I weakly smiled up at him. "I'm sorry," I said quietly as he got off me.

He didn't smile or laugh at it either. It made me feel bad. He looked over at me. "Kendall, there's nothing to be sorry about," he admitted. I didn't believe him though. I know that he wants more. I can't control that thought. I looked away from him as he moved back over to me.

He's now lying beside me, looking down at my face. I'm still not making eye contact with him. I got up out of his bed. "Where you going?" he asked curiously, his eyes following me around his room as I went to my bag. I reached in and grabbed my pajamas out.

"To change," I said as I went in his bathroom, closing the door behind me. I got changed and then got myself under control as I wiped my eyes dry from all of the tears. I had to force myself out of the bathroom to face him with my nerves still running wild inside me. I didn't look at him, though, as he was still on the bed. I went back to my bag, setting my other clothes inside. I know that he is watching me, and I feel uneasy.

I walked back over to the bed. Micah sat up to me, sitting back down now in shorts and a comfortable shirt. They matched, being polka dot. I lied back down cautiously. He knew that I was upset. "Do you want anything before you go to sleep?" he asked, trying to talk to me.

"No, I'm fine," I said quietly, not being able to face him yet.

He didn't move any closer to me yet until a minute or two later. He got right behind me and rolled me over slightly to look up at him as he was about to speak. "I don't' care that I want to. I don't want to ruin this by forcing you, Kendall. I can ignore it," he said as I still looked away until the end.

I was happy to have him then more than ever. I smiled at him a little, not really knowing how else to express how I felt. I put one of my hands in his hair. He smiled because of it. I gripped it between my fingers and just stared at it. I love his hair. "We good?" he asked, looking down at me as he was propped back up on his arm.

I nodded and smiled at him.

"We should go to sleep then," he said as he lay back down against me. I rolled over to face him. I got against his chest so there was no space left between us.

"How many girls have you been with?" I wanted to know.

He didn't say anything for a few seconds. He could tell that the question was bothering me. "You want me to really answer that?" he asked back. I didn't say anything back as I clenched to him. "A fair few," he admitted.

I had one of my arms under his, wrapping around his back, and my legs entwined with his as I fell asleep with ease.

MICAH

Chapter 14

The number is different, and I hope it's the right one. The last four calls have been awkward, and I'll be sure to let Shailene's brother know how many on the list I had to go through to find the right one and give him an earful. He's supposed to be good at this kind of stuff, and right now, I'm not too convinced with the reviews.

I dialed the numbers on my cell phone after making sure they wouldn't be able to call me back and pressed send after looking at Kendall once more before closing my bedroom door gently and walking down the hall into the kitchen and opened up a beer, again being quiet, not wanting to wake her. The phone still rang and eventually went to a voicemail that belongs to an old man. I cursed quietly and took another drink of my beer and looked back down at the list and dialed the next number. This better be it, or I'm giving up. They'll survive without me ever calling and getting in touch with them ever again. But would we? I don't want to lose what I've found. What I've discovered. With this connection, I feel that this—my discovery—will bring our connection closer. Kendall needs someone that at least doesn't look like such a screwup. Yes, I know I came off that way. I only wanted to sleep with her and leave in the morning. That's why I was so insistent on following her home that night. That's all I wanted. Back then, I could tell she was unused, innocent, and inexperienced. But I wanted that. I wanted to take it. It would be something different, something new for me, and I was getting bored with the whores who were so willing.

When I went to her house that morning, I had planned on doing exactly what happened. It went so smoothly with her mother, and I was anticipating on seeing her that night—on that date. The longer that day went on, the more excited I became. I thought about it a lot when I was with Corey and Johnathan, and we smoked a couple of joints. They said I was acting like a pussy and was just going to be a good shag because she just won't know what to do, so it'd be more amusing for myself. I told Corey to fuck off after he'd said that about her.

Then I questioned it.

Why would I do that?

I had no idea why, and now I think I do. I liked her. I mean, I actually liked her. And on that night, I was trying to ignore it and push that dark feeling down as far as I could. But with each word she spoke, each nervous breath that emitted from her mouth, I couldn't fight it anymore. That's when I planned the second date . . . and the third . . . and so on, and so here we are, and here I am in my kitchen, beer in hand, calling all these annoying people to find the people who truly messed me up—maybe unintentionally, but still. I'm not going to sit here and whine about that. I never have, and I won't start right now. That part of my life is over. Maybe now it will be different? No, probably not.

"Hello?" a sleepy voice answered the phone. I paused and wouldn't answer. I already recognize her voice. "Hello? Who is this?" Yep, this is her.

"Uh . . ." Crap. What do I say?

"I'm hanging up."

"No." I rushed. "Don't do that."

"Then who is this?"

"This . . ." Nope, it's not coming out. "This is, uh . . . This is . . . well . . ." Still not happening. Come on. "This is . . . this is . . . Micah." There.

"Micah? Well, Micah, I think you have the wrong number. I don't know a . . ." She got it. "Oh . . ." She sounds shocked. Is she shocked? Hell, I'm shocked. "Micah," she whispered. Here come the questions. "Where are you? Micah, where are you?"

"Candice," I spoke back.

"Where do you live?" Let's get this over with.

"Over in Hillsborough."

"Should I come? It's only like three hours away?"

What the hell? Whom am I talking to? This can't be Candice. "Slow down." I couldn't help but laugh at her.

"What? Slow down? Micah, it's been years." She's loud now. Yes, this is her.

"We can meet tomorrow."

"What? When?"
"I'm skipping work so . . ."
"You have a job?"
"Yeah."
"Where are we meeting again?"
"Uh . . . at that coffee shop an hour from the house if you haven't moved."
"Okay, I know which one. Grandma took us to it."
"Yes."

***

When I sat down in that coffee shop, I didn't order anything. I just sat there. I feel sick. I don't want to be here. Right when I was standing up to leave, I saw them. I froze and then I sat back down to act like I haven't seen them yet. I don't want to see them. I don't want to be here. They're not going away now though. They know where I live now, and I've let myself feel weak again. It was too late when I felt there eyes find me in the booth at the back against the wall, and I started to hear my own heartbeat.

I glanced up when I heard them walking toward me. Candice seems taller, and my mother's hair is shorter and thinner, and she's gained some weight. Her eyes are glassy already as well as my sister's. Oh god. Don't start crying. I'm not good at comforting people and never will be. I should never have called them.

This is for Kendall.

This is all for Kendall.

I stood from the seat and hugged my sister. This is so weird. It's been years, and now, we haven't even said a word to each other, and we're just hugging in a café. "Micah." Her voice cracked. Here we go. She looked up at me after pulling away from me and just stared up at me. "I've missed you so much." She weakly smiled. I just tried to grin back, still without any words said from me.

Then it was my mom's turn. She just stood in front of me. I think she's . . . mad? I'm not sure, but she looks mad. Maybe sad? Upset? Confused even. But I can tell she's at least a little mad. With me? *Of course, dumbass.* That thought leaves my mind when I start to think back to more reasons why I decided to leave that place they seemed to call home, and apparently, it was mine too. I couldn't live with them anymore. Since I left, I've only had one panic attack, so I think I'm better off anyway. But now they're back and this one is on me.

"My baby." My mother latched herself on to me. After a moment of her arms wrapped around me and her face buried in my chest, I started to hug back, not trying really though. Why should I hug her, this woman who let that monster do all those things to me. That man who . . . I need to stop thinking right now.

"Don't start crying." I let go.

"What, after all these years you're going to be mean to me?" She's hurt. Don't think. Maybe they'll leave.

"Can we just sit down?" I sat at the booth as they slid in across from me.

It was quiet as they both just stared at me and glanced at each other, then stared at me some more. "You look so different," Candice spoke first. "Your hair. Your body. Voice. Just everything. What happened? Micah? Why? Why would you leave us?" She was reaching across the table for my hands and eventually held them in hers, but I only stared down at her small, bony fingers with small tattoos on them as well as her hands and some on her arms. I can even see one coming out of her shirt on her chest. No, I remember that one. It's a rabbit. I don't know what it means. Probably some dumb shitty idea when she was drunk at a party. Probably some dare.

"Candice." I breathed and took my hands out of hers, which caused her to recoil her arms on to her lap as I ran mine through my hair another time. "I didn't come here to answer a load of questions." I breathed. Relax. My heart rate is speeding up. I need to calm down. Kendall. This is for Kendall. Her lips on mine. That's comforting. Her smile. Her laugh and tender touches. Okay. Okay. I breathed in and out deeply.

"Micah." Candice rushed. "Are you all right? Are you having a—"

"No." I cut her off. "I'm fine."

"Well, then you can answer some questions, Micah," my mother chimed in. "Where the hell did you go? How did you get way over here all by yourself?"

"I left."

"We know that much. We're the ones that woke up and searched for you everywhere. Everywhere. Where were you? What you get to go dye your hair and become a different person to leave us behind because we're not good enough for you? What, you're some hotshot now? Is that it? You look like a punk."

"Mom!"

"Candice, don't. You cried for weeks, months even, over . . . this."

"Okay, I get what you're doing." I rolled my eyes. "You think I'm some punk? You think I look like some punk?" She nodded. "Really? That's what you think?"

"That's exactly what I see in front of me."

"Well, this punk has his life together more than you ever have."

"Stop yelling," Candice pleaded to us.

"She started it," I spoke next.

"Mom, he's not a 'punk.'" She looked at both of us. "He looks good. He's doing well. He's alive. He's safe."

"I am your mother. You just left us."

"I know what I did."

"Who is she, Micah?" Candice is serious now. How can she tell though?

"What?"

"Oh, come on, just spill it already. Who is this lady you got? Or man."

"Candice, I like women."

"Then who is she? I'm not going to be an aunt . . . am I?"

I shook my head, looking down and laughing a little. "No."

"You have to tell us."

I laughed again. "Her name's Kendall."

"And?"

I shrugged. "She's eighteen."

"When did you meet her?"

I shrugged again. When was that? "I don't remember."

"What were you drunk or something?" Now she's laughing while my mother is still not able to take her eyes off me. "Since when do you drink though, Micah?" She scolded.

"Oh please. Not from you. I didn't come here to be yelled at."

"Or what? You'll leave?" my mother asked.

Candice rolled her eyes and adjusted her white tank top. "When can we meet her? That's why we're here, isn't it? So she can meet us sometime? You're embarrassed to be a runaway."

"I never said that."

"What do you do?" my mom chimed back in now.

"Work? I'm a boxing trainer. A fitness trainer."

"At eighteen, and you became all that?"

"I didn't have anything when I first left really. I worked up to it."

"You couldn't do that with us around?" More eyes were watching us like a new reality TV show.

"You know I couldn't."

She stared at me.

"Look, that doesn't matter, Mom. I'm good now. I don't want to talk about that past."

"You left us, and now you're just here. I don't want to be mean to you, but I can't help how angry I feel. You just left us. My son was gone one morning, and I couldn't find out where he went. My baby boy."

"I'm not going to apologize," I admitted quietly.

"I didn't expect it, honestly."

"You want us back in your life so that your girlfriend can have this illusion of a close, happy family."

"She knows what I did, Mom. I tell her things."

"Okay then."

"Okay."

"I should get going, actually," I spoke up.

"Where?" Candice rushed.

"Work."

"Oh yeah. Right." We stood up, and I hugged my mother again. She told me she loved me and that I do look good and kissed my cheek, and I even whispered back, "I love you too." When Candice hugged me, it lasted two minutes, it seemed, and it was a strong hug.

KENDALL

Chapter 15

"Kendall?" I heard a male's voice say as I was nudged. I moaned, not wanting to wake up yet. "Kendall," he repeated.

"What?" I asked, still with my eyes closed tiredly.

"Don't you have to work?" Micah asked.

I took a deep breath before I opened my eyes and looked over at him. He wasn't lying on the bed. Instead, his hair was wet, and he had a towel wrapped around his waist. I closed my eyes quickly. He laughed, finding it amusing. "Kendall, I don't mind." Well, of course, he doesn't. There's a hint of something in his voice though. He seems different.

I took the sheet up and rolled over. "Come on." I felt uncomfortable as he got in front of me. "You have to get up now," he said, nudging me again as I held the sheet over my face. I felt the mattress shift as he sat down on the edge of the bed right beside me. I tried to roll over, so I won't be facing him. He snaked his arm over my hips to hold me in place. "Kendall." He laughed again.

I opened my eyes, but I only looked right up at his face as he looked down at me. I noticed as I looked up at him that he had a pair of shorts on. He leaned back a little and set one of his hands on the other side of me. "Okay, okay," I said, pushing his arm away as I got up out of his bed and grabbed the outfit I had packed and went into his bathroom to find the mirror all steamed up.

When I came out, he was gone. I set my pajamas down into my bag and looked around the bedroom for him. I peeked around out of the door and looked both ways for him. I heard his voice coming from the living room. I began to walk over to go and see him. I heard the familiar name: Candice. He sounded upset with his sister. I walked in as he saw me. I walked over to sit on the couch by him, and he just watched me as I did.

"Look, it's not until tonight, and I'll be fine," he told her as he paced away from me.

They were talking about the fight tonight—the illegal fight. I stood up and walked over behind him and wrapped my arms around his waist. I rested the side of my head on his hard back and closed my eyes. He smells so good, fresh from a shower, and his musky cologne.

He reached one of his hands down to hold on to both of mine as they stitched together at his belly button.

"Yeah, she's here."

"Am I interrupting?"

"No, no, we weren't doing anything. We have to go now. I'll talk to you later," he said, trying to end it.

"Where are you guys going?"

"Kendall has to go to work, and so do I."

"Okay, I'll call you later."

"I'm busy later too." He hung up.

Micah slid his cell phone down into his short's pocket and then unlatched my hands from him and turned within them to face me.

"Why'd you do that?"

"Do what?"

"You were being rude to her."

He shook his head. "So . . ."

"She's your sister."

"I know my sister. She'll get over it. That's what she apparently does." I rolled my eyes when I put my head down to avoid him noticing.

"You ready then?" he asked, looking down at me as his arms wrapped around me.

I smiled. "Yeah," I lightly replied. He lifted me to be at the same level as him and kissed me.

While he was driving to my job, I couldn't help but say something about the fight. I decided to not try and talk him out of it but just talk about it with him. "Who are you fighting tonight?" I asked curiously, peering over at him.

He glanced over and grinned. "Uh, his name's Shaun," he answered.

"How do you know him?"

"You always want to know more . . ." He sighed, talking under his breath and then continued. "We used to be friends, I guess you can say, and then I don't know . . . stuff happens." I didn't know what to say to him. What happened to them?

"Just be careful." I looked down at my lap.

He reached over and grabbed my hand into his as he drove with the other on the wheel. He never did answer me when we arrived at the bookstore, and he came over and opened the door for me. I didn't get out immediately. I didn't care that I was a few minutes late. He looked at me, curious to what I may be thinking. I looked up into his eyes, trying not to think about anything else. I can't help but worry about tonight. I shifted over in the seat so that my legs hung out.

He walked with me inside and into the backroom where I got prepped for work, and then he kissed my cheek. "I'll see you later." I don't know what's up with him.

"Bye," I said, pecking him again.

I watched him walk off to and back into his car and driving away to go to his job. I walked past a few customers and Brandy. I went to the back to Ben getting a drink. I smiled at him. "Hey, you decided to come in after all," he said as I was putting my phone into my pocket.

I looked over at him. "I'm only a few minutes late . . .," I answered back awkwardly. My wrists were showing, and I know he was now staring at the marks of Micah's hands still barely there.

"Kendall?" he asked, looking up at me in shock.

I looked at them and then took them down to my sides. "It's not what you're thinking," I said as I went to the door.

"What else would it mean?" he asked louder.

"Ben, it was my fault, okay? Drop it," I snapped back at him.

"Kendall, how could that be your fault? Look at your wrists!" he said louder. I looked at him to shut up. "He's not allowed to hurt you," he said quieter.

"Ben, you don't know what happened. It wasn't on purpose," I tried to tell him.

"If I see it again, I'll call the cops on him," he stated as I just walked out.

He wouldn't call the cops.

Would he?

The day went on with Ben trying to talk to me about Micah, but I just ignored him. "Brandy," I said, standing beside her to get her attention.

"What is it, Kendall?"

"Uh . . . I have to leave just like half an hour early today," I told her nervously.

"You already have plans?"

"Yeah, I'm sorry." I was nervous as I held my hands together.

She shook her head. "Just stop coming in late." She sounded mad and irritated. "You can go."

I smiled. "Okay, sorry. Thank you," I said happily, not knowing what order to put my words into.

I went to the back and grabbed my bag and walked outside. Micah's fight doesn't start for two hours, but I want to go home and get a shower and actually fix my hair before tonight. I walked home quickly as the sun was just going down. It's around six thirty. I went inside and got a snack from my kitchen, making something quick to eat for myself, and then I heard a car pulling into the driveway.

I looked out of the window before I noticed who it was. I opened the door and went out to see her, my mom. I sort of didn't really mind that she wasn't around this whole few days because I was just with Micah the entire time. "Hi," I said happily, hugging her tightly as she did the same.

"I've missed you," she said, smiling.

***

What do you wear to a boxing match, I mean?

I looked through all of my drawers for something that may seem right to me. My mom then came upstairs. I was wearing a dark gray boyfriend sweatpants and a lighter gray tank top. "Hey, I have to take a shift tonight, so I won't be home till late or in the morning sometime. I'll text or call you," she said to me from the doorway.

"Okay."

"You going to be okay?" she asked.

I nodded. "Yeah, I'll be fine."

She grinned at me. "Okay." She looked at me curiously. "Are you going somewhere?"

"Yeah, I have plans with Micah, actually."

"What are you guys gonna do?"

I shrugged. I can't tell her what is actually gonna happen. She'll keep me away from him for sure. "We're just gonna hang out."

"Kendall, I need you to talk to me. Don't you have any questions?"

Where is she going with this? "About what?"

She looked at me seriously now. "About being safe. Kendall, don't be stupid. I know he's older than you and that you two are probably—"

"Mom!" I cut her off. "We aren't." Why did she have to start this?

"Don't lie to me. I want you to be open with me. I know I'm never home, and you could be doing whatever." She started to explain while I begged her to calm down and told her that we don't do anything like that. "I want you two to be safe just in case you do anything at all. I don't want him to hurt you."

"Mom!"

"Kendall, I'm serious. I'll kill him if he hurts you. No matter how cute he is."

"Okay! Bye!"

Now she was smiling. "Nice talking. Bye. Love you."

Now I was laughing. Then she closed the door, and eventually, I heard her car pull out and drive away.

I just continued my search for something to wear. I decided to just text Savanna about it.

She responded about a minute later, saying, "I don't know, but since when do you like boxing?" I responded back that Micah is boxing tonight, and I don't know what to wear. She just texted back, "ha-ha sorry just check online," with another happy face. I shook my head.

I sighed as I fell back on to my bed.

After a minute, I just got up and tossed my phone to the side and grabbed a pair of light gray skinnies and a white shirt with pink sequence sleeves, only a little half way down, lining out the whole shirt.

I was pleased with my choice enough to fix my hair nicer. I didn't curl it to make it really curly, only to leave long waves in it and some messy curls mixed in, making it look thicker than it really is. I applied some dark mascara and some foundation and ChapStick. I then brushed my teeth. I sat and just lay there on my bed for a few minutes with the TV on. My phone buzzed with Micah's name coming up, telling me that Josh is on his way to pick me up and that he is just finishing up a few things. I just replied back an okay. About five minutes later, Josh came and got me and took me back to the gym as Micah was just walking out. I got out of Josh's car and went straight over to him, taking him into my arms quickly as he was unprepared by the action. He paused and laughed a little at it before hugging me back.

I didn't want to let go of him. I don't want him to fight, although I understand why he wants to do it so bad, and I can't stop him from doing so. I buried my head into his hard chest, lacing my fingers together on his back as I was right up against him. I wasn't smiling either. I don't want him to fight.

"It's all right, Kendall." He laughed.

I knew that Josh was right there, but I didn't care. He rubbed one of his large hands around my back to try and calm me down. I knew he was smiling. I had my eyes closed as my arms were still wrapped now tighter around him.

"We should go," Josh said, feeling awkward most likely.

I felt Micah move from me. "Yeah," he replied. He was happy. He's looking forward to this. I can tell now more than ever. He took his hands to his back, grabbing on to each of mine and unlocking them, but he still held on to one of them, holding me now only to his side. "We'll take my car," Micah told Josh as we all three went to where he was parked. Josh didn't wait for the awkwardness of who would sit where. He just knew to get into the back, letting us both have the front.

From the outside, the building looks rough and out of shape in some way. I looked around out of the window. I got confused at first when Micah turned and drove down a dirt road in the woods. Now, I'm just scared and shaking. This isn't a boxing match. Micah wasn't nervous at all, at least not from what I could see. He kept me close as we entered with Josh behind us. He kept his arm around me, holding me tightly to his side. Thank God. The smell isn't the best inside either. It's horrendous. I was surprised, though, by the number of people who occupied the terrible big building. Some of them came up to Micah and wished him luck, completely ignoring my presence with him. But he held me tight, letting me know that I was safe with him. I didn't doubt it either. It was loud, and the noise was everywhere, bouncing off the walls, and more voices joined in—screaming, shouting, yelling, and chanting all at once in the space where they all seemed to be crowding. I tried to see what the fuss was about. Well, I know there's a match. But where is the boxing ring? What's going on? Some people started yelling louder, and then it went down a little, and I could hear Micah talking to someone on his other side.

A loud man's voice rang loud and clear next, yelling into a microphone, announcing a man's name. People cleared a line and were still shouting, of course, while two men held a guy up, his arms slumped over their shoulders, and they were carrying him away. His nose was dripping blood, his eye swollen and black, and his mouth hanging down while he could barely keep his eyes opened. When he glanced up and made eye contact with me, a cold chill breezed up my body.

It was weird inside as we went more to the back and through a door that lead into a hallway, and then we turned to the left and down a short hall before we entered another room.

Where the heck are we?

My hands were sweating, and my eyes scanned everything around me. What kind of place is this? I clutched his side tighter, squeezing his hand tighter at the same moment. He glanced down at me. I saw from the corner of my eye. I know, though, that if I look up at him, I'll ask if we can leave, and I'd feel pathetic and embarrassed. There were a few other guys in the room. One of the men had tattoos littering his body completely from what isn't covered that I can see, another having a few, two smoking, and one looking like he couldn't care less about what is going on.

He led me to the back of the room. The walls were white and dirty. "Just hang out back here for a while. I'll be back in a few minutes. You're safe." He sat me down on the wooden bench that lined the filthy wall at the back. My eyes widened, and my grip on his hands holding mine tightened drastically. I shook my head quickly while staring up at him, crossing my legs when the other guys in the room looked over at me. Two of them smirked. No! No!

"Micah," I spoke quickly to try to get him to take me with him or stay with me.

"You're safe. I promise you. You think I would leave you if I thought something bad would happen?" He bent his knees to my level, cocking a dark eyebrow up at me for the answer. I nodded. I'm still pleading for him to stay here with me. Hold me. Leave. "Just sit here, and I'll be right back. Just keep an eye on her for me." He looked at Josh as he nodded a second after.

It made me feel weird as if I were a small child with a babysitter. Josh came over and sat beside me. I tightened up when I heard someone say in the room that the match would start in fifteen minutes. Micah disappeared out of the room. I was left only with Josh now and a few other men whom I don't know. This is uncomfortable.

"He'll be fine, Kendall."

I looked over at him. "How could you know?"

He smiled as he was about to reply to me, but he was taken off by a few other guys entering the room, roughly messing with each other. One of them held in his hand a girl's hand as she was dragged alongside him. She looked in place too. She was pale and had piercings that covered her entire ears. Her skin was tanned really dark, and her outfit revealed a lot more than it should. It made me feel unwelcome. She looked over at me, and her eyes skimmed me down head to toe.

I want to go. I want to march down that hallway with confidence and burst through every door until I find that damned Shaun and plead for him to call off the fight. I don't want this to happen.

"See you out there," Josh said.

Micah looked down at me as he was a few feet away from me, and Josh was now in the doorway. "She's staying with me," he told Josh.

A few seconds of quietness passed as Josh just walks away, leaving us. I looked over at Micah who was now removing his shirt. I felt awkward and oddly numb as he tugged down his jeans. Once off, he put on a pair of navy shorts. I was now sitting on a small table against the white wall. He strolled over to me as I let his hands set on my knees, allowing him to go stand between my legs. His large hands went to my back now, tugging me a little closer to him as he smiled down at me.

His hair brushed the top of my face as he dipped down onto it, setting his forehead to mine. I smiled, closing my eyes and setting one of my hands on the nape of his neck. His lips then went to my ear as he paused for a second. "I promise I'll make it out alive." He joked, laughing a little at it.

I didn't laugh. I just hummed in indication to him that I was listening. He kissed my cheek, surprising me. He drew back and locked his eyes with mine as he leaned in to kiss me. I closed my eyes though. I don't know how to exactly explain what I'm feeling. I feel everything all at once, and it's making my head fuzzy and my lips quiver with too much emotion surging through me at once. I don't want him to go out there and fight. I do have faith that he can win. But there is always a chance. I know I'm not at a boxing match but at a fight club. And yes, I know how brutal they can be. I've read and watched enough movies to know how dangerous they can be. How much can happen with so little rules. Why did he have to get involved in something so dangerous? Why? He paused when his face was centimeters from mine. My eyes stayed close. I know that if I look at him, I'll lose the small thread that I'm hanging on to, to control my tears. I must keep them shut. I heard and felt his sigh against the side of my face, making me shiver. When his lips placed a soft, wet kiss on the corner of my mouth, my eyes opened. "Okay," he whispered. His lips, still softly pressed against my skin, glided soothingly up to my cheek to plant another moist kiss, then retracting suddenly and stepping away from me and going to the table. I watched him closely with each move he took with ease like he's done it at least two dozen times. How many times has he fought at a fight club?

I stood up straight and wiped my eyes and took a few calming breaths. He looked back at me after gulping down half the bottle of water and clutching it in his hand loosely at his side. Before I knew what I was doing, I was standing in front of him again. He gazed down at me expectantly, listening intently to whatever is about to come out of my mind. "Good luck." He nodded once. It's the only thing that would come out. I wasn't even thinking to say that. It just came out. I know in some way that it's not exactly what he wanted to hear. Maybe he did want me to wish him luck, but not like that. Not this way. How am I even acting like this? I feel terrible and anxious and sad and angry with him. I think it's dangerous how alive he makes me feel.

"I'll be back. I hope to see my girl out there though." His shirt was lifted over his head and laid on the worn-out and ripped-up couch, his jeans sliding down his legs to be replaced with a navy pair of gym shorts that hung in a delicious way from his hips. He walked out of the room with the door left open wide as I heard his footsteps down the hallway now, getting further and further away, and in my head, a million voices were screaming for him to come back and for me to run after him. How could I turn them down? They're me.

My heart went wild, thumping uncontrollably in my chest. I couldn't let him leave, at least not like this. My head shook. I didn't want him distracted about me as he was about to go into the ring. I got off the table quickly. I stumbled quickly over to the door. My anxious gaze instantly found Micah's naked back as he walked down the hall.

"Micah!" I shouted as I went quickly, following after him as he walked barefoot. What is it about men's naked feet? He turned to see me approaching, my eyes spilling a little. My hands went to the back of his neck as I leaned and brought him down to my level, kissing him desperately. He wrapped his big arms around me, holding me tightly to him. We both drew back perfectly at the same time. "I'm sorry," I whispered as our foreheads were pressed together.

He took my hand gently into his. "Please, please, be careful, Micah," I softly pleaded to him. "I don't want you getting hurt. I can't bear to see you beaten. I don't want to. Don't do that to me. That's all I'm asking." I would have never pictured myself being this intimate with a man. I always thought it would be uncomfortable and weird and plain awkward on both parts. But the strange part of all of it is that you don't know until you meet someone like my Micah that makes your thoughts stop and the words and actions to go whichever way without your control, and once it happens, you have the ability to think of your next move. This is my first. Once it happens, you can never control it.

"I'll be okay, Kendall. I'll see you out there." He grinned, kissing me once more and turning to continue walking.

***

It was loud and smelled slightly awkward. The ceilings are high with the flimsy ropes, making a ring in the middle of the floor of the vast room. A vague thought keeps flowing through my mind of what this place maybe once was. I felt uneasy and queasy at the thought of people betting on this fight, on who will win tonight. I sat in the front row with Josh beside me on the one side, and then a girl came over and sat on the other side, Shailene. It was because of her. This whole mess was because of her. She smiled at me as I looked over at her. I can't help but feel mad at her. I should have a right to be mad at her. I knew that she felt awkward sitting by me, knowing as well that it was her fault. Her hand patted my shoulder, knowing how I felt at the time. But before we could talk, both Micah and Shaun were up and ready to kill each other.

Everyone was loud and excited with their entrance, but for me Shailene, and myself, we found it hard to watch him just stand up there. I tried to read their lips as they both talked to someone in their corners. I couldn't though. It was too hard, and it was distracting with everyone surrounding us. "I didn't want him to do this either," Shailene spoke, pulling me a little closer to hear her. "He's just so stubborn, Kendall," she added.

I looked at her. I just stared at her for a second. She was being sincere to me. I didn't want her to feel anymore hurt, so I nodded, smiling at her as she smirked at me. I know Micah well enough from these last three weeks to know that when he gets determined, he protects women because of his experiences in his past. There is no stopping Micah from anything.

I looked back up at the ring and saw Micah staring down at me, even though his coach was talking to him. I had to smile to keep in my small giggle as the elderly man slapped him gently to get his attention back to him as he spoke. All eyes were then on both Shaun and Micah as they got ready, going to the middle to meet. Micah glanced back over at me as he got closer to Shaun. Shaun looked over at me, making me freeze. I saw Micah see his eyes on me as he grinned over in my direction. Micah said something to him, and Shaun just laughed at him, making Micah's blood boil.

We watched them shake to start the fight. As soon as the referee backed away out of the ring, Micah's fist hit Shaun's face harshly, his head snapping to the side in a vicious jerk. They were hitting back and forth. I tried not to watch when Micah was hit hardly in the face and chest by Shaun, but it didn't faze him much, as he recovered quickly, hitting his opponent back. Ouch! I knew Micah wasn't new to fighting and that he is good at it when sober. I didn't think, though, that he would be doing so well out of his weight class, especially with someone like Shaun who is bigger than him. I believe in him, though, and when I encourage him, I know that he can be even better. Micah was quick with the blocking as Shaun tried to hit him with a sharp blow, ducking away and going around out of his enemies reach. I grabbed on to Shailene's hand at her side tightly as Micah took a powerful blow to the side, making him look in pain for a short moment. Oh no. How long can I watch this? People screamed and shouted. I knew that she looked over at me with my tight grip on her. He proceeded to take heavy and strong punches from Shaun.

Why did he slow down?

I want to scream at him to fight back, but I'm afraid to. Finally, I just shouted a simple no. I desperately looked over at Shailene. Josh was shouting out to Micah in the fight on my other side. "It's all right, Kendall!" Shailene yelled to me over the other's loud voices around us. I looked at her. "He's just finding his weakness."

"I don't know boxing," I told her.

She smiled. "It's just a flaw. Everyone has one to take them off guard. He needs to find it to win."

"Well, can't he do more not to get hit so badly?" I asked desperately.

She laughed at me. She didn't respond, being too much into the fight happening in front of us. I looked back up at Micah as he was hit again in the side of his face powerfully, sending him tumbling back to the old rope. I couldn't think of what his physical flaw would be. It had me completely at a loss. I can't seem to think of any.

At first, I was very scared to be around Micah, and now it feels happy and easy to talk and look at him as he looks at me. I know now that all he wants is someone in his life to truly care about him and to love him even if he doesn't admit it. The more that I thought about it, Micah is my main weakness as I now have the thought that I may be his. The tall blond male that had somehow forced himself into my life, making me now never wanting him to leave it. I need him. Just then, Shailene and Josh got considerably loud as Micah acted as if he'd found something and had to destroy it quickly.

She looked at me, smiling as I glanced over, not fully understanding at all what is going on up there or around me. Micah set one hand on Shaun's shoulder and began hitting him repeatedly on the side just below the shoulder. Shaun's right then hit Micah unpleasantly, making him stumble back a few steps. I looked uncontrollably as Shaun approached him again, setting his filthy hands on him as he spoke something in his ear. I was silently screaming in my head for Micah to attack him and defend him, but he didn't. The referee went over to them to break them up and continue as the crowd booed. Micah's face was filled with anger, his breathing rising with the looks of his chest heaving up and down at a fast pace. Shaun was pushed away from him. Micah's fists hit against Shaun's chest, shoving him away further. I sat frozen as Micah looked over at me. He just stared at me for a very quick second. I don't know what was just said between the two, but whatever it was has provoked him dangerously. His jaw tensed and his breath seemed to be increasing even more. I saw his muscles all tense. Shaun started screaming at him in the ring as Micah just looked at him full of hatred. People were shouting for him to do something and cheering for Shaun. He lifted his arm to wipe his forehead, taking away the sweat to only be replaced by another layer of it. Shaun was smiling as he gave me a quick glance. I then had the thought that maybe whatever was said may involve me in some way. I didn't know what to be thinking of, or if I should say something as Micah aggressively walked to Shaun. I couldn't watch anymore, knowing what was about to happen, but Micah could still get beat up even worse the second he may let go of Shaun. I can't stay here as I felt my stomach turning inside me, feeling sick with the sight in front of me in the ring. I can't watch. This is too much.

"I-I can't," I said to Shailene as she watched.

I knew that she looked over at me as I stood up out of my chair. I shoved through the crowd, standing, and past Josh. I heard them yell my name a couple of times as I exited. I had to leave though. I had to get out of that place.

Around twenty minutes or half an hour has passed now as I'm just sitting outside behind the building on a rail. There is only a small and calm breeze flowing through the air, relaxing me a bit. It feels good too after being in the clammy space inside with all those people, although it's a large building.

I turned my head to the sound of cars starting. I knew that the match was finished. I'm too nervous to walk over there right now. I'll wait for him to come out.

I got goose bumps as I trembled at the thought of what may have happened after I left. I felt a few tears run down my cheeks with the thought of Micah lying on the ground unconscious and beaten badly. No. No. I wiped my face with my hands, trying to stir the thought out of my mind.

I jumped a little as a hand was placed on my shoulder to get my attention. I swung around quickly and hit the person in the stomach to what I'd say was pretty hard. The man bent in the pain, hands on knees style.

"Oh, Josh, oh god, I'm so sorry," I said, getting up and setting my hand on his back as he groaned.

He smiled as he shook his head. I had hit him in the lower part of his stomach, considering his height. "I'm so sorry." I sort of laughed.

He shook his head. "No, no, it . . . it's fine," he tried to say without sounding in pain.

"Are you okay?" I asked, still with my hand on his back, trying to somehow apologize even more.

He got up fully as he sort of strained from it. He smiled at me, trying not to let his still painful lower part show. I laughed a little. He then noticed my cheeks a little red from the tears.

"Are you okay?"

I nodded, knowing that I cannot trust my now immediately shaky voice. "Kendall?" He pried.

I didn't do anything except look up at him. He walked closer to me, hugging me and trying to make me feel a little better. "He wanted me to come find you. He wants to see you," he told me as he let go of me. I looked at him, worried about what he was saying. "He's fine." He laughed. "You had him worried when you left."

Josh led me back into the building and down the corridor and to the door. He grinned sweetly as I went in to see what Micah may look like. I didn't want to walk into the room. I was too scared to.

I stepped in and shut the door behind me and looked to see Micah sitting with another guy, talking and smiling at something the other said as Micah held an ice pack to the side of his face. I just stood there awkwardly, not knowing what to do to let him know I was there. He turned, feeling someone behind him, I'm guessing.

He smiled quickly as the man patted his bare back and got up and nodded to me as he left the room. I looked at Micah as he sat down, looking up at me. He had blood still coming out of his nose and a slight black eye, his lips busted, and his face bruised along with a few nasty cuts and bruises on his chest and one on his right side. Then he smiled up at me. I'd imagined worse of what he would look like after the fight like he would be unconscious, laid out and not breathing, or just drenched in blood. I was so scared each day leading up to the fight.

I don't want to lose Micah. I feel that I need him in my life, and I don't know how to live without him. At the same time, I am too nervous to be around him sometimes because I feel that I may appear too clingy, and I know some of his history with women from others talking about him negatively.

I walked across the room in long strides, neither I nor he taking our eyes off each other. I stood in front of him and got down in. He stood when I got closer, and I just launched myself at him. He's here. He's fine. I wrapped my arms around him as if he'd disappear if I didn't hold him securely. "Hey," He smiled once he pulled back, wincing a little.

"Sorry," I shyly replied. I started to inspect his face further.

"Why?" he whispered, wiping my cheeks with his thumbs.

"I couldn't watch." I shook my head, looking down at my feet now. His hand gripped my chin and tilted it back up to meet his green gaze. He shook his head.

He held on to my hands as he leaned back and sat down on the wooden bench behind him. He pulled me even closer, indicating for me to sit on his lap. When I sat down, I did it carefully, not wanting to hurt him.

I leaned in to his warm body, sitting sideways. He winced as I put all of my weight up against his chest. "Oh, I'm . . . I'm sorry," I said as I removed myself from his chest.

He smiled. "No." He said as he laughed a little. I smiled at him as I leaned to him and kissed him. "Don't you want to know how I did?" he asked as I was kissing him. I didn't care. I didn't really want to know. As long as he's okay, I don't care. I shook my head against him. I felt his smile spread across his cheeks as I placed delicate kisses on him. "I won, Kendall," he whispered to me while his arms were set around me gently.

"What?"

He chuckled for a second, still smiling though. "You don't believe me? Have a little faith," he boasted proudly to me, showing off.

I just looked at him as a smile erupted on my face. I felt completely comfortable with Micah then. I wasn't nervous at all around him anymore. I felt safe and content with him now.

I didn't know what to say to him, so I just leaned in and kissed him with my confused thoughts with no words coming out, being careful with his lip. I felt him having trouble with the pain, as I was on his lap, trying to block it out. I drew back and stood up. He got up with me. "Kendall, I'm fine." He tried to tell me.

"No, you're not," I whispered to him as he stepped closer to me and set his large palms on my hips.

The door opened then with Josh and a few other guys entering. I pulled back from him because of their appearance. Josh looked over at us. "Oh, sorry about that man," he said, smiling and knowing that he was interrupting.

Micah smiled over at him, as he was very happy. I was embarrassed by them walking in. "Hey, uh . . . you wanna go out, Micah?" one of the men asked him.

"Where to?" he asked back as he stepped over to where I stepped away, knowing that I was uncomfortable.

"Just out, you know," the man whom I don't know said. "Celebrate," he added as he sat down.

He looked down at me as he stood right in front of me. "You wanna go?" he asked, looking down at my eyes.

I shook my head. "No, it's with your friends," I told him. I don't want to intrude with what is clearly just meant to be a guys' night out.

He just stared down at me. I felt the others' eyes on us both as we talked over it. "Oh, come on," he said, smiling down at me.

"Micah, just go. I'll be fine. Go with the guys," I said softly to him. He nodded, sort of taken off by me rejecting him. "Go." I encouraged him.

"What time?" he asked, looking over at Josh. They all smiled while two of them cheered. I laughed at them. They seem to be a lot of fun.

"Whenever you're ready," Josh answered.

"Okay, just let me take Kendall home and get a shower," He said to them as he held me close.

"Okay, we'll go to my place until," one of the men said.

"Okay, I'll come over after," he told them.

***

Once I was home, I just went upstairs. My mom was not home yet. It's ten o'clock now. My mind kept drifting from the movie and back to Micah. Oscar came up into my room and began whining. I figured out that he had to use the bathroom, so I went down the stairs with him right behind me. I opened the sliding door to the fenced backyard.

Oscar went running out and went to the tree. I followed him to just get some air. Oscar then turned to face me, and he began wagging his tail. I smiled at him, confused by what is making him so happy. He then barked. I walked closer to him and sat in the cool grass with him as he began to play around.

We both sat there for a while. It's like ten thirty now. Oscar sat on my lap and laid his head down as he got tired. His head propped up suddenly, looking behind me. "What ya doing?" I asked him as he began to wiggle off my lap and run behind me. I turned to see where he was going. It was to Micah standing behind me. He was in a different pair of jeans and a blue T-shirt, smelling fresh from a shower. Oscar jumped up as Micah picked him up from the ground, saying hello to him.

"I thought you were going out with your friends?" I asked, looking up at him.

"I wanted to spend my time with you," he said, coming up behind me and kissing me passionately as I leaned my head back. He set Oscar down as he started squirming. He started running around and messing with us as he came and sat on the grass with me. Micah sat in front of me and got close—really close. He put his hands at the hem of my top and lifted it until it was under my breasts. My breathing instantly hitched rapidly as his hands folded it up there. I could only stare at him in pure awe and amazement. He was so relaxed and confident with each move he made. He was being sweet and caring. I didn't know what to do when he lifted it, so I just sat still. He plucked a small white flower from the grass as Oscar went and lay up against his leg. I laughed at him nervously. My heart was beating fast all through my body. All I knew was how much I have grown to care for this incredible man. How much I will always care for him no matter what happens.

He plucked the stem off and slid the delicate flower slowly up my stomach and placed it into my belly button with his index finger. I looked down as he did it. I couldn't keep my eyes off him. He kissed just above the new decoration after he set it there softly. "You're so beautiful," he whispered as he laid me back. I smiled. Oscar got up and just stared at us and began trying to get Micah to play with him.

He laughed in our kiss as Oscar began tugging at his pants' leg. I felt too comfortable with Micah at that moment. It made me feel a little worried about what I started to think about.

Is this really what I want? Yes.

I knew it then. It had to be Micah. I know it's him. I want it to be him, and I'm sure of it. He lifted one of his hands to my chest. "I love that that's for me," he whispered as he went to the crook of my neck, kissing slowly and barely scraping his teeth against my skin as goose bumps started rising suddenly at the contact, and I shivered.

It was only ever him that made me so nervous and calm at the same time. It's an indescribable feeling I get. I absolutely hated and despised him when we met. I still don't really know him, but right now, I couldn't care less. I'm too fond of him. The only other time my heart was ever racing was when I had my first kiss. Cal Harrings. It was awkward and uncomfortable. It was a long kiss, but I don't think it ever meant much to him. To me, it was everything. It was the highlight for two years of my life. Hell, today, I still sometimes smile at the mesmerizing memory. His hands weren't near as masculine and perfect as my Micah's, but they seemed perfect at the time. He held my hips gently and then moved them up to my face. It was loud and cold that night. There were others who saw it happen. It was when everybody my age hung out at the varsity football games. It seemed like everyone was getting their first kiss behind the concession stand. We only dated for a few months. He said I was becoming too obsessed with him, and he just didn't like me as much as I liked him. I didn't love him. I realize that now. It was only from him being my first kiss/make-out session that made me feel so attached to him. I thought he would have been my first sexual experience as well.

My second boyfriend, Roy Walker, I thought that too. He was only a few inches taller than me and a year younger than me, whereas Cal was three years older and about a foot taller almost. His hands weren't big at all. His lips weren't as full, and his hair was always in a messy style. I, still to this day, don't know why I ever agreed to be his girlfriend in eleventh grade. Nothing ever seemed to get serious, though, with either Cal or Roy. Micah is everything though.

The pressure I felt in my mind was overwhelming. I have to say something to him. Let him know what I want. I trust him. I pushed all of the negativity to the very back and lifted his head from my neck to look at me. He looked down at me, wanting to know what I was about to say that interrupted him. His knees were on both sides of me as he sat over me. I lifted myself to him until I was near his ear and whispered, "I want to make love with you." He watched me in silence for a few seconds before his dimples showed. He looked like a small boy who wasn't sure of anything that was going on then but never been so happy in his life at the same time. It was like he couldn't believe what was going on. Why not exactly?

"Are you sure?" he asked softly, still with his eyes locked on mine. He looks scared and worried. Oscar relaxed and was now just lying by one of Micah's knees against it. I nodded to him slowly. His expression changed a little with what I said and replied to him. He just stared into my eyes.

I'm not naïve to the fact that he's had sexual relations with a girl before. He told me that flat out on our first date. But for a relationship, I don't think that he has ever. I ignored that fact that sort of troubles me about all of the other girls that he "knows" and set my hand around his neck as I sat up with him. He took my forearm and lifted me from the ground with him, the flower falling to the ground as I stood. I pulled my top back down to cover my stomach.

He paused for a moment as we made our way back to the backdoor. I noticed that Oscar followed. He stayed close to Micah's legs. He stopped at the door and made it so he was going inside first, turning us. His back was to it as he stopped and kissed me as he reached his hand back, sliding it open. Oscar ran in first. I smiled.

When we got to the top of the stairs, he switched us so I would enter before him. He shut the door behind him, not letting Oscar follow like he wanted to. I stood there, nervously twirling my thumbs, not knowing what to do next. I got confused, and my heart seemed to stop for a quick second as he reached into his back pocket and pulled out his phone. He switched it off and set it down along with his wallet and keys by my bed. Micah quickly took off his shirt with ease and dropped it to the floor. His back and front all bruised up from the fight and a couple from Anthony. I stared at his chest unable to take my attention from each mark and scar.

He slowly made his way over to where I stood, still nervous. He took me in his arms as he kissed me slowly. "It's all right," he whispered. He slid his warm and large hands up my shirt slowly, his thumbs massaging as he went up. I took over, taking my hands at the bottom and slipping it over my head. I sort of struggled with it as I heard him laugh and set his hands over mine and lift it over my head, throwing it to the floor. I looked down where it lay. It feels a little uncomfortable now that I'm going through with it. What am I supposed to do? Now, I wish I would have watched these kinds of scenes in movies. How does this kind of thing begin and end?

He brought my chin back up gently with his hand. "Shhh," he said quietly as he kissed me again. This time the kiss still only started out as gentle and patient. After the second one, though, his tongue was prying my lips open. He took my face in his hands, caressing it gently and sensationally. I couldn't breathe. I need air. How doesn't he seem to? I pushed back his chest just enough to break the kiss. His face went into horror and panic. "I . . . need to . . . breathe," I said in between gasps of air. He visibly relaxed from my explanation. He sighed and took another deep breath.

He took my face back in his hands and started kissing my cheek. "Sorry," he lowly mumbled as he continued his heated actions on my skin. I gripped his wrists lightly with my trembling hands and closed my eyes in pleasure as he continued kissing my right cheek. He moved to the other side and placed a few kisses there, then a single peck to the tip of my nose, causing me to giggle breathlessly, as well as he.

"You have such beautiful skin, Kendall," he said lowly as he started kissing down my neck while his hands gently caressed my sides. "Smooth and so soft." I moaned in response as I held on to his forearms, my head rolling back without my control. When he looked back up at me in the eyes, we just froze for a second and stared at one another.

He could tell how nervous I was about this and tried to calm me with every action he did. I took my hands to his back and to the top of his jeans. I took them to the front to the belt he wore as my hands shook, trying to get it unlatched. He chuckled lightly as he took over, undoing it himself. He didn't take them off though. He just took his large hands over to the button of my jeans. He got the button undone quickly and started to take them off me as he helped me step out of them. He stopped then and skimmed down my body now just about bare.

"You're so gorgeous," he commented, his voice husky and needy sounding. I blushed at him. I kept my arms around him as my hands began to get warm and sweaty. I took them up into his hair to try and cover it up from him. I would embarrass myself further. "It's all right, Kendall," he whispered. "You shouldn't be so insecure." He kissed my collarbones in a passionate way. "Especially about your body."

My heartbeat quickened.

My grip got tighter around Micah. He sensed my fear with what was said, and my pulse rose. As long as I have Micah, I will always feel safe no matter where I am. "Are you okay?" he whispered, kissing my neck.

He pulled back to look at my face after he asked it. "Yeah," I responded, looking up at his green eyes. He grinned down at me. He went slowly down my body, his hand starting at my sides and slowly making their way down past my hips and over my underwear, his lips following along slowly. He stopped and squeezed my hips on his knees in front of me. I threaded my fingers in his hair lightly, tugging at the thick strands. He rubbed his lips just above the tiny bow in the middle of my panties. He gently pressed his lips down, kissing me across my stomach.

"You want this?" He stopped, which made me feel suddenly very irritated. *Don't stop!* I pulled at his hair a little tighter.

"I'm sure."

He pressed his lips on my left hip bone. I sucked in a sharp breath as he ran both of his hands down the outside of my thighs, squeezing gently, the back side of them and over my butt where he stopped momentarily. He wrapped his arms around the back of my legs and curled his hands around my legs so they were spread on the inside of the top of my thighs now. My legs started to shake, and I didn't feel like I could stand any longer.

"Micah . . . please," I pleaded with him as my legs felt like they were going to fall off any second now. An intense feeling started erupting in the pit of my stomach. "Ahhh . . ."

"No. Kendall, you have to hold on. It'll be better later."

I can't stand. My knees started to buckle, and I leaned forward in to him slightly, looking for any sort of support. "Micah, please."

He chuckled at me. What was he expecting? He slid back up my body after placing a soft kiss on top of my right thigh, just below my panty line.

He began to walk me back slowly to the edge of my bed, with his feet no longer with shoes or socks. Micah's naked feet. He smiled as I opened my eyes from the last kiss before he encouraged me to lie back on the mattress. I took a silent deep breath. I closed my eyes after I was on my back and bit my lip. Micah got on me as we rested at the top of the bed.

I didn't even know that my eyes were closed until he kissed the corner of one of them. I opened both of them to see him above me, staring down at me. He straddled on top of me as he grabbed my wrist and began removing my bracelet and setting it on my nightstand. My mind was interrupted by the sound of scratching at my door. It's Oscar. He looked back at the door and then back down at me and smiled. I smiled back up at him as he lightly laughed, leaning back down to kiss me again.

He lifted me smoothly and unlatched my bra very easily. I felt insecure when he did, so when he let me back down, I turned my head, not wanting to look at him to see his reaction. "No." He laughed. "Look at me," he added, turning my face back to him so that I was looking up at him. "You just have to relax, Kendall," he said, making me calm a little. He wasn't pressuring me at all to do anything.

He leaned back down to me as I was pressed against his chest now, both bare. I set my hands on his back, moving them gently, careful not to touch any of his bruises. I kept my arms wrapped around him, kissing at his left shoulder gently. "It's all right, baby," he whispered, feeling my hands shaking as I still had them placed around his smooth back. "You're okay. You're safe." His head goes down and his lips press just above my right breast. His lips travel down my sensitive skin. His hand glides over my left one and I lift my back up so I press myself into his touch. His hand squeeze and pushes my back down against the bed once more. His hips move against me. I point my toes at the sensation, my eyes closed.

"Mmmm . . ." I involuntarily moan.

He leans up enough to undo the button and unzip the zipper on his jeans and pulls them down his long legs, disposing them to the floor. All too quickly, he was at the foot of the bed, grasping my knees in his gentle, rough hands and prying my legs apart. I tried actually holding them together. "We don't have to if you don't want to. You know that, don't you?" he asked, removing his hands from mine.

"No, no. I-I want to," I spoke quickly as I sat up on my forearms to gaze down at him. His eyes searched mine. "I'm sorry . . . I'm just nervous." He nodded, his eyes clouding with something, but then he quickly shook his head with some memory that I won't ask about, especially right now.

"Just relax though, baby." He tried again, pulling my legs apart. He reached his arms up and pressed down on my shoulders for me to lie back down completely. "Just try to keep still for me," he says loud enough for me to just hear him. The next thing that I feel is the cool and moist sensation of his lips connecting with my burning skin on the inside of my thighs, each one getting the same attention as the other. How am I supposed to stay still?

"I can't keep still." I breathed loudly as my legs stretched around.

"Just try for a minute. For me, please." The temperature has risen drastically all around me. The only relief is the feeling of his lips on me. I started clawing at the bed sheets beside me, trying to get some kind of relief. "Kendall." My skin is on fire everywhere down south. Everywhere else just feels only a little cooler. I start wiggling again beneath him. He stops and pulls his lips away.

"No . . .," I whine.

"You can't be moving round, Kendall."

"I can't . . . can't control . . . help it."

He slid his hands up over my lacey underwear and up my burning stomach and chest, stopping at my breast.

He dipped his head, placing gentle kisses all over my chest. His hands pinched carefully and squeezed and kneaded my breast as I was practically falling apart and dying underneath of him. He moaned and groaned as I lifted one hand back into his now unruly hair that tickled at my chin. He spread his palms over both of them and cupped for a few moments, sliding his hands up past them and down my sides, and he blew cold air from his mouth up my neck. I turned my head to one side to allow him better access to do so, which he took full advantage of. I couldn't last any longer. I don't even know how I've been holding it in for so long. However long it's been.

"Micah," I gasped loudly as his teeth slid down my neck.

"You can let go, Kendall. I've got you."

My whole body stiffened for a moment, my toes curled up, and my head arched toward the ceiling. My eyes squeezed shut as I held Micah as close as I could. My breathing started getting heavier, and just like that, I felt instantly and amazingly relaxed.

My breathing slowed down and then hitched again, and my whole body caught on fire as he slid his hand down the side of my panties and started sliding them down my legs. "We can stop at any time, baby," he whispered as they got to my ankles, and he slid down my body. I was somehow relaxed with him seeing me fully naked. I just seemed completely comfortable with him like it's a natural thing.

I opened my eyes to look down at him as he softly caressed my hip. "Have you ever done anything yourself?"

"What?" I leaned up a little to get a better look at him. "Oh no." I understood.

"You're all right, yeah?"

I nodded, not able to speak. I was speechless with everything that is going on. "Okay." His voice was low but deep. He leaned up and stretched his arm out to retrieve his wallet from my nightstand. I stared up at him as he unfolded it and opened the back of it, pulling out a light blue square packet. He held it between his fingers while leaning on the same arm to use the other to grab the waistband of his briefs. I set my hands over his as he started trying to get them down. I aided him in getting them all of the way off. I was shocked to see him naked on top of me. I started shaking as I stared at him for a moment. When he leaned back down and the small thud of the wallet falling on to the floor from the mattress sounded, I sucked in a sharp breath and closed my eyes for a second. He kissed me again before tearing open the packet with his fingers.

"I don't want to hurt you, Kendall."

"Please, Micah."

Small tears spilled out of my eyes and rolled down my cheeks once he rolled his hips down. "Don't cry," he pleaded as he leaned down and kissed away the salty drops. I clung to him as he adjusted slightly, and I sobbed quietly at the uncomfortable feeling got even more intense. "I know, I know," he spoke softly and desperately as he placed soft and gentle kisses on my cheek. I knew he was trying to distract me with the featherlight kisses, but nothing could distract me from what is actually happening right now.

He held the position for a minute to let me adjust to the foreign feeling. The longer he seemed to stay still, the more uncomfortable I started to feel, and the pain was becoming annoying.

"Please, move." I squeezed his sides.

"No," his raspy voice strained in protest.

He bent down and kissed me hard. His tongue breaking open my lips immediately as it entered my mouth. I started to roll my hips slowly, desperate for him to move for more contact. The more I moved, the more comfortable I seemed to get. "Micah," I whined when his mouth left mine. "Please, I want to feel you. I need you," I whispered.

He took another deep breath before he continued moving. It made me irritated. I want more of him now. I feel like I'm going crazy everywhere inside my body. The feeling is strange, but I fell in love with it as he continued to meet his hips with mine.

His breathing was going faster. I could feel his heart pounding in his chest as he lay down against me. The temperature was still rising. His forehead was starting to sweat. His lips were suddenly pressed against mine in a heavy and seemingly urgent kiss, the sounds emitting from our mouths caught by one another. I slid my hand up his back and into his damp hair and fisted it between my fingers. He groaned in response.

"Kendall." He breathed breathlessly. He slowed down when he saw my eyes were swelled again with unwelcome tears. "You like it slower then?" he whispered, breathing heavily. I nodded slowly. "Sorry, it . . . it's just been a while." I didn't understand what he was talking about, then it hit me. That's not something I wanted to hear. Him talking about the last time he had a one-night stand while he's on top of me right now. He closed his eyes, realizing what he'd said. He shook his head. "It's only you, Kendall," he whimpered, kissing my cheek again sort of playfully. He groaned loudly as he encouraged my head to the side to get access to my neck. Small sounds escaped my lips as he playfully started kissing and scraping his teeth up and down my neck. His nose nudged my cheek to get my attention, and the second I turned my head, I was met by Micah's plump, swollen lips in a loving and sweet, tender kiss. It reminded me that none of the other girls have never actually seen him like this. They had him differently. "Does it still hurt?" he mumbled.

There was no point in lying to him. I don't want to anyway. I nodded slowly, feeling guilty for not lying. His brows furrowed and his lip got caught between his teeth. He started kissing me again as he continued to move in me slowly, massaging the area with each movement of his hips. He shifted slightly, causing me to release a heavy breath. I felt his cool hand slip down my body, and I reacted quickly, grabbing his wrist and bringing it back up, and held it in mine instead. He looked at me in confusion. "Please, don't."

"I don't want it to hurt. I only want to make you feel good."

"It's just too much right now."

"I only want to keep you safe." He pressed his forehead to mine, nuzzling his nose with mine sweetly. I felt him retracting his hips, starting to pull out of me carefully.

"No," I spoke desperately, grabbing a hold of his hips tightly, trying to keep him from moving any further out of me. "Don't stop, Micah. I want this. Just keep moving, please." I sounded desperate and out of breath. He looked down at me, still apprehensive to comply. "I want you." I leaned up quickly, kissing him and bringing him back down into me fully. I bit down on his bottom lip, causing him to moan loudly in approval. I could tell somehow that he seemed more desperate for the contact. His kisses became heavy and more heated. I wrapped myself around his body, holding tightly on to him, clutching. His naked body shielded me, making me feel like we were the only two in the world. Nobody or anything else mattered.

"Kendall . . .," he moaned. My breathing hitched in my throat as I felt him twitch inside me, releasing his warmth into the condom. The thump of his heart beating against his chest matched mine as our bodies were pressed tightly together. I started kissing lightly down his neck as he rode out his orgasm. He laid me down slowly back on to the pillow. I felt sore and exhausted. He sweetly kissed my lips a few more times, his sweaty body pressing down against mine.

***

I tried my best to ignore the pain that was pulsing throughout my body as Micah then lay beside me. He got up out of the bed after a minute after he gave me a chaste kiss. I turned my head, feeling weird to look at him as he acted completely comfortable with the situation. "Kendall, I don't mind." I heard him laugh. I didn't feel right to look at him, though, even after what we had done. I felt him grip my sheet and take it away. I figured that he was going to cover himself up, so I turned my head back. He didn't though. He only threw it into the hamper. Not quick enough, though, before I could see some of the blood stains on them. He picked up his boxers in his left hand and walked toward the bathroom door. I blushed and grinned, watching him walk, his muscles moving with each step. I only kept my eyes on his naked back, still holding bruises and scrapes all over. They didn't seem to hurt him the entire time as I was gentle as well though.

When he got to the opened door and turned and smirked at me, my cheeks heated quickly. I couldn't take my eyes off him, knowing now that I no longer hold the title of virgin, and he is the reason why. I feel so connected with him. I gave everything I could to Micah, and I don't regret any of it. I couldn't help but feel my cheeks heat more, knowing I was part of the reason for his unruly sex hair that's a little patted down and somewhat a little waved at the ends. When I heard the water for the faucet turn on, I got up out of bed quietly and picked up my undergarments and slid them up.

I got back into my bed, pulling the quilt over me and lying down comfortably. I don't know what to say to him when he comes back out. I feel speechless. The door opened with him walking out in his boxers only on him, then walked over to his clothes and bent down to pick them up. "Can you stay?" I asked, peering down at him as he was grabbing his jeans.

He set his jeans back on to the floor and looked over at me with his dimples indented on both cheeks. I just watched as he walked back over to the side of the bed that he once lay at. I scooted over a little as he got in and under the quilt. Micah kissed my nose gently and lay down beside me.

"Are you okay?" he asked softly with his hand now tugging me a little closer so that I was now right up against his warm body. I ignored the sharp pains bursting through my body from my hips. I don't want him to know what he did. I gulped down the pain emitting, not wanting him to feel guilty for doing what he did to me.

I just grinned. I answered his question in just a small nod. Micah held me a little closer to him even though it seemed impossible to be even closer and to have more pain shoot up my body and down, but I didn't let him see my discomfort.

"I'm sorry. I'm just used to leaving . . .," he spoke quietly as he held me to him.

I knew what he meant. Before, it was nothing more than just a shag to him. None of the women ever meant anything to him, really. Micah began to move his hands around, grazing one of them down under the quilt, but I giggled a little, pulling it back up for two reasons. He just grinned in humor. I just watched as his eyes came back up to meet with mine.

"You don't have to walk away anymore." I held on to one of his hands. He looked down between us and then back up at my eyes.

"Anyone else would have been out the door by now."

I looked over at my door with the thought, even though I could never leave him. "I could still make a run for it."

Micah smiled and chuckled a little but not loudly. "Kendall, I think we both know you can't outrun me."

I just grinned at him with my cheeks flushing again. I know I have Micah to always protect me. He leaned his head down and kissed the top of my lips. The worrying thought then rushed through my mind that I hold a bigger connection with him than he does for me. I was able to hold it back as a small tear crept out the corner of my eye, slowly making its way down my face.

"What's wrong?" he asked with his tone a little deeper in worry. I proved successful in holding back the other weeps from coming out to upset him.

"Nothing." I shook my head lightly.

Micah stared at my face as he leaned over me and kissed the corner of my eye where it came from and then where the tear ended, kissing it away. It made me smile with my eyes lightly closed.

"It's late, Kendall. Go to sleep, baby," he said sweetly as he kissed my lips again softly in a good-night version. I entwined our legs. I began to wiggle my toes, feeling Micah's hair on his legs tickle at mine. I couldn't help my loud giggle as he mirrored my actions, wiggling his as well with his dimples popped.

Micah still held me to him even when he fell asleep. I lay awake for what seemed like hours, my mind racing, desperately trying to figure out what happened to my normal life. Micah.

***

I was asleep by like an hour as Micah passed out in a matter of minutes. I was awoken by his louder snore. After a minute or so, it got quieter, but it was still there. I got so relieved when it finally stopped after like two or three minutes of having to just lie there awake against his limp, heavy body. I can't just get up and go down to the couch though. I can't leave him. One, because he managed to like tangle himself against me securely as if he was afraid I would leave him, and two, I just can't leave him even just to go to sleep on the couch more comfortably.

Micah has his legs entwined with mine tightly, but his upper frame stretched out from mine. I felt a movement as I looked to see his large hand around on the sheet where the quilt was moved down a little more. "Kendall," I heard him mumble in his sleep. Is he dreaming? I realized that his hand was in search of mine. I reached one of mine down to meet his wandering one. I took it in mine. He entwined our fingers awkwardly and uncomfortably. He's still fast asleep. He mumbled my name again even more quietly. I just stared down at our hands connected. His hand is warm and clammy. Why?

His lips tugged up in a small grin, still in his heavy sleeping state. He held me closely to his warm body until there was no room but only a small bit left between us. He was scared of me leaving him sometime in the night. His chest is warm and feels good against me, comforting against my soreness. I slid my hand a little lower that stayed in his hair where he left it to move some of the strands hanging just below his eyebrows. I leaned my face closer to his, kissing his cheek, happy to have him beside me.

He still has his legs mixed up with mine under the quilt. I jumped a little when one of his legs moved against mine, causing a little pain from his being of more weight, now resting a little on top of my ankle. I managed to wiggle it off, making Micah moan in his sleep. What's he doing in his sleep, making him do this? I just held in my laugh as his breath hitched a little louder as his legs moved a little more as if he were walking. Thank God he isn't running.

I should try and go back to sleep before his snoring starts up again. Then I'd never be able to sleep. I closed my eyes gently, but I don't feel tired. I had to force my eyes shut again. I don't want to take my eyes off him. He's everything to me now. I never imagined becoming so involved with a guy, especially with someone as incredible and breathtakingly beautiful as Micah. I feel so lucky. He has everything that I would want. I never want him to leave. The feelings I have developed for him are almost too much to contain, and I don't want to stop them.

At first, I hated Micah and resented him for forcing me into his life that I wanted absolutely no part of. But now, I'm glad for his pushy demeanor, as I slowly fell for him, and now, he's lying beside me after the most memorable night of my life, thinking back to when Micah won the fight against . . . and then this, and everything. I now trust him with everything.

Then, as I was falling asleep, a question appeared in my mind that really is puzzling to me. I remember thinking of it before but never asking what the answer is. What were Micah and his "friends" doing at a graduation party? I brushed it to the side and eventually fell asleep with my arms and legs holding on to Micah's body.

Micah stayed with me the whole night as he held me close to him. I lay awake as he still slept. I lay facing him and looking at how he still looked perfect passed out. I raised one of my hands into his hair. He snored lightly with one of his arms wrapped around me. "I think I love you," I whispered very quietly to him. He was too asleep to hear me. The way that he held me was as if he were afraid that I'd leave him but more so protectively. I wouldn't though. I couldn't.

I want to get up and go eat. I feel so hungry, but he has his legs wrapped around me like a vine. I gently tried backing up from the bed. I heard him moan a little but still fully asleep. It took me a few minutes to finally get out of the bed as I quickly picked up his shirt and put it on after and then grabbed a pair of boxer shorts from my drawer. I went into the bathroom firstly and just stood there with the door closed. Why do I feel so different? I don't look any different, do

I? I don't know. There's a strange glow to my skin, and my cheeks are flushed a deep shade of reddish pink. Or maybe I'm just imagining it. I touched my fingertips to my cheek to feel the coolness to my warm and inflamed skin on my face. I took a deep breath. What is it about what we just did that is making me feel this way? I feel . . . happy? Special? Pretty? I can't pinpoint it. Something about me is definitely different. Everything, yes, was uncomfortable in a way, but . . . it felt normal, and I feel so connected with him now. More so than before, that is. I flicked the light off and walked back into my bedroom.

I looked back at him before I opened my door, and Oscar ran into my room. He slept right on the step the whole night. He ran in and jumped onto my bed, not disturbing Micah. It's seven thirty in the morning.

I walked down the stairs into the kitchen and to the toaster to make some toast. After it was done, I grabbed it out and set it on the plate I had ready and unplugged the toaster. I didn't even know that Micah was in the kitchen until I felt his arms wrap around me as he leaned down and kissed my cheek. I smiled. "I don't like waking up alone," he said.

"Oh I . . . I, um . . ." I looked back to the front door to see my mother standing there, not knowing where to look. My eyes got wide, and I quickly took my hands off Micah as he just smiled over at her normally as he stood there without a shirt and only in his bottoms.

My mother went past us awkwardly. I looked up at him in my nervous state and embarrassment. He just smiled. I had forgotten about my mother. I felt so ashamed I guess. "Oh god . . .," I said quietly, looking to where she walked off to.

Micah just acted completely normal with the situation. He doesn't care that my mother just saw us. He just smiled at me as if he were going to laugh. "You should put a shirt on," I told him seriously as I pushed his stomach. He looked at me. He smiled at me then as he grabbed the bottom of the shirt I wore.

"You're wearing it," he said, looking down to where his hands grabbed on and started pulling it up slowly.

"Micah," I said, trying to get him to stop as I laughed. He took me in his arms as I lightly screamed in laughter. "No, no." I laughed as he lifted me. "Micah, no, stop." I kept laughing as I spoke.

He set me down. I hit him playfully as he laughed at me.

MICAH

Chapter 16

Kendall went into the living room to talk to her mother. I stood in the kitchen and just took one of the pieces of toast. After a few minutes, I went upstairs to get my phone and other things that I left. I walked up her stairs and entered to see Oscar still just lying there where I was before. He woke up and looked up at me. I went over to the side of her bed where I set them and picked them up and shoved it all into my back pocket of my jeans from last night. I reached on the floor to grab my belt. Once I looped it around all of the loops, I felt someone walk into the room.

I looked up from latching it to Kendall standing, looking over at me. She smiled to me. I just grinned. "I need my shirt," I told her as I stepped closer to her front.

She blushed, looking up at me. I set my hands on her hips to lean in to her, but when I did so, she whimpered. I lifted my shirt up and over her head to put it on myself. "I should have been more careful."

"It's okay," she whispered.

I didn't know what to say to her as she told herself that she was okay. I didn't want to ruin it by telling her that it wasn't, so I just backed away from her touch. She covered her chest, still not acting a hundred percent comfortable. I laughed. "Kendall." I stared down at her. She's so beautiful. "You . . . you don't . . . ya know . . . regret anything?" I took a deep breath. "Do you?" She looked down, her cheeks still a bright pink, her hair wavy. "Kendall?" my voice cracked, embarrassing myself. It seemed to make her smile though, which I tried to return, and she shook her head.

"No."

She grabbed a loose shirt from her drawer nearby to cover herself from me. "You're leaving?" she asked, looking over at me.

I smiled. "Yeah, I have to go," I told her as I closed the distance between us. I wrapped her in my arms as she giggled when I began to kiss around her face. She grinned at me as she brushed her delicate hands over my hair. I just stared down at her, blushing a little as she smiled to me, even though I feel like I ruined this all slightly.

"Kendall!" her mom suddenly shouted from downstairs. She looked back to her doorway and then back at me. She reached down and took my hand as we went to the door and down the stairs. When we got downstairs, her mother was in the kitchen. She looked over at me and smiled. I grinned back at her. I didn't feel at all uncomfortable around her—or really around anyone. I don't care.

Kendall wouldn't touch me at all around her mother. I turned on my phone and saw the missed calls and texts from Corey and Jared and one call from Candice. I looked down at it in a plain look. I felt Kendall's eyes go to me as she talked with her mother about something that I wasn't paying attention to. She kept her arms away from my body, crossing them over her chest instead. She is obviously uncomfortable around her mother with it. I looked up to her and grinned, and she looked at me curiously to what I was looking at on my phone. I took my arm to her shoulder and pulled her in, locking my phone first so she wouldn't see what I was looking at. I hugged her to say good-bye.

"I gotta go," I told her as I then kissed her and let go of her shoulder.

I felt her mother watching us as I walked to the door. She followed me. "Micah?" she asked as I opened it. I turned to her and kissed her again. "You okay?" she asked, wanting to know why I was leaving. I'm not going to tell her though. She shouldn't know. It's not her business. I know that she won't like it both if I do, and she would just be mad at me.

I looked down to her as I held her to me. "Yeah." I lied. I kissed her again. She tried not to smile but failed.

"Okay," she said, sounding a little upset with me leaving her already.

"I'll call you later, Kendall," I told her, kissing her cheek and looking back at her as I walked out. I went over to my car and got in and looked back to her as she stood in her doorstep and watched me leave her. I did feel a little bad for leaving her, but I have to. I have to go now.

***

I arrived back into my driveway and got out quickly. I grabbed my keys out and went to my door as I looked over to my neighbor looking over at me. They don't like me very much. I looked away and fiddled with the keys until I found the one to unlock my door. I went inside and flicked the light switch. I set the keys down and went to my bedroom. I opened my drawer by my bed and moved the clothing to lift the compartment.

I grabbed the bag filled with the substance and just stared down at it. I thought of Kendall. I felt a little ashamed if she would know how I got on my own. I don't feel comfortable with telling her anything of my past. It's too much for her to know yet.

The craving was killing me inside. *No.* But I have to. *No.* I bite down, clenching my jaw. I can't control it. I took some of it out, storing a little into a small baggy and hiding it down in my vent to the side, keeping a little out for myself as I quickly lit it up and inhaled. I sit on the edge of my bed and relax my shoulders with my eyes staring straight ahead of me. I took a deep breath once I finished it. I got up and turned on my ceiling fan and opened my window a little to air out the smell in case someone would stop over. No. I do feel kind of ashamed, but I don't care right now. Nothing is bothering me, really. I was good for an entire few days, but I just ruined it.

I grabbed my bag and then walked out of my room and picked my keys back up after setting the bags into my bag and setting it over my shoulder. I went back out and into my car as I pulled out quickly. I looked over to my neighbor who was still on his porch with a little girl. He glanced over to me. I drove down to where I was supposed to meet Corey.

When I got to the pier, he was waiting with another man whom I don't know. I walked over to them with my bag, making sure that I didn't see anyone that I knew. I went up to them both as they turned, hearing me approach. Corey looked over to me. "Who's this?" I asked, looking over at the other man with light hair and blue eyes.

He looked over at him. "This is Eric," he answered. Eric nodded. "He'll get it to the buyer today," he added.

"Okay," I answered, handing him the bag I carried.

Corey smiled at me. "Jared told me that you were mad about this all."

I scratched the top of my nose. "Yeah," I told him, looking over to his face from Eric's.

"Why would you want to quit?" he asked.

"I have an actual job now, Corey," I told him.

He just looked at me. "I don't think that's all there is," he told me. "You've had that job a while."

"Just give me my cut so I can go."

He smiled to Eric. He then reached into his pocket and pulled out my share. "Nine hundred," he said, handing me the stack.

I took it quickly and put it into my pocket. "You can never just walk away, Micah," he said. I just looked up at him and then turned to walk away.

I walked down to go back to my car. As I was walking quickly, I looked over and noticed a girl that seemed to look familiar. I looked away from her as she talked on the phone. I only looked at her for a quick second, but I saw her naturally blond hair and her eyes that stood out in a light blue. I walked quickly to my vehicle and got in and picked up my phone to check it. I had a text from Kendall asking again if I was all right. I looked at the text for a moment before I saw the girl again outside walk past down the sidewalk and look over at me as if she knew who I was. I just ignored her as I went to Kendall's name and clicked call and backed out of the lot.

Kendall's mom stayed home with her on Saturday, so I just called her before she went to sleep instead of intruding on them spending time together. I woke up alone in my bed, stretched out across it. I got up and got a shower.

She stayed again for the whole day of Sunday. I made sure, though, to contact her at least every few hours by a simple text or call. I didn't want her to feel at all used. I really like her.

It's Monday now. I woke up again alone in my bed and got ready for work. I got to work and texted Kendall that I was there, and I could pick her up after to take her home, but I have plans with Candice for the rest of the night. I lied about that though. I went in a few minutes late. The whole day, I felt distracted, thinking back to when I took some of it and hid it in my room. I want it again now. I had to shake my head a few times to the strong thought of it.

When I decided to take a break for a few minutes, Josh came up to me. He came and sat by me. "I know you're still doing it," he told me.

I looked up at him. I sighed, being annoyed by him always patronizing me about it. "It's not that easy to just walk away," I snapped at him.

"Well, I can't have you working here if I know this much," he told me. I looked up at him. "I'm not firing you. Just get done with it,

Micah," he said as he then got up and walked away. I just ignored him and got back to work. I had Kendall on my mind during the whole day though. She acted a little weird each time that I talked on the phone with her. It bothered me if she regretted being with me.

***

After work, I just went straight to see her. I walked inside the shop to see Ben standing, talking to some girl. He looked over at me. "Kendall here?" I asked him as the girl turned to me.

The girl had blond hair, and I recognized her from Saturday. I looked down at her surprised. Who is she?

"You're Micah?"

I looked a little nervous and confused, I guess, to her as she sort of giggled. "Uh yeah," I said back to her.

"I'm Emily," she told me. "Kendall's friend," she added, knowing that I was confused.

"Oh," I said back. I felt weird. She saw me that day. I just looked down at her.

"It's nice to finally meet you. She really likes you." She smiled to me. I grinned to her. "So don't get her hurt," she added seriously. Kendall then came out of the backroom.

She soon saw me standing with her friend and Ben. "Micah?" she asked, smiling, coming over to me. I smiled at her, meeting her halfway and kissing her. She looked at Emily. "I'm sorry. What was it you wanted to tell me?" she asked her friend.

"Oh." She looked at me as I looked down at her from holding Kendall to me. "I, uh . . . You know what, it's nothing really," she said it glancing up at me as she looked a little frightened.

I looked at her a little confused.

What was she going to tell Kendall? About me?

I know that she saw me. Kendall just smiled at her. "Okay then. I'll see you another time."

"Bye," Emily told her, taking her sight off me.

Ben looked completely lost to what's going on. "Bye," Kendall replied back as she left.

"You ready?" I asked, trying to make it not seem awkward anymore.

She looked over to where Emily left at and then up at me. "Yeah," she said, confused by what just happened.

I could tell by the way she acted when I grabbed on to her that she was still in a little pain. Ben just stood there awkwardly.

Kendall and I went outside to my vehicle and got in. She wasn't acting weird anymore. It relieved me a lot. When we got in the car, I knew that she was thinking about something. "Wonder what she wanted?" she asked out loud. I knew. I'm not about to tell her though.

I just shook my head. "I wouldn't know," I told her as I glanced over. She smiled at me.

She came over and sat as close as she could to me in the seat. I reached my right hand over with my left still on the wheel and let her hands entwine with it on her lap. I can tell that she's different. She seems more comfortable with me and not so nervous like before. It makes me feel better. The thought came back into my mind. I want to go home.

We got back to her house. "You said that you were going out with Candice?" she asked as I walked her to her door.

I looked at her as she held on to my side. "Yeah," I answered.

"Can I meet her?" she asked, holding on to me.

I looked down at her as we got to her door.

I nodded, not trusting my voice for some reason. "Yeah, of course, I just don't want to mess any of this up."

She looked at me confused and then smiled up at my face. "You won't," she told me sincerely.

I looked at her for comfort after that. "I just don't want to fuck this up like I do with everything else," I told her honestly. I always mess up everything no matter whom it's with. She came in and hugged me. Her door then opened with her mom standing there, surprised to see us. "Oh sorry. I was just going to work," she said. "Hi, Micah," she greeted, smiling at me.

"Hi," I said back, my voice a little deep from being a little taken off guard. She then turned to Kendall who loosened herself from my body. "I have to go, but I'll be back tonight," she said, looking at us both. I laughed, but Kendall didn't.

"Okay." she said. "Bye," Kendall told her mother sweetly. I leaned down and gave her a kiss. Her mom then went to her car and got inside. She seemed to be waiting, though, and I knew what she was doing.

"Bye," I said down to Kendall, still holding her to me, but her hands barely on me because of her mom being around. I leaned in and kissed her again.

"Good night," she said as she let go of me.

I looked at her as she closed her door with the pressure of her mother now pulling out, trusting Kendall. I walked back to my car across the street. I don't know what they talked about, but her mom still seemed to like and have respect for me. I drove home quickly.

KENDALL

Chapter 17

My mom took me to work that morning. I said good-bye to her and thanks as I went inside. It still feels a little weird to be around her. It makes me feel bad. The day seemed to be going so slow. Micah texted me a few times just to see how I was doing. I smiled at every text. I don't understand exactly what I am feeling though. I'm still a little confused with him. I want to know more about him. I want to meet his family.

Brandy came over to me as I stood at the counter after I was done with a customer and handed me some stuff to put on the shelves. I went over and started to set it all up. I looked to see that Ben and Brandy were both absent from the store part. I looked back and continued my job. I glanced over at the windows to the blinds being pulled down, and then I remembered that Brandy had closed those moments earlier when we first closed up, the door only having the sign flipped over to Closed.

We had just closed now, and I was just finishing up my part before I would leave. I heard the door open and close to the shop then. I didn't turn around to see who it may be. "We're closed!" I yelled to whomever just walked in. I heard a clicking sound after and came to the conclusion in my mind that it was the lock.

I just thought it was Ben or Brandy. Then I heard the sound of heavy footsteps coming closer to me. I got a bad feeling, a knot in my stomach that just kept on twisting. "Hello, beautiful," the deep voice said from behind me.

I tensed up as my hands got shaky and warm. Usually, that type of saying came from Micah. But something seems different with the tone. It's only a deep one and doesn't have the same sound. My stomach tightened even more into a more tangled knot. I dropped what was in my hands as my mind went crazy with what's going on.

Who is it?

I could feel his breathing, the heat hitting the back of my neck.

It's not Micah.

I didn't move until my wrist was taken harshly to to turn my body around. My eyes widened and my body trembled at who it was. His face still looks beat up from the fight. Shaun. He was intimidating to look at. His height only a little taller than Micah and his arms large, he used it all as an advantage against me. I had no desire to be here. My mind went crazy to going straight to Micah. He isn't around, no one is.

"Aren't you happy to see me, Kendall?" he asked, smirking down at me. It made me feel sick.

He held my wrist tightly in his large hand. It made me disgusted to look at him. "Don't touch me," I said loudly to him, yanking my arm from his grip and back to my body. He laughed at me.

"You still are feisty," he said, coming closer to my body as it shook. His eyes went from my face down my body, stopping at my chest. I felt even more disgusted, knowing what he's doing. I was mad at myself for wearing a V-neck. I stepped back as he tried to take his hand to my face, denying him. My heart is thumping quicker, my pulse racing, not completely knowing what he is planning.

Shaun is going to kill me.

I know that he planned this if he won the fight or not. He doesn't like Micah for some reason that I don't know. I'm sure he knows where Micah is now and how close he is. That's how he wants it most likely, to have him know that he was only a few roads from me when it happened, to be so close.

When he smiled, it sickened me further to the point where I now feel as if I will vomit at any second. I looked up at him with glassy eyes about to spill. He was enjoying my state of fear of him.

Shaun stopped me as I jolted to make a run for it to the door for some sort of help, knowing that I can't outrun him. I had the outgoing thought that I could make a run to find Micah at work but no. He took me harshly to the wall, pinning me between him and it. "Scream for me," he said softly as if trying to be sensual, looking down my body and back to my face, only glancing up every now and then to see my reactions as he had his mouth to my neck, harshly biting at the skin, raising the blood as I tried to bat him away as hard as I could. "I want Micah to know that you screamed for him," he added as tears spilled out of my eye, running down my cheeks quickly with the others following. "Come on," he tried to encourage me to do what he demanded. He settled one of his hands on my hips firmly, and the pain set in. I don't want to listen to him. I will be his next victim. "I want to mess up your pretty face for him," he whispered in my ear, setting his hands all over me. I closed my eyes tightly as the tears continued with his words.

I don't like it. I can't stand it anymore with people making me feel physically powerless. His touch makes me want to gag. I lifted my arms in defense to block his fist that was sure to knock me to the ground. I was left against the wall, and he backed up from me. It made me wonder what was going to happen to me next. He took his arm up, hitting me across the face hard. I stayed on my feet surprisingly with the powerful blow. The pain was bad. His frame stalked closer to me after. The moment that he got close enough, I hit him back, my palm catching his nose at an angle. My eyes widened as I took my hand back.

What did I just do?

I regretted doing it immediately. It just came out of me. Blood poured from both of his nostrils. He's filled with anger. I don't know how I hit him so hard, but the thought crossed my mind that I may have just broken somebody's nose. "You dumb fucking bitch." He cursed at me and lashed his fist to my face, knocking me to the floor. His shoes came into my vision, as I was now on the floor. I was then in contact with his foot to my stomach. I scrambled up to my feet, sobbing badly. I was never beaten up before, maybe one punch, but it wasn't hard. This was all new, and I don't know how to exactly react to it happening now, especially from an older man. I don't know if I can explain how painful it is.

My plan was to just dash out of the door. I could be with Micah in five minutes if I ran fast. He could help me, protect me. I don't know if anyone else could besides maybe Josh or someone else he worked with, but I want Micah. I cried for him, not saying his name though. I couldn't find the strength to fight back against Shaun like he may want me to, making him even angrier. When I tried for the door, Shaun grabbed me in his arms.

"No," I cried out over and over. I don't want to. My hip collided with the counter as he shoved me off him. He spit out the blood that was in his mouth from his nose. I'm bruised badly. I can already tell with the pain happening. I don't know what kind of damage I have taken because all of the pain is mixing together at once, not making it hurt so badly all over.

Shaun hit me again and then another time. "Kendall!" I heard the voice coming. I know who it is immediately as it comes into my hearing. Ben. He rushed from the backdoor, running over to help me. I looked at him as he came closer. I felt so relieved to know that Ben didn't leave yet, staying to wait with me for Micah. I felt so close to him then. I could barely see Ben as he attacked Shaun. I blacked out for a few minutes, I guess, as I heard a loud voice shouting, holding me behind me, and I knew it wasn't Shaun. Thank God.

I held on to him with the small amount of strength that I still had, clenching his pant leg tightly as I cried. "Get out of here!" he yelled, which I assume is to Shaun. I looked over to see Shaun wiping the blood still coming from his nose. He looked to me.

"You keep your fucking mouth shut," he told me as he pointed directly in the position I held on the ground. He held me captive in his vision. "Or I'll kill your little perfect boyfriend as well," he added.

"Who was that?" I heard Ben faintly ask me, not knowing where I am right now.

It feels like about five minutes has passed since Shaun has now left, leaving me alive. I smiled that I was safe now thanks to Ben. "Is this all your blood?" he asked. I tilted my head down to where he looked. My hand was covered in dried up blood. I cried a little harder from looking at it.

"You have to help me wash it off." I panicked. I can't let Micah know what happened. Shaun will kill him.

"Kendall," I heard Ben say as I hurried to get the blood off. I was in the bathroom in the back, sitting on the counter. I was carried in by Ben. I washed desperately.

I didn't look in the mirror yet though. "Ben!" I cried out for his help. Within seconds, he was at my side.

"Okay, okay," he tried to reassure that he was there to help me. He took my hands from the running water and turned me to him, rolling up my thin sleeves. He then guided my hands back under the water. I saw the bruises that litered my arm now. I sobbed as he scrubbed me clean from all the blood. The cold water felt good washing over me. A towel was tugged then, and Ben lightly dabbed it over all of the marks that Shaun put on me. When he came to my face to help it, I got scared that he was going to dab my bottom lip with the towel to try and help.

"Please, don't," I pleaded quietly. He withdrew the towel. He nodded, looking at me face as I had my head facing down now. He took my hand as a kind gesture to try and make me feel a little better.

"This had to do with Micah, didn't it?" he asked, looking at me, but I didn't look at him as he stood in front of me. I was sat on the countertop of the sink. "The guy who did this to you was because of Micah," he said as he already knew the answer. I know that Ben and Micah don't get along. Micah doesn't like him the most. He hates that I work with another man. "You have to tell him then," he said after a little more softly.

I took my head up quickly to look him in the eyes. "No." I shook my head desperately to his words.

"No? Kendall, he could have killed you," he said loudly. "I'll just call the cops then. You know who it was, I know," he said calmly to me.

"No." I shook my head again. "Shaun said . . ."

"He's not good for you. Because of who he is, it's going to hurt you again or get you killed," he said, looking into my eyes as I stared at him. A few tears came out from my eyes. "He's dangerous," he added, trying to convince me. "You're too good for him."

"No," I cried.

I took my hand from his as he tried to get me to leave Micah. "For fuck's sake, Kendall, look at your face!" He broke loudly. He took my chin and turned it to the mirror. I looked in defeat. I don't care how badly hurt I am. I just want to protect my Micah. I was shocked as I absorbed the image I now carried. My eyes got filled again. I covered my mouth with my hands as I turned back around. "He caused this," he said sharply.

"Stop it!" I cried. "You don't know anything!" I added as I got off the counter to go home.

"Kendall!" he shouted as I walked out of the room and back into the store part.

I grabbed my bag with me. He followed, rushing behind me. I heard my phone then vibrate in my bag. I grabbed it out, wiping my eyes first. It's Micah saying that he'll be over in a few minutes that he had to stay a little longer but he can send Josh to get me.

Ben stood beside me now. "You don't want to risk him seeing you," he said calmly. "I'll take you home," he added.

The tears came out as we then hugged, and I sobbed into his much less of a chest compared to Micah. I can actually fit my arms around him. My phone then rang. Ben looked down at me as I looked at the screen to Micah calling me because of not texting him back after the two minutes that passed. He worried. I pressed the green button to answer it.

"Hi, beautiful," he greeted. My heart feels like it stops and a chill runs through my body. I know that Ben could hear him with my raised volume on my phone. Ben looked at me as my eyes got filled up again. I thought to Shaun being the last one to call me that. He would have ruined Micah's greeting, making it only in his voice that I could remember if I'd died then.

I took a deep breath to try and get my tears under control. I looked up at Ben as he watched to see what I would say. "Hi," I said, shaking.

"Kendall?" he asked his voice worried. "Kendall, baby, are you all right?" he asked, now more worried with my silence. I can't let him know. He sounded a little confused.

I gulped down loudly. "I-I'm fine. I just . . . um . . ."

"What is it?" he asked desperately.

"I . . . uh . . . I'm just not feeling too good," I said with my voice shaky. I heard a door open and close on his end.

"I'll come get you right now," he said as he was leaving his work.

"No, no, Micah," I told him anxiously.

"What?" he asked as I heard the wind outside.

"I'm . . . uh . . . already home."

"Micah!" a voice yelled to him when he was standing outside now.

"I can't wait to see you," I told him with a tear coming out as I lied, trying to calm him down and convince him to believe me.

I could tell that he was smiling. His voice sounded happy as he spoke again. "Well, can I come over after work to see you?"

My eyes widened. I have to keep him away until I heal. Shaun's threat came into mind. I have to protect Micah even if I have to lie to him. "No, um, actually I have one of my friends over with me," I told him after thinking of it, hoping that he would believe me.

"Oh okay."

I felt bad making him feel like that. All I want to do is hold him in my arms and have him talk to me in person. But I can't. "I can come by when she leaves?" he sort of asked and stated at the same time.

"She's staying, actually."

"Kendall? Are you sure that's it? I . . . You sound really upset about something."

I got myself under control. "Uh, just a bad day at work," I admitted. Ben was watching me closely as he then let out a girly laugh to go with my lie. I looked over at him quickly with my eyes wide. He just grinned a little to me. I can't imagine what Micah must have thought of that, so I just tried to ignore it.

I could tell that he tensed up. "Is it because of that guy from work?" He sounded mad.

I squeezed my eyes closed. Ben was listening to everything right beside me. I heard him lightly laugh from Micah's statement.

I looked up at Ben. He never upset me. "No, just forget about it," I told him.

"All right. I'll come see you tomorrow then," he said softly.

I smiled with my eyes closed. I can't convince him not to come.

"I have to go," I told him, lifting one of my hands to my hair, moving it out of my face.

"Okay, I'll talk to you later."

"Bye," I whispered back after a few seconds, making sure I wouldn't cry to him.

"Bye, beautiful."

I took my phone away from my ear and hung it up, putting it back into my bag.

***

Ben drove me home. I hoped that Micah wouldn't drive past us the entire time and see that I lied to him and was with Ben. He parked in front of my house as I saw that my mother wasn't home. She's already left for work. My face hurts a little worse now. "Thank you," I said with my head down. I looked up at him after and gave him a weak smile before I got out of his car.

"Yeah," he said quietly. I can tell that he feels good that he was there for me and not Micah. "Just be careful," he added as I shut the door after stepping out.

I looked back at him and gave another weak smile to reassure him. "Night," I said, not saying good night because it's not a good night.

He didn't respond. He just waited in his car until I reached my door and was safely inside. I heard him pull away as I stood against the door with it locked right away from fear that Shaun could have followed us.

I didn't get out of bed for two days. I called off work, telling Brandy that I'm sick. I lied to Micah and told him that I went to work yesterday, but I avoided him every time he tried to come see me. I prayed that he wouldn't just show up and ignore my texts from telling him that I was busy with my friends or mother. He never did thankfully.

I jumped at the sound of my phone vibrating in my bed. I moved the sheets around to find it covered. I picked it up to see Micah's name popped up, calling me. "Hi, beautiful," he said as I answered it after it rang a few more times. I really wish that he'd stop saying that to me nowsince Shaun has tainted it.

"Hi," I said back, wiping my eyes.

"You didn't tell me that you were still not feeling good," he said right after getting straight to the point.

It caught me off guard, and I didn't know what to say. "What?" I asked back like I didn't hear him.

"I went to see you at work today and Brandy told me you called in sick . . . again." His voice was annoyed.

"Uh . . ." I paused, trying to think of what to say. "I'm sorry. I should have just told you. I just didn't want you to worry."

"Well, how are you feeling?"

"I'm okay," I said back happily to hear his voice caring about me.

He didn't answer for a minute, making me scared to what he was going to say to me for lying to him. "Well, I can stop by after work to see you. I can take care of you," he suggested sweetly but a little demanding at the same time.

"No, I'm fine," I told him, frightened.

"Kendall." He laughed. "I'm going to come see you," he added humorously, but I know he's being serious.

"I-I'll come to you."

"You sure?"

"Yeah, yeah, I'm fine. I'll see you later."

"Okay, bye," he said, sounding a little confused by my tone and anxiousness.

"Bye, Micah."

I figured that if I went to his house, I will have more time to get ready. I got out of my bed to look in the mirror in my room to inspect what my face looks like now. I looked into it after taking a deep breath to see marks and bruises that still remained there. I gently set my hand over each of them as a tear came out. My eyes were a little puffy from all the crying I did. I haven't really had to face my mother yet, though, because of her schedule.

I got my makeup bag from the other end of my room and took it over to the mirror as I stood looking at myself, at my face. I figure that

I can just wear long sleeves and jeans to cover up the other markings. I took some of the concealer to my finger and began to rub it over the bruises, and then I covered it with more of the makeup.

I feel awful. I don't want to leave my bed. I took one more glance in the mirror before I headed downstairs to go to Micah's house. It scared me to death that I have to walk over to Micah's house alone. I don't want to run into Shaun or have him attack me again. I can't bear the very thought of him hitting me again. I don't see how Shailene ever liked him or any of the other girls he has been with.

How did she get her scar? How did he do it?

I shook my head at the thought, trying to rid of it. I continued to walk quickly with my legs holding some pain as I did so. I then reached his turn in the sidewalk, and I went down it quickly. I knew that he'd be waiting for me. I'm glad, though, that his house isn't even a mile away so that I can walk. I thought that on my way to his house, I would have some time to think about what I would say to him but no. The only thing that I could think of was if Shaun saw me and if Micah would be mad at me.

My heart got faster. I was only a couple of houses before his came up. I stepped up his stairs slowly. I only knocked once before I heard him rushing to the door. I smiled with his anxiety to see me. He paused at the door before he opened it. He stared at me quietly, as I didn't want to look at his face as he studied mine. I couldn't help myself. I have to look at him after two days. I couldn't stand to be away from him. He moved sideways for me to enter. I looked behind me before I stepped in carefully. I walked in a few steps before I turned to face him.

He stared at my face sadly. I stood there in his sight nervously, holding my hands in one another. He looked down and then back up at me as if he didn't want to look at me. His eyes were frostylike as if he's upset. Upset for what though? Micah stepped in front of me so that he was against my front. I looked up into his glassy eyes as he moved my hair away from my face. He looked to where I covered one of the larger bruises and then away, biting his lip as if to control himself.

"What happed to your face?" he asked after looking back at me as if he were building up to talk to me. I smelled the strong smell of liquor on him then, and it made me shake. I just looked at him as if I didn't know what he was talking about. I didn't cover it well enough. He tilted my head to the side to look at the mark better. "You tried to cover it," he said almost in a whisper, looking over at my eyes. My eyes got full of fear as I looked at him, and they filled up quickly.

I spoke quickly then, trying to give him an answer. "I didn't want you to worry . . . I fell," I said, trying to reach for his arm to hold for some sort of comfort. But he moved it away as he looked away from my lie.

"You don't think that I'm dumb enough to believe that bullshit, do you?" he snapped.

How does he know?

My hand fell from trying to reach out to him and trying to get him to understand. His breathing got uneven as he looked away from me and then back down at me.

His height just made me feel worse. I can't have him against me. "I don't know what angers me more, the fact that you didn't tell me yourself or who the fuck I had to hear it from." he said, looking down at me. I couldn't find my voice because of him knowing about it. I didn't know how to respond to him, so I just stared up. "Kendall, you were attacked," he said, looking down at me. Then he clenched his jaw. "He fucking hit you!" he screamed with his voice deep and made me jump. I freeze up and stare up at him. His raise in volume made my eyes barely spill out. "Do you know who told me?" he asked, looking down in my eyes. I shook my head. "That fucking guy from your work, Ben," he told me. I've grown accustomed to Micah always cussing, but in this situation, it made me feel worse. Ben told him after he knew that I didn't want him to say anything to anyone.

Micah then stocked past me, brushing against my arm, leaving me in the hallway. I followed him slowly to see that he went into the kitchen. I stood in the doorway, setting my hand on the frame. He was by the sink. His head bowed down as his hand was tightly holding on to a glass cup, half empty with some clear liquid. He picked it to his mouth and drank it all. After cursing, he spoke again, "I need another fucking drink." He turned and grabbed the bottle of vodka from the counter by the fridge. He's not drunk though. Micah filled the cup and then drank it all again.

He didn't look back at me as I watched him drink more of it. It made me scared as he turned and looked at me. I didn't know what to do. His house smells weird today. I don't know how to describe the smell completely. I just know that it isn't completely all from the alcohol. What is it?

I think he had finished the whole bottle by himself. He set the glass down roughly, slamming it on the counter. My pulse began to race. His eyes locked on mine. He looked so angry with me, and I knew that he is now drunk by drinking the entire bottle. I feel terrified. I don't know what is going on in his mind right now. "Micah?" I asked, trying to understand what he's doing.

He just stared at me though. He looked away from me and around the room as he took his one hand up and just slid it down his face and looked at the floor afterward. I didn't feel safe enough to approach him, so I just stood there shaking. "Don't be scared of me," he said, looking back up at my face. I didn't answer as he walked into my direction closer. I took my arms across my chest as he approached, not knowing what else to do. He looked at my bruises again. He lifted his hand and set it against my cheek lightly. I'm scared of him right now. What's he going to do?

Tears started to run out of my eyes without my consent. "Don't cry," he whispered as I just took my arms around him and cried into his chest. I'm overwhelmed. He waited a few seconds before taking his arms around me with his chin pressed lightly on top of my head.

"What are you going to do?" I spoke once I calmed myself down a little.

He didn't answer for a few seconds. "I don't know yet," he responded quietly. He let go of me after that completely. "I'm still angry with you."

I knew that. "I know," I responded back to him as he stared at my face. He then just walked away from me, leaving me alone in his kitchen. I turned to watch him go into his bedroom. I wiped my eyes and took a moment to compose myself before following. Right when I walked in, the awkward smell of marijuana was separated from the alcohol. I don't want to ask either. I feel too scared to ask him any questions right now. He went over to a stack of clothes and pulled out a pair of sweatpants.

I looked away awkwardly as he stripped off his clothing completely, not caring if I watched him or not. He's never embarrassed by his image. I looked back to see him then change from a buttoned shirt to a normal one. He usually would just leave his shirt off when he would go to sleep around me, but he put one on.

I watched him then climb into bed, not caring what I was doing. He looked stolid as he did so, but I ignored my thoughts and just got in bed as well. I thought back to when he said that he'd never let Shaun touch me, and if he did, he'd kill him, and when I said I don't fancy visiting him in jail. I don't want to think about him being locked away from me.

I didn't lie by him, only staring over at the wall. I felt him then grab me and then he pulled me over against his body. I wrapped my arms around his chest as he lay down by me. He didn't do it out of any sort of compassion though, only for his own need to have me there against him. "Micah, please, please don't—"

"You don't get to decide," he interrupted after. "You have no fucking say in what I do." I sobbed quietly as I held on to him tightly. "You understand?"

I looked up at him, and he looked down at me as I nodded in response lightly. I don't know how long I lay awake before I got too tired to keep my eyes open. I didn't want to fall asleep though, I was scared that if I did, I wouldn't wake to feel Micah get out of bed and go to Shaun. I tried to hold his hand at one point in the night, but he denied me of it. It made me feel bad for not telling him, but I knew that I couldn't. I pondered over the thought of telling him how I felt, but I couldn't find the strength to do so. The one person that I depended on for some kind of comfort had shut me out. I sobbed against him silently, not because I felt bad or I let the pain get to me, but because I don't feel that I have more feelings for him than he does for me. I can't ignore that.

MICAH

Chapter 18

When I woke up, I couldn't feel anyone else in the bed with me. Where is Kendall? Did she leave already? I'm still angry and intoxicated from last night. Her decision to keep this to herself is something that I cannot understand. How does she expect me to protect her if she kept a secret like that from me? My mind is tainted with the picture of how Shaun must have hit her. I know how he did it. I got the covers off and stepped out. I looked in the bathroom, but she wasn't there. I opened my door and looked around before I left. It's only nine. Why is she up? I walked down the hall to the kitchen, but she wasn't there. Where the heck is she? I decided to look in the living room. I looked in, but before I was just gonna go back to bed, I saw her sitting in the dark on the chair by the window.

Her legs bent to her chest as she is just looking blankly out the window with her head laid on her knees and her arms wrapped around her legs, holding them as she watched the world outside. I don't want to talk to her. I feel so mad at her that I don't know how to explain it. How do I control myself with her anymore? How am I supposed to be able to trust her? I don't want her afraid of me, but I can't help what is going to be said from me with the rage bursting through. I noticed after a second that she was wearing one of my shirts. One of the light blue button-up ones. She has to roll the sleeves up to her elbows due to the much longer length.

How does she expect me to protect her if she won't tell me anything? Why didn't she tell me what happened?

She could have been killed, and still, she felt it best not to tell me about it. I bite down, holding my jaw tightly. I then started to walk over to her. I don't want her sad, but I don't want her thinking that she can just do that to me. She turned quickly to hearing me approach her.

I don't know how to comfort her and make her feel better. I looked at her face as I sat down on the window sill. She looks bad but still beautiful. Her bottom lip is still busted. It looks painful. I don't know how she put up with Shaun's punches to her face. I have to admit that he can hit hard, but I can block it out better than others. She still has a darkened spot on the side of her face. It doesn't look as bad as it must have when it was fresh. I want to leave and go fucking kill him right now.

I can tell that she is sad by the way that she is just staring at me and wondering what I'm going to do about the situation. I took a deep breath, still observing all of her marks from Shaun. I don't know what I am going to do now though. All that I am longing for is to have Shaun held down and do worse to him than he has done to my Kendall. I want to kill him. But I'm not letting it show, knowing how she will react.

"Micah," she said quietly as I looked back at her from glancing outside. I clenched my jaw again as I had to look at her face. It took me a second before I could make full eye contact with her. She lied to me, and I can't just let that go. I'm confused with her. If she won't tell me something as serious as this, what else isn't she telling me?

Why wouldn't she tell me that another man beat her almost to death or what was intended to end with her dying?

I know that all she wants me to do is hug her and tell her something to make her feel better and cuddle. I can't do that though. Something's stopping me from getting any closer to her. She's broken. I can't look at her face anymore from only being able to see what Shaun wants me to see, her split lip and bruised-up jaw and cheeks, and slightly black eye. It's what he wants, and it makes me want to just kill him even more. She cried all night. I don't know if she even slept for more than an hour or maybe only a few minutes. She just lay against me last night with her face on my chest with tears wetting my shirt as she sobbed but not making it obvious with sound.

I still can't do anything to comfort her. I watched her as she leaned to her side and grabbed a cup to her lips, sipping. I watched her closely as if something bad would go wrong while she did it. It was quiet between us until she broke it. "You had hot chocolate . . . I made some for you too." I wasn't watching her until I heard her stop talking, and then I looked up at her into her eyes. I can't look at her face anymore. "I-I didn't want to wake you," she added, still quiet.

"Thanks," I answered her back quietly, staying with her tone. She smiled. She just wants me to talk to her and let her know how I'm feeling with the tone I use. "Why'd you get up so early?" I asked after a few seconds to just talk to her as she gripped the mug close to her.

She blushed at me as I tried my best to smile at her. She looked down and then back up at me and smiled more. "You were snoring," she responded, smiling while she said it. I grinned at her.

KENDALL

Chapter 19

Micah took me home later that morning, saying that he was busy for the day. I didn't say anything to him or ask any questions about it. I acted shy with him. I can't help but constantly wonder if he loves me back. I know that I love him. I just went upstairs to my room after he walked me to my door and waited by it until he heard it lock securely. I do wonder what it is that he has to do, but it doesn't bother me as much as Shaun does right now. He said that he would kill my boyfriend if I told him.

I just slept all day, avoiding my mother for the past few days. The next day after work, I was somewhat surprised that Micah came to pick me up. He was waiting for me in his car when I walked out. Ben didn't come to work. He knew that I would be mad at him for telling Micah what he didn't need to know.

He drove me back to his house in silence. None of us talked the whole way. I wasn't uncomfortable like you might have expected, though, and I trust Micah now. By now, I am completely fed up with the way that Micah is handling this situation by giving me some sort of silent treatment as if I'm a young child. He's the one acting childish. I can't handle it with him if he is going to be this way. I can't leave him, though, no matter how childish he may treat me. I love him.

When we were back at his house, he was still acting immature. I walked inside and stood in the hallway, looking back at him as he turned his back to me and locked the door with both of the locks.

Would Shaun come here? Why is he acting like this?

After he did that, he just walked right past me and into the kitchen. I followed him slowly. He still won't take the time to talk to me properly, so I just decided right there that I'll handle the situation myself.

I know that he is going to yell at me, but that's all that he'll do. I know he won't hurt me. I won't take another day of tiptoeing around the subject and letting him ignore me and just brush me to the side like I'm not really there.

I stood in the doorway, struggling to find a way to start what I want to say to him. What do I say? I'm not afraid of how he will react with me. I know that he won't hurt me. Will he? I watched him as he drank more of some of the alcohol he had on the counter. I'm not familiar with the type. I stood against the wall, thinking that he may say something. When he turned and began to walk to the doorway to walk away from me yet again, I blocked him, mirroring his actions so he couldn't get by. He looked down at me, irritated to what I'm doing to him, blocking him from leaving me. I can tell that he is angry, his tall frame shadowing over me as I just shook my head to him. He's trying to intimidate me, but I'm not letting him.

"Talk to me," I demanded

He just stood there as he relaxed his shoulders. His jaw tensed. "Move . . . or I'll move you," he threatened.

Why is he being so mean to me when I need him?

I brought my eyebrows together as I stared up at him with my arms crossed at my chest. I held back my tears that were lingering in my eyes. "That's not what I meant," I said back to him quietly in a frown.

I knew what he was doing as he took his large palms to my waist. I struggled in his hold, not letting him do what he wanted to—move me away or to just lift me out of the way for him. I stumbled back a step and then closed the distance between us, shoving him away in annoyance.

"Stop!" I cried to him as I shoved him away again, punching his chest weakly. "Stop doing that! I'm not just a child that you can pick up and brush to the side just because you don't want to talk to me!" I said, trying to sound mean, but I cried when I spoke, my voice sounding weak and pathetic.

My chest began to rise and fall quickly with my heart racing. He took no notice of my sadness, though, with him acting like this. He is acting fatuous. I squeezed my eyes closed as he bumped into my arm, leaving me with my darkness. He did it lightly, knowing what a fragile state I am in now.

I followed him as he went into the living room and took a seat on the sofa. He has to be kidding? I watched him in disbelief as he turned the TV on and settled the channel on a football game.

"Micah!"

He wouldn't take his eyes off the screen, though, pretending to be watching it just to not talk to me. I went over and stood in front of him, trying to win this.

"You don't make a very good window," he said, looking still in the same way that he looked at the TV as if he was still watching it through me.

"I don't care." I stood my ground. Don't back down. Don't back down. You can do this. I took a deep breath.

The sound of the TV was making me more irritated—the voices behind me, mocking me, taking his attention away from me. Am I jealous of a TV? Yes. It was driving my patience thinner more and more. It gave me a startling chill when he made eye contact with me, so I turned and switched the TV off from the button on it, too scared to snatch the remote from him.

"Talk to me!"

"Why didn't you tell me! Why should I talk to you! You didn't talk to me!" He boomed, standing from the couch and staring down at me from the few feet away that he is.

His raise in volume made me scared, my heart race, and my hands shaky. I just wasn't prepared for it. Don't back down. He won't hurt you. I want to believe my conscience, but right now, while he's in this state, I honestly don't know right now.

"Because I wanted to protect you!" I started out and took another deep breath. "I want to keep you safe for once! He said that he'd kill you if I told anyone," I spoke back, keeping my tears under control, not letting any slip out. But my body betrayed me, letting unwanted tears start to come out. The thought of Micah being gone just kills me.

I hastily wiped them away, gaining control again. I took a step back in fear, remembering that Micah just drank nearly half a bottle. I still can't comprehend how frightening he can become when he wants to be or not sometimes.

"I can take care of myself!" he shouted back.

I became aggravated with him as more tears slid down my cheeks. He just doesn't understand. I have been fine with looking and taking care of myself before I ever met Micah.

"I didn't tell you because I couldn't bear to have anything happen to you!" I yelled back. Oh no. Stop! Not like this! "For goodness' sake, Micah, it's because I'm in love with you!" Too late. The words tumbled out of my mouth uncontrollably as I tried to stop them as I knew it was going to come out. Micah's eyes were wide with what I said, unprepared to hear it, mortified even. His mouth parted a little as if he were about to say something, but nothing came out as I stood there waiting for some kind of response. What have I done?

The silence is killing me more than ever. My bottom lip began to tremble. I swallowed the lump in my throat as I then headed to the door to just leave. I unlocked the door in panic. I couldn't seem to get the last lock, though, as my hands were shaking uncontrollably without my consent. I looked back at him as he stood in the hallway now as if he were trying to say something, but I beat him to it. "I want to go home," I cried.

"Kendall," Micah said as I heard him begin to walk over to me, so I panicked to leave faster. I can't talk to him now. I just told him that I love him in a fight. I ruined us. I fell against the door in defeat. I struggled as I finally unlocked the door completely. I felt him now right behind me. "Kendall," he said as I cried against his door, my forehead pressed against the hardwood. "You can't love me," he barely spoke, which let me know I wasn't even meant to hear it. He set one of his hands on my hip as he stood against my back, holding me to him. I was expecting him to say something to me to try and make me feel better but no, nothing. Not a single word for a few seconds that seemed to pass by like hours.

He let go of my hip a little as I could tell he was leaning away to grab something. "I'll take you home, baby. Please don't cry," he said softly, moving me from holding my hip to the side so that he could open the door.

The fact of how he just talked to me helped a little. I still cried, though, as he held me to his side securely as we walked outside to his car. I glanced over for a second for some reason and saw his neighbor watching us. He saw that I was crying and Micah holding me tightly to him. He acted a little curious to who I am because he has saw me a few times leaving and coming to Micah's house, most likely knowing some of his past.

Micah opened his door for me and then shut it after I was inside. He's acting a little better with me just telling him how I felt about him. But he is still acting immature and stubborn with the Shaun situation and also how he never said anything back.

He didn't say anything to me as he drove me home. I glanced at him a few times, picturing him just pulling over and coming up against me and kissing me and apologizing and maybe just going to the cops about Shaun attacking me. But none of it would ever happen, not with Micah. I just sat still against my door, looking out at everything that we drove by.

When we got to my house, Micah walked over to my door, but I got it myself and got out beside him. He held me against his body as my eyes were still glassy, but I didn't let myself cry anymore around him. It was too much already. I kept my head against him as I leaned in to his figure as we walked across the street to my door. When we reached it together, I didn't even think about my mother.

She opened the door in a hurry. "Oh sorry. I'm just heading to work," she said, smiling at us. Micah grinned politely at her. "Kendall?" she asked, looking down at me from looking at Micah with suspicion. "Kendall, honey, what's wrong?" she asked. I held on to Micah, fisting his plaid shirt tightly, letting him know that I don't want my mother in on this at all. She stared at us both intently for an answer. "Kendall, where were you the other night?" she asked, wanting to know something.

"She stayed at my house. She wasn't feeling too good, and so I just invited her over so she wasn't alone," Micah answered collectively back. "I just picked her up from work a while ago. I brought her home because she said that she feels too sick that she wants to be home," he spoke, trying to convince her with the lie that I was only feeling sick, which I am actually from all the crying. My stomach is strained.

"Oh well, are you sure? Should I stay home?" she asked, looking down at me with her hand now on my shoulder. "You're welcome to stay here, Micah." She then looked at him.

He smiled at her and then looked down at me as he held my body to his much more firm one. He nodded to her then. "Okay, well, I have to go. Just be good," she said, looking down at me. I weakly smiled to her comment, knowing what she was talking about. "Bye. Thank you, Micah," she said, going past us and into her car and leaving us.

"Thank you," I said softly to him as he let go of me to go inside.

"Yeah, just go to bed, Kendall. Just get some rest to clear your head," he told me as he still had one of his hands on me. Clear my head?

I looked at him in a little confusion. I felt guilty for saying that I love him now. I wish that I didn't, but I'm glad I got it out of the way, not wondering and stressing over the idea when I might tell him. "You won't come in?" I asked, wiping my eyes another time.

He stared down in my eyes and then at my house. "I have something I have to do." He always has something to do. Wait. I haven't seen him smoking any cigarettes in a while. When did he quit?

I looked at him in sadness and just nodded. I thought of Shaun. "Micah?" I asked with a lot of worry in my voice. He looked back up at me from the ground and stepped closer to me as I stood inside the doorway. He leaned his head in to mine. I didn't close my eyes, only for a second or two when he was pressed to me.

"Don't worry about me," he spoke seriously. "Go to bed," he told me as he got off me and walked away back to his car. I felt broken as he didn't even kiss me good-bye. He stood, and I knew he was waiting to hear the door close with me safely inside and the lock latch together, encasing me safely inside the house. So I did it. After I locked the door I heard Micah's car go away down the street fast.

I slid down my front door to the cold, hard flooring as Oscar came running and tried to say hello to me and be friendly, but I ignored him as I took my face into my hands and down on to my knees, which were folded up into my chest as I just thought about Micah. I don't want him hurt or jailed or, worst of all, killed. I cried into my hands, sobbing loudly.

I just lay in my bed until I drifted off for just a quick minute. I can't help but worry about Micah. I can't help that I love him even if he doesn't love me back. I sat and just played with Oscar's ears as he lay up against me. There's nothing I can do to prevent anything bad from happening to Micah. I am helpless against his will to do anything. No one tells him what to do. He tells them. He loves the control.

I figured that I would just try and go to sleep. As my eyes began to close by themselves from how tired and worn out I feel, I jumped at a knock on the door—well, more like a pounding, really. I got up quickly as Oscar did as well as he ran barking at the door downstairs. I followed after him, thinking it to be Micah coming back to me. I felt so excited that I smiled as I neared the door. The knocking and pounding continued as if he were hurrying.

I hurried over to the door, unlocking it and opening it quickly.

"Josh?" I asked confused as I looked up at him.

He looked tired as he huffed and puffed quickly. "Kendall," he said, looking down at me quickly.

"What is it?" I asked after my voice filled with worry as I thought the worst in my mind. "Where's Micah? What happened?" I asked quickly, not taking any breaths.

"You have to come with me," he spoke quickly as he grabbed my forearm, trying to take me with him. "I'll explain on the way," he added, taking me outside.

I went with him willingly. I was scared the whole way over to his car as we both rushed over and hopped in quickly.

"Josh, what's going on?" I asked as he started the car. He ignored it as he drove quite fast down the road. "Where are we going?"

"It's Micah."

"What? What about Micah? What happened?" I paused. "What has he done?" I panicked.

"He lost it. He was with me drinking and then just completely went insane and went after Shaun," he told me, not taking his eyes off the road. Oh god, he's drunk.

"So what am I doing?" I asked after a second. He looked over at me after I asked that in confusion. "Josh, he doesn't—he won't even listen to me. I can't say anything to stop him. He doesn't care what I have to say to him," I spoke louder in panic.

He glanced back over. "He cares."

I shook my head. Micah doesn't care. He drove for a good ten minutes. It only gave me more time to worry, and my imagination got the best of me of what has happened. He pulled up to an unfamiliar bar-looking place far outside of town.

"Josh?" I asked as he got unbuckled and took the keys out.

"He's still here," he spoke almost to himself as I looked to where he was looking. It was Micah's vehicle parked like thirty feet away from ours uncaringly.

Josh got out of the car quickly as I followed him into the awkward aroma. Inside was loud and very different from anywhere else I've ever been. It smells of different alcohol and smoke as women dance on poles in the back. I grabbed on to his hand scared to where I am now and what I might see of Micah or Shaun. He seemed a little off guard as I hurried to his side, holding on tightly with my hand. He looked around only for a second before we both saw what everyone else was yelling and shouting and cheering for.

Chapter 20

My eyes widened by seeing him. I can't really see him through the thick crowd of people surrounding him though. I just know he's the one attracting all of the ruckus and attention. I gripped Josh's hand even tighter, although it seemed impossible to do anymore. He started lifting his head to see Micah as he pushed people out of the way. I held on to his hand as tight as I could as he dragged me right behind him through the rough, odorous crowd.

When we reached the front of the swarm, I realized how different Micah can be and how he changes around certain people. He has Shaun against the wall, punching him over and over repeatedly. He was kneed by Shaun, but it wasn't hard due to how beat up he already was. I still winced at the sight. He quickly recovered from the slight pain and threw Shaun to the ground, kicking him hard. I caught a glimpse of Micah's eyes driven with anger and revenge. He doesn't look like himself. He looks scary to everyone else—to me. I was taken back.

"Micah!" Josh shouted as he gripped my hand in his more securely.

I stood in shock. I expected bad, but not this bad. I can't bear to look at Shaun's face even after what he did to mine. Micah violently shoved Shaun to the wall beside them. I heard Josh curse as he pushed through everyone to the front, letting go of my hand, trying to keep me away from Micah and Shaun's fight now. My eyes widened in shock still. I didn't think that Josh would leave me alone in a bar like this.

Once Josh made it to the front, I followed him, even though I know that he doesn't want me to. Heck, if he thinks I'm staying in there with that crowd. I am not staying in that place alone. Well, with no one I know I can trust. None of the crowd followed outside as

Micah shoved Shaun outside. There were three cement steps till the dirt ground of the long alleyway. I ran out behind Josh to see Micah having Shaun pinned to the ground, on top of him while punching him. Micah got off him as Shaun got up slowly. Micah wants a fight, not a simple one either for some odd reason.

Within seconds, Micah had Shaun against the wall. "What kind of man hits a woman!" he yelled in his face as he kneed him against the building. Shaun grunted in pain, and his face in nothing but agony. "You're a waste!" Micah yelled as he let go only to punch him even harder.

"Josh!" I spoke loud. I want him to do something to stop Micah from being a murderer.

"Who hits a girl!" Micah screamed in his face. It made me feel smaller that they were kind of fighting over me. I feel powerless.

He looked back at me as I stood behind him. He then left me on my own as he rushed to Micah. "Micah!" Josh yelled beside him, trying to help me out. "Micah, stop!" I screamed from my spot still frozen with fear.

I began to cry, seeing who can be sweet and gentle, and then at the same time, possess this within him, this anger and strength to do this. What if he ever turned on me? I would never stand a chance. This can't be happening. I never wanted anyone to get hurt. I just want a normal relationship for now but no. I can't have that with Micah. I never will. But I still love him and can't control that. Josh looked back at me, crying, only now doing this for me as he grabbed on to Micah's shoulder and pushed him.

"Stop! You're scaring Kendall!" he yelled to him, yanking him off Shaun. Right when he was off Shaun, he fell to the ground. Josh pinned Micah. I never would have guessed that Josh could take control of Micah like that or have that power over him. "If you don't stop, you're going to lose her! You will lose the best thing that has ever happened to you!" he yelled in his face, holding him down strongly.

Micah actually struggled to get free from Josh's grip on him. Shaun stumbled to his shaky and unsteady feet and began to wobble down the alleyway, knowing Micah's intentions. "Get off me!" Micah bellowed up to Josh.

"Look at what you're doing!" Josh yelled back down to him harshly. "Stop this!"

Micah sort of relaxed under Josh. I had my hands by my face in a praying position, but I wasn't. I just held them below my nose as I cried alone in the darkness of the alley. Josh got off Micah, knowing that he did something to calm him mostly. Josh looked at me and stepped away from Micah.

"Why would you bring her here!" Micah shouted to his friend. I understood why he would ask that, though, so I didn't feel threatened by it at all. Awkward? Yes, definitely. I know when I'm not wanted.

I just stood, unable to take my eyes off Micah as he was angry. I saw it then, the way that everyone else looked at Micah, the way that I used to look at him. I realized then how much I truly love him because I was the only one that ever really saw the best side of him. He wouldn't show me that side if he didn't care for me, right? I know that all he wants is someone to love him, but now that he does have that, he doesn't know what to do with it due to never having it before. He's blind.

Micah's dangerous. That's why though. It's what everyone saw of him—only danger and his past with fights and other wrong things. Adding the fact that most women only see him as a sex symbol, using my angel for his body. It sickens me to think about what he's been through. I saw it in his eyes when he looked over at me, holding my gaze captive in his own. I saw the danger, but at the same time, the man I have fallen in love with and given everything to. I know that if it wasn't for Josh and I, Shaun's only exit from here would be zipped up in a body bag.

I stood there for a few minutes as Josh talked to Micah, but he was barely listening because his gaze kept coming back to mine as I couldn't take my eyes off him. I felt different as Micah then began to walk to me. My feet instantly took a step out of his reach, only three feet or so. Josh stepped by my side closely, blocking Micah from me.

"I'll take her home," Micah spoke softly.

I don't know what happened to me as I became afraid of him as I stepped more behind Josh's body, shielding me. He looked hurt and broken up as I was taking refuge behind any man besides him.

"She's too shaken up," Josh spoke calmly to Micah.

Josh then leaned forward a little and sat his hand on Micah's shoulder reassuringly. I saw a glimpse of something that I've never seen Micah's eyes hold: fear. "Let me say good-bye to her," he instructed to Josh. "Josh, she's still my girlfriend," he demanded.

I don't know why Josh seemed to be holding me back from Micah. Why? I felt exposed as Josh stepped to the side, leaving me uncovered in Micah's sight instantly on me. Threatening tears waited in my eyes as I caught a glimpse of Micah wiping his bloody knuckles on his pants. Moments later, he was right in front of me, lifting my chin.

I don't understand how he still looks like an angel, perfectly put together, but holding so much within him. How could so much hatred come from someone like my Micah?

As I inspected him a little further, I saw Shaun's and maybe a little of his own blood splattered on his clothes. I denied his kiss, only leaving his to lean his face against the side of mine. Instead, he just pressed his lips to the side of my mouth as I closed my eyes tightly, still feeling too shaken up. I'm literally shaking.

I didn't know what he was doing as he slid his lips up my cheek to reach my ear. He stopped as he reached the area right above my ear. "I love you, Kendall," he whispered. My breath seemed to hitch to hear him say it. My cheek brushed with his face as we were very close to one another. I went completely numb and breathless with his words. I never had anyone else besides family to say it to me. He pressed a little harder to me lovingly. "Say it," he quietly begged to me in a whisper. "Please . . . tell me . . . tell me that you love me," he added sadly as if he was going to cry. His voice was sad and depressing to hear. He sounds so broken, so scared and terrified.

I flinched a little when his large hand took hold of mine, rubbing some of the leftover blood on to my skin unknowingly. I desperately looked over at Josh who stepped a little closer knowing my uneasiness with Micah. Micah's touch then slid away from my hand in defeat. Josh stepped in gently, grabbing on to my shoulder and taking me away from Micah as he tried to get my attention. I couldn't help but keep wandering my attention back to the bloodied angel.

"Go wait by the door," Josh instructed me. I did what he asked.

I went, and I didn't make him believe that I was listening to him to go by the door. I stopped at the corner to listen to them. I began to listen as closely as I could to their conversation.

Micah cursed loudly in frustration. "I've lost her," he cried softly. No, don't cry. My heart is shattering.

I closed my eyes tightly, thinking of his pain for thinking that he has lost me. No, he hasn't. "No, she's just shaken up. She'll come around."

"She's scared of me. I could see it. She didn't want me even near her. She didn't want me touching her." He pouted, his eyes red rimmed and swollen now.

"Kendall will be fine."

There was a pause.

"I love her," Micah told him softly as his hand tangled in his hair stressfully. I never imagined Micah to be one to cry when I met him until I saw a tear slip from the corner of his right eye before he acted quickly in wiping it away with his left wrist.

I turned to look at them, peering around the cold bricks. Micah's head was down until he took it back up to look at Josh's gaze. I froze as Micah's gaze found me. He looked hurt, unsure of what to do as I saw his eyes glassy with sadness. He has no clue what to do.

"Call me when she's home safe," Micah said, staring at me only.

Josh nodded. "Of course," Josh told him softly.

Micah went back to Josh's attention. They hugged then.

"Don't worry. Just go home and clean yourself up, man," Josh told him as he left the embrace, and Micah wiped his face, and Josh patted his shoulder. "Sleep it off."

I watched as the two men said good-bye to each other, and I came from the corner. Josh met me halfway, coming up to me and instructing me to turn away from Micah as he set his arm around me. "Come on, Kendall," he said, turning me as I went with him down the alley back to his car in front of the building.

I can't leave. I won't leave Micah like this. No. He had spent too long searching for something that no one was brave enough to give him—love. My fingers slipped away from Josh's hand. Josh spoke my name out in confusion when I did. I ignored him. I don't care. I rushed back over to the tall figure standing alone in the dark now. He had tugged his hood over his head to conceal himself. I rushed to him. His eyes were watching me closely as I took his hood off and ran my fingers through the thickness of his fake blond hair. There's no point in being timid anymore with the man that I've come to have fallen so deeply in love with. I love him more than anything or anyone that has ever loved anybody. I hooked one of my hands to the back of his neck, getting up on my tippy toes as I never left his sight. I kept him in mine as I leaned up in to his face and placed a delicate kiss to his lightly bruised warm cheek.

I looked him back in the eye after. "I love you," I told him again.

He curved his full lips from my statement. "I love you," he said sincerely, happy that I came around back to him, relieved for the most part. He held me to him. We didn't kiss, although I longed for it. He just held me in his arms, holding me to his chest.

When he let go my feet, he carried me back to Josh who was waiting for me where I left him in the dark alleyway.

***

I lay in bed that night and every other night, not being able to sleep, relieved and so happy that we'd both said it to each other. That was three days ago though. That final minute together is still tattooed in my head. It's strange how three simple words can have such an effect on someone. "I love you." How? How do they do this much to a mind? What's the significance?

Micah saying those words to me gave me a whole new feeling and strength that I never knew possible. Then a heavy pile of fear jolted in my stomach as I heard footsteps running up behind me as I walked home from Savanna's house. I don't have any sort of protection on me, thinking that Micah got rid of my only enemy, the only one to hurt me. Did he?

I reached into my bag, remembering my small can of pepper spray that my mother gave me last year. I always had it in my bag, thinking that I'd never use it though. I grabbed it quickly and pulled it out just in time to face the person behind me and point it in their face where I knew the eyes would be.

"Whoa," the tall blond figure said as I pointed it at his face.

"Micah?" I asked, taking the pepper spray down. "Don't sneak up on me!" I scolded him loudly. I was angry with him, although I do love him. It upset me that he didn't contact me for a whole day and then just texting me, "Good night," and "Have a good day," the other two days, acting too afraid to talk to me.

He didn't react mad with me though. He smiled largely at me as he looked right down to me. "I won't make that mistake again."

I tried not to let his smile catch, but I failed. I laughed with him awkwardly. We haven't talked in three days after saying I love you. It is strange. Then we both just stopped and looked up and down at each other. I have his picture memorized in my mind, but I still wait to see him with my own eyes every morning I wake up. I then tried to contain my smile of happiness for seeing him tonight as my eyes filled up. I can't believe that he is here.

He saw me as I was about to cry then. He didn't say anything. He just closed the distance between us and hugged me, burying his head in my shoulder as I did the same to his chest with mine. I wrapped my arms around him instantly. I missed him so much.

"I didn't think that you'd want to see me," he said quietly to me.

I held on to him tightly after that, squeezing him to show that he was wrong. "Why would you think that?" I asked back. Why would he think that I don't want to see him after he told me that he loved me?

He shook his head, releasing me in his arms. I let go of him as well, but I still stayed close to him. He kept his hands on my hips as I held them there and looked up to his face grinning. "I missed you," I said quietly to him.

He didn't reply to it. He only smiled down at me in response. "What are you doing on the street?" he asked as if it were humorous to him.

I looked at the ground and smiled between us as he held me close, and then I looked back up at him. "I was walking home."

He didn't laugh with me at his question and my answer. Instead, he just looked at me. "I'll drive you now," he spoke. "But will you go somewhere with me?" he then asked suddenly, gripping my hips playfully, tugging me closer.

I looked up at him curiously. Where would he want to take me? "Where are you talking about?" I asked, blushing up at him and glancing around us.

He smiled. "Well, Tyler's having a little party."

"Tonight?" I asked, as he was sort of rushing me in his tone.

"Yeah," he told me. "I'll take you home if you need to do something though," he told me.

I smiled at his gesture. "I have to feed Oscar," I told him as I looked at his face, still having a small cut on his top lip from a punch from Shaun, I think. "What happened to your lip?" I asked, looking right at it.

He lifted his hand over it. He didn't know it was there as he was confused by me asking him what happened. "Oh," he said as if he were thinking about something and trying to think of something to tell me. "Shaun hit me, and I guess I still have a mark from it," he told me. I tried to calm down from the name he just said: Shaun. "Come on, let's go," he said, grabbing on to my hand as I gratefully accepted it. He walked us down the street some ways and then to his car of which he still opened the door for me to get in and rushed back over to his side and got in and drove me the rest of the way home. My mom was still home.

I knocked on the door, which she opened for me. "Hi, Kendall," she greeted from the kitchen. "Oh hi, Micah," she then greeted as he walked in with me.

"I thought you left?" I asked her.

"In a little. I just wanted to clean up first," she told me.

She then looked at Micah for a second because she knows that we haven't seen each other in a few days. "I'll be right back," I informed them both as I went upstairs, leaving Micah with my mom. I went up into my room quickly and grabbed my phone, unplugging it off the charger. I then ran back downstairs to see Micah sitting down at the island, talking to my mother.

"Just take care of her," my mom said as I heard the last piece of what she was saying.

"Yeah, she's safe with me," he reassured her. Only when I'm with him most of the time. I smiled as if I didn't hear that coming up behind them.

"Okay," I said behind Micah as he was sat down.

"Ready?"

"Yeah," I said back, answering him.

"Where are you two going? I can make something to eat," my mother sort of insisted.

"Um, my friend is having a small party."

"Okay, well, have fun," she said as Micah stood up beside me. He looked back and smiled at her. I didn't have to feed Oscar because she was still home and can just do it before she leaves. Micah and I went back outside to his car and got in. I scooted up to his side in the seat after. I knew that he heard when I said it as he gave me one of his hands on my leg. He then grinned, still with his eyes on the road.

***

About fifteen minutes later, we arrived at Tyler's house.

We walked close together as we walked to the front of Tyler's house this time. You could barely hear music coming from only inside and nobody in the pool area that you can hear at least. Once we entered, Micah was greeted by one of his friends Brian, Tyler's cousin. Shailene, of course, came over, greeting us nicely, and we really all just hung out for a while. I sat down with Shailene while Micah left to get us a drink. After a minute of talking with her and her continued sipping from her can, a man came over and sat beside me.

"You're Kendall. Yeah, I know a lot about you." He grinned.

I looked from Shailene to him as she stood up, walking quickly toward the kitchen, leaving her drink on the glass coffee table. He looks older than Micah by a few years. I noticed Brian and Johnathan watching us closely. "Um . . . yeah. Yeah, I am." I was confused.

"I'm Keegan." He smiled. "Micah." He looked up, smiling.

Chapter 21

I looked up seeing Micah, his eyes full of anger. They were darker instantly. "What are you doing here, Keegan?" he demanded.

"Kendall's a lovely girl." Keegan scanned me over again, more closely as Micah gripped my arm, lifting me from my seat to behind his body quickly.

"We're leaving."

"We haven't talked," Keegan told him. "We got another job for you," he added as Micah was about to turn us around to just leave. *Job? What are they talking about? What do they want to talk about with Micah? What kind of job?*

"Micah?" I asked, looking up at him.

"Keegan, you should leave, man," Tyler spoke, causing Keegan to look at him little surprised.

"We're leaving," Micah said firmly as he turned us around.

"We'll talk soon!" He yelled at us as we walked away.

"Where are we going now?" I asked, a bit worried.

He got us in the car quickly and then started it, driving off. "What time's your mom coming home?" he asked.

"I—I don't know. Why?" I asked, concerned with why he is acting like this.

"We'll go to my house."

"What's going on?" I asked, trying to understand what is going on. He just set his hand on my leg as if to calm me down. "Micah?" I asked. He didn't answer.

***

Micah took me back to his house as he stayed close to me the whole time until we got inside.

"Can you tell me something?" I asked, irritated with him. *What's going on?* He locked the door carefully.

"Micah?" I asked as he then turned around with me against the wall. "What's going on?" But he didn't answer as he kissed me.

He set his hands on my hips and kissed me again, more passionately. I smiled after. *What did he just do?*

"Micah," I said, smiling, trying to get him to stop a little and tell me what's going on. He didn't say anything more.

"It'll be all right," he said softly as we kissed again.

I took my arms around his neck as he lifted me. I know what he's doing now, and he's distracting me, he's distracting himself. I'm not fighting him about it at all though. I haven't seen him in three days, and before those days, he was ignoring me. I was desperate for him to come back to me. He took me from the wall and headed down the hall into his room.

"Micah," I said quietly as he continued trying to keep the subject about Keegan and Brian and the job off my mind and talk about it with him.

He set me down to stand on my feet as he removed his shirt quickly, chucking it to the floor. I blushed when he started to unbuckle his jeans. "Kendall," he whispered as I slid his boxers down. I never really looked at him naked, and he knew that it made me somewhat uncomfortable still. "Kendall."

"It's okay," I reassured him. I love him it doesn't bother me anymore. When he began to back us up to the mattress, I noticed that he stopped, hesitating. "I trust you," I whispered to him. He closed his eyes and then gripped my hips a little tighter. "Micah," I whispered to him again. He smiled shyly down at me as he continued. He laid me back on the mattress quickly and slid us up, so my head was now lying on the pillow comfortably. He started panting heavy. He kissed me roughly and in a hurry like fashion. My hands fisted his hair, tugging at the roots a little, wanting to hear him groan in response.

"Kendall?" he breathed.

"Mmmm."

"Are you sure?"

"Yeah." I nodded, continuing to kiss him in return.

He started kissing down my body, both of us completely naked together. He slid down my body at a slow pace, kissing and caressing me everywhere as he went. I love him so much. My body shuddered as his lips met the skin on my inner thighs. "I'll be gentle," he whispered.

I blushed at his words, his voice deep but quiet. He kissed even closer, his hands prying my legs apart slowly as he continued connecting his lips with my burning skin. "Micah."

He groaned as I cried out in surprise. My body clenched all my muscles. My legs were shaking drastically with each touch and kiss he emitted on my body and inside it. My feelings for him continued to grow and grow every time we do or say anything together. Whimpers continued to fall from my parted lips. "Mmmmm." He kissed just below my belly button.

His chest was rising and falling quickly at a rapid pace. "Does that feel good?" He glanced up at me, almost sending me over the edge. He parted my legs more. "Kendall," he demanded. I couldn't find my words. How would I be able to? I've never experienced anything like right now, not even the first time we had sex. It still wasn't like this, and this is different. I stretched my arm down, his hand meeting mine halfway and gripping it, curling his fingers around my palm. Instead, I just squeezed it in response. The pleasure I was feeling in my body was becoming too overwhelming now. I stared finding it difficult to keep my eyes opened fully. I wanted to watch him, how he seems to love my body and thinks it's so perfect, although it's not even close. He makes me feel comfortable with the way he talks to me, comfortable enough to let him take my virginity and lie here with him in his bed completely naked while he does this to me.

I glanced down quickly to see his lips quirked into a smug smirk. "Micah," I whimpered loudly, powerlessly. He took his finger to his lips. I was barely even able to watch him any longer. The room got hotter and hotter with each passing second.

My eyes widened when his plump lips took his index finger past them, sucking on it, his eyes closed seductively. When he withdrew it, his tongue glided out, wetting his pink lips slowly. "Oh god," he whispered. He reached down and started stroking himself with the opposite hand, the other resting on my leg. He tilted his head up toward the ceiling, his jaw clenching tightly. He looks so incredibly hot right now, not that he doesn't all of the time but right now is different. I assume he still has his hand on himself as he lowered his head, his opposite hand giving my thigh a squeeze. His hair tickled my inner thigh, causing me to giggle. He looked up at me again.

"What's so funny?" He smiled his dazzling smile.

I shook my head quickly, still giggling. He raised one of his eyebrows, only causing me to giggle even more that it became unstoppable. "I would love to know why you're giggling. Especially right now, Kendall."

"It just . . ."

"Don't get all coy on me now."

"It tickles," I admitted shyly. *Why am I feeling shy now all of the sudden?*

He stared, chuckling along with me, his smile wide and bright. "Sorry." He continued smiling while pushing his hair back. I can tell he hasn't had it cut in a while. Even though I like guys with shorter hair, Micah still looks breathtaking with his hair a little longer. A gasp escaped my lips as he nipped at the inside of one of my legs. I felt his hot breath fan over me, causing me to shiver. He looked up again, smirking, and shot me a cheeky wink. A few seconds later, my whole body shuttered and quivered as his warm and moist tongue licked up my center. Both of his hands gripped both of my thighs to keep me still. I couldn't control myself at all. I started shaking and whimpering out of my control. He hummed against me. "I want to hear you scream."

I didn't know what to do with my hands other than fist the sheets at my sides. I shrieked as he nipped at my skin suddenly. He seemed to like my reaction, as I swear I felt him smiling against my most sensitive area. His nose brushed me, causing me to gasp even louder and suck in and let out a few deep breaths, trying to contain myself. My back arched off the mattress in pleasure as it shot through me. "Micah," I whimpered again. He started sucking, his plump lips soft and warm against me. I jolted with the new sensation being erupted.

"No," I whined as he slid back up my body, on top of me again, his chest pressed against mine. I watched as he licked his lips, grinning. His now swollen lips pressed to mine desperately, his tongue forcing itself into my already-parted lips. The kiss was wet and amazing, definitely one of the most intimate we've shared so far. While one of his hands stayed on my breast, the other slid down my side and gave my hip a playful squeeze. We both laughed about it. He watched me intently as I struggled to breathe beneath him; he seemed to find it not only amusing but also satisfying. I felt his hard and large erection pressed against one of my legs. The skin was brushing against me as he rolled his hips down, his finger sinking back down.

"Is that good?" he said demandingly.

My eyes were closed. His touch was everywhere, overwhelming me all at once. Teasing and pinching and rolling, sucking, sliding, wet, and smooth. "Open your eyes . . . I want to see you."

I opened my eyes to his command. "Yes, yes, Micah."

It was so intense and sensational. Everything went blurry for a few seconds, and then he caressed my face, his fingers rubbing my cheek. I leaned into his touch, wanting nothing more than to feel him. "You're so beautiful, Kendall." His lips went to my ear, nibbling at my lobe. "I'll always keep you safe. You know that, don't you?"

I nodded.

I grabbed a hold of the back of his neck as he started kissing a soft spot behind my ear. "Ahhh. Micah."

I had never felt anything like that. My toes started curling, tipping me over the edge again. I released broken gasps as my lips parted wide. I couldn't close them even if I wanted to. "I want you so bad." He kissed the corner of my mouth. "Are you okay?"

"I'm wonderful," I whispered back.

He smiled against my mouth as he kissed me. "That's good."

"Mmmm."

He kissed me passionately while he reached his hand over off the bed and opened his nightstand drawer. I heard the crinkling of plastic. He had to break the contact with my mouth to see what all he was grabbing. "Sorry," he blushed. I smiled back up at him. He leaned his body half off the bed as he continued flipping things around in the wooden drawer. Finally, after a minute, he came back to me. He quickly ripped open the condom and rolled it down his length, the head of his penis the same pink color as his lips. I watched him as he positioned us both better. "I don't want to hurt you again." I looked down to see what he was doing. I watched as he flicked a small bottle's lid open and squirted some of the clear liquid on to his digits. He glanced up at me. "It'll take away some of the pain, even though you're already really wet."

"Micah." I batted his arm, blushing like mad.

He smiled while rubbing his fingers together with the liquid now on two of them. He pressed against me down there, making me tense up, spreading the liquid. He looked back up at me before he looked back down and concentrated on his task, squirting more liquid on his fingers and spreading it all over his rubber-covered length. He tossed the bottle and wrapper on to his bedside table and then grabbed a hold of himself and positioned the tip between my legs. I watched him as he looked back down at me and then slowly eased himself in. I gasped and tilted my chin toward the ceiling. We should have turned on the fan or opened the window first when we walked through his bedroom door. His hands quickly became entwined with mine as he pressed all the way inside of me. His jaw clenched as he gave me time to adjust. There was still a slight pinching happening. The pain wasn't that bad compared to the pleasure that is.

"Is that okay?" he asked, concern clear in his voice.

"Yes, it's good."

"Does it hurt that bad still?"

I shook my head, opening my eyes. "Not really anymore. I'm okay though, Micah, really." He looked down at me a little confused but didn't fight me on it or try to stop us from doing this again. He pressed his already-sweating forehead down against mine as he kissed me a few times and then began to roll and rock his hips down into mine. That pace was calm and steady, neither of us in a hurry. It's perfect. He drew out deep breaths and sighs with each time his hips collided with mine. I bit down on my lip, wincing some and squeezing my eyes shut.

"You're so beautiful, Kendall." He breathed as he rolled his hips again, squeezing my hands at the same time. "I love you so fucking much," he said hoarsely as he grunted, giving me a heavy thrust. I winced. It didn't hurt; it was just that I wasn't expecting it. "Sorry."

"It's fine," I reassured him.

"I love you more than anything," He said softly, his eyes closed as he rolled his hips again. I watched him above me, concentrating. I got the curiosity and looked down to where we lovingly connected. It made the pit of my stomach erupt. He was pressed all the way inside me, the end of the condom showing slightly. "I'll only ever want you," he admitted.

I lifted my face to connect my lips with his. "And I love you, Micah," I spoke after I broke the kiss. He grinned, still with his eyes closed.

"Is there any pain still?"

"No. You don't have to keep asking either. I will tell you."

He nodded, his forehead still resting on mine. It feels so romantic. So perfect and amazing, incredible and mesmerizing. Extraordinary. He rocked his hips a little faster. He was close, I could tell now. He whimpered and panted. I watched in awe as he came undone above me, opening his eyes and squeezing them shut, and opening them again. He placed a heavy wet kiss on my mouth and then down my chin and neck, still holding on to both of my hands on either side of my head, our fingers entwined with each other. "Kendall," he panted.

Micah and I had gotten half dressed in the middle of the night, giving me one of his T-shirts to be more comfortable. His heavy, musky scent filling my senses. I gripped it in my hand to smell it better. Micah. I grinned. I'll never get used to his scent. When I finally awoke, I was lying on Micah's chest with a pillow beneath me.

He held one of his arms around my back with the other stretched out when I opened my eyes. I scrunched my hands together against the pillow before I got up to look at him, still sleeping with a light snore. I smiled down at him. The man that I love loves me back, and I can't go a second without thinking of that.

"Micah." I laughed, trying to wake him up. "Micah." I tried again lightly, pushing down on him, trying to shake him awake.

He moaned with his eyes still shut; he's awake but doesn't want to get up yet. "What time is it?" he asked with his deep voice.

"It's time to get up." I smiled.

He lazily opened his eyes, taking his stretched-out hand to wipe his eye as if to see well. He then smiled up at me as I sat up to look at him directly.

"Or maybe it's time for you to get up and make me something to eat."

"You're serious?" I asked, raising one of my brows to him as he opened his eyes again. His dimples popped out in his cheeks.

"I love you," he said, trying to get me to get up and make him something to eat.

I smiled at him. "Awe, I love you too." I kissed him after. "What do you want?" I gave in to him.

He smiled, knowing he won me over. "Waffles." He smiled up at me. "Please."

I sighed loudly and humorously as I got off him and onto my feet of his floor. I heard him laugh as I left his bedroom to go to the kitchen. I know how to make waffles, and I really don't care making him some.

I patted my feet down the hallway into his kitchen. He surprisingly did have all of the ingredients and supplies to make them so far. I heard what I guess is Micah just getting out of bed, so I ignored it. I then went to the fridge to grab the eggs. I grabbed the carton and opened it in the fridge to just grab two of them. It was empty. I smiled. I should have known that he would set empty things back like someone else would throw them away for him.

I grabbed the egg carton and threw it in the trash can. I then went to tell Micah about the dilemma. I went down the hallway to see him standing with his back to me with a pair of dark grey sweatpants pulled up to his waist.

"Micah, you're out of eggs," I said as I approached him from behind.

When I got to his side, I had no time to prepare myself as a pair of arms was taking me into a tight hug. I hesitantly hugged the older woman back awkwardly not knowing who she is. I looked up to see a younger woman standing in front of me.

"Thank you so much for bringing my baby back to me," the woman spoke as she held me. I didn't know what to say back to her. *What's she talking about? Who is she?*

"Mom," I heard Micah say as I began to get confused by what she just said. "Mom," he said again, prying her off me. She's his mom? I smiled at the women as she backed up to the younger one of them both. I looked at the younger girl's eyes to them being the exact green color of Micah's. She's his sister, she has to be, and his mother.

"Kendall, this is my mom, Jennifer, and my sister, Candice," he said as I looked at him and then at the women that stood in front of us. Micah then took his arm closest to me to tug him against his side, putting his arm around my back to hold me there telling how nervous I suddenly became.

"Hi, it's nice to meet you," I said to them nicely but also a bit shy. This was so unexpected. And I am only wearing his shirt that comes far down on my legs and my bra and underwear. I felt embarrassed, as he had his bare chest, showing still with some light bruises. *When did he get those? They can't be from the fight with Shaun still at the bar? Where did they come from? How come I didn't notice them this morning or last night?*

The women smiled at me as Micah held me close to him. I didn't know what else to do with my arms but let them dangle.

"You're both still in your pajamas." She laughed.

"Mom, we just got up," Micah replied, smiling at her.

"It's twenty till one, honey," she told him, smiling.

I saw his sister smile at the conversation. "Well, they probably weren't doing much sleeping last night," she blurted out, her tattoos coming into view.

My cheeks immediately flushed with her sudden comment that was the truth. Micah rubbed my back a little with his large hand, which took up most of it any way, to try and relax me. I feel so uncomfortable now. "Well uh, just give us a minute to go get dressed then. Just make yourself at home," he told them as he guided me back to his room still with him arm around my back.

When Micah and I got into his room, I put my hands over my mouth and just fell on the bed. I heard him laugh. "It's okay, Kendall," he tried to say without laughing and in a serious way but failed.

I sat up. "No, it's not, Micah. We were just pointed out by your sister, and it's not exactly the best first meeting," I told him, being more serious.

"Well, I didn't know they were coming," he told me honestly. He came up by me and set his palms down on the front of the bed, that's where I now sat in front of him. "Don't worry so much. They'll love you because I love you," he said with his face practically almost touching mine. I blushed at his words that still have an overwhelming effect on me. He then leaned further down and kissed me. "I'm going to get a shower." He then informed as he got up and began walking to the bathroom.

I got off the bed quickly. "What am I supposed to do then?" I asked, panicking.

He laughed at me. "I don't know. Just go talk, or you can join me," he suggested, still smiling at me. I rolled my eyes at him as my cheeks flushed again.

"About what?" I asked, going up to him. He's crazy. I wouldn't do that while his mom and sister are here and for the first time meeting them.

"I don't know . . . Girl stuff."

"Micah."

"Go get 'em," he said playfully, lightly slapping my bum before he walked into his bathroom.

When he closed the door, I sighed. I don't know what to talk to his family about. I have no clue at all. I leaned over and grabbed my jeans and shirt from yesterday and put them back on, setting his shirt in what I guess is his dirty clothes. I feel so nervous. I don't want to face his mother and sister alone and awkwardly and a mess from just waking up.

I went to the door slowly and opened it to walk out to the living room to see them. When I walked in, they were both just waiting for us to return. I stood in the doorway, awkwardly looking at them. "Micah's getting a shower," I informed them, not knowing what else to say to get their attention.

"That's fine. Come sit," Candice said, getting up and grabbing my arm and taking me over to one of the couches.

I smiled shyly at her. I don't know what to do. Candice is so pretty. Her hair is light brown and curled, and her eyes hold the same charming green color as Micah's do. She sat beside me. I feel intimidated around her because I probably look awful compared to her. "So you're eighteen?" she asked, trying to find out more about me.

"Yeah," I responded.

"You don't have to be nervous." She smiled, trying to sooth me.

"I'm sorry I just wasn't expecting this," I told them, trying to contain my excitement the best way I can.

"We can leave," her mother suggested, only being nice.

"No, no, don't. Please don't. It's amazing to meet you, really. I just get nervous," I told them quickly. His sister smiled at me after I looked down at some of her ink-covered skin. I have to think of something to say or asked quickly to not make this awkward.

"He already has you making him breakfast does he?" his mother asked, laughing.

I blushed at her. "It's fine. I don't mind. That would have been the first time I did," I admitted, smiling at them and laughing a little.

His sister laughed before her mother broke in. "Does he still fight? I mean, besides the boxing?" his mother asked me seriously.

I looked at his sister, not knowing how to answer. I bit my lip. "He does, but not like for no reason," I told them both as I curled my legs on the couch.

"He always had anger problems," his sister teased.

I smiled. "I know."

"Do you know why he may have dyed his hair?" his mom asked.

I shook my head. "It was like that since I met him. I don't know."

His mother and sister both looked at each other. "Does he do anything else besides working at the gym?" his sister asked.

I looked at her, confused. "I don't understand."

"I just don't see how he's doing so well only on that," his sister said as soon as I stopped talking.

"What was he like when he was younger?" I asked, trying to keep it going.

They were quiet for a minute. "He used to have panic attacks," his sister blurted out.

I took my attention tight to her when she said it. "Really? You mean because of . . . um . . ." I stopped myself. "I'm sorry I shouldn't have . . ." I apologized, feeling guilty for bringing it up.

His sister shook her head. "Don't be," His mother told me. "I'm guessing that he's told you?" I nodded to her. "It's nice to know he has someone to talk to about it."

We sat and talked for a good ten more minutes, laughing about a story Candice told me about their trip to Hawaii when Micah went skinny-dipping with a girl, and she went down and stole his clothes, leaving him to go in the elevator naked back to their room. But she apologized for talking about him with another girl. I told her that it was fine though, and it doesn't bother me at all.

"What's going on?" I looked back to see Micah standing in the living room, wondering what we were laughing about.

I got up and went over to him and got on my toes and kissed him, feeling completely comfortable with his mom and sister being right there. He kissed me back gently, while he set his arm around my back. I stepped off to his side. "Do you want to go somewhere?" he asked them as he held me to his side.

"Yeah, sure, that's fine," his mom answered.

I looked up at him. "Where?" I asked.

"To eat. I don't have anything to make here, really, just to do something. You look great don't worry," he said, smiling down at me, knowing why I was asking as he squeezed me closer to his frame.

His mom and sister got up as I smiled at them. "Okay," Micah said as he then turned us. He walked us over to the front door. "My keys are in my room with my wallet too. I'll be right back," he said leaving us. His sister lightly laughed and covered her mouth, knowing that it would make me feel nervous.

"Candice," her mother scolded her.

"It's not a secret," she told her, smiling.

Micah came back in a minute with his keys, wallet, and phone along with my phone as well. "Here," he said when he handed it over.

He put his wallet in his pocket but stared at his phone screen, as it lit up. I looked over at his sister and then at Micah. "Everything okay?" his mother asked.

He hesitated before answering her. "Yeah, it's fine. Just a friend," he told her. I don't know if he was letting me look at the screen or not, but as I stood at his side, I glanced over to see the text from Brian saying to come and meet just him and Walter tomorrow night at some address that I don't know.

"We going?" I asked, tugging at his arm.

He grinned down at me. He then opened his door as we all got out of the house, and he locked the door securely. We took Micah's car. I sat in the back with Candice, while his mother got in the front with him. I didn't mind, she's his mother. He glanced back at me every few minutes or so, and his sister found it amusing to herself how he acts around me.

**

We arrived at a restaurant by the boardwalk. We went in and were seated, and I sat beside Micah, while he every now and then would skim his hand on my leg to reassure me to relax. I looked back to a familiar voice to see Emily. Micah looked back to see her as she saw us all sitting. "I'm going to say hi to her. I'll be right back," I told him as I got up and kissed him good-bye for a minute only.

I walked over to Emily who was just standing there, waiting for something or someone. "Hi," I said as I got to her.

She smiled. "You wanted to tell me something the other day. What was it?" I asked, getting right to it.

"Oh I," she said, looking over to Micah who glanced back at us. "I'm sorry about that. I need to tell you this though. Just don't get mad," she said, looking at Micah a few times.

"What is it?" I asked anxiously, wanting to know what it is.

"It's about him," she started. "Well uh . . .," she said, grabbing my hand and pulling me away from Micah's sight. "I saw him. He was doing something."

"What? What do you mean?"

"I can't be a hundred percent sure about it. I saw him though with I guess his friends."

"Okay. What are you trying to say?"

"Kendall, I think that he's a drug dealer. Like he's involved somehow in it all," she told me quickly. "I'm just saying that I saw him hand over a few bags of . . . stuff to a couple of men, and they gave him money," she added.

I didn't know what to say. "I just met his family," I told her sadly.

She just looked at me in sympathy. "I'm sorry I should have just called you about it. I just wanted to tell you."

"No, thank you. I—I have to go back though. Thanks." I thanked her over and over. I am grateful that she told me. I didn't care how long she waited as long as she told me. I don't know what to think. I somehow guessed that he got money from something else rather than the gym, but drugs never came into my mind. I understand it, though, why he would be involved. But he doesn't seem to ever be on any, and it makes me feel better knowing that he isn't doing them, I think.

I went back over as he smiled at me. "Was that Emily?" he asked as I sat back with him.

"Yeah, I just haven't talked to her in a while. Her mom was with her, and she sort of dragged me over," I lied.

He just grinned at me.

Chapter 22

We went back to his house and said good-bye to his mom and sister as they then left. I called my mom and told her that I stayed with Micah, and I would be home later.

Micah took me home in an hour or two. He walked me to my door as my mother let us inside. "Are you guys hungry?" she asked as we walked through the kitchen.

"We just ate," I told her.

I want to say something to Micah about what Emily informed me and Keegan and Brian, so I just took his hand and dragged him up the stairs to my room with Oscar following us, saving him from a conversation with my mother.

He went over and sat on the edge of my bed. "You okay?" he asked, looking over to me as Oscar jumped on my bed and lay by Micah's leg.

I just stared at him as I then walked over to him and stood in front of him. It took me a second to realize that he wouldn't hurt me if I say anything about it and especially with my mother downstairs. I kept my door only a little cracked from my mother telling me to keep it open when he's here. I walked directly in front of him and sat on his lap as he then smiled and just put his arms on me.

"Emily told me she saw you," I told him as we both made complete eye contact. "You know what I'm saying," I told him in case he tried to tell me a lie.

"Her mom wasn't there," he said out loud, knowing that I lied to him a while ago. "You lied to me."

I shook my head. "I couldn't say anything there," I said, grabbing his hand that sat on my leg into mine. I stared at him to say something, to tell me. He looked away from me and smiled, shyly, obviously not wanting to say anything to me. "Micah," I said, getting his attention back as I rubbed my thumb against his knuckles as I held his hand. He looked down as I did the action, trying to relax him as his hand got warm. "Please," I said to him softly. "I love you."

He held me a little closer with his other arm still wrapped around my back and his other hand holding mine in it and my other hand holding onto them both. He set his forehead against mine and then took it back. "I just transport it to Brian," he told me finally. "I'm trying to get out of it though, Kendall." I believed him. I gripped his hand a little more, trying to calm him. I know he isn't telling me everything though.

"Since when?" I asked him, wanting to know when he started this.

He paused. "Why does it matter?" he snapped a little.

"Because . . ." *Why does that matter to me?* "Because I love you, and I want you to be able to tell me things." I leaned into him with my head on his shoulder. "I understand why," I told him. He rubbed his hand on my back up and down a few times. "So why are they like mad with you?"

"Cause I want out, and I'm a part of it. You can't just walk away like I want," he snapped. "And don't sit there and say you understand why because that's a lie, and you know it."

I don't know what to say to him. I sighed and reopened my eyes. "What's the meeting about?"

"I don't know. I just don't want you involved with it," he sounded irritated.

"Micah."

"They know who you are now, and I don't know what to do anymore," he sighed heavily.

"I don't care. I just don't want you to go away." I sounded needy with my eyes glassy, not as much sad though but glad and happy that he trusted me enough to tell me what I know he hasn't told anyone else besides maybe Josh, practically, the entire system.

"I should go," he said as he pressed his head to mine again.

I got up as he did off my bed. Oscar stayed on the bed, as he fell asleep. Micah walked me back to my door, holding my waist. "I won't lose you," he whispered as we went downstairs.

My mom wasn't in the kitchen anymore. I don't know where she was. When my front door was opened and Micah stepped out, he turned and kissed me. "Love you."

"I love you too," I told him back, returning the favor.

"Don't say that."

"What? I do love you."
What's he talking about?
"Not that." He smiled. "Too."
"I don't get it."
"It just sounds like you're agreeing with me when you say it like that." *Oh, Micah.* I pulled him into me and leaned against his chest while going on my toes to reach his face better. He looked irritated and stressed out. *Oh no.* "I love you." I looked him in the eyes and kissed him, hard. My tongue swiped across his lips and pushed through, rubbing against his in a desperate greeting. I held him closer as he tilted his head and continued massaging my mouth. His hands slid slowly up over my breasts, making me heart quicken even more and pound loudly all over my body. My legs are now literally shaking against his, making him smile, then continue in the heated action.

***

Ben was back at work the next day. I didn't say anything to him about the fight or Shaun. I just ignored the whole thing and acted normal. At the end of the day, I waited inside, feeling scared that maybe, they would take me if I stepped outside without Micah or someone else to be there with me. Ben stayed with me the extra five minutes. Micah pulled up, and I went out with Ben with him locking the door behind. Micah got out of his car and walked over to me.

He looked at Ben with just a plain look but at the same time to go away. I let him guide me to the passenger door and opened it for me to get in. I did.

Micah got in and leaned over to kiss me. "You have a good day?" he asked normally as he kept his eyes on the road.

"Micah," I said, looking over at him. *Why's he acting normally? How?* He looked over a little confused. "Why'd you dye your hair?" I asked without thinking as I moved closer to him while he drove.

He smiled over at me. "Is it bad?"

I shrugged, teasing him, so it was evident.

"I don't know. I did it when I moved, well, ran away, and I just kept it." He paused and turned the wheel. "So how was your day?" he asked again.

"It was good," I answered him finally. "Yours?"

"Fine," he answered almost immediately.

"Are you meeting them tonight?" I jumped back into the subject that I know he didn't want to talk about though. He took a deep breath in annoyance and gripped the wheel tighter with his one hand he had on it. "Just be careful," I told him, letting him know that he doesn't have to answer me.

He nodded, not looking over at me as if he were embarrassed by it all. "I'm not going." He smiled but still kept his eyes on the road, not looking over at me at all.

I looked up at him, confused. *How can he just blow them off? I don't get it. I know he can't. It will aggravate them more if he does. It's best if he goes, or stays?*

"What?" I asked, very confused.

"I'm not gonna go. I thought that would make you relieved?" he sounded confused and disappointed.

"I—I am. But is that a good idea?"

"It'll be fine, Kendall, really." He reached over and set his palm on my knee, squeezing gently but with obvious intention. With each second, he slid his warm touch up my leg, higher . . . and higher my blood was working overtime to keep up with my mind. My eyes were closed, as every piece of me was now only focusing on this one area where his hand dominated. Higher. Higher.

"You're driving," I breathed quickly.

"Mmmm. I've done much more while . . ." He stopped himself while realizing what he was saying before he could control it, leaving his now-pouting lips. My eyes were opened now and fully aware of every part of my body, the moment tainted with the faces of other random women taking up with Micah's hand. His hand went back to my knee and patted before awkwardly going back to join the other, and he drove with both on the black steering wheel. The air was now thick and awkward, neither of us not knowing how to break it.

***

Micah drove me back to his house, and we went inside. He locked his door and then turned to me. "I didn't mean to say that . . . in the car."

"I know," I spoke quietly.

"No, Kendall, seriously. I wasn't thinking." He was pleading. "It's only you—"

"Micah, I get it," I snapped.

He stayed silent, unsure if he should talk anymore. So now he's thinking what to say. "Let me make it up to you."

"Mi—"

"Shhh . . . Stay tonight." He stared down at me, his arms now wrapped loosely around my hips.

"Mic—"

"Please." It wasn't a question. His eyes looked different now. He wasn't angry or disappointed but . . . worried? Upset? I can't decipher, but something's getting at him I know.

I nodded.

His arms moved down and lifted me in the air, my legs wrapping around his torso, his arms on my lower back. His lips went to my neck, kissing gently, nothing fast or harsh in anyway but just like small pecks. Sweet and passionate. "I love you."

"I love you," I barely spoke.

He turned and walked down the short hallway and pushed the door open to his bedroom, the cool air coming out and breezing past my back. It felt good against my hot skin, soothing. My heart was pounding by the time he laid me back on his bed. "I want to make you feel good," he whispered against my lips as he hovered over me, his lips ghosting over mine, only brushing. I didn't say anything in response; I couldn't. My voice isn't working. He doesn't need my permission; I'm his. His touch seemed to be everywhere when I closed my eyes. His fingers moving agonizingly slow down my arms. I shivered at every movement he made on me. I let out a deep breath I hadn't realized I was even holding in. His lips were cold as he kiss just below my ear and then down my neck, peck after peck. My hand went to his back and squeezed his T-shirt with my fingers.

"Off," I barely spoke, my eyes still closed as I demanded him.

"Impatient Ms. Starla?"

I grinned already, knowing that he held that cocky smirk and his eyes were glowing with amusement without even having to look. He started sliding down my body. His fingers hooked into the hem of my skinnies, and he started easing them down my body after undoing the zipper and popping the button. I was motionless the entire time. "You gunna help me out down here?" he laughed lightly. I smiled, my eyes still closed as I lifted my lower half off the bed, and the jeans came off quickly and were tossed to the floor. *Oh god, what underwear am I wearing? I don't even want to remember right now.* I heard a slight laugh from Micah. "I see you're well prepped for the occasion." He snickered playfully.

"Shut up." I was barely audible, but I could feel him listening intently to my words, a light laugh erupting, loud in the silence. His hot breath broke all of my thoughts of his smile. He breathed teasingly slow on my underwear. I can't even worry about what I'm wearing, he's taken all of me with him in the last two minutes not even. I reached my hand down. I can't take it anymore. I gripped his hair tightly in my fingers. It was somewhat of a relief on my half, and I hope to stay the same for him. His cold hands went to my upper thighs as he spread them further apart and his fingers hooked into the top of my boy shorts, the color blue coming into my range of sight as he slid them slowly down my legs and on to the floor. I sighed as a cold air hit me. "Can y—you . . . open . . . the window?" I was craving for some cool air to blow on me. "Please." It was still more of a demand.

I felt him slap my thigh lightly, making me lazily smile, my eyes still closed. I knew once the window was opened, the cool breeze flowing through the now heated room. "Better?" I opened one eye to look at him, his smug smirk and glowing eyes painted on his face as he walked back over to me. He came back to me and got on top of my shaking body. He rubbed his hips against me forcibly. His breathing came fanning over my neck, burning my already-flaming skin. My legs started shaking, and the now familiar pressure started in my lower stomach. My mouth opened involuntarily. I came at my own will intensely. "Kendall," he scolded, lifting his head from nipping at my neck just under my right ear. His hand now cupping me, making me shiver, and try to suck in more air, making me cough lightly. He brought his lips up to mine and set a wet heavy peck at the corner of my lips, only leaving me wanting more.

I feel exhausted already and out of breath, as I tried to suck in more air too quickly at once. "Relax." He set his hand over my chest. Yeah, that'll make my breathing slower. My conscious snickered, fully naked and ready now. "Open your eyes," he spoke seductively into my ear, tugging on my lobe. I opened them only to see the top of his head. His hair was sticking up everywhere and tangled-looking from the perspiration. His forehead sweaty like mine feels right now. I couldn't resist as my hands went into his hair, detangling it carefully. The friction building and building between our clammy bodies. I rested my head on his hair like a pillow as he continued kissing me sweetly on my neck, moving down to my collar bones. "Ahhh . . ."

"Lower your voice . . . as hot as it is. I don't want to give my neighbors the pleasure to hear you moaning." I swatted at his back. "Hey, it was your idea to open the window."

He lifted his backside off me a little, then his hot breath was fanning out heavily panting on my chest. I opened my eyes again to look down to see the source of loss of contact. His bottoms were pulled down along with his briefs, while he held himself in his hand. His thumb was rubbing circles over the swollen pink tip. Oh my. He groaned, his mouth coming up to mine and brushing his now puffy lips against mine. His green eyes boring into mine for a split second before squeezing shut. His warmth spurted out on to my clothed chest. "Kendall." His breath was hot against my face. His lips pressed to mine in a wet loud kiss before he rested his head against mine, kissing above my eyebrow. "I love you so much."

When his hand pressed against my chest again, it was warm and sticky. He pressed another kiss to my face before I felt his smile against my skin. "Sorry for being annoying."

I combed my fingers through his hair, soothing it back.

***

I woke up which feels like really early, but I know was later. I must have rolled around in my sleep because I was back to my position before I woke in the middle of the night. I looked behind to Micah being absent from the bed. I sat up, wondering where he is. I got out of bed, removing the thin sheet from my body that I sort of tangled myself up in sometime last night in my sleep.

I walked past his bathroom to it being empty and just opened the door to the hallway and walked down it to the kitchen to find him on the phone. "No, I told you it has to be today if you're going to do it." I heard him as I walked in. He turned to see me quickly and just gave me a smile. "Okay, just do it. I gotta go." He ended the call. "Good morning." He smiled before he took another drink.

"Good morning," I replied back as he came up to me and gave me a slight hug. "What time is it?"

He clicked his phone to see. "It's eleven forty."

"What time did I go to sleep?" I asked quickly.

"I don't know. I was talking to you and I looked over, and you passed out." He laughed.

"I should probably go home," I said softly to him.

"I called your mom. I told her that you just fell asleep last night, and you'll be back tonight."

I just looked up at him. "Thanks for that." He moved closer to me.

"You hungry?" he asked.

"Yeah, I should get a shower first," I informed him.

"Okay," he said, setting his hands on me.

"No, no, no." I laughed. "Alone."

He laughed as he held me against him. He leaned down and kissed me. "I'll go to the store and get us something," he said, releasing me a little.

"Oh okay."

"You're okay alone?"

I nodded. "Yeah, I'll be fine." I smiled to him, a little confused why he would ask that.

"Okay, I'll be back in a little bit," he said, kissing me again and then walking off.

I went into his room after he left and looked around first. I feel so at home here actually. It's comfortable. I went into the bathroom and got a shower and then got dressed and went to my bag and applied some makeup and sorted out my hair, fixing it with my mini straightener. I then just went out and sat in his living room and started watching television.

I didn't realize how long Micah had been gone until I heard a familiar voice enter the house. "Hey, Micah, we still going?" he asked loudly. I know who it is—Josh. I sat up in the couch to look over to see him walking in, wearing a dark pair of jeans and a blue plaid shirt. He must have a key or something, or I forgot to lock the door when Micah left.

"Going where?"

He jumped and cursed under his breath. "Oh god, Kendall. I didn't see you there," he added, catching his breath.

"Sorry." I sort of laughed.

"Is Micah here?" he asked, getting back to why he came.

I shook my head. "Nope."

I stared at Josh to say something more why he is here. His jaw tensed. He looked annoyed and confused at my answer. He cussed quietly. "He said he'd wait for me," he complained.

"Where were you guys going?"

"Not being mean, Kendall, but I don't think that Micah would want you there." His statement only fused my curiosity even more.

"Why?" I felt like a small child having to ask questions to everything he says to me and Micah. *Where the hell is Micah?* He obviously lied to me about where he was going, but I'm sure he would have stopped on the way back if he didn't do it before just so I wouldn't know where he really wanted to go. "Take me with you, please," I begged, getting up.

"What?"

"Wherever you're going, I want to come," I demanded Josh as he stood there baffled as I slid on my shoes. I strolled past him right out the front door.

"Micah's going to kill me," he said, following me outside.

Josh drove for about fifteen minutes until he pulled over in a different neighborhood. "There he is," he mumbled to himself. We got out, and I stayed close to Josh, not knowing where we are or why we are here still. We stood behind a white car parked by the curb.

As we walked down the sidewalk, I stood close to him still but not going unnoticed by a few of the residents giving us some harsh looks. "Micah," Josh said to get Micah's attention.

He turned to hearing his name. He saw me, and his face got really confused as he then looked up to Josh. "What's Kendall doing here?" he asked.

"She can be very persuasive," Josh explained to him.

I walked up to Micah and grabbed his neck to take him to my height and kissed him as he took his arm around my back, holding me close to him, and then lifted me off my feet with them to curl around him. "Hello to you too, babe." He smiled.

"Yeah, I'm still right here," Josh murmured to us as I kissed Micah's neck. I felt Micah laugh as he then gave his friend the middle finger most likely with a smirk on his face.

"Okay, that's mature," he grumbled, laughing.

I felt pleased to see Micah although we were barely apart for only like thirty minutes. He set me down back to my feet. "What were you looking at before we came?" I asked, staying close to his figure.

Micah looked over to Josh who still stood behind me a few feet. Micah took my hand and guided me over to a gap between the cars parked beside us. He stood closely behind me with us both peering around the cars to look across the street. He directed me to look at an older-looking home that looks somewhat dirty. "What is it?" I asked, looking back at him.

"Just watch." He instructed for me to turn back around. Then I began to hear sirens coming in our way. I fell back a little into Micah's body behind me. I heard him laugh lightly. "It's okay." He laughed.

He put his arms around me as I held his hands on my chest. Three cop cars then appeared and stopped in front of the house. My eye followed as the cops went to the door and inside, then a minute or two later, two of the cops came out dragging a man down the steps with them, struggling to hold him. He was shouting things at the cops. I then examined his face, and I stumbled a little more back into Micah still holding me though.

"It's all right, Kendall," he reassured as Josh stood by us.

"That's Shaun's brother," I said sort of quietly. "Micah, what's going on?" I asked frantically.

"Shhh." He calmed me to stop talking. "Just watch."

Police cars lined up the curb on that side of the road, and more of the officers hurried about. More of them went in the house and pulled out another man. Multiple hands were needed to hold him back as he stumbled down the steps within their grip. They were both handcuffed tightly as they continued to shout. They looked furious. Seconds later, Shaun displayed his strength by knocking one of the cops to the ground hardly.

I jumped a little as he was then thrown on his chest against one of the cars. I looked around me to see other people just watching. The two brothers were then thrown into two different cars, and the doors shut. The tension had died down a little.

I turned to face Micah. "Why are they being arrested?"

He then made sure we were hidden behind one of the cars as Josh just continued to watch the men be arrested in the cars. "You know that Shaun and his brother supply drugs," he retold me. I thought of making a remark like "and so do you," but I kept it to myself. "They were careful enough though to not keep any in their house," Micah paused then, "until now."

"Wait, what?"

"The police may have been given a report off to find quite a large amount of stuff in the premises," He told me sort of proud like.

I pointed to him. "You . . . did . . . What did you do?" I asked seriously.

"I didn't do anything." I followed his sight as he looked to his left to see a man with his back on his car, leaning on it for support and watching the men as well getting arrested.

"Who's that?"

"He's a friend," he answered.

"What did he do?" I asked, trying to understand better.

"I'm gonna go," Josh said as he passed us after.

All of the teasing banter between the two was gone. Micah's friend sensing that it was time for the conversation. I almost didn't want Josh to leave us though. "All right, see you later," Micah shouted back to him as he headed back to his car.

Once Josh was gone, I took my attention back to Micah. He seemed to look a little unsure how to handle this as he fidgeted. "Before, I . . . got on it, I used to collect money. That's how I met that man."

"Money for what?" I asked, confused. *What does that mean? I understand what he means by "it" and "that man," I know, but what about money?*

I harshly swallowed down the lump in my throat, waiting for him to answer. Micah's anxiety rubbed off on my face. "Debts mainly," he answered after a minute.

I understood it then. Like rent. "But what if they couldn't pay it Micah?"

He looked away and then back down to me. "That's where I came in," he said softly.

It wasn't just to go and get the money; it was to beat them up for it, to force them to give the money if they had it or not. Micah was the man to get the job done and get the money, and they wouldn't be late on it twice with him around.

"I don't do that anymore," he reassured.

A kiss was pecked to my lips. I still stood, half frozen though. I thought that drugs would be all for Micah besides his abuse as a child and early teenager years, but no, he did worse. But I still feel the same warm affection with him.

"I love you," Micah whispered, taking my chin up to look at him as I looked between us, speechless.

"That's a lot to take in," I said back with little emotion as he loomed down still holding my contact.

I'm not sure how I feel. Although I know that I love him, something is holding me back. I'm confused. I let all of Micah's shadowy past sink into my mind. That's only what he has told me, is there more to it?

"I know," he said softly to talk to me more. "I didn't want to frighten you, Kendall," he added sweetly. I took hold of his hand. "We can go now," he said as he then led us to his parked vehicle and let me in, and then he did the same and drove us back to his house.

I looked over at him as he was driving at one point and just couldn't find it in my mind to even think of something to scold him with about himself. Every time I look at him, I fall in love all over again. He's perfect the way he is now. It all just adds up to him—the fights and the bad past. I love everything that has made him into what he is now today. I love everything that he hates about himself. I believe him too when he said he was done, and the time when he told me he is trying his best to get out of it because you can't make the same mistake twice, because the second time won't be a mistake, it will be a choice. He is done, and I don't hold anything against him.

I felt bad for not returning the words back to him when he whispered it to me in the strange neighborhood when he got rid of Shaun for us and his brother. I just couldn't find the words although they are there. I do love him. I don't know what is holding me back.

He took me home later that night, and yet when he kissed me good night, I still couldn't say it. His past lingering in my thoughts, playing pictures of him in fights, giving me nightmares. I don't know what to do. *Why does this have to happen now when it all seems to be perfect? What's happened? Why does Micah have to have such an awful past behind him?*

I lay in bed with Oscar at my side asleep, stretched out fully across my bed with his legs. I could only find the reason that he has to there being something in the future for him, but what is that? I don't remember when we met; it wasn't a night that I wanted to remember, even today. That night, I was terrified to be around him and his "friends." I don't want to remember that time. I'm glad for his pushy demeanor though, it adds to him and how we were forced into falling in love. It's a lie that you can't force love.

I can't find it in my mind to fear him anymore. I never will again even if he ever struck me. I mean, he's my first for everything, and I can't just let that mean nothing to me.

I finally fell asleep.

***

My face keeps feeling wet, as if someone is dabbing me with a moist rag. I got irritated and annoyed with it as I scrunched up, my body and face pushing it away from me, fluffy. I opened my eye fully to witness Oscar standing in my face. He was waking me up by licking my face. I wiped my face, shoving him away playfully.

"Oscar," I mumbled, closing my eyes, wanting to go back to sleep and for him to leave me alone.

He just whined, and I figured that I should just get up now anyways. I couldn't seem to find my phone under my pillow, on my nightstand, or in my sheets, so I just gave up trying to check the time. I got out of bed as Oscar still just stood on the mattress and stared at me closely.

"Come on," I told him as I instructed it with my hand as well for him to follow me downstairs to let him outside.

Oscar and I went in the kitchen and to the sliding doors that I slid open for him to go out. I let the door cracked only enough for him to come back in though. I watched him for a second as he just ran around. I got bored watching him, so I just walked back into the kitchen with my arms crossed and then into the living room to the bathroom and then all around the house. *Where is she? Where is my mom?* I walked back into the kitchen in thought that maybe she left me a note. I looked at the countertop, but nothing.

I walked toward the front door to see a sheet of notebook paper lying on the small table by the door. I rushed over to it in my night shorts and oversized tee and picked it up from its place. She wrote messily that she'd had to go to the store. I set the note down. It's Sunday today, so I don't have work.

I don't know where my phone is, and it's driving me crazy. What if Micah texted or called? If I don't know where it is, I can't reply, and he might think that I'm angry with him. I don't want that, and it's driving me even more up the wall.

I heard Oscar run inside, so I went to close the door completely now. I walked over, watching him as he ran upstairs for some reason almost running into my leg as we crossed paths just about. I looked and gave a confused smile as he ran up. I grabbed the handle and slid the door shut, locking it. I went back upstairs and looked for my phone again for five minutes I'd say. "Where the heck is it?" I asked myself, becoming more frustrated. "Micah's," I said to myself quietly. I don't know how else to get there but walk though. I have my license but no vehicle.

"Uhhh," I sighed loudly as I rummaged through my drawers to find an outfit to walk to Micah's house in. I went back downstairs and grabbed my house key out of the drawer and went outside to start my sort of long walk to Micah's house.

I walked quickly, scared that someone would possibly hurt me. But at the same time, I felt safer thinking back to Shaun and his brother being thrown into the police cars and taken away to jail.

I wore a pink half-sleeved slouchy sweater with a pair of mid-thigh jean shorts and my navy sandals due to the awkward weather today. I continued to walk quickly down the sidewalk even as I neared Micah's street. I walked with my head down for a minute or two just watching my feet hit the sidewalk. When I looked up, I heard my heart thumping in my head and my legs stopped abruptly and my eyes widened with my heart then skipping a few beats.

I watched the four men all dressed in black and with white masks on run down Micah's steps and go quickly into a car that was parked outside that I never saw before and then accelerate down the street. The worst possible thought rang out in my mind as if I was screaming it, but I'm not, and it makes me feel insane.

Chapter 23

"Oh my god," I said to myself.

Once they were gone, I don't know how, but something gave me the strength to run as fast as I could to Micah's front door in only a few seconds. I stopped at the door with my heart going insane in my chest and then just opened it quickly. "Micah!" I shouted loudly to where he might be. I didn't get any response though. I don't know what's going on. *Who were they? What were they doing in Micah's house? What did they do?* I opened the door quickly and went inside. The place was a wreck from what I can already see. I stood in his hallway just looking around. *Where is he?* I took slow steps, looking into his bedroom and walking in; it's a mess.

"Micah?" I asked when I walked in. I looked over to his bathroom. He's in there and looking in the mirror with one of his hands up to his face with a small towel pressed to it. He turned to me and locked eyes. He's surprised that I was there. I silently started thanking God for him still being alive.

"Kendall," he said to himself. "What the hell are you doing here?" he panicked.

"Oh my god," I said, rushing over to him as he stood in his bathroom doorway. His eye is black and swollen, and his eyebrow split above the black eye. He has a large cut on the side of his face. His bottom lip is cut, and his top busted on the edge.

"Sorry about the mess." He tried to joke about it.

"Oh my god. What the hell happened to you?" I asked frantically. He just grinned at me, but I could see that he was only doing it to hold back the pain. "Micah!" I sort of yelled, trying to get him to tell me. "What the hell happened?"

He put his hand on my side as he just stared down at me as my eyes filled up. I can't look at his face and be happy; it's broken. "I was coming to your house, and I was shoved back inside," he spoke.

"Who?" I asked quickly.

"I—I don't know," he said honestly. "I couldn't tell really. I think, one was Keegan," he said as he held me to him.

"But why . . . Why would they do this to you?"

I couldn't help my sight, as it kept going to the large cut on the side of his face, just above the cheek and a little over. "Shaun and his brother got busted," he said softly.

"This has to do with that? But why would they come after you for it?"

"Who else?" he responded.

"You need to go to a doctor."

"I can't."

"Micah, look at yourself!"

"They'll ask what happened and then just get the cops involved."

"Well, you look like you need stitches." I tried to persuade him.

"I can't go to them." He stuck with it.

"Well," I started to think about how I can help him. "My mom," I blurted.

"What about her?"

"She can. She's a nurse. She can help you, Micah."

"She won't ask?"

"She won't get the police involved."

He shook his head to the suggestion that I hoped to be the solution. "No. No, I can't go to her for this."

"Well, what else are you going to do?" I asked him loudly and irritated of how stubborn he is. My mom can help him. *Why won't he just go to her?* He didn't answer as I watched the side of his face continue to bleed, but he held a small towel over it again, feeling it bleed and maybe more of seeing my gaze locked on it unable to look away. "Micah?" I asked for some kind of answer to what he is thinking of doing about this.

He shook his head. "I don't want your mom not to like me."

"What do you mean?" *Not like him? Why would he think that?*

"I don't want to lie to her, Kendall," he answered louder to get it through my head.

I just looked up to his eyes and nodded a little. *But what's he going to do to the large cut?* I can't stitch. Micah walked back into his bathroom and looked in the mirror as he switched towels and held it to the thick opened cut. *What happened?* "Can you go get my phone?" he asked, glancing to me but focusing on the slit.

"Where is it?" I asked, stepping toward him.

He grinned to me. "I think, the living room." He thought, not really knowing the answer himself.

I just looked at him for another few seconds before I left him alone and went in search of his cell. *Why does he want his phone? Who's he going to call?* I entered the room and searched in a hurry to find it desperately. I finally found it after a minute and rushed back into his room to find him still in his bathroom, holding the cloth firmly to his skin.

"Here," I said as I walked up beside him.

He turned. "Thanks," he said softly as he took it. I went and just sat on the edge of his vast bed and watched him as he scrolled though it and clicked on a number and then held it to his ear. I watched him curiously. *Who is he calling? Do I know them?*

He walked into his bedroom still with the cloth tightly to his side of his face. I was close enough to him to hear the person on the other end say, "Hey," a man's voice that does sound familiar, but I'm not really sure who it can be.

"Hey, are you busy?" Micah asked as he went over to his dresser, pulling out some gym shorts and a different tee, and began to take off his pants and slip the shorts over his hips. I watched him with my head turned, seeing the marks on his skin from Keegan and the others who attacked him. It pained me to see how badly he was abused by them. He's known them for so long. I went over and started to help him put his shirt on as he still continued on the phone as the one on the other end was saying something to him. "Well, I'll be over in a few. I got a problem."

He laughed a little as I aided in getting the shirt completely on him, carefully, not hitting any of the bruises inflicted on his smooth skin. "What happened?" I heard the man ask.

"Just wait till I get there," Micah told him.

He hung up his cell a moment later after exchanging a few more words with the man and set his phone into the deep silky pocket. "Where you going?" I asked and sat back on the edge of his soft bed.

He looked over at me as he kicked his bloodied clothes into a pile with his feet. "Josh's," he answered.

"He can fix that?" I asked, looking to his large cut.

"Yeah." He nodded.

"How'd that happen?" I asked through my curiosity.

He shook his head. "I don't want you to think about it."

I grinned a little up to him as he then reached for his car keys. After he snatched them up into his hand, his eyes went to across the room. *What's he looking at?* I followed his gaze to him looking at his vent in the floor. I looked back to him to what he is really looking at. "Micah?"

He shook his head to change his thoughts. "You okay?"

I looked at him, confused. "Can I come?"

He just stared down at me for what seemed like the longest second of my life now and then grinned to me before nodding gently. I sat up and walked with him out of his bedroom and out the front door.

"You okay to drive?" I asked worriedly.

"Yeah." He chuckled a little.

***

Micah drove for a good ten or so minutes before pulling up to a well-set-up home from the outside. "Okay," he mumbled before stepping out. I rushed out of my side and tried my best to help him. He laughed as I slid my arms around his back, helping him out as he still held the cloth to him tightly. I ignored his humor to me as I still held on to him, taking him to the front door step. I only had to knock on the door one time before it was opened quickly by Josh as he grinned quickly to me before going to Micah.

"What the hell?" he asked in pure confusion as he helped Micah in getting up the step with me just holding on to his free hand following inside. I stayed right behind them as they went into his kitchen. Josh's house is nice, tidy, and well set up, still leaving me a little in surprise. Micah was sat into one of the barstools by Josh, taking over as if he were his parent. I just stood right beside him. "Move the towel away," he said to Micah as he obeyed him, lifting it gently off him. Josh looked at it carefully. "You gonna tell me what happened, who?" he asked, going to the cabinet under the sink and grabbing some kind of kit and opening it out on the counter.

Micah just looked up at Josh quickly after he asked. I held my hands on his arm. "Micah," I said to him, indicating for him to tell Josh the truth now.

"Keegan and a few other guys got me when I was leaving for Kendall's, pushing me back inside," he answered.

Josh looked somewhat worried when he spoke the name Keegan. "Well, they really got you this time." He kind of smiled.

This time? I looked frightened at the sight of the needle and other things that Josh got out and looked over to me just like looking at my face. "Can you get some ice?" he demanded more like to me.

"Yeah." I almost whispered going over to his freezer and grabbing the carton of ice and giving it to him. Josh bashed it off the counter top, knocking the ice cubes loose and for a few to fall out on to the top. He picked two of them and set them by the cut on Micah's face. "What are you doing?" I asked just curiously.

"I have to numb it first." I watched Josh as he held the cubes from place to place. "Can you feel it anymore?" he asked Micah.

He moved his head a little to shake it. "No," he answered him softly.

After he had it numbed, he pulled out a shot needle and injected Micah with it. Micah only tensed a little bit from it like he was unprepared. After that, he got a small moist rag and cleaned the area around it, dabbing over it gently, and then holding the ice to the skin again.

I hate any kind of needles and find it even hard to just see them about to inject me or not. I couldn't look away when he injected Micah for some reason. I just felt like I had to watch. Micah didn't really flinch from it going into his arm, only tightening up. Josh looked inside of the cut.

"It's clean. How'd he do it?" he asked, looking back to Micah's eyes.

"I honestly don't remember much of it."

When Josh got closer to his face with the stitching needle, he looked over at me and signaled for me to hold on to Micah, I guess. I looked at him sadly as I held Micah securely to my chest to try and help best I can. Micah tensed as Josh began to sew him up. I bit down on my bottom lip for a second, feeling Micah hold my hand tighter as he wove it through his skin and tugged a little on it. Micah was obviously not able to hold back this pain. I regrettably watched Josh for only one time, thankfully, as he tugged it through his skin again but quickly looked away back down to Micah's legs as he continued his job to help his friend.

It seemed to take forever for Josh to finish. I looked over to him cutting the string and setting them back down. "You're all good," Josh said to him as he set the stuff down.

"How long they have to stay in?" Micah asked calmly.

"Just several days. Seven, I think, at the most."

"What if they come back?" I asked quickly. *What if they do come back? What will they do to him then?*

Josh looked over to me but didn't say anything.

"You can just stay here," Josh told him as he packed the stuff away, walking back to the cabinet.

"Keegan knows Kendall," Micah said softly up to Josh.

Josh looked from Micah to me. "What? How?"

"We ran into him one night."

I thought back to the night I met Keegan. He seemed fine to be around, but no, he isn't at all it seems to be. I don't see how Micah was ever friends with them all. *How was he? How did he once trust them?*

"They know where she lives?" he asked about it as if concerned. *Why? What do I have to do with this?*

"They shouldn't," Micah answered.

"What—what's going to happen?" I asked quickly.

Micah held my hand a little tighter. Josh held an ice pack to Micah's eye, as it was swelling quickly, as he then made Micah hold it there himself as my fingers carefully ran up and down his toned arm, trying to comfort him in some way.

I felt a little uneasy as Josh just looked up to me and then going back down to Micah's as he set the bandage over the slit in his eyebrow when the small amount of blood was wiped off for it. I still didn't want to look at Micah's face. Knowing who had done this to him only caused me more pain and stress. I kept my hands on his large arm as his other hand reached across his chest to set on top of both of mine.

I watched Josh as he walked back over to us with a few things in his hands. He looked up to me and then to Micah more seriously. *What's going on?* I can tell by the look in Micah's eyes that he does feel some of the pain even with the needle's liquid. Whatever it was, I'm just guessing it was to help with the pain. I don't want him in any kind of pain.

"You wanna lie down?" Josh asked Micah.

I gripped Micah's arm a little tighter, as I felt him lightly chuckle under my touch. He can tell that it was a desperate action for not wanting him to leave my sight. Micah nodded to him in response. Josh had to help Micah to stand completely on his feet and then to walk as the sudden rush of weakness was pursuing through his muscles and entire body.

I held his hand until he was fully on his feet. Josh took him to the extra bedroom he has on the same floor, through the kitchen and to the right. So it wasn't that hard to lead Micah to it. It has its own bathroom as well, making it an even more easiness for Micah.

After Micah was laid in the medium-sized bed, his eyes were barely open due to the drug that Josh injected him with. I know now that it was something to help him go to sleep just by my observations of how quick he got tired so that he can sleep better and not have to feel the pain, thankfully, until he wakes up again and hopefully not for a while too. I sat on the end of the bed but with no room really for me to lie next to him, and I filled with disappointment. The bed is smaller than mine and Micah's where we were able to lay with the other beside us. But even though I would be able to fit in the small space and deal with it just being able to lay with him, he has his arms and legs all stretched out, and with him just about passed out and in so much pain, I don't want to disturb him from going to sleep and bring back the pain to him, and plus, he's too heavy to move. I just want to lie next to him but no.

Josh left the room moments later. I brushed my hand across Micah's sadly. "Good night," he mumbled in a very quiet voice as his eyes began to close tightly. I leaned in close enough, pressing a light kiss to the side of his lips. He moaned a little under my touch as my palms were set on his sides. I don't know how to tell if it was out of pain or appreciation, so I just took it off him gently after I took my head back up. I laid my hand beside his body on the soft mattress and then stood to my feet. *Where am I going to sleep?*

I left the room reluctantly. I don't want to leave him. *What if something happens? What if he wakes up thinking that I left him? But where will I sleep?* I don't want to leave Micah here. I walked out after looking back at him from the doorway and walked back out into the kitchen. I want to turn back and just force myself under Micah's arm to lie next to him on the bed. The lights are all off. *Where is Josh?* I walked carefully, feeling awkward to make any noise for some reason.

I trust Josh since Micah does. I know for him to trust you, it is a good sign. I just feel weird and nervous still even as I keep saying that in my mind, it's not my house, it's the house of my boyfriend's best friend. I just want to ask him if I can stay here to be with Micah. I don't want to leave him. I walked straight into the living room from hearing the faint sound of the TV being on.

Josh was sitting on the couch with the volume low, his legs crossed on his coffee table. How old is Josh to have his life to be so under control? He looked over quickly as I stood in the doorway with my hands clammed together shyly. I looked at him, trying not to look so nervous. I just feel weird. I don't know why. It's not like I want to be. I can't help it. I wish I wasn't as much as I long to lay beside Micah.

"You can come in." He smiled over at me.

I shyly grinned back as I walked over slowly to him as I sat on his comfy couch, a cushion apart from him on the other side. He looked over at me.

"What time do you have to be home?"

I smiled a little, looking down from his gaze to my crossed legs. Josh and Micah both seem to make me feel younger than I am. I laughed a little to myself quietly. *Why do they treat me like such a child?*

"You can stay here, with him," he added sweetly.

He got that I wasn't answering because I don't know how to answer him if I can stay over his house. I nodded to him. "Thank you," I said back softly to him with my hands tucked under my legs comfortably.

He smiled with it, tugging further upon his right side more than his left. He nodded. "I'm guessing he's told you about Keegan and them . . . What they do and stuff?" he asked intently to me.

I looked over to him. "Yeah," I responded quietly.

"I've tried helping him. He just can't stop it."

"What do you mean?"

"I tried to get him to stop doing it so many times before. It's just like none of my words ever sunk in his mind."

I don't know what to say to him. *What's he really talking about? What's he mean?* I trust what Micah told me.

"He told me he doesn't do that anymore," I said back like defensively to Micah.

Josh just paused and looked at me for a moment. He almost looked as if he were giving me a look of understanding. *An understanding of what though?* I trust Micah. I don't care about his past, only now, since it's affecting him but only that part. I just want them to go away.

He gave me a weak like smile as if he were trying to comfort me now. "Well, my room is messy, so I hope you don't mind sleeping on the couch," he said nicely to me as he stood up.

I shook my head. "I don't mind." I knew that Josh would never make a move on me completely then, not only because he and Micah are best friends but also because he was more leaning on me sleeping on his couch than his bed in his room. I trust him.

Josh walked over to a wicker chest he had by the closed window with the blinds and curtains pulled to enclose the room. He opened it, pulling out a folded quilt and walking back over to me as I just sat watching him. "Here." He handed it to me.

I took it from his hands. Josh didn't give me a pillow though as he then walked away. I feel so out of place right now I don't know what to do. I just sat there in silence and alone in his living room. I looked behind me just in time to see Josh closing his bedroom door at the end of the hallway. I looked over into the kitchen in Micah's direction. I don't want to sleep out here all by myself. I am closest to the front door, while they are both behind closed doors in a secure and comfortable bed. The two men that I depend on left me to be on my own. Although I don't believe Micah had any say in it being he was drugged to go to sleep, I don't think that he would be able to protect me if they come after us here due to his injuries. But knowing him, he would try.

I settled into the couch more to get comfortable and then laid back on to just the single soft couch pillow draping the single patterned quilt over me. I gripped my phone in my left hand, holding it while I thought. *Should I tell Micah's mom or his sister? Do they deserve to know?* I pulled it out and unlocked it, going to my contacts and scrolling down to Candice's name. She gave me her number the day that I met her just for anything. I just laid there, staring at the screen. I set the phone down quickly, as I heard a noise of someone approaching me from behind the sofa. I sat up quickly, looking over to see Josh. He has a pillow against his wrist and side, holding it there. He grinned at me.

"Sorry, I forgot," he said with a hint of laughter in his voice.

I shook my head. "It's fine. I was fine," I said quietly back to him as I took the pillow from his hand.

"You good then?"

"Yeah, thank you," I said, replacing the uncomfortable pillow with the much softer one Josh gave me, I'm guessing from his bed.

"Okay, night," he said, going back to his room.

"Night," I whispered back as he closed his door to his bedroom, and I heard the bed faintly as he got in. I looked over to the kitchen in the direction to where Micah is passed out heavily. I want to be there, not here. I can't. I have to stay here. I feel too scared to get up and walk to the room. I don't feel comfortable being here. I do trust Josh, and I think he's a nice man, but I just can't feel comfortable staying the night on his couch. I don't know why. I laid back down and got comfy and just forced my eyes closed.

I didn't realize I was still sleeping until I started to hear voices. It took me a moment to distinguish who they belong to, and I realized

I wasn't dreaming, as I was now awake. I opened my eyes wearily and just looked up to the plain ceiling. I yawned before I remembered that I'm not home or at Micah's. I'm at Josh's. I looked to the side to see the TV still on, but the volume all of the way turned down. *I didn't do that. Who did?*

I don't feel right to just stand up off the couch and walk to the voices that seem to be coming from the kitchen. I just laid there with my eyes and ears open to hear Josh and Micah talking about something. I don't understand the conversation though. I heard footsteps walking over to me. I sat up quickly to see Micah. His face all screwed up with bruises, scratches, and stitches, black eye, and spilt eyebrow with the slim bandage covering the cut underneath. I didn't smile, grin, or blush to him I just watched him as he came over to me. I looked down to his lips—the top cut and the bottom busted.

He leaned on the back of the couch close to me, grinning. "Morning," he spoke softly and yet so sweetly.

I smiled to him. I just studied his face. "Morning," I said back, still quietly.

"You hungry at all?"

"No."

I couldn't seem to look away from his stitches. They're red and look a bit swelled. They just look gross. I don't like them one bit, but then, on the other hand, I'm sure that he doesn't like them either. I was too late to look away without him noticing what I was staring at. He grinned to me shyly. "I'm sorry, I just . . ." I tried to say, but he cut me off.

He laughed a little. "No." He shook his head humorously. "I know, they don't look good. Looks better than before though." He smiled.

I smiled a little at him. "Yeah," I said really quietly, telling him the truth.

"Sorry," he said softly in a whisper as he leaned a little further down until his lips met mine in a soft and light kiss. He had to be gentle. I had the feeling to slide my hands into his hair and pull him down again, but I can't. I don't want to hurt him, this time, physically. I pondered over the thought that I can actually hurt him now, not mentally but physically. I have the urge to protect him best I can because if I'm able to hurt him like that, it probably wouldn't hurt much. Imagine what someone stronger and bigger than me could do to him.

"So what's going on?"

Micah looked back, as Josh was making noise over in the kitchen. He looked back into my direction and into my eyes. He opened his mouth as if he were going to speak, but nothing came out at first. "I can't drive. I'm too lousy, so Josh is going to take you home."

"What? Why?" *Why does he want me to leave him?* I don't want to leave.

"Kendall, you need to go home. I'll be fine. You don't need to worry. I'll call or text you later. Okay?"

I nodded. "Okay." I stood up off the couch. Josh came walking over.

"You ready then?" he asked, holding his car keys in his hand, messing with them with his fingers, making them jingle.

"Yeah," I said it softly because I don't want to leave Micah.

Josh grinned to Micah. "Okay," he said, walking over to his front door.

I looked over to Micah as I stepped over to him behind the couch and hugged him gently. "I'll see you soon, princess," he whispered before kissing the top of my head.

I took a deep breath. "Okay," I mumbled into his chest, as I didn't want to let go, but I did. He winced a little bit when I let go. "Oh sorry," I said, a little embarrassed.

Micah gave me a weak smile. "It's fine." He laughed a little before setting his hand on my side and moved it up and down a few seconds. "I'll call you later, Ken."

I nodded and then walked past him after letting go of his hand and following Josh outside to his vehicle and getting in the passenger's seat as he drove me home.

***

"Kendall, I'm leaving for work now, sweetie. There's food on the stove you can warm up later." My mom called over to me as I was slumped down in the couch just watching the TV screen as "Ridiculousness" was playing, but I kept the volume low with my phone sat right on my leg.

"Okay, bye, love you," I shouted back.

"Love you." Then the door shut, and I heard her locking it from the outside with her key. I looked behind me, as I heard Oscar running through the house quickly and coming over and jumping onto the couch beside me.

I set my hand down to rest on his back as I scratched it for a few seconds for him, and he relaxed and fell asleep against my side. I set my head back comfortably as a few hours passed, and I still kept my phone on my lap and the televisions volume down as the marathon continued on MTV. I started to drift off to sleep after I set the empty plate on the coffee table, and my eyes were getting heavy when my phone started vibrating on my left leg, opposite to where Oscar was lying.

I moved opening my eyes quickly, trying to wake myself up as I picked my phone from my sleepy leg and looked at the bright screen, blinking a few times. I looked at the screen to see that Micah's name popped up with a sideways smiley face. I felt disappointed as it was only a text and not a call from him.

> From Micah:
> Have a goodnight Kendall. Sorry, I couldn't call I'm not feeling well enough to talk on the phone. I'll call you tomorrow babe, night, love you, goodnight Kendall.

It was weird but sweet at the same time. Not being rude or anything when I say it was weird, but Micah never sends long messages to me, usually, just a simple "good night, beautiful." He didn't even say that. That's what makes it weird. He repeated himself and didn't even say his usual "compliment." I couldn't help but have something go through my mind that something is wrong with him. I don't think that he would go and get drunk, so he is probably just drowsy from some medication Josh gave him for some of the pain. I just ignored it and answered him back. "Okay, good night, love you too."

After I texted him back, I tugged the small blanket up the couch and spread it over me after laying down and getting comfortable. I felt too lazy to walk up the steps to my bedroom and get in my bed, so I just slept downstairs on the couch that night.

Chapter 24

I waited outside the door for Micah to come and pick me up at work. A new guy started working here a few days ago, Matt. He's a little awkward with a few tattoos on his arm and his upper back that peak out of his shirt sometimes, and I can't help but try and figure out what they are of and what they may mean to him. I've never said anything about them though. He's nice. He also has a piercing on one of his ears. I haven't told Micah about him yet though, which makes me worry about how he is going to react with this.

He had texted me saying he'd be like fifteen minutes late, as he had something to do first. Of course he does. I didn't bother asking what though. I crossed my arms over my chest while clutching my bag in one of my hands. I looked up and down the streets, hopefully for him to hurry up. After another minute, the shop's door opened with the bell dinging, and Matt stepped out.

"Hey." He started shuffling around in his front pockets until he pulled out a small box of cigarettes and started tamping the pack on his opened palm. The noise it caused instantly started annoying me.

"Since when do you smoke?" I laughed, thinking back to Micah and when he used to smoke.

He looked over at me. "Two years ago."

I just looked at him awkwardly, probably making him think that I was a little crazy. I sort of am since I met Micah though. He's changed me, but I like the new me. I watched Matt as he took out one of the sticks and held it to his lips then pulling out a small red lighter and igniting the white stick as he smoked it. After he took one puff, he held the carton in the air at my height and moved it closer as if asking if I wanted one.

"No, I—I don't smoke," I answered nicely to him, flashing a smile.

He just grinned. "You can."

I smirked nicely to him as if saying "no" as I shook my head at the same time. After another minute passed and I was so eager to see my Micah I couldn't help but think what it is that he had to do before he came and picked me up? I mean, it must have been important. *But why couldn't he pick me up and just take me with him?* I looked back over at Matt's face. I watched closely as he smoked the cigarette, taking from and to his heart-shaped lips. I took a deep breath, looking back down the street and then back to Matt.

"On second thought, I think I'll have one," I said quietly, sort of regretting as I said each word to him although I'm not embarrassed.

He smiled at me as I glanced up to his eyes for a second, the light green that they contain always makes me look at them longer than I should, reminding me of my tall blond. He held the box back out and with the lid part flicked open. I reached two of my fingers in and picked one out and pulled it out of the carton. I remembered everything that he did in order to do it correctly as he handed me the lighter.

I took a deep sigh as I took it to my lips, feeling the round fold, and lit it. I closed my eyes sort of tightly and coughed, taking it out of my mouth. It felt a little hard to breathe, as I coughed a little more. I heard Matt laugh a little but tried not to. It made me feel retarded to hear him laugh as I desperately tried to stop the coughing as I tried to keep my cool.

"Just relax," he said quietly. I looked over at him as I made another attempt, only causing me to cough more. I laughed a little nervously after that. Then I tried it again. I did it that time. I took it to my mouth another time, inhaling and exhaling the smoke of it. I never tried anything like it. I felt sort of accomplished once I got it down and was able to do it normally a few times, blowing the smoke out but not without a little coughing. As I took another breath of it, I felt a little light headed suddenly. I blinked my eyes and then looked over at Matt.

"Good?" he asked, grinning at me.

I nodded toward him and hummed because I wasn't able to answer, scared that I would start coughing once more. Then I started to feel different as I felt a little happy and excited at the same time, making me smile as I smoked it again. My mind went back to normal for just a quick few seconds, but that's all the time that I needed as I threw it to the sidewalk and squished it with the bottom of my flip-flop. "What is it?" Matt asked, confused.

"I can't. My boyfriend is coming to pick me up, and he'll be here soon," I spoke quickly.

He laughed. "I didn't even know you had one." He grinned as I looked back at him still smoking.

"Yeah," I answered quietly.

"What's his name?"

I know he was only trying to avoid an awkward silence and be nice. "Micah."

"Micah who?"

I paused, thinking something bad like I shouldn't tell him, but why shouldn't I? "Harlan. He's a little older than me though." I shrugged.

As I was talking, though, my throat has this weird and uncomfortable feeling as if I have a sheet of sand paper in there, like I was at the beach and swallowed some sand or something. I set my hand over my throat and gagged a little. "Oh, that's . . . that will go away," he referred to the feeling in my throat.

I nodded, removing my hand. Not even a minute later, we both saw Micah's black vehicle pull up in front of the shop.

"Bye, Matt." I waved, walking toward where Micah parked.

"See ya," he yelled back.

I opened the heavy door and hopped inside on the black leather seating. "Hi, Micah." I smiled, leaning in and kissing his still purple and dark bruised up cheek. When I pulled back, he grinned, showing his deep dimples, and then glared around me as his arm relaxed around my back.

"Who's he?" he asked. I looked back to see him looking over at Matt as he put his cigarette out and walked back inside.

"That's Matt. He works with me now. And no, you don't have to worry about him."

"Well, I don't want him smoking around you." I couldn't look away from his stitches.

"Micah." I just said for him to shut up. "Have you gone back to your house yet?"

He started up his car and began to drive off. "Well, no, not really."

"Not really?"

He glanced over, smiling. "I drove by."

"Oh," I whispered to myself, looking out the window the rest of the way.

"I still have some things that I have to do today, Kendall. How about we just go out to dinner or something on Saturday?" he suggested, pulling into my driveway, as my mother wasn't home.

"Why two days away?" I was confused why would he want to wait two whole days to take me out?

He looked over at me, confused. "It's usually the other way around that the girl remembers, and I would forget." He laughed. "It's been four months, Kendall."

I looked over at him. "Oh my god, Micah, I'm sorry." I felt so bad so fast. He remembered, and I forgot. "I just . . . I wasn't—"

Micah interrupted me. "Kendall, it's fine," he said softly. I could tell though that he was upset.

"Will those be out by then?" I pointed to the stitches on the other side of his face.

He smiled and laughed a little. "I don't know."

"Is it just going to be us?"

He looked over after rolling his window down for some reason.

"That what you want?"

I shrugged my shoulders. "I don't mind really."

"Then yeah, just us."

I grinned back at him after tucking my hair behind my ears and leaning over to him across the middle of the console in the center. I started kissing his face, making him a little confused thinking that I was only going to his lips. "I'm so sorry," I said as I sprinkled kisses around his face and then to his lips twice. Micah smiled, kissing my cheek after.

"I have to go, okay."

"No." I wrapped my arms around him.

"I'm sorry, I really do though."

"No, you don't." I squeezed him tighter in my arms.

He moaned loudly as I felt his chest vibrate against mine. Micah reached back and grabbed his keys out of the ignition. I smiled against his shoulder, thinking that I won, and he would stay for a while. I heard his door opening, and then he stepped out and grabbed me with him carrying me over his shoulder as I sort of screeched along with it. I heard him laugh and then set me down at my door step. For a second, I actually thought that he was going to leave me at my door step and just walk back to his car and drive away. Micah wrapped his arms around my lower back and then lower. At first, I didn't really know what his intensions were until I realized he was just sticking one of his hands into one of my pockets to search for my key. When he finally found it, I just laughed and smiled up at him as he turned and unlocked the door.

"Okay." He motioned for me to get inside. "In ya go."

I shook my head, grinning, trying not to laugh really hard.

I thought with the disgusting stitches on his face that I wouldn't be able to act like this around him. It's still my Micah. And despite what he's been through, he's still the same loving and playful guy that I love.

"Kendall, get in the house."

"No."

"Kendall," he warned again, seriously.

As soon as I tried to shake my head again, he hoisted me up over his shoulder again and ran me through the house and up the stairs into my room and tossed me on to my bed.

"Now stay." He held his hand up.

"Don't leave," I pleaded, sitting up on my knees to, no, not really be to his height just yet but closer.

"I have to, Kendall. I have plans already."

I wrapped my arms around his torso, trying to pull him onto the bed. He stumbled a little to try and let me think that I was going to win but then stood right back up. I slid my hands down to his hips on his navy colored shorts. We both turned our heads toward my door as we heard another car pull up. Micah peered over to my window.

"Your mom's here."

I groaned. "Where are you going?"

"Nothing you'd be interested in, Ken."

I wrapped my arms all the way around him for once and felt my other hand. Wow. I've never really been able to fit my arms completely around him as if he's lost weight. *What happened?* My face was really confused as my elbow then bumped his silk shorts pocket. *What's in his pocket?*

I looked from my face being buried in his chest to peak down into his pocket. I ceased my eyebrows together as I was able to look down to see what's down there. It was some kind of plastic baggy full of some kind of green stuff. I tried to look at it closer, but I wasn't able to. It's like round balls of green. They look sort of fuzzy or fluffy. Marijuana.

I let go of him and pulled back, sitting back down with my legs bent underneath of me. I looked up at him and grinned weakly. *What's he hiding from me?*

"Micah?"

He looked back down at me.

"What's wrong?" His tone was confused and deep.

"Where are you going?"

"Kendall."

"No, Micah, where?"

"Kendall, you don't have to worry. You can still text me if you feel that nervous about it."

"Why can't I call?"

"I never said you couldn't, Kendall. What? You don't trust me?" He turned to walk out.

"I never said that," I raised my voice.

"Then stop asking me so many goddamn questions!"

"I'm not!" I yelled back. "I just don't want something to happen to you!"

He just stared at me angrily. He took a deep breath before going down the stairs and leaving. After a few minutes, my mom came upstairs. I wiped both of my eyes quickly, as I felt a few tears escape.

"Kendall?" she asked as she walked in.

"Yeah?" I asked, sitting down normally on the edge of my bed.

"What's going on?"

"What do you mean?" I tried to act like I didn't know what she was asking about.

"Well, Micah just drove off looking pretty mad." She seemed concerned.

I shook my head. "I don't know what's wrong with him, honestly." It's true though. I have no idea why it made him so mad that I just wanted to know where he was going. Apparently, I'm not allowed to know that much.

"Are you two okay though?"

I nodded. "Yeah. He's just . . . upset about something, I guess."

She nodded, slightly looking at me. "Okay, well I got food for you when you come downstairs."

"Okay," I responded weakly like I was crying and sounded pathetic.

After my mother went downstairs, I started looking around my room. *Where's Oscar?* I haven't seen him in a little bit. It's strange. I stood up and looked in my bathroom to under my bed. "Oscar?" I called around my room. *Where is he?* "Hey, mom?"

"Yeah?"

"Is Oscar down there?"

"I thought he was with you."

I looked around again. "No!" *Where did he go?* I ran downstairs and looked absolutely everywhere. I mean everywhere for him. After a good fifteen minutes, I walked back over to my mom who was cleaning up the kitchen. "Oh god," I whispered to myself.

"What is it, honey?"

"The door." I paused. "Micah and I left it open." I looked right at her as she looked right back at me from across the island as she stood in front of the sink.

"Kendall," she whispered, "he must have ran outside." I put my hand over my mouth and bit my lip. Oscar hasn't even been away from home except if he was on a leash, and that was only like a few times. He's always in the backyard that is surrounded with a tall brick wall. "You have to go find him."

I groaned in annoyance. How could I be so careless? Oscar's only a year old since a month ago. I ran back upstairs and looked around for my phone. I finally found it and quickly unlocked it. I went to my contacts and went straight to Micah's number. *Should I call him?* I kept my thumb over his name for a minute before I just decided to only text him, as he may get angry if I call him, thinking back to earlier.

> To Micah:
> Hey, sorry for bothering you if you're oh so busy but did you see Oscar run out earlier?

I waited with my phone in my hands, staring at the screen for a few minutes until he texted back.

> From Micah:
> No. No I didn't see him. I. don't know. I don't. Remember. Where. Is HE%?

I stared at his message for a long second. "What the hell?" I whispered quietly, so nobody else could hear me. *What's wrong with him? Is he drunk?* No. He said he's done with all of that. *But?* But I saw it. I know what it looks like. *Why would he have it? Is he high?*

I wiped my hand over my face. Why would he lie to me?

> To Micah:
> I don't know, that's why I'm asking you.

> From Micah:
> I think I DID see Him run out when I took you upstairs;)

Is he serious? He's going to act immature about this making a joke like that.

To Micah:
Are you okay?

From Micah:
Why wouldn't I be*?# Look I'm busynqlnd LOve you goodnightt

    I don't even want to text him back. I can't go looking for Oscar right now. I'm tired and too scared to walk around outside at nighttime since Micah was attacked, and they know who I am. *Would they attack me?* I don't know. All that I can really think of right now is that I want a cigarette.

Chapter 25

I walked through the door to the back room to get my stuff to leave early today because I have to go home and get ready for dinner with Micah. He only called me yesterday saying that he was sorry, and he was with Candice. I wasn't completely convinced by it though. I don't know what to think right now. I know what I saw in his gym shorts pocket. Marijuana. I feel broken that he lied to me. He isn't off it. Yes, I do believe that he has tried or maybe, just maybe, is still trying to get off it. He isn't doing such a great job of that.

I grabbed my bag, and then I looked over to Matt's stuff, sitting in his opened locker space. I moved my head to get a better look and saw two cartons of cigarettes. I want one so bad. I'm so stressed and angry. He gave me one yesterday too on a break. We took it out back because Brandy got mad at us for being out front doing it. I looked to the door and then quickly, quietly, and carefully reached my arm over and snatched one of the boxes and quickly threw it into my bag. I walked out of the shop normally, and Emily was there in a minute to pick me up.

"So where is it he's taking you?" She kept her eyes on the road.

"I'm not sure. He only said to dinner."

"Well, that's not too helpful."

"No." I laughed.

I've been keeping Emily updated with everything Micah and I do. No, not about his "habit" or his past because that is only between him and me. She knows where he works, what his house looks like, and what we do and did together. Yes, I told her that because she is my best friend.

"Have you found Oscar yet?"

I looked over to her as she glanced. "No."

I did look for him yesterday, and when we were talking on the phone, Micah said that he was sorry he left the door open, that it's his fault. I tried to reassure him that it wasn't, but he didn't believe me, although it is kind of his fault. But it's mine too. I could have told him to close it or just not be the way I was with him that day, stubborn. I was just flirting with him though.

When Emily dropped me off, I said thanks and good-bye and ran up to my room. My mom texted me that she left for work. I got undressed, closing my curtains first, of course, and then picked out a blue skirt and lace shirt to go with it and just a pair of sparkly sandals. I went over to my bag to find my phone incase Micah texted me something. In the struggle to finding it, I fumbled over the pack of cigarettes. I pick it up, holding the box in my hand and thinking how bad I just want to hold one between my lips again. I open the box and look at all the ends, staring up at me, and grab the one on the top in the middle. I hold it to my nose for a second and take in that bitter scent of tobacco. I moaned, realizing I don't have anything to light it with. I hurried downstairs and rummaged through the drawers in the kitchen to finally find a lighter. I run back up to my room with the lighter and with the white cigarette in my hands. Then I slip it in between my lips and light it. I inhale thick scratchy smoke, and I feel as if I can almost not breathe, like my chest got hit by a truck. By the time I remember how to exhale and inhale again, I am overwhelmed with the feeling of light headiness and dizziness, so I have to sit down. I take another drag, and it is a lot smoother and manageable. I finish smoking the cigarette and feel fine, other than the slight feeling of sand in my throat. I picked an old can of sprite on my bedside table and tossed it into the hole and tossed the can into my small garbage bin.

***

I made my hair to be in loose waves and applied some makeup to match. I frowned, looking around and not seeing my Oscar anywhere. A tear escaped my eyes along with it, bringing a few more until I was actually crying, sitting on the end of my bed. My phone started vibrating, and I wiped my eyes off before picking it up.

From Micah:
Hey, I'll be there in a little bit to get you. I have to stop at my house to get showered and stuff from work. See you in a little bit:)

To Micah:
Okay, I'm at my house. Em gave me a ride.

From Micah:
Oh okay well see ya soon, love you

To Micah:
Love you.

Chapter 26

Micah planned this all out I could already tell. There was a vase of roses at the table against the wall. It was beautiful. I took my hands over my mouth and awed quietly to myself. I looked over to Micah, grinning like an idiot, quite pleased with himself. We both sat at the booth. I smiled over at Micah. But now I have that small voice in my head that keeps growing in my head.

A minute later, the same girl that led us to our table last time came walking over with a notepad in her hands as our waitress.

"My name's Karley, and I'll be serving you today. What can I get you to drink?"

"I'll have a water," I answered first. I accidently glanced up at Micah's stitches though after.

I looked over at Micah as he was still looking down at the menu intently. *What's he looking for? Just pick a drink already!* The lady grinned at me and then over at Micah. "Just a glass of Cold Springs," he finally answered. *What the hell?*

"Can I see your ID?" she asked, looking at the stitches on his side profile.

Micah lifted his hips a little as she watched very carefully. He's mine this time, lady. Back off. You can watch his hips buck all you want, but that's all mine. He pulled out a thick leather wallet and opened it, slipping out his ID. I was able to see down the middle where you put the money to see that it was actually filled. Like literally. *What? How does he have so much?* I want a cigarette.

Karley smiled and walked away as Micah ticked it all back into his jeans pocket. "What's Cold Springs?" I was curious and trying to get my mind off a cigarette and all of the money and his addiction that I think he has. Hypocrite.

"It's a red wine." He looked up.

"Oh," I responded quietly, looking down at my menu.

"You are hungry this time, right?" He smiled.

It took me a minute to realize what he was saying to me. He remembered. After all those months, he remembered. I giggled at him, and my cheeks felt red. "Yes." I smiled.

***

After we ate and Micah had two glasses of wine, he seemed tired after yawning a few times and a little dizzy by just the way he was acting. "Here's your check." Karley handed him the black packet. Micah rolled his eyes, and I laughed a little when he had to move his hips back up to retrieve his wallet. I watched him as he looked at it and then set the money inside and put it back onto the shiny wooden table.

Soon enough, Karley came back and got it and her tip and, then we got up and walked out together. I could tell that she remembered us by the way she actually smiled at me, realizing that he is taken, and she can't have him. Micah reached down and took my hand in his light. I have to say something to him about it. It's bugging me so bad. I don't want Micah getting back into all that, not saying that he has ever stopped now that I think more about it. His behavior sometimes makes sense to me. The way he is right now isn't really him. He's tired and wore out from not doing anything but eating. He didn't even have a big appetite for food really. Micah and I got back into his car as he started driving off in the direction of his house I realized. I reached down and texted my mom that I'm staying at Micah's tonight, and I love her.

"What about Oscar?" I blurted out once he got closer to his house.

He stopped at the red light. "Fuck," he murmured quietly.

I had to say something to him and Oscar came right into my mind, and I just spoke it right then and there. "Micah—"

"No, we can drive around a little bit and look. I don't have any idea where he could be though. The pound is closed, so . . ." He trailed off as the light turned green, and he sped off.

***

Despite all of our searching for a whole fifty minutes, there was absolutely no sign of Oscar. A tear ran down my face when Micah pulled into his driveway for the night.

"I am sorry, Kendall," he spoke softly, removing the keys.

I nodded, looking down while wiping my eyes. Micah got out and rushed over to my side and opened the door as I slowly got out. When my feet hit the ground, he planted a heavy kiss to my cheek. I didn't respond quickly to it. It's our anniversary though I have to give him some sort of attention, right? I put my hands on his waist and nuzzled my face into his muscular chest. I took a deep breath before I let go and took his hand in mine. He smiled down at me, dimples popping in his cheeks deeply. I grinned back up at him as we started to walk to his steps, and he locked his car up. When we did get to the door, Micah stopped us.

I looked down to see a cardboard box all taped up very securely. "What the hell?" I peered up at him as I clung to his left arm.

Micah let go of me and reached down and turned the box around, looking for some indication to whom it is from. *Why is there a box? Where did it come from?* All I want is a cigarette.

"Who's it from?"

He held the box in his arms, still investigating it. "Doesn't say."

"That's odd."

"Yeah." He laughed, looking back at me.

"We can just open it in the morning though." He flashed his dimples back at me while unlocking his door and stepping inside. I followed him inside, holding my purse in my hand.

"So when do your stitches come out?" I asked as he turned his light on and set the box down on the small table and looking back at me, smiling.

"They really bother you that bad?" He laughed.

I just stared. "A little," I answered nervously.

He came closer to me and wrapped his arms around my lower back while leaning down to my height right in front of me. "Well, lucky you, Josh said they can come out tomorrow."

I blushed at him and then leaned in and kissed him sweetly. He moaned into the kiss while holding his arms under my butt and then lifting me with no trouble and having my legs wrap around his torso. I can't help but always giggle a little when he lifts me, which he always seems to do. Micah though didn't start moving us down the hallway to his room. *Are we going to do it right here? In the hallway? The wall?* "What's wrong?" I asked, as he stopped completely only with his hands holding me up.

He looked at me nervously. "Uh . . . can you give me a quick minute? My room's a mess," he said a little nervous.

I opened my eyes to look down at him, as he's holding me taller than he is. I nodded while giggling a little. Micah set me down carefully and kissed me another time, sliding his arm back up and taking them back. I watched Micah as he glanced back at me, smirking while going into his bedroom and closing the door behind him. I ceased my eyebrows in confusion. He only gave me time for my nerves to take over.

I stood there awkwardly for a minute. I decided to take off my shoes. I slid them off and set them by the doorway, standing back up straight. After five minutes, I got even more confused. After ten minutes, I couldn't wait any longer, so I took a few steps down the narrow hallway quietly. I feel nervous and scared. I don't know how to calm myself down without a cigarette right now. I want one so bad. I shook my head to get off that subject, squeezing my eyes closed for a second. "Micah?" I asked, getting closer to the door. I took a deep breath before I heard a snorting sound. I got scared, but the only thing that came to my mind is that he is feeling sick from something like allergies. I pushed the door open but didn't see him right away. When I took a step closer inside, I saw his arm stretched out into view as he was sitting on the carpet on the other side of the bed with a bottle in his hand, half empty. "Micah!" I rushed over. *Did he seriously go in there just to get drunk?*

I rushed over to him on the other side of the room and got on my knees. "Micah?" I shook him. He looked over at me as if he didn't have a care in the world. "What are you doing?" I didn't yell it. I couldn't; I was in shock. "What the hell are you doing?" He just looked away, giving me the sight of his stitches. He wouldn't answer. I looked down to the floor on the other side of him to see a mirror-type thing with white powder spread all over it. He just stared at me. My eyes widened. I've seen movies and went to a public school long enough to know what it is. There was like a razor on the mirror as well. I fell back on my bent legs and looked away from him. He lifted his hand and caressed my face. "Micah." *How could he do this to himself? To us?* He's too perfect to me though to think any less of him. I don't want to remember him like this. I shook my head and threw his hand off me.

"What is wrong with you?" I shouted in his face.

I wanted to cry. He ruined this. He ruined our night just because of his addiction. I have to face it now. He has a serious problem. Not just an addiction with one single drug but multiple.

How? How is he still doing this when he told me that he was finished? Why would he lie if he loves me as much as he used to seem to?

Tears slid down from the corner of my eyes.

"Don't touch me!"

He tried reaching his hand up again.

"How could you do this?"

I was freaking out. All of my stress was going on him. It was all because of him though. He needs someone to yell at him. He probably always just did whatever he wanted without his mother there to teach him different.

I looked at him in disgust. I got up and walked out of his room. I grabbed his phone off his dresser by the door before I walked out and slammed it shut.

I went to his contacts going down to Candice's name and called it. It's around ten o'clock though, so I don't expect her help really tonight with him. I have to get him help though. It took around six rings for her to answer.

"Hello, Micah?"

"Uh no, no. This i—is Kendall." I lowered my head and put my hand over my face. I sounded sad, listening to my own voice.

"Kendall? Where's Micah? Is everything all right?" She was instantly worried.

I shook my head as I started crying. "No. Mi—Micah needs help," I cried.

"What? What are you talking about?"

"He—" I was cut off when Micah came into the room, looking so angry and upset, ripped the phone out of my hand.

"She's just sad because she lost her dog. Good night, Candice." He hung up the phone.

I stood up in his face, looking directly into his dark eyes. He tossed his phone on to the couch and looked back at me furiously. "What the hell, Kendall? I'm supposed to trust you! And you go behind my fucking back?" He took a hold of my wrists, bending my arms against my chest, pinning them.

"Micah?" I asked softly in pure terror.

"This is what I get? Huh?" He started shaking my body. I started sobbing.

"Micah, stop it!" I cried harder.

"This is what I fucking get for everything I do for you! You go and tell my sister I have a fucking problem! Huh?" He shook me again.

"Micah. No, no. I—I just want to help you. I love you." I sobbed between just about each word.

"You think you're better than me? Is that it? You want me sent away?"

"No, no, no." I cried even harder.

Micah threw me on to the couch. As soon as I tried to get back up, he pushed me down by my shoulders.

"No. Micah!" I screamed. "Stop it! No!"

He pushed me down on to my back with both of his hands. Let's face it, I can't fight Micah off if I tried with all of the strength I have. He's huge compared to me, and it's all muscle. Well, recently, he seems to be a little less muscular. He slid one of his hands down my side while he sucked harshly on my neck after, yanking my hair out of the way. I was crying too hard and was too scared the entire time to even try and stop him from doing this. It's not him though. He's drunk and high. There's nothing I can do to stop him. That just makes me cry even harder. "No," I whimpered with my eyes closed. I don't want to look at who he is becoming.

His hand went to my skirt and lifted it and started yanking it down my legs furiously. The feeling of his hand was rough, nothing intimate or loving about the gesture. And all I could do was lie underneath of him while he crushes and violates me harshly. After that, he started kissing my mouth with even more force with his eyes closed. He slid his knee under my leg to spread them. I tilted my head back in defeat. *Why does this have to happen and on tonight? Just why? How could he do this to me?* I cried and cried. His hand then went to my lace shirt and started tearing it away with his hand, attacking the hem angrily. His hand slid up my trembling stomach and underneath of my bra, moving the cup to the side and squeezing my breast, pinching my nipple hard, causing me to cry out, literally cry, nothing pleasuring about it. "Stop it, Micah. You're hurting me," I cried, trying to get him to stop. He slid his hand roughly back up my leg and tugged at my lacy underwear I bought for tonight. He gave me no sort of warning before two of his fingers shot straight inside of me. I cringed in pain. It's too rough. He started grinding his hips forcefully. It hurts so badly. I could never get used to something like this. I don't want this. It hurts far too much. "No . . . no . . . no," I cried. I'm completely helpless.

He mumbled into one of the kisses. I didn't kiss him back at all though. I can't. It's not my Micah that's doing this to me; he's gone. I squeezed my eyes shut when he bit my bottom lip and forced his tongue down into my mouth. I put my hands on his sides and then got courage. If this fails though I don't want to even think of how he'll react to it. I pushed it all back, thinking back to how he is going to rape me. I bit down on his tongue hardly, causing him to pull back, his fingers yanking out of me, causing me to make an unpleasant sound. As soon as he sat up with his legs in between mine, I moved my one leg into position and kneed him in his enlarged crotch. He cried out in pain. "Fuck." I shoved him off me in his weakened state. This is my only chance. I threw him on to the floor and grabbed his phone and then got off the couch and ran. If I run outside, I can only think of where am I going to go? It would waste time if I tried unlocking his door again, which always proves unsuccessful when I'm in a hurry. The only idea I had was running into his room and closing the door and pressing the lock in and then rushing, searching around the room for something to defend myself with. I grabbed the vodka bottle from the short, long dresser and then ran into the bathroom and closed the door and locked it.

I tried not crying best I could, to try and keep calm. But I couldn't do anything to prevent the tears that ran down my cheeks. I moved over to the sink and broke the bottle, causing the rest of the liquid to rush down the drain and the glass to shatter, leaving me with a knife-type weapon. I held it tightly in my hand and just stared at the closed white wooden door in fear as I was shaking. My hand started bleeding. I felt the liquid drip down on to my feet. I didn't care though. My mind is too focused on that door swinging open to not think of the pain in my hand. I heard his bedroom door open, and I cowered back until my feet hit the edge of the tub. I moved the curtain out of the way and got into the cold tub. I sat in it. Then it hit me. The phone. I left it on the sink. I reached over and grabbed it.

"Kendall, babe, open the door." Micah was outside the door. I didn't move. I froze. I wasn't comprehending anything while I sat in Micah's bathtub with blood dripping from my hand and going down the drain and with mascara running down my cheeks and my hair a bird's nest. My legs were shaking, and I only have on my ripped up shirt and my lace underwear. "Kendall, open the god damn door!" he shouted and started hitting the door. My eyes grew wider when I heard a clinging-like sound on the other side, and the lock turned. I got up as quick as I could, still holding on tightly to the broken glass and cell phone. I ran into the door as soon as he tried opening it. "Kendall!" he shouted as I somehow shoved it shut with my back against it.

"Go away!" I shouted back at him.

With that, I only pushed his anger deeper, and he shoved the door open with all his strength. I stepped back in pure terror as he entered the bathroom. I held the glass in my hand as if I were going to cut him with the sharp edges. "What? You going to kill me?" he asked and then came even closer quickly and took my wrists in his hands. I cried out with his tight grip holding me down.

"Micah, no!" I cried loudly. He threw my wrists to the side, shaking me until the glass was thrown out of my reach. He turned us around, so my back was closest to the door. He started walking us back. I looked up at him. His eyes were dark and different looking. They were wide and a little glassy, and his breath held the smell of alcohol and the vodka. "Micah, please, stop," I cried, looking up at him.

He looked over at me, lifting his head from my neck. He stopped like he had no idea what he was doing. I was still scared, but I have to talk to him. "What are you doing?" he asked, inspecting my body and becoming confused when he saw me only in my underwear and shirt with blood on me from my hand. I just stared at him, confused. "What have I? No." It was like he wasn't even here the whole time. I still had tears sliding down my face when he decided to let go of me. He backed up a little. I cowered back, dropping his phone to the ground. His eyes were wide and looking around as he stood against the wall with his knees bent only a little, so he was slouching. "You need to go." He looked away from me. I ran off into the living room and found my skirt and then slid it back up my legs. I don't want to be here no matter how bad I feel for him. *How am I going to get home?*

I picked my bag and then looked back in Micah's bedroom to see him at his nightstand, digging in the drawers frantically. I just watched him but didn't stay in his doorway long enough to see what he had found when he stood fully up and seemed happy with his find. "Micah," I whispered, making myself stay a few seconds longer to check on him, I guess.

He turned his head around quickly, holding a baggy in his hand. "I told you to leave! Just go dammit!"

I stared at him as he turned back around as if waiting until he would hear his front door close. I turned and started walking down the hall. I only glanced at the box and then opened the door and stepped outside and just looked around for a moment. *How am I going to get home? Yes, I can walk, but is it safe?* I dug my phone out of my bag and pulled it out going to Josh's number. He answered a minute later after like seven rings. I don't know who else to call because I know he'll know something about Micah being on drugs, and I don't want to call one of my friends or mother because I would have to say something to them, and I know I can't.

"Hello?" He sounded tired like he just woke up.

"Josh, I'm sorry it's late, but could you pick me up?" I tried to sound like I still wasn't crying.

"Kendall?" He paused, probably seeing what time it was. "What? What's wrong? What about Micah?"

"He's . . . uh, he can't drive, and I want to go home. Now." I sounded sad even to myself, which I regretted.

"Idiot." He laughed. "How did he even get that drunk? You guys just went to dinner." He found it a little funny. "Sorry he did that to you." He sounded like he was stepping out of bed and getting dressed or something.

"Yeah," I cried a little when I said it.

"So besides that, how'd it go?" He sounded interested. He acts like he's Micah's father figure a little, which made me smile.

It wasn't that great really, but I didn't want to tell him that we went back to his house and were making out when he walked off and got drunk and high instead and tried to rape me. "Um, not that great actually."

There was a pause. "Well, he was probably just nervous, so he got drunk. You're his first girlfriend he's been with this long."

"I hope so," I said back softly.

"I'll be right back, baby. Go back to sleep." I heard him saying to someone else and then a kissing sound.

"Sorry, it's so late. I didn't mean to interrupt." I felt bad for ruining his night too.

"What? No, you didn't. I was just sleeping." I heard what I guess is his door closing.

"I kind of heard you talking a second ago." I blushed.

I heard him laugh a little as I think he got into his car. "We were just sleeping." He laughed.

"I didn't even know you had a girlfriend." I tried to keep up a conversation, so I wouldn't start crying.

"I don't. I have a wife," he answered back.

"What? I didn't know you were married . . ." I've never even saw a ring on his finger.

"Yep. Just like eight months now." He started up his car.

"Well, congratulations." I smiled.

He laughed a little more. "Thank you. Sorry, where'd you say you two were?"

"Oh um, I—I'm at Micah's."

"Oh. I thought you two . . . You saying he got home and got drunk?" He found it a little amusing.

"It's not just that," I cried a little.

There was a pause. "Okay, well, I'll be there in five minutes."

I hung up and set the phone back into my bag and just waited on Micah's steps, sitting down. I heard Micah still awake and just ignored it. I don't even know how to describe how I'm feeling right now. I can't leave him. I still love him. I just sat there for the whole five minutes, looking around me. I felt scared if Micah would come outside and be mad that I'm still here. After about almost ten minutes, I'd say a car pulled up. I got up, putting my bag on my arm, and started walking over to where Josh parked in front of Micah's house. He got out though and walked around.

"So uh, what happened? Why you outside waiting?" He was concerned.

"Josh, just please take me home," I asked, looking up at him.

I realized he was staring at my face. Oh. I must look like a sight. I remembered I have blood and mascara all over me.

"What the hell happened to you?" He sort of shouted. I just shook my head. "Kendall, you have blood all over your right side." He was in some shock.

"It's not what you're thinking. Just get me home, please." I pushed against his chest for him to go back to the car.

Once we were in the car, I buckled up, and Josh just drove away. "You look like you got mugged." He tried to laugh nervously. I looked over and grinned at him.

"So uh, what's your wife's name?" I changed the subject. I don't want to talk about it.

"Bailey," he said normally.

"Sorry, I ruined your night." I looked down, ashamed of myself.

"I told you, we were just sleeping. You didn't ruin anything." He glanced over. I just grinned, looking down at my hands. "You sure you want to go home? I mean, is your mom home?" I felt his eyes keep glancing over at me.

I shook my head. "She works nights," I whispered loudly.

"You can stay at my house, if you're uncomfortable being alone."

I grinned and looked over at him. "I think I'll be all right. I need some time to think."

"Okay. So uh, well, di—did you two break up?" he asked nervously.

I shook my head again. "No."

"Can I know how this happened? I mean, you're literally a bloody mess."

"When we got back to his house and got inside . . ." I blushed. I heard him let out an awkward laugh.

"You can skip that." He looked over, smiling and chuckling lightly.

"It didn't happen. He told me to wait a minute, so he could clean up, and after ten or so minutes, I went in his room to find him." I started crying. "He was sitting on his floor against the bed with a bottle in his hand and . . ." I started crying harder. "I don't know, I'm not sure what it was really. I don't know drugs. It was some kind of white powder-like stuff, a lot of it." I sobbed.

I looked over at Josh to see his face planted on the road with his eyes wide in some shock. "I knew he was still on something. I never thought he would be on that though." He was completely disappointed it seemed like.

"He freaked out." I paused again. "He held me down on the couch and . . ." I whispered. "So I kneed him and ran, and the bottle broke, and that's where the blood came from." I breathed carefully to try and calm myself down.

"I'm really sorry, Kendall." He shook his head. "I don't want to defend him, but I know he didn't mean to. He can't help it . . ."

Just then he pulled up in front of my house. "Thank you," I said, opening my door and getting out quickly.

"Yeah." That was all he said as I closed his door and started walking to my door. I got the key out of my bag and opened my door and got inside safely. I looked back to see Josh watching me as I then slowly closed the door shut and locked it. I remembered though that Oscar is gone, and I'm completely alone now.

MICAH

Chapter 27

I sat on the edge of my bed with my elbows resting on my knees, and I took the Bourbon whiskey back up and sipped on it with my eyes opened the whole time. I just stared at the dresser in front of me. I looked at all of the powder still there and just stood up from my seated position and walked over to it only taking one hit and then set the bottle down. I lifted back and sniffled my nose again. I blinked tightly and opened again, feeling a little better. *What happened last night though?* I can't really remember what it was, but for some reason, one little part of me is sad and feels bad for something. That's why I just keep drinking and filling my nose up, so I won't feel like that completely. *Why should I have to suffer?*

I walked out of my room and go into the living room to look for my phone to call Corey for another order. *Where the hell is it?* I looked in the living room, throwing everything out of the way to look for it. I don't care. I just need more. I don't want what I already have. I want something else, something different this time. When I walked back into the hallway, I saw a box lying on the table where you first walk in. I ignored it. *Where's it going to go?*

I went back into my room but still couldn't see my phone. I just went and laid back down. I looked at my floor, and then I saw it there. I jumped up and walked over to it, smiling as I did so. I went back and laid back in bed. When I looked down at my phone after pressing down the home button, I just stared at my background of Kendall and me. It was of me kissing her cheek and her just smiling, holding me closer to her. I couldn't take my eyes off it. Then I just forgot completely what I was doing. I went over to my messages and went to the ones I sent to Kendall. I smiled while typing to her.

To Kendall:
Hey lovely :)

I just sat the phone on my stomach with the bottle of whiskey by my side and lifted it and chugging a little down. I set it on my nightstand and then laid back down, happy to have Kendall in my life. I folded one of my arms up behind my head and then held my phone in my other hand resting on my unclothed chest. *Where's my shirt?* I waited and waited for it to vibrate to hear back from her or to have her call me. *Should I call her?* I don't know. I laid there until I fell asleep, staring up at the ceiling. I love her so much that I don't know what to do. Eventually, I was completely knocked out.

***

When I woke up, I still had my cell phone in my hand. I picked it up and let my eyes take time to adjust to the light as I clocked the button down and saw that I don't have any messages back from Kendall. I was confused. I threw my head back on to my pillow and looked around the room from there. I've ruined it again. I always fuck everything up in my life. I clenched my fist tightly, thinking as hard as I could about the night before the last, our anniversary. I can't think of anything really. Her smile. I remembered that she smiled. We went to dinner. It was nice. Two glasses of wine. We kissed. It was going good. We came back to my house. We were kissing again. I was holding her up, her legs wrapped around me. There was more. Her skirt. She looked beautiful. Her smile seemed brighter when I looked up at her from kissing on her neck gently. She seemed so happy. *What did I do wrong? Why's she mad?* I focused more, giving myself a headache. I remember.

No. I couldn't off. I came in my room. It was a mess. I was embarrassed. I thought of Holly. I cleaned up a little. I set my dirty clothes in a pile and then looked at my dresser, the powder was laying out. I left it lying around. I'm so stupid. I had to get rid of it. *How? How do I hide it?* I told her. I told her so honestly that I was quitting it. That I did. I looked over at the other end of the dresser. Vodka. *What the hell?* I rolled my eyes as I grabbed the plate of cocaine and then the bottle and started chugging some of it down. It stung a little going down my throat. I sat on my floor and took the metal plate up closer to my face. I closed one nostril with my index and then closed my eyes and started one of the rows up. I shook my head and did the next row. I opened my eyes and suddenly felt confused and different. I was gone now. I forgot why I was in here. I don't care.

I tried even harder to remember what happened next. *What happened next?* I had her down. She was talking about me to somebody. My hand. I slid her skirt down. Her face. She was crying, shouting for me to stop. No. *Did I? Was I that gone?* I held her down. I forced my tongue in her mouth harshly. She wasn't enjoying herself. She bit me. She kneed me. The pain. I barely felt it. But I was overreacting, something I had no control over at the time. I was on the floor. I knocked the door open, busting the lock. My vodka. She took my bottle. It made me even madder. The coke, the vodka, and my anger all working together. I had the key to the bathroom though. In case a sleepover would occur, and she, whoever she was, at the time locked the door to get a shower. I got it off the top of the door and unlocked the door. She fought me. Blood. There was blood on her, dripping down her smooth and delicate and petite body. I shook my head. *Blood? What from?* Her hand. Glass. Sharp glass. I yelled at her more. I shook her. She was sobbing uncontrollably. I ruined it. I tried to rape her. Rape. *How could I let myself get so out of control?* And to her, my love. I did that. Then she was gone. I told her to leave. Her voice. Her voice came back. She was there, behind me. I found what I was looking for. My lighter and bag of pot. I hate myself. I let her go. I told her to leave again, to just go. I was too freaked out with everything, so I kicked her out, on her own, with herself a mess. She still looked somehow very attractive to me. I couldn't even look at her, not trusting myself as she was only in her lacy shirt and black lace underwear. I love her so much that it honestly does hurt. But I wouldn't trust me either.

I started crying, and then I got mad. At myself. I went to my fridge and grabbed a beer out of it. I drank it. I stumbled around and then was too drunk and high to do anything. I went back to my room and passed out. Another thing. A box. We came back and there was a box all taped up. *Where is it?* The table.

I got out of bed after wiping my eyes and jogged over to the front door. It was there. I stared at it and then took it all in. *Why would someone give me a box? Who gave me a box? Why?* I shook my head again for myself to stop asking questions and just open the damn thing. I unwrapped the duct tape and got it off. I opened the flaps after turning on the hall light and looked inside. A piece of paper.

Micah,

I know you stole from me all those times. I need my money back for all of it. 4,000$. Don't slip up again or you know what comes next.

-L

I was a little confused. I got it. I opened my eyes wider. I moved away the newspapers as I set the paper down on the table. Then once the papers were all removed and now laying on my flooring, I froze. No. Oscar. Not all of Oscar but Oscar. One of his front legs. I felt warm tears slide down my cheeks. They killed him. Little Oscar. I loved him. Kendall loved him. Her only pet that she's had not that long, and he's gone or with only three legs. No. *What am I saying?* They killed him. Or they cut his leg off and then killed him or let him suffer like that. *Why would they care?* They want their money.

They knew. They knew about Oscar. They knew he belonged to my Kendall. They were watching her, watching me. They stalked us, her. She isn't a part of this! I shouldn't even be. This is all my fault.

I tossed the paper back into the box and the letter that Lucas wrote me and opened my front door, taking the box with me. I went to the front of my yard and tossed it down by the trash can angrily. It's all my fault. *How do I tell her that? That because I owe some money they butchered her dog? And that he may have been alive in the process. How? How do you tell somebody that? Anybody?* No. You shouldn't have to. Nobody should have their dog cut up like that. Those assholes. That's just pathetic. They should've just came after me. Not after her heart. Not to take her dog away from her. I'm not the biggest animal lover out there, but I respect them and especially Oscar. He was nice and loved me for no reason. I never understood it. He liked me from the start, which is what I wanted from everybody to just give me a chance. Josh, Kendall, and Oscar were the only ones to ever really think more of me and, maybe Kendall's mother, but I don't know.

I sat on my couch and just pretty much cried and cried the rest of the day. I couldn't even look in the mirror at myself. *How could I of done this? To her?* I just, I just don't know what to do anymore. I want to just die right now. But I can't leave her behind me. Even though she would probably do better without me anyways, I love her too much. She gave me a chance when nobody else did, ever. No wonder nobody else ever did though.

I curled up closer to myself on the couch and just hid my face for the last few hours. I haven't really moved at all. *Why should I? Where* am I going to go? Sure, I could go to Kendall's, but why would she talk to me after what I'd done to her or tried? And even if she did give me a chance to talk to her, how do I bring up about Oscar? I can't.

***

The next morning, I got off the couch and started cleaning around my place again. It's a mess, and it smells awful. I picked the pieces of glass in the sink slowly, not wanting to cut myself, to stay with Kendall. I cleaned up all of the garbage lying in my kitchen and tossed it into the bag and all of it from each room. I really just let it go the last few days. Well, since Kendall and I weren't really hanging out here, I guess I just didn't care or have the time. Once I was finished, I gripped the black trash bag and opened my door to set it in the can. I set it into the can and then looked down at the box just sitting on the ground.

"I'm sorry, Oscar." I looked down at it, stared actually.

I looked around then to see if anybody was watching me. I slid my hand through my hair, probably making it stand up, but I didn't mind and then went back inside. I went back, threw my bedroom, and then got in the shower. Once I was done with that, I put on fresh clothes that didn't smell at all of any sort of the drugs or alcohol; I made sure. I figured that since Kendall is still with me, she still loves me. That's the only sentence I could tell myself in order to get in my car and park in front of her house. Her mother's car is in the driveway. It's only six thirty.

I was so scared. *What if she breaks up with me tonight? What's going to happen?* I got out and walked up to her doorstep, feeling so guilty when I didn't hear paws running on the floor to the door when I knocked.

"Oh hi, Micah." Her mother smiled.

I grinned at her. "Hello. I—is Kendall here?" I asked nervously, scratching the back of my head.

"Yeah, she's up in her room, honey." She smiled as I walked inside.

"Okay, thank you."

"Are you hungry? I just made dinner. I can make you a plate?"

"Oh no, actually. I'm fine, thanks." I walked upstairs after giving her a nice smile, being kind.

When I got to Kendall's door at the top of the steps, it was closed. I was too scared to just waltz in like everything is normal because everything is not normal. Nothing with me will ever be normal. I knocked on the door instead lightly with my knuckles.

There was no answer from her.

I knocked twice more. "I said I'm not hungry, Mom," she said plainly.

I just decided to open the door to at least apologize to her hearing how sad she seems. When I walked in quietly, she was lying on her bed, her back against the headboard with a book in her hand. I looked over to see she had the stuffed dog I'd won her a while back on one of our first dates at the fair. She had it on her bed still. One of my jackets covered her upper and some of her bottom half from being too long for her. I let her borrow it one night when we were outside, and it was windy. Her hair looked a little damp like she got a shower just a little while ago.

"Kendall?" I asked, trying not to scare her.

She jumped up and scooted back a little. "Micah," she said, surprised. "What are you doing here?" she whispered, now sitting against her wall, as her bed was up against it. Scared.

I just stared at her. I shook my head and closed my eyes for a second. "I'm so sorry." I sounded weird like I was going to cry. I looked away from her. "I just wanted to apologize to you."

When I turned around to leave, she stopped me. "Micah." I turned back around.

"It wasn't me. I didn't. I couldn't control myself. Kendall, I just . . ."

"Please, shut up."

"Kendall . . ." I looked down.

"Shut up," she snapped. I stood frozen. If her yelling at me is what it takes to forgive me in some way, then that's what I'll stand here for, even just to be in her presence is what I'm happy about. I expected her to throw me out and make me leave. I expected her to hate me. "You lied to me." Her gaze was cold, but she was still looking and thinking of me. "Micah, how, how long have you been . . . doing . . . the stuff that you were the other night?"

I looked up and met her glassy gaze. I looked down at her hand to see a bandage wrapped around it. That's my fault too. "I'm sorry about your hand." I stared at it. She tucked it into her lap and then looked back up at me.

"I asked you a question." She was serious.

I looked around her room. "Three weeks." I looked nervously down at the floor and tightened my jaw. I shouldn't have to discuss this with her. *Yes, yes you do.*

I looked back up into her eyes. They were confused and angry. "Why? Why would you get yourself involved even deeper when you said you were quitting? When you told me you were quitting." She sort of shouted.

I opened my eyes wider to her shouting. *What if her mom heard this?* Kendall sighed loudly in frustration and got up and off the bed, as I was sat on the edge now. I watched her as she went and closed her door and came back and sat in her spot again, trying to hide the stuffed dog away from my sight. It was like she was embarrassed. Ashamed.

"It's not as easy as it may sound when I say I'm quitting, Ken. Have you even stopped smoking? You know the urge when you want one, right?"

She just stared at me. "Don't change the subject, Micah," she demanded. "Why are you still doing this? Answer that. You said it was over with! I don't want to leave you. Is it because of me? Am I not doing something here?" she said in a loud whisper. "Why?" She cried a little, wiping away the two tears that spilled out of her eyes.

"What? Of course not. I don't know. I love you so much that I don't believe it, and when I . . . do it, I feel like I'm in my reality again. That's the life I grew up in. I can't just walk away like how you think. I can't do everything you want me to do. Sorry, I'm not so perfect like you." Her eyes grew wide and wild.

"Excuse me? You think that I'm perfect? I'm with . . ."

All the blood drained from my face. My mouth went dry, and I froze. "That's it then. You're with me, so that's what makes you not so perfect." I paused and stared at her as she looked down.

"I didn't mean it," she whispered. "Micah . . ."

"No. You meant it. I know you did. I know that it's true though." My voice cracked.

"No, Micah, please. Forget what I said."

I shook my head. "You want me to forget what you just said to me?" I scoffed. She looked down nervously.

"Why did you come here? Just to apologize? Well, I'm not going to forget what you did and said to me."

"I know," I spoke after a few seconds of silence.

She stared at me, glanced away, and then back at me. "Micah, I'm here, and I love you. I want you to get help though. That's all I can say. It's either that or I don't know if I can constantly try this all the time with you. And it hurts me to say that to you, honestly. You're not killing only yourself but also me, us."

I just stared at her. Besides Josh, nobody has ever tried to get me clean. What Kendall said really hit me as weird as that may sound. Like it really got to me. It made me think about my future.

"Kendall, I love you so much. Believe me when I say I never want to hurt you. It's like it's not me when it happens. Don't be scared of me, Kendall. I'm sorry." The look of hurt in her eyes wasn't as much after I said that to her. They lightened up and looked only a little sad now.

"I'm not scared of you. Micah, I'm scared of losing you through your actions." She shook her head as if I should shut up.

Kendall leaned forward from her spot and wrapped her arms around me from the side. I lifted one of my hands and held hers as they were stitched together across my chest. I turned my head back to face her. She pressed her forehead against mine. I leaned back against her warm body. "You won't lose me," I whispered to her with my eyes closed. I felt her cold lips make contact with my jaw bones, as she kissed the area gently. A year ago, I would have never pictured my life the way it is today. It's better with her in it, and I want her to stay. One day, I want to honestly say I made it somewhere in life. With her arms draped around me and her face pressed to me with her smooth and delicate body against mine, that's it. That's when I realized to treat life as a gift because that's exactly what it is, never ignore it or take it for granted.

I turned my head more and gently pressed my lips to hers momentarily. "Can you stay?" Kendall asked, pulling back a little bit.

I held her tightly to me. I want to feel her body next to mine, not look at it from across the bed. She giggled a little when she tried to pull back again, but I just pulled her right back. "Don't," I whined as she tried again, but I held her arms around me, forcing her to stay.

"I'm just going downstairs. I'll be right back." She kissed my cheek playfully, and I finally let her go.

"What for?" I asked as she stood off the bed.

"Get us a movie and a snack or something."

I smirked at her. I watched her as she opened her door and walked downstairs. I looked around her room as I retrieved my phone from my back pocket. I went to my contacts and deleted Corey's number and messages. I sighed as I sat up to set it down on her nightstand. I put my hands over my head and closed my eyes as I rested my elbows on my knees. I want something so badly already.

Kendall came upstairs about six minutes later and put a movie into her DVD player and came back after turning her lights off.

Kendall came back over on to her bed as I pulled her back down. I crawled on top of her and just stared down at her in her eyes. She blinked, looking up at me. I leaned down and pressed my lips to her nose. She grinned up at me with her eyes closed. "I'm gonna quit."

Kendall's eyes opened with my words, and she took her grin away just looking up at me. Kendall started to wiggle underneath of me. "My mom is downstairs." She sort of laughed when she said it.

"We're not doing anything," I protested, smiling.

She rolled her eyes. "It sure looks like it."

"Kendall, I wouldn't do that when she's down there." I sounded mean. I'm not trying to be though. It just seems like so long since I've had anything.

Her eyes got a little wider, sensing my frustration with her. "Okay, okay." She sort of sounded upset and shaken up.

I shook my head. "Sorry. I just, it's been a while . . .," I admitted.

She sighed. "So you're staying tonight?"

I looked down between us and then back up at her. I want to go home and get my stuff. I want it so badly. I closed my eyes and looked back up at her. I want to go home to get it. I want to call Corey to meet up with me, so I can get some more. I sighed and looked away again. Kendall's hand brought my mind back down to her. She caressed my face carefully, forcing me to look back down at her, knowing what I was thinking about most likely.

Just as I was about to say something to her, my phone started vibrating on her nightstand. I looked down at her and sighed. I leaned back down on top of her, so my chest was against hers and my arms wrapped around her. I don't feel like answering it. "Micah." She laughed.

"No," I said, kissing her neck gently.

"Answer it." I just moaned in response as I reached over and picked it up and leaned up so my hips were below her knees. I looked back down at her before answering it without even looking at who it is calling.

"Hello," I greeted in a friendly manner even though I was angry that they interrupted me.

"Wasn't sure if you were going to answer." His voice spoke right when I looked back down at Kendall as she was watching the TV and then glanced up at me.

Why's he calling me? "What the hell do you want?" I asked, getting off Kendall and sitting on the side of the mattress.

"I just wanted to make sure you got your package." He sounded amused.

"You sick fuck. What is wrong with you?" I got mad with the picture of Oscar's leg popping into my mind.

I closed my eyes and looked down only to look up and notice on Kendall's TV stand a few framed photographs of her and Oscar as he was a baby and fully grown.

"So I take it you got it, yeah? You're the one that owes us some money now."

"I would have gotten it to you. You didn't have to do that. What in the hell were you thinking?"

"You know Lucas doesn't play around. You're the thief."

"I'll get it to you."

"Micah?" Kendall came up beside me.

"She's with you, isn't she?"

"Who is it?" She mouthed quietly as I looked over at her.

"Look, Johnathan, I'm gonna get your god damn money. Just don't bug me about it. And don't you even think about fucking touching her."

"Just take it to Keegan's when you get it in a week. By the way, I saw Kendall today with her mom. Her ass looked great."

"You stay the fuck away from her," I said back sternly.

"I'll talk to you later then."

With that, I took the phone away from my ear and hung up before him. "Micah, what's going on?"

"I'm staying tonight." I looked over at her.

"What's going on?" She seemed a little scared.

"Did you see Johnathan today?"

"What? I only saw him at the grocery store, Micah. He didn't say anything, just acknowledged me." She sat back on her legs.

"Just stay the hell away from all of them okay?"

"Why? What's going on? They're your friends?"

I looked away and then back at her. I set my phone down on the bed, and then Kendall's door opened up. "I just wanted to tell you that I'm leaving for work now."

I smiled over at her mom politely as she returned it. Just as she was about to leave again, Kendall spoke up. "Mom, is it okay if Micah stays with me for the night?" She sounded a little nervous asking it.

"Yeah, of course. Can I just talk to you for a moment?" Kendall released her touch from my back as she stood up and walked out of her room with her mother and closed her door behind her, leaving me. I heard some of their conversation about me staying as she just told Kendall some things regarding personal things. I laughed a little but made sure it was quiet. Kendall then came back into her room and rolled her eyes about her mom, and I smiled at her, probably showing my dimples.

"Sorry." She blushed, walking over to me and sitting back on the bed. I just shook my head looking over at her, well, having to look down a little. "Now can I know what's going on, please?" She smiled, leaning closer to me.

"I . . . I owe some money to them," I admitted quietly to her.

She looked confused. "Well, how much?" She was scared to ask.

"Four grand." I looked down. I didn't need to look over at her to know she was in a little shock with her eyes widening with the information. I bit my bottom lip, waiting for her to answer me in some way. I couldn't take it anymore. I don't want her to say anything, and I don't want to wait for her answer. "Can we not talk about this?" I looked up at her nervously.

She nodded lightly. Kendall wrapped her arms around my shoulders and kissed my cheek. "I still love you." She smiled, leaning her head against my left shoulder.

"I don't know why." I kept my eyes down and out of her sight.

"You need to stop talking like that. You know that I love you, but you still act like I'm lying." There was a pause. "Micah . . ."

"You know what I'm saying, so don't act so clueless." I couldn't hold myself back. "I'm not blind when I say you shouldn't be with me. You know exactly why you shouldn't be with me, yet you still overlook everything for whatever reasons like I'm some science project to you. I don't understand why I'm still here with you after what happened last night. What I did to you . . . Yet you're still here saying you love me."

"Because I do love you."

I shook my head. "You don't understand."

"No, I don't because you don't tell me everything."

"You know more about me than anyone."

"It doesn't always seem like it. You leave me in the dark, and you know it. You do it on purpose."

"You don't need to know every little detail of my fucking life. You don't need to hear about it."

"I want to."

I shook my head slowly. "Why can't you just trust me when I say you're better off not knowing the entire truth about me? You want to know something about myself? Do you want to hear something about me?"

"Yes, I do."

"Fine. How about the time when I walked in on my father raping my mother? Or how about when I almost beat my sister's boyfriend to death? Then there's when I got my first punch at seven . . ."

"Micah, stop!" Kendall shouted. "You can stop. I'm sorry, okay? I . . . I didn't know." Her eyes were swollen with fresh tears as they slid down her red cheeks. I couldn't help but stare at her now. She's so beautiful and pure, and yet she's wasting all of her love and what's left of it on me. Thanks to me she is like this. She is crying and broken and guilty for no reason. It wasn't her fault what had happened to me in the past or the decisions I had made. It all had nothing to do with her. I didn't want her hearing any of it, but I sort of feel relieved that she does know a bit more as selfish as that sounds. She shouldn't feel the way she does about me.

"Don't feel guilty." She shook her head with her face buried in her hands while she wept and I'm over here, standing in the middle of the floor after getting up to shout at her for no reason, and now she is crying alone when I should comfort her in any way, but I feel I need to give her some sort of space.

"I shouldn't have . . . made . . . you say that." She sobbed. I walked over so that I was on my knees in front of her and gripped the jacket adoring her body.

"I love you, Kendall. I should be able to tell you these things. I know that, but I just don't know how to tell you everything without it turning out like this . . . I just need some time to still get used to this whole thing between us."

"I understand." She wiped her face as I stared up at her now. "I just don't want to be kept in the dark if something is going on or bothering you. You have to tell me things."

She looked at what she was wearing, and then her cheeks were tinted a shade of pink. She shook her head a little in embarrassment. "Sorry, you can have it back. I was just cold. It was out and—"

"It's fine." I smiled at her.

"Sorry, I can't sleep in pants." I sighed, getting up and undoing my belt and shimmying my jeans down and stepping out of them and then taking my shirt off and throwing it on her floor next to my pants. I heard Kendall giggle. I looked over at her and cocked an eyebrow, causing her to laugh even more. I got back on my side and got closer to her. I couldn't keep smiling though because I kept thinking of Oscar.

"What's wrong?" She looked over as my arms were wrapped around her stomach.

"I'll be fine." I said back quietly, nuzzling my face into her neck. "Just go to sleep."

I felt her rest her head over on top of my hair, flattening it down. I closed my eyes tightly.

***

I don't remember what I was dreaming about, but it caused me to jolt out of my sleep quickly and sit up a little. Kendall was taken by it. My nose was feeling, I don't know, different. I lifted my hand as Kendall was flipping around to face me. When I took my hand back to look at it, there was a dark liquid. Kendall sat up on her elbows, looking at me. I got the covers off and got out of bed.

"What is it?" she asked as I was walking toward the bathroom.

"Just, my nose is bleeding," I said as I kept walking. I got into the bathroom and flickered the bright light on. I looked at my nose as it was still bleeding a little. I turned on the water and then started washing off my entire face. I feel awful right now. Once I dried my face off, I looked in the mirror again. I backed up a little bit to look at my torso. I turned to the side and then inspected myself. My ribs are slightly showing. I'm never hungry though as much as I used to be. I called in sick the last three days for work too. I looked back up into the mirror to see that the sudden nosebleed had stopped. I walked out of the bathroom and turned off the light before I left the door only cracked, walking back over to the bed with Kendall.

"You okay?" she asked tiredly, looking up at me as I got back in bed.

"Uh yeah, yeah, I'm fine." I kissed her forehead. *Why was my nose bleeding?* I stayed awake, just stared at Kendall's back with my hand on it just rubbing it back and forth for some random reason, but she didn't seem to mind, as she faced the other way. I couldn't fall asleep though. I feel so awful, like a sick feeling. Sometime after like two hours of just lying there, I was finally able to just pass out.

KENDALL

Chapter 28

When I woke up, I was facing the wall. I opened my eyes and then tried turning over, so I could look over at Micah, but he's managed to hang on me like a vine. I remembered in the middle of the night last night that he got out of bed because he woke up with a nosebleed. When I flipped over, he was still sleeping with his face flat on the pillow with one of his hands under it while he snored. Thank god he wasn't snoring bad last night. His eyes are moving like he's dreaming, I smiled a little, wondering what he's dreaming about. I sat up and crawled over him and got off the bed. I could have just got off at the foot of the bed, but I'd rather take the chance of waking him up, so we could both be awake.

I looked back at Micah before I went and cleaned my teeth. When I walked back out, he was still sleeping. I still feel bad every single morning without Oscar getting up with me to run down the stairs to go outside. I tried to ignore it, knowing that he'll come back sooner or later. I went downstairs and remembered my mother won't be back until like eleven thirty. It's only ten.

I grabbed a water from the fridge and then grabbed my phone from the coffee table in the living room from the other night. I jogged back up the steps. I unzipped Micah's jacket once I got to the door then walked in. I was hoping that Micah would have awaken, and he did. He was sitting on the edge of the mattress with his feet set on the floor and his head buried in his hands, elbows on knees. He was fisting his own hair in his large hands.

"Morning, Micah." I smiled, walking over to him just thinking he just woke up, so he's still a little drowsy or something. He just fisted his blond hair a little tighter in his fingers. I walked over to him and got down on my one knee and looked up at him from there. "What's wrong?" I whispered.

He sniffled his nose and then looked out at me. He stared at me for a few seconds. "I don't feel too good." He barely even whispered.

I got concerned as if I had a motherly instinct at that moment. "What? What's going on? What's wrong?" I know that if you wake up early, you could be getting sick, and Micah did. He just hid his face again from me. "You're head hurt?" I grabbed a hold of his arm gently, my hands probably somewhat cold.

I heard him make some kind of noise like he is in pain. "A little," he admitted quietly.

"What else?"

"I just feel sick . . ."

"So you feel like . . . irritable?"

"I guess . . ." He sounded so sad and lonely whenever he talked back.

"I'll get you some medicine," I said once he moved his hands away and looked over at me as I kissed his cheek. I went back to the stairs and hurried down and searched the cupboards for some medication for headaches and irritability. I moved some things around, trying to remember when the last time I was sick, because it was behind the TUMS and some sleeping pills. Once they were moved, I found it right behind them. I looked back at the colorful tablets before closing the door and then grabbing him a water and taking the unopened medicine back upstairs with me. Micah was still sat at the edge of the bed when I got there. "Okay," I said as I set the water down by him, and he watched me carefully. His eyes looked bad like he's still tired and just different. The usual darkish mossy green replaced with a paler shade. I undid the cap and got the cup sealed onto the top of it and filled it up, giving him the amount needed. "Here's some Advil."

Micah looked at it before taking it and tilting his head back, drinking all of the liquid. "Thanks," He whispered as he took the water then.

I got more curious. "Micah, when's the last time . . . well . . . that . . . that . . . you did it?" He knew what I was talking about. I know that he does. He has to know. *Is this just withdrawal?*

He acted like the floor had become very interesting to him then. He blinked a few times before looking up at me. "The day after you left." He couldn't look me in the eyes. I got up and sat beside him on the bed.

"You know how dangerous this is, ya know. Micah, you have to quit it."

"I know . . ." he admitted, leaning into me.

"No. Micah, I'm serious. You need like professional help. I mean, you're addicted. It's serious."

Micah just shook his head. "I'm not going to a doctor," he sounded irritated now as he leaned off me, obviously annoyed.

I shook my head and sighed. "Well then you're staying here until all of this goes away."

Micah shook his head again. "I can't do that. I'll be fine. Just stop talking about it." He groaned. "Just shut up about it right now at least."

"No. You're going to listen to me, or I'm kicking you out. We have to talk about things together, especially things that are serious. This serious."

"Okay, fine. You want to know something? Do you? I owe them four grand. You want to know something else? I have to give it to them in a week." He finally spoke, his voice low but deep like he was admitting something that was locked away.

"How?"

"I have some saved, only like $1,000 though. It's still not enough."

I paused. The idea came right to me, but I was afraid of how he'd react but more afraid of him possibly dying or being killed over this all. "How much of it do you have?"

Micah looked back up at me. He shook his head. "Why?" I think he already knew though what I was going on.

"Because you know how to deal, Micah. You're going to fucking sell it and get the money." I was so serious. He clenched and unclenched his jaw, looking at me. He finally nodded. It's a win-win if this all works out. "I need to be there though."

"What? No, Kendall!"

"Micah, can you say that you won't take it instead?" He just stared me in the eyes. I know he would do it in the opportunity of having it right in front of him.

"Okay," he answered softly.

"Today's Tuesday, so . . ."

Micah looked away from me. He was just staring at the floor but looks like he is thinking about something.

***

Yesterday, Micah stayed at my house again and had two more nosebleeds. We just stayed upstairs pretty much the entire day and watched TV together. Micah only has four days to make $4,000 now. I don't trust him to go back to his place again alone. No matter how scared or nervous I may feel about going with him, I have to unless I want to lose him again. I just want him back.

I moved out of the way from the water when it started burning my back too much. I had to shake the conditioner bottle a few times harshly for it to finally come out on to my hand. I took my hands to the top of my head and rubbed it all through my hair, massaging, and jumped slightly and tried to cover myself when my curtain was pulled open slightly, and Micah stepped in with his head down. I watched him closely as he wouldn't look me in the eyes as he took my wrists and moved them away from my breasts from him. "Please don't hide, not from me," he whispered, his voice thick with sleep. He set his large hands on my hips, still not making any eye contact with me, and switched places with me, so the water cascaded down his naked body now. I couldn't help but stare at him in all his glory. I'd never get tired of this. I don't want to lose him. While the water hit his body, I stared at some of his scars down to the one on his hip then wandered down his oh-so-happy-happy trail. He grabbed my chin and tilted my chin up finally looking me in the eyes. Something more is bothering him this morning, but with the look in his eyes, I'm scared to ask not knowing what kind of reaction or mood I might trigger.

He turned me around before I could do or say anything to him, and before I could turn back around, his hands were in my hair, massaging my scalp and conditioning it further, while I closed my eyes and savored this moment of pure serenity with my Micah. Once he decided it was good enough or either he was bored, he switched us, and I washed his hair for him, and while he rinsed, I couldn't help but wrap my arms around his waist and hold him as physically close to me as I could muster. When his arms didn't go around me in return, I gave him a squeeze but still nothing as I pressed my cheek against his chest. Finally, when I accidently let out a strangled sob, his hand patted my back, and then his arms followed in, wrapping around my back while he rested his head on top mine.

Once Micah and I were both showered and ready, he grabbed his keys after I gave him more Advil, and we left to go to his house. He just acts so anxious today and jumpy.

When Micah and I got back to his house, he got out first and came to my side and opened the door for me. This is gonna be weird I can already tell by the sudden way his attitude has changed and mood has shifted. Micah and I walked up to his door side by side but not holding hands. He unlocked the door, and then we walked inside. He turned on the hall light, and then I grabbed his hand into mine. He closed and locked the door behind him as he leaned down and kissed me sweetly. I could tell that he doesn't want me here or around any of it. But I have to be here, and I have to go with him.

"Where is it?" I turned and faced him.

"My room . . ." He sounded ashamed. "I don't want you involved."

"Micah, I am. I have been since they met me. Well, since I met you, I guess."

"Okay, but you will stay in the car the whole time."

Micah and I walked into his room as my eyes quickly found the powder laid on his long dresser. I looked up at him to see him staring at it. "Is that all?" I looked around.

"I . . . I can package the rest up and . . ." He paused and looked down at me.

"Micah, we have to do this. You need to get their money, so they just leave you alone, and you can get clean."

He looked down at me still and looked so guilty for something. He nodded. "The vent . . . off to the side in it." He pointed. I gave him a reassuring grin before I walked over to it, while he went to the powder and started to get it all together. When I got on the floor and took the vent off, I couldn't see it at first.

"This is how you hid it from me?" I asked, looking down, and saw the bags. I lifted them as they were well concealed. Micah never answered me as I kept looking back to see him resisting to take any of it. Once I got all of it out of the floor, I just laid all five bags out and stared at them. *How could he do this to me?*

I looked over at him as he pulled out an old-looking backpack and started putting the stuff into it. He looked over at me and then spoke. "The nightstand . . . under everything," he said, trying to avoid eye contact with me. I nodded, giving him a weak smile, as I felt my eyes get cold with tears, but I didn't let any escape.

As I opened the drawer and started moving stuff out of the way, I couldn't help but feel disgusted with some of the things he has in here next to his bed. I don't care if he is a man, it's gross. I have to start some kind of conversation, so I can try and distract myself. "So uh, you did quit working . . . for . . . for Keegan." I glanced over as he stopped his movements to look up at me.

"Yeah."

"But you still bought from them," I concluded, looking over at him.

He nodded slightly as he looked back up at me. "Only from Corey, but I'm sure they found out. I was still giving them money though, so . . ." He let out a nervous chuckle.

I weakly grinned over at him. I put my eyes back into the drawer as I finally found it. The bag was long and filled just about all the way. I mean, it was a big bag. I picked it up and just stared at it only to reveal that there was another but completely filled one in the very back. I set them both down on the side of his bed. Micah came over beside me and grabbed them both and set them in the backpack. He looked down at me as I looked up at him. "We're getting rid of it." I set my arm around his back and moved my hand around on his other side, rubbing it up and down and leaned a little into him compassionately. Micah then left my side, as he went and got the other filled bags off the floor.

"How do we sell it?"

"You're not dealing anything." He sounded annoyed, and I know by his tone he's not to be argued with. "I know what to do." He looked up as he finished packing up the bag and then walked over to his other dresser. I watched him carefully as he picked a beanie from one of the dressers and slipped it over his unruly hair from the shower a little while ago and didn't really fix it after. And plus, it's actually a little chilly outside today from usual, so I still have on his jacket.

"There's more?"

He shook his head. "You always have to take something with you," he said, opening a drawer on the top. I watched as he pulled something out and turned around as he started loading a small handgun.

My eyes widened. I never knew he had a gun before. He looked up to, I guess to see my reaction. "Protection from what?" I asked, kind of loudly in shock.

"Kendall, it's just a revolver. You just never know who you're selling to. You just need a small one, so you can hide it, so they don't suspect anything. It makes it more okay."

"Okay? Micah, I didn't know you carried a freaking gun around with you!"

"Ken, it's for my safety."

"Have you ever shot someone?"

He nodded. "I didn't kill them if that's where you're going with that. I'm not a murderer, Kendall. I couldn't kill someone."

"When was this?"

"Just like a year ago, and the year before that."

"What?"

"You didn't know me then. I was with Brian, and it wasn't for no reason."

I nodded. "And the other time?"

"Shaun and his brother and I were attacked," he answered casually as he finished loading the small silver weapon. Micah looked at me again.

"Is . . . is that all of it?" I asked, walking closer to him a little shaky. "Micah."

He just stared at me. "Just go wait by the door." He leaned down and kissed me on the forehead, momentarily setting his hand on my back as if to convince me better to just wait out by the door.

"Micah."

"Come on," he said, leading us out of his bedroom with the gun in his hand and backpack slung over one of his shoulders. He left me in the hall as he walked into his living room, but I watched in the doorway from the hall as he opened the vent beside the couch and pulled out a bigger baggy completely full and bigger than the other bags. My eyes widened. He stored it in the backpack.

Micah walked back over to me, and I followed him back to the front door as he slid his phone down his back pocket and then tucked the gun away after switching the safety on and swinging the backpack over his shoulder once more. He then blindly took my hand into his and we walked out of his house. I feel so nervous now. I wasn't really thinking about what I am really doing until now.

My hand got sweaty, and I felt Micah's eyes drift down to me as he walked me over to the passenger's side. Micah opened the door for me as I walked over and stepped up inside on the leather seat. I think Micah knew how nervous I had quickly become. I was proved correct when he leaned inside of the vehicle, staring up into my eyes with his very serious and mature look right now. It made me freeze and just sit still in the seat.

"Nothing is going to happen to you, okay? I wouldn't let anyone hurt you if something happens. Don't be scared." I just stared back down at his hand as it rested on my thigh and then nodded, looking up to meet his gaze again. "I know what I'm doing." With that, he took his hand off my trembling leg and closed the door and then getting into drive on his side.

"Where are you gonna go?" I asked quietly while peeking over at him as he drove down his road and out of the neighborhood.

He just looked over. "Don't worry, Kendall." Was all he responded back as if I can't know? *Is that a good thing?* I turned my head after watching his face a few seconds and stared out of the window. I must have fallen asleep at some point because Micah started shoving at my arm lightly with his hand.

When I turned and looked at him, his dimples were indented, and he was smiling over at me. We were parked. I just grinned back at him. "Do you need anything?"

"What?"

"I have to get gas. Do you want anything from inside?" he said, turning the car off.

"Oh um, I'll go in with you," I said, unbuckling myself.

"I can just get it." I ignored him, while I just got out of the car and walked up beside him. He laughed a little before nodding. "Okay." He smiled while taking my hand in his.

I went to the back to get a drink, while Micah stood in the line. After I got my drink, I started to walk back up the aisle. I met up with him when it was his turn, and he paid for the gas and my water. I couldn't help but look up at all of the cartons though. I bit down real tight to fight the sudden urge I got from just looking at all of the unopened packs. My mind though was quickly shot back to Micah as he gripped my hand and led us back outside, and I got back into the car. I knew I was caught. I looked over at Micah as he pumped the gas and was leaning up against the car's side. He looked back at me and winked, causing my cheeks to flush. I heard his laugh faintly from me looking away shyly. I watched as a girl with short brown hair stepped out of the car parked opposite of us and said something to Micah to get his attention. He sort of ignored her as she was saying something. Like a minute later, Micah got back into the car and leaned over and pressed his lips against my cheek. I felt like he was sort of showing me off. I just laughed a little and smiled over at him as he started the car back up and drove away.

***

I don't know how much time passed before Micah parked somewhere that didn't look familiar to me at all. I looked around out the window with my eyes wide. *Where are we?* There was an old apartment building in front of us. It looked bad. I looked over at Micah as he reached behind him and grabbed something from the bag and slipped it down into one of his front pockets. He then got the gun and sat up, slipping it down the back of his pants, and then opened the console in the middle of the seats, pulling out a small blue can like thing and handed it to me. "Just use this if someone bothers you," he said as I grabbed it carefully out of his hand. I looked down at the small can of mace and just looked back up at him. "I'll be back in a few minutes," he said, leaning over and kissing my cheek. Micah got out of the vehicle and went to the wooden steps after locking the doors and jogged up them. I watched him as he looked at each door before knocking on one of them and then saying something before the door was opened, and he stepped right in like he was friends and comfortable with whoever it was in there. I looked around nervously. I'm scared.

As more time passed, I got more worried. *What's taking him so long?* I want to get out of the car and go up there. But I'm too frightened to unlock the doors let alone walk up those steps alone without Micah, so I would feel more protected with this little can of pepper spray. *How could he just leave me down here by myself?* I kept looking around nervously and back up at the door he went into. After like a whole ten minutes of worrying, the door finally opened. I stared at the opened door for what seemed like forever, just staring at Micah's back as he stood there and then smiled at someone inside and then closed the door and came walking back normally.

I never took my eyes off him as he jogged back down the stairs. I jumped a little when he unlocked the doors. I saw him smiling a little, knowing it scared me when he did it and then climbed inside and started the car up and pulling out quickly and driving off. "Micah?" I stared at him still.

He glanced over. "What is it?" he seemed concerned.

I shook my head. "Who were they?"

He glanced at me twice. "Do we have to talk about that?" He sounded different now, like ashamed, I guess.

"No, I, I just . . ." I started, but Micah talked over me, interrupting.

"It's all right, Kendall. We had to come this far because someone would say something to Keegan."

"Yeah," I answered back softly that I could barely even hear myself say it.

"So uh, how much?" I asked nervously and sort of smiling.

He looked over at me, smiling with his dimples indented in his cheeks. He then reached in his pocket and pulled out a stack of cash and handed it to me. I took it in some disbelief and feeling bad about myself at the same time. I was just involved in a drug dealing. I took the money and undid the rubber band and took out the few hundreds and fifties and started counting. "There's two thousand there," he said to me.

I looked up at him. "That was fast . . ." I said back quietly.

"You feel bad or something?" He seemed a little worried with one hand taken to the corner of his mouth, glancing over at me again.

"What makes you think that?" I stared at him.

"You, I don't know, seem sort of sad or something . . ." I didn't answer. I just looked away, as I felt his eyes on me again.

"What do we do now?"

Micah didn't glance at me like he always does when we talk in the car; he just kept his eyes on the road still. "We make two grand more."

"That's all you have to do ever?" *Was it really that easy for him to make money?*

"No." He laughed. "I wish."

***

I watched out the window just about the whole time, sometimes glancing over to see Micah with one hand on the wheel and the other sitting on his leg. I looked over at him again and then back out the window as houses started to pass by, and the area wasn't as junky as it was a few miles down the road we came. I got a little confused but even more confused when he pulled into a driveway and parked.

"Where are we?" I asked, looking around and then over at Micah.

Micah killed the engine and then looked over at me. "My mother's," he said normally.

I got more confused. *Why are we here?* "What? Why?"

"You don't like my mother?" he asked, sounding a little amused.

I just gave him a look. "I never said that. I'm just wondering." I was a little defensive.

"I'm just messing with you."

Micah then got out of the car, and I followed. I went up beside him as he took my hand in his. The house isn't big, but it's not small. It's clean outside, and the grass is a dark green. Micah went up to the front door and then looked around before knocking gently. After a couple of knocks, the door opened. I feel nervous even though I've met his mom before; I still get an awkward feeling. Candice was standing in the doorway, and her face lit up right when she looked up at Micah.

"Oh my god, what are you doing here?" She smiled, hugging him.

"Candice," he said as she was hugging him tightly.

"Sorry, you . . . you feel a little smaller." She smiled, looking up at him. She looked over at me then. "Kendall, hi, it's so nice to see you both again." She smiled at me and then wrapped her arms around me as I returned the hug to her.

"You too." I smiled at her.

"Oh sorry, come in." She moved out of the way.

"Mom here?"

"Yeah, she's in the kitchen." The house was neat and smelled nice. When you first walk in, there's like a platform and then a staircase; off to the right is a living room it looks like. Then there's a hallway off to the left with a few doors down the way of it. We went to the right and then took a left from the living room and then entered the kitchen. Candice walked away from us when we got up the steps, and Micah seemed to know where he was going. I mean, well he did live here for most of his life.

"Hi."

She turned around quickly like he startled her. "Oh hi, Micah, Kendall. What you two doing here?" she asked, walking over and hugging her son and giving me a few second hug as well that made me blush a little.

"Um, I was thinking that we could stay tonight?"

"Yeah, of course. Your room is still the same," she continued cooking something.

"You still have my room?"

"Of course, I do. I couldn't just get rid of all your stuff."

"Oh god." He sighed. I smiled over at him as we were both sat at the small kitchen table. I laughed a little. *What's in his room that he'd be embarrassed about?*

"I've cleaned it out, Micah." She looked over her shoulder. I tried not to laugh but failed. Micah's face was a little red when his mother said that. "You two hungry?"

Micah looked over at me, and I shook my head, crinkling my nose at him, which he found a little funny. "No."

They talked for a while, and I just listened and laughed at some things, and she asked me some questions, getting to know me better even though she and Micah have already talked about me before. After like an hour, I started to yawn. It was around nine or ten o'clock by then.

"We're gonna go to bed," he told her, standing up.

"You sleeping in your room? You sure you're both gonna fit on your bed? I can fix up the couches?"

"Yeah, Mom, we'll fit." I guess his sister was just staying here or still lives here even though she's older than Micah I only know by a few years, but he's twenty-one. Micah led me down the hallway to the left past a door that I'm guessing is Candice's bedroom and then to the other door of which he reached over and opened after kissing my neck, causing me to giggle. Micah's room was tidy. Well, probably because he hasn't stepped foot in it for like four years. But it was cute like an average teenage boy's room would look. But it's not like he had posters of half-naked women or anything, but you could just tell that it belonged to a teenage boy. The bed cover is dark blue and matching sheets with like a pale wall and one window on the side with dark curtains covering it. It made me feel special really, knowing that I'm the only girl who he's ever brought home or met his family for that matter.

He looked around his room with his hands in his pockets. His facial expression changed as he looked around the small space. "You okay?" I asked, standing behind him.

He turned around with his dimpled smile and just stared at me for a moment. He then came closer and took his arms undermine and reached back and pulled the door closed. His arms wrapped around my waist as his face went to my neck, and he started kissing it gently. He brought his face up and met my eyes. "I'm fine," he answered and then leaned down further and placed his lips against mine. When I didn't kiss back, he got confused. "Are you okay?" I looked down, away from his mossy eyes as my hands fisted his thin hoodie, adoring his torso. "What is it?" By this time, we were only hugging one another closely. "Who you are is not where you've been. Kendall, you're still innocent," he whispered. I closed my eyes tightly, holding my arms around him tightly.

It did make me feel better for what I did today, to hear his deep and yet so smooth voice say that to me. I pulled back and leaned in and kissed him back as he was slightly smiling down at me, proud that he won me over. I knew where he was going with this, as he acted more anxious. "We can't." I laughed, pushing him away a little. He came right back though and wrapped his arms back around my hips.

"We're in your mom's house," I protested, my eyes wide and hands placed firmly against his muscled chest. I laughed as he came back again and just tried once more. I giggled quietly when he set his index over my mouth, signaling for me to just be quiet. "Micah, I can't." I moved his hand away.

He sighed before just looking me right in the eye. "Okay." He smiled, kissing me one last time. "You ready to go to sleep then?" he asked, still with one of his hands on my hip. I nodded, feeling a little guilty that I know he is a little disappointed. "Well, I'll go get us another pillow."

"What, you only had one pillow?" I sort of found it weird as I looked over at his made bed with only one pillow.

He shrugged. "It was only me." He patted his hand on my hip, causing me to smile at him and hold back my laughter as he went and opened his door back up and walked down the hallway. I didn't know if I should follow him or not. Once he was gone for a few seconds I guess, I just got curious to see the entire house as I walked out of his room with my arms crossed and looked down the dark hallway and started walking quietly.

I walked past the staircase into the living room and then heard Micah in the kitchen. When I walked in though, it wasn't Micah. He turned around whenever he heard my footsteps. "Oh I, I'm sorry. I didn't . . ."

He smiled at me. His hair is dark black, and he's tall. "It's fine. You must be Kendall?"

I smiled shyly. "Y—yeah."

"I'm Calvin." He introduced. "Candice's friend," he explained.

"Well um, did Micah pass by here?"

"Yeah, he went into his mom's room I think."

I looked behind me down the opposite hallway of which I guess is his mother's bedroom. "Oh okay, thank you."

He nodded with the pop can opened in his hand as he left the kitchen through the other doorway on the other side. I feel awkward. I looked at the kitchen before stepping out and looking down the other hallway to where Micah is. I'm not going in his mother's room while they're talking. I went down the other way. I tried to picture the night that Micah beat up his sister's boyfriend. Sure it's easy to picture him beating somebody up, but I just can't picture it now. I walked back down the hallway to Micah's bedroom. I pulled out my phone to see a few texts from Emily and Savanna, and my mom called me twice. I unlocked it and texted my mom back, saying I'm with Micah and staying at his mother's with him. I sat on the edge of his bed until he came back.

When Micah walked back into his bedroom, I smiled at him. He had with him an extra pillow for us. He set the pillow down from the other side of the bed at the top and then came back over to me and set his hands down on either side of my lap, so he was at eye level. Then his door suddenly opened. Micah and I both looked to see his sister standing there.

"Oh my god, sorry, I was—just wanted to say good night," she said, quickly closing the door again. I felt the warmth rush to my cheeks even more as Micah got up and opened the door, and I guess, Candice was standing out there or something.

"Good night, Candice." I heard him say as he was peeking out the door while holding it.

With that, he closed his door and then reached over for a chair and propped it up on the doorknob. I was smiling, trying not to laugh when he turned back around. When Micah and I both lay down, his bed squeaked, and I laughed, and his cheeks went red. I took my arms around his chest. He took it as something else and rolled on top of me. "Micah, no." I laughed. He just groaned in response and laid his head on my chest like he was going to sleep. I know why he wants to now though. He never got to bring a girl home before. "Is this the first time you've been back?" I whispered to him.

He brought his head up and looked like he was thinking. "Well, inside, yes."

I gave him a confused look. "Inside?"

His dimples popped as he looked down at me. When he leaned down to kiss me again, I knew it was only as if saying good night, but I didn't stop. I felt his chest vibrate against me as he moaned into the kiss. "But you said we're in my mother's, and you don't want to . . . ?" he said, still kissing me.

"I know . . ."

I felt Micah smiling as he reached down and took his shirt over his head, setting it down by the bed along with sliding down my yoga pants and his bottoms quickly but quietly. We weren't even thinking about anything as he continued kissing me, leading to us being both bare on the small bed. His tongue came through my lips slowly and lapped over mine. I kept my eyes closed as he kissed down my neck and behind my ear, nibbling, scraping his teeth, and licking a stripe back down my neck. "Ahhh."

"Shhh. As much as I would love to hear you screaming, you have to be quiet here." He took his hand off my mouth after whispering to me. I nodded wearily, not being able to speak. He breathed through his nose heavily as he pressed into me. I struggled not to make any noises. I bit down on my lip to keep my muffled noises inside. "You good?"

"Yeah," I whispered back quietly.

He nodded back, kissing my forehead before slowly pushing himself fully inside of me. I let out a sigh and relaxed my body. He buried his head in my neck, kissing every few seconds as he continued rocking into me slowly, so the bed wouldn't squeak. It felt so much different, like I was closer to him in some way. "I love you so much." It almost sounded like he was about to cry.

"I love you."

I knew he was smiling even though I couldn't see it. "I'm gonna get us outta this mess. I promise you that."

"Mmmm."

He laughed a little. I threaded my fingers through his hair. He delivered a few quick thrusts, the bed squeaking two or three times loudly, and then he started twitching inside of me. He squeezed me as close as he could to his bare and beautiful naked body above me, filling me to my extremes. "Please don't ever leave me, baby."

I shook my head, still not finding my voice. His breathing hitched in his throat, and he groaned loudly, too loudly. I tugged at his hair, pulling at the roots before I felt him come inside of me. He bit down on the pillow and pulled at my hair some to keep from yelling out. He was buried so deep inside of me when he came that it felt strange, good, just different. It's different every time though. I came around his length a few seconds later, barely able to breathe.

***

When I woke up, Micah was lying beneath me, surprisingly not even snoring a little bit, so I just went back to sleep. The next thing was Micah was moving me off him on to the side of the bed. We both got dressed again sometime in the middle of the night. "Micah?" I asked still with my eyes closed, as I felt him get off the mattress.

"Just go back to sleep, babe." He kissed my cheek. "I love you so much," he whispered quietly.

I still kept my eyes closed as I smiled and blushed. I felt him kiss my cheek again. "Where are you going?"

"Just stay in bed, Ken," he whispered back as I heard the door open.

Yeah, like I'm going to stay here. I got up slowly and brushed my hair out of my face with my hands. I stepped out of the bed and walked out of the room with my arms crossed over my chest. I heard the front door open and close, so I walked a little faster over toward the staircase. I stepped down them carefully, trying to follow him. I opened the door and stepped outside and saw his vehicle still parked in the driveway, so I just looked around for him. "Micah?" I called out but not loudly. *What is he doing?* I heard somebody then that sounded like out back. I went around the house into the backyard. When I got back there, Micah was digging a whole with a shovel. *What's going on?* "Micah, what are you doing?" I walked closer to him.

He kept digging though and only stopped when he heard my voice. "I came back a while ago and buried some money here." He looked at me.

"What? Why? How much?" I walked over beside him as he crouched down and pulled out a box that had a dash on the corner and then his name.

"Six thousand."

"What? Why would you bury so much money?" I was being quick with my words.

He looked up at me. "Just in case," he said calmly and opened the box. It seemed to be all there. There were stacks of money in small baggies. "Okay."

"Okay what?"

"I have to give them their money." He paused. "I need you to stay here."

"What? Micah, you can't go by yourself," I whisper yelled back.

He paused, looking at the ground again like he was thinking something over. "We'll wait until tomorrow then." I nodded. Micah got up and handed me the closed box as he covered up the hole.

***

Micah's mom and Candice insisted that we should stay longer, but we had to go. Calvin apparently had left sometime in the middle of the night, and when I asked Micah about him, he doesn't know about him yet. *Why is that?*

"I take it you want to come back to my house?" Micah asked as if he already knew the answer when the light turned green.

"Yep," I said it normally as I kept facing forward.

I heard Micah sigh, and I looked over at him and raised one eyebrow as he found that a little funny.

***

When Micah pulled into his driveway, he came over and got my door for me and then got the box by my feet. Micah and I didn't really do anything that day, and I already have some clothes there from previous visits, so all I had to do was call my mom and tell her I'm at Micah's.

"You want to borrow some of my clothes?" he asked as we both went into his room to go to sleep after watching *The Wizard of Oz*.

"Yes, please," I said sweetly as I walked over to him. Micah reached behind him, pulling out a navy pair of boxers and a grey T-shirt for me and handed them over. I took them from him and started walking toward his bathroom.

"Where ya going?"

I looked back at him and held the clothes up a little. "To change."

"I don't mind if you do it in here."

"Micah."

"I just don't understand why you're so embarrassed. I mean, it's not like I haven't—"

I hurried up and cut him off. "Micah!" I sort of yelled.

"Okay, okay." He raised his hands up in surrender.

I pointed my finger at him as I turned around and went into his bathroom. After I got dressed, I walked back out, and Micah was already lying in bed. He was already covered with the blankets when I walked over closer. I walked around the bed on my side and crawled in and up against him. He sighed heavily when I put my arm across his chest. "I don't want you being embarrassed with me with your body, Ken. You're beautiful." He paused, one of his arms wrapped behind my head, his fingers playing with my hair lightly. "You have flawless skin all over. You're gorgeous in every way," he whispered, kissing the side of my head. "I love you, Kendall. Don't ever leave me," he spoke quietly, his chin lightly pressed against the top of my head as I snuggled closer into his warm body.

"I don't plan on it." I giggled. I felt him shift a little.

"What's so amusing?"

I snuggled back into his side, sliding my hand up his chest slowly. "I don't know." I started giggling again. He put his other hand on my arm stretched out on his chest and slid his fingers up and down my forearm slowly. "Just don't ever think that I'll leave you. It's silly of you really."

"You think I'm silly?" I didn't even have to look up at him to know he had that smug smile plastered across his face.

"Mmmmm." I lifted one of my legs and slid it between his, my foot going under his other leg. "I still don't want you going by yourself to deliver the money." There, I feel better, more relieved.

He rubbed his nose against my hair. "You smell good."

"Micah, seriously. Don't change the subject. I'm being serious. I don't want to have to worry about you."

"I'll be safe, Ken. You don't have to worry."

"Yes . . . I do."

"I don't see why you do," he spoke quietly.

I lifted my head from against his side and looked him straight in the eye while leaning up on my hands. "Why would you say that? Micah, I love you. I've told you over and over."

"I don't deserve you, Kendall. I don't know why you do," he whispered. "I am nothing without you . . . But you are everything without me." He wrapped his arm around my back, holding me closely to his body.

I shook my head. "They are both lies." He didn't say anything in return. He only stared at me. I laid on his chest, my legs between his. "You're everything to me." I leaned my forehead against his, closing my eyes, and speaking softly against his lips as mine brushed his softly. I gently pressed mine against his. I looked up at him through my lashes and his were closed tightly as I pressed them against his a second time, and his tongue slowly entered past my lips and into my mouth, rubbing against mine smoothly. I reached my hands up into his hair, tugging at the roots to hear him grunt. His cold hands slid up the shirt I wore and slid up my back. They slid under my bra clasp and unclipped it. I leaned up from his chest to take it off. His eyes stayed in contact with mine the entire time. I tossed it off the bed as I leaned back down against him. His hands didn't go to my chest as

I had thought they would though; instead, he cupped my face as we continued kissing slowly, his tongue still claiming my mouth.

He stopped abruptly and just held my head against his. "What's wrong?" I whispered, confused.

He shook his head. "Nothing."

MICAH

Chapter 29

I was relieved when my alarm didn't wake up Kendall who had rolled over away from me sometime after we fell asleep, taking with her half of the blankets like usual. I got out of the bed carefully, doing my best not to disturb her like last time. I slept in my clothes, just so I wouldn't make any noise getting dressed.

I picked my phone up and saw that it's just 6:50am. I looked at Kendall again as she was curled up in the blanket and heard her sighed, mumbling something incoherent. I smiled as she moved over in my spot and laid on my pillow, hugging it close to her body. I turned around and walked out of the room, grabbing my keys on the way out and the box. When I pulled out, I hoped that she didn't wake up.

I drove the half hour all the way to the warehouse in the woods. I grabbed the box and got out of the car seeing Corey's, Keegan's, Johnathan's, and Lucas's cars all parked by the trees, while I just did it in the open. I took another deep breath. I tucked the small handgun in the back of my pants and closed and locked my car up as I began to walk to the backside of the building. I walked right in to see Johnathan and Corey at a table with their backs to me.

"That's real safe," I muttered.

They both turned around quickly—Corey with a joint hanging between his chapped lips, Johnathan's hair sticking up a little. They both looked tired and somewhat wore out or maybe just a little too high for this early in the morning.

"What're you doing here?" Corey asked, taking the joint from his mouth to in between his index and middle fingers.

I held the box in my hand tightly with my other hand in my pocket. "Lucas here?"

They both just stared, and Johnathan looked over to Corey. "Yeah," Corey answered.

Corey started to walk away, but I knew to follow instantly. That's how it goes. I walked past John, giving him just a stare; he knows why. He just looked away like he was afraid of me, and I continued following behind Corey. This is going smooth so far. I took another deep breath. We walked up the steps to the top floor. When we got to the door of which I know Lucas is in, Corey held out his hand, moving his fingers, knowing that I have a gun with me. I sighed, pulling it out of the back of my pants and handed it over to him. He patted my shoulder before going back down to Johnathan. I went in the room without even knocking.

"Lucas," I said to get his attention.

He turned around from doing something. "You have my money, I assume."

I nodded as he was looking back down. I walked over and set the box down on the table. "There's an extra grand to leave me the hell alone."

He looked up with his eyebrows raised a bit and nodded once. He took the box, opening it, and started taking the uneven stacks out and counting. After he was done, he set them down back into the box. I wanted to kill him right then. He killed Oscar.

"You killed Oscar," I said in disgust, looking at him.

He paused. "That wasn't my idea entirely." He looked me in the eye.

"Then who's the fuck was it?" I sort of shouted back.

"Keegan's. We saw him and knew who he belonged to, so he said I know how to get our money back. You can ask your buddy Shaun how we knew you were stealing," he remarked. My eyes felt a little glassy as I stared at him, thinking back to Oscar running over to me each time I'd visit Kendall and now only seeing his cutoff limb being tossed into a box. "You going to cry?" He laughed. He stood up and walked over to me. He got close to my face. I would have attacked him right there, but Corey took my weapon. Even though I know I can take him with just my hands and then Corey and Johnathan, Corey has the gun, and I'm sure they all have one, including the producers in the basement. "I admit you can beat the pulp out of someone, but you're still a pathetic kid that can't control your emotions like you should," he said quietly before looking me in the eye. I clenched my jaw, getting my eyes under control.

"We done here?" I asked, holding my fists at my sides, as I saw him glance down at them. He nodded. "We're done, no more from me? I'm finished with this fucking shit." He nodded to the side.

I started to turn around and opened the door, but before I stepped out of the room, he spoke again, "Have a nice life with your whore." That was it. I clenched my jaw and already came up with a plan. Kendall is not a whore. Nobody has the right to talk about her that way. I was able to hold myself back for a moment as I ignored it and walked down the steps with the closing of the door behind me. I went back down to Johnathan, and Corey was gone.

"Here, Corey left." He handed me my gun. I looked at Johnathan. I have to do it if I want to kill Lucas. He smiled and turned back around. *But where is Keegan?* The more I thought about it, he's probably downstairs. I took it from his rough hand and then began to walk out. I stopped in my tracks and turned around suddenly. I went up behind Johnathan who was probably high on something and clubbed him in the back of the head. He fell down with a thud but not too loud. I looked down at his body. If he isn't dead, he is knocked out pretty bad with the force I used. I looked around me and saw the hatch to the basement. I can't go down there. I went back up to the top floor and entered the room again without Lucas noticing me.

I want him to look at me. I want to see him die. "Lucas." He turned around. With that, I already had the gun held up and aimed at his chest. I pulled the trigger back before he could even react. It went straight to the top center of his chest, and he lifted his hand over it as the blood started to pour down out of the wound. He slid down the wall as blood trailed down the white with his body. I didn't even take the time to grab my money as I ran back down the stairs. I regretted it when I dropped the gun to the ground on my way down after hitting into the railing. Everybody already heard the shot and would be prepared, so I ran outside and unlocked my car as fast as I could and started shaking as I put the keys in the ignition. My breathing picked up considerably fast, and I feel like I'm having a heart attack. I know what it is. I know what is happening. Calm down. Breathe. One . . . Two . . . Three . . . Four . . . Five . . . I need to get myself under control. I'm trying to remember what Candice would always do and set my palm on my chest and watched it go up and down with my breathing. I thought of Kendall's face. I'm all right. I'll live as long as I get the hell out of here right now before they come out to kill me next and bury me somewhere in the woods. As I drove, I could only picture myself going back to Kendall and holding her tight to try and get this hideous memory out of my mind.

    I just killed a man.

KENDALL

Chapter 30

The sound of a car pulling into the driveway woke me up all of the sudden. Then I remembered where I am. I got up quickly, stepping out of the bed as the front door was opening. It was cold in his house for some odd reason. It's never cold when I'm here. I heard footsteps going down the hallway. I grabbed Micah's jacket from the foot of the bed and slid it on. I stepped out of the room and went into the hallway of which the lights were all off. *Where'd he go?* I walked straight into the living room to seeing the TV's light being on. I stepped in and instantly saw his messy blond hair. I grinned, walking over to him.

He has his head bawled and his arms lying on his legs, hands connecting. "Micah?" I asked, getting in front of him. He jumped and looked really relieved when he looked up and saw me. I didn't feel the need to ask him where he was. I already know he must have got up early and gave the money away. "Everything go okay?" I asked, getting down to his level.

He looked like he was thinking about something. "Everything went perfect." He stood up, hugging me quickly, holding me tightly in his arms.

I was happy. It's finally all over with. He's clean so far that I know of. "So what happened?" I asked, letting go of him to look at his face.

"Everything that needed to," he said softly as he looked down at my face.

I was confused. *Really?* Somehow that just seemed too unreal to me. *How could everything just go okay?* I smiled, looking back up at him. As I observed his features, I could tell he wasn't telling me everything that happened. I know for sure everything didn't go "perfect" like he says it did. It just couldn't have. I mean, come on, honestly.

***

For two weeks, everything seemed to be back to normal. I put up some posters of Oscar just in case someone may see him around. It's strange that he ran away like that. Then again, I guess I understand because we always keep him at home, and he probably just got caught up in all of the new smells. Micah though seemed to be happy like he didn't care about anything as much as before, although he never really cared at all. Shailene and I went shopping one day, and we dragged him along with us. It was funny all day long. He tried getting me to try on this dress. Well, I did end up grabbing it and walking to the dressing room. When we got there though, he refused to sit in the waiting area for me to get it on and show him. Now, these are his words, "No, I'm not letting some creep get off to seeing you in this. I'm coming in with you." Instantly, I said he couldn't, and that's when he pushed us both into the stall and locked the door. I was really uncomfortable in that lighting, while he watched me undress in front of him. Once he noticed I was nervous, he stood from the chair in there and undressed me himself. I know I've put weight on, I can just feel it. When he kissed my shoulder and zipped the back of the dress up, I laughed, and he twirled me once. I can still tell that he's hiding something from me, but I don't want to bring anything up.

As the week went by, I felt different. When Micah dropped me off at my house after we dropped Shailene off, I gave him a kiss and said good night. I looked back at him as I unlocked my door to my mom already left for work a little bit ago. There was still no sign of my Oscar either. Micah always tried to avoid the topic of him. For some weird reason, he didn't want me talking about him. I think it's just because he doesn't want me to be stressed out like he thinks he'll come back on his own when he's ready to come back home. I went up to my room all alone without my furry friend and got changed. Thinking back to the time when I barely didn't even know Micah and laughed to the memory when he texted me, I should shut my curtains before stripping off. I peeked out the curtain to see him gone though. I went into the bathroom to clean my face and brush my teeth.

After I brushed my teeth and looked at them in the mirror, I stepped over to my cabinet on the other side of the bathroom to grab my face wash. When I opened it, my face dropped. The small box instantly catching my attention. The pink and black color to it making me forget everything else. I just stared and swallowed the lump in my throat. *How long has it been?*

The box wasn't opened yet and made me worry more. It took away the thought of maybe I just forgot about it the last time. No. No. No. This isn't happening. It just can't be. *How could I?* No. I don't want this. Micah won't want this. I know he won't. I thought back to the last time we ever did anything so interment. His mother's house. I bit my lip in between my teeth roughly as I thought back to it. *Did he?* I can't remember. "Oh god . . ." I whispered. I sat back against the sink counter. I looked away as my eyes filled up. He didn't. I felt nauseous just thinking about it. Tomorrow is my birthday, and now it's ruined because I'm going to have all of this on my mind the entire time.

I feel so sick now just thinking about it. I went and sat on my bed with my legs curled up by me. I wrapped my arms around them, holding them close as I put my face in between my knees. I started crying. I feel so scared and alone right now. I calmed myself down a little and lifted my face and wiped my eyes. "It's just one week, just one," I told myself as I wiped my eyes drier. "Okay." I calmed myself. I looked over at my phone, thinking about Micah. He's the only guy I have ever been with. This is his fault.

My attention was brought back to my phone when it lit up and vibrated twice quickly. I hesitated before I reached over and picked it up from the nightstand. Micah's name was there.

> From Micah:
> Night Kendall. Xx

I stared at the screen for a few moments before I got up to responding.

> To Micah:
> I'm not going to sleep yet.

It took him a few minutes for him to text back.

> From Micah:
> Oh thought you'd be in bed by now?

> To Micah:
> I'm not that tired. So what are you doing?

From Micah:
With Josh having some drinks. You okay? You can put that dress on and I'll pick you up

No, no, I am not okay. No, I'm never putting a minidress on again. I'm fucking late all because you were careless! The embarrassing and uncomfortable conversation I had to have with my mother after the first time we had sex and she came home seems like it was for nothing now. Then again, I did nothing to prevent this either. *How could this happen to us? How could he ever want children?* I don't want to ruin his night.

To Micah:
Yeah, I'll be fine. I'm just bored I guess.

The next thing I knew, my phone started vibrating, telling me someone is calling. When I picked it back up, Micah's name was there. *Why's he calling?* I don't want to talk to him. I can't just ignore him though. I answered it.

"Hey, babe."

I could hear music fading in the background. At least he didn't lie to me.

"Hi." I mentally killed myself for letting my voice let him know I was crying.

"So what's wrong? You sick or something?" He was worried.

I shook my head, containing my tears and the words that I'm late. "No, I—I'm okay."

"Kendall, I'm not stupid," he said, knowing I was lying to him. I laughed a little at him but didn't say anything back to him. *What do I say?* "You want me to come over?" I still didn't answer. I do, but I don't. "I can be over in twenty minutes, Kendall?" he asked again.

"No, Micah. Just stay with Josh. I'm okay. Just believe me, okay."

He didn't say anything for a few minutes it seemed like. "Just call me if you want to talk again."

"Okay." I nodded at the same time.

"I don't know . . . You sure you're okay?"

I laughed lightly into the cell phone. "Micah."

"Why don't you invite somebody over if you're alone?"

"Look, Micah, don't worry about me. Go back to Josh."

"I don't want to now."

"Micah." I laughed again. Now look what I did to him.

"I'm coming over there."

"No, Micah, don't."

"Let me just tell Josh, and I'll be right there."

"No, Micah. Micah." I heard him walking back into the bar as the music was sort of loud. "Micah, listen to me!" I shouted into the phone this time.

"What?" he asked, laughing at me.

"Stay with Josh."

"I wanna be with you now though."

"We can hang out tomorrow, Micah." I smiled. He just groaned into the phone. I could tell he was taking a drink as I heard it slam down as if he was asking for another. I could hear Josh's voice, but I can't tell what he's saying. It made me mad. What an asshole. He's out partying pretty much while I'm sitting here, worrying about if I'm pregnant or not with his child. "I'm gonna lie down now, so night."

"Wait no!"

"We're not even talking."

"What do you want to talk about?"

"Micah, I'm going to bed now. Night."

"Okay." He pouted. "Night, love you." I heard Josh and a few other voices coo at him loudly and make other remarks. *Who all's he with?*

I blushed a little from his words. It took me a moment to be able to say them back. "Love you." I hung up right after, which probably made him confused with me. I don't care though. I threw my phone to the other side of my room and looked over to the picture of Micah and me on my nightstand. I lifted myself and grabbed the frame and threw it down on to the floor. I lied down crying until falling asleep. *What if that's the last time he ever says those words to me?* The thought kills me. He doesn't want a child.

I walked down the steps and into my kitchen. When I turned the corner, my mom, Emily, and Savanna were standing there.

"Happy birthday!" Savanna yelled when she saw me. I smiled, looking back at her.

"Happy birthday," Emily said after.

"Good morning, sweetie. Happy birthday." My mother cheered. I went over and sat at the table with my friends. "What do you girls want to do today?"

I looked down at the table only thinking about last night. I looked up to see them all staring at me for an answer. "Oh I—I don't care. Just whatever."

Emily sighed loudly, and Savanna rolled her eyes. "Oh, come on, Kendall!" Savanna yelled at me.

"Yeah, we never see you anymore. We have to do something."

"I just don't know what to do."

"She just wants to go over to Micah's is what it is." Savanna smiled. I got embarrassed with my mom standing right there in the kitchen.

"I'm going back upstairs," I said, standing up and going to the staircase.

"You do that." My mother laughed as I heard my friend's footsteps following me.

When I got in my room, I just fell on to my bed as Savanna sat on the edge of it, and Emily went and sat in my chair. "So what's going on?" Savanna asked honestly. I sat back up and looked at both of them. I wiped my eyes.

"What happened?"

"I have . . . something really serious t—to tell you, guys. Only you two. That's it. You can't say anything," I started off. I have to tell them. They can help me somehow with getting rid of it before Micah finds out.

They both stared at me with their mouths slightly opened and their eyes wide and fixated on me. "What is it?" Emily asked seriously.

I bit my lip and looked down nervously. I can't. No. *What if they say something? What if my mom hears us?* No. I have to. I moved my hair back and looked down at my blanket as I held in my hand tightly. "I . . . I might be, uh, well . . ." I paused. "I might be pregnant," I said softly. After a few seconds, I looked up to see their faces.

"Are you serious?" Savanna asked.

I just nodded, looking down as my eyes started watering up and spilled over. "What? Since . . . since when?" Emily asked quickly.

"Like a week I think." I cried silently as I spoke.

"Have you said anything to him?"

I shook my head. "I can't."

"Why not? You told us he says he loves you so . . ."

I shook my head. "Why would he want a baby?"

They were both silent. "Well, are . . . are you going to keep it?"

"Savanna, she doesn't even know yet."

I looked back and forth to them as they spoke. "I don't know what I'm going to do . . ."

"Okay, okay." Emily came over on the bed with us and calmed me a little. "You don't know yet. But if you are, you have to say something to him. You can't just get rid of it without at least mentioning it to him."

"How do I bring that up?"

"Well, are you sure he's the father?" Savanna asked. Emily gave her an "Are you serious?" kind of look, while I sort of laughed and threw a small pillow at her.

I looked over at Emily as she was thinking as well as Savanna.

"I don't know. Just say something like . . ." Emily started.

"Oh! I know!" Savanna yelled. I shushed her quickly. She smiled. "Sorry, but why don't you guys just go for a walk, and then if you see like someone with a baby, just be like all 'awe' or something and then see what he says about it." She suggested.

I thought about the idea for a while. "How could you get a test, ya know? I'm sorry, but I can't buy one for you," Emily said honestly.

"I understand." I glanced at her.

"This just seems so crazy . . ." Savanna said softly as she stared down at my bed.

"You can go to the doctor to make sure you are or aren't," Savanna added quickly.

"I can't. My mom's a nurse. I don't go to the doctor because I always just had her."

"This isn't good . . ." Savanna looked at me.

"Wow that helped me a lot."

"So uh . . . How was your anniversary?" Emily asked sort of shyly.

I'm definitely not telling her anything about his drug use or trying to rape me and getting drunk all at the same time, and I had to call his best friend to come pick me up and take me home. I shrugged. "We only went to dinner, and I came home."

They were both confused. "Then when . . . when do you think this happened?" she continued to ask.

I looked away from them. "Like two weeks ago, and I'm like two weeks late."

Savanna moved her mouth awkwardly and looked away from me.

Then my phone started vibrating. Savanna saw it across the room before me, as she got up and ran to it. I didn't even move from my spot. I don't care right now.

"Hello, hello," she said happily into the phone.

"Who is it?" I whispered.

She just smiled. "This is Savanna, her friend." She stood there, listening to whoever is on the other line. "So you're wanting to talk to her?" She joked.

"Savanna." I whispered. I mouthed who it is again.

"Why don't you just come over here and talk to her in person. I mean, because it is her birthday and all." Emily and I both looked at each other like oh god. She hung up the phone and then walked back over to us. "By the way, Micah is on his way over." She winked.

My eyes instantly widened. "What the hell? No!" I panicked. "I can't talk to him with this on my mind!" I sort of shouted.

"Since when do you curse? He must be rubbing off on you. You two need to talk though, seriously. This is serious."

I sighed, falling back on my bed. My mom then came up, opening my door without knocking. "Everything okay?" My friends nodded. "Well, there is stuff downstairs and some money for you if you decide to go somewhere, but I really need to work tonight, so I have to go. Love you and happy birthday again, honey."

"Love you," I muttered quietly. With that, she left. "This is such a great birthday," I said sarcastically.

I saw Emily shrug, sitting beside me against the wall. "I think it's interesting."

I couldn't help but laugh. But laughs soon turned into me sobbing a little bit. "Hey, hey. You can't start crying now. He's coming over, Kendall." Emily picked me up. "Did he say how long?" she asked Savanna.

"He said he would be like twenty minutes or so," she answered normally.

"Should you fix yourself up?" Emily asked.

I just groaned loudly. "I don't care right now."

I saw Emily looking at her phone. "I'm so sorry, Kendall. I have to go though. Happy birthday." She hugged me. Then she went downstairs.

Savanna and I eventually went downstairs. We went from talking about Oscar running off to what she's been doing, but it always made me go back to the possibility of a little person growing inside of me. It's scary to think about. I don't want to go through that kind of pain. I have considered having children, but I'm nineteen. My life should just start beginning not coming to a closing of one. I bawled my head in my crossed arms on the counter while we were eating, just thinking about the possibility of having a child in nine months. I can't do this.

The knock at the door got Savanna's and mine's attention right away. I looked over at her and gave her a sad face. I don't want to talk to Micah in person. I can only picture him yelling at me if I say something about me maybe being pregnant. *What if he denies himself being the father? Or if he tells me it's over? Maybe he doesn't want to be a dad? Why would he?* I walked slowly over to the door as he knocked two more times.

When I unlocked and opened it, he immediately lifted me into a hug, making me feel sick all the sudden. "Hi, beautiful." He kissed me before setting me back on my feet. Micah came with me into the kitchen. I started feeling nauseous, but I swallowed it all down quickly.

"I don't know if you two met or not, but this is Savanna." I introduced, sounding a little nervous probably. But I'm not nervous. I might be pregnant. It's not nerves; it's fear.

"Spoke on the phone earlier." Micah laughed as he sat on one of the barstools. I saw Savanna smile and laugh a little before she looked at Micah like in a sincere look and then at my stomach as I gave her a mean look like don't you dare. For some odd reason, she found it a little funny. I stood beside Savanna, just about hip to hip with her because I feel so scared right now. Then Micah leaned up and handed me a long wrapped pink box. "Happy birthday, princess." I took it from him, smiling and blushing.

I knew Savanna was watching closely as I took it and started unwrapping the box. When I finally opened it, I found that he bought me a bracelet. It's so pretty actually. My eyes widened. The whole way around is diamonds, not big but still. They all looked like they were woven together so perfectly. I looked over at Micah. "You got me a diamond bracelet," I said, sounding funny in amazement.

He smirked at me, facing me directly while he sat in the barstool. He leaned over and clamped it on to my wrist securely. "It's so pretty," Savanna commented.

"It's gorgeous. Thank you so much." I leaned closer to him, giving him a light kiss on his warm and calming lips.

"Well, I don't want to impose. I'll leave you two." Savanna smiled, bumping my hip.

"Oh no, you don't have to leave," Micah told her even though I think it sort of made him a little happier if we were to be alone.

"I should go anyway. Bye, Kendall, Micah," she said her good-byes, but I ran to the door after her. I stopped her when she was walking down the sidewalk. I grabbed her into a tight hug as she hugged me back. I cried a little on her shoulder as she rubbed one of her hands on my back. "It'll work out somehow, Kendall," she said softly as I loosened my grip and finally let go. I wiped my eyes and watched her as she got in her car and left before I went back inside.

"Everything's okay?" Micah asked as I came back inside and sat beside him.

"Yeah, I'm just really tired for some reason." I yawned at the end.

"You want to go to your room? Or you can come over and stay with me." He looked over at me and winked.

"I want to be home tonight."

"Kendall, don't be scared to tell me things. That's fine." He set his arm around me. "You want me to stay with you?" I smelled something on him then. I don't want him to leave though. I know the smell of marijuana; that's what it is on him. I don't want to say anything to him though. Now that I smell it and really pay attention to his eyes, I can tell he's a little high. I thought he was done with it completely now . . .

MICAH

Chapter 31

Kendall and I went up to her room. She seems like she's a little on edge. I don't understand why. I just brushed it off. I kept thinking that there was something on my shoulder, as I kept on flinching from it. I set my water bottle on her nightstand; my mouth is really dry this time. That usually never happens. Usually, I just get headaches or maybe feel a little nauseous. I feel a little dizzy as well. Kendall changed from yoga pants into a pair of loose jogging pants for some reason and then put on a bigger T-shirt.

"Where you that uncomfortable?" I laughed at her.

She just shrugged a little as she came over to her bed of which I sat on, waiting for her to join me as the TV was silent but still on with some TV show that I don't know. "I'll be right back." She got right back up, going into her bathroom and coming out a short minute later. I have a pair of jogging shorts and a soft navy T-shirt on, so I'm good to just sleep in this. *Did she smell it on me? Is that why she is acting like this?* I don't really think she did. I sprayed myself a lot before I came over.

I started buying from this guy Logan like a week ago. I couldn't stand not being high anymore. I needed it so badly. I know how transfers and stuff go and how you act when you are waiting for someone, so I knew right away he was a dealer, but I've never seen him before that day. I haven't done anything else though besides pot since I sold it all. I used that thousand dollars and some of my pay from the gym to buy her a bracelet. Well, Shailene picked it out for me, while I just followed her around.

I laid back with Kendall as she fisted my shirt in her small, cold hands, burying her face in my chest at the same time as she kept her body curled up. I pulled up her quilt over top of us and then her extra purple blanket over top of her small frame as she seems just so cold. "Can I have the other side actually?" she asked, lifting her head.

"You want on the edge?" She always just sleeps on the side with the wall like she was scared she would fall off. She just stared up at me.

"It's fine. I'm okay here anyway." She sounded sad as she buried her face back into my chest.

I got up and got on top of her, straddling her whole body under me as she just stared up at me. I leaned down and kissed her cheek. "Good night, babe." I laid on the other side by the wall this time. She kept turned toward the other way, leaving me with only the sight of the back of her head. I took one of my arms around her and placed it on her stomach as she tensed up with the movement for some reason. "You okay?" I asked, as she seemed to be breathing quickly as my hand stayed there. She seems like she's so nervous to be around me tonight. She took a minute before connecting one of her hands with mine on her fit stomach. She let out a deep breath as I stitched our fingers together over her quickly rising and falling tummy.

***

I kept hearing an awkward noise. It kept me awake for a few minutes now. When I flipped over on the bed, I reached over to wrap my arm around Kendall's body, but she wasn't there. I was confused. *Where is she?* I opened my eyes. I sat up in her bed with the blanket on my lap. I looked around until I saw the bathroom light on, and the door is closed. It sounds like she's throwing up. I reached under my pillow and grabbed my phone—8:20 a.m. I threw the blankets off and set my phone back down.

I got off the bed quietly and walked over to the door. I knocked on it with my knuckles. "Kendall, you okay, babe?" I asked, still half asleep. I yawned again. "Kendall?" I heard her crying. I turned the knob, and it's unlocked. The light felt like it was blinding me.

When my eyes finally adjusted, I saw her curled up beside the toilet, just crying. I rushed over to her. "No, don't come in here," she cried at me.

"Kendall," I said as I lifted her a little.

"No." She just kept crying.

"What's wrong?" I asked, holding her.

She pushed me away as she bent over the toilet again and vomited. She stayed there. "Get out of here," she cried again.

"I'm not leaving you," I said as I began to rub my hand around her back. She fell back on her bum on to the tile flooring as she kept her hands covering her eyes as she cried. I feel so bad for her. Whenever I got sick, I didn't have anybody. Sure before I ran away, I had my sister always beside me because my mom was constantly working just like Kendall's. I pulled her against me. "You feel okay now?" I asked her. I felt her nod against my chest as I stood up with her in my arms. I walked her out of the bathroom after she flushed the toilet. I kissed the top of her head as she wrapped her legs around me, and I carried her like a child back to the bed. I laid her down as she wouldn't stop crying. "What all is wrong?" She just turned the other way, so her back was to me. I didn't understand. *What's wrong with her? Is she that embarrassed?* I just stared down at her. "Kendall?" I asked as she then scooted over to the wall for me to have room to get in.

I got on the bed with her but propped the pillow up, so I could sit against the wall comfortably as I pulled her closer to me, and she instantly put her arms across my chest and rested her head on my stomach. Eventually, she just cried herself to sleep as I kept my arms around her.

KENDALL

Chapter 32

When I finally woke up, I still feel somewhat nauseous. I sighed. I already had tears coming from my eyes, and they hurt from crying so much earlier this morning. I fisted whatever was close to my hands until I felt something hard under the fabric. I froze. I felt a hand rub my back lightly. "You up babe?" he whispered. His voice sounds so tired and worried at the same time. I fisted his shirt tightly as I held my head against him. I made like an awkward crying noise as I curled up closer to his warm body.

"Sorry, I woke you up so early," I said back softly, still sounding like I'm crying.

I heard him lightly laugh. "It's fine. I have to go to work though in a little bit."

"What time is it?"

"It's ten now. I already told Josh I'd be a little late because you weren't feeling well." I couldn't help the tears that ran down my cheeks when he reminded me of how I woke up so early and vomited a few times. I cried so bad and long after that. It scared me so bad. I don't want to be pregnant yet. I don't feel ready for that kind of pain. I don't think that Micah is either. *Will he leave me?* "Are you feeling any better?"

I took another deep breath to try and get my normal voice back. "Yes." I still sounded pathetic.

"I can stay if you feel too sick?" he asked as I sat up and looked up at him.

"No, I don't feel that bad. Can I go to your house though?" I planned on saying it to him later after he got off work.

He paused like he was actually thinking over letting me got to his house. "That's fine. It's just a mess." When he said that, I couldn't help but have the feeling again to cry, thinking of the last time when he said his room was a mess. He looked at me as I felt a tear run down the side of my cheek, but I quickly wiped it away. "Something else wrong?" I was about to just spill it all out and say that I think I'm pregnant, but I held myself back.

"Yeah, I just . . ." He stared at me for an honest answer, but I don't know what to say to him anymore. *How do I bring up a conversation about pregnancy to him?* I thought over about what Savanna said about taking a walk to see a baby and talk about it somehow, but I just don't think that I can do that. I'm too afraid to go through with it now. The more that I think about it, the more nervous I get. "I'm okay," I said calmly this time.

He grinned and leaned over, pulling me halfway, so he could kiss the top of my head for a long second. I knew he was avoiding anywhere near my mouth, and it made me so embarrassed.

Micah got up and picked his phone with him. I got up a minute later and went and got a quick shower and got dressed and everything, while Micah went downstairs to eat. After I was done getting dressed and just straightening my hair, I looked back in the mirror. I don't look so good. I look so tired and just not myself. I put on some light makeup to look a little better then joined Micah downstairs, and we left. Every time I go somewhere, I always feel the need to stare out of the window just in case Oscar would be passing by.

I was so nervous to say anything to him the whole way to his house. "You just want to wait at my house until I get back?" I looked over at him after he said it.

"That's fine." I looked over at him and then back out of the window.

"I know you're lying to me, Kendall." He sort of laughed as we both looked at each other. *Does he know why though?*

I just shrugged. "I don't want you worrying at work about me," I said quietly.

"Well, it's too late." He kept his eyes on the road as he pulled into his driveway.

"Just go to work," I said as he was getting dressed, and I was just sitting on the other side of the bed from where he was getting dressed.

"You're not still sick anymore, right?" I nodded. "Okay. I'll text you on my way home. I love you."

I smiled as I felt my eyes fill up a little, but I didn't let myself cry now. "I love you," I said back softly as I stared at his green eyes as they stared back at my face. Micah leaned in and kissed me. His warm lips against mine calmed me a little. It made me feel more comfortable with the situation and relaxed a little better.

"There's some food and stuff," he said, walking out of the bedroom. I heard the front door open and close as I looked around being alone now.

I have to get a test done to be sure about this before I say anything to him. I'm too nervous to say just a maybe. I grabbed my phone from my pocket as I made my way into the living room to watch some TV or find a movie. Emily had texted me, seeing how I was doing, and I told her I'm okay, just waiting for Micah to get back from work to say anything.

How am I going to find out though? Then the name hit me. I don't want to ask his family to help me or Josh for that matter. Shailene. I scrolled through my phone and clicked on her name. She answered almost immediately.

"Hey, Kendall." She sounded okay with me calling her this early.

"Hi, Shailene," I greeted back, sounding a little sad that made me bite my lip.

"Everything all right? What's going on?"

"I need to ask you a serious favor . . ." I started out.

There was sort of a pause. "What sort?" She sounded like she was listening closely now with her full attention. It helped a little more.

"I don't know who else to ask and my friends can't do it, so you're the only one I think—" She cut me off.

"Look, Kendall, what is it?"

I took a deep breath as she spoke. "I need you to buy me a pregnancy test," I said quickly.

There was a longer pause. "What? Are you serious? Oh my god." She sounded excited. I didn't answer her, as I cried a little. "Okay, okay. Have you said anything to him?" She calmed herself down.

"No," I said, holding my head in my hand as I slouched over on the couch, still crying but not bad.

"Don't cry. I can do it for you."

"Really?" I didn't actually believe it.

"Yeah, of course. Anything for you two."

"Thank you so much," I cried happily now.

"Yeah, where are you?"

"I'm at his house, while he's at work."

"Okay. I'll be over there in a little bit."

"Thanks again."

"You're welcome." She sort of laughed. "I'll see you in little, just relax."

"Okay."

"Okay, bye."

Like twenty or twenty-five minutes passed before I finally heard a car pulled in. I got up and just hoped it wasn't him coming back early. Then the light knocks on the door let me know it was her. I practically ran to the door, opening it. She smiled at me and was taken off guard as I pulled her into a hug.

"Okay." She sounded amused. I let go as she came inside, closing the door behind her and turning the lock. I looked up to her face. She's a little taller than me, well, everybody practically is. We went into Micah's bedroom by the bathroom as she dumped the bag out on to his bed. "So I didn't really know which kind to get, so I bought like one of each." She smiled.

I just looked up at her as I looked at all of the boxes she bought for me. "I can pay you back." I looked up at her as she sat on the bed.

She just shook her head. "Oh no, of course, you don't, Kendall. It's fine. I don't mind." I just smiled at her nervously as I looked back down at the purple, blue, and pink boxes. "So how long has it been?" she asked.

I looked back up at her. "Two weeks." She nodded in understanding. "I've thrown up in the mornings too." Her eyes widened with the information.

"Okay. Well, let's just be sure about this," she said. I picked one of the cardboard boxes and took a deep breath. "Do you want it?" she asked softly as she was staring at me. I just shrugged without even looking back at her.

"Okay," I said, taking the box with me into the bathroom. I did what the instructions said and then set it on to the sink counter and opened the door back up to see Shailene looking around his room, checking everything out. She turned around and looked at me.

"You set a timer?" she asked. I held up my phone with the right amount of time it said to wait. I sat on the bed.

"Can I ask you something?" I looked up at her nervously as she came and sat on the bed with me.

"Sure."

She's just so pretty and nice I don't understand how she and Micah only stayed just friends. "How did you and Micah meet?"

She smiled and looked down; she knew what I meant. "It wasn't like that." She laughed awkwardly. "We were neighbors. I met him when he was eighteen," she said, smiling. "But to be honest with you . . . we have . . . hooked up a couple of times only. And that was only once when he was nineteen and another when he was twenty. It was never anything serious."

Then before I could speak, my timer went off. I bit my lip harshly as I got up and went and looked at it. I closed my eyes before I picked it back up in my shaky hands and then opened them. A small pink plus sign. I just stared at it. "You should try them all just in case!" Shailene shouted from the bedroom. I got relieved as I went back into the bedroom with the test. "What is it?" she asked as I had the small stick in between my fingers, staring down at it as I walked closer to her. I looked up at her. She knew that it was positive by just the look on my face. "You need to try them all, then we can see the difference with all of them. Here," she said, handing me the next one. "Just whenever you're ready to go again." She smiled as she looked away from me.

Two hours passed, and I had finished up with all of the tests, after forcing myself to urinate on to each and every single one. There on Micah's sink counter lie seven positive and two negative tests. The odds were against me. I have to face it now completely. I'm pregnant on accident with Micah's child. I threw away each box into his bathroom garbage can, so if I wimp out on telling him, he can just go in the bathroom to figure it out. I left the bathroom and joined Shailene in the living room where she was watching the TV. She heard me come in and looked up at me as I then sat beside her.

"He doesn't want a baby in his life," I said sadly, looking down at my hands as I tangled them together on my lap.

"What?" she asked, sounding really confused. "How do you know that?"

I shook my head, avoiding eye contact. "You really think someone like him would want a baby?" I stated.

"Kendall, I can't believe he's never said anything to you," she started talking again. I looked over at her, confused.

"What do you mean?" I asked, wiping my eyes as I sat back.

"He's talked about having a family before. He wants children."

I sort of do believe it actually as hard as that may seem or even insane. But he can't be a father yet. "Not in his condition," I said back strongly.

"What condition?"

"He's an addict!" I sort of shouted as I looked over at her.

"What?" she whispered.

"You've had to of known something from knowing him this long."

"I know he does stuff, but I wouldn't think of him as an addict," she defended. She's defending him . . .

"I've seen enough to know he is," I said back softly, not wanting to argue with her over this.

"Well, I'm sorry about that. But he's a good guy though. He wants a family."

"He's said that?" I looked over at her as I was silently crying.

"He's always wanted a kid." I smiled in relief. "But do you?"

I haven't even really thought about what I want, only what he would want. I don't want to lose him. That's really the only thing I've been worrying about if I am surely 100 percent pregnant with his child.

"I'm just scared," I admitted quietly.

"I'm sure everybody gets scared with this, but if it's what you two want, then congratulations."

I smiled and laughed a little at her as she smiled. "Thank you." I smiled. "I'll text you what he says," I said as she got up to leave.

"Okay, well good luck, Kendall. Sorry, but he'll be back soon. I think I should go."

I nodded. I got up and hugged her tightly in my arms. "Thank you so much," I said before letting go of her. I walked with Shailene to the door and watched as she pulled out and left. My phone started buzzing as I sat back down on the couch. I picked it up.

From Micah:
Hey I'm on my way home now see you in a little bit

I smiled as I read his words. I'm excited now to tell him. Like fifteen minutes passed before I heard the door open and close. I got up and met him halfway in the hallway. I smiled running up to him as he looked really baffled to the way I'm acting. I'm so happy. I can give him something that he's always wanted, a family of his own. I held him in my arms tightly as he lifted me a little in his arms. I smiled with my eyes closed as I buried my face in the crook of his neck and shoulder. I squeezed him tighter in my arms.

"Can I know what's going on now?" I nodded into his neck. "I take it that it's good news?" I nodded again as I kissed his neck a few times and then his cheek, then one light kiss to his warm lips. He raised his eyebrows to me as he sat me down. "And first of all, you're feeling a lot better?" He laughed. I nodded again. "So what is it?"

I held his hands in mine as I looked down nervously. As I opened my mouth to speak the words, I was interrupted with the sound of sirens getting closer and closer. Micah got confused as he turned. They were as close as there was a loud banging at the front door.

"Open up!" A man shouted.

"Micah?" I asked as he looked down at me in confusion. He shook his head. I started shaking, and my voice was trembling. I held his hand tightly in mine as he turned around to go to the door. He opened the door, and then my heart sank. There were four cop cars parked outside with the lights still on. There were officers with guns pointed at the house. "Micah, what's going on?" I asked frantically as I gripped his shirt tightly in my hands, trying to hold him closer to me.

"Put your hands up now!" The cop yelled, pointing a gun right at Micah.

"What's going on?" he asked, staying as calm as he could.

"I said put your hands up now!" he shouted again. Micah put his arms in the air as commanded and was now facing me. "Turn around!" I held on to Micah still, fisting the front of his shirt as he stared down at me wide-eyed. The man gripped his arms and yanked them down and hand cuffed his wrists together.

The officer then pulled him away from me. "No!" I shouted as he yanked him down the stairs. "Micah!" I tried running after them.

Micah didn't fight the men that held him away from me. He didn't break his eye contact with me as he was tossed into the backseat of one of the police cruisers. He just stared at me. This seems unreal to me, like it's just a dream. It's not a dream though I wish it was, a nightmare really. Micah is being arrested right now in his own yard. He is being taken away from me. With that, the cops left. I was left alone and scared on his front porch as he was driven away in the back of a cop car.

I grabbed his keys and went quickly to his car, starting it up and backing up from the driveway, then I went to the jailhouse. When I got there, I quickly parked and went inside after turning and locking the car and taking the keys with me.

I rushed inside and went to his front desk. "Uh . . . Micah Harlan was just arrested. I want to know when I can see him," I said sort of nervously.

The dark-haired woman looked up at me. "You said Harlan?" I turned to see one of the cops from the house standing there, coming up to me from the hallway.

I nodded. "Yes."

"Well, not just yet. He's in questioning right now. Just wait here until he's done, or you can leave and come back tomorrow." His voice deep, his hair dark.

"I want to see him today." I looked him in the eye as I turned and went and sat on one of the hard-cushioned seats against the wall. He looked at me, and I looked at him. "I'll tell you when you can see him."

I nodded. "Thank you."

MICAH

Chapter 33

I sat handcuffed to the chair and desk as one of the men sat in front of me. "Can you tell me now why I'm here?" I demanded really.

"There was a report of a gunshot by a man walking his dog in the woods the other week," he started seriously. "You've been arrested for many counts, Mr. Harlan." The one said in the corner.

They both exchanged glances before putting their attention back on to my face. "We know everything about you now. What you do every day, where you work, who you're with, everything."

"I work at a gym, I go to work and talk to my family and girlfriend, and I'm always with her," I said, a little confused.

The one sitting in front of me across the table smiled and laughed a little, looking down. "Not that life," he said, still finding it funny. "What about buying and selling any kind of drugs, working with drug dealers, and being with Keegan Thomas and Lucas Franc?" I just looked from him to the other cop. I shook my head, not wanting to believe what's going on. "Sound familiar?"

"You have any proof?" I said, looking back up.

He nodded to the side. "We have your friends Keegan, Corey, Jared, Anthony, Johnathan, Walter, and Brain. I can go on. Oh, and Lucas's body in the morgue. We know you shot and killed him. We have witnesses for everything, photos, and videos. You're going away, Micah. We have everything we need to put you in jail for a long, long time."

I looked at them in disbelief. "Excuse me?" I said, not believing them although I do.

He smiled again. "We have men at you're house right now, searching for some more evidence."

I buried my face in my hands, sighing heavily. "You understand us?" The one walked over. "We have more counts that they've all said you've done."

"Wait, what? What the hell did they say?" I shouted at them. *Did they really tell a bunch of lies about me just to have me locked up longer? Where is Kendall? How is she?* They just looked at each other. "I didn't do anything!" I shouted. "They're all lying to you!" I was freaking out now. I calmed myself down somehow and set my wrists back on the table. "Okay." I calmed down. I opened my eyes and lifted my head back to see the two men with the arms crossed.

"What do you say?" One asked.

"Okay, well, I got with them when I was younger and I got out of it this year but I owed them some money, so I went there and paid him."

"Who's him?"

"Lucas. Anyway, we argued, and then I shot him and just left. That's it." I have to lie. I have to lie. "Look, he was going to kill me. I had to kill him." *Would he of really came and killed me after I paid him?* "I just wanted out of the whole mess. That's it. I just wanted it to be over."

"I do believe you there because Johnathan was saying if you didn't kill him, then he was going to." I stared at him wide-eyed. *Really? He would kill someone?* "You're other friends Shaun and Kevin are serving seven years added together just for their possession and a murder. Shaun killed a woman. You knew that probably already, yeah?"

I shook my head. Liar. "They're not my friends."

"No?"

"No."

"These photos say otherwise." He opened a folder of which had pictures of Shaun and I from like two years ago that I recognized right away.

"That's from a few years ago. We stopped being friends."

"But you still talked?"

I looked away and then shrugged. "Sometimes." My voice was small and weak.

"And what did you talk about?"

I stared at him and then glanced over at the other man. "I—I don't remember everything."

He grinned. "So what do you remember?" I just put my head in my hands again. "You sold drugs together, marijuana, cocaine, heroin, secondly. There's more. What other kinds can you think of?"

I looked back up at him. It's all true. All of it. My jaw tensed just hearing the word cocaine. I kept my elbows on the table and looked at him seriously. "I want a lawyer." The man smiled and looked over at the other man and then back to me.

I couldn't get her off my mind though. I looked down at the table. *What was she so happy about? What was so exciting that she wanted to tell me about? What was she going to tell me?* I was too focused on her words that I could barely hear the officer speak again. "Okay."

KENDALL

Chapter 34

I don't believe that I'm sitting in here. This just doesn't seem real to me. Micah has been arrested. I have to wait to see and talk to him. It's been almost two hours just sitting in here. I looked up quickly when I heard footsteps coming closer. "Come this way if you'd want to talk to Mr. Harlan now." I got up quickly after wiping my eyes again. I walked behind him for a minute until he stopped. He took my bag from me before letting me into a room. I looked back before the door was closed. I looked in front of me to see Micah sat.

"Kendall," he said, surprised.

I went and sat in the chair across him. I just stared at him as he stared at me. I looked down. "What's going on?" I asked, looking back up at him. "What'd you do?" He put his hands on the table and extended his arms over to me. I gave him my hands, and he squeezed them. *He's going to jail, isn't he?* The father of my baby is going to be behind bars when he or she is born. I can't do this anymore. I can't tell him now. It will only make things worse. I felt the cool tears sliding down my cheeks as I just looked at our hands as we both held each other tightly.

"I'm so sorry," he whispered.

I took a deep breath. "What'd you do?" I shouted. I feel so mad right now I can't even think clearly. My head hurts. He isn't answering, he's only staring at my face. "What did you do, Micah?" I spoke more demanding now.

"I . . . I killed Lucas . . ."

My eyes widened. "Lucas? Who was Lucas?" *What? He didn't.* No. Micah wouldn't kill someone.

He looked away as tears were in his eyes, but he wasn't crying. "He was the one that was really in charge of everything. Keegan's the boss really, then he became mine, then I was in charge of some stuff." This is all some kind of sick joke. Micah isn't a murderer.

I just stared at him. "So . . . they're . . . you're going to jail?" This can't be happening.

He looked at my eyes carefully. "I don't want to ask you to do it for me, so I just want you to tell my mother what's happened, and I need a lawyer."

I nodded. "Okay." No, I don't want to do that. I keep looking around for someone to jump out and tell me this is all just a charade.

He then sort of smiled like something was still making him little happy. "So uh . . ." He looked down, losing his smile and then looked back up at me with the same happy smile. "What was it you were going to tell me earlier?" He's smiling? Why does that make my head hurt even more?

I looked away before making eye contact with him. I was so happy to tell him. Now if I tell him, it will hurt him. He won't be able to handle it. "Um . . ." I can't say it. I looked down at my belly, thinking maybe he would get the hint. No. He didn't. I looked back up at him as he was still staring at me to what I was going to say before all this. *How do I tell him now that he's going to be a father?* I just can't do that now.

"Kendall, what is it?" He got serious and scared.

"Look, you know what, um . . . just forget it. It wasn't anything really."

"Are you sure?" He furrowed his brows.

Then the door opened, and I was said to leave now. "I love you," I said softly, getting up. Micah watched me as I walked over to him. I have to hug him. He turned his chair, he can't get up, and his feet are cuffed to it at the bottom. I leaned down to him and wrapped my arms tightly around him. The cop watching us started hitting his hand on the glass, meaning for us to break apart. He buried his face into my neck as I could tell he was biting his lip at the same time.

"I love you, Kendall. Don't leave me."

I shook my head. I pulled back and placed a gentle kiss to his trembling lips. "I'll see you soon," I said, looking at his dark green eyes.

"Okay," he whispered back softly. I walked away out of the room only with the awkward thought of our child growing up without a father.

***

I had to tell Micah's mother what happened to her son over the phone because I started crying and I knew I would, so I couldn't find myself to tell her face to face. I had to tell her the whole story—well, what Micah told me at least. Now I have to tell my mom something, not just about what has happened to Micah but also to me.

I went down the steps as I heard my mother moving around in the kitchen. My mind hasn't been right since four days ago. I haven't heard or seen Micah for four days, and it's literally killing me. "Hey, honey." My mom smiled as I walked into the kitchen. It's around six thirty right now. "I'm gonna be going to work in a few minutes." I just nodded to her. I looked down away from her as I sat in the barstool Micah sat in the first time he was inside my house. "Everything okay with you and Micah?"

It took me a minute. I don't want to have to tell her all of this, but I have to. I need her help. She needs to know. "Mom, can you stay home a little longer?" I barely asked as my voice was trembling.

She got confused. "What's wrong?"

"I . . . I need to talk to you about something serious."

"What is it?"

"It's about Micah."

"Okay," she said, as she was willing to hear more.

She came closer to me. "He's been arrested," I whispered, looking down again.

"What? What did—why?" she asked quickly. "What'd he do?"

"He didn't do anything wrong," I said instantly. "He had to do it," I said to myself. He had to do it. He had to do it.

"What happened?"

"Mom, Micah ran away from home when he was still young. He got into bad things to make money. He's not a bad person," I cried uncontrollably. I glanced at my mother as she set her hand on my back. "Mom," I cried. She instantly grabbed me in her arms, setting her purse onto the counter. "I love him so much." I continued crying as she held me tightly to her.

"Shhh . . . Kendall." She tried to help in some way. "How long ago was this?"

"Four days." We both just stared at each other as if she knew there was more to the story.

"So what's happening with him?" She was concerned with my problems I was having with him. She cares about Micah. I hugged her tight. We both let each other go as she sat beside me. "Does his mom and dad know what's happened?"

"He, he doesn't have contact with his dad." I wiped my eyes with the back of my hand. "I called his mother and told her." I calmed down. That's not all that I have to tell her though. I don't know how to tell her that I'm pregnant now. "There's something else I have to tell you." I looked down at my lap, well my stomach.

"What, what is it honey?" She stared at me, waiting for my answer. "You can tell me anything." I looked back up at her, her eyes filled with tears and worry.

"I . . ." I sighed in embarrassment. "I, uh, I believe that, that, I'm pregnant." I somehow managed to say. My voice was low and depressing as I spoke it.

Her face was just staring at me in some shock. "Did you take a test?"

I nodded, looking away again as she held on to my upper arms caringly. "I don't know what to do," I cried.

She didn't say anything. She sighed and looked down, shaking her head as she did so. "I knew something was going to happen," she spoke quietly while wiping her forehead. "Have you said anything to Micah yet?" She composed herself. Well, that wasn't what I've been expecting.

I shook my head, thinking back to when I was about to tell him, and he was ripped away from me and put behind bars. "I was before they came to his house," I cried.

"Okay, okay. Just relax. We can get this all figured out."

"What's going to happen to him?" I kept crying. "I don't want to raise a child by myself."

"Hey, nobody said you were going to. You don't know a hundred percent that you are or what's going to happen to him. Just relax. We can take you to get a real test. Then we can help Micah out, get him help."

I looked up at her in some shock. "You're gonna help him?"

She nodded in some confusion. "If you love him enough and want to have his baby."

I nodded quickly. I never thought of not having the baby if I am pregnant. *How could I think like that? But how hasn't that ever crossed my mind?* Micah. Even though I love him, I don't think he is fit to be a father just yet. I don't know what else to say about him.

"What's his charges?"

I shook my head. "I don't know. We were at his house, and I was about to say something about this." I gestured to my tummy. "There were pounds on the door, and then he was taken away, and I took his car to the station and waited forever so I could only talk to him for a few minutes in a small room, and I couldn't tell him then. How could I do that?"

My mother only nodded. "How old is he again?"

"Micah's twenty-one."

She closed her mouth and looked at me sadly. "I'm so sorry, honey." She grabbed me into another hug. I can only think of Micah though. He's in jail. I haven't had any contact with him in four days. *Have his mother or sister?*

Waiting for the test results with my mother was awkward to say at the least. I'm turning nineteen in five days on June 22. So I'm going to start my life when I'm just nineteen. It doesn't feel right. It feels impossible to think about. *Am I going to be a mother? What's going to happen to Micah most of all?* I thought over all of the questions the woman had just asked me over and over and over. *Am I having a baby?* I don't know what I want any more with this question attacking my thoughts.

Chapter 35

Then the results came in. "Well uh, Ms. Starla, your results are positive. You are pregnant." I stared at the doctor with wide eyes, not even thinking of how to reply only, on the small life growing inside of me. I wasn't even able to control the single warm tear that slid down my cheek. Micah can't be a father, not yet. As much as I want him to have what he wants for one time in his life, he isn't ready. He is in jail. He isn't even here. He's not here. I am. I am the only one here. I'm the one that's going to have this baby. He would only be there to watch mostly anyway. *When he is out, who's to say that he's going to stay clean?*

No matter how many thoughts like that go through my mind, I still love Micah more than anything or anybody in my life ever. I can't explain my connection with him. He's perfect to me but wouldn't be perfect for a child growing up. Whenever we were in each other's presence, I would always be sharing his body heat. His arm would drift around me, drawing me in even closer to him, our fingers sometimes unknowingly entwining. Even asleep, Micah was like my extra blanket, his lashes brushing against my cheek as he would hold me impossibly close. It was like we didn't have a care in the world besides each other. I know he will never let me go. *So why would I ever do that to him?*

I won't.

I stared at my legs. The only response I could muster was to silently nod as I stared down. I blocked out my mother as she was talking, so I could only think back to when I first saw Micah. I hated him. He was pushy and arrogant. *How did he get like that? Why did he open up to me the way he did?* I can't just leave him because of his past.

After the doctor left us, I looked over nervously at my mother as she was sat in one of the chairs by the wall. "I'm sorry," I whispered.

I glanced back down at my legs. "Don't be sorry, honey. It's not like you planned this," she said calmly. "You don't have to have the baby," she added a moment later in the same tone.

I looked at her quickly. "I can't do that!" I sort of said loudly.

She just stared at me. "I'm just trying to help you out."

The ride home was mostly silent. My mom was a little taken back that I want to keep this baby with everything that is going on. I haven't thought much of having a baby of my own.

When we got home, it was quiet. "Are you still looking for Oscar?" I didn't look over at my mom as I sat in one of the barstools as she spoke.

I nodded, looking at the counter. "I don't understand why he would run away is all?" I looked up at her as she made her way to the fridge.

"I . . ." She shook her head slightly as she opened the door. "I don't know either. Maybe he just . . . I don't know." She looked over at me as she set the orange juice on the counter and got a cup from the cupboard above the counter lining the wall.

"I didn't think he would. I wasn't even thinking when the door was left opened," I said quietly, messing with my fingers on the counter.

"Don't stress yourself out. He's probably just nosing around somewhere," she said after pouring the drink and putting the jug back into the cold confines.

I just hummed back, still looking at my fingers as they tangled with each other. "What's going to happen with Micah?" I looked up at her as she took a drink.

"I, I don't know. You can't just go about a pregnancy without saying something to him though before you decide anything."

I just stared at her. "His friend said he wanted a baby." I looked at her and then down.

There was a minute of silence between us before I heard my mother taking another drink. "But do you want a baby? Kendall, it's a lot of work, ya know? I mean, it's not like Micah is here to help anytime soon. He's in jail, honey. You need to realize that. It's not like I won't be here for you or anything, but a baby needs a father figure in their life. Are you really sure you know what you're doing?" My mother's voice was calm and collected as she spoke the words carefully that she obviously thought over in our awkward minute of silence between us. She was concerned with what I was thinking.

"I don't know how to tell him, Mom. I can't just waltz into the jail and say I'm pregnant. That would kill him!" I sort of shouted back as

I stared at her a little mad. I don't want to accept that Micah is in jail. I haven't seen him in a few days, and that's killing me.

"Well, the doctor said you're almost three weeks, so you have some time to make up your mind. Just be careful, honey." She was still keeping a calm voice somehow.

I stared up at her. "Okay," I whispered as I sniffled my nose.

"Do you need me to stay home from work? Like, do you feel sick or anything?" I shook my head, avoiding any eye contact with her. "Okay, well, I love you. Just get some rest."

"Love you," I said, glancing at her.

Then she left. I looked around the kitchen and then turned in the stool, so I could look into the living room. I was all alone now. The TV was on as an episode of *How I Met Your Mother* was playing, the volume low. I just watched the screen as I seemed to just stare into space for a minute. The thought of Oscar came into my mind. I miss him. *What happened to him? Where is he?*

I took a deep breath as I looked down at my stomach as I ceased my eyebrows. I slowly set my hand on my tummy. It was still slim and tight. I sniffled my nose. I have to go see Micah. I need him now. I reached my other hand up and wiped my eyes, as tears were escaping them unexpectedly. "Time for bed," I whispered to my stomach. It made me smile. I do want a baby. I don't understand why, but I already feel so connected to the small baby growing inside of me. I love him or her already. I can't imagine getting rid of the child. *How could anybody do that?* I just can't picture it.

I got up from the barstool and strolled over to my staircase. I went up to my room without any problem and opened my door as it was cracked open only a little. I looked around inside before I went over to my bed and just laid down, already in jogging pants and a loose T-shirt. I laid down and looked over at all of the pictures of Micah and me on my nightstand. There are some more over on my TV stand as well. Also some of Oscar and some of me with him. I have three of Micah and me on my nightstand that are framed and one of just Oscar that is in a frame with dog bones and hearts. I got back up and took off my shirt and walked over to where one of Micah's shirts is laying on my chair. I sort of took it when I went back to house and cried my eyes out before I had Shailene take me home.

I picked the jacket and slid my arms through the long sleeves. It came down to my mid-thighs, maybe a little longer due to Micah's height difference compared to me. I rolled the sleeves up a little so that my hands would be showing. I reached down and gripped the zipper and tugged it up. After that, I just stood there. I wasn't even thinking really. Then the memory of the last time I saw him wearing this jacket came back to me. It wasn't that long ago. I walked back over to my bed.

It's weird to think that Micah and I will be parents, that Micah is going to be a father, and I'm going to be a mother. I reached over and grabbed one of the framed picture of Micah and me with his arm draped over my shoulder as I held him tightly in my arms. I took it on my phone and got it printed out and framed. I turned the frame over and unlatched it and took the photograph out and set the frame back, upside down on the nightstand by my lamp. I laid down by the wall and curled up with the picture in my hands. I pulled the sleeves back down, so I could grip them from the inside with my fingers as I still held the picture in my hand and eventually passed out after crying a little.

***

I reached over and picked my phone from my nightstand, as it started buzzing as I was just lying in bed doing absolutely nothing. Candice's name was popped up on the screen. I answered.

"Hi, Candice. What's going on?" I asked quickly.

"Well, we got a lawyer for Micah and stuff, but it's still not going all that great."

"What'd you mean? What's happening?"

"It's his charges. He says he didn't do half the stuff they are charging him for."

"What?" I paused. "What are they saying?"

"Well . . ." She paused, sounding sad. "They said murder, theft, drugs . . . rape." She sounded like she was crying.

"What?"

"That's what I said. I know he couldn't have done any of those things either. I know he didn't." I just stayed silent. She doesn't know anything about his drug habits and selling. "You still there?"

I thought about it for a few seconds. I have to tell her the truth. "Micah, um, well, he, he does kinda have a . . . drug problem. He's done a lot, Candice. He when, well, when he told me that he left, he met a guy, Walter, and that's when he started when he was like eighteen." I was shaky the entire time I spoke.

There wasn't any talking for another few seconds. "What, no. No. Micah. He doesn't. He just can't. He isn't involved in all of that Kendall, he can't be."

"Candice," I just whispered.

"No, Kendall."

"I wouldn't lie to you. When I got to talk to him the other day, he did tell me though that he did kill Lucas."

"What? Who, who is Lucas?"

"He was uh, the, oh gosh, all he told me about him was that he was the main guy in charge of it all."

"Oh god, this can't be happening."

I took a deep breath. "I'm pregnant," I blurted out quickly. *What the hell did I just do?* I couldn't control my words. They just came tumbling out.

There was like a slight laughing noise from her. "Wait, what?"

"Mmmm."

"Ar—are you serious?" She stopped giggling.

"Yeah."

"Well uh, oh gosh, this is . . . is exciting." She sounded happy once she said the last word. "Were you guys trying to have a baby?"

I laughed a little as I wiped my eyes. "No. He, he doesn't even know."

"What? Well, when did you find out? How long are you?"

"Um, I guess like five or six weeks."

"So uh, Micah's trial is in a couple of weeks. That's why I called." She sort of laugh, cried at the end.

"How's he doing?"

"Um, I guess how you'd expect he would be. He acts fine and all, but, yeah . . . he always asks about you." I smiled. "Are you coming to his trial?"

Am I going? I know that I'm going to cry at some point while I'm there. I took another deep breath. "Yeah, yeah, of course." I set my hand over my stomach.

"His charges are just so serious. I don't know what to think is going to happen," she cried softly as she spoke.

I shook my head. "I don't want to believe that he's done the other things."

"No, he couldn't off. He wouldn't ever do those things." She sounded like she was holding back sobs.

"So when are you planning on telling him about the baby? I mean, are you going to keep it?"

I bit my lip. I don't want to get rid of it. "I can't tell him, Candice."

"What do you mean?"

"He's in jail. I can't just be like, hey."

"So you do want the baby?"

I nodded as tears slid down my cheeks. "I don't think I could get rid of it."

I knew that she would be smiling on the other end. "He sometimes said when he was younger that he wanted to be a father just to know he would never be like ours," she said back softly.

"He's never said anything to me about kids."

"Well, do you need anything? You need some kind of help?"

"Um, well I have my mother. She already knows and she loves Micah and understands everything, so she's good with it."

I heard her "awe" on the other end. "Well, that's good. Wait, are you saying that she knows about his drug use and everything?" she spoke quickly. "Like everything you've told me?"

I shook my head. "She doesn't need to know that. She'd think I was doing something."

"I just can't picture him ever doing something like that."

"He gets crazy when he's drunk too," I said softly, sort of regretting it after. I couldn't help it though. The words just escaped.

"What? What do you mean? What's he do?" she spoke quickly again.

"He, uh, well, he drinks a lot whenever he does drink. It's never just a sip."

"Kendall, what'd he do?" she asked quietly like she was afraid of the answer.

"He's attacked me," I managed after a few seconds of silence.

There was a pause. "What, no. He hasn't done that." She protected him.

"It was never like a full-on attack. He just gets really mad or aggressive and shouts and grabs me. It's never Micah I know though." I held back my tears. She didn't need to know about our anniversary.

"I just, I don't know how to take that. I don't know. I never thought that he would even start drinking." She paused. "Well, I have to go."

"Oh, Candice."

"Yeah?"

"Uh . . . please just don't say anything about my pregnancy. I want to say it. I'm so scared, but I have to tell people. Please?"

"Of course. I'm sure it'll make him so happy though. Bye."

"Thanks, bye."

Chapter 36

My mother made my breakfast this morning. The whole week I just prayed that Candice didn't blurt something out to anybody. I gulped down the scrambled eggs quickly. I was so hungry lately. I seemed to be eating twice as much really. I felt fat and sad all the time. I am sort of fat now though. "Are you going to see him today?"

I nodded. "I don't know what to say to him . . ."

"I don't know either, honey," she whispered. "He needs to know though, Kendall. This is between you both. You can't keep this kind of secret from him. He deserves to know."

I stayed silent. "I know," I whispered back, finished my eggs and toast.

***

I took my mom's car to the prison. I wore one of his hoodies that was loose and bigger on me. I tucked it into my shorts because it went down to just above my knees. I parked. My hands were shaking as I removed the keys from the ignition and swallowed hardly. I'm literally shaking so bad. Micah's in jail right now. I don't want to believe this anymore than he probably does. I haven't seen him in weeks.

I locked up the car and walked through the big doors leading into the prison. It was a weird feeling being inside here. I looked around as I put the keys into the hoodie's pocket in the front. I walked up to the front desk. "Um." The officer looked up at me from the computer as I was still shaky. "I—I'm here to visit Micah Harlan." I told him, my voice shaky.

"Oh, okay then. I'll need to hold on to your cell phone and car keys for that matter, please." I smiled politely as I fished out the keys and my phone and handed them both over to the young dark-haired man behind the desk. "Now, just take that hall, and you'll be searched back there before you are able to see him." He kept his attention on the computer screen while he pointed to a hall to his right.

I just looked at him and then the direction he pointed to before walking away and down the short corridor. I was searched thoroughly by a female officer before I was lead into a longer room where there were other visitors talking to other inmates through glass windows with phones. "Just take the next empty seat, miss."

I looked back at her as I went and sat in the next empty stool. I looked around, still shaking. I never imagined that I'd ever sit in a place like this and wait for my boyfriend to join me on the other side of the glass. A few minutes passed before a door opened on the other side of the glass, and there he was. Micah was shoved into the plain and boring room with his wrists handcuffed. My heart ached as I watched him give the cop an evil glare, and he shoved him again into my direction. His eyes lit up when he saw me. My eyes began to get glassy, and I just stared at him. He sat and stared at me. He picked the phone as did I.

"Kendall," he whispered. His hair was sticking up a little, letting me know he hasn't even tried to fix it. The blond is fading away, letting it look like he just has a few highlights now. His eyes look tired, and his facial hair is growing thick.

"Hi, Micah," I said back, holding in my tears.

"Oh my god," he said while he wiped his face with his hand. Before he said anything else, he looked at the other prisoners to his right and then back at me. "Where have you been? It's been so long." I shook my head, looking down. *What do I say?* "Did your breasts get bigger?" he asked quickly as I saw his eyes on my chest.

My eyes got wider. I can't bring myself to tell him now that I'm just about three months pregnant with his child. I am showing a little, but his hoodie is hiding most of it. "No." I laughed weakly.

He blinked a few times before he took his eyes off my chest and back to my eyes. He smiled awkwardly. "Sorry, I just haven't seen you in so long, I guess. I didn't think you would ever come really." He grinned happily. "I thought you'd given up." Oh no, Micah, don't ever think that.

"Why would you think that?" I asked immediately.

He shook his head. "I don't know. Josh came, my mom, Shailene, Candice, just not you."

"I'm sorry. I just—"

"It's fine. I understand why. I was just upset is all."

"I did want to come see you. I just couldn't bring myself to. I don't know why. I don't want to see you in here, Micah." I wiped my eyes.

"Hey, hey, please don't cry, Ken. I'll be out soon enough."

I don't believe what he's saying to me though. "I know your charges," I said softly as I looked away from him.

I looked back up at him after taking a deep breath. He was just staring at me. "I didn't, I didn't rape anybody, Kendall. That was Anthony. You know I wouldn't do that!" I just stared back at him. He tried to once to me. I want to believe him. "Kendall, I need you to just trust me, not anything anyone else is saying. That's all bullshit," he whispered.

"I do trust you."

He looked down and hid his eyes from me. When he looked back up, they were glassy, and his lip was trembling. "Oscar's dead," he whispered as he wiped his eyes.

"What? Why would you think that? He just ran away, Micah."

"They killed him."

My eyes got wide, and then I covered my mouth with my hand. "What? Who—who killed him?"

"Johnathan and Lucas. I'm so sorry. It's my fault, Kendall," he cried a little. I never thought that I'd be looking at him crying and not to do anything about it. I bit the inside of my lip. Oscar's gone. He's dead. I didn't let any tears, but one rolled down my cheek. "I'm sorry what I'm putting you through," he whispered.

I have to tell him now. *How do I say it? How will he react to it?* I'm too scared to say anything. I looked over as the other visitors started to leave. I have to go now. I looked back at Micah. I looked down and then back up at him.

"Miss, visiting hours are over." I looked over to see a guard getting my attention that I had to leave.

I looked back at Micah and then just grinned while my eyes started to water up. I looked back down. "I'm pregnant," I said loud enough that I know he heard me. After that, I just got up and walked out to go back home.

MICAH

Chapter 37

"Come on, Harlan!" The guard shouted as he lifted me out of the chair. She was so nervous to tell me. I know now. That's what she was going to say to me the day I was arrested. I knew it was something, and when she said it was no big deal, I just didn't want to push her into telling me something that she was scared to say to me. When Candice came and visited me, she was trying to hold back her smiling. Same with Shailene. She must have told them. *Why would she tell them all except for me? Who else knew before me?*

She should have just told me in the first place. *Was she really that scared to say something like that to me? Did she not trust me?* Sure I haven't told her anything, but it's not like I would be pregnant. That's serious. The guard took my arms behind my back, holding my wrists tightly behind me. I kept my head turned and watched Kendall as she passed by the guards to leave. I'm going to be a father.

I did think about it before a year or two ago about having children, but I never pictured myself with a girl that would actually stay with me like Kendall has. I was nothing more to any of them but one night or half a night really. They always left right after. I would never leave Kendall. Even when I would go to their place, I would make them something to eat in the morning or wake them up or write a note saying I was leaving. I wasn't an asshole like most of them were toward me. I still respected them enough to say something nice afterward.

But the reality that my girlfriend is actually pregnant now makes me feel so much older for some reason. Just to think that I'll be a dad just gives me the chills. It's weird. I wasn't planning on having a son or daughter anytime soon really. I don't feel ready.

That's why she was always sick in the mornings and crying more. She knew and was scared to tell me. *Why did I make her scared?*

I was tossed out of my thoughts as the guard shoved me back into my cell. I looked up at the top bunk at my cell mate, Levi. We don't talk much. I don't make myself look weak to anyone else. You don't do that. The only other times I've been arrested I was released that day or the next. This is different. It's been almost two months, and I still haven't had a trial until next week. I looked away from Levi and then sat on the bottom bunk with my elbows on my knees. I wiped my face, still in shock.

"Who visited ya?"

"What?"

"You don't get much visitors really, so who was it this time?"

I laughed lightly. "You trying to make conversation?" I laughed, looking up at him as he held his book in front of his face.

He just shrugged. "Why not? Might as well get used to each other if we're gonna be here awhile."

"My trials next week."

"How's your lawyer?"

"An asshole really, but I guess he's supposed to be."

"Most of 'em are." He laughed. "So . . . who was it today?"

I paused, thinking if I should really tell him the truth. "My girlfriend . . ."

"Girlfriend. I thought you said she didn't want to see you?"

"I don't know what's going on really. She said she wanted to come. She was just scared to see me in here, locked up, ya know?"

"Armed robbery," he suddenly said.

"What?"

"That's why I'm in here." I had asked him the first week why he was here and a few other questions that were just random, but he just told me to shut the hell up, that we're not here to make friends. "You?"

"I thought you sa—"

"I know what I said. Just answer the damn question. You asked first."

"Murder, drug usage, selling, theft. I didn't rape anyone though."

"You sure about that?" He laughed. "I didn't think you out to of killed someone."

"Yeah, me either. No more talking."

I laid back on my bunk and put my hand behind my head as I closed my eyes. I just feel so stressed. Kendall is pregnant. *How could I of done this to her? What if it's not what she wants and feels that I would be mad at her if she got rid of the baby in some way?* Dammit. You know. You know that if you have unprotected sex, it ends up with pregnancy. You know that! *What the hell? How could I of done this?* I practically made her do it that night. She didn't want to. *But she came back and acted like she did. Is this what she wanted to happen? Did she plan this?*

***

The lights were turned off, and the noise was loud. "Mommy," I whispered as I turned to look around the corner.

He hit her across the face. "You fucking whore. Do you really think you look pretty in all that makeup?" He yelled in her face. It's their thirteenth year anniversary. I was supposed to stay in my room until Candice came home to take me to the movies with her and her friends. Her friends are funny and nice to me, so it's not awkward.

My eyes widened in panic. What do I do? Can I stop him? "Get off her!" I sort of shouted as my eyes welled up.

My mother was sobbing badly as he let go of her neck to stare at me in somewhat a little shock. He's drunk. "What the hell did you just say to me?" He asked, walking over to me.

"I . . ." I paused in shock as I backed up from him as he got closer and closer to me. I almost tripped over my feet when I took just a second to look over at my mother as she watched us both. "Leave her alone," I whispered as I stumbled against a table against the wall in the hallway toward my bedroom. My heart rate was quick, my hands, lips, and face all shaking with terror of what's happening, what's going to happen.

"No, Ethan, don't hurt him. He didn't mean it, honey." My mom started pleading while she held back her sobs best she could. Then the front door opened.

"I'm home!"

My eyes let tears fall down. My da-Ethan turned around to see my sister in her blue button-up knee length dress with her thick hair straightened and her bangs pulled back. I stared at my sister as she saw me and mom and the broken glass that caught my attention to why I came out here to check on my mother. My mother ran to her as my da-Ethan started walking over to her. My mom grabbed her by the shoulders and ran past him as fast as she could, shoving her into me quickly as she shielded us from him. Candice grabbed on to my arm and dragged me down the hallway into her room with the only door with a lock for some reason. She locked it and shoved her longer dresser in front of it quickly. I stood in the middle of her bedroom in my pajamas.

"Candice," I whispered as I started to cry and wrap my arms around myself. There was crying and somewhat quiet screams coming from my mother

on the other end of the door. I stood in the middle of her room, shaking. She came quickly over to me and grabbed a hold of me, her arms wrapping around my small frame of a fourteen-year-old.

"I got you," she whispered as she took me over to the other side of her bed and into the corner and kept her arms around me as we sat against the wall. She stayed right against me the whole time, trying to calm and soothe me with reassuring words as my mother was still crying and yelling for my father to stop and just leave us all alone while he just told her to shut up. My breathing got the best of me. My heart started pumping faster and faster and faster. What's happening? I started panicking, reaching my hand over my heart as I still cried and started to feel sweat trickling down my forehead. I can't breathe. "Micah?" I barely heard her ask frantically.

My eyes opened quickly.

I blinked quickly a few times. "Harlan! Get up. Time for breakfast." Levi shook me awake. I sat up even quicker. I wiped my forehead, as there was sweat coming down from my hair. I brushed my hands through the brown and blond streaks a few times before standing up, still with the memory of my first panic attack happening.

This happened every single night though, nightmares. Not always a faint memory replaying itself in my head, but they scared me every night. I usually wake up in the middle of the night with sweat downing my face and body, massive migraines, and just tiredness. Almost every night is hell inside my head. I would kill for a hit or gram of really anything right now. The craving is too high. They put me on some kind of medication though to help me with the cravings I get of it. I can't say though that it never takes my mind off it. Because when I take it, I remember why I'm taking it. As the pill goes down my throat, all I think of is Kendall and how I'm getting clean.

I got up and stood beside Levi and stretched my arms at my sides. It's not a big cell. I have to pee. I looked back at the toilet and just stared at it. The cell door opened, and the guards stood around all of them as people exited. I bit the inside of my lip and just ignored my bawls and went out with Levi.

Kendall. She's all I care about, not my needs. Our baby. I want the baby. *Does she though?* I'm too scared that I'm going to end up like my father. I'm afraid that I'm going to hurt her. I can't control myself all that great when I'm intoxicated. *What if I end up like my own father when the baby is born?* I don't understand how he ever lived with himself. I couldn't live if I ever hurt my Kendall or the baby. I would rather die than ruin their lives.

We were all sat in the cafeteria. The grey ray just sitting there in front of me as I sat there. For the whole couple of months I've been here, I guess I've gotten respected. A few remarks here and there, but most of them knew who I was and were afraid of me and spread the word around. Nick sat across me, gulping down his food like he always does. Kyle to my left speaking about something annoying to Jerry on my right. I feel so annoyed.

"What's your problem?" Dale asked, sitting on the right of Nick.

I looked at him normally. "My girlfriend's pregnant." I pushed the tray away from me.

I can't picture Dale for being the person everyone sets him out to be. He seems kind and friendly. I just can't picture him for kidnapping a child, holding him for money. The thought about it now though sickened me, thinking about it being my own child. *How would I react?* I would have killed him. I would kill anyone who tried to take my kid away. To think of someone doing that to their parents, taking them away from them.

The way he looked at me when I answered him. "How far long?" I didn't want to answer him. The way he asked so casually while finishing his food made me feel sick, and anger build up inside of me.

"Why do you want to know?" I bit back, causing Nick to look over at him while chewing his food and to get everyone else's attention at the long table.

"Just asking," he remarked, still in a casual tone.

"I'd rather not tell you." I said it back seriously as he was looking down at his food and then lifted it to look back up at me.

"All right, Ted Bundy, fine. Keep it to yourself." He smiled.

"The fuck did you just say?" I asked back loudly.

"You're the murderer and rapist. How'd you meet ya girlfriend?" He smiled.

I couldn't take it anymore. I went up to throw my tray in the can. I walked to throw it away behind him and turned around quickly and slammed it into the back of his head, causing it to jerk forward. I threw it to the ground when he turned around and felt the rage build up inside of me. Someone implying that I've raped Kendall and compared me to someone like Bundy just made it even worse. I blocked out everyone yelling and shouting as I repeated punch after punch to his face, kneeing his stomach and crotch after a few more times of my fists colliding with his face. I couldn't stop even if I wanted to. I want him to die. Why would I even want to stop is the point. He took somebody's child away. A boy? A girl? It doesn't matter. That was someone's son or daughter. I would kill him if it was my child as soon as I saw him. He's pathetic, a waste. I punched his face repeatedly. The hands gripping my biceps finally pulled me off. The guards shouting and yelling as I stood up to admire my work to his face.

Blood. His face smeared with it completely. It gushed out of his nose like water. His nose shaped in a different angle now. His eye swollen and black already. His cheeks cut up as well as the sides of his face. Black and blue. I was taken away, but I didn't care. I felt better.

KENDALL

Chapter 38

Micah's trial was pushed from today to two more days on the fourteenth. I took a deep breath as I sat on the couch with my hand sat gently on my belly as my mom made dinner. I quit my job. I'm too tired, and I took the past week off because of all that's been going on. They didn't mind all that much. Ben texted me a few times just joking with me, trying to cheer me up.

I don't feel all that good at all today or yesterday. "Hey, Mom?" I asked, walking into the kitchen with my empty plate.

"Yeah, honey?" She looked over. "You okay?"

"Yeah." I smiled. "I, uh, I'm gonna go over to Micah's house and just clean up a little for when he comes home."

She just stared at me. "Nobody's been over there since?"

I shook my head. "Well, his mom and sister live like an hour away, and I don't think his friends would be into cleaning, so . . . I just wanna do it for him."

She nodded. "Okay, sweetheart. The keys are on the hook." I walked to the door and grabbed the keys. "Be careful!" she yelled as I walked out.

I looked over at his older neighbor as he sat on his porch and just stared at me as I went up and unlocked Micah's door with my key he gave me. I walked in, taking off my shoes at the door and walked down the hallway and turned on all the lights. I gasped at what I saw. The place was a wreck. I immediately thought that maybe the cops ransacked the place, looking for some kinds of evidence. The longer I stood there though, the thought that maybe it was just someone he used to work with looking for something to keep away from the cops, maybe Josh, got into me.

It hurts to look at his bedroom like this. His drawers opened with his clothes unfolded and wrinkly now. I remembered why I was here when I felt the cold tear running down my cheek. How somebody just turned his whole house upside down. I rushed over to the clothes on the floor and started folding them quickly and fixing the drawers. I didn't even realize I was crying until I tasted the tears hitting my chapped lips. I just stared at the blue shirt in my hands. I rubbed my thumbs over it as I held it in my palms. I unfolded it and put it on over my tank top. I finished cleaning up his bedroom from the mess of clothes. I went over to his nightstand next and opened it and started rummaging through the entire thing. No weed, nothing.

I bit the inside of my cheek, thinking where else did he ever hide anything. *Did the cops find it as evidence? Is that why it's not in here?* I tucked my hair behind my ears as I went to where the vent was, but there was a chest over it now. *When did that get here?* I have never even seen it before. I stared at it for a moment. It looks so familiar. It was at his mom's house in his bedroom. That's where I know it. I hurried up and slid it away from over the vent. It was heavy. I got on my knees and lifted the vent and reached my hand down and felt around the walls. I pulled out a bag. I looked down at it to see the green clumps. They didn't find it. I held back my tears, knowing that he's still on something. I jumped and dropped the baggie on the floor when there was a few knocks on the door.

I went over to his window and peeked out. Josh's car was parked in the driveway. I walked out of the room quickly, closing the door behind me and going to the front door and opening it quickly.

"Josh, hi." I smiled while wiping my face of the tears.

"Hi? Sorry, I was, I went to your house. Your mom told me you were here."

"You were looking for me? What's going on?" He smiled before reaching into his back pocket and pulling out an envelope. "What's this?" I held it in my hand, looking up at him.

"I visited him the day before the fight, and he wanted me to give it to you. He says just to take it and leave, and he'll take care of the rest for you." I looked at him confused. "I had to promise not to open it. So uh, how long are you?" He poked at my belly.

I slightly laughed. "He told you?"

"That's all he talked about really." He laughed. I smiled and looked down at the envelope. "Is it a wreck in there?" He pointed inside.

I rolled my eyes. "Yeah, I cleaned his bedroom, but I haven't even looked at the other rooms."

"You need some help?"

I grinned at him. I looked behind me. I sniffled my nose, looking back up at him. I nodded.

He followed me into his living room. It was a mess. Everything just thrown around. I put the envelope in my purse by the door before we went inside the room. We started fixing up all the couch cushions first. "So how long are you again?"

"Oh sorry." I laughed. "I—I'm just thirteen weeks next week."

He just nodded and looked back at me. "Wow. Uh well, congratulations." He smiled.

I grinned back at him. "Thanks."

"Yeah."

After we straightened up more, I knew something was missing. The photograph. "Where's the picture that was there?" I asked, looking around for it.

"Oh," Josh said, noticing it was gone. "Maybe it fell under something." I went to get on my knees to search under the couch, but he stopped. "I'll look. You should just sit down or something."

"Josh, I'm pregnant, not crippled."

He laughed. He just sat me on the couch and got down and started looking for it. A minute later, he pulled the broken frame out from under the couch. "Okay," he said, setting it back in its place. "So how have you been?"

I rolled my eyes. "Terrible." I paused, feeling awkward with being alone with Josh in Micah's house although I know I can trust him just as well as Micah. "Sick, just a mess."

He snorted. "Well, sorry to hear that. He told me to look after you while he can't, so if you ever do need anything or if your home alone or whatever, you can always come stay with Bailey and me."

I smiled. "Thanks, Josh." He nodded. "How are you two so close?"

He looked confused a little. "Micah and I?" I nodded. "I don't know. I've known him since he was eighteen, and I was twenty-three. He's like my brother, I guess." He paused, looking around. "I should go now. I'll leave you to do whatever." He laughed.

"Okay. Thanks so much." I stood up and walked with him to the door.

When he was outside, he turned back. "He wouldn't rape anyone," he stated, looking at my eyes.

It took me a few seconds to realize that he's trying his best to make sure Micah and I make it. "I know," I whispered.

He walked to his car and left. I walked back inside, bringing Micah's shirt closer to my body from the sudden breeze that came in from the door closing. I walked a little down the hallway until I remembered. I rushed back quickly over to my bag on the table in the hallway. I rummaged through it until I found the white envelope and pulled it out. I walked into the living room with it in my hand. I stared down at it, looking for some kind of writing on the outside for no reason really, just curiosity.

I sat on the couch and started opening it. I unfolded the flap and pulled out the folded piece of white paper. I tossed the envelope on to my lap and began to unfold the white paper.

> Kendall.
>
> I'm so sorry I can't be there with you during all this. I know what's going to happen to me and I need to at least help you in any way I possibly can. I love you too much to leave you without any sort of support. I want to be there with you when the baby is born. I can't. I know I won't be there and that will always be there is haunt me.
>
> Go to New Bucking. I have a friend there that held some money for me. Take it all. Newton. If I knew him well enough he'll be in a place called blazer's bar. Don't be scared of him. Don't anger him either. Just say Micah Harlan sent you and he'll know what you're talking about and probably take you somewhere more private. He won't hurt you, trust me. He knows you'd be mine. Take the money and just leave as fast as you can. No talking further more. Don't give him any information just say I sent you to get the money. Leave right after. Go home. Take all the money. Take care of yourself and our baby. I'm sorry for all you've put yourself through and I just wish I could kiss you good-bye or have one of your hugs right now.
>
> Let our baby know how much I love him or her. I won't go a day without you in my mind I don't think. Thanks for the chance at least to change for you. I don't know how else to put it but im sorry.

Don't come to the trial. I don't want you to be there when im cuffed and taken away. It won't help either of us. Don't come visit me either. It'll be easier on me. To not see the baby growing or any pictures. It won't help me. It will distract me from being in here, I can't risk that. It's dangerous at a prison for you to visit me. Just don't do it darling. You can buy a house with that money. You can do whatever you want with it. You'll do better with it than I would have. I took it away from myself. I hope all goes well. I want to be with you, holding your hand when our child is born. To hold the baby. Just forget about me.

Love you

I stared down at his sloppy handwriting. I don't know what to think. I understand everything he is saying to me, but I don't want to. He doesn't want me there to visit him, to see photographs of the baby. *Is he breaking up with me?* I let my eyes let some of the tears back I was holding in. I wiped them away quickly. I shook my head. I'm not giving up on him. *How could he say to just forget about him?* I'll never be able to do that. Sure I'm mad as hell at him. I'm furious at what he's done. *How he could continue smoking weed?* Although it's not as bad as a drug or cocaine, he said he was quitting, and then he finds another to buy off it? That pisses me off more than anything. *But how could I hate him?*

I set the letter down and looked around his house. New Bucking, Blazer's Bar. That's where I have to go tomorrow. Newton, I have to find Newton. Ask about the money for Micah Harlan. Okay. I can do this for us. All three of us. *How much money? I can get him out maybe?* No. I can't get myself too worked up over this. I might just end up disappointing myself. I set my hand on my growing stomach and just soothed it around, looking straight down. I'm not doing everything he says.

After I got dressed and fixed myself up, with my hair in a bun and comfortable clothing on, I jogged down my steps carefully with my hand caressing my stomach the whole way down. I tucked the letter in my back pocket. I found my mom in the kitchen like always making something to eat for us.

"Hey, Mom?"
"Yes, sweetheart?"
"Can I borrow the car for a little to visit Em?"

She looked over her shoulder. "Isn't Micah's trial today? At two, isn't it? Kendall, it's already twelve. I don't think you should go anywhere." I just looked down. I held back my girly sobs as I looked back at her. I shook my head. She just stared at me. "I understand," she said sympathetically. I just walked out the front door and got in the car ready to drive to New Bucking.

The drive to New Bucking took two hours. Now I have to find Blazer's Bar. *Should I of told someone where I was really going today? Should I of brought someone along with me?* The place was trashy looking. I looked down everywhere. *Where is this place?* After fifteen minutes of driving around looking for it, I saw a bar. I inspected it closer to see the name. On a sign, it read Blazer's Bar. I drove into the small parking lot and parked the car. I looked around at some of the people entering and exiting, not the kind I talk to. But if Micah told me to go here, I have to.

I took a deep breath and got out of the car and grabbed my purse with the letter, my phone, and a pepper spray. I closed and locked up the doors. I walked carefully to the entrance. The music was playing but not blasted like the other places Micah has took me. I looked around, clutching the bag tightly to my side. A few eyes inspecting me as I walked around looking for somebody to ask about Newton, whoever he is.

I don't know who to ask. They all look too intimidating to me. I'm scared to ask anyone for where this guy is. "Can I help you, babe?" I turned around quickly as I felt a large and rough hand take my wrist gently.

I smiled nicely. "Um, actually, I—I was just looking for this guy—"

"Forget about him for a while, sweetheart," he interrupted. He smiled as he stroked his thumb over my skin slowly while holding on to my wrist. I looked down and sort of blushed and quickly felt bad for doing it. I pulled my hand away from his gentle warm touch. I laughed awkwardly. "Do I frighten you, sweetheart?" He lowly chuckled.

I looked at him wide-eyed. That's what Micah asked me on our first date. Maybe they know each other. I shook my head. He's tall like Micah's height with black hair swept to the side mostly, some of it sticking up, his breath holding a little bit of an alcohol stench. I grinned. "No, sorry, umm, do you know Micah Harlan?"

His eye brows rose a little. "Harlan? Haven't heard from him in a while." He grinned, looking away for a second. "Yeah, I know 'em a little," he spoke quickly.

I got excited. "Oh great! Well, maybe you know this guy Newton I'm looking for?"

He smirked. "Newton? You're looking for him?" I nodded. "He comes in 'ere all day time."

"Is he here today?"

He lifted his arm with the beer bottle in his hand, indicating where he is. When I turned my head and looked back at the man, I wasn't met by his gaze though; instead, his eyes were staring down at my grown breasts intently, just staring. I got a little upset for some reason and felt a little too emotional. "You Micah's girl then?" he asked, glancing up at my face for a few seconds.

I just stared at him. "Yeah."

"Lucky man." He smirked at me and turned to walk away.

I was confused until I got disgusted at what he was saying a little. At least he didn't notice how fat my stomach has gotten.

I walked over to where he lifted his hand to see a few men sitting at the bar. I got shaky and just really nervous. I have to do this. It's okay. I set my hand on my tummy for a second and sat beside one of the men on the side. The bartender came over asking for my ID. I shook my head that I wasn't gonna get a drink anyway. I tapped on the man's shoulder beside me.

He turned his head. He grinned when he saw me. "Hello."

"Hi." I smiled. "Sorry, but do you know a Newton?"

"That's me, young lady." He smiled, turning fully around to face me.

"Micah Harlan?" I questioned. He got a surprised look on his face.

"What about him?" He looked at my chest for a moment.

"He, he s-sent me for some money," I stuttered.

He took a drink from his glass. "Yeah? How much?"

I took a minute to answer. "All of it?" That's what Micah said to say, so . . .

He raised his brows, finishing his drink completely now. "Who are ya to him?" He looked over curiously.

I took a long moment. *Do I tell him?* "His girlfriend."

He looked over, surprised. "Oh, young man finally found a pretty lady I see." He smiled. "So where's Micah that he isn't here tonight?"

"He's, uh, he's, he wasn't, and he just sent me to get the money for him."

He tilted his head. "Any confirmation of that do you have on ya?"

I gritted my teeth. I brought my bag around on to my lap and started digging through it. I grabbed my phone and went to my photos and showed him a couple of Micah and me together. "He looks better."

"He's been better."

"That's it? Just a few photos, and you expect me to give you all of the money he has with me?" He was serious. I opened my mouth to speak, but the words were lost. I went to my messages and scrolled through them with him looking at them all. "So you texted? How's that supposed to convince me of anything? Call him."

I furrowed my eyebrows. "He doesn't have his phone right now."

"And why's that?" He laughed.

I have to tell him. *How else am I supposed to get his money for him?* "He's in jail," I spoke quietly as he ordered a few more shots. He heard me.

He looked over. "That's not really a big surprise. How long you two been together?"

Micah said no conversation. Just get the money and leave, just go home. "He wrote me a letter to get all the money. I really need it."

"Where's this letter now?" He drank the second shot. I stared at him for a moment. I reached in my bag and handed it to him. He read over it. He laughed a little. "He knows me, all right." He laughed. He looked down at my stomach then and up to my face. He read all of it. "Okay." He handed the letter back over.

"You believe me now?"

"I believe you, Kendall." He smiled. He turned to the few guys beside him and said that he had to go take care of some business, and they seemed to understand as he stood up and looked at me. "Come on then."

I stood up and followed him. I followed him behind the bar and through a door. The bartender or nobody else looked at us weird or stared. There was a man sitting at a table. He gestured him over to me. "Against the wall, miss," the man told me. I looked at Newton worriedly.

"We have to search you," he reassured me nicely.

I got against the cement wall. "Spread your arms and legs, please," he instructed. My eyes got glassy, as I was so nervous. I did what he asked, still shaking, being hesitant. He patted his hands all over my body and then set them on my sides.

"She's pregnant, you sick basted," Newton said to the guy. I looked over at Newton as my eyes were still glassy and filled with worry and nerves.

He patted his hands where they were. "All good." He stepped away. Once I got off the wall, the stranger took my bag out of my hands without even asking.

He started taking things out and setting it on the table while he looked around in it. I looked over at Newton. His brown hair is a little curly at the ends, but it's not long. He stood there with his hands in his front pockets, watching the large man search my bag carefully and non-caring. He glanced over at me as I was looking at him sadly and quickly looked away, not wanting to make any eye contact. After the guy searched my purse, he threw everything just back inside, including Micah's letter. He took the pepper spray and slid it into his pocket. He picked my bag and shoved it back into my arms.

"You're not Harlan's type?" He looked over me. "Not usually, since those are for the baby." I just glared at him. Asshole. Newton put his arm over my shoulders and led me through another solid doorway.

He flipped on a light switch and walked to the end of the small room. I stood in the doorway. Now the door shut on its own. The room was cement and with an older-looking wooden floor with a single light in the middle of the ceiling. The wall had a few safes lining it. Newton went to the one in the middle on the back wall and started putting in the combination. Then after a few minutes, he turned around, closing the door gently and gestured for me to open my purse. I placed it to my front and opened it up. I watched him as he put around ten envelopes into my bag carefully. My eyes probably looked like they were popping out of my head and mouth touching the floor. *How much money did he just give me?*

***

I ignored mom asking me questions if I took my vitamins today. I take them right when I wake up every morning, yet she still feels the annoying need to ask. I ran up to my room and closed my door gently after returning her keys to her. After I got the money, I just walked straight out of that place and drove right home. Newton only told me to take care when I left and to say a greeting to Micah and laughed.

I threw my bag on my mattress and plugged in my cell phone and changed my outfit in pajamas. When I went back into my bedroom,

I paused, looking at my purse on the bed. I walked over to it slowly. I picked out all of the envelopes. I took a deep breath before I looked over at the picture of Micah and me. I latched on to his side as the moment was saved.

I opened the flap to see the tops of green bills all neatly sat in the white paper. My mouth fell agape. I pulled out the wad to see all hundreds. I grabbed on to the next envelope and opened it up quickly. The same thing. Not as many hundreds but fifties. I grabbed the next one. Fifties and a few hundreds. I grabbed the fourth one. All hundreds, same with the next one, and the next one. The rest mostly fifties and hundreds.

I separated all of the money on my blanket, each bill stacked with the same amount on it. I sat Indian style as I stared down at all of the stacks. I'm scared to count it. *How did he get all of this? What did he do?* I took a deep breath as I reached down to pick up the wad of hundreds, but the knock on my door caused me to seize my moments as I quickly pushed it all under my blanket. "Come in!" I shouted after.

"Honey, is everything all right?" My mom asked with a concerned look plastered on her slightly wrinkled face.

I nodded quickly in response. "Yeah, of course."

"You're feeling okay? Are you just hungry? What's wrong?"

"I'm just tired."

I saw her look at the lump of my blanket and my discarded purse on the floor with stuff spilled out of it from when I quickly lifted my blanket to hide the paper. She looked down at my stomach and just smiled. "Okay." I walked over to grab my phone off the charger when she pulled me into a loving hug with her arms over my shoulders and her face on her arm. "You're going to be an amazing parent, sweetie. Don't stress."

I just held my arms around her, not knowing how to respond. *What do I say? Thank you?* No. I'm not worried about being a good parent and loving my child. I'm scared that my baby will grow up without a father. I need Micah here, now. I need him to be standing here, hugging me, saying those words, not my mother. I know she'll help me with everything. She's stayed home a day just to be with me and make sure I'm all right. I've been to two doctor's appointments, and everything is just fine with the baby and me already. I had to start eating more though for the baby. Making me fatter.

She finally let go. "I'm so sorry about what has happened to Micah." She looked me in the eye.

I just stared back at her. "Did you hear about his trial?"

She nodded silently. "Well, he's pleading not guilty to the rape charges, and his friend—oh, I forgot his name—is looking for the women that were said to be the other victims by the one girl that is charging him, and then we'll see. But the other ones, Kendall . . ." She paused, looking at me sadly. "He's not fighting them, sweetheart." Her eyes were full of concern and sorry.

Chapter 39

At each doctor's appointment, I didn't even try to picture Micah in the baby's life. He gave up. He's not trying at all that I know of to get out of his mess. He going to jail, and he's accepting it. That's why he sent me to Newton. That's why he sent me to get all of his money, so I can support myself and the baby. I hid all of the money in my bedroom away from my mother. I haven't told her yet.

Everything was still going fine with the baby, and I'm now twenty weeks along. Em and Savanna are always stopping by to see me, and it's fun. It takes my mind off things, for a while.

I slowly got ready to go to the doctors to have my twenty-week ultrasound. I'm not excited at all really. I don't want to go all that bad. Micah won't be there. He won't be there when the baby is born, and I won't get to see him as a father holding his child for the first time in the hospital and holding my hand. It's never going to happen.

I held back my tears of those thoughts raging through my mind as I bit my bottom lip and got dressed. I opened my drawer and picked my bracelet that Micah bought me. It took me a minute to get it on. I don't like sleeping with it on my wrist because I'm afraid that it will break somehow.

***

"Okay, do you want to know what the gender is?" my doctor asked as he continued to move the scope over my belly.

My mom looked at me to answer. I wasn't even really paying any attention. I was just staring at the ceiling. "I guess," I said back softly although they both heard me perfectly clear.

"Alright then. Just one moment . . ." he said as he continued to move the scope over my cold stomach slowly before stopping, and a wide smile appeared on his face. "Okay, I found it." He looked over at me.

My mom came over closer and put both of her hands on top of mine as it just lay still on the bed. I felt my mother looking down at me as I kept my eyes focused on the ceiling, counting each tile and every dot inside of each one. "Aren't you gonna look, honey?" I turned my head on to the screen to see movement. Micah's baby moving around inside of me. I looked down at my stomach for a short second.

"It's a girl." The doctor's voice rang out into my ears.

I looked back over to the screen and grinned slightly. A girl. The image of Micah holding a baby girl. The thought of when she'll be older and a guy would ask her on a date came into me. How Micah would react. I giggled a little but quickly stopped myself. The doctor looked back at me. "Congratulations." He smiled warmly.

I just smiled back as I looked back up at the screen. "You sure it's a girl?" My mom asked as I just stared at the screen, trying to forget about Micah.

He moved it around again in a circular motion. He pulled his bottom lip in between his teeth as he studied the screen once more. "Yeah, yeah, it's a girl. I'm sure." He took the thing off my stomach. "It's a girl," he stated again, giving me a small smile as we wiped off my belly, and I was able to get up. My mom helped me a little although I don't need it. If someone's going to help me around, I want it to be Micah. "You want pictures printed out?"

He looked down at me as I nodded quickly. "Yes, of course," my mom answered. He smiled again.

The car ride home was silent. I just stared out the window. When I would glance over at my mom, she had a big smile on her face. "Gonna be three girls." She looked over at me, smiling like an idiot.

I gave her a look of disgust. I didn't care if she saw me although I know she didn't. *How dare she say that to me?* I'd rather take the sixty grand and buy my own house far away from her than have her say those kinds of things to me. I just want to go home and eat something and pass out.

MICAH

Chapter 40

"Micah never raped me." I looked up at Ashley as she looked over at me and then the lawyer questioning her.

"Well, there are statements that you were the victim. If it wasn't Micah, who exactly was it?"

She looked down, not wanting to answer. This is my third trial already, and I haven't seen Kendall for a while. She actually listened to me for once. I felt Ashley's eyes land on me once more. I looked up and met her gaze while I was chewing on my lip nervously, my elbows rested on the wooden table. "It was Anthony Collier."

"Anthony Collier? Are you sure about that?"

She nodded. "Yes, sir, I am."

"Now we have witnesses saying it was indeed Micah over here." I gave him a dirty look as he pointed over at me.

"Well, they're lying. I think I would know who raped me." She spit back at him. I chuckled a little, causing my lawyer to nudge me with his elbow, and I tried to stop. That was just Ashley though. I felt a few eyes on me, giving me disapproving looks, but I didn't give a fuck.

The lawyer questioning her rose his eyebrows as she raised one of hers right back at him, which I grinned at, trying to hold in my laughter. "Okay, okay, how long ago did this happen?"

"Last year at the Roxie's."

"The strip club?"

"Yes."

"Where you work?"

"Yes."

"So you were a stripper when all of this happened?"

"Yes. I used to be. I quit sometime last year."

"Why'd you quit?"

"I got raped."

I tried holding in my laughter again, but one escaped, causing a few to look over at me again.

"Can you replay what all happened that night, day?"

"Night. Yes."

"Can you share with us?"

She looked over at me like she was scared to say it. I knew why when I looked at her eyes glancing over at me. I gave her a weak grin. She nodded. "Well, it was like eight thirty, and Micah just left the place—"

"Micah was there?"

"Yes, he came by for an hour or two and hung out with Karol and me before we were closing."

"Micah never tried anything that you two would say no to?"

"No, sir. He's not like that."

"Has Micah Harlan ever threatened you at all or anybody else at the Roxie's?"

"No, of course not . . . Micah would never hurt a woman. He's a gentleman all the time I've spent with him."

"You've spent a lot of time with Micah Harlan?"

"I guess so."

"Did you have a close relationship would you say?"

"Friendly, yes. Not an actual relationship."

"Friendly as in sexual?"

"Object your honor."

"Please, continue your story."

"We walked Micah to the front door, and his friend picked him up because he was drinking. When we went back inside, well, we started getting dressed again to go home. We both turned around when we heard a few knocks on the back door. We both looked at each other because no one was supposed to be coming over for anything, and we were the only ones there. Karol was already in her clothes, so she went to the door. Next thing I knew she was shoved back into the back dressing room with me, and Anthony was there with a small gun in his hand. He tied Karol up when he raped me and then tied me up when he raped her." She wiped her cheeks and eyes as tears rolled down them. "He threatened to kill us if we ever said anything," she whimpered a little. "So Karol killed herself a few months later when she ended up pregnant."

My eyes got glassy as I put my head down in embarrassment and put one of my hands over my forehead as I thought about Kendall.

How big her stomach must be growing. She doesn't need me though. She has her mother and her friends. She doesn't need me.

Two hours later

"Would the defendant Micah Harlan please stand."

I got up slowly, the chair screeching a little as my legs pushed it behind me. I watched as a member of the jury stood up too and glanced over at me with a serious look on her face as she looked at the judge. "Read us the verdict." I closed my eyes for a second with the memory of Kendall snuggled up against me, the first time she actually made a move on me. I have to say good-bye to that, her smile, her arms wrapped around me, holding our baby and being there when he or she is born.

"Yes, your honor. We find the defendant, Micah Harlan, not guilty on all counts of rape."

"Theft?" the judge asked.

"We find Micah Harlan, guilty."

"The use of selling and taking illegal drugs."

"Guilty."

"For the murder of Lucas Franc."

"Guilty, your honor."

The judge sighed as I was looking down, hearing each word read off the paper from the woman in the long black skirt. I already knew my mom and Candice would start weeping as soon as my sentence was declared.

"Well, Micah Harlan, with that, I have no other choice but to send you to jail. But with the circumstances of the threats by Lucas Franc here, I'd say it was self-defense. Now, with that all said, I sentence you to a total of eight years."

I heard a noise that my mom made. I just kept my eyes down as the officer came over to me to take me in. When he turned me around and I put my hands behind my back, I looked over at my mom and sister with just a plain expression on my face. My mom had tears running down her cheeks. My sister just looked stunned. I looked away when the cop pulled at my wrists, and another one came and grabbed my other arm as I was pulled through a door and down a small hallway.

KENDALL

Chapter 41

I just got off the phone with Candice. Micah was just sentenced to eight years and was guilty for only drugs and theft. I have eight years until I get to see him again. Candice was so happy that I'm having a girl, and she told her mom. I told her after she told me the bad news, and she sounded like she was crying, so I cheered her up a little bit. I haven't said a word to anybody about the money or to my mom on how I'm planning on moving out in like a year with her granddaughter.

Six months now, Micah's been gone. I had to try and keep my mind off him at least. My mom and I went and got a crib and a few things for the baby yesterday. I just got done texting with Candice asking if she and her mom wanted to come over and help set up some stuff for the baby. She said her mom was at work, but she'd come over as soon as she could. I waited for an hour and a half until someone pulled in, and there were a few knocks at the door.

"Mom, I got it!" I tried to rush to the door before her. Candice was standing there.

"Hi." I smiled.

"Oh my goodness." She smiled, bringing me into a hug.

"Come in."

I watched Candice as she looked around my home, still smiling when she saw my mom. "Hi, it's nice to see you." She went and gave my mom a hug.

"You too. Well, I have to go to work. Just be good you two." My mom waved us off. "There's food on the stove."

I grinned at Candice, feeling awkward as we both just stood there in my kitchen. "Micah, h—he didn't look that good the last time I saw him," she said softly as she stared at me. I just looked down and laughed a little. I brought my head back up and wiped my eyes with the backs of my hands. "Is that the bracelet he bought you?" She came over to me.

"Oh yeah." I smiled, showing it to her.

"He mentioned buying it for you. It's so pretty." She examined it. "Wonder how much he paid for it." She smiled, looking up at me.

"He's crazy." I laughed as tears lined the insides of my eyes, ready to spill.

"I'm sorry, I just . . ."

"I know. I'm always emotional. Come on, my room's upstairs." I led her over to the staircase and into my room.

"Wow, your room is huge."

I laughed a little. "Yeah . . ."

"They took this one girl on the stand that was like a stripper, and she was saying all this stuff about her and Micah getting together, like bragging and shit, and I just wanted to punch her." She walked over to where a few pictures of Micah and me were framed.

"A stripper?" I asked just to have a conversation.

She just looked over at me and grinned weakly. "Sorry, I just, this is a little awkward . . ."

"I know." I laughed at her. I sat on the edge of my bed with her. "Oh, I actually . . . I got something for you." I rushed over to my nightstand and opened the drawer and pulled out one of the photos of the baby.

"I—is this . . . Oh my god . . ." She stared down at it, smiling. "This is for me?"

"Your mom too. I got an extra printed out for you to keep." There were a few minutes of silence.

"How're ya feeling?" She looked down at my swollen belly.

I just scrunched up half of my nose and shrugged. Then an awkward feeling started in my stomach. It felt like I was hungry at first, like my stomach was rumbling, but I don't feel hungry. Then I thought more about it. I'm just about twenty-eight weeks pregnant. It's the baby. It's like a goldfish swimming around in there or like popcorn popping.

I sat up a little, my hands lifting a little from the mattress. "Something wrong?" I smiled. I grabbed Candice's hand and set it on my lump. "What—" She smiled.

"You feel it?" I asked, smiling.

She nodded. "That's so cool." She was staring at my tummy while glancing up at me. "Does it hurt?"

I shook my head. "Feels like popcorn just popping." I giggled. "Or something fluttering, like butterflies, I guess." I chuckled at myself.

She moved her hand around. She looked up at me seriously. "You'll be a great mom." I smiled at her.

I took my lip between my teeth as I started to stand up. Candice instantly grabbed my arm and back, helping me hoist myself up better. I walked over to the dresser on the far side of my bedroom. I opened the drawer and grabbed the ten envelopes and started walking back over to Candice and sat on the bed slowly and set them all down on to the soft quilt.

"What are these?" She looked at them and then me, puzzled.

"Micah, he sent me to this guy. He ha—was holding money for him. He told me to take it all and keep it for the baby and me."

"What—"

"It's sixty grand." I looked down at all of them.

"Wait. What?" She said, laughing awkwardly.

"I've counted it several times. I didn't believe it either. He wants me to move on. I guess he thought I'd listen." I handed her the letter from him. "Josh delivered it to me." She opened and began reading it closely.

"What're you going to do?" she whispered.

"I'm not moving on, Candice." I smiled.

She leaned in and hugged me. "Am I supposed to be helping with something more than a crib here?"

I shrugged my shoulders. "I just don't know who else to tell . . ."

"Where the hell did he get all of this money?" she asked quickly as she went through a stack of it.

I shook my head.

"He never said anything about this Newton guy?"

"Not before the letter, no. He looked like four or five years older than 'im too."

She rolled her eyes.

***

After like an hour, Candice and I were actually able to set up the furniture for the baby. "Have you thought of any names?" I didn't look up to meet her gaze on me. Honestly, I've never thought of it. I never wanted to. If I wanted to discuss names, I wanted to do so with Micah. What names would he and I agree and disagree on.

"No," I said quietly.

"Not even thought about it?" I shook my head. There was a moment of silence, almost like she understood why. "Any names you can think of right now."

I shook my head again. "I just never had the time to think about it, I guess."

"Anything else to do?"

"No."

"Okay, well . . . you're good while she's at work on your own?"

"Of course. I'm just fat is all really."

Candice giggled a little at me as I just smiled.

"Okay, well, I should be going then." We both walked to the front door. "Thanks for inviting me to help out." She hugged me.

I walked slowly back upstairs still with the awkward fluttering sensations in my belly. *How am I going to raise a baby without Micah there?* I almost don't even want my mother to help at all. It may help the baby and all, but not me really.

I couldn't take my eyes off the crib and stand we set up with the pink cushions and animal print blankets. I curled my lip between my teeth. I felt my eyes swelling up slowly. I furrowed my eyebrows. The thought of Micah never seeing his daughter in person as a newborn eating away at me. He'll never have the chance to hold her when she's a small baby. He won't be there to hold my hand when she is born. He won't be there for her first birthday party.

I sat on my bed and just looked over at the picture of Micah and me. That's when I lost it. His hair now completely back to brown. I won't see it for years. Three damn years I have to wait to wrap my arms around him and say I love him again to his face. The last time I saw him, his eyes were dull and lifeless, his skin pale from lack of sunlight. His face lighted up when we met gazes, but that was it. He was already gone, changed. I just cried myself to sleep uncontrollably.

Chapter 42

Nine months without Micah went by slowly. It's gotten harder to walk. Everything has been set up for the baby around the house. I think my mom is more excited than me though. *How could I be enjoying myself though?* Sure there are things to look forward to, but without him being able to be there, how can it seem exciting? He's missing out on his daughter's life.

I still haven't thought of a name yet. Every name I choose that I really like, I think about what Micah would think about it, then I just try to pick another. Just every name I pick I have second doubts about. None seems to fit. Then again, I can't picture Micah saying anything to our daughter.

I haven't said a word to anyone yet besides Candice about the money in my bedroom. *How do I tell my mom everything I know about Micah's past?* Even then, I don't know how Micah had $60,000 in cash stored away with some guy at a bar.

The kicking is more frequent every day. I like feeling it, it's like a part of Micah was left behind for me. Every night, the only way I could seem to fall asleep was by crying unit I just eventually passed out. I just wasn't able to cry tonight, like I haven't got any more left in me to cry. *How am I supposed to sleep now?*

I've seen this before. Where am I? Micah's bedroom. His bedroom at his mother's house, the house he "grew up" in. It's spotless. I looked to the window, my vision blurred until I focused on one thing. I looked down at my feet, then a crying sound erupted. "There's mommy, yeah?" *A baby's voice said, but it wasn't a baby, it was a man's trying to sound like a baby.*

I looked up in the direction. His back was to me. Dark brown hair laying messily on top of his head. It was like a jail jumpsuit the man was wearing. Who is he? Micah. My Micah. "Micah," *I cried out.*

"Mommy's behind me, isn't she? She was lucky to have you, I ruined her," he talked again with his head down, his back still to me as he sat on his small bed with his feet up, facing the headboard.

"Micah?" I whispered, feeling confused. His head lifted, and he turned it slowly around until his eyes met mine. They were a darker shade of green to me. He just stared at me. I started walking closer, aching to wrap my arms around him and feel his lips against mine, their warm touch on my skin . . .

He looked back down. Once I got closer, he stood up from the bed. He had like something small wrapped up in a blanket. He turned but didn't face me as he set it on the bed. "There you go, sweetheart." I noticed then the small hands. They were moving around, reaching out back to Micah to hold her. Her small giraffe blanket fell from covering her body from her wiggling so much. She was instantly beautiful to me, precious. She's just so small. I started walking toward her. She was just making random noises, whimpering. An object stopped me from picking her up.

"Micah?" I got confused when his arm prevented me from getting any closer.

I looked up at his face. Sadness. Disappointment. I looked back down at the baby quickly. She wasn't moving. Limp and lifeless. There was blood suddenly drenching her pink outfit, her small plush blanket, and where she was sat. I felt warm tears tickling my skin, as they slid down. I looked back up at Micah. He was covered in blood. He looked like he was holding back tears. "I didn't mean to," he said softly as he cried. He lifted both of his hands. A sharp-looking blade in one hand, both covered in blood. "She just wouldn't stop crying, Ken. I didn't know what else to do." He wept. He rushed closer to me as he took me into a hug.

"What have you done?" I tried to scream at him, but the words just didn't sound loud enough.

"Shhh . . ." He wrapped his arms around me tightly. "She's not crying anymore. Don't worry about her," he whispered as he lifted his head from my shoulder to place a kiss to the side of my head, pressing down hard against my hair and scalp. I refused to hug him back as I shoved him away. His looked angered and confused like I triggered something within him. His eyes seemed to turn a darker shade of green as he stared at me. "Don't you love me?" I just stared in shock. I want to go home. I thought about clicking my heels together and saying over and over again there's no place like home. I would just look stupid and silly if that didn't work, but who's the one who just stabbed their own daughter to death.

His face instantly softened by looking at my face as I cried. "I was just trying to help . . ." He let the tears fall down his cheeks.

I didn't have any time to respond to him, to do anything as he grabbed ahold of my shoulder tightly. The next thing I knew there was a throbbing and unbelievable pain shooting all through my stomach, up and down.

"Kendall! Kendall!" I suddenly shot up, my mother hovering over top of me. "Honey, are you all right?" she asked frantically. "You were screaming."

"Mom?" I asked quickly as I sat up but felt a pain in my stomach as I tried. My stomach hurt so badly. I cried out in pain, while my hands stayed planted on my throbbing tummy. "Mom . . ." I cried, feeling scared. "Something's wrong," I cried quickly over to her.

"You may be in labor."

I looked at her, terrified. "What? No? No, he, he just stab—" I stopped myself. It was only a dream.

"What?" She shook her head, realizing I was just having a dream. No nightmare to me would ever have Micah in it. It just couldn't be a nightmare. "We have to get you to the hospital."

She helped me all the way to the car; it was hard. The pain came every ten minutes or so. The drive seemed to take forever as my mom made some calls on the way. I wasn't paying any attention to who. I couldn't.

The pain was too strong for me to take anymore.

***

When I woke back up, a nurse was standing there. "Oh, you're up." She walked over to me. "How do you feel, Ms. Starla?"

I wiped my tired eyes. "Better." I laughed tiredly.

"That's good. First time for me to have a patient pass out after giving birth." She laughed. I just smiled back to her.

"I—is she, well . . . yeah, okay and all? She's healthy and all?"

"She's wonderful. She's perfectly healthy, miss."

I smiled in relief as I closed my eyes. "Where—where is she?"

"Would you like to see her?" I nodded, an uncontrollable smile erupting on my face. The nurse smiled and walked out of the room.

I want to see her and know that she's all right for myself. Just Micah popped into my head right then. He stabbed me, her. No. I shook my head. No, he didn't. It was only a dream. You have weird dreams when you're pregnant I know. *But what did all that mean?*

The pain giving birth was horrible. I had my eyes closed most of the time, squeezing them shut. As soon as I heard a faint cry, I just let myself pass out. I let out a brief laugh, making fun of myself.

My mom walked through the door a moment later, the biggest smile on her face as the nurse walked in behind her with the baby in her hands. She placed her down gently in my arms. I already knew how to hold her. Once she was all settled into my arms in her small blanket, I had the chance to actually study her. She was the spitting image of the baby from my dream. Micah was holding her as a small baby. I looked around the room not seeing him and felt awkwardly sad and relieved at the same time.

I smiled down at her as she stared up at me and giggled. "I noticed that she has Micah's eyes," my mom said softly as she looked down at her. I looked up to her eyes. The same mossy green as Micah's. They were beautiful on her.

"Yeah," I whispered.

"Do you have a name for her?" I looked over at the nurse who was waiting to ask it.

I looked up at her, biting my lip. I looked back down at the baby in my arms. I couldn't think of anything for a minute. Candice walked in with her mom. I smiled over at them. I looked from them back down to the baby. One just suddenly came to me. "Mia." I smiled over at the nurse.

"That's a nice name," she said as she wrote it down. "Last name?"

I looked over at Micah's mom, questioning. She nodded with a smile on her face. "Mia Harlan." I looked up at the nurse again.

Micah's mom held her after my mom did for a few minutes. "Hey, Mom, can you call a few numbers for me and tell them?"

"Yeah, who?"

"They're in my phone. Just go to Shailene, and then can you call Josh? They're Micah's friends."

She just nodded as she left the room. Micah's mom looked so happy with Mia in her arms. Candice was smiling over at her, grabbing on to her hand and laughing. "She's beautiful, Kendall." His mom looked over at me.

I smiled. She was so small I wondered how much smaller she would look in Micah's arms while he smiled and told her she was beautiful. I was shown how to nurse and cuddle her into her blanket with the nurse and my mom's help. I wanted Micah's mom and sister to be there with Mia as long as they wanted.

Shailene, Savanna, Emily, and even Sadie came an hour or two later, and we talked for a while. My mom went and got some things ready and said she'd bring me a change of clothes for tomorrow. The nurse came and got Mia for a few things. I thought I was going to sleep good tonight. I closed my eyes still with the same silly grin on my face every time I look at Mia.

The room seemed darker when I opened my eyes. I felt a cold sensation on my arm. I looked over to see the brown messy long hair looking down at my arm. When he looked up, I instantly knew it was Micah. He had facial hair now. It looked like he hasn't shaved in months. His eyes still dull and lifeless-looking. "Do I frighten you?"

I shook my head quickly.

"You're a bad liar." *I looked down at his hands. Red. I looked over past to the door, praying that someone was going to walk in. He was in his jumpsuit still from the jail. It doesn't really look like him all that much anymore, but it is. Micah was gone when I looked back over to where he was standing. I looked around frantically, panicking. I looked over by the window. He was there in one of the visitor's chairs, his head in his hands. He looked up at me, his eyes swollen from sadness.* "I was just trying to help," *he whispered while crying at the same time. My eyes widened.*

"What did you do?" *I screamed over at him.*

"She's so beautiful," *he whispered.*

"Kendall, honey." I felt a shaking on my shoulder. My mom.

"Mom?" I looked up at her.

"Um, your, Micah's friend, Josh, is here with his wife." I sat up in the bed. "Are you okay?"

"Yeah, yeah, I'm fine." I looked over at the chair by the window.

"You want to see them?"

I nodded quickly. My mom walked away into the hall, and the nurse walked in with Mia in her arms. She handed her to me to feed her. "I told them she has to eat first, then your friends can come in. Unless you want to see them now?"

I laughed. "They can wait."

After Mia was fed, the nurse went and told Josh that he could come in.

Mia wrapped her small fingers around my index finger as she was lying in my arms. I was so caught up in watching and smiling at her that when Josh spoke, I looked up quickly but smiled. "Sorry." He laughed.

I shook my head, smiling at him. "This is Bailey." I looked over at the girl beside him, smiling.

"Nice to meet you." I smiled.

Josh and she walked over closer to me. "You too."

"Her name's Mia?" He looked up at me from her.

"Yeah," I whispered. Mia wrapped her hand around Josh's finger that caused him to laugh.

"Starla?"

I shook my head. "Harlan."

"Thanks for calling us." He looked up at me seriously.

"Yeah, of course. I want you both in her life." I smiled down at her.

"She looks just like him." I looked up at Bailey. I grinned. She closed her eyes when she shook her head. "I'm sorry, I shouldn't of . . ."

"It's fine," I reassured her honestly. I looked back up at Josh. "You wanna hold her?"

He looked surprised. "Oh." He looked sort of scared. "No. I've never—"

"It's easy." I giggled. "Here." He bent down and held out his arms a little.

"Okay," I said as I handed her off. Josh brought her close to his chest.

Mia let out a little whimper as she threw one of her small hands up, acting a little fussy. Josh laughed at her as he cradled her small body. "She's gorgeous." He glanced up at me. "Hi," he cooed down at her. Bailey came over and sat on the chair beside me.

"Micah's lucky to have you."

"How did you two meet?" I asked curiously as I watched Josh walk around the room with Mia in his arms.

"I, um . . ." She thought about it. "It's not the way you're probably thinking." She laughed. "I guess it was like in the same week he left home. He came asking my friends and me what town he was in. He looked so different then." She looked down, smiling, remembering the moment. "He was so shy." She laughed. "So . . . uh . . . he knows about her then?" She looked over at Mia and Josh.

"I . . . yeah, he knows I was pregnant."

"Oh, I told him." We both looked over at Josh.

"What?" I asked quickly.

He got confused, looking. "I, yesterday . . . after your mother called me, I was on my way to visit him, and . . . I told him you had your baby yesterday."

"What'd he say?"

"Did you not want him to know?"

"Josh, what'd he say about it?" I asked again.

"He, he just stared at me and then smiled and asked about it and everything. He was happy . . . He wept a little."

I shook my head a little, looking down, knowing that I was acting crazy. "I'm sorry. No. I wanted him to know and all . . . I just never . . ." I stopped as my eyes got glassy.

Before Josh and Bailey left, she took a picture of him holding her. Josh gave me a hug too before they went.

"How you feeling, sweetie?" I looked up at my mom as she grabbed my bag for me.

"I'm okay." I shrugged my shoulders. "Just . . . sore, I guess." I felt a little embarrassed. My mom and I walked to the nursery area to get Mia to take home with us. "Josh said he told Micah about me going into labor and having the baby before he came," I spoke awkwardly as my mom and I got to the nursery.

"Is that okay?"

"Yeah." I paused. "Of course, it is . . . She's his daughter."

Mia slept the whole car ride home, which I was glad for. I haven't really heard her cry yet. Right after she was born, I passed out, and she was well calm and pretty much peaceful the entire time I've spent with her at the hospital. She only really fussed a bit after Josh held her for a few minutes.

I was glad how happy Josh seemed to hold her and speak like a baby to her, smiling the whole time in the process.

Chapter 43

The first night with Mia in my room was hectic. She seemed to wake up every ten minutes. After a week, it was still bad but not as bad, as she got up to a half an hour. After a month, she was up to an hour. I was tired every day, and late at night, I would just start crying. I wanted Micah to be here with her and for him to get up before me to tend to her.

After changing Mia, I set her down in the crib. She started wiggling around and giggling. She is three months old now. Mia was still almost as tiny as she was when she was born. When I laid down that night and every other night, I just laid there and tried to picture what Micah looks like now. *Raggedy? Hairy? Older? Bad? Good? Sleepy?*

I looked back over at the crib, and she started making some noise. It was like ten thirty when I looked at my phone. I got up and walked over to Mia and looked down at her. I reached my arms down and scooped her up against my chest and cradled her in my arms. I started walking around in my room while holding and looking down at her sweet face. She was just making a whimpering sound like she was about to cry.

"It's okay, little baby. It's okay, Mia honey. Don't cry, sweetheart." I smiled down at her once she relaxed better. "Why're you sad, honey? It's okay. Don't cry." I sat on the edge of my bed with her. "You miss daddy?" I paused, thinking if I could even say his name to her without losing it. Probably not. "It's okay, honey, daddy will be home before you know it. He loves you so much I know." She stared up at me. "His name's Micah." She giggled, which made me smile. *Why do people mock or laugh at his name?* "Don't you like his name? It has Mia in it." I giggled back at her, which made her only do it more. "You have his pretty eyes, honey."

"Kendall. Oh, I didn't mean to interrupt anything." My mom smiled in my doorway.

I wiped my eyes quickly and looked up at her. I shook my head. "What is it?"

"Someone is at the door for you. He, well, kind of came inside. I don't know who he is." Her voice shaking.

"What? You just let them in?"

"He said he really needs to talk to you." She paused. "I've never seen him before."

"Here, just take Mia. I'll go."

"No, honey."

"Mom, none of the guys who associate with Micah have ever lied to me. He needs to talk." I handed little Mia over to her. She still followed me down the steps though.

When I walked into the kitchen, there were three men standing there, looking around. I swallowed the nerves, so I could talk. "Hello." I got their attention quickly.

"Kendall," Newton turned around, smiling.

"Newton? Who—what ya—you doing here?"

He looked over at one of the guys, still smiling. When he looked back over, he looked over into the living room. "This your baby?"

I looked back to my mom and Mia. "Yeah," I whispered.

"Can I see her?"

"Why are you here? I got the money. What you want?"

He looked a little shocked at me. "Kendall." He laughed.

I looked back at my mom and walked over to her for Mia. She was holding her close, while she just looked around, sort of smiling. "Kendall? Who are they?" she whispered.

I looked at her seriously. "Mom, it's okay. They won't hurt us." I grabbed on to Mia. "Come on, sweetie."

"Does this have to do with him?"

I just stared at her for a moment before I walked back into the kitchen with Mia in my arms. Newton smiled at Mia, which had her giggling. "Mia, this is Newton." I looked from her to Newton's face.

"She looks a lot like him." He smiled at her as I held her closely to me.

I just grinned back. "Who are you two?" I looked over at the other men with Newton.

"This is Logan Blanch and Aaron Flincher."

I looked at both of them. Logan stared at me like he already knew who I was. "Flincher?" I looked back at Newton.

Aaron laughed a little. "He was just my cousin. We weren't really close."

I weakly grinned for a quick second, still holding Mia as close as I could possibly to my body. "So what was it you guys wanted?"

Newton looked at both of the other guys before looking back at me. "I didn't fully believe that you were with Micah. The letter just didn't sound at all like him." He laughed a little. "I visited him in jail. And um . . . wow. He looks like another man." He chuckled. "He's turned into a different man from when I knew him."

"So what's going on?"

"I told him about a visit from a young pregnant lady and told him that her name was Kendall and showed him picture of her, turns out I can trust you and little Mia here." He smiled. "I came here to give you the rest of the money."

I paused in a little shock. "Money? What'd you mean? You gave me the money?"

"I did, I know. Sixty grand of it."

"You're saying there's more?"

He smiled in amusement. "Who's this lady?"

"Kendall, what's going on?" She took Mia from me.

"This is my mom."

"Nice to meet you." Newton smiled.

"What's going on? What do you men want?" Newton and Aaron both looked at my mom, a little surprised as Newton smiling at her. Logan just kept staring at me for some reason, making me even more uncomfortable.

"How much more money?" I sort of whispered to Newton.

He grinned with his hands in his front pockets. "Kendall, what's going on? What money?"

"Forty."

"Forty? Forty what?"

My eyes got big and mouth fell slightly open. "Aaron." He turned toward him. Aaron grabbed a briefcase and set it on the counter. I looked from it to Newton. He was only grinning. "We'll be seeing you." Newton smiled to me as he began walking toward the door. "Mrs. Starla, Mia."

That only caused my mom to hold her granddaughter even closer to her body protectively as if someone was going to rip her away from us. Aaron smirked at my mom, while Logan seemed the most normal out of all three of them. When they stepped outside, the slight breeze blew Newton's jacket back a little bit to reveal that he had a gun on him. *Would he of killed me? Why's he edgy around me?*

As soon as the door closed and the sound of a car pulling away, my mother looked at the counter. "Kendall, honey, who—what's going on?"

"Micah left me money," I whispered. "He gave me all of his money he had saved."

"What? How much? What do you mean?"

"We have a hundred thousand dollars now."

"What?"

I looked up at her.

I showed my mom all of the other money, and she counted it all a few times because she was just shaking. I showed her Micah's letter, everything. One word I can think of to describe her state right now is just shock. I took Mia upstairs to go to sleep. I started rocking her in my arms, my eyes welling up. "Daddy cares about you so much."

She closed her eyes to sleep right when I slid her small blanket over her petite, pudgy body. I looked over my shoulder quickly when my phone started buzzing. I walked over to where it was. "Hello?"

"Kendall? Kendall, are you okay? Are you all right?"

"Josh, what's going on?" I chuckled a little.

"Micah gave me a call today. Is a guy named . . . uh . . . Newton there?"

"No. He just left actually."

"What'd he say?"

"What'd Micah say?" I asked quickly but quietly to not wake Mia.

"He told me to go to your house and to bring your mom, Mia, and you to stay at my place."

I didn't understand what was really happening. *What did Newton and Micah really talk about?* "Josh, what's going on?" I whispered.

"He just wants you three to be safe. Kendall, he was serious."

"He just gave me the rest of his saved up money. He brought two other guys with him. He met Mia and stuff . . . When he was leaving, I saw a gun on him."

"He didn't hurt any of you?"

I shook my head. I closed my eyes to stop myself from breaking down and waking Mia back up. "No," I cried a little.

"Well . . . he thinks he will. How much of the money did you get?"

I took a few moments to calm myself down. "A hundred thousand."

"Hell." He laughed. I laughed back, smiling as I sat on the edge of my bed. "Mia sleeping then?"

I nodded, wiping my eyes. "Yeah, for a while now."

"You said that Newton came to your house?"

"Yeah."

"Did you tell him where you live?" I froze. I didn't say anything personal to him that one day. Micah told me not to make conversation really, so I didn't. *Did he have someone follow me? Did he have me tracked down?* I started crying softly.

"What am I going to do? I can't just move." I sobbed quietly into the phone.

"Kendall, it's okay, you can—"

"You don't want us there with you and Bailey. We have Mia. She'll wake you both up through the night."

"We wouldn't care. Micah's like my brother. We'd do this for him to keep you all safe."

"Josh, we can't just pick up and come over. Just . . . I don't know. We'll talk tomorrow."

"Everything's going all right?"

"Yeah, yeah, everything's fine. You should have seen my mom's face when she saw all of that money." I laughed.

"She knows?"

"I've told her enough."

Chapter 44

Mia's eight months old today. My mom and I just decided to take her to the park for a while. I finished packing her small bag of anything she might need and strapping her into her car seat. My mom and I took pictures of her in the baby swing and a few of her and me. I was just sitting on the bench now, going through some of the pictures we took like half an hour ago. My mom had her on the swing again. I looked up every minute or so to see Mia still giggling while my mom spent time with her.

I looked around for a second and then back down at my camera, clicking over to the next photo. I paused. I looked back up slowly and looked around again. I glanced down at the camera, setting it back in the bag. I stared at the man for a quick few seconds. I zipped up Mia's bag and stood up and started walking over to him. *Who does he think he is? Micah is gone, why is he harassing us?* He has no right to be here.

I stormed over to his parked car where he stood there, staring me down while he leaned his back against the closed front door. "What the hell are you doing?" I asked angrily while crossing my arms over my chest and waited impatiently for an answer.

He just looked from Mia and my mom back over to me and smirked. "Just keeping an eye on you all," he said casually, still with the twisted smirk plastered on his face.

"What the hell is that supposed to mean?" I raised my voice, probably catching my mother's attention.

"Nice seeing you again." He smiled while turning around and opening his car door to climb in.

"No! You're telling me why you are here right now!" I stomped closer toward him, catching his broad shoulder in my small hand tightly to turn him around. He stared at me plainly. I know he has to have some kind of weapon with him, but we're in a public place, giving me more confidence to do or say what I want. He ignored me, only staring at my face. "Logan?" I got more and more impudent with him.

"Newton will take his money back if you don't leave soon," he said softly, a hint of pity in his blue eyes.

I got confused immediately after he said that. "Excuse me? That was never Newton's money to begin with. It always belonged to Micah. Newton only held on to it for him."

He sighed. "What's Micah going to do about it? How much time is he spending in that pigpen? Ten years? Good luck with the problems he left you with." He slammed his car door and started his engine.

I stood at the curb as his car sped down the street. *What's he talking about? Did he come here to warn me? Or to actually keep an eye on us? But why?* I licked my lips before I turned around. I walked quickly back to my mom and Mia who were standing by the bench, Mia cuddled up against her chest. She started smiling and giggling when she saw me and started leaning over to me for me to hold her instead. I picked her bag and slung it over my shoulder.

"Who was that, sweetheart?" My mom's voice spoke behind me.

"We have to stay at Josh's for a few days."

"Josh? Micah's old friend? What's happening?"

"They're still friends," I said while taking Mia into my arms, and my mom walked by my side as we walked back toward the car.

I opened the backseat to strap Mia in. She wouldn't stop wiggling and whimpering like she was about to cry. "Come on, Mia, you have to hold still, honey." I tried again to slick her belts together.

She just kept moving her body around being really fussy now. "Mia!" I shouted, getting too irritated at her as she started pouting.

"Here, sweetie, I got it." My mom grabbed my shoulders lightly, getting me out of the way.

I stepped aside as my mom took over, trying to strap her in safely. Her crying slowed down and got quieter. "It's okay, honey." My mom kept soothing her. "Mommy's not feeling good is all." I tucked my hair behind my ear. My mom finally got her strapped in, and she only snuffled her nose a few times after she cried for like ten minutes.

My mom turned to me as I got into the front with her. "Kendall, we can't just go stay with Micah's friends. If they're after you, you have to go to the police! Not just run."

"Mom! You don't understand, do you? Micah was a drug dealer! People fear him. That's where he gets all of his money from! Newton was his partner, I guess. They won't just take the money back, Mom! If they know we went to the cops, they'd kill all of us! Not just me. They'll take Mia away and sell her or something and probably kill you! We have to go to Josh's. I can trust him." She just stared at me, her mouth slightly hanging open. I was sobbing quietly now as Mia started making noises like she was speaking, but it was only mumbles of nonexistent words. "We have to!" I spoke loudly.

"Have you talked to Josh about this yet? Where does he even live?"

I calmed down knowing that I've convinced her. "He did the other night. He told me that Micah told him to move us in with him. He offered it to me already. I can ask him for his address."

***

Packing to go to Josh's was hard. We didn't want anybody seeing us packing bags into our car. Logan would drive by at random times of the day as well as a few other men that you just know who they're working for. *How did Micah get involved with them?* I carried Mia down the steps and set her in her play yard in the living room. "Stay here, honey." I told her before walking into the kitchen.

I walked in to see my mom getting Mia's bottles packed up and getting some formula ready for her next feeding. "I got most of her stuff ready, just whatever is in your room, I guess."

"Okay, thanks."

My mom turned and looked at me seriously. "How long do we have to stay?"

I just looked down at the counter and shrugged. "Until we find somewhere else to go." I kept my eyes glued to the counter, counting the specks in the granite. "I'm sorry," I whispered.

"For what?"

"I got us into this," I admitted quietly.

"This is Micah's fault, not yours."

I looked up at her quickly. "Are you trying to say that he did this on purpose?" I raised my voice. "You think that he planned all of this? That he would want this? Are you serious? You have no idea what he's been through! He doesn't deserve to be where he is!"

She just stared at me in shock. By now, my eyes were barely watering. It wasn't because I was yelling at her but because of what she just said about Micah. "He knocked you up and left you with all these people to worry about. I'm glad you have Mia and all, but look where she is now. She is going to grow up without a father now, Kendall, all because of what Micah has done."

I just stared at her. I took the bottle of formula and went back into the living room and picked Mia up into my arms. She was crying now. I patted her back gently, while I walked up the stairs. I sat on the edge of my bed and cradled Mia in my arms while trying to give her the bottle. She just kept pushing it away.

"Mia, stop it. Just take it." I tried to not raise my voice at her. I tried giving it to her again, but her hands shoved it away again. I stopped for a second. "Mia, please," I whispered. She actually seemed to calm down a little more. I tried one last time. She finally accepted it. I sighed as she started drinking it down. "Daddy didn't do it on purpose sweetheart. He loves you."

I packed some of mine and Mia's clothes while she took a nap. I packed enough for two weeks for both of us plus some of her toys and a few packs of diapers and some blankets. Josh would be here in ten minutes to pick us up to go to his house.

When he got here, he help my mom and I put some bags into the car along with Mia's car seat into his backseat. He made sure that nobody was around before we left. I kept the money just in one of my duffle bags in the backseat beside me. When we got to Josh's house, we already had a crib set up in the guest bedroom that Micah had to sleep in before. After everything, my mom was already asleep in bed, Mia passed out in her crib in only a minute.

"Everything okay?" I walked out into the hall to see Josh standing there.

I bit my lip as I just stared up at him. I wanted to just break down right there and crawl into the corner. Instead of doing just that, I just wrapped my arms around him. It felt so different compared to hugging my Micah. His muscles were defined but just didn't feel like Micah's. He wasn't as tall and broad in the shoulders, making me feel safer, although I doubt that Josh would let somebody just kill me. "Thank you," I mumbled into his chest. I felt his arms go around my back as he kissed the top of my head.

"Everybody's sleeping," he whispered. My eyes instantly widened as I pulled away quickly.

"I'm sorry." I shook my head, closing my eyes in shock.

I heard him chuckle lightly under his breath. "Kendall."

"Look, Josh, I, I—"

"I wasn't meaning that. You have a kid with him . . . I was just saying that I was just checking on you and seeing how you were and all." He laughed. I sighed in relief. I laughed at myself for being so stupid.

Mia started crying. I looked over at the clock. Five forty-five. My mom was sound asleep. I got up, tossing the covers on to her still body. She was getting good at sleeping through the night. I lifted her and started rubbing her back to try and soothe her. She just kept on crying. I looked over at my mom as she was mumbling something. She has to get up early. I left the spare room and walked around into the living room with her. She had calmed down in about ten minutes after I gave her a bottle.

***

Mia started crawling when she was five months old. I wish I would have thought of recording it. I walked out with her in my arms when I woke back up at eleven, and my mom was already gone for the day. "I was confused last night when I heard her crying." Josh laughed.

"Sorry." I looked down, a little embarrassed as I finished getting Mia's next bottle ready. "I'm looking for a place today." I readjusted Mia on my hip slightly.

"Oh no, I didn't mean it that way. I was just saying."

"So where's Bailey?" I changed the subject quickly.

"She left for work this morning."

"Oh." I cleaned up my mess. "When do you have to go to work?"

"Twelve. I have a client, so I actually have to leave in a minute."

When Josh left, I was all alone with Mia. I had her sitting in her play yard in the guest bedroom, while I had my laptop out on the bed, looking at apartments for sale. After a good two hours, I did find one that I really like. It looked cozy. Some of the walls were brick, and it had two bedrooms right beside each other. The kitchen came with appliances and wooden countertops. It was twenty-five grand. I don't think it is a too high of a price really for what it is. I looked through all of the pictures more than ten times before deciding that it's the one that I want. Every time that I did go through them though, I only thought about Micah and how he'd like it.

MICAH

Chapter 45

I missed her first birthday and her second. She and Kendall are all I can seem to think of even two years later. Two years. I haven't been able to see her in two years. I can't just sit in the corner and cry about it though, not here. I don't feel like the same guy really being in here. Six more fucking years I have to still spend in this hellhole. There isn't all that much to do. You don't make friends, you make allies. As weird as that sounds, it's true.

The guards are all complete dicks and fucking showoffs. They don't seem to mess with me. I've been working out every time there were weights or anything to use by me. It gets boring. After two damn years, it still doesn't make anything more fun, maybe a little more comfortable. Something that will never seem more comfortable though is the damn bed I have to sleep on. It's pathetic really. I never really thought about how special my actual bed was until now. Well, that's not entirely true. Before Kendall, when I'd go to a girl's house, their beds weren't always the best. That was just another reason for me to leave, not like what I told them though. I would wait until they were asleep. I never wanted anything with any of them so what was the point in staying the night in the first place? I mentally killed myself after Kendall and I had sex and it was her first time, and then I picked my clothes up from the floor to get dressed and leave. *How could I do that to her?* She can't even be compared to a whore like the other girls. I could tell that she'd never even seen a naked guy before. Her expression was actually kind of funny. I didn't laugh to make her any more nervous than she already was. Her breathing was so heavy, her heart was pounding, and her hands were shaky.

That's why I wouldn't always wear a shirt around her. I loved the reaction I got. Her eyes would get wide, and she would fidget around.

I did it the first time because I started to really like her. I wanted to know if she was used to see a guy's chest. I never got that reaction before just by doing something as simple as taking my shirt off.

Thinking of that guy at the party where I first saw her makes me sick to this day. Not exactly with the reminder of his hands forcing themselves to move around on her body. It's the reminder of what I was thinking about. It had nothing to do with actually saving her from him. I could care less about her. She was just another girl to me at first. I only wanted her on my bed and not his. The thought just makes me nauseous now. *How could I ever let myself be like that? To think that way about somebody as innocent as Kendall is?*

Last week, Josh was here just to say a few things. He just told me about how the gym was going and asked how I was doing and other boring things. After we both laughed a little, I got serious. I couldn't even make eye contact with him when I asked how they were doing. I got another picture of Mia from him. It was from her second birthday party. I put my hand over my mouth and looked up at Josh as he stared at me, wanting to see my reaction. I wiped my eyes. She had on a light pink dress with dark pink polka dots. Kendall had her on her lap as the picture was taken by somebody who Josh said was her cousin. She's just beautiful, they both are. Her hair had little curls in it. Her eyes were a mossy green like mine. She was smiling as where Kendall wasn't even looking. It looked like she was talking to someone else beside her.

There seems to be some kind of fight every week really. I just stand by and watch normally. When I first got here for the first year, I was on a medication to help with my addiction. My nightmares started to die down from it, which helped me sleep a whole lot better. Now just to get a new damn bed, and I'll sleep almost perfect.

One of the worst things about being on the inside is that your life is mostly controlled by people who are ignorant or stupid and that could care less if you live or die. When I first got here, it was almost fight after fight, each one just ending with me having a bloody nose. One of the worst things really besides the bed and toilet placed right beside it is that the prison becomes like your universe. On the outside, there are different faces every day to look at. In here, it's the same damn people, every single day.

Another thing that really sucks is when they finally give you food that you actually really like. Like this one chicken we were getting, and then one day, they decide they're not going to be serving it any longer. *What the hell?* I loved that chicken. It was a big deal, and a few almost tried to kill the people who just serve the food. On the outside, you can simply find another place with something similar, if they sold out in the store, and you can just wait until the next shipment. Not here. It's gone, and it's not coming back. One thing that you may like, it's like they know that, and they take it away just for a laugh at us, to have the power to control how people eat and what they're allowed to do. That's their problem.

I haven't been in a fight in a whole year. That's hard especially in here. Being in here with the same idiotic people who are murderers, rapists, robbers, and just sick people. One guy, Richard, has two kids, one only two like Mia.

I sat at dinner just thinking about Mia. Everybody was prattling. It gets annoying. They sound so stupid and annoying the more they go on. One guy, sixty-three years old, is a dumb bastard. I hate him. At first, you think he's a nice guy. His head is bald on top, and his eyes are dopey. He looks just like any other sweet old man who's had a rough time to the naked eye, but underneath, he's disturbing. When one man told me about what he'd done to a few little girls made me feel like I was mind raped. I looked at him differently after that. Others say he's innocent, but he couldn't get a good enough lawyer, and the girls' father was extremely wealthy and made sure the old prick was sent for seventy years to life. I don't really know what to believe, but since I have Mia, I can't even consider talking to someone who may even have just a bad rumor about him going around like that. No father would, I don't think so. He tells jokes every day though at lunch. His eyes are always watery every day. He was married, and his wife left right after she heard about what supposedly her husband had done, and they had three sons and a daughter who had just had a daughter herself at thirty. I always listen to him even though I don't want to talk to him. Every time we would look at each other, he would give me a weak smile. He was eating his food just like he always did and was talking up a storm to everyone around him; they were his new family. He's nice and listens to everyone. His oldest son, Henry, sends him mail every week with a new joke on it that he shares, some he writes when we're all locked up back in the cells. He's pretty damn good too. They're funny actually, seriously, they crack you up. Or maybe it's just because you don't hear them often, and they seem funny, or some are just trying to be nice because they feel bad, or next time we're getting shower, they think he'll ram his dick into your ass from behind and rape you for not laughing at them the correct way.

"So what's so funny today?" one asked him.

I tuned out after that and looked back down at my plate that only consisted of a slice of ham, a biscuit, and a sandwich. Richard sat across me eating his although he didn't seem to like it. "What'd you do?" I looked up at him.

He stopped chewing. We never really talk often, so it was weird. "I—I, uh . . ." He sighed. "I helped rob a bank."

I rose my eyebrows. "Wow." I laughed.

"Yeah." He smiled, rolling his eyes. "The mother, she's your wife?"

I didn't understand what he was talking about. *My wife?* Nobody ever thought of Kendall to be my wife. I don't even know if we are still boyfriend and girlfriend after two years of no face-to-face contact. I gave Josh a few notes just with a simple "I love you" on it. She never replied in any sort of way, which I sort of expected but hoped she would do something. I was expecting her to just come and sign in to visit me, ignoring my first letter for her to not come and forget about me. No. She listened for once.

I shook my head. "No, she isn't." I looked down, smiling at the thought. "We only dated for a few months before . . . this." I looked around.

"Past tense?"

"I don't know. I haven't heard from her in about two years."

"She have money for the baby?"

"Yeah, hundred grand," I said quietly.

His eyes went wide. "Well, god damn! You really were a good dealer." He smiled.

"I guess."

Would Mia want me as a father? A fuck up? To have others knowing what her father did to her? What I've done in the past? Where I am or was? She does need father I know that. *But what kind of father would I be to her? What good would I do? How would I ever tell her stories about when I was younger? What if she asked about her grandpa? What would I tell her?* I wouldn't, but I wouldn't ever lie to her. I need to be there for her. I just wait for the day until she's in my arms. *Does she know who her father is? Does she know she has one? Would Kendall even ever let me around her? Would I even be allowed around her at all?*

I'm going to be there for her even if Kendall won't let me around her; she is still my daughter. I don't care if she screams at me to leave, I'll hold Mia. I'm still her father, and I still have every right to be there for her. I'd take her. No. I wouldn't hurt Kendall like that. The way her arms were wrapped around Mia. I couldn't take that away.

KENDALL

Chapter 46

"Mia, no." I walked over to her again. She just threw more of her cereal on to the tile floor. "Mia."

She only continued to giggle at me, which had me smiling but still irritated with her. I was living on my own at nineteen with a two-year-old. I sighed, picking her up out of her chair and walking her into the living room. The TV caught my attention. I picked the remote and changed the channel from the news to a kid's channel where Dora started talking. "There." I set her into her play yard. She stood up and held on to the edge while watching the screen.

I went into the bedroom and heard Mia making noise at the TV. I ignored her words as I opened the small closet and moved the hanging clothes as I crouched down and started entering the combination. I only took out $50. I closed and locked it back up, closing the closet doors and walking back out to Mia. "Dora, go!" she shouted. She always only talked loud when we were at home. In public, she's too shy to talk to anybody. I went and grabbed my purse from the kitchen and put the money in it. I went back and picked Mia, which she didn't like very much.

"We're just going to the store, honey, then you can watch Dora when we get home."

"No, stay!" she shouted back.

"Mia."

She only laid her head on to my shoulder and started moving one of her hands in my hair, playing with it a little. I slipped my purse over my shoulder as we left the small apartment. I locked the door while having Mia on my hip. "Get cereal."

"If you'd stop throwing it on the floor, you'd still have some." I laughed at her, which she started giggling at. "Okay." I sighed as we started walking over to the steps.

"Why no elevator?"

"Because I have to stay in shape a little, honey," I answered her as we passed the neighbor's door just as it were opening.

"Kendall." He smiled.

"Hi, Carter," I greeted as we stopped.

"Hi Mia." He waved and smiled at her.

That only caused her to bury her head into the crook of my neck. He laughed, and I smiled. "Honey, say hi back."

"Hi," she mumbled, still hiding her face.

"We're going to the store," I informed him as Mia wrapped her arms around me.

"Oh sorry. I didn't mean to delay you." He smiled, and I smiled back at him.

"No, it's fine." I laughed. "We'll see you around." I smiled while walking past him.

"Bye."

"Mommy," Mia whined when I started walking down the steps.

"What is it, honey?"

"Where Uncle Josh?"

"Uncle Josh is at his house."

"Why he there?"

"Because that's where he lives, sweetie. This is where we live."

"Where's Grandma?"

"She's at her house."

"Both of 'em?"

"Yeah, they're all probably home."

"And Aunt Candice too?"

"Uh . . . I don't know."

I walked out of the building and started toward the car. "Does Candice like cereal?"

I started buckling her into her car seat. "I'm sure she does." I laughed.

"Did daddy?"

I paused for a moment. "Mia."

"You don't like cereals."

"I know."

"So I like daddy?"

"I guess so," I said quietly while wiping my eyes.

***

I had Mia holding on to my leg as I wiped down the seat in the front of the buggies for her. "Mommy."

"Okay, okay, I'm done." I threw the wipe into the next cart. I lifted her and set her in.

"Want that one!" Mia said loudly while pointing at a cereal box.

"This one?" I grabbed the blue box.

"Beside it."

"Okay. This one?" I grabbed the next one.

"Noooooooo," she whined.

I started laughing at her. "This one?" I grabbed another.

"No." She kept giggling.

"You know what." I sighed before I started laughing with her again. "This one?"

"The other one."

"This one?"

"Nope."

I went over to her and lifted her. I held her close the shelves. "Pick the one you want." She calmed her giggling before grabbing on to a box and hugging it to her chest. "Throw it in." She tossed it into the cart. "Yay."

After I got everything we needed, we paid, and I put her in her seat and loaded the car up. On the drive home, Mia fell asleep in the back. I didn't wake her as I unbuckled and lifted her, taking her back up to our home on the elevator. When I got to her bedroom, she started whining about something that I couldn't understand, so I just kept telling her it was all right. After she was tucked in, I went into my bedroom and went to the safe and put the change inside.

Only a certain few know where I am. My mom and Micah's mom and sister along with Josh. None of them ever really can visit though in case they would be followed. So nobody ever comes by. After moving in here, my mom stayed the first night only. She had to go back home and go to work and all. I was left with Mia alone. It was hard. She was always crying. I only ended up staying with Josh and Bailey for a week before ending in this place. After a few days of her constant crying, I just started crying with her. It took a while for me to get myself together.

For her first birthday party, we went to my grandma's house. She found out about Mia when she was seven months old and immediately started hating Micah. She didn't want to hear about him at all after she knew he was into drugs. She started yelling at me about how dumb I was but somehow lucky that Mia doesn't have any health problems because of him. After she screamed at me for a minute or two, she moved on to my mom, screaming on how she could let her daughter around someone like him.

I couldn't stand it after a good ten minutes. Micah wasn't here. He wasn't able to make it to his daughter's first birthday "party," our daughter's first birthday. I handed Mia to my grandfather and just ran to the bathroom. The way they were talking about him and judging him right in front of me made me sick, literally. I threw up right when I got to the toilet. Then I just started bawling my eyes out for a few minutes. It was a long day to say the least.

Her second birthday was easier. We had it at my uncles in Georgia. I held back my tears. I was occupied the whole day with something to not have any time to think about how her father is in prison. Josh and Bailey came surprisingly. He only lived two hours away, and he said that he and Bailey need a little vacation anyway, and he wanted to be a part of Mia's life like she was family. He said that they did try to have a baby last year but found out that she couldn't get pregnant. That included him telling Micah about it and what his comments were. He said he wanted to be a father but only like in ten years or so, also how he said he was fucking stupid to want a baby right after you got married. He told me about their wedding day and how Micah was kicked out for getting really drunk, and he started singing on stage with a microphone, also getting into a fight with Bailey's father because of Micah being the one to introduce Josh and his new wife. He was mad at her for hanging around someone like him. Bailey just rolled her eyes, which had me laughing.

Her third birthday was a lot better than the first two. I didn't have to fight the urge to cry although the thought of Micah did surface every now and then. It was just my mom and Mia and me. We didn't do anything that special, only taking her to the beach for a few hours.

***

"Choco Puffs."

I poured the chocolate cereal into the small Styrofoam bowl and handed it down to her. "Don't try to eat the bowl again," I told her as she walked back into the living room with it in both hands. My phone caught my attention as I was cleaning up the counter. I wiped off my hands and walked over to it. I set it back down after recognizing the number calling me. What caught me off guard next was a light knocking on the door.

"Mommy!" I walked over to Mia and lifted her quickly. Of course, like always, her cereal was on the floor. I held her closely to me as I just stared at the door. I've told her to never answer the door and just to let me know when someone is here. "Mommy is who—"

"Shhh . . ."

Chapter 47

The silence seemed dangerous. As if one sound would be made on either side would alert the other on either side of the red wooden door. I didn't move as I held Mia right against me. *What if the floors creaked or I stepped on a piece of cereal she threw on to the floor?* Something I'm completely still dumbfounded of why she always does that and why I keep giving it to her. I couldn't keep us here though, standing in front of the door. That was just stupid and careless. I have to get Mia somewhere safe.

I looked at the door as everything stayed silent and then down at the floor. I moved only one of my feet slowly toward the right, to the kitchen, to get my cell phone. As soon as I moved both of my feet, I snapped my head back up to the door when I heard a few knocks lighter than the first few. There's no way in hell I'm risking anything to open that door.

"Kendall, you home?" I jumped when I heard Carter's voice on the other end. I sighed in relief as I rushed over to the door after setting Mia back down where she was previously. When I opened the door, Carter was on his way back across the hall.

"You wanted something?" I asked, wiping my eyes quickly before he turned around.

He turned on his heel quickly and gave me a weak smile. "Yeah, I do actually." He walked back over. "You okay?" He came over worriedly.

I nodded. "Yeah, of course. Yeah. I'm fine. I just—"

"Is something going on?"

"What, what do you mean?"

"Oh, come on, Kendall, don't you dare lie to me."

My eyes widened with his language. I turned and peeked my head around the corner.

"Mia, I'll be right in the hall, honey. Just one minute."

I closed the door and walked right back up to him as he stood there staring at me and looking down both ways as if something was coming.

"What the heck is wrong with you? Don't you ever yell at me like that when my daughter can hear you." I shoved him backward.

"Who are you?" he whisper shouted right back.

"What are you talking about?"

"You have bad people out to get you, Kendall. Men are looking for you for some reason."

"What?" I was stunned as I just stared blankly up at him, eyes wide.

"Why do you live alone? Nobody ever comes to visit you. You don't go hardly anywhere. Who are you hiding from, Kendall?"

I just stared. "Where are you getting at?"

"Kendall . . ."

"Who did you talk to?" My eyes started to well up.

"I was just at the bar last night, and these guys kept saying stuff. I was playing pool with 'em. They sounded like they were describing you. It sounded just like you. They said she has a daughter now with that loser Harlan, and she's hiding out somewhere around here. Kendall, they are looking for you."

I just looked down the hallways again before grabbing on to his wrist and opening my door again and dragging him inside. I let go of him once we got inside. I locked up the door—lock after lock just like I always do. I stared up at him for a second before I walked back into the living room, and he followed behind me.

"Carter!" Mia cheered. I lifted her. "Mommy . . ." she whined.

"Mia, it's nap time, sweetie." I carried her into her bedroom and tucked her in.

When I walked back into the living room, Carter was looking at the books on the small bookcase. "Who were the men?" I demanded, crossing my arms at the same time.

"Who's her father?"

"I need to know who you were talking to . . . now."

"Micah Harlan. He's the father, isn't he?"

I just stared at him. "That is none of your business, Carter."

"You're like eighteen, Kendall. What the hell were you doing with a piece of shit like him?"

"Don't you ever talk about him like that. Ever. And don't talk like that when my daughter is around. Do you hear me?"

He looked more than angry and shocked at the same time that it became harder and harder to read his expressions as they changed from one to the other. "I'm sorry. But seriously, you know what I mean. Do you even know who he is or did he just fucking sleep with you and then get you into all of this crap by knocking you up and leaving?"

My blood was pumping even faster now, my heart beating out of my chest. "Who. Were. They?"

"I don't know. Just some guys at the bar I was hanging out with. Drug dealers, I guess. I don't know. We only played some pool together then I left after getting my ass butt kicked."

"Micah is not a piece of shit," I whisper shouted at him.

"He left you with a baby? How could you defend him like that?"

"You've never known him, Carter. People talk. But I need to know what those men looked like. I need to know now. I'm not messing around with you either. Now."

"I think one's name was Johnathan."

"Are you sure?"

"Yeah, that's all I know."

"Okay," I whispered, sitting on to the couch. I took a deep breath while burying my head in my hands.

"I think I have a right, being your neighbor and all. I should know who I'm living next to."

"He didn't leave me. He's in prison." He sat next to me. "What have you heard about him?"

"I've heard he's in fight clubs and a dealer, trafficker, just about anything."

I shook my head. "He wouldn't sell women. I know him more than anyone. He was my boyfriend for a long time before he was arrested. Mia was an accident, and he knows about her and all. He gave me money to take care of her since he can't. He's not a piece of shit. He was a dealer. He had to kill his boss though, or he would have killed him. He's not a bad man, Carter."

When I turned to look at him, I realized he was staring down at me as I spoke. He was listening the entire time and just staring. "You still deserve better, Mia deserves better, and you know that," he whispered, moving a piece of hair from my face slowly.

"Carter."

His cold hand cupped my face gently while he rubbed his thumb back and forth and keeping eye contact with me. He moved his hand down on to my thigh and started rubbing it slowly. I couldn't react to any of it. I was just frozen. His hands weren't as massive as to what I'm used to and what I like. He doesn't smell the same as compared to Micah. He's minty and smells like AXE. He had a close shave and was more mannered. I didn't feel pressured. I don't know what I'm feeling.

His lips weren't chapped as Micah's always seemed to be when they connected with mine. His arms didn't feel as comforting and protective as they wrapped around me and the kiss was deepened. He didn't seem to care if I wanted this or not like Micah did mostly. There was no smiling into the kisses. His heart wasn't going crazy inside his chest as he laid me on to the cushions, his chest pressed against mine as he kept his eyes closed. Every time Micah's face came back into my mind, it was replaced immediately with Carter's.

"Mommy!" I leaped back up at the sound of Mia's voice like she was crying. Carter got off me quickly as I pushed on his chest, and he sat normally on to the couch. I got up quickly and looked over to see Mia. "Mommy," she whispered while wiping one of her small hands across her tear-stained face, the other hand holding a small stuffed Dalmatian.

"Mia. Mia, honey, what's wrong?" I lifted her and held her close. "Sweetheart, what happened?"

She just cried into my shoulder. I knew he was watching us. "I want daddy."

"Honey, daddy's not here."

"I want daddy." She continued to cry while squeezing her dog with her hand on his plush paw. I just started shushing her.

"I'll be back." I looked over to Carter, and he nodded, looking a little concerned for Mia and sad. I patted Mia's back as she continued to weep on to my shoulder, and I walked back into her bedroom.

"Mommy," she whined again as I laid her back down and put her blanket over her body.

"What is it?"

"Why he here?"

"He just had to tell me something, honey."

"Talking?"

"Yeah, that's all, sweetheart. Why are you crying?"

"I bad dream."

"Honey, it's all right." I tucked her hair back.

"She okay?" he asked when I came back into the small living room.

"Yeah, she just had a nightmare."

There was a silence as I just stood there awkwardly. "Has she ever met . . . him?"

I shook my head. "His mom and sister."

"How does she know she has a dad?"

"They've talked about him before. His sister has showed her pictures from when he was younger . . ." He got up and walked closer to me and set his hands on to my waist and stared down at them. "You have to go," I whispered.

He took a deep breath before nodding slowly. "Okay."

"Just . . . I—if you hear anything else, please tell me."

He nodded and walked over toward me as I stood there awkwardly. "I will," he whispered while holding my arms. I kept them crossed, not wanting to touch him at all. He leaned down and kissed my cheek before leaving.

What the hell have I just done? Why am I feeling this way? Micah isn't my boyfriend anymore. I haven't seen him in three years, yet here I am feeling guilty for making out with my neighbor. I walked over to the door and locked it back up. I ran my hands through my hair, sighing heavily. *What the hell have I just done?* Whore. *You have a child with one man, and you're making out with your neighbor?* That's a whore. Shut up! That stupid, lonely voice in my head. *She'll never shut up will she?* There's always something she has to add.

The walk back to my bedroom seemed to take forever. *Why am I crying?* It's all his fault. Micah. It's kind of amazing though how a person who was once a stranger can suddenly, without any warning or sign, mean the entire world to you, making it like you can't live without them.

MICAH

Chapter 48

I hate hearing something that absolutely kills you inside, and then you have to act like you don't care. That's all over. Three years. It's better than my actual sentence at least. I feel as if I'm waiting for something to happen that I still just know isn't going to. She won't want me, not after this. Every day, I looked at the photograph. Mia. Kendall. Mia sitting on her lap at one of her birthday parties, while Kendall was looking to the side talking to someone. I fell in love with her because she loved me even when I couldn't love myself.

 The best love is the one that makes you a better person without changing you into someone other than yourself. Kendall. She did make me into someone better I'd like to think. She got my mom and sister back to me. I had to change. But we all get addicted to something that takes away everything else. I couldn't stop. It's been three years since all of that. I'm twenty-four now and never met my three-year-old daughter.

 I want someone who will not leave no matter how hard it is to be with me. People change and often become the person they said they'd never be. Every day is a new opportunity to start over I'd like to think. When I met Kendall, all that went through my mind was bad things about myself. No self-control. None. Nothing. Pig. *Why would she ever like me back?* Nothing is going to come of this, so just sleep with her and move on. That's all this kind of attraction is. It wasn't though. She wasn't flirting with me from the second I started talking with her. It was the complete opposite of that in fact.

 How can one person make you see everything so differently? But in the face of true love, you don't just give up. *Did she actually ever love me?* Not as much as I did her I know at least. I hid it all from her until I was too fucked up to even care. You have to respect yourself enough to walk away from something that no longer serves you, grows you, or makes you happy. It was being with her that made me happy. Some people only pretend to try and help you. Walter. He did help me. Without him, I don't know what I would have done for money back then. In prison, there seemed to be a lot more time to think. I didn't want that for the rest of my life.

At first, it was fine. It was even fun. It made everything seem like it didn't matter. It made everything better and more fun. It's just, after a while, things just really get to you.

I was zoned out the entire time Josh was driving. He's been talking the entire time it feels like. Three years. It wasn't anything about anything I wanted to hear, only meaningless, little things. It was boring, and I just didn't care at all. I didn't want anyone else to know I was out early. *What do I say? What will they say?*

"Micah?"

"Mmmm."

"Have you been listening?" He laughed but sounded annoyed at the same time.

I shook my head as the trees continued to pass outside the front passenger's window. Three years. "What were you saying?"

"I asked you where I am taking you."

I opened my mouth to speak. *Where is he taking me?* "Just take me to my old house."

"Okay."

"You kept it good for me?"

"I did."

"Good."

"Why don't you want anyone else to know you're out?"

"Because."

"Don't give me that."

I smirked, and it turned into a smile, and then I started laughing lightly. "I don't know."

"I told Bailey I was going to get a lamp."

"A lamp? That's all you could think of?"

He just shrugged. "It's just the first thing I looked at. I didn't know what to tell her. Her face was funny though." He laughed to himself.

"I'm sure."

"Why couldn't I tell her?"

"Because."

"Don't start that Micah!" He laughed.

"Because I know how Bailey is."

"What's that supposed to mean?"

"You know what it means."

"She's not as annoying as you remember."

"I believe you." I looked back out the window, trying to hide the smile.

"She's not bad."

"If you'd of told her, everybody would've known."

Josh took a deep breath. "Is it safe at your house then?"

I just sat there. "You went the wrong way."

"You're coming to help me buy a lamp."

"Not again with the lamp bullshit."

"We need a new lamp."

"You're such a jack off."

"Not a lying one."

"Just go in and buy your damn lamp since you're so scared your wife will beat you for lying."

He laughed while shutting the door and going into the store. It took him fucking at least twenty minutes to come out without a doubt most likely the most hideous lamp they probably had. "Can we go now, or do you have to buy her some and yourself some tampons?"

"Screw you." He laughed as he started the car back up.

***

"I would've went home, but this guy wouldn't let me."

Bailey only laughed at my comment as she gave me some fresh blankets. "Why wouldn't you let him go home?"

Josh's face was in shock. His eyes went wide as he stared down at his young wife. "Because, he, he just, ya know . . ."

She just gave him an even more confusing look than before. "Okay then." She turned to leave the small guest room. "Good night, Micah."

"Night, Queen Slater." She only turned around and raised one eyebrow.

"He's just being an ass."

I just laughed at them both as he set his hands on her shoulders as they walked out of the room together, him behind her closely. He turned his head to look at me like, now look what you did.

After I was under the pink fluffy blanket and the blue-covered pillow Bailey gave me, I stopped smiling and laughing all together.

What the hell are you doing? Why are you here? You have a daughter out there that you have never met, yet here you are, joking around with your friend and his wife and sleeping at their house. I just tried to ignore it and go to sleep. Kendall doesn't want me. I gave her a hundred grand. That should be enough to keep her and Mia good for a while, and she can get a job and start a new life.

I have to find Mia, I have to find them both. Maybe if Kendall lets me at least just meet Mia without saying I'm her father, then she'll realize that she wants me in her—our daughter's life, and I'll get to come around more. Maybe. That's why you were such a pussy in prison to get out early, you moron. You're going to see your daughter whether or not Kendall permits it.

Does Josh know where they are?

Whether he does or not, at least I don't have to sleep in that damned small slim mattress anymore. This bed isn't great, but I'm not complaining. The color. That same stainless steel grey color I had to look at every day. That "bathroom" too. Those beds. The bunks. I got the top due to my cell mate getting out after five years. I only had to deal with him for a few months, thankfully, and had the bottom bunk the whole time thinking that I would want the top, but after he left, I just couldn't do it. *Isn't it more comfortable on the bottom?* I tried sleeping on top for a while, but it never worked out for me in the end. The picture of Mia and Kendall was on one of the bricks that the bed was against. After a while though, I took it down and just put in under a pillow. I really missed my pillows. And yet even though I'm out, I have to deal with Josh and Bailey. I didn't want anyone looking at what I had waiting for me. *Was she ever waiting for me though? Did she just take the money and leave?* She never contacted me back after I gave Josh small letters to give to her. *Did he ever give them to her or just lie about it? Why would he lie? Does Mia even know that she has a father?*

***

"You know where they are."

"Micah—"

"No. I deserve to know where they are!"

"I don't think it's the best idea."

"I don't care what you think. Tell me where they are!"

"You know how much you've put her through? She had to move by herself with a baby."

"You think I wanted that?"

Why won't he just tell me where the hell they are? Why is he so involved? Why does he care if I see them or not? He looked at Bailey for a moment and then back at me. "Micah," Bailey started softly. "We haven't heard from her for a while."

"What do you mean?" My eyes were glassy now.

"We haven't been in contact is all. Kendall moved away. She got rid of contact with all of her friends, Micah. I don't know what she's been up to really."

"Wha—what about . . . Mia?"

"She's good. Last time I saw her, she seemed happy and all."

"Does she even know about me?"

He shook his head. "Not that I know of. I think Candice has told her about you, what you look like, and that kind of stuff."

"Kendall never said anything though?"

"Micah, I don't know." He sighed. Bailey announced she had to go to work and gave Josh a quick peck on the lips before walking past me and patting my shoulder sweetly. She smelled nice like vanilla. Her larger breasts were being supported nicely and her legs being shown off with her dark blue dress that hung on her curves almost perfectly. Her walk was in a hurry as her heels clicked against the wooden flooring toward the door. Her butt wasn't swaying but only moving naturally with her legs. She didn't have to show off to anybody. The only thought that was cruising through my mind was the memory of the night I took her virginity.

I had told her when we got back to my new home that I didn't want anything with her, and she didn't seem to care, well maybe because her underwear was off and my hand was against her. The next morning, she was nervous and embarrassed, which I hated. I didn't want to make her uncomfortable at all. She was one of my best friends that had just spent the night is all. It wasn't a big deal to me. There was nothing wrong with it. She was way too skinny then. Now is a different story. No, she isn't fat, she is in shape just like her whipped husband that is now my only male friend. I came into my bedroom to find her covering her body with the blue sheets. She was almost ready to cry. She was frantic, wondering what happened the night before. I had rushed over to her and sat on the side of the bed.

"Don't cry."

"What did I do?"

"You feel bad?"

She only looked over at me. Her eyes were wide, and her hair was a mess, which I told her otherwise. She looked back down and nodded slowly. "We're just friends."

"I know."

She only broke out into a small sob. "What if I'm pregnant?"

I chuckled at her nervousness. "I know you're not."

"How would you know?"

"Bailey, I was safe. It's okay. I wouldn't do that to you."

"Maybe it happened, ya know?"

"It didn't. I'm not a moron. I know how to use a condom, I know . . ." I stopped myself quickly.

She paused and just stared down at the blanket. "Okay."

"You weren't bad. You were amazing, Bailey. Why are you embarrassed?"

She shrugged. "I don't know. I feel like a whore."

"That was your first time. You're not a whore. It's not like I'm some stranger to you." She nodded and then looked back up at me.

"So you don't want anything . . . to happen between us . . . at all?"

"Bailey."

"I should go."

"No, stay awhile. I drove you here. I'll take you home later."

"I want to leave."

"Come on." She stared at me a few moments. I reached my hand up and cupped her shoulder gently. "You okay?" She nodded. I grinned politely to her. "You're gorgeous, Bailey. Don't feel embarrassed in any way." She leaned into me. I wrapped my arm around her back and held on to her as my chin rested lightly on top of her soft, wavy hair. She set her hand on my bare chest and moved it around curiously. There was never any sort of intimate touching with all of the other girls, not even Shailene. It was only to "get the job done," and then that was it. She was only expressing her curiosity as she lowered her hand down further to the small trail of hair disappearing into my boxers. She looked up at me as if asking for permission. I didn't stop her. "Are you hungry?" She looked up at me in shock, wide-eyed. "I made breakfast." She giggled and nodded.

"Micah, my wife isn't available. She's married . . . to me." I looked back at him, smiling. "I don't see how you went three years."

"Yeah and don't ask." His face went to disgust and humor.

"Maybe I'm the one I should remind you she is married."

"You sick freak. I have a hand." I waved it.

After a few hours, I left Josh's house and took the bus back to mine. It was a wreck to say the least. Not that it was trashed, just dusty inside. I walked though each room a few times and went into my bedroom. I changed my clothes into gym shorts and just a green tee. I went back out to the mailbox and took everything out. Josh stopped paying the bills with the money I gave him two weeks ago. I went back inside and sat on the couch and started calling them all in.

After an hour, I felt exhausted. I leaned back in the chair and closed my eyes. It's already four thirty-five. I sighed loudly before getting up out of the chair and going to get a shower. The water didn't seem to be hot any longer than five minutes, but it was a hell of a lot better than being in the shower with more than twelve other men.

Looking in the mirror, I felt different. Hell, I looked different. Three years ago, everything seemed to be going normal. Kendall and I seemed fine. There were no more debts to be paid. Keegan was gone. They were all gone. Then everything got fucked up just like it seems to always do.

I picked at my brown hair with my fingers and, after a few minutes, styled it a little and walked back into my bedroom. I shaved every week in prison. It's been two weeks since I shaved though. I can't take my hands away from my face. The stubble is just too addicting to rub the pads of your fingers back and forth against it. I just put on the outfit I had on before I got washed up. Mia. I have to see her. I have to meet her. She's my daughter. I could care less about what Kendall thinks. The more I think about it, the more I could care less about her. That's if what I'm thinking is true about her not wanting or allowing me to see my daughter. *Will she?* No. Maybe.

***

"Look, Mom, I'm sorry. We can have dinner another day together. I'm too busy today though."

"I haven't seen you in so long though."

"It's been a week." I laughed.

"You know what I mean, honey."

It was the second day since I've been out, and I was just glad she called me to ask to have dinner with her tonight and just stay there instead of just showing up. I don't want to deal with anyone right now until I've dealt with Kendall. I'll just snap. I have to see them. Her. I don't feel like going all of the way back to Josh's house almost a half hour away. I know who would know that only lives down the road. It was windy and cold out, so I pulled on my orange hoodie and shorts and left.

I just sat in my parked car across the street from Linda's house. As soon as she stepped outside in her work clothes, I got out and hurried across the street just when she got to her car. "Linda." I grabbed on to her shoulder lightly.

She turned quickly and kneeled me right between my legs. I mean, with some force too. I grunted loudly, cursing under my breath. It's been about two years since I was hit there. Someone trying to get into my pants is a big difference, especially if it's another man that hasn't been with a woman in twelve years and was extremely lost in the head. I set my hand over where she kneeled me hard enough for my whole body to feel the pain. The strong burning and throbbing sensation being sent up and down me causing me to just stay in place for a long moment, only grunting, and whimper coming from my mouth.

When I composed myself a little better and was able to tolerate the pain enough to stand up straight, I looked over at her. She only stared at me though. A hard, lifeless stare at that. Her eyes were glassy for a quick two seconds at the most. Then all of her anger came to surface. "You heartless bastard." She spat as if she couldn't believe that I was standing in front of her.

"Look, Linda, I'm sorry. I ju—"

"You're sorry? You're sorry? I'll tell you who's sorry! Me! I let you around my daughter, thinking it would be good for her to have a boyfriend! I'm sorry!" She slapped me, hard.

I could only look at her. She composed herself and opened the door to her car to leave.

"No!" She slammed her door shut and started the engine. "No! Linda! Linda, please. Please, please. I have a right!"

She looked over at me. "A right? You're going to ask me where my daughter lives, so you can ruin that child's life. I already let you ruin one of my girls' life. I won't let you ruin another."

"Linda, there was nothing I could do. It's not like I asked for any of this. I never wanted to hurt her."

She took the keys out and bit down on her lip in concentration. "Micah, you took my only child practically away from me. You had and still may have men after her. And now, my granddaughter can't even hang out with her friends unless Kendall is right beside her."

"I need to know where they are. Please. She's my daughter."

She nodded. "I understand."

***

The building looked old and not that nice at all on the outside. It was tall and not that clean-looking. The red bricks were turning a darker color. I couldn't believe that Kendall moved here when her mom told me. She said it was the only place that was cheap enough, and it has enough room. I paused outside the main entrance. *What do I say to her?*

I opened the door slowly.

I should just come back tomorrow. No. She'll be mad. I have to do this today. I looked in the mirror hanging on the side and fixed my hair a little better. *Does she miss me? Would she actually want me around as much as I do her?*

I didn't want to buzz in. I looked at all of the names until I saw Starla AP. A17 written on a strip of white tape by a button. I went straight up the stairs. I think I stared at that door longer than I've ever stared at anything in my life. Every crease and nick in the wood was imprinted into my mind. *Is she even "home"?* I knocked loudly on the door two times and stepped back and looked down the hallway toward the elevator and the stairs. My attention was instantly back to the door when it opened slowly.

Chapter 49

My eyebrows furrowed, and my mind went blank. My jaw clenched, and my body went numb. *Who is this? Who is he?* She isn't here. She doesn't live here. *Where is she?*

"Can I help you?"

"I must have the wrong apartment."

"Someone ya lookin' for?"

"Uh, Ms. Starla actually, if she's here?"

He paused. "Who did you say you were again?"

"Who are you?"

"Carter?"

I couldn't take my eyes off him. *Carter?* I looked around his frame to see her. She was skinnier and her hair longer. Kendall. I let out a breath I was holding in. My eyes went glassy, and my hands started shaking. I looked back up at the man. Kendall was still frozen to the floor. "Who are you?"

His eyebrows rose in amusement. "Excuse me?"

"You get away from here."

"Why don't you? Get out of here before I call the cops, right now."

I wanted to knock him out right there whether Kendall was there or not. I shoved him as hard as I could muster. He stumbled back into the door frame. He recovered quickly and punched my jaw. I gripped his collar and spun him out of the doorway and on to the wall in the hallway.

"Micah!" I let go of him and turned. Kendall. "What are you doing?" she screamed as her cheeks were already covered in tears and redness from the dampness. "Who do you think you are? You can't just show up here!" She shoved me.

I could only watch her. She looked so fragile and scared. She needed rest it looked like. "Who is he? Who is this?"

"That's none of your business!"

"Bullshit!" She shuddered back. "What, are you screwing him? You're sleeping with this loser now? Is that what you do?"

The man grabbed on to me and threw me to the ground harshly. "Get out of here!"

"Carter! No!"

He turned and looked at her. "Kendall?"

"Don't hurt him." She got down beside me. "Go home, Carter."

"What?"

"I said, go home. I'm okay. You need to leave, now."

The guy only went to the door a little down the hall on the opposite side of Kendall's and closed it powerfully. Her cold hand grabbed on to mine and helped me up.

I looked down for a second and looked back down at her. She was only staring. She took her hand from my wrist and back down to her side quickly.

Neither of us said anything for a minute. "Kendall, we should talk."

"Talk?"

I nodded slowly. "Yeah, talk."

"About the three years you spent in a cell, and I was changing diapers and being tracked down by your old friends?"

I took my eyes off her while my hands rested on my hips. "Can we just go inside to talk?"

She turned and walked in, and I followed. I closed the door behind me and stepped into the living room with her. "Kendall," I whispered when I looked back down at her, her arms crossed.

"I was alone."

"Where is she? Where is Mia?" She paused and just stared at her pink socks covering her feet. "Kendall?"

"She's not home."

"Where, where is she then?"

"Why do you care? You left us."

"I didn't leave." I raised my voice. "I went to prison. I had no choice!"

"Don't come here to yell at me."

"I wanted to see you two." We finally made normal eye contact for a few seconds. "But apparently, you already had enough company today. Is that why she's not home? So you could whore around the building? Did you blow all the money, and now you do that?"

"Excuse me?" Her mouth was wide along with her eyes. "You think I would lower myself to that! We're friends. I need some friends—"

"Yeah, friends."

"Don't interrupt me. I still have around thirty grand of your money. I'm not a whore." Tears started streaming down her cheeks now. "I am not a whore."

I took a deep breath and sat on the couch. A moment later, she sat on the opposite side. I didn't spend three years locked away to get away from her. I slid over beside her. I set my hand on her leg and held on to her hand. We didn't even look at each other. She was still crying. "I'm not a whore," she said softly, still looking down. "He told me people were talking about me at some bar, and he found out about you and me," she cried a little harder. "We kissed, and it just kinda happened."

I rubbed my thumb across the back of her hand. "You look so different." I felt her eyes on me, so I looked up, sort of laughing. "I never really saw you with facial hair." I shook my head. "Are you hungry?"

I nodded. She stood up and walked over into the kitchen and started rummaging around. She's been with another man. *Is he the only one?* Every time I looked over at her, she was already staring.

"Where is she again?"

"She's with her friend down the hall."

"Who's her friend?"

"Evan, and he's four. I know his mom. He has a seven-year-old sister."

"Evan?"

"Yes, they're just friends." Just the name got to me. A boy. She's already hanging out with them. "She'll be home in a few minutes."

I buried my face in my hands and leaned my elbows on to my knees. I almost jumped out of my skin when the sound of the door opened, and the soft sound of a child filled my ears.

"Mommy!"

"Hi, honey." I looked over to see Kendall with a small girl in her arms for a short second before they parted. "Thanks for watching her."

"Oh, it was fine. They had fun. Even passed out though."

I blocked out everything that was being said between the two young women as the little girl found me in her sight. She was holding on to Kendall's leg. I didn't realize when the other woman left. "Mommy, who man's this?"

I looked up at Kendall. She bent down beside Mia with her hands on her arms. "Sweetheart, this is Micah."

"Hi, Micah." She smiled warmly while swaying in her mother's arms slightly.

"H—hi Mia." I tried to keep calm as I stared at her.

"Mom, food?"

She took all of her attention off me as she rushed over to the kitchen counter. Kendall stayed where she was. I got up to my now even more shaky legs. I walked as normally as I could over toward Kendall. She set her hand on my bicep.

"She knows that her father is away."

I nodded, still staring at the small beautiful girl now seated on a pink flowery chair eating mac and cheese. Her dark hair falling in loose waves down her back. The small pink sparkly bag strapped across her chest. She looked back at us, Kendall. "Mommy, there no milk?"

Kendall didn't say anything more to me before going to the fridge and getting Mia chocolate milk in a Disney Princess cup. After she sipped down some of the milk with both hands set on the sides, she looked back over at me. "Mommy? What's Micah doing here?" She looked at Kendall as if she was uncomfortable.

Kendall looked back over at me as Mia just stared at her mommy. "Honey, Micah is here to have dinner with us. He's a good friend of mine. He's nice, sweetheart." She blinked over at me and grinned widely. I looked back over at Kendall, just trying not to cry. Mia got up out of her seat and walked over to me. The soft sensation and tingles that ran throughout my body and mind made me go almost in a state of shock. She walked me over to the table and got me to sit in the chair next to her.

"My friend's dad has a beard too," Mia spoke as she shuffled the mac and cheese into her mouth, and Kendall walked over and sit across me. "Carter doesn't though. He one my friend too."

"Mia, just eat your food."

She nodded and took another spoonful into her mouth. "He comes over a lot too."

"Mia," Kendall spoke firmly and angrily toward Mia. I looked down. I heard Mia start sniffling before she got up from her chair and walked away through the living room and opened a door and closed it gently. I looked over at Kendall. "Sorry," she whispered.

"Sorry?"

"I'm sorry I've changed, but you've changed too."

"I've changed? How have I changed? You're the one that has my daughter around that sleaze ball."

"Don't say you're not different from when the last time I saw you."

"Yeah? What, three years ago? The last words you said to me were that you were pregnant. That was it. That was the last thing you ever said to me. I lived with that for three years."

"Don't talk like that when she is just down the hall."

"Look," I calmed myself down, "I fell in love with her from the very first photo Josh gave me. I need to be in her life. What we have," I stopped myself quickly and briefly shook my head, "had, I don't want it to end. I don't. I've done terrible shi—things throughout my life. I went through hell growing up. I got out of that and moved on to that dang life and then met you, and everything started to get better for me. Then that crap happened. I spent those three years bunking with murderers and rapists and showering with them all at the same time, having to put up with their crap, literally. I'm out of that now, by being a baby to get out early. But I'm going to make the rest of my life the best of my life."

"Micah—"

"I'm not the best guy. I know that. I do. I tried with you, even if it never seemed like I loved you enough all the time we spent together. You have no idea how much I cherish our time we've had together those years ago. I loved you every second since you gave me the chance and went on that second date with me. I thought it was too good, so I had to keep getting high. We all get addicted to things that take the pain away. Then when you actually said the words to me even though we were fighting, that was one of the best nights of my life practically. I am not the best guy, but I promise I will always love you with all of my heart even if you never give me another chance, Kendall." I sniffled a little.

Her lips were trembling, and her eyes were prickling with tears about to spill over down her rosy cheeks. "I never stopped. You don't know what I've went through either, Micah. I went through just about the whole pregnancy without you. I forced myself to picture you in the room every checkup and that you were holding my hand. My mother would have put me on medication if she could have. You don't know how scared I was through the whole thing. And I didn't have you there with me. Raising a baby is the hardest thing any woman goes through, and I went through that without you. You did miss out, that's not a secret. But I never stopped loving you either."

We just stared at one another from across the small round kitchen table. I took a deep breath. *What's supposed to happen now?* Even though she's right there in front of me, pouring the truth out to me how much she still loves me, I can't get a grip on reality as if I'm dreaming, and I'll wake up soon. "I am clean. I admitted my problems to them at the first place I was taken to after I was arrested and told them what I did. They got me clean. I did try to quit every time we talked about it. That only got me started on something else though. I couldn't say good-bye to it then even as much as I wanted to. Now it seems easier to say no though." As I talked, she looked as if she was thinking the whole time and walked over in front of me.

After I finished speaking to her, she just stared up at me. "I don't want her to be without a father any longer. I don't want to be without you either."

I nodded back to her understandingly.

***

Her couch isn't the most comfortable thing to spend tonight on. She gave me a quilt and pillow from her room. She said I could sleep in the same bed with her, but I declined. Cage, or whatever his name is, has slept in there with her. She's had him undressed on those sheets, and she thought I would sleep in there with her in that same bed.

After what seemed like fifteen minutes or so, I was finally starting to doze off even with how uncomfortable I am still. The sound of feet patting down on the wooden floor makes my eyes open slowly to see a small figure for a second before they close automatically again. The feeling of something hitting against my upper arm makes me groan sleepily. "Micah," she whispers. That sweet, angelic, and delightful voice whispered has my eyes snap back open quickly, and all of the sleepiness just seems to disappear and leave me wide awake.

"Mia, what's wrong, princess?" I sit up quickly. In her arms is a stuffed Dalmatian.

She didn't say anything more at the time, she just sat on my lap and wrapped her arms around me, surprising me. I set my hand across her small and delicate back gently. "How know my mom?"

"I've known her a long time actually."

"You my daddy?"

I stared down at her. *How would she guess that? Would Kendall want her to know who I am to her in her mind? Who cares?* "Yes, sweetie. I'm your dad." I buried my face in her hair. I kissed the top of her head. "You want to go back to bed now?"

She shook her head and tightened her arms around my chest.

There was no room on the couch all night after she came to lay down and sleep there with me instead of her bed, but I didn't care. It only meant that she was closer to me. It was easier to sleep with her right next to me on the cushions. She didn't complain either.

I missed out.

I had to kill him though. If I didn't, I would still be dealing with his shit. I might have still been working for him. No. No, I wouldn't. I wouldn't put her through all of that shit again. I was such a dick to her. Because I was too damn lazy to just get a normal job, I made her suffer when she was with me and then go through the entire pregnancy while I was in prison.

***

"You look so different."

I only nodded back. "I didn't have much access to hair dye."

She grinned even more and continued to stare up at me. "I still recognize you though. Your eyes."

"Don't do that."

"What do you mean?"

"Don't act like you still love me."

"Micah . . ."

"What? Since I wasn't here, you thought it was better to just start bedding your neighbor and pretend he's the father of our daughter?" I pointed toward my chest and leaned closer down toward her small body.

Her eyes widened, and her jaw dropped. "That is not what happened." She pointed her finger.

"No? It's not? Then please, please Kendall, explain how my story is wrong. I'd love to hear that I'm still a screwed up liar from you. How many times I've lied to you. Go on, tell me I just told a ridiculous lie."

She only stared dumbfounded. Her jaw tensed, and her eyes were in slits as she only stared with her arms crossed. "I wasn't saying you were lying, Micah."

I scrunched my nose in disgust. "You whore," I said in almost a whisper, not even believing the words that were coming out, but I couldn't control them, even as hard as I was trying to contain myself. "You go to the next loser waiting for you and pretend he's the father? Is that what you're trying to do? Get rid of me? I will not have some lowlife like him help raise my daughter."

"Who are you to talk about someone? You just spent years in prison for being a lowlife." We stared hardly at one another by the door.

"I'll be back soon." I looked down and talked lowly, not making any eye contact.

"Do you still have your house?"

"I'm staying with Bailey and Josh."

I knocked more than five times already on Josh's door. *Why isn't he answering the door?* "Josh, god-dammit!" I heard his feet running across the floor before the door was unlocked and opened quickly. "What the hell?" I shouted, which made his dumb grin wipe off his face instantly.

"Where were you?" I stalked past him. "Micah, you can't just stay out all night. You were released early. You can't just go out like that."

"I was at Kendall's." I went into the kitchen where Bailey was coming out of the bedroom in a pink silky robe and her hair cascading over her breasts in loose waves. She gave me a sweet and innocent smile, which I dismissed as innocent when I put the pieces together in a quick second.

"I guess that didn't turn out for the best," he muttered as he joined us.

"What gave you that impression?"

"Are you hungry?"

I laughed at her. "He's not a child, Bailey."

"I was just being nice," she yelled back sternly. "He's not in the best right now."

"You know you have to come back to work tomorrow."

"That'll be fun."

"You don't realize how lucky you are to have gotten out so dang early."

I turned and looked back at him as he was leaning on the kitchen island. "Well, maybe if I was still in there, I wouldn't catch her with the neighbor while my daughter is just down the hallway." I snickered back like a child and walked into the spare bedroom that will be mine for a while. I went straight into the connecting bathroom and turned on the shower and waited for the entire room to steam up until it was quite hot enough.

After washing my hair and body well enough, I just stood under the heat and set my palms on the tiled surrounding wall. The longer I stood there with the scorching water drenching mostly my back at the time, the more I realized that I have to move on now. She has.

I swallowed hard. I need to go somewhere different. I don't know what I was expecting before I went to her mother's and then to Kendall's. It sure as hell wasn't what I got. I wanted to hold her tight after those miserable years of having men too close to your junk and trying to get even closer after years of not having any women. I had to throw them down and kick their faces a little when they started getting touchy and too perverted with the way they would approach the subject of slamming into me. They approached the offer as if it were normal for men to do that to one another, to grab on to one another's cocks, and to bang each other from the rear. Never would I do that. I shook my head at the reminder of the first time it happened in the showers. He just came up behind me, immediately, of course. I turned and kneeled him right in the crotch, hard enough to make him bleed a little, have him crying on the floor. The fucking came up behind me and set his hands on my hips, a disgusting son of a bitch at that. I had every right to beat him down in front of everyone. I was just glad a big fight didn't break out. That would be a very unsettling and disturbing sight. I sure wouldn't stick around to watch or join into it either.

I shook my head and ran my hand through my drenched and warm hair as it laid over my forehead. I turned off the water slowly but stayed leaned against the hot tiles for another few minutes. Those sick bastards. *Who thinks it's okay to grab another man unannounced like that?* The first thought I had put together in my mind was that when he grabbed me, when I turned to take him down, he would hit me back, and hard, and others would join in, and they would . . .

I had nightmares just about every night, worse after that. They brought up things I forgot about my childhood with my father. Things I've never told anyone, not even Candice or my mother.

I shook my head slowly at the reminder. I wiped my hand down my face before opening the curtain and grabbing the towel sitting on the closed toilet lid, drying off a bit, and wrapped it around my waist before going back into the bedroom to dress.

"I'll be home soon, Micah. Candice should be about an hour or two. She's at a friend's house, doing some kind of project."

"Okay," I whispered.

"You'll be okay then, yeah?" She looked down at me as she finished with her hair in the bright mirror. I only stared up at her.

"Do you have to go?"

"Sweetheart, you know I do. I already told your aunt I would meet up with her for a while tonight."

"I don't want you to go."

She walked out of the bathroom, patting my shoulder as she left. "Your father's here with you. There's no need to be scared, honey."

"Can't I come with you?"

She giggled as she went through her drawers. "You're much too young to go to a bar, sweetie."

"Mommy—"

"That's enough, Micah."

I sat on her bed quietly, swinging my legs on the end. "I don't want to stay with daddy." I stared at her and looked away as she got changed into a different outfit. "Please, don't leave me here."

She bended down and kissed the top of my head. "I'll be back. I love you."

She walked out. I ran after her down the hallway. When she opened the front door, I stood there as she started going through her purse for some reason.

His hand.

"You're meeting with your sister, that's right?"

"Yeah, I'll be home at around eleven."

He rubbed my shoulder slowly but painfully as they talked, and I only stared at her. Begging. She just didn't get it. "Love you, honey." They kissed before she left.

After the door was closed, he looked down at me before walking back into the living room and disappearing into the kitchen.

I ran.

It was the longest still that it ever took to get into my room. I had lost count of how many times it had happened before tonight. I've blocked it out so much. Ignored it. Even as a ten-year-old, I just found it easier to ignore it than to make a big deal out of it and have them fight and him start drinking again. I closed my door behind me and got beside my long dresser and pushed and pushed until it was in front of my door and ran into the corner and squeezed my eyes shut while at the same time covering my ears as I started to hear him pound at the door.

"Open the damn door!"
The dresser was shoved to the side, and he stood there. His—
"No!"

I sat up quickly in the bed. My eyes wide. My body trembling and my entire body drenched in sweat. I was only able to sit there and stare straight ahead at the black screened TV. I wish Kendall was here.

Chapter 50

It was easy at the beginning to fall asleep after my shower. After that, not so much. Every time I seemed to just blink, his face was there, and I was sitting in the corner. The next time I shut my eyes, my shorts were being torn off me. The next . . .

When I walked out into the kitchen, I could tell right away that they both were trying to not stare at me. My eyes were swelled and had bags the size of Texas under them. They had to of heard me last night too. *How could they not?*

I'm looking forward to going into work. I'm glad too that Josh was able to get my job back for me. I don't know where else I would want to go besides there, especially now. It was tiring doing the same routine over and over again in that place. To go somewhere that I haven't been for years just makes me feel so relieved that I'm back.

The gym didn't look that different, a few new posters here and there, new members, that sort of things, little things really. I followed Josh into the back room where people were in the ring, boxing in the middle of the floor.

Kendall.

I swallowed the lump in my throat. But I'm glad to be here. I have to be here is the thing that's making me uneasy actually. "Just go back to what you always did before," Josh said as we walked into the room.

"I know that."

He gave me a look before going off to his job. I had a client to train, not boxing though like I prefer. I went to my corner and started setting up. I turned to get a drink of water at the table behind me.

"Micah." I turned to see a girl. She was familiar. I know her. "Sorry, I'm a few minutes late for our session."

"Excuse me?"

"You don't remember me, do you?"

"Uh . . ." I know her. I bit down on my lip, thinking about it. *Where the hell do I know her from?*

"I think I do." I laughed. I couldn't help my eyes as they wandered down to her chest, full and not well covered, obviously by choice. "Miranda."

"Yeah." She smiled. "You had me worried."

"You—you said you were late?"

"You're my trainer."

I raised my brows. "Trainer? You—you're my . . ."

"Yes, silly. Can we get started or what?"

"Yeah, yeah, of course, we can. You're all ready to start then." I turned back and set my water back down on the table against the wall. "We can go over here and start—"

"Shouldn't I stretch?"

I stared at her. She's being obvious of why she is actually here. I nodded. "Yeah, you're right." I tried to laugh, which she found funny. She laid down on the mat to start her stretching. "Just do fifteen leg lifts each to start off?" She smirked up at me as she lifted her left leg first and started out. "Try to bend it as far back as you can, Miranda."

"Can you show me what you mean?"

"You know what I mean."

"Calm down, killer. Just help me out down here."

Killer.

I inhaled and exhaled quietly but deeply. She is obviously already in shape and is just pretending that she doesn't know how to stretch out properly. I know that from experience already. She knows what she is doing. She knows why she is here. I know why she is here. Maybe she's just flirting right now though. I bent down on my knees beside her, and she laid all the way down on the blue mat. I grabbed her ankle and wrapped my fingers around it, squeezing for a second, not making any eye contact with her. I heard her breathing hitch for a second as I lifted it for her. "Up," I instructed as I looked down at her chest, rising and falling, spilling out of the top of her cami. "Higher." I lifted it even higher, she's still flexible. "One." I set it back down. "Clear now?"

"Maybe one more time? I wasn't listening very well," she spoke lowly, biting her lip and gliding her tongue along her bottom lip slowly to wet it. I think? No, definitely not for that reason. My crotch spoke for me as I leaned forward and then sat back on my feet again.

I closed my eyes as I exhaled deeply, gripping her ankle again and lifting to her chin then slowly back down.

"So you look different."

"Yeah, I've heard."

"I heard you were in prison and just got out." I looked down at her. "That must have been terrible for you. But you probably don't know how much that turns me on."

"Miranda, why are you actually here? I have to work."

"I haven't seen you in three years. Why do you think I'm here?"

I looked over at Josh as he was boxing with some guy that I don't recognize. I looked at the table by the locker room. The table. Kendall. "I think you're here to waste my time." I looked back down at her. "You need to leave."

She blinked slowly before sitting up, her face mere inches from mine. She looked down at my lips. Her makeup was perfectly set on her face, her eyelashes long and black, and her lips full, shiny, and plump. How amazing they would looked wrap—

No. It's not going to happen.

"I like you demanding." She slid her fingers up my arm, slowly, her nails barely scratching the skin as goose bumps started rising from her cold touch. "It's really attractive."

"Miranda, you should go." I breathed.

"We can meet later."

"No, we can't."

"Why not?"

"I have plans."

"I know that's not true. We both do." She leaned in closer. Her lips even closer as she had her mouth barely opened. I wasn't thinking at all, my mind shut down, and my body took over for me. Her lips were warm and smooth just like I knew they would be. They molded into mine. Her tongue pried my lips apart. I wasn't able to break it no matter how wrong it felt. It's been so long, way too long for any man. *What kind of man am I?* I feel terrible and pathetic. *What am I doing?* She's a dumb whore who's here to see if I'll screw her later just like she did three years ago before I met Kendall. I moaned as her tongue lapped over mine, going deep in my mouth. I tried to just picture Kendall over and over with each second that came and went. I was becoming harder and harder with each second that passed, and our lips were locked. She won. *Why am I doing this?* Stop! Stop, now! No! I couldn't stop myself. Three damn years. Three years. I can't just keep jerking myself off and expect to be satisfied, and I don't really have

Kendall on my side right now, so I know nothing will be happening with her anytime soon. I waited a long time while we were dating until she was ready and brought it up to me that she wanted it. I was willing to wait because I fell in love with her from the second date with her. She doesn't know that, of course; she hated me. She hates me now. Miranda is here now and throwing herself at me, literally. I had to grip her fingers and dig my hands into her flesh to hold her back a little, so her breasts were pressed against my chest. If that happened, I might have already had my pants down and have her on the floor screwing her from behind, so I won't have to look at her and feel even guiltier about this all going on.

"Micah." I pulled away quickly. My eyes shot to the figure standing a few feet away from me, a small hand clasped in the hand of the taller one. I gulped down the excess from mine and Miranda's mouth as I stared into her brown glassy eyes.

I stood up quickly. No. No. No. God, no. She lifted Mia into her arms quickly before turning and leaving.

"No." I started walking after her. I have to talk to her. Now. Before this is completely ruined. I can't lose her. I need to have her in my life.

"Micah?" Miranda gripped my arm tight enough, so I was forced to turn to her. "Where the hell do you think you are going? You're walking away from me to go after some tacky, stubby monster, and what looks like to be a mother when I'm trying to get you to just lay down?" she said loudly.

"You think that a whore is better than her?" I turned back around.

"What did you just say?" She pulled me back around.

"I don't want anything to do with you anymore. We never had anything, only sex. Stay away from me, Miranda."

Her eyes widened. "Micah—"

I turned and shoved her back, and she fell against the mat. *What did I just do?* I opened my mouth to say sorry, but honestly, I don't feel sorry. No, I should have never done that. I know that. But I couldn't help it. She stared at me in disbelief, close to tears. A few guys rushed over to her, giving me disapproving, angry glances. She'll live. I have to get to Kendall. I turned on my heel and ran toward the front entrance of the building. I rushed through the front glass doors and looked frantically left and right, trying to look for my girls. "Kendall!" I ran toward her car parked across the street, cars beeping at me. "Kendall! Wait." I ran to where she was buckling Mia in on the right side in the backseat. "Kendall." She looked up in tears.

"Go away, Micah. I was wrong to come here. I knew I shouldn't of." She kept her voice steady as she finished strapping Mia in.

"Kendall, no. It really isn't what you think."

She stared at me. "Don't use a line as silly as that as an excuse to me. I'd rather you didn't say anything right now and just go back inside to where you were clearly tied up before the whole gym walked in on you."

"Please, please, Kendall. Let's talk. I need to talk to you about all this."

She shook her head at me. "I don't want to talk to you."

"You came all this way. You brought Mia with you. You want to talk to me. I know you do."

"I thought I did, but it was a big mistake apparently."

"No, please don't say that to me." Tears were rolling down my cheeks, and people were staring at us. I couldn't help it. She was slipping out of my fingers like string, and I couldn't catch her. "Kendall," I pleaded. "I need you in my life. I need you both in my life. You have no idea how much I love you both. I don't care about her. I don't. She kissed me. I couldn't pull away. I'm not lying to you."

"Stop making a scene. I have to go now." She walked over to her side to drive away from me. No!

"Kendall." I grabbed on to her and forced her to look at me, which made her gasp. "I want this to work again. I'm her father, and you're my love. Don't leave me." I calmed myself down a lot now. Nothing is working anymore. She doesn't want to talk to me anymore. She's leaving me and won't listen to anything I am trying to say to her to make her stay. Kendall! No! Stop! Mia! "Kendall." I ran around the car where she was opening the door to get in. When she turned around, our eyes locked for a split second. "Marry me?" She looked at me in shock for a second and then as if I was really doltish. "You know I love you. Just marry me, Kendall."

She shrugged my hand off her arm. "Just go back to work, Micah. We'll talk later."

I stared at her. That's good enough for me. I'll have more time to think about what I'm going to say to her. *Did I just ask her to marry me?* Yes. *Do I really want her to marry me?* Yes. *Really?* Yes.

"Go back to work, Micah."

"Bye."

"Bye, Micah."

I smiled back at Mia as she wiggled in her car seat. Kendall looked back at her as well. "Bye, Mia. I'll see you later." I looked back up at Kendall. "Thank you."

She nodded, sniffling her nose. "Yeah." She got in her car. I closed the door for her once she was all of the way inside and buckled up. I watched her as she drove off.

When I was back inside the gym, Miranda had already left. Josh looked over at me when I walked back into the back room and me at him. I'll have to talk to him at lunch. The day seemed to go slower than it did in a cement box I shared with another man who hasn't had a woman in years. I worked with an older man to help get him in shape. Apparently, loads of people aren't that enthusiastic about having somebody who just got out of the slammer and is now on parole training them, but this man didn't seem to care. Mr. Jerald. We talked to each other a lot it seemed like. He joked about me being locked away, and it was actually funny. He told me about his wife, Mary, and his two daughters, Jane and Courtney, who are twenty-three and twenty. It just came up in conversation; I didn't ask. He was very open with me. And now I'm going to be seeing him three times a week after that all.

When Josh and I got back to his place, Bailey was already home and in the kitchen. He went up behind her and wrapped his arms around her waist, low, and his elbows resting on her defined hips. "Hi, how was work?" she asked, glancing back at me, smiling. I rolled my eyes, which caused her to giggle.

"It was . . . interesting." Josh looked back at me.

"And . . . how's that?"

She looked at both of us to try and get an explanation. Josh and his big mouth talking when it should just be pressed against hers, so we wouldn't be being interrogated right now. "It's not sure really you'd be interested in. Gym things really."

"Okay." She continued cooking.

I got up and started walking back into the guest room and heard Josh start to blab now that I'm out of the room about what really happened today at work. I plugged in my iPhone before going to get a quick shower. I closed my eyes under the hot water and just breathed slowly, trying to think of what exactly to say to her. I need them in my life. I don't need time to think about that. They have to be here to stay. When I got out of the shower, I stumbled getting my briefs and pants on. I spent about a few minutes on my hair and washed my face again. I took a deep breath before calling Kendall.

"Hello?"

"Kendall?"

"Yes."

"It's Micah. I just wanted to call and ask you if we could go somewhere tonight. I know it's late and all, but—"

"Where?"

"Dinner? If that's okay and all with you. You can pick."

"That's fine," she spoke after a few seconds. "I'm already at my mom's, so you can get me around eight."

I smiled. That was quick. "You don't have to."

"I want to."

"I'll see you later then, yeah?"

"Yeah. Bye."

I didn't actually think that that really happened that quickly at first. It took me a few seconds to comprehend how simple that task seemed to be. I finished up getting ready and headed out of the room, grabbing the keys to leave. "I'm going."

"Where? You're on parole."

"I'll be back, damn. I gotta go."

I got into the car and drove quickly over to the house of Kendall's mom in twenty minutes. I sat in the car for a few minutes before getting out and going up to the front door and taking another long moment before knocking three times "One moment!" Her mom shouted.

When she opened the door, she stared up at me, not in the best way either. "Grandma!"

She held my sight captive still as Mia started yelling inside. "Hi."

"That's not an appropriate phrase for someone like you."

"Mom." She came over and placed her hands on her mother's shoulders to scoot her to the side. "Come in, Micah."

"Kendall." I smiled as she pulled me inside by my arm. Her fingers were clean feeling and slightly cold. They felt more than nice, and I felt myself having to calm myself down from her innocent touch.

"Daddy!" Mia got up off the floor from her coloring book and ran over to me quickly. It caught me off guard as she wrapped her small arms around my knees, hugging tightly.

I laughed while smiling as I looked up at Kendall. "She's been talking about you a lot." I lifted her into my arms, and she giggled. I brought her back down to my chest and hugged her to me. "I color." She wiggled to get back down. I sat her back on to her feet, and she ran back to her books and crayons on the floor.

When I looked back over at Kendall, she was staring at me. I gave her a weak smile. Her eyes were glassy, and a few tears slipped out and slid down her cheek quickly. We only stared at each other.

"Today was—"

"Don't. Just don't say anything right now. Let's go have dinner, then we'll talk about that kind of stuff, please?"

I nodded. "You okay to go?"

She nodded, looking down to wipe under her eyes. "I'll just be right back." She giggled, making fun of herself. I smiled at her as she turned to go into the bathroom to the side.

I looked down at Mia and sat with her on the floor. "What're you coloring?" I looked at the book. She didn't glance at me or anything as she continued with the red crayon. I bent one leg and folded my arms across it and supported my chin on my elbow.

"It's an Elmo."

I smiled. "You like Sesame Street?" She nodded quickly. "I always have too," I said quietly.

She turned and smiled at me. She held out a yellow crayon for me. "You can color Big Bird." She tried handing it to me.

I shook my head, declining her sweet offer. "You do it. It's yours, honey." She continued smiling and went back to her coloring, not pressing hard at all. I watched her color in and out of the lines for a few minutes before the sound of Kendall's came into my hearing range. I looked over my shoulder to see her talking to her mother, wiping her makeup once more under her eyes. Her mother embraced her warmly for a minute before letting her daughter go, and she started walking toward Mia and me.

"Are you ready?" she asked, looking down at me.

I glanced at Mia, and then we both looked up at Kendall. "You look so beautiful." She stared down at me and grinned happily and sort of shyly. "Yeah, I'm ready." I started to get up, groaning as my back cracked.

"Mia, sweetheart." Kendall got her attention. Mia got up on her feet and went into Kendall's arms, which I watched intently.

"You're leaving?"

"We're gonna be back in like two hours, okay? Daddy and mommy are just going to dinner. It's going to be boring you wouldn't like it." She scrunched her nose, making Mia start giggling loudly. I laughed with her. "You're just gonna stay here with grandma until we get back, and maybe we'll just all stay here for tonight if it's too late, and you're already asleep."

She nodded. "Okay."

Kendall smiled at her as she kissed her cheek, and then Mia kissed hers back quickly, and they hugged. "I love you, Mommy."

"I love you too." She unwrapped her arms from her mom's neck and leaned over in my direction.

"I love you, Daddy." She wrapped her arms around my neck. I took her from Kendall's arms and into mine. I hugged her back. She got her head off my shoulder to kiss my cheek. "Bye." She wiggled. I set her back on to the floor.

"Love you," I whispered.

"You'll be back soon then?" We turned to her mother.

"Yeah, we're just going to dinner is all," I answered back.

"Okay. Well, I have her to bed and everything probably when you're all done. Just take your time . . . both of you."

I gave her a grin, and Kendall nodded. I looked down at her before we started walking to the front door. I opened it, and she closed it behind her. I don't know whether or not I should try to take her hand in mine. It was an awkward twenty-five feet to my car. I opened the door for her and closed it, staying quiet when she was inside securely. I jogged over onto my side and got in quickly, closing the door once I was seated. She looked over at me the same time I looked over at her. She smiled. "This is really awkward," she admitted.

I laughed. "Yeah."

"Déjà vu."

"That's what I'm getting." I smiled at her. I started to remind myself about the first time I picked her up for our first date. "Try not to look so nervous, Kendall." I laughed at myself. She found it funny too.

"So how old are you?" I started driving and replaying that night.

"We're really doing this?" She giggled.

I nodded seriously. "Yes, yes we are." I continued driving through town.

"Well, I believe that I asked where we were going first of all, Micah."

"Then, please, take the lead, my lady."

She was still smiling from ear to ear. "Where are we going?" She was facing me in her seat, the strap against her breast tightly when I looked over. She has great breasts. I remember every little detail of them still from the first time I saw her naked, laid out on her bed before we made love the first time three years ago.

"Just to dinner."

"Yeah." She laughed. "But you were acting all like mysterious, like a bad boy and all." She recalled, still laughing and smiling like an idiot when I glanced over again.

"I am Mr. Mysterious."

"I was so terrified of you." She laughed.

"Terrified? Really? What'd you think I was going to do?" I laughed.

"I have no idea. I had no idea. That's why I was so scared of you. You were a closed book with no words still if you flopped through every single page. You were so closed off."

"That does sound mysterious."

"And all you did was smirk at me, and I went crazy in my head thinking, what the hell am I doing?"

"Sounds like you really liked me."

"I hated you. When we were at the eating place—"

"Restaurant." I smiled.

"Yeah." She laughed harder. "I went into the bathroom even though I didn't really have to go and seriously, like really seriously, thought about climbing out of the window to get away from you." She continued laughing.

I looked over at her wide-eyed. "You're not serious. A window? You were that scared like I was planning to kill you?"

"I am dead serious. Excuse the pun, but seriously."

"I never knew that." I looked back at the road.

"I can't believe I just told you that." She sort of laughed a little more. I felt her staring at me.

"You're staring."

"I know." She paused, her voice was quiet. Then normal volume. "I can't believe how different you look without your blond hair. You have stubble on your chin. You never had any stubble on your chin when we were together."

I looked over at her. I rubbed my hand over my stubbly chin. "My fa—" I stopped myself. "I don't like having facial hair."

"You remember a lot about your father?"

The space seemed to get smaller and hotter in temperature. I nodded. "I do."

"When he lived with you, did he—"

"I don't want to talk about that pathetic waste," I shouted. I heard her take a deep breath. "I didn't mean to yell," I whispered.

"I understand."

I shook my head. "No, don't say that because it's not true." The rest of the ride was silent. I noticed her legs shift uncomfortably all of the sudden. Her dress moved a little more up her thighs as she stared out the window. I swallowed deeply as I pulled up into the parking space. Neither of us said anything or looked anywhere different than where we have been staring for the whole thirty minutes. "I don't mean to make you uncomfortable. I never want to do that. I want you to be as comfortable with me as you were before . . . before I went deeper in hell. I do still love you, and I love Mia. You know that. I know you do. I thought about you every day."

"I never slept with Carter." I looked over at her, and she looked over at me. "When we kissed the few times, he never compared to you. It didn't feel right. I still love you. I thought of you almost every day. But most days were too occupied with Mia. I wished and prayed to God that you were there with me to watch her grow and to hold my hand. You just weren't."

"I couldn't."

"You killed him . . . Whoever he was I forget. You really killed him dead, didn't you?"

I nodded. "I thought it was right at the time . . ."

"I don't know what it was . . . I didn't know what to think after I heard you say you killed another man. I cried and cried and cried. I hated being pregnant really, but I'm glad I have her. I just wish it would have all went about differently."

I nodded. "Me too."

"When you first kissed me, I was angry with you, thinking how mad it made me feel that you thought you were that good, you were that good."

I held in my laugh; instead, I smiled widely, and I knew my dimples were showing. "I was trying to sleep with you."

"That's a way to put it." She laughed as did I.

"I'm just telling you the truth." I paused and looked over at her, facing her as she faced me. "I saved you from that man for two reasons."

"I get it now."

"I didn't think you were that innocent until our first date. You were feisty."

She snickered. "So I remember somebody saying."

"Let's go in now."

I got out and ran to her side, but she opened the door first. "Oh sorry. We could try it again?"

I shook my head, laughing. "I'll win."

"You're such an ass."

"You still have a nice ass."

"You're not so bad yourself." She walked beside me inside of the place. The music was soft and the lighting dim when you walked in. It was calm and romantic.

"May I help you?"

"Harlan." I looked at the hostess.

"Ah yes. A table for two. Is that correct?"

"Prefer a booth actually."

She nodded. "I believe I have a few available. Right this way, please." She led us toward the back of the restaurant and to a booth against the wall. Kendall sat first on one end and me on the other. "Your waitress will be with you in a minute to take your drink orders. Her name is Catherine. Have a nice dinner." She looked at me before leaving.

"You didn't have to bring me to such a fancy place, Micah. You don't have to try to impress me."

I shook my head. "I do."

"There's a lot I think we need to talk about."

"Kendall—"

"No. Micah, you know we have to talk. That's why I've agreed to tonight. You know that, I know."

I nodded. "I know. You're right."

"Hi, I'm Catherine. May I start you off with something to drink for tonight?"

"Just a glass of water, no lemon," I answered.

"A glass of Beringer."

"Yes, I'll bring that right out." She walked off, giving me one last glance. Her walk was obvious to catch my attention, and she succeeded. I didn't look for long, so Kendall wouldn't notice. I can't help it. I need some actual relief. It's been three years. I know I won't be able to go slow once it starts either, like the way I remember Kendall and I always did it together. I liked going slow with her though. Every other girl, I was fast and mostly made them turn over and hold on to something, so I wouldn't really have to look at them, and I did it fast and hard, wanting it to be over, but it felt so good. I don't want to think of Kendall as one of those girls. I have to control myself . . . if anything happens.

"So . . ." We both made eye contact from across the small polished wooden table.

After my water and Kendall's wine was brought out, we ordered the food. It was delicious to say the least. It felt like the first time I've actually ate. I tried to eat slow and look polite the entire time, but for the most part, I couldn't control myself. It tasted so good to me. Even if the food wasn't that great, I would have been completely and utterly oblivious to it. I paid when we got the check, which she tried to intervene, saying she could do it. It was fun. We laughed and talked the whole time it seemed like, besides when I was busy stuffing my face, which she laughed about.

"Have you seen your mom yet?"

"Tomorrow."

"But you have to stay at Josh's, don't you? I thought you would have to be under house arrest or something for . . . you know."

"Parole. I do have to stay at his house for a while, which really sucks." She laughed.

Kendall nodded. We just stared at each other for a long minute before the waitress brought back my card, and we got up to leave. Outside was windy. "Thanks for dinner," she spoke on our walk back to the car.

"You don't have to thank me." I opened the passenger door for her, which she clambered in, smiling gloriously. I walked over and got in as well. We rode in silence for the first few minutes awkwardly.

"This doesn't seem real to me." I looked over at her quickly then back at the road. "You being here, I mean. Like it's a dream, and I'm still asleep . . . And I don't want to wake up." I smiled.

"It does seem weird."

"I don't know what to say . . . Well, yeah, you won that one."

I rolled my eyes. "You didn't have to shower with a room full of other men. I wouldn't even call half of them real men."

She was quiet. "Why didn't you just tell me you killed him when you did, Micah? Honestly, I'm just curious to know why."

I didn't want to answer. "Why do you want to know that?" My wrists were starting to turn white from my grip being so tight on the steering wheel.

"I'm said I'm only curious," she snapped. "Maybe, if you would have told me about it, things would have turned out differently, and you wouldn't have had to waste three years of your life and ruin your daughter's first few years of life. You missed out on everything, Micah. All because you kept something from me."

Is she serious right now? She starting a fight with me right when we were getting along just fine. *She wants to ruin this?* Here, I was ready to throw her in the backseat with me on top. "Are you serious right now?" I shouted, looking over at her for a second and then back at the road again. "You really want to fight with me about the shit that went down three years ago? I didn't tell you because why would I? I had just killed a man who was threatening us, Kendall. I was starting over with you, and they wouldn't let me, so I fucking shot him. I put one of my oldest friends into a coma from hitting him in the back of the head with the same gun."

She was in shock, I guess, because the rest of the ride was quiet. I wanted tonight. I needed tonight to relieve myself and have a proper release, but I guess not, and now I don't have Kendall on my side anymore. I still love her too much. I just don't know about her right now. I wanted to kiss her and forget about everything bad that is still happening. I just want to hold her face in my hands, her looking up at me. Her eyes looking at me. I waited three years to have her here with me again. It's not going as I thought it up to be. I don't really remember now how I was picturing this all going down. Yes, I did know there was bound to be disagreements, arguments, and fights with plenty of shouting happening in them. But now that it's happening, I don't know what to think about it anymore.

When I pulled up in front her mom's house, we both just stayed silent, staring straight ahead out of the windshield to the dark street where the lights were barely shining down for light.

"Mia's most likely already asleep." I looked over at Kendall as she spoke.

"Just . . . Kendall." I looked over at her silently, lost for words.

"It's just me, Micah. We were so comfortable. We still should be."

"I don't see that the same way as you do," I whispered, staring at her still as she twiddled her fingers on her lap and glanced up at me occasionally. "You don't even seem to believe yourself when you talk anymore."

She nodded. "You know I still love you, and I want you. I'll always want you, Micah. I want you to be her father. I know you'll be a good fa—"

"Don't give me that bullshit."

"What bullshit?" She raised her voice. "You don't believe that I still love you?"

I only stared straight ahead. I took in and let out a deep breath and looked down toward the dashboard. "I've thought about Mia and you for the entire time I was in that place. I don't want you saying to me that I've ruined her life so far. I'm the one who ruined my life so far, Ken. If you want an example of a father ruining the first years of their kids' life, go ask my old man." I bit down on my lip and looked down. *I did not just say that, did I?* I did. Dammit. I could feel her staring at me intently, listening for anything else I was going to blab out to her. I don't need a fucking therapist right now.

"Micah?"

"Just drop it," I snapped.

"No. I can't drop something like this?" She paused. I took another deep breath. "Is this what this is all about? Mia? All because you didn't have a good father? Micah, you're nothing like him. I have to believe that. You're a good man."

"Kendall. I don't want a lecture."

"You need a lecture, Micah. I never knew your father, and I don't think that I want to. I just know though that you are a better man. You can't be like him, and you never will be. Mia loves you. I love you. Don't be scared to be her father . . . because I'm gonna need your help with this." I still didn't feel right to look over at her. I know she's still looking at me though.

"I would like to just go to bed," I said suddenly.

"What did he do to you?" she asked timidly. I shook my head. My eyes were getting the sensation in them that the tears were coming, and I wouldn't be able to stop them once they arrived. "Micah?" she asked, seeming really concerned. "Do you want to just stay here? You can stay here?"

I shook my head. "I have to go back."

"Thank you for tonight, Micah."

"I'll walk you up." I got out and went over to her side and opened the door and walked up to the front door of her mother's house.

"I really did miss you. I don't know if you believe me, but I did every day and night." I stared down at her.

"I missed you." My voice sounded really deep, trying to hold myself back from looking too pathetic right now.

The next thing I did was freeze. Kendall had thrown herself at me, wrapping her arms around my neck and tilting her head up, kissing me, hard. I was too shocked at first. Her tongue pushed past my lips, her hands threaded and fisted through my hair, messing it up surely, but it felt so good. I had her close to me, pressed against my body just the way I've been imagining since I was first locked up in a cell. Away from her. No Kendall. I kissed back with more force, my tongue going all throughout her mouth that I remember well, and my hand quickly making its way to her breast. Her breathing was heavy through her nose as well as mine at this moment.

She pulled away suddenly. "Sorry," she blurted out, embarrassed. "I didn't mean to . . ." She laughed at herself. I smiled down at her. "Do you . . . do you want to . . . you know, come inside?" I laughed but then got serious. *Do I really want this to happen? To make it look like I was just planning on sleeping with her the first night we spend time together?* No.

"I don't think it's the best idea right now, Ken. We should wait," I spoke quietly.

She nodded. "You're right." She shook her head, looking down, and her cheeks enflamed a brilliant red that made me want to kiss her even more.

"I do want to," I whispered. She nodded.

"I'll be back at my apartment tomorrow."

"Good night, Kendall." I kissed her on the corner of her mouth.

"Night, Micah," she said softly before going inside and turning the lock.

When I pulled into Josh's driveway, I just sat there with the key out of the ignition and in my right hand. I just stared outside. When I kissed her, it was amazing, beyond incredible to feel her soft pink lips pressed onto mine with such passion and love. The face I saw though, when I pulled away, was her damn neighbor's face, Carter. His lips pressed against hers. She said they didn't sleep together, but I don't know. I want to believe her, of course. The image of his lips on her sweet and innocent ones, his tongue exploring through her mouth, going deep. That asshole. I clenched my jaw. She got with him. She had to of. I shouldn't think that way, but my mind is not something I can easily control.

I put the keys right back into the ignition and backed out of the driveway.

Chapter 51

I went to the only place I could think of: Balzer's Bar. The music wasn't loud. It seemed to be packed at every table and pool table. I went straight over to the bar and pulled out a stool and plopped down, resting my hands on the polished bar. "Micah Harlan." I looked over beside me. "Haven't seen you in years," the man spoke.

I stared at him. "Hi, Frank." He's wasted.

"You do remember me!" he shouted triumphantly.

"I don't think I'd forget you that easily."

"Yeah, I know we screwed."

I gave him a disgusted look. "No, we didn't." I laughed awkwardly.

"So now you're denying me?"

"We didn't fuck. There were a few girls between us. Mine was never near yours."

He shrugged. "That was a good time."

"It was weird." I looked at him crazily.

He laughed. "Soooooo where have you been?" He slurred, taking another sip of his glass after talking.

"Not around." I waved the bartender.

"That helps," he said quietly. I looked over smiling. "You have a kid now, don't ya?"

I froze and glided my tongue over my bottom lip and looked to my right back over to Frank. "Where'd you hear that?"

"The men were talking about it a few days ago when I was here. A daughter, isn't it?"

"Who?"

"I don't know. I think Newton."

"Well, what were they saying?"

"What can I get for you guys?" I looked up at the blonde behind the bar asking for my drink order. She was leaning down, giving me a perfect view of the top of her chest, her breast practically spilling out of her top as she leaned on the counter in front of me.

"Ummm . . . just give me a Sloe Screw, more vodka than usually added though, please." She raised one brow at me, adding a small smirk and then going to make my drink.

"So what're you tryyying to for-get?" Frank asked, sitting down beside me with a thump of his arms onto the bar.

I looked over at him. I'm sure as hell not sharing anything that's been going on or that's happened to me with this freak. I'm the freak. I sighed. "Screwing you." He laughed loudly.

"Okay, don't tell me then, just drink up," he said as the busty, curvy, and tall blonde set my drink down in front of me. I picked it up while Frank hit my back, still finding that what I said was funny. It was literally the first taste of liquor I've had in years. I know I'm not supposed to be drinking and getting mad drunk. Right now, though, I can care less about everything I am not supposed to do. That's why I'm here in the first place. The blonde and I stared at each other as I chugged some of the drink down. She bit her lip, fixing her hair so it was only cascading in waves down her one shoulder. When she started walking over to another customer yelling, "Bartender!" she turned and gave me a brief stare. Her body seemed amazing. I just can't tell if it's me, the liquor, or my hormones telling me that she looks incredibly sexy in her black leather pants and matching vest, with obviously no bra under, and a V-neck-type thing at the top that comes just above her belly button. I stared at her ass as she bent onto the counter, talking to the other man who kept glancing at her chest as she rested them on the counter. She looked back at me over her shoulder again. I didn't care that I was caught staring at her body. I liked that she noticed and got the slip from my eyes and not my mouth. "Don't overthink it and try to woo her there, big guy." Frank laughed beside me. "She'll mount just about anyone, and right now, I think you've already made it to the top of her 'to-do list.'"

I just looked down before taking the glass back to my lips, swallowing every bit of the liquor as it burned slightly flowing down my throat. I welcomed it, though, and I needed it. I deserve the burn. By the time I finished my third glass, everything was bright, and the music was blasting, pounding even, my ears thumping with every beat the band played. Everything became funny. Everyone looks funny and is spinning somewhere, never staying in one place, never staying still. I sat back down after doing . . . what was I just doing? Who cares? I went back and sat at the bar with Frank and some guy—what's his name? I don't remember, and honestly, right now, I couldn't care less about this guy. Why should I care? Plus, on the bright side, he's been buying me a few more shots of something that I can only describe right now as strong but delicious. Everybody was shouting and laughing right in my face, and all I could do back was laugh with and at them. I'm definitely smashed.

So why do I feel so bad right now? What have I done?

Kendall.

I wanted to curl up in the corner and just hold my legs to my chest and weep, just to cry my eyes out until I get dehydrated and just dry up somehow, and maybe just die. Mia. She's so beautiful, and I'm so incredibly in love with her when I don't even know her.

I don't know her.

I bit down on something in my mouth and jumped, then laughed, of course. Somebody slapped my back. I laughed. I laughed and laughed when I should be screaming, sleeping in my car, kissing Kendall somewhere, even holding Mia in my arms while she sleeps. I should have never come here in the first place.

"Micah, that's enough. I'm cutting you off, no more."

"What the fu——no. I-I-I know what I am a doing o'er air." What am I saying again? Who am I talking to? The bartender. Breasts. Her ass. "You're so hot." I stared at her dumbly, I imagine. She blushed and said something. I was too busy ogling her breasts.

Kendall.

Mia.

Stop!

No!

"I want you sooooooo b-ad."

"Excuse me?" She laughed, still smiling.

I reached out, and I don't even know what I was touching. I started curling my fingers. At first, it looked like I was caressing her face, but then there was nothing. I was just waving my hands around in the air. I spun around, pointing randomly. "You." I pointed to somebody with a short haircut and a small gut, their T-shirt tucked into their jeans. That's all I can make out.

"Hey!" The person cheered. Frank?

I narrowed my eyes. "Frank?" I tried looking and stepping closer, hitting past people and tripping, falling into somebody. They caught me, thankfully, and I stood up again. "Frank." I smiled, embracing him in my arms. He was laughing and cheering.

"Micah? Micah, you awake?" I tried opening my eyes. "How many has he had?"

"Like three glasses and like . . . I don't even remember how many shots of tequila and vodka."

I heard a distant sigh and cursing. I know him! I know I do. Who is it?

I reached my hands up to feel for his face; I know his bone structure. I started laughing. His face was all swirly whirly. "Who?" I tried yelling, but my voice was a near whisper and inaudible even to me.

"Micah?" There was a clicking in front of my face. I smiled.

"Kendall, shhhhh, Mia's sleeping," I told her.

"No, Micah."

"Shhh. You don't want to wake her."

"Micah, you need to stand somehow. I can't carry you."

"I love you so much."

"I need to take you to the car."

"Can we go see her?"

"Who?"

"M-my girls. I love them so much, ya know? They're so beautiful . . ."

"Yeah, yeah, sure. Just come on now. Stand. One. Two. Three."

I was helped to my feet, wobbling around outside. It was so windy now. I started laughing again. "It's four in the morning, Micah."

"So?"

"We'll go see . . . your girls tomorrow, okay?"

"Mmmm."

I was ducked down and into something cold and smooth. Leather. Car ride! Then everything just went black suddenly. I had no control as I just slumped over.

***

I groaned, turning over. It's soft. What the hell is it? A bed? Yep, that's what it is. A bed though? How am I in a bed? I opened my eyes. Holy fuck! My head hurts so badly right now. What happened last night? Oh yeah. I went out to Balzer's. I got so hammered there. How did I get back? I'm back at—Wait, where am I? This isn't Josh and Bailey's spare bedroom.

"Micah? Micah, sweetheart, you awake?" the light flickered on above me.

"Oww, what the?" I said softly, covering my face with my hands. Mom?

"Sorry." She laughed a little. The light switch was flicked back down, and the lighting disappeared, the room suddenly becoming covered with a blanket of darkness. Mmmmm, that's better. But this is not what I deserve. I deserve to have the light inflicting pain on me and giving me a monster headache like I'm being hit in the side of the head with a ball bat. "Turn the light back on!" I just groaned. She walked over and sat on the side of the bed. I slid my hand down my face slowly and opened my eyes slowly, squinting to see her sitting beside me on the small bed.

"Sorry." I felt bad all of a sudden for cursing around her.

"I shouldn't have turned the light on." Her eyes were watering.

"Please, don't cry."

"I just haven't seen you in so long, darling. I love you. I didn't mean to hurt you in any way."

I stared up at her. "I love you," I whispered. "How'd I get here anyway?"

She wiped her eyes. I reached down and placed my hand over hers on the blankets. "Some guy brought you here and said you got mad drunk, and you weren't coming back to his place like that and apologized that it was so late. I didn't care though. Candice and I brought you to bed."

"I'm sorry. He should have just left me there instead of waking you two. I'll call him in a little bit about it all."

She shook her head. "We were happy to see you, even at four in the morning, and you were, like, passed out."

I shook my head. "I didn't mean to get drunk. Maybe I did but . . ."

"You don't have to explain. I brought you some orange juice. Sit up." I sat up, and she set my pillow against the headboard and laid back against it slowly. My head was still spinning and pounding. Bam. Boom. Click. Tick. Boom. Thump. Thump. Thump. Thump. Smash. Boom. Boom. Boom.

I set one hand on the side of my head and gripped the cool glass containing the half-empty juice on the other. I tilted my head back slightly and poured the cold orange juice into my mouth. It was delicious. It made me feel good in a way, and I drank almost all of it. I started to feel dizzy, and my head felt light, a sickness overcoming me suddenly. I took the drink away from my face and covered my mouth, as I felt like I was going to vomit everywhere on my bed and mother sharing it with me partially. After the feeling subsided, my throat was still very dry. I drank the rest of the drink and handed it to my mom, which she took.

"I'll bring you some medicine, and you should feel better in an hour or so."

I shook my head. "Don't care for me like you did him."

She turned before opening the door. "You're my son, Micah. I'll always care for you."

"I don't want you to bring me anything. No medications."

"You're sick."

"It's my fault, don't worry about it," I whispered. "I deserve it anyway. Just go away from me."

"Excuse me?" She sounded like she was going to start crying again.

"Mom."

"No, Micah. You are not your father if that's somewhat of what you are referring to. You are a good man who just was in some trouble. Don't you dare ever say that you deserved to be sent to prison or anything bad that has happened to you, Micah."

I just laid back down. "Sorry." I breathed. "Just please, stop talking right now. We'll talk later."

I faintly saw her nod before my eyes closed again, and I heard the door close gently. I don't deserve her at all, and she nor Candice deserve to have any bad people in their lives.

***

"Do you still love her though?" she whispered.

I looked over at Candice. She started showing me some of her pictures of Mia she has with her, and then Kendall came in to talk after that. First, it was about me getting wasted, which she couldn't find herself to believe until, of course, I told her the entire story, minus some parts about your sex life that are understakable to keep out of conversation. "Candice."

"Micah." I laughed a little. She smiled when I did. "It's just a simple question: yes or no?"

I shook my head, not making any eye contact with her. "I don't think she loves me."

"Are you kidding me?" I looked over at her staring at me while we sat on the couch together, hip and hip. "Yes, she does, Micah. I know she does."

"I don't know."

"Stop being so stupid right now. You can't act like she doesn't love you, when, in fact, you know she does. I know you know that."

I grinned at her. "Every time I've been around her lately, all she does is start something and start yelling, and I just let her go."

"You can't just walk away because you're fighting." She got serious. "Seriously, she has your daughter, my niece."

"I'll be right back." I stood and walked into the hallway along the kitchen. I pulled my phone out of my pocket and went to my contacts and clicked the green call button.

"Hello?"

"Hey, I need to talk to you."

"We can start with, where the hell are you? You know you can't just leave and stay the night somewhere else. You'll go back. Micah, you're on parole. You have—"

"Wait." I waved my hand. "What are you talking about? You dropped me off at my mother's."

"What?"

"What?"

"I didn't see you at all last night, Micah?"

"But . . . are you sure?"

"Yeah, I'm sure."

"Then . . . who?"

"You said somebody dropped you off at your mom's house?"

"Yeah."

"Who were you with that you don't remember what happened?"

"I got hammered, and I guess I passed out sometime. I swore I thought I was talking to you . . ." I froze. Kendall. "Josh, I'm gonna have to call you back." I hung up before he could answer me with any words and went straight to Kendall's name in my contacts.

"Micah?" She sounded different.

"Kendall, Kendall, are you all right?"

"Micah, what's wrong?" my sister whispered beside me. I put my hand up to silence her.

"Kendall?"

"Yeah, I'm fine. Are you okay?"

I shook my head. "Where are you?"

"Still at my mom's. I'm packing Mia up to take her back home."

"No, don't do that. Stay where you are. Don't go outside. Is your car there?"

"My mom picked us up, no."

"Okay, that's good. Don't go outside, please. Just stay where you are, and don't go by the windows or anything, please, please."

"Micah?" She was now in panic.

"Please, Kendall, just listen to me. I'm going to come to you. I'm at my mom's, though, so it will be awhile."

"You have to tell me what happened. We have to tell each other things if this is going to work. No secrets. Okay?"

I sighed and wiped the continuing sweat from my face. "I think I was drugged last night at the bar."

"You went drinking?"

"Kendall, that's not the point here," I raised my voice.

"I don't understand. You left me to go out partying. Are you serious?" She was crying, I think.

"Don't be like that. It wasn't my intention. It just happened. Just listen to me this time."

"Who would have drugged you?"

I thought about it. "Frank," I whispered.

"Frank? Who's Frank?"

"I'm coming to you. Just stay inside."

I hung up quickly. "What's happening?" My mom and sister were staring at me.

"I have to go get Kendall." I rushed to get my shoes on. "I have to go now."

"Would they come here?" Candice asked quickly.

"If they would have wanted you guys, they would have tried when I was locked away. They didn't know where Ken and Mia were."

"Be careful."

"Love you."

Chapter 52

I kept my eyes on the road the entire time. I ran two red lights, already knowing I'll be getting tickets in the mail and probably something said to me by my parole officer, who is a total dick, and the other classes about getting out early that I have to go to. Right now, though, I can't give a fuck about any of that. Mia. Kendall. I have to get to them.

"Move out of the way!" I kept shouting at everyone who was actually going to the speed limit. I don't remember how many cars I've passed already. No drive was ever as long as this one. As soon as I got there, I looked around when I was on the same street. I didn't see any signs of anybody I know. I parked right in front of her house and ran to the front door. As soon as I knocked, I hurried up and wiped my forehead with the back of my wrist. It was drenched in moisture. I took a deep breath and knocked again loudly.

"Kendall!"

The door was opened quickly. "What is going on?" Her mother rushed. "What the hell are you doing, making us panic like this?" I saw Kendall holding Mia in the kitchen as she slept in her arms. "Who the hell do you think you are?" she asked loudly.

"Is everything okay?" I closed the door behind me. My eyes stayed on Kendall and Mia, being cuddled closely to her chest.

"Yeah, what's going on? What happened last night?"

"I don't know. I don't know why they did that . . . I just thought . . . I just . . ." My voice was cracking, and my eyes were watering.

"Micah?" Kendall walked closer over to me.

"I'm so sorry." She shook her head. Mia stirred in her arm.

"Daddy?"

Mia lunged for me in her arms, and Kendall handed her off to me to hold her. I took her and brought her small body to my chest and kissed the top of her curly hair as she wrapped her arms around my neck. "Don't cry, Daddy." Her small, soft lips pressed against my cheek.

I closed my eyes for a second. I don't ever want to let go of her now. "Are you hungry?" I looked over at Kendall's mom. "I just finished cooking." I nodded, still cuddling Mia in my arms as she rested her head on my shoulder. Kendall placing her hand on my back brought me back to reality from my peaceful moment in time.

"You wanna sit down?" I nodded and reached and grabbed her cold hand into mine and led us into the living room. Holding her hand again made me feel relieved. I still have her. When we sat down on the sofa, I brought Mia down on to my lap to sit instead. Kendall kept her hand in mine on my knee.

"I don't know why they did it? I don't know who."

"Where were you?" she asked quietly.

"Balzer's."

Her eyes widened. "Why would you ever go back there?" She got angry.

"I wanted a drink . . . it's just where I ended up at I guess. I just don't get that drunk that fast. I had two drinks and a few shots . . . I don't know when they even could have spiked it."

"He—or whoever it was just took you back to your mother's house though?" I nodded. "They didn't hurt you?" she whispered. When I looked up, she was staring down at Mia on my legs. "Can you take us home after dinner?"

I nodded. "Of course."

***

"Thanks for the food." I gave Kendall's mom a quick hug. She only nodded and said her good-byes and love to her daughter and granddaughter. I watched as she bent down and Mia put both her hands on the sides of her face and leaned up giggling to give her a kiss.

"I just have to get the car seat transferred from my mom's to your car then," Kendall said before walking out the front door, closing it behind her.

"You just make sure you always take care of my girls, Micah. It is good to see you again, to see her like this again." She gave me another hug again, a sincere and gripping hug, in which she squeezed me tightly, lovingly like my mother would and still always does to me.

"I will," I whispered. "Of course I will," I added softly.

"Where are going, Daddy?"

"I'm taking you and Mommy home now."

"Home? Where do you live?"

"I'm staying somewhere else."

"Else?"

"Yes, I have to stay with someone for a while."

"Why?"

"Why not?" I smiled down over at her. She buried her face in the crook of my neck and had a fit of giggles. I held her close to me as I stepped down the few steps.

"You got set up?"

"Yeah, it's good."

I stood beside Kendall as she buckled Mia in, who didn't exactly want to be set in her seat. I opened and closed the door for Kendall on the passenger side and then got in myself. We didn't really talk on the way there, and when Kendall was getting Mia out of the car, I just stood on the sidewalk, looking around. I kept just staring at stuff, like the park across the street, but my sight always brought me back to a truck parked right across the street from Kendall's building. Why does it look so familiar?

"Micah? Micah?" Kendall waved her hand in my face.

"What? Yeah?"

"You okay?"

I shook my head, looking away from the truck. "Yeah." I nodded. "I'm fine."

She laughed a little. "Yeah, okay." Mia started laughing a little too, which I didn't understand.

"Mommy, Daddy's silly." I heard Mia whisper as they walked in front of me to the front entrance of the building.

"Yes, yes, he is, darling" She glanced back at me smiling. I smiled behind them both. On the way up the stairs, Mia looked back at me from Kendall's shoulder, where she set her chin down on.

"Mommy? Where Dad stay?"

"He has a friend to stay with."

"Can stay with us?"

"That would be up to him."

"He stay again?"

"I don't mind."

She looked back at me again, and I was trying not to laugh at her excitement to be around me. It made me feel . . . different I guess would be the word. It made me feel happy in every way possible.

"Don't you have to stay with your mom or Josh until your parole is up?"

"I do," I answered as she unlocked the door. She walked in, giving me a weak smile. Right when she stepped inside, she gasped loudly.

"Oh my god . . ."

I gently moved her to the side to see inside of the apartment. Holy fuck. "Wait in the hall."

"Daddy," Mia pleaded.

"Just let me look inside, sweetie." I looked back at her. The whole place is thrown upside down completely. My mouth was barely hung open, and my eyes felt like they have been open for ages.

"I didn't know if I should have been expecting you to come in instead?" I looked over into the kitchen to see Newton. He was wearing a black hoodie and jeans.

I just stared at him. "Micah? Micah, is it okay now? Should I just call the police?" She walked in beside me. She made a surprised screech and not a delightful one at that. "Micah?" She was horrified.

"I was hoping it'd just be you and me, Kendall . . . alone, of course, that is."

"Shut your mouth."

"Mommy . . ."

"No, I have a few things to talk to you both about. I think it's better if you're the one to shut your mouth."

I reached my arm behind me and grabbed on to Kendall's arm to position her and Mia's body behind mine, where they would be safer. With her opposite hand, she fisted my T-shirt tightly, shaking. "What are you doing here?"

"I was wondering the same thing when I saw you step inside, Micah. It's been a while since I've seen you. You just got out, yeah?"

"What do you want? Why are you here?"

Kendall's hand held on even tighter as he stood up fully from noticing that Newton leaned on the counter, and his gun in his left hand became visible. "I wanted your lovely girlfriend to be bent over this table handcuffed . . ." He shrugged.

"You go to hell."

He smirked back at me. "I never did like your attitude. You're too much like Walter in that way; you never shut up. You keep your women to yourself . . ." he looked behind me at Kendall. "Frank must've not really known what he was doing when I told him what to do with you," he added coolly as he stepped even closer to us, and I could hear Kendall's faint sobbing behind me as she kept fisting my shirt and holding Mia as close to her body as possible, I assume. I clenched my jaw as he took another step toward us. "As I can't have her." He waved the gun toward Kendall. I moved to the side more to cover her from his range of eyesight to shoot. "I'd like to have all my money back. Today."

"It was never your money to begin with. I made it, you held it is all."

He raised his brows at me. "You would have never had any money if it weren't for me, you know that." He paused. "I didn't want another man added into our group. There were too many to begin with. Walter really liked you. You ratted him out though. He saved you from the streets, I remember." He looked around and then back at me. "You ruined the whole operation. You bankrupted so many men just because you got whipped by this slut."

"You had to make this big of a mess just for some money?"

He smiled again and laughed a little. "I would have no greater pleasure right now than to kill you like you killed my business. How 'bout in front of your daughter?" He lifted the weapon.

"Just put the gun down, Newton!" He shook his head.

"You ruined it all, every bit of the business. You got rid of all of my employees. They quit because you gave everyone else up, a bunch of cowards apparently I had working for me."

"Newton, god dammit, put the gun down now!" Mia by now was crying louder than Kendall, so he could hear her clearly. "Just put it down." We stared at each other for a while. He started to lower it, and Kendall breathed a deep sigh behind me, not holding on as tight but still tight as hell on to my shirt.

He lifted it again, and the noise went off. The next sound was screaming, crying. Mia. Kendall. No! What's happened? Everything was blurry, and my arm felt like someone was twisting a knife around inside of it. "Ahhh!" I screeched. The pain was horrific in a simple word to describe it. It's like someone has cut you open and is pouring salt into it. I gripped where the bullet went inside of me and just squeezed.

"Micah! No!"

"Daddy!" There were faint screams and cries. I leaned down, feeling Kendall at my side, Mia balling her eyes out so much that her entire face was red in my eyes.

Another bang.

More screaming.

More crying.

"Micah!" There was a pause of uncontrollable sobbing beside me, above me, all around, and everywhere. "Help! Somebody help us!!" She screamed. There wasn't that much pain that I was feeling to tell where anything hit me, only a burning sensation in my stomach. There. I swallowed loudly. I tried grabbing on to anything: skin, arm, Kendall.

"Kendall!" I tried yelling. Is it her? Who's above me? It's hard below me, cold in a way.

"Micah, I'm here. I'm right here, darling, right here."

My body was going somewhere else. There were hands and noises all around me, spinning around. "Ken-d . . ." I couldn't speak.

"Dad!"

"Mi—"

There was a slam. It jerked, and the feeling of movement started below me. I kept cringing. There's not that much pain. There was something put over my face. "Micah, Micah, can you hear me? Can you see me?" I tried opening my eyes to see whoever is shining a little light in my face that keeps growing and growing. "Can you hear me?" I was barely able to nod up to the black man with the shaved head. He's wearing gloves and looks in a hurry.

"Ken?"

"She's right beside you." My hand felt a squeezing sensation.

"I'm here. We're here, honey."

I tried smiling, I don't want to know what it actually turned out to be though. I heard a small giggle beside me to my left. Mia. There was still sobbing. There was a shift beneath my body, and I was lifted somewhere else. "We have to take him into surgery now if he's going to live!" Shouting. There was even more sobbing and crying. I tried to reach over to touch her face, to just smear away and kiss away each tear streaming down her face. There were big bright lights one after the other above me. Then there was a door or two shoved open quickly. There was talking, a lot of talking, needles, and men in hats before there was complete darkness.

***

There is pain. My arm. It's an awkward burning type of pain. On the side side of my stomach, there is even more pain. More pain, and more. Where am I?

"Will he wake up soon?"

"He should, yeah. He is just resting right now, just sleeping, ma'am." There's a cold feeling on one of my . . . hands? Yes. That's what that is. My hand. I moan.

"Can you hear me, sweetheart?" Mom? I try to fight the sleepiness and exhaustion, at least enough to open my eyes, but it isn't enough. I fail to do only that much.

"Why wake up, Dads?"

"I'm not sure, sweetie," Kendall's voice cracks.

"I'm going to get a coffee. I'll be right back." My mom.

"I'll come," Candice spoke. Candice.

"Momma, I getta cookie?"

I heard a slight sob. "Yes, honey. Just go with Aunt Candice and Grandma."

There were rushed footsteps and a door opening and closing.

There was again a cold feeling grasping my hand. Kendall. She rested the side of her face on my left arm. Then my strength felt like enough to open my eyes. Her hair has been pulled up messily, and she has tear stains covering her cheeks, her lips pressed against my warm skin, startling me at first.

"Kendall." My voice was small and hoarse.

Her head shot up immediately. "Micah." She smiled, her eyes watering again. She gave my hand another tight squeeze. "Oh my god, thank God." She sobbed lightly while barely leaning into me.

"I'd hug you if I-I could," I stuttered.

She giggled. I started trying to laugh with her, but when I tried, my stomach felt like someone was standing on it, and my throat started throbbing with thirst. I started gagging a little, not even able to cough. I winced as the pain shot through me again. I clenched my jaw, not being able to do anything than accept and endure the pain consuming my body. "I'm going to call in the nurse for you now." She reached over and pressed the button. I kept my hand on her smooth arm.

"I've missed you." She reached up and moved my hair off my face.

A nurse came bustling through the entrance. "Well, good afternoon, Mr. Harlan. I'm Nurse Paula. I'll let the doctor know that you are awake now." She comes up beside the bed, by Kendall who moves politely for her but hesitantly at the same time, still gripping my fingers in hers. "Do you know where you are?"

"Hospital."

"He's said he's thirsty." I looked down at Kendall, who shot me a quick glance after speaking up.

"I'll get him some water after the doctor has examined him thoroughly." I watch as she gets a blood pressure cuff and wraps it around my arm. "So how are you feeling? Do you have a lot of discomfort?"

I nodded, sucking in a sharp breath and then regretting it and making an awkward coughing noise. "Okay, okay, just relax. That's normal after you've been shot twice, especially where you have been hit. The bullets, though, were successfully removed, and the surgery went well." I watched Kendall as she sat on the very edge of the bed, careful not to hit into my body at all.

"I just feel so . . . drained and exhausted I guess. Just terrible . . ." I spoke softly.

"I understand. I'll tell the doctor all that. Your blood pressure is okay, Mr. Harlan. I'll just go get the doctor now for you and see about that water." She smiled kindly and patted my shoulder lightly before leaving.

"I thought I'd lost you," she whimpered. "You were barely conscious. Mia was crying so hysterically the entire time. I didn't know what to do so I just started screaming for help . . . and Carter came rushing as fast as he really could." She smiled. "Sorry, I was just so relieved when the ambulance came, and they started doing whatever to save you on the way here. You did lose a lot of blood . . ." she stated softly, not breaking eye contact with me the entire time she spoke as if she would break at any second.

"Where is he? Newt-un." I coughed again.

"He was arrested a while ago, I was told," she whispered.

It started becoming hard to swallow, and I was just so damn thirsty. Nurse Paula came back in the room with a little Styrofoam cup and walked over to my side. "Just take small sips now," she instructed before handing the cup off to me.

Kendall scooted up the bed closer to me and helped me with the cup. "He'll be in in a minute."

"Thank you," Kendall told her sweetly before she left the room again. She helped me tip the cup back for another drink and then retracted it again and set it down on the tall, slim nightstand beside the bed. "Better?"

"Better." I smirked. We stared at each other for another moment. "I'm so sorry. I know it won't change anything and just drive you further away from me, but for what it's worth—"

"Micah, you're here, you're alive, and you're good. I'm here, and I'm not going anywhere nor would I want to be anywhere else." She gave my hand another squeeze.

When the door opened, both of our eyes shot to it, startled by the sudden movement occurring. A man that looks to be in his thirties or early forties strides in, wearing a white doctor's coat and black glasses. "Well, it's nice to have you awake, Mr. Harlan. Welcome back. I'm Dr. Greene." Kendall and he exchange a few words, and he checks and examines me thoroughly by shining a little white light in my eyes and checks on a few other things that I didn't really pay any attention to at all, keeping my sight on Kendall as she watches the doctor closely, and they talk a little. Kendall gets up out of the nurse's and then Dr. Greene's way and goes to make a few calls in front of the bed by the door while they both work on me.

"Now the bullet that hit down here." He barely touches his fingers over it, and I wince and look like a big baby as I squeeze my eyes shut and clench my jaw while biting down on my tongue, even though it just makes it hurt even more like hell. "It did do some pretty bad damage. It was removed successfully, and your stitches should be out in a few weeks. The one that hit your arm will heal quicker than the other, although it will have to be cast until those stitches come out. I have pain medication prescribed to you." He stopped for a little bit, taking a pause while flipping the papers on the clipboard to the next one. "Just really take it easy, and if there's any bleeding or anything that seems abnormal and loads of pain, just call us." He nodded. I nodded slightly back. "I think you should stay one more night to just keep an eye to just make sure it's all good."

"Okay," I whispered.

"Thank you." Kendall thanked him quietly.

He grinned at Kendall, and I glared, but she only glanced at him and then back at me, her hand lying over my leg, though it was covered with a cream-colored cable-knit blanket. "Your family is waiting outside," he said before exiting with the nurse.

My mom, Candice, and Mia all came in, and Kendall's mom came a little later. Mia kept trying to climb up the bed and lie down with me, but someone stopped her every time. I wanted to lie with her more than anything, to hold her as close to me as possible, even though it would hurt tremendously. I think it hurts more to not have her up here with me to lie down. Josh and Bailey only stopped by for a little bit to see how everything was going. It made me sick, literally throwing up when I thought back to the incident and how he was in her apartment with a gun, having the upper hand. What he said he wanted to do to my . . . Kendall just made the sickness worse. The things I've put her through. The things I've done to her myself makes me want to just leave her, but she's still here and won't leave my side. She didn't want to leave, so her mom took Mia with her when she left, and she just left and went home with Candice. My mom left about half an hour after everybody else was gone.

It was hard to sleep, but once they gave me some medication to help, I feel like I passed right out. Kendall. Mia.

I walked into her apartment. Why am I here again? What am I doing here? How did I just walk inside like that? Mia was in the corner, screaming and crying. The walls were folding over, as if they were melting, and with each step I took closer toward my sweet little Mia, my feet made a big booming type of noise, as if I weighed a thousand pounds, and you could hear me coming from a mile away. Loud. So much noise was all surging through my ears. I bent down in front of her and tried to reach out to take her trembling body into my arms and take her home with me. Every time I reached out to grab on to her, though, the distance increased, and she just got further and further away. The room got bigger and longer. I was only able to watch her from afar as she cried and cried, covered her ears with both hands, and kept her eyes sealed shut. I stared and then for some reason stood to my feet, and they carried me past the living room as everything drooped over again like melting ice cream. When I got to the kitchen doorway, I was frozen on the spot. He came dragging her in by her hair as she cried and screamed, holding her hair as he gripped it to relieve some of the tugging and pulling pain shooting through her scalp.

He pulled out a pair of handcuffs and put one around her wrist harshly. She shouted in pain for him to please stop, to just please, please stop hurting her. Don't hurt my daughter! No! And all I could do was watch. No matter how hard I tried to move, my body just wouldn't, like I was glued to the tiled floor. My brain was screaming, but my body just wouldn't listen to it. I was going absolutely mad inside. He put the other cuff around the table leg and threw her across the table top, pulling her jeans down her legs along with her underwear. He held her down by keeping one of his hands on the center of her back and the other held her ass tightly, squeezing and rubbing roughly. He smacked her hard. It was already beating red from such impact on the skin. All she could do was cry now and just wait for it to be over with. It will never be over in my mind, though, after this. It will never stop replaying like a tape. The image will always be there. The pictures will always be stuck in my mind. The thoughts will always be there. No, the facts will be engraved in my brain. This is my fault. My eyes felt glassy, but nothing was coming out.

"Kendall!" I screamed it at the top of my lungs. He undid his belt quickly and tugged down his pants, immediately shoving his cock through her. She screamed in pain, and I tried to lunge forward to bash his head into the flooring until he hits the lobby. Nothing. Nothing was happening. No part of me would move. Move! Nothing. It's like I'm not even here. None of them can hear me. He pulled on her hair like reins and just kept moving faster and harder. She just cried and bit down on her bottom lip, her tongue, or anything that could help her I guess. Finally, my arms moved up, and the tears came pooling out of my eyes rapidly. My feet flew across the room. When I should have been tackling him away from her pure body, they disappeared. They just vanished just like that. They were just gone. The room was all black: walls, appliances, and all. Then there was Kendall when I stood back to my feet. A knife was thrown into the center of her chest, just below her breasts, which were covered in bruises and scratches, and cigarette burns even. How? When did this happen? How is this even at all happening? I looked around. Mia? I rushed over to Kendall's body, slumped against the black, pealing wall behind her, the only thing around. Black. Darkness. Oblivion. A whole lot of nothing. I tried to stop my crying, no noises but the tears streaming down my face. "Kendall . . ." I whispered. She's still here, she's still alive, and she's still with me. "Kendall? Can you hear me, darling?" I whispered, my voice cracking at the end. I got right in front of her, and her head moved from resting on her shoulder to look directly at me.

"Daddy?" I looked into the doorway. Behind her short frame was only darkness. It's so dark here.

"Mia," I cried. "Mia, come here, sweetheart."

She turned and ran into the darkness after I said that. I looked back at Kendall. I wasn't able to move anymore. I was glued back to the floor. She was watching Mia, now only staring into that direction. When she looked back at me, her corneas were pitch black. "Leave us alone," she said softly, calmly even.

"What?"

"I'm not staying with you anymore." I was in shock, only able to stare into whatever is taking her away from me now. She looks so helpless and lost, confused in a strange way, even though I know she knows what has just happened to her. How long ago? She has to know. She's sitting on the floor with blood around her wrist from the cuff, her naked body showing the obvious signs of rape. Yet despise it all and what all she's been through, she still manages to look effortlessly beautiful like she did the first time I saw her that night at the graduation party. *Myself. No! No! No! Kendall! Mia! Don't go! Not now! Not ever! Stay! Stop!* I wanted to scream, to pull my hair out, and to get shot a billion times just to never hear her say those words to me that I've been terrified to hear since I've met her.

"No. No, you can't. You can't."

"Good-bye." It echoed, over and over again.

"No!!" I cringed as my stomach started throbbing, and I screamed loudly. I couldn't help myself from starting to cry. It was so real, but at the same time, it wasn't. It wasn't. It wasn't.

It started to really annoy me now that I couldn't move one of my arms. I pulled the blanket further up my cold and shivering body to be warmer and just cried myself to sleep with the horrific film playing over and over in my head. I don't know how I fell asleep for a few minutes, that is, but I was glad it was a few minutes. I was spared from the hell that is my mind and thoughts.

I've been awake for a few hours now, and I can't wait until someone comes to pick me up from this place. I can't stretch. I can barely go to the bathroom on my own. I have to be helped up out of bed to the bathroom's door, and then they still insist on helping me. My mom came while they were giving me breakfast, and she was able to help me go after that. It was still incredibly awkward. She couldn't stop trying to help me, constantly carefully hugging and kissing my cheek, saying how much she's so thankful for me to still be here. Little does she know I'm already gone.

When I was finally discharged to go home, the doctor told me to stay home off work for a while and to take some medications and a few other things as well. All that was going through my mind at the time he was talking, though, was that nightmare from the night before. My mom wouldn't stop saying how happy she was and was just about in tears the entire time. "I can't imagine what Mia is going through," she whispered while wiping her eyes.

I just looked over at her dully while she drove back to her house, and I guess mine now again for a while, that is. "Just, please, shut up." I didn't want her talking about that, the darkness engulfing her. She accepted it though. She ran willingly into it, a small grin appearing on her face before she turned around, embracing it in a way. She was happy to go when I told her to come here. She came to me. I stared out the window. What the hell did I just think? She wasn't ignoring or running away from me at all. She was listening and running toward me. That can't be it? Can it? Most likely not. It's just all the drugs they gave me for the pain.

"Well, they're coming over the day after tomorrow since you'll probably just be sleeping all day tomorrow, and you'll feel as lousy as you probably feel right now because you lost a huge amount of blood like all the doctors said," she sniffled again. "I'm so happy you're still here with us," she whimpered again.

"Mom."

"Thank God Kendall and Mia weren't there."

"Just . . . stop it."

"I know how much you love them, sweetheart. They both love you too darling. Don't doubt that ever."

"I want to go to sleep."

"We're almost home."

***

Candice was there when my mom pulled in, and they acted like they had to help me do everything. I mean everything. I got mad and yelled at them constantly, to the point where they were just really uncomfortable, and I just went into my old room to go to sleep and wait until tomorrow is done with to see my girls again.

Mia and Kendall didn't come today. She called my mom and said that Mia was refusing to come because she is scared. I didn't get it at first. Why would she be scared to see me? Once my mom and sister thought that I'd gone to bed, I took out my cell phone and called Kendall.

"Micah?"

"Hi, sorry it's kind of late."

"No, no, it's fine. It's good to hear you."

"You too. Look, I just want to see you so bad. I miss you, Kendall."

"I miss you."

"It's not like that, Kendall." I paused. "I want you back so bad," I spoke quietly. The line stayed silent for what seemed like hours. "Kendall?"

"I'm here."

"Say something, please . . . I need you. Please, just stay. I don't want to ever let you go. I want you in my arms forever."

There was another pause. "I don't want to talk about this over the phone."

"What's wrong?"

"I just don't know what to say to you anymore."

"I don't get what you mean?"
"You're different I guess. I don't know."
"You really don't love me anymore?"
"I've never said that, Micah. I do love you. I always have. You were everything to me. I wish that wasn't over. I do. I do still love you very much. It just doesn't feel the same anymore since you've come back. I guess it's just because things have changed."
"You mean since I knocked you up."
"I wish I had more time with you."
"You regret anything?"
"No, of course not. I love Mia, and I'm more than glad to have her in my life and to have you as her father, to have given you a daughter. I just wish we had more time together is all. I always wanted to be with you when I wasn't."
"I wanted to be there so bad when you told me you were pregnant. I couldn't. I had no other choice than just to picture myself there with you like I still do, but it only makes things hurt more."
"I want you," she whispered.
"In what way?"
"Every way. I want you to be in my life."
"Are you at your mother's?"
"Mmmm."
I took a deep breath. "Can I come over?"
"What?"
"I want to see you and Mia."
"Micah—"
"Please."
"She's just really shaken up right now. She won't really talk . . ."
"I just want to see her, please. Kendall, please, I love you."
There was a long pause. "Can you even drive?"
"I can always drive." I barely even laughed at myself. "Kendall?"
"I'm here." She giggled. "It's late . . . are you sure?"
"I'd rather be there with you."
"I'll see you in a while then. Bye."
"Bye."

I waited until my mom and sister were passed out in their rooms before I went out and left on my way.

When I pulled up into her mother's driveway, I just stared at the front door for about five minutes.

<u>From Kendall:</u>
You coming in? (:

I smiled down at my phone. She's probably been watching me since I pulled in, just staring. I got my keys and got out, locking it up while I walked up the steps. The door was opened quickly but quietly. She held up her finger to her lips, telling me to be quiet.

"Why?"

"They're both sleeping, and Mia has had trouble sleeping since . . . she just passed out a few minutes ago. She wouldn't sleep at all last night. It was awful," she answered in a whisper. I followed her inside.

I limped around until she stopped in the kitchen. "You thirsty?" She turned to me at the fridge, her eyes going directly to my stomach. Her eyes were already glassy, and with the light, I could see that her eyes are bloodshot and are red around and black underneath.

I shook my head. I limped over to the barstool and got up to sit down on it. "You okay?"

"I'll live." She nodded, grinning at the same time. She sniffled her nose and looked away to blink away her tears. "Please . . . don't cry. Not for me, Ken."

"Why do you always talk like I don't care for you?" I only looked down and back up at her. "Micah, I love you. I don't understand why you think you deserve any of this. You almost died," she spoke a little louder.

"I just can't . . . you're the one . . . he was planning—going to hurt you because of me. If anything would have happened to you or to her, I wouldn't be able to live with myself not after all of the other shit I've done to you."

"Nothing happened to neither Mia nor me."

"And thank God for some reason of that, which I was there."

We stared at each other for a long minute it seemed. Her eyes gave way finally, and her tears just flowed down her cheeks. "I don't know what I'd do without you." She started walking over to me. "How bad are all your stitches?"

I shrugged at her. "Stitchy. I don't know. They're okay I guess. They hurt every now and then . . . I was shot twice."

"So I've heard. They hurt badly?"

I shrugged again. "Just sore . . . why?"

She took a deep breath in and out and then looked away before looking back down at me. "Because I want you to make love to me," she spoke in a whisper.

Chapter 53

I was muddled with her. "What?" It was barely even a whisper.

She nodded. "I want you."

I stared at her with my brows stitched together. I took her hand on the counter and stared down at it. I looked back up at her after squeezing her hand in mine tightly, rubbing my thumb over the knuckles. "I've waited so long to see you again. To be able to have you in anyway. If you're just in my life as a friend or the mother of my child . . . I thought about it, and I only want you one way, and that's mine."

"I am yours."

I took both of her hands and pulled her closer to me so she was standing in-between my legs. We pressed our heads together, and I tilted my head up and placed my lips barely over top hers. I finally kissed her completely but stopped after one. "What's wrong?"

"I'm sorry." I looked down. "For everything. I've only put you through hell."

"Being with you three years ago was the best decision I ever made . . . I didn't even have to make up my mind. I wanted to be with you, Micah. You've done nothing but good since you came into my life."

She fisted my hair from both sides and brought her lips back down to mine slowly. The sensation of her soft lips placed between mine was heavenly. She moved her hands slowly up behind my ears while our lips stayed interlocked. Then they went back up into my hair. Our tongues were reunited after so long. I savored her taste, closing my eyes in bliss. Our breaths stayed as one until neither of us could breathe any longer. Her legs began to shake between mine as she pulled away, her eyes looking deeply into my lustful ones, keeping her bottom lip in-between my teeth. "I don't think it would be slightly appropriate for me to take you in your mother's kitchen . . . or anywhere else where we don't have a lockable door in this place."

She blushed a brilliant bright scarlet color and looked down slightly embarrassed. How is she ever like this with me still? Well, ever really. I stood from the bar stool and backed us up so we were in the living room, her lips still connected with mine, continuously brushing each other. Her soft, plump, and pure lips are against my dried-up, cracked ones, and yet she still can't stop connecting them back together. I was already rock hard by the time we reached the stairs. Dang stairs . . . It's a bit hard to navigate yourself up a flight of steps while you're turned the opposite way of them, let alone if you have a crap load of huge stitches in you, one of your arms not able to move at all. "I'm not good with steps right now." Her hands went to my shoulder as I spoke, brushing against my cast.

She smiled brightly with her arms wrapped around my neck, carefully not bumping into my lower tummy or cast-up arm. She turned us so she was going backward up and started helping me up each and every single step up to her bedroom. I started to laugh at what a sight we must look right now, she helping a man who can barely even walk and not have any use of his arm up a flight of stairs.

"Where's Mia?"

"She went to bed with my mother."

I nodded into our kiss as we reached the top of the stairs and I walked backward into her room. Her hands went to the hem of my shirt.

"Ahhh . . .," I groaned as her fingertips hit the patch on my stomach.

"Sorry." She rushed, looking back up at me.

I shook my head. It was dark, and she didn't see; her lights are turned off. She made another attempt, going slowly to ease my white shirt over my head. After it was over, she stared down at my chest, her hand moving slowly over my more defined muscles now since prison.

"You look different."

"There's not much to do in there really," I whispered back, explaining to her. I reached down with my one arm and gripped her tee. She grabbed over my hand with both of hers and pulled it over her head, exposing her braless chest. I slid my hand over her belly button and up between her breasts. So soft. I leaned my head down to her newly exposed skin. When I kissed just below her collarbone, she twisted one of her hands into my hair, tugging at the roots. I moaned, kissing her again just below the spot before, wrapping my arm around her back and bringing her closer to me, making it easier as I closed my mouth around her nipple, making her gasp into my neck. Her breasts didn't feel the same as before, though, softer around them and harder and much tougher in the center.

"Mi-cah," she spoke loudly.

"Shhh . . ." I smiled against her skin as I slid my face back up her chest. "We'll have to be quiet, remember?"

I felt her smile against my neck. She stumbled into me as I bit down on her earlobe, making me stumble back as well from her hitting into my cast. She laughed breathlessly. "What's so amusing to you?"

"I—"

I felt up her chest and cupped her breast in my hand while kissing at her neck, my teeth scraping over the skin.

"You what?" I laughed.

"I feel like . . . I'm going to br-break you." She giggled again.

"You're the only one who ever could do that." She kissed my neck when I finished speaking. The feeling was getting to be too much. It started to hurt now. My breathing increased as the pressure started to become more and more intense, my member now throbbing within the tight confines of these dang boxers. "Kendall." I almost sounded like I was begging. When she finally started to undo my belt, my jaw clenched, and I felt exhausted already dealing with this anxiety.

Right when my belt hit the floor, she slid her fingers into the top of my jeans and pulled them to my feet so they pooled at the floor, and I stepped out of them. With the jeans off, I felt more of a relief, and I sighed, but the tightness was still there with my underwear. She gripped my shoulders to sturdy herself as I unbuttoned her shorts and started to tug them down with my one hand. She aided in taking them off her legs and kicked them off. She looked up at me after, and I looked down at her. I lifted my hand. Her cheek was so smooth against the pad of my thumb. "You're so beautiful." She leaned her forehead against mine.

"I was going to try and take it slow with you . . . stay away from you somewhat."

We both smiled at each other. "Well, that didn't turn out very well."

She started giggling. "No, not at all." It was infectious, and I started laughing with her. "We have to be quiet." She calmed herself.

I nodded, still smiling like an idiot from ear to ear. I stumbled into her, making the back of her legs hit the footboard. I felt way more than relieved when my boxers hit the floor, and I pushed them aside. I cursed and groaned in pain. Not pain from the gunshot wound or her accidently skimming her fingers over the bandage again but because the friction was finally gone. It felt so good to be out that it actually brought pain. The realization that this is actually happening pained me. Just as easy as she was taken away—I being taken away from her could possibly happen again pained me. She said she wanted some sort of distance from me when I got out. What if after tonight, she finds that that was the true way to go and she wants me to leave her alone? That's what truly hurts. Kendall is the only person in this world who can truly hurt me, and it will be the kind of pain that will last an eternity in my mind.

The first time she told me she loved me was the first time she hurt me. Yes, loving me might sound all nice and sweet and romantic in a way. In my mind, though, it was all pulled apart from those silly words. Her confessing her love for me only meant that I truly did have something to lose. I loved her long before she told me. It was odd though. I tried staying away from her by getting high and shooting myself up to realize something maybe when I came to. It never happened though. I couldn't stay away from her physically or mentally. She was there to stay. I figured, though, that if I never said a word to her of how much she really meant to me, how much in love I'd fallen with her, she would get tired of me and leave. When she did finally avow her love, I figured it was because I took her virginity, and she was addled that she thought she was in love with me. She had to love me. The only thing that I try to keep telling myself, though, is that I do love her, and I will never be able to stay away from her in any way.

A tear slipped down from the corner of my eye. Don't start now. Don't you start crying and ruin this! You're finally here, and you're going to make yourself like chewing gum if you start the waterworks. I sniffled very attractively I'm sure, and sure enough, it caught her attention.

"I don't mean to keep bumping into you. Sorry," she spoke quietly. "If it really hurts that bad, we should stop."

"No." I spilled the word so quickly I didn't even know I had said it at first.

"I don't want to hurt you."

"My, how the tables have turned." I smirked, trying to lighten the mood.

She smiled fondly up at me. She walked us over to the side of the bed. Awkwardly and very slowly, she helped me sit on the side of the bed of hers and lay back with my head on the pillow then asked me a few times if I was comfortable. I was dying with anticipation to finally be inside of her again. "Kend?"

"What is it?"

"My pants . . . front right pocket. I'm gonna need the condom this time."

She blushed vermilion, with that beautiful reddish and a hint of a sort of orange, making her face light up even in the darkness of this room. She got to my pants and dug up the square silver packet. Why did I even bring that? Habit. My hopes of this happening. She walked back over to me and slid her pink skivvies down her legs before gently straddling my waist, just above my erected penis, which leaned against her backside now. She leaned down, the packet being held between her pointer and middle finger, as she held the side of my head.

I couldn't help clenching my jaw, biting her lip or wincing every time her thigh or hip would even just barely brush against my lower stomach on the side. Even when she started rocking her hips against mine, my arm ached. "You're gonna have to take it easy on me." I smiled but was serious with my words.

"Now, if I can recall, I heard just about those exact words before our first time, do you?"

I smiled at her recollection of that night that neither of us are sure to forget. One time, when I was lying in my bunk at prison in that plain cell with the old, fat man who—what did he do? I can't remember, but I do remember what I was thinking of how I thought about Kendall. I had thought that she was forgetting about me, about all of our firsts. Apparently, I was wrong after all.

"Believe those were my words." I smiled into our kiss. "Seriously, though, just take it easy up there on me."

She nodded, blushing brilliantly once more down at me while we continued kissing, her tongue in my mouth. I could tell she was having thoughts about being on top this time since she'd never done it. I grabbed her hip with my only free hand and ran my thumb on her back as I held on to her. "You just have more control." I confirmed with her thoughts. "I would top, but there might be some technical difficulty with me even getting up there. Then these will probably tear open again." I looked down at my stomach.

She nodded shyly with a serious face. She bit open the packet and rolled the condom down my length. Only she could make me this hard. I hissed when her nails slid back up to the head. I'd forgotten the feeling of her hands on me somehow due to how much I've put mine around myself in these past three years. To think that I could have lost her, that she would have told me to stay away from her like she had planned . . . I could have lost this, and I'm not talking about what we're doing but what we have.

I watched her closely as she concentrated to fully connect us. She was having some obvious trouble. I soothed my hand up and down her back and back down to her hip to relax her a bit. "Just take your time." I couldn't help but smile up at her when she looked down at me with her serious face.

"Don't mock me." She tried to be serious. "Ahhh," she groaned as she finally sunk on to me. I sucked in a sharp breath and closed my eyes for a few seconds, taking her all in. She leaned back up, coming off me, causing me to become confused and hungry for more with her sudden departure. "Sorry," she quietly apologized when she looked back down at me. "I'm just—it's been a while," she spoke quietly, nervously.

"It hurts?" She bit down on her lip and nodded sheepishly while looking away for a second timidly. "Put your hands on my shoulders." She did as I told her cautiously and leaned down on me, not taking me inside of her though. I reached my arm down between our bare bodies, sliding it slowly down her stomach causing her to quiver under my touch. I brought my hand back up. "Suck." I held my index in front of her slightly swollen lips. She leaned her head down on to my finger taking it into her mouth, swirling her tongue around and sucking on it, holding on to my hand and staring into my eyes, almost making me combust by just batting her lashes. "You can lean on me, Kendall." She grinned and glanced away from me, obviously feeling embarrassed. I leaned my head up at the same time. She put more of her weight on me, and our lips met. Her warm sweet breath continued to flow into my mouth as her luscious lips stayed interlocked with mine. Our moist tongues met each other in the middle, connecting with one another, exploring every depth of the other.

Her heart was pounding as her breasts stayed pressed against my chest, and my hand skimmed down between us again. "Just relax." My voice was deep. She took a deep breath and visibly relaxed above me as I helped her. Her fingers dug into my shoulders as I drew it out before sliding it right back inside of her. She was quivering by now. "I think you're good now," I spoke in-between our lips. I put my hand on to her hip, encouraging her. She leaned her hips off me and held on to my hips as she slowly sunk back on to me, biting her lip in concentration as I filled her completely. I clenched my jaw and sucked in a sharp breathe. Her fingers dug into my chest as she started to grind her hips.

The pain started again as she continued to move her hips down against mine, taking charge. I don't want her to stop though. The pleasure is way better than the pain. Not even after a couple of minutes of her moving her hips rhythmically against mine, I felt myself building up. "Micah," she whispered, already out of breath.

I pulled her head back down to mine and took claim of her mouth. She continued to grind her hips down, holding on to my shoulders for support. The pain from my stitches bit in again. Her eyes were closed and her mouth stayed open after she pulled away from our kiss. "Open your eyes. I wa-want to see you." She obliged and opened them slowly to gaze down at me. That was enough to tip me over the edge. "Kend-all." I tried to tell her that I couldn't hold on any longer.

She moved her hips a little more forcibly down on to mine, so I went deeper inside of her, kissing at my neck. I squeezed my eyes shut as I came quickly into the condom while cursing under my breath at the heavenly release. I put my arm around her lower back as she laid on top of me, carefully, of course, avoiding my stitches at every movement she made. She kissed my cheek and raised one of her hands up to my forehead.

"It's hot in here," she whispered.

I nodded, my eyes still closed.

"You're that tired?"

I nodded again with my eyes closed, smirking.

"I'll turn on the fan."

I wrapped my arm tighter around her.

"Micah." She giggled. "I'll be right back."

"Nooooo!" I whined, my voice laced with sleepiness. "What time is it?"

I felt her arm move to retrieve the time from her phone I assume. "Two thirty," she whispered. "I don't get how you're so tired. You didn't even really do anything but—"

"Hey." I interrupted. "It's a more of a workout than you think." I opened my eyes a little to look up at her. "I don't see how you're so talky now."

"I've waited to talk to you for so long is all . . ." She spoke after a few seconds of silence besides our heavy breathing. I rubbed my hand up and down her back slowly, still grinning like mad.

"I have to go," I whispered.

She sat up alarmed. "What? Are you serious? Why don't you just stay?" I smiled larger than anything. "What's so funny about that?" she snapped.

I tried not to laugh loudly. "I have to piss."

I knew she was staring at me. "I hate you." I smiled wider, trying to hold in my laugh. I bit down on my lip to try and ignore the pain as I pulled out of her to sit up. "Do you need help?" I shook my head, sitting on the edge of the bed now. I clenched my jaw. I definitely feel like I've torn something open. I set my palm over the patch and just sat there for an extra minute. "You okay?" I ignored her and waited for the pain to subside. She came up beside me and put her hand on my shoulder. "I'll help, just one sec." I felt the bed shift as she clambered off on the other side. I knew something was different about this bedroom. The opening and closing of some drawers came to my ears before she appeared in front of me now clothed.

"Kendall, just give me a minute, and I'll be fine," I snapped a little. I didn't have to look up at her to know she was frowning. "Sorry." I reached down and pulled the condom from around me and tossed it into the trash bin. "You should get on birth control because I hate those." I heard her make a noise and looked up to see her staring down at me. "What?"

"Now you say something." I laughed with her for a second and then regretted it, clenching my jaw. I struggled but stood to my feet.

"Just lay back down. I'll be out in a minute." I closed the door, amused with her persistence to help me pee. I washed up a little after using the bathroom and flushing. I looked down to the patch covering my stitches to see a little bit of blood but not much. They must've only torn a little. I shrugged it off. I don't feel like making a fuss over it, even though the pain is tremendous when I stretch. I'll change the bandage later. My whole arm feels numb. I tried lifting it, and it just stung. After I was done in the bathroom, I walked slowly over to the bed limping, and Kendall watched me with a worried look itched on her face the whole time. When I sat down, I made sure to make a noise like I was in a lot of pain that had her right there right away. I smiled.

"You're mean." She swatted at my back.

"Owww."

"I'm so sorry." I turned my head around to grin at her while holding in my laugh. "Just go to sleep," she demanded.

I laid back down, pausing momentarily. When my head hit the pillow and sunk down into it, I sighed, feeling relieved that I was finally lying back down, and the pain eased up and went away, not just the pain of the stitches in me but also the pain of not having Kendall next to me when I sleep. I stared up at her ceiling. She shuffled closer to me and picked up my arm and draped it over her shoulders and rested her head back on it while holding on to my hand. "You okay?" I looked down at her.

I nodded. "Insanely." I bent down, and she met me halfway. Her swollen lips pressed to mine. One of her arms went across my chest and held me closer to her to deepen the kiss. "I've missed you," I whispered when we pulled away.

"Mmmmm."

"Are you okay?" I fought to keep my eyes open.

"I'm fine." I kissed the top of her head before closing my eyes.

"What time do you usually get up?"

"Whenever Mia does really, but since she's with my mom, maybe a little later." She paused. "You should get dressed if she comes up," she added seriously. I hadn't even thought of that. I moved to get up, groaning. "I'll get your clothes for you." She got up quickly.

"I'm not helpless—"

"Stop it, okay? I'm helping you." She got irritated while picking up my clothes for me. "You just want your boxers?"

"Yes, thank you." She handed them to me and helped me sit up. I didn't say anything to her about it, even though it killed me not to tell her to stop, that I could do it. I felt helpless like she thought less of me in some way. *Unmanly*, I suppose, is the word, even though it sounds weird. "Kendall," I groaned again as she moved the sheet away and lifted my legs and slid the boxers up them slowly until they were to my hips. "I was shot, not paralyzed," I told her after she laid the sheet back on top of me.

She looked up at me while her hands rested on my hip closest to her. "If it wasn't for me you, wouldn't have been shot at all."

"What?"

"You know it's true," she spoke so quietly that if I wasn't actually really listening, I wouldn't have heard any of it.

"Kendall, what are you talking about? You think this is your fault? Have you gone mad?" I sat quickly to be face to face with her.

"If it wasn't for me, he wouldn't have been there to shoot you. I started a lot between you and ruined your relationships with everybody you were friends with," she whimpered. Is that really what she thinks? Is she serious?

I stared at her. What am I supposed to say to persuade her the truth? "Kendall." I started out at a loss of words. "You can't be serious?" I laughed. She looked down nervously. "If anything, if it wasn't for you, I'd still be in hell with all those fucking losers." She looked back up at me. "They were never my friends, maybe at first, yeah. I depended on them for my life. That's the way it was. But . . . but they . . . I chose to be with you because I fell in love." Why do I feel so nervous with her now? "I wanted to be with you, and I realized that what I was doing—what I did was wrong . . . it was bad and hurt a lot of people. What happened to me was my fault."

"You almost died right in front of me, Micah, in front of your daughter." She broke. Her tears came racing down her pink cheeks in a hurry. "I never felt so lost when I was holding you and there," her voice cracked.

"Hey." I wrapped my arm around her to pull her against my chest.

"There was so much blood," she blabbered on through her tears, her words were barely audible through her crying.

"Please, stop it." I kissed her cheek. I laid back down with her still held in my arm, and she leaned against me still being cautious. "I'm here." She fisted my tee shirt in her hand while sobbing into my side. "Stop crying. I'm here with you now. I'm fine. I'm here."

She shook her head. "I can't help it. I love you so much."

I held her waist against me tightly. I don't want to let go ever. I want to hold her forever. I need her. "Shhh . . . just take a minute to breath." I can't think of anyone else I'd rather be with, but the words of how much I love her just wouldn't come out. The words don't seem like enough to show her how much I truly do love her. She deserves more than words. She didn't say anything more. She only held me as tight as she could against her until I felt her arms relaxed, and she passed out still holding me to her, her leg between mine.

After she fell asleep, I closed my eyes too. How could she think anything was her fault? Where could she get any idea that it was ever her fault? It was all 100 percent my fault. I put her through so much. I can't believe she is still here lying next to me, saying that she loves me. It seems impossible. It should be in fact. Anything that I've learned in being with her is that anything is possible. She loved me when I finally accepted to hate myself and try to drive her away, but she always got back under my skin and showed that she is not leaving, and now she is the mother of my child, and she still loves me. How? I can never answer that question. I have no idea how she thinks of anything that goes through her mind.

***

"Where's Mommy?" There was a voice.
"She's still in bed."
"Can I go to wake her?"
"Just let her sleep, Mia."
"But I want a see her," she whined.
I opened my eyes and squinted while the sun beamed in. I looked over at Kendall. She was still sleeping. Her cheeks were all red and puffy from crying. She still looks beautiful as always. "I love you," I whispered and kissed her warm, red cheek. I sat at the edge of the bed.
"Who car outside?" Her sweet and girly voice sounded again.
"Your dad came last night and stayed."
I smiled. "Why?" She sounded different. Wait? She's talking? When did she start talking again?
"He wanted to, I'm guessing. Just eat your breakfast, angel."
She didn't say anything else for a couple of minutes. "Where he sleep?"
"Upstairs."
"With my mom?"
"Yeah, he's your dad, honey."
She stopped again. "I'm full." I heard a plate slide. "I want Mommy." She pouted. I stood to my feet and winced as the pain shot through my body from the stitches. I took a few seconds before I went into the bathroom to relieve myself and headed down the stairs after putting my jeans on and got fully dressed. When I walked into the kitchen, Kendall's mom gave me a warm grin.
"Morning, Micah."
I grinned. "Good morning." I looked around.
"She's watching TV now." She read my mind. "Hungry?"

"Y-you don't have to—"

"It's already made. I wouldn't mind anyways. How are you?"

I stared at her for a few seconds. "I'm okay."

"Here, just sit down, and I'll get it." She pulled the stool out for me." I laughed.

"You both act like I'm helpless." I smiled up at her after I sat down, and she started filling a plate with scrambled eggs and minisausage.

I stared at it a little strangely. "It's what Mia wanted. She always wants the same things." She laughed.

I grinned up at her. "Thanks."

"She's still sleeping?"

I finished chewing my mouthful of eggs before answering. "Yeah."

"That's good." She started cleaning up. "She needs some rest."

"Yeah," I spoke quietly before shoveling more of the food into my mouth. I'm so hungry I feel drained. The awkward feeling of only being able to use one arm, not even affecting me like it usually does. "Kendall said she wasn't talking?"

She looked back at me. "I guess she changed her mind this morning." She shrugged. "I want to thank you."

I shook my head. "You don't have to ever thank me." I finished the plate.

She gave me a sweet grin, and her eyes got glassed over. I stood up and walked the plate over to the sink. "Thanks." I gave her another small smile before exiting the kitchen. I walked into the hallway and peaked into the living room. Where is she? I looked around the room confused as a cartoon continued to play on the screen where a pudgy little girl with a purple backpack talked to a big red chicken.

I took my time going up the steps because with each step I took, it hurt a little more. When I got to the top, I looked over to Kendall's bed to see her sitting up in it, Mia on her lap as the TV played in front of them. Kendall looked over at me as I stepped inside and the floor made a noise. She smiled. "Hi." I grinned and looked at Mia as she sat in her mom's lap and looked comfortable, but when she saw me, it looked the opposite. "Your mom and sister called you. Mia answered, though, when your sister called for you." She smiled at the memory.

I walked over, grinning widely at them both. "What'd she say?"

We both waited for Mia to say something, but she kept her focus on the television. Kendall set her hand on my back as I sat down as if it would help, and in some way, it actually did. She cocked an eyebrow like she was asking if I was in pain. I nodded, taking a deep breath. "Well, anyway, she was wondering where you were, and when she heard Mia's voice, she was like, are you okay? It was funny. I told her you were with me at my mom's and were eating all my mom's food downstairs." She laughed.

I crinkled my nose at her. "It was one plate."

"Sure it was."

I smiled at her before looking at the TV where the same cartoon that's still on downstairs probably is playing. I looked down at Mia, well aware of how closely Kendall was watching me admire her as she tried to say the words in Spanish the same way as the little cartoon girl did. Before I knew it, my hand was softly caressing her head in my hand and brushed through her hair. She stilled in her spot and stopped talking. I took my hand back promptly, not wanting her to be uncomfortable on my account. My lip trembled as I looked down and then back up at the TV. Cartoons I guess are something I'll have to grow on. I hope they will be anyway.

"Mia, what's wrong?" They both looked at each other when I glanced over.

She shook her head.

"Why are you acting afraid of him, sweetie?" She waited for an answer. "Mia, it's all right. It's Daddy." She looked up at me. She looked over at my arm that was cast up next. "Don't ever be afraid of him . . . he's a big baby," she whispered, and Mia started giggling. I looked up at Kendall and tried not to laugh at her. Mia looked up at me smiling now. She leaped off Kendall's lap and ran over to where a pink chest and a small table and chairs sat on the floor and ran back over and jumped onto the bed holding a stuffed spotted dog. She clambered around on the bed until she was sat between Kendall and me.

"This is dog." She tried climbing onto my lap now. Kendall acted quickly and grabbed her and pulled her on to her lap, and her legs rested on mine.

"Daddy's hurt, honey."

"What's wrong with 'im?"

"Somebody hurt him a while ago, and he has stitches now."

I looked up at Kendall confused. Doesn't she remember? She doesn't understand you, dumbass. She's nearly only four years old. Four years. "Stit-ches."

"Yeah." I smiled.

She shook her head, her long hair swaying from side to side. "I don't get what stit-ches is?"

"Stitches are like . . . string, sweetie. They're holding him together where there are holes."

"Holes?"

"Yeah, someone was very mean to him."

Her mouth dropped open, and she looked over at me. "Who would hole him?"

"Just a bad person."

I reached over. I want to hold her. I don't care if I have string holding me together where I have holes right now. I need to have her in my arms, to be able to feel her heart beating, to feel her in my arms like I've been craving for years, so much that I've missed out on already. I lifted her and brought her over on to my lap. I ignored the feeling of them stretching and sat her small petite body on my legs as they dangled off the bed now. She started talking about the stuffed dog as if it were alive and her best friend of all time and how much it means to her. I listened intently the entire time.

"I'm going downstairs to get a drink." Kendall kissed my cheek out of nowhere and ruffled Mia's hair, which had her giggling and went off the mattress and walked down the steps. The next five minutes while she was gone, Mia talked and talked about everything and anything that came to her mind. Even when Kendall came back upstairs, she continued jabbering on about all of her toys and bringing them over to me and telling me about all of them in detail. She loves them like her own family it seems. It's adorable.

Kendall went back downstairs for a few minutes to take down her trash bag and brought back up some water for both of us and Mia a juice box and some pop tarts.

Kendall came and sat on her bed with me with our legs hanging off while Mia played with a dollhouse across the room happily. "You know I can't stay all day." I kept my sight on Mia's small back as she sat on the floor with a doll in her hand, making her dance across her lap. I knew she looked over at me.

"I don't want you taken away from us again."

I nodded, looking down. I bit the inside of my cheek before looking over at the side profile of her face. She looked over after a few seconds as I stared at her. "You know I don't want to go."

"Then you can't stay here. Did you tell your parole officer you were leaving your mom last night?" I shook my head.

"The last time I spoke to him is when I moved from Josh's to her home."

"How far are you allowed to go away from her house without reporting?"

"Fifty miles."

"Micah," she whined.

"Don't fret about it, Kendall. It'll be fine. I'm not going anywhere."

"We'll just come to you sometime this week."

"Sometime?" I smiled, amused with her.

"Well, I want to get a new job now that all those as——bad people are gone now, right? Who else was there?"

"Kendall, I don't know. It's never just one little circle of 'em. There's a chain, and if you take away one piece, the whole thing goes to——messes up. I didn't know everybody involved. Sure, I saw others, but I don't know. I don't want to talk about this here now."

"You have your sister's car?"

"Yeah." I stared at Mia on the floor. "I should probably get it back to her before she flips."

Kendall seemed amused by it and shrugged. "You're going then?" I nodded, not wanting to actually say it. She leaned over to her nightstand and handed my phone over to me. "She was trying to play with it," she explained with a smile.

I grinned as I took it from her hand, making sure to touch her as much as possible in the process of retrieving it. I leaned up a little and shoved it into my back pocket but not before seeing a few texts from my sister. I stood from the bed and stretched a little, still feeling wore out. "I still don't understand how you're the one complaining." She stood up from the bed as well while looking at me.

I sighed. "Three years," I reminded her. She only grinned and then looked back over at Mia.

"I know," she spoke back quietly. "Mia, we're going downstairs. Daddy has to leave now." She turned and got up from her spot on the polka dot rug and ran over with a stuffed elephant in hand. She ran to Kendall, and she picked her up into her arms and sat her on her hip while I walked first down the steps . . . slowly. I was so relieved when I reached the bottom and Kendall got my keys for me from the kitchen table.

"Why go?"

I scratched the back of my head. How do I answer that in a way she'd understand? "We'll go see him soon, sweetie."

Mia leaned from Kendall's arm to try and reach me, her fingers trying to grab on to my arm. I reached my arm out without Kendall's consent and set her on my hip, my one arm wrapped around her back to hold on to her. She wrapped her small arms around me. I kissed the top of her head and held her closer to me and closed my eyes momentarily. "Love you," I whispered. Kendall reached over and took her from my arms and handed her off to her mom who took her into the living room with her.

I looked back at Kendall and grinned before opening the door and stepping down the steps. She followed me down, and I unlocked the car door. I turned back to say good-bye, and she stood there with her arms crossed across her breasts, a small grin plastered across her sculpted lips. "I'll see you soon."

She stayed still and just stared at me and gave a small nod. "Yeah," her voice cracked when I turned to get into the car. I stopped and turned back around and hooked my arm around her waist and buried my head in the crook of her neck breathing in her sweet smell. Her arms finally wrapped around me, and she fisted my shirt in her hands, holding me tightly. "Call when your home safe," she spoke, her cheek pressed firmly against my chest.

I lifted my head from her shoulder and kissed her cheek for a few seconds, holding my lips to her sweet, smooth skin. I kissed her again down her cheek and to the corner of her mouth. Her lips twitched a bit and reached over in the direction toward mine. I paused with my eyes barely closed, my head against hers. I leaned down and gently brushed my lips past hers and then connected them. I started to kiss her slowly. She gripped my shirt tighter and pulled my closer to her to deepen it, our breathing both rising as my tongue pushed past her lips and started to massage hers. Her breath was fresh from a recent cleaning. Minty and delicious. I moaned uncontrollably. Is this really happening? Yes. She's here. She's really here. Her lips leaving mine brought me back to reality. She really is here. She just laid her cheek back against my chest, pressing it against me forcibly as if I'd disappear in a way it feels. "I'm here," I whispered.

She nodded and sniffled against me still, her arms wrapped around my back to hold me closer. She still was careful about my stitches though. "I know."

"Please don't cry." I rubbed my hand up and down her back.

"This just seems . . . I don't know—"

"Shhh . . . Just relax, sweetheart." I kissed the top of her head. She started giggling. "Something amusing you?"

"You." She laughed.

"Me?"

"You called me sweetheart." She giggled and rubbed one of her hands up and down my back a little as if to say she wasn't mocking me, that it was good humor.

"Sorry." I smiled.

"No." She paused. "Don't apologize. I've waited three years for my arms to be wrapped around you and to hear you say those sorts of things again."

"That's my fault."

"Don't say that. It isn't your fault. It never was." I just held her with my arm. "Are you crying?" She sounded surprised in a way.

"What?" I sniffled my nose.

"Micah." She tilted her head up. I hadn't realized tears had ran down my cheeks and on to her hot skin. She reached her hands up and sat them on either side of my face and swiped them across my cheeks and cupped my face afterward.

"I have to go," my voice cracked.

She nodded. "Call whenever. We'll come by."

I nodded back and gave her a chaste kiss before clambering into the vehicle and pulling out once she was back on the porch and waved to her while grinning, my eyes swelling with fresh unwanted tears as I drove off.

When I finally pulled into my mom's driveway, I just sat there and stared at the garage. At first, my thoughts were only focused on my night with Kendall, and I was smiling with my head fallin' back on the leather seat. Kendall. I open my eyes back up to look at the garage blankly. The faded memory came to surface of the first time I ever took a hit to the face. I don't remember exactly what I'd done wrong . . . the more that I think about it, though, I probably didn't do anything wrong.

I got out of the car while letting out a loud sigh.

"Micah." Candice opened the door and walked down toward me. I grinned at her and hurried in wiping my eyes underneath to try and hide my recent breakdown. She wrapped her arms under my armpits and squeezed me.

"Okay, okay." I tried pushing her away. "I want to go inside and lie down now." She smiled and kept one of her arms wrapped around me to help me up the steps inside where the sensational smell of my mom's cooking made my mouth water, and I was reminded of my hunger and was instantly starving.

After dinner, I went and sat on the couch, feeling wiped out. Candice came and sat with me while I laid down, my legs resting on her lap with my head on the pillow. She flipped through the channels quickly until landing on a show that she insists is the best on. I rolled my eyes but watched it anyway with her.

With both my mom and Candice telling me goodnight, I went into my old room and laid down. Once I was closing my eyes after thinking, my door opened, and Candice walked in.

"What?" I groaned.

She gave a polite and apologetic smile as she came and sat on the edge of my bed. "I think I should tell you something," she spoke quietly, not making eye contact. I stared at her as if to tell her to continue and spit it out.

"What?" I let out a sigh. I just want some fucking sleep. "Can't it wait?"

She shook her head. She tucked her hair behind her ears and took a deep breath. "She told me not to tell you." She sounded on the verge of tears as she sniffled.

"Candice? Who?"

"Mom."

"What do you mean?"

"Dad." My heart stopped, and I couldn't take my eyes off her. What? Dad? "She went out with him while you were gone." When she finally looked over at me, it was a look of uncertainty and terror.

"What?" my voice cracked.

"She said I'll be back in a little and then she came home. Someone picked her up, and when she came home, he was with her. It was him." I only stared at her. "He tried talking to me all normally and came inside. He looks different, but it's him. It was him, Micah." She paused and composed herself. "I just—I don't know . . . I had to tell you." She looked over. She got up and left after that.

I want my old home back. I hate being here. I only like seeing Candice. There's too much that has happened here for me to like it or feel comfortable being here at all. And now this shit. After over twenty minutes of just lying on my back, staring at the white ceiling, I passed out soundly, with my medication kicking in and taking over.

At breakfast, I never felt more uncomfortable. It was easier when Kendall came here with me. She comforted me in a way, and I felt at ease with her. I always feel easier with her by my side. I looked up at my mom. How can she sit there like nothing has ever happened to us? How has Candice never said anything to her? Why do they act so normal for Christ's sake? I shook my head a little and stared at her as she ate.

"Micah?" Candice's voice piped up.

I didn't take my gaze off her. My mom looked up. "Something up, honey?"

"Is something wrong?" I cocked a brow. "Is something fucking wrong with me? Why don't you go and ask my father?"

"Excuse me?"

"Don't you dare," I barely spoke. "Don't you sit there and act like you have no idea what I am saying to you."

"Micah—"

"No! How could you?" I stared at her as all eyes were on me. "How could you bring him back into this house and let him just hang out like that's normal?"

"You have no right to judge me. He is your father. He heard what happened to you, and yet still, after all the stuff you've done to him, he wanted to check and see you if you were doing well. He heard about being a grandfather."

My eyes popped out of my head. "I have no right? How can you say that to me after everything he has done to you and Candice? After what he's done to me? And don't you ever think that he's ever going to meet my daughter."

"He hit you, Micah." She sounded calm. "He was a drunk. He didn't know—"

"You're going to defend him?"

"He didn't know. He was a drunk. He's sober now."

"That's no fucking excuse!" I screamed. "He... I just can't believe that you're defending him after everything that's he's done!" My eyes were pouring by now, and hers were wide. Candice was staring at her own lap, where her fingers stayed stitched together, and then glanced up at my mother. "I wouldn't have ever came back if I knew this would happen!" I waved my arms around. "You let it happen. You left me." I couldn't even talk anymore. I set my hand over the stitches as I turned to go back to my bedroom and pack.

Chapter 54

I started just grabbing all my clothing and tossing it into my suitcase. I kept having to sniffle my nose, but at least my tears had finally stopped by now. My eyes are probably bloodshot as hell. When the door I opened, I jumped. I looked up at see my mother standing there with her arms wrapped around herself. Her eyes were still wide and glassy when I made eye contact with her still figure before she started walking over toward me. "Micah," she croaked.

"I'm not staying here." I turned my attention back to my packing.

She stared at me and watched me pack. "Micah, darling. I'm sorry… I just … I don't know." She wrapped her arms around me, and I winced. "I'm so sorry," she sobbed heavily into my chest. "Oh no," she cried harder now.

"Mom," I said normally and put my hand on her back.

"Micah, my baby." Her hands dug into my back, holding me tighter to her. "I just don't want to be alone." She was shaking. She pulled back to look at my face. I stared down at her wide-eyed, her hands rubbing up and down my arms slowly, above the one with my cast. Her eyes closed, and her face scrunched up.

"You can't just leave here whenever you want, Micah."

"You think that I don't know that?" I busted. "I'm the one that spent three years of my life in that hell!" I stormed out.

I took Candice's car and got a few gallons of gas for mine and filled it back up in my mom's driveway. After that, I left. I don't even know where I am going, just away from there. My phone started going crazy, buzzing in my front pocket. I finally pulled it out, and Candice had called me twice already. I'll talk to her later. Then it started buzzing again, and I quickly just pressed the green button at the bottom of the screen.

"I'm not coming back!" I shouted.

"What?"

"Cand-Kendall?" I pulled the phone away from my ear, and Kendall's name with a heart next to it was on the screen. "Sorry, I thought you were someone else." I sighed.

"Something happen?"

I gripped the steering wheel tighter. "You want to have dinner? You and Mia?"

"Micah, what happened?"

"Did you already eat?"

"No. But what happened? Why are you mad?"

"I'm not mad with you . . . I just don't want to deal with my family."

"Where are you?"

"Is Daddy?" Mia's small voice came into my ear.

I smiled.

"Do you want to have dinner?"

"Yeah, sure. What time?"

"I can be there in, like, two hours."

There was a pause. "Yeah, okay, but Micah, you have to tell me things." I shook my head. "What'd they do to you?"

"My dad's back," I spoke quietly, afraid to say the words out loud.

"Back? What'd you mean? Where?"

"My mom and he are hanging out," my voice cracked.

"Oh, Micah." Her voice was sincere.

"I don't know what to do." I broke into sobs. "He knows about Mia." I paused and tried containing myself. "I don't want him to ever see her."

"Don't you think that's a bit harsh? He's her grand———"

"No. It's not. That bastard doesn't deserve to be anywhere near my daughter."

"We can talk about it tonight or something, okay?"

"We'll see."

She laughed. "Okay, well see you in a little. Bye."

"Bye."

The drive gave me time to compose myself. By the time I'd pulled up into her driveway after telling my parole officer where I was going, I was all put together again. I took a few deep breaths and faced the mirror toward me. I blinked a few times. I don't look like myself. My face is pale, my cheeks flushed with a deep red shade, and circles under my eyes and slightly swelled around them. I looked down at my phone. Five fifteen. *Okay. Okay. You're good.* I opened the door and started walking up to her front door, fixing my shirt a few times and running my fingers through my hair. I knocked a few times before the door was opened. Kendall's mom smiled at me. "Micah, hi." She put one of her arms around my shoulders and led me inside. She took her arm off when we got into the kitchen and patted my back gently. "Kendall's upstairs with Mia."

I grinned at her. "Okay, thank you." I waved awkwardly and went up the steps slowly. When I got to her door, I heard them both talking with obvious smiles on their faces. I creaked open the door slowly. I couldn't see them though. I opened it completely while walking into the room. They were off to the side where a dollhouse sat on the floor and dolls laid scattered around them with tons of clothing to dress them with.

Kendall's head snapped toward me after her floor creaked. "Hey." She smiled.

"Daddy!" Mia stood and ran over to me. I bent down easily and wrapped an arm around her as her arms wrapped around my neck.

"What were you doing?" I asked as she took my hand and led me over to where she and Kendall sat on the floor.

"Mommy, play Barbie with me." She sat back down, and I did the same, crossing my legs. Kendall was staring at me when I looked over. She gave me a weak smile, still knowing something was up.

I grinned down at Mia as she started to slide a golden dress up the blonde bombshell's body. I looked back over to Kendall as she sat the one she was holding back down. "You two ready?" I reached my hand over to rest on her knee.

She nodded. "Mia, it's time to go."

I watched as she strapped Mia into her car seat after transferring it into my vehicle in the back behind my seat. The dinner was good and lasted an hour and a half. Mia was probably the most well-behaved kid I have ever seen in a restaurant. She and Kendall sat across from me in the booth. Kendall carried her back to the car when we left because she was tired and passed out once she was strapped into her seat, a blanket she brought with her spread across her lap with the stuffed dog held limply in one of her hands. When the light turned red, Kendall spoke, "Can you stop at the store? I need a few things." I looked over at her.

"Yeah, of course. What'd you need?"

"Just a few things, not much."

"Yeah, okay," I spoke back quietly. I pulled into the lot and pulled the keys out. "What do you need to get?" I asked, opening the door.

"Oh, I can just go in."

"Kendall, just tell me what you need?"

"I'll just be a second." She leaned over and kissed my cheek before clambering out of the car and jogging inside.

I looked back to Mia who was now opening her eyes. "Where Mommy?" She wiped her eyes.

"She'll be back in a minute." I reached one of my arms back and moved her hair out of her face.

She looked out the window and then back at me. "Where we?"

"Parking lot."

"Why?"

"We're waiting for Kend——Mommy."

"I want my mommy," she whimpered.

"Hey, hey, don't . . ." I unbuckled and leaned back.

"No," She whined.

"Mia—"

"Mommy. I want Mommy." She cried and held her dog closer to her body, squeezing it and leaning toward the window. "I don't want you, want Mom." She started crying harder. *Fuck.*

I stared at her. "She's coming," my voice cracked. "Hush, princess. Mommy's coming back." I stroked her side. My head snapped to the passenger door as Kendall clicked her knuckles a couple of times on the rolled-up window. I stretched an arm out to unlock it, and she climbed inside and sat.

"Mommy," Mia cried out.

"Awe, don't cry, my darling." She put the grocery bag behind my seat and started talking to Mia. I watched the encounter closely, how much Mia loves Kendall, how close they are. Mia started sniffling but calmed down a lot and wasn't crying anymore but just pouting quietly from the outburst. I didn't know my eyes were glassed over until I saw the sincere look Kendall was giving me when she sat all the way back in her seat. She set her hand on my thigh and rubbed it. She lifted her hand and put it on my bicep. "She's just cranky, Micah. She's tired is all. She's always like this. It's not you." That's just the problem that she's blind to though. It's not me.

"We'll be home soon, sweetheart, then you'll be in your bed." Kendall looked back at Mia, who still continued to pout and whine tiredly. I kept looking into the mirror to watch her move about in her car seat. When I pulled into Kendall's driveway at her mom's, we both looked at each other at the same time. "You okay?" she asked quietly. I nodded reassuringly to her. "Thank you for dinner." She smiled.

"We had fun. It was nice." She grinned now. "I should get her to bed." She giggled softly. I gave her a lopsided smile in return. I opened my door and got out with her. While she grabbed Mia up, I took the bag from the back and walked with her up into the house. Mia was passed out in Kendall's arms, her head on her shoulder. "I'm going to put her in bed, just one minute." She excused herself, going up to her bedroom. I went and sat on one of the stools at the counter and took out my phone to find multiple missed calls, mostly from my mother. I put it back in my pocket, not wanting to deal with either of them, and watched as Kendall appeared back in the room.

"Diapers?" I asked, out of my control, as I pulled them out of the small blue transparent grocery bag. "She still needs diapers?"

"Yes," she sounded harsh, protective at the most. "She still wears them. She is your daughter." She bit back more.

"She's not potty-trained though?"

Her eyes bored into mine as if she'd pounce like an animal to a threat. "It's only when she's asleep. She has no control over it."

I stared at her. "I just—I didn't know . . . it's just a reaction."

She started at me, now holding the box of diapers made for nighttime. "What was wrong earlier?"

"I don't want to talk about it."

"Micah," she sounded upset. "We have to talk to each other, that's the problem with us. It always turns into something bigger just because you don't trust me for some reason."

"It's not that I don't trust you."

"Then what?"

"It's-It's not exactly stuff that I want to say to you. You don't need to know everything that's happened to me before."

"Excuse me? What, so you're scared of what I'll think of you?"

"No, I don't know. It's just stuff you shouldn't hear." I shouted a little too loud. "Sorry." My side ached from straining. I can't wait for next week to get these damn stitches out.

She was staring at me from across the island. Her eyes held something as we locked. Anger? Confusion? Pain? She was hurt most definitely from me keeping things from her. Why should I tell her though? Oh hey, by the way, my father molested me when I was younger, and now he and my mom are seeing each other again. I have to tell her about my dad eventually so that she understands. He can't see her. "My dad knows about Mia." I bowed my head before looking over at her. Her eyes were confused now and her lips opened.

"Y-your dad? I . . . Micah, er . . . did you see him?"

I shook my head, not looking over at her. "My mom told me he wants to meet her," my voice was rough.

There was a pause and a loud intake of breath from her. "What do you think?"

My head shot up, and I looked directly over at her. "Don't you ever, ever let him near her. I mean it, Kendall."

She seemed more confused now. "Micah, you told me that he would hit your mom, that he was a drunk. But . . . maybe he is different. Your mom is, you said, seeing him, so maybe—"

"What? No. No. Kendall, don't say that. He isn't changed at all. He can't change."

She walked over to me and set both hands on my thighs as I sat. "What did he do to you that was so awful?"

"Everything, Kendall. What he didn't do is an easier question."

She searched my eyes. "Just tell me one thing." I sucked in my bottom lip and looked down at her hands and placed mine on top of hers.

I blinked my eyes a few times before talking. "Can we just go to bed?" I looked up at her. She stared at me before giving me a light nod in response. My wounds didn't hurt as bad as before since they're healing, but it's still fucking annoying having to deal with them with everything I do every single damn day. There's a twin-sized bed by the opposite wall where Kendall's is with short railings on the end, her dollhouses sit in the front, and toys still spread out from earlier lie in front of them. In the bed is Mia sleeping soundly facing the wall, her hair a beautiful mess across the pillow, pink pajamas with white clouds covering her small body. I stared at her as Kendall patted quietly to her dresser and grabbed sweatpants and a tank top and disappeared into her bathroom. I walked over to the small bed and knelt down and smoothed out her soft hair with my hand. She moved slightly but didn't wake.

When Kendall emerged from the bathroom, I was already sitting down in her bed, the cozy soft quilts covering my legs as I leaned against the headboard with a pillow behind me. She walked quietly over to me and climbed into bed beside me so she was near the end and not the wall where I took place. She adjusted her pillow and laid down, facing me as she laid on her side. I placed one of my hands on her shoulder and rubbed it a little around. I didn't look down at her to know that she was looking up at me as I watched Mia's little body move up and down peacefully as she slept. Kendall moved closer to me and leaned against my body. "She's precious," she whispered. I nodded and bit my lip, still staring at her unconscious body.

I shook my head slowly while keeping my gaze across the room. Don't you fucking cry. "I can't believe I missed it," I whispered, my voice thick and deep.

"Micah—"

"Don't try to comfort me in any way. I did miss it, and I can't go back to see her. I wanted to be there every second." I stared. Her hand rested on my rising and falling chest flatly, her fingers spread about. "What was it like when she was born?"

I looked down at her excited sort of feeling to hear what she would say back to me. She was grinning but not looking up at me. "I passed out." She giggled.

"What?" I smiled.

She shook her head. "I remember the pain. No mother can forget that pain. But once I heard her first cry and she was in the doctor's arms, I felt like I was in heaven, like I almost had everyone I needed in my life." She fisted my shirt. "I just passed out after that. It was too much I guess, and I was beyond exhausted. Birth is hell."

"Was your mom with you in the room?"

"Yeah, of course, she was." She was calm.

I grabbed and squeezed her hand in mine. "I sometimes try to picture it actually. I never thought that you passed out though." I chuckled. She smiled.

"I didn't even have a name picked out for her . . . it took me a while to think of one that day." She smiled at the memory. "Then it just hit me."

"Did you breast-feed her?" I scooted my pillow down to be at her level. She grinned.

"Sometimes, not that much. I felt more connected to her in some strange way, though, when I did. It just . . . felt a bit odd is all, so I just used a bottle after the first few times." She adjusted herself better. "When do you get these stitches out?"

"Pretty sure next week. They don't hurt as bad."

"That's good." This seems like our first normal conversation.

"I think I should tell you something. . ." I felt too ashamed to make eye contact with her with what I am about to tell her.

Chapter 55

I lifted my hand over hers, lying on my chest, and squeezed it as I took a deep breath. "You're sorta scaring me . . ." She whispered. I shook my head, still staring straight up at the ceiling. "Does it have to do with why you are staying here tonight and not your mom's?"

I shrugged a shoulder. "Sort of." I was barely audible, but I know she is listening intently to every word. I kept moving my hand along hers, slowly rubbing my thumb around. "I don't want you to think . . . I don't know. I don't want you to ever consider ever letting that man near our daughter ever. He's never allowed to see you either. I don't want to go back to prison either because if I see him . . ." I stopped myself.

"Okay," her voice was small.

I don't want to tell her this. I have too, though, if I really want things to work out. I have to tell her everything. Everything. "When I was younger, my mom used to go out with her friends a lot." I breathed. "And . . . she would leave me at home with my dad." I stopped for a moment and glanced up at her after softly pressing my lips to her hand that I'm still holding on to. "At first, I didn't really mind because he never hit me yet, and he would just yell occasionally, but I'd seen him hit my mom and sister already so I knew to be scared. My mom just didn't see any harm in leaving me alone with that monster." I sucked in another breath. My heart starts to pound, and I feel like I may start to have another panic attack.

"Micah, relax."

"I didn't think he'd bother me if I just stayed in my bedroom all night and wait for Candice to get back. She would always stay with her friends real late . . . I never really had any friends because I usually wore the same T-shirt a lot, and nobody liked me at school really." I stopped myself for another fresh breath. "I was the smelly kid." I try and lighten the mood but it doesn't seem to work.

"Micah . . ."

"No. Anyway, he came into my room one day, and I had the shirt lying across my bed and was trying to read some book, and he picked it up and saw a stain. He was just so mad, Kendall. I couldn't stop shaking once I saw how mad he was. He started yelling . . . then he slapped me across the face. That was the first time he ever hit me . . . It stung so badly, and I started crying beyond my control. I just couldn't stop . . . so he yelled at me more and was screaming down at me," my voice cracked a little. "He told me to grow up and stop being a pussy, then he pulled me off the floor and smashed my lamp against the floor. I did nothing but cry and he hated it so he would hit me more. . ."

"Micha, you can stop. I'm sorry I asked." She leaned into me more. "No, I'm sorry. I'm so sorry." She nuzzled her head in the crook of my neck, kissing me tenderly with her soft lips. "You're safe now, sweetie." She wrapped her arms around me. "Hush," she whispered, and with the thought, I squeezed my eyes shut. "Open your eyes." I couldn't find the strength. "Micah, look at me." I squeezed her hand and opened them to find her hovering over my face, sitting up on her arm. "Don't torture yourself. Please." She caressed my cheek. Her face was falling, though, and she looked weak like she would burst any second.

"It hurt so badly." I barely spoke while squeezing her hand.

"Shhh, I've got you now, Micah. You're safe."

"Don't cry for me."

She shook her head. "I can't help it. I just love you so much. I can't think of what you went through."

"I never had any girlfriends. I did have a few friends, but after they met my father, they weren't allowed over anymore." She rubbed her thumb over my cheek as she still held it softly.

"Well, they missed out, darling." I looked over at Mia. "Just look what you have now." She giggled, making me only squeeze her hand tighter. "And pretty soon, I'm not going to have a hand anymore," she added still giggling quietly.

I let off on my squeeze and just stared at Mia as Kendall kissed my cheek and laid her head on my shoulder. "Love you."

***

There was a sound. It woke me up. My vision was blurry, but I blinked it out, and I could see clearly now. It was a quiet yet strained sound. I lifted my head to look over at my side, Kendall still latched on to my side sound asleep. I looked over at Mia's bed. The blanket was half on the floor, and she was missing. I got confused and looked over to the closed bathroom door to where the light seeped under the door. Is she crying?

I gently removed Kendall's arm from around me successfully without waking her and stood up slowly as my back cracked. I walked quietly over to the door and lightly tapped my knuckles on the white painted wood. "Mia?" I spoke through it. "Honey?" She went quiet. "I'm coming in." I opened the door and looked in to see her sat in the corner against the wall in front of the tub. "Mia?" I walked over to her after sliding my hand over my tired eyes. Am I dreaming? Her eyes were bloodshot and swollen. "What's wrong?" I crouched sown in front of her. "What happened?" I asked quickly.

She shook her head, still crying, just not as loud as before. "I w-wet the b-ed," she cried. I went to her and wrapped my arms around her small waist and held her as she cried into my shoulder.

"Didn't Mommy put your pamper on?" She shook her head. "Okay, okay. Relax, baby." I rubbed her back. "Calm down. Nobody's mad at you." I clenched my jaw at the reminder of me when I was younger, and I used to be the same as Mia. She took after me in this situation. "Hey, hey." I pulled her away from my chest. "It's okay. I was the same way when I was younger." She stared at me and wiped her eyes with the backs of her hands. Her cheeks were puffy and adorable, even red and tearstained. Her hair laid a mess on top her head. Her eyes are rimmed with tiredness and redness from crying. They looked just like mine, and if I think about it, this is probably how I looked when I was younger, and I'm Candice. Mia's just the girl version of me in a way. Besides, she's incredibly beautiful when I'm nothing close. "Let's get you cleaned up." I turned on the water for the tub to fill up a little. Once it was, I turned it off and checked the temperature with my hand. I gulped uncomfortably, even though she's my almost four-year-old daughter, as I lifted her small shirt over her head and set it next to her and then slid her wet pants down her legs. She grabbed on to my arm to steady herself when stepping out of them. I lifted her and sat her down in the warm water and grabbed the washcloth and soap.

After she was all cleaned up, I reached over to the closet and grabbed a pink fluffy towel with butterflies on it and lifted her out of the tub beside me and wrapped it around her and started drying her body off. "You're all clean now, sweetheart." I kissed her soft cheek. "Don't cry no more. It's okay." I hugged her to me. I carried her back into Kendall's bedroom after draining the tub, throwing the dirty clothes into a pile and turned the light off. I set her down by her dresser while she hugged the towel to her body. I looked through a few of the drawers before looking to Mia and asking where her PJs are kept. She pointed over to the other dresser by the window, I figured. I walked over and looked for a matching set with paw prints on it, and she grabbed my arm again for support while stepping into the pants after I slid her diaper onto her. I slid her shirt over her head and then set her on the bed with Kendall against the side where I left it warm. She blinked up at me before I kissed her cheek and told her to go back to bed.

Her blankets weren't as bad as mine always were. I stripped the bed and carried the sheets and blanket downstairs with me along with her pajamas and put them in the washer. When I got back upstairs, Mia was still wide awake as she watched me walk over to the bed where Kendall slept and she laid. She looked worried . . . scared? I don't know. I tried to ignore it and just smile at her while lying down on the edge, with her in-between Kendall and I. "Go to sleep." I kissed her forehead and got comfortable on my back. I closed my eyes.

He was drunk, I think. I recall a glass of dark stinky liquid sat on the work bench against the wall. His fist collided with my jaw, and I fell over. I was eight. I cried like never before. The tears wouldn't stop flowing from my eyes. Finally, my mom came in.

"What the hell have you done?" she shouted at him as she rushed down to me, lying on the cold concrete floor.

"Oh, shut your damn mouth, wench. He deserved it." He finished his drink after that. The glass hitting back down was so loud I remember. My mom had picked me up and cradled me in her arms. "Just leave him on the floor. It'll toughen the pussy up." I had cried even harder. I remember fully now. I just wouldn't stop. I wanted to be tough. I wanted to show him that I am tough.

I remember the bright light being turned on in the bathroom and my mom setting me on the sick, and tears started flowing down her cheeks as she cleaned out the cut left on my cheek from his hard fist. "Shhh . . . Shhh, my angel. It'll be okay. You don't have to go to school tomorrow, Micah. Don't worry." I had dreaded school. I was the odd one out mostly, except in gym. I wanted to try out for the wresting team, and my father called me a faggot. The coach was disappointed when I told him my dad wouldn't let me. My mom, I remember, argued with him that it would be good for me. He disagreed and took it out on her. That night, I couldn't sleep. When I did fall asleep finally, I woke, and my sheets were soaked. He was going to scream at me again and hit my mom. No! I got out of bed quickly but carefully. My jammies were stuck to my bum, and my cheeks were red, and I was shaking as I walked down the hallway to my parents' room. There were noises coming from behind the door, but I creaked it open anyway.

My mom's hair was a different color as she laid on her back on the carpet. She was naked, and her mouth gagged, and her eyes were rimmed with the same colors as my crayons. He was on top her, calling her a bitch, and moving quickly. I was so lost and confused and scared.

"Mommy," I cried out. They both looked up at me. A pair of arms wrapped around me and lifted me off the floor. "Candice," I cried harder. "Mommy," I whimpered as Candice took me into her bedroom and sat me back down.

"Micah, you have to learn to go to the potty before you go to bed."

"I did," I cried.

"Okay, okay." She rubbed my back. "Relax, I'll go get you more pajamas." She stood.

"No." I reached for her to stay. What if he comes after me? I don't want to die. She studied me and then went to her drawers and pulled out a T-shirt and then a pair of her gym-like shorts. She walked back over to me and undid each button on my dinosaur shirt and slid it off me. I stepped out of my bottoms when she had told me and held on to her shoulders. "I should clean you up." Once I was naked, she picked me back up and took me into the bathroom across the hallway with the clothes in her hand, my head buried in her neck as I had my arms wrapped around her. She gave me a quick silent bath and kept giving me a reassuring smile when I did make eye contact with her. It burned where he struck me. He left a cut on my face. She used a sponge to clean my entire body but didn't wet my hair. She wrapped the cold towel around me and dried me off. She put me into her bed after dressing me and went and took the sheets off the bed and threw them in the washer.

"They won't find out," she whispered as she climbed into her bed with me. I wrapped my arms around her.

"You promise?" my voice was hoarse.

She nodded and sniffled her nose. "Yes, I promise, Micah." The bedroom door swung open, and he was there and angry as hell.

"Micah!" I opened my eyes quickly. Kendall's eyes were wide, and worry filled them. "Micah?" She gripped my shoulders. "You all right?" She swiped the back of her hand across my forehead. I looked around. I'm not at my mother's or in my sister's bedroom. I'm with Kendall.

I leaned up and pulled her into me. "Hush," she spoke quietly when I started to take a deep breath of relief. "You're okay now." She wrapped her arms around my back while still standing, her hair damp from a shower. "Do you want to talk about it?" I shook my head while hugging her tightly to me. "You hungry?" I nodded into her neck.

"What time is it?"

"Twelve thirty, sleepy head." She unwrapped her arms when a voice from downstairs started yelling. "Mommy!" She smiled. "I'll see you downstairs. My mom already left for work a few hours ago."

I watched her walk all the way to her staircase, an obvious show being put on. I cursed quietly when I removed the blanket to see my growing erection. I can't go down there with this with Mia around. I debate whether or not I should call for Kendall to help me out with this situation, but what if Mia comes up instead or with her? How did this even happen? She barely touched me, and it wasn't even sexually. Because she's Kendall, and this is what she always does to me without even trying. I want her. I open my mouth to yell but stop myself again when I hear Mia's voice.

"Daddy, Daddy." She rushes through the doorway, and I throw the blanket back over my lower half as quick as I can. "Mommy want know when you come for breakfast." She laced her fingers together behind her back and rocked back and forth on her feet while standing in the middle of the floor.

"Umm, I'm going to get washed up a bit then I'll be down."

"Okay." She smiled then came over to the bed and climbed over my legs. She went to the corner and lifted the pillow to reveal the stuffed dog that I remember winning at the fair on the boardwalk for Kendall almost four years ago. She grabbed it and then clambered off the bed and went downstairs again. I sighed. She still has that thing?

I got out of bed and into the bathroom. The sink water turned warm in a few seconds, and I washed my face and rinsed through my hair and dried it with a towel and fixed it better. I looked down at my lower region, but I was still hard. I bowed my head. Fuck. I looked at the door then back down at myself. I took a deep breath. Nothing's going to be the same. Kendall isn't just mine anymore. Mia is always going to be there and she's always going to need Kendall. She can't just leave her downstairs to come up here so I can fuck her. What's done is done, and I can't go back in time to remind myself to wear a condom. This is the part that will always suck. It's not that I regret and wish Mia was ever conceived. I just wasn't ready to share my Kendall yet. I have no choice now, so I have to suck it up. I love my Mia. I'll never wish that I didn't have her or have done anything different, minus the imprisonment.

I have to take my mind off Kendall right now if I ever want to go downstairs. It had eased up on me a bit, but I still felt that desire, keeping me hard. Dammit. I opened the bathroom door and went down the steps and into the living room. Mia was sitting on the floor with her toys spread around her. She has a lot of toys. I mean it seems like hundreds and it's probably true. I have to think, though, that half are actually Kendall's that she kept. I sat down on the couch, figuring Kendall will come in to get her soon.

She didn't seem to mind me being there while she talked to her toys and made them talk back in sweet voices. I smiled as she continued their dialogue about going to the park all together. She put her toys down after telling them that they were getting a new pet today and started running behind the couch. Not a few seconds later, there was a thud. I don't think I ever leaped up faster from sitting to rush over to her. "Daddy." She pouted loudly when I picked her up, laying her head on my shoulder. She kept pouting, getting louder and louder until she was about screaming.

"Mia, you're okay, you're okay. What hurts?" She didn't answer, only kept crying, her tears seeping through my thin T-shirt and soaking it.

"Mommy!" she yelled, and I turned from facing the wall with Mia in my arms, wrapped around her securely.

"Oh my god," Kendall sounded terrified. She hurried over. "My baby." She put her hands around both of Mia's sides to grab her from me. I shot her a confused look but decided that Mia would probably calm down better in her mother's arms and better words.

"I was just trying to help," I spoke quietly. Her eyes shot up to meet mine, and they looked different, holding some sort of emotion. What though? I can't tell, and I'm not sure I want to the more I think about it. She finally sighed and started rubbing her hand up and down her daughter's small back, swaying her body with her eyes closed, head resting against Mia's.

"Mommy," Mia still cried, lower now.

"I know, princess, calm down. What happened?" Kendall opened her eyes to look up at me.

"She tripped," I answered.

A thorough inspection was done on her, not a single scratch on her smooth, soft skin, her cheeks now puffy while she nibbled her breakfast.

Watching how Kendall handles Mia, I know she's the perfect mother. There was no doubt in my mind before that she wasn't, but just seeing it now, it really means something. At least I was able to give her something that she loves and for her to cherish her entire life. I can't think of any other life that I want than one with my girls. I want to wake up every morning and have their faces not far away. I need my girls. I did ask her to marry me. I don't think then that she took it serious because of that whore Miranda trying to sleep with me in the middle of the gym.

Would she ever consider marrying me? I don't know anymore. There was a very short time before I was locked away in those stone walls when I thought she would be thinking about it once or twice. Look at all of the shit I've put her through though. Will she want anything else to do with me? She's here. She's here with me now. That's what matters. I don't want the now-to-ever end though. I'm too selfish to give her up and have another man father my child, my angel, everything. I want them. I want them both in every way humanly possible. I want to hold them and never let go. My love will always stand tall and strong for these two beautiful girls that have somehow found their way into my screwed-up life. Even Kendall's mother has become a woman in my life that I've come to love, and I know how great of a mom and grandmother she is. She raised the perfect daughter that no matter how many times she pisses me off and takes me over the edge to make me madder than hell, I'll always love and cherish her more than anything.

Mia calmed down, and Kendall seemed to visibly relax with her daughter's sudden change in mood. "She's okay," she spoke softly, calmly now as she sat beside me on the couch, and Mia finished her breakfast and sat now on the floor with a few toys in hand. I could stare at her all day.

Kendall leaned her head on my shoulder as I took a deep breath. "I love you," I whispered setting my hand on her knee and rubbing my thumb over it soothingly.

"How long do I have to worry about you being on parole?"

I sighed. Her and her constant questions. "Just don't think about it. It's my problem."

"Well, you don't seem to be too concerned about it." She sounded annoyed now. Great.

"Kendall, I don't want to talk about my problems right now. It's not like I'm gonna go back to jail. I'll try to follow the rules well enough."

She gave a weak ha-ha back at me. "You better," she demanded.

"After it's over and you've accepted my proposal, we'll move to a nice home and settle there, and I'll still work, and you can have my dinner ready every day for me."

She lifted her head from my shoulder suddenly. "What proposal?" I didn't look at her.

"I think I was yelling loud enough that day for you to hear me, Ken."

"I-I-I didn't . . . I didn't know you meant it . . ." When I looked over, her eyes were wide and held something in them. What? Fear? Love? Confusion?

"Of course I meant it."

"Micah—"

I leaned my forehead against her. "Nothing would make my life better than to be spending the remainder of it with Mia and you." I looked up at her.

Her eyes were brimming with tears. "I never thought you would ask of marriage in my mother's living room." She barely spoke, a tear sliding down her cheek. Now she's crying.

"Maybe you could make me dinner sometime."

"Maybe. Is that a yes?"

She smiled.

Epilogue

"What all are we getting, Daddy?"

"Well, it's Mom's birthday tomorrow so . . . I don't know." I sighed.

"Why not cake?"

"You want to make her a cake?" She nodded quickly. "Okie dokie." I turned the shopping cart around and went down the baking isle.

"Chocolate!" Mia shouted.

"Okay, okay, calm down." I lifted her from the buggy and sat her on her feet. She rushed to the shelves. I rubbed my temples as she grabbed different tubes of sprinkles and colors of icing. "Hey," I walked over to her. "Do you need so many colors?" I leaned down to her. She ignored me and tossed them into the cart that was already packed with junk food that she insisted she needs. "Mia," I said sternly.

I sighed. "Mommy likes colors." She smiled, three of her top teeth missing.

"Everybody likes colors." I finally just snapped. She avoided eye contact with me and bowed her head sadly. "Okay, fine. We'll get every color. You need the mix now." I grabbed the chocolate and held it in front of her. "This one?" I asked. She looked up and wiped her eyes. "Hey, no more crying. Today's Mommy's birthday. No crying, baby." I put my hands under her arms and lifted her, throwing the mix into the buggy with the other healthy foods. Kendall's gonna kill us. No, she's gonna kill me. I held Mia against my chest as she wrapped her arms around her neck. "Do you need anything else?" She nodded against my neck as she nuzzled me and sniffled her nose.

I sighed. "Like what?" I had to laugh now.

"Ice cream," she barely spoke.

I pushed the cart and carried Mia all the way to the other side of the fucking store to the freezer section and opened the door to grab the container. "Chocolate?" Mia nodded. "Okay." I adjusted her in my arm. "Okay, we're done now." I told her as she tightened her grip around me, and I waited in the damn long ass line to pay. I sighed and rolled my eyes, as only three registers were opened and there was a ton of people all paying at once. If I didn't have Mia with me, I would just leave and order a cake at the bakery down the street. I know she would blow up pouting, though, because she needs everything in the cart and wants to make her mother a cake by herself, she insisted.

When our turn finally came, I sat Mia down and told her to just stay right there, and she grabbed on to my pant leg with her small hands and waited. After swiping my card and receiving my $250.30 receipt, Mia stared tugging on my leg quickly, almost pulling down my jeans the last time. "What is it?" I tucked my wallet back into my back pocket.

"I have ta bathroom," she whined.

"Okay, just wait a minute." I loaded the bags into the buggy. "You have to go really bad?" She nodded, bending her knees and making a face like she was in pain, biting her lip. I hurried up and ran to the restroom. One thing I hate more than anything is when Mia has to pee, and we're in public, and Kendall isn't here. I parked the cart by the restroom and lifted Mia, carrying her inside. Two guys stood at the urinals as I held Mia's head down against my shoulder as I passed them quickly and went into one of the stalls. I covered the toilet seat with paper like Kendall taught me when I take Mia out and then helped her up and held on to her so she wouldn't fall. "Okay, Mia."

She still held it in. "Don't listen," she whined.

"I'm not listening." I looked away.

She finally started and then finished. I had to help her clean up and held her up to the sinks to wash her small hands. I'll never get over looking at how tiny her hands and feet are. I've already saved a pair of her socks in a small box that holds a lot of her things that I stole or that she gave to me from her that she hasn't noticed so we can look back at them in the years to come hopefully.

Once the car was loaded and Mia was strapped into her car seat, I buckled myself in and drove back home. Once in the garage, I took Mia inside and turned on the TV for her and went back out to get the ton of grocery bags. I set them on the counter and then had Mia wash her hands again, which she whined about. I poured all the ingredients into the bowl and handed Mia the whisk to mix it all up. She sat up on the counter and pounded the whisk into the bowl loudly. I went back over to her and showed her how to do it, and she complied.

"When's Mommy get home, Dad?" she asked after I took the cake out of the oven, well what was left after Mia ate, like, ten spoonful of the chocolaty mix when I went into the restroom for a few minutes. I got it out of the pan successfully and laid it out for Mia to decorate.

"In like ten minutes." I looked at the microwave.

"I'm finished," she announced with pride, eight minutes later.

I took Mia into the bathroom quickly and washed her up, getting all of the icing and cake mix off her skin, and then changed her clothes and brushed her hair. A minute after I finished and kept her away from the cake, the front door was opened, and Kendall walked in. Mia went running to her mother, hugging her legs tightly while smiling and laughing.

"Hi, darling." Kendall lifted her, planting a kiss on her cheek. I walked over and wrapped one arm around her and kissed her cheek. "Hi," she greeted me. I grinned.

"How was school?"

She shrugged. "School. I have so much to get done tonight. Are we still going to dinner tomorrow right?" She looked up after taking off her shoes and walking into the kitchen.

"Yeah, of course."

"Okay, I was just wondering. What all did you get for dinner tonight?"

"Cake!" Mia shouted.

"Cake?" She looked to me.

"We-well, Mia made you a birthday cake." By now, Mia was bouncing up and down and dragging Kendall over to the counter to her masterpiece.

"Looks delicious." Kendall smiled and laughed and glanced over at me.

"We got Chinese take-out for dinner too." I smiled.

"How romantic."

I shrugged and kissed her cheek again then she grabbed my face between her hands and planted a quick, feverish, wet kiss upon my lips and raised a brow at me then got back to Mia who started singing Happy Birthday, and I joined in.

***

Kendall lied underneath me while she continued to kiss at my neck and right shoulder. I moved my hips again, slowly causing her to bite down on my skin, and I squeezed my eyes shut. I moaned as I retracted my hips and rolled back down. She gasped and tugged at my hair again. "Micah," she moaned quietly.

"Shhh . . ." I kissed her neck.

"It's been too long," she complained.

"Ye-ah," I gasped.

I started moving quicker, and she tugged my hair again, harder this time. I love it when she does that. It had been a whole week since I've felt her around me. I see her naked almost every day, but there's never enough time for anything especially with her in college. "I've missed you so much." I breathed and hit into her harder a few more times until I felt her legs stiffen up and clench tighter around my waist, the heals of her feet started to dig into my lower back at just above my waist. "Let go . . ." I breathed, my voice deep and strained.

"Ahhh . . ." She groaned as she came around me heavily.

I clenched my jaw and cursed while I held her even closer to me as I felt my own release. I stayed on top of her, riding it out in heavy breaths. I found myself at ease and satisfied after a long week. I kissed her neck and continued to trail my lips up to her mouth and kissed the corner.

"What time is it?" she whispered, her eyes closed. She sounds exhausted.

I glanced to the digital clock beside the bed. "One thirty already." I paused and kissed her nose for the third time. "You're not going tomorrow, are you?"

She combed her fingers through my hair, her nails scratching the roots. Mmmmm. "No, I'll stay home for my birthday. I take it you're not going to work either?"

I shook my head. "I'd rather be home actually." I sat up, smiling down at her.

"Aren't you sweet?"

"You're sweeter, babe." She turned her head, her cheeks inflaming a deep shade of embarrassment.

"I don't think I'll even warm up to you talking like that." She giggled.

"Baby, you're always warm." She laughed again.

"You're a pervert." She smiled, still laughing.

"Don't insult me." I smiled bigger while forcing my hips down so I went deeper inside her. Her eyes squeezed closed, and her laughter stopped. She took in her lower lip and tilted her chin toward the ceiling.

"Ahhh . . . oh my." She strained each breath. Her face twisted in a weird way, and I had no idea how to tell what she was feeling. I gave her a few more seconds to get accustomed to whatever she was now feeling.

"What happened?" I breathed. She shook her head, her eyes still barely shut now. If she doesn't tell me now, I'm gonna go insane trying to figure her out. "Kendall."

"Nothing . . . it just fel——it felt deeper is all." I smiled.

"Stop smiling at me like that, Micah. It's late. We need to go to bed and be rested if we're to put up with Mia tomorrow."

I laughed lightly and kissed her nose, her cheek, the other cheek, the tip of her nose again, the corner of her mouth, and her lips. The second time, I pressed my lips to hers, which she slowly kissed back. "Don't tell me you're falling asleep on my baby?" I grinned.

"I'm exhausted, and honestly, I don't mind at all going to sleep like this. It's bliss, Micah."

I sighed and pressed my forehead against hers, and we both closed our eyes. I can't stay inside her like this all night, though, no matter how happy it makes her feel. It's my bliss to be this connected to my love. I finally lifted myself with my arms on either side of her head and retracted myself from her confines. She sucked in a sharp breath when I was finally all the way out of her. I let out a deep breath while I tossed myself on to the other side of the bed and took a few seconds of silence before sitting up on the edge to put my feet on the floor.

"You okay?" Kendall's sweet, small voice spoke.

I nodded, even though her eyes probably aren't even open anymore again. "I'm really good." I stood from the bed. "You want a drink or something?" I asked, pulling on my plaid pants. I looked back at her to see her watching my every move. "Enjoying the view?" I smirked.

"I'll never get tired of watching you, Micah." I grinned lazily. "Did Mia really make me that cake or just decorate it? Or the other way around?" She leaned on her elbow while it rested on my pillow.

I shrugged. "She wouldn't let me help. I just did the oven thing. What, you don't think I can decorate a cake?"

"I just think she inherited your decorating abilities, and now I'll never know the truth." She smirked back at me.

I looked down and then back up at her. "You don't want anything?"

"Some water would be nice." She stared at me as I stared at her.

I came back a few minutes later after devouring a slice of cake. It's not bad actually. The icing is really sweet and makes you cringe at first. I walked back into the bedroom and peered into Mia's bedroom to see her still passed out and oblivious to what her mom and I were doing it appears. Good. I left her door cracked while I opened our bedroom one open and laid back down. Kendall had stayed awake. "Took you long enough."

"I was hungry."

"Of course you were. What'd you do, eat the whole cake, ya pig."

"No, not the whole thing, a large slice, yes. Why?"

"Well, because you have a glob of icing on your face, and it looks delicious right now." She set her empty glass on the nightstand on her side.

"Does it?" I leaned closer to her. "What are we going to do about it?"

"We? You're not going to do anything, big guy." She crawled over to me and wiggled herself onto my chest, her legs between mine. "It's a dirty job, but I think I can manage," she whispered in my ear and then grazed her teeth along my jaw and then started kissing up the icing from the side of my mouth. "I think you're good." I smiled again at her words.

"You're still sweeter, baby." I squeezed her hips and slid my hand over her backside.

"It's bedtime." She slid off my chest. "Should I get dressed, you think?"

"I'll get up with her in the morning. You can sleep in naked, baby." She swatted my arm.

"I don't want to be lazy, Micah. I'm still trying to shed all that baby weight."

"Honey, you're not that fat." Her mouth hung open, and she slapped my arm hard this time. "I'm sorry, princess. You're not even close to having a centimeter of fat on your gloriously perfect body. I can feel your ribs when we hug and see them we you stretch in the morning. Don't worry at all about your figure. What you do need to be doing is gaining weight. We're losing my fun bags, sugar."

She giggled. "I love you." She kissed my cheek. "You really think I don't have any breasts though?"

I looked over at her chest as she lay exposed to me completely. "I think they're still intact pretty well." She giggled again.

"So umm . . . I wanted to ask you something."

"Hit me."

"I already have a few times." She paused. "On our honeymoon, when we finally do get married . . . are we taking Mia along with us wherever it is we're going? I don't want to leave her, and she thinks she's not—"

"Kendall, don't stress over it. We don't have to get hitched right away. It's already been a year, and it can be another. Just as long as I can call you mine, I don't care how long we wait. Do you want to take her?" She shrugged. "I think it will be good for us to spend some time alone and relax in a paradise for a few weeks, right? I want to have you every night and . . . we won't be able to. I hate saying that about my daughter, but it's true. I know it's disgusting to think that way." I lowered my voice.

"We'll figure it out." Kendall snuggled against me, her hand resting on my hip, head on my arm as she held me to her comfortably.

"Yeah, we always will."

***

I sat in the kitchen, waiting on Kendall to finish getting Mia ready to go bowling with us for a small birthday party of just the three of us. I leaned against the countertop in the kitchen while Dora still played on the TV. Why do I always catch myself still watching this when she isn't even in the room with me? Better yet, where is the remote? Before I could even begin to look for it, the bedroom door opened, and Mia came out in Kendall's arms, both their hair curled with Mia in a black sparkly tee and shorts and Kendall in ripped-up skinnies.

Once Mia had stopped fussing and let me get her strapped into her car seat, which Kendall found amusing while looking back at us in the front seat, I buckled myself in because I have to set an example for her. Like Kendall says as well as her mother who is constantly telling us things we should and shouldn't do. Once we arrive at the bowling alley on the boardwalk, Kendall said she'd get Mia out since she preferred her mother to do it anyway, and I refuse to let her know how I feel about that because it's what she wants, and I'm trying not to be as selfish and try to pull her away from her mother. After I had found out that my mom was not only speaking but fucking my father again, I quit speaking to her for a few months, but Candice would always stop by and one time brought mom, and we talked. I had nightmares every night of things I didn't even remember happening until they reminded me. I guess I had blocked them out, but they wouldn't stay hidden forever. Mia would get scared in the middle of the night when I would wake up screaming and crying, covered in my own pathetic sweat. Kendall would explain that I was having nightmares, and they both would hold me, even though I wouldn't go back to sleep. Instead, I just watch them and wrap my arms around them, wondering how I got so lucky with my beautiful girls.

Once we were in the bowling alley, the music was loud, I recognize the song playing as one of the singer Lucas Fischer. I had to shout to the woman behind the counter, wearing no makeup, the shoe and ball sizes three times. Kendall handed Mia over to me as she changed her shoes, and I did Mia's for her while she examined her surroundings. I held her hand as we walked over to the open alley and got the sides pulled up so it couldn't go into the gutters. We both showed Mia how to do it, but in the end, she ended up just barely rolling it down, and it took two minutes to hit into the pins, knocking down five total, and then two the second time. The excitement and smile she displayed was enough to get us all into the game. Kendall and I took pictures of her and got one of ourselves, and I took one of just them two when they didn't realize and kept it as my background. "Daddy, help." Mia caught my attention as she tried to reach her ball while Kendall went to get us water.

I got up, but right when I got to her, a young woman was already handing the pink ball down to her. "There you go, sweetheart." She smiled as Mia thanked the stranger. When she looked up at me, she grinned. "Your daughter?" She smirked. Oh god . . .

"Uhhh . . . yeah," I spoke awkwardly.

"Your wife is a lucky woman."

"I'm not married." Why'd I say that? I don't need to be answering her in any way.

"Well then, we could have a little fun later." She arched her thin dark brow not even acknowledging Mia.

"No." I shook my head seriously. "I'm engaged." I walked with Mia over to her lane and bent down behind her and showed her how to put her fingers in again and toss it down the middle, which she took very seriously, and got a spare, which had her smiling even brighter. When Kendall got back, she was grinning at us both as Mia chugged down her refreshment. I glanced over for some reason and made eye contact with the overfriendly stranger who helped Mia. And she was staring already. "I love you." I kissed Kendall lightly, and she smiled while blushing.

"I love you, Micah." She put her arm around my waist and kissed me again.

I beat them both at bowling three times, where they both countered I was cheating, which was amusing to both Kendall and I. Mia was asleep in my arms as I carried her back inside and into her bedroom and kissed her tucked her in goodnight. After which, I met up with Kendall back in our bedroom.

Paradise in Silence

Twenty-four months later, it happened, the greatest and most relief flushing moment in my life. She's mine, completely and utterly mine in every way possible. She's there and is always going to be there. From the moment she walked down the aisle and she and my beautiful daughter were at my side, I knew I was happy with how my life turned out. Don't ask how it turned out this way because I have no clue. I don't even want to ask myself that right now. I'm enjoying myself in this sun too much.

Kendall's hand reached over onto my chest, sand rolling down my side. "As long as you stay in shape, I'll be a happy wife."

"As long as you have my dinner ready every day, I'll be a happy husband."

"Whoever is home to make dinner has to keep that one up."

"Deal."

"It's settled then."

I opened an eye as I kept her hand caressed on my chest. "I don't want to go back."

"We live at the beach already, you moron."

"This is different."

"My mother is even here. How's it different?"

I shook my head. "It's a beginning."

"It's always been a beginning with you."

I grinned. "Thanks."

"So you do have manors?"

"I can take it back and carry you back up those three steps."

"There's more than three steps, Micah."

"Not when I'm in a hurry."

"Are you threatening me?"

"Am I, Mrs. Harlan?"

Her hand squeezed mine. "I don't mind what you do to me. I'll always love you."

"I love you." I rolled to my side for a quick second to plant a kiss on her warm cheek, and she grinned from ear to ear.

We had waited for Kendall to finish her last two years at college to get married. Mia choked me practically while we boarded the plane to New Zealand. I had let Kendall choose wherever she wanted to go while I saved up sixty grand. I took her to the Southern Cook Islands, and it's still worth every penny. We brought Kendall's mom along to babysit with Mia. Almost every night, we all go out to dinner somewhere together, sometimes just Kendall and me, but we'd rather take Mia and her mom with us so we can get more photos like Kendall says.

"I'm exhausted." Kendall sighed as she flipped on to her stomach.

"Mmmmm."

I watched her as she opened her eyes to me. "We only have two days left."

"Yeah."

"You're not very talkative today, are you?"

"Nope."

"Mommy!" We both turned our heads to see Mia in her one piece, running over to us with small sand toys in hand, a pale, and a red shovel. She sat down right between us, and I groaned, making Kendall laugh.

"What, princess?" Mia dumped a pale, and shells clattered everywhere. "Oh wow," Kendall gasped. "You grabbed a lot."

"Aren't they pretty?" Mia spoke, picking one up and setting it on my back.

"What're you doing?" Kendall asked Mia as she continued to put shells all over my back.

"Making Daddy pretty."

"What's that supposed to mean?" I looked up at Mia as she giggled.

"You need makeover."

"Yeah, Micah." I glared humorously at Kendall as she tried to keep a straight face.

Mia ruffled her hands through my hair, swaying it to the side in front after parting it. "Now you're pretty, Daddy. Like a mermaid."

"I'll show ya a mermaid." I wrapped my arms over her body and lifted her from the sand and running down to the clear blue water. I ran through it as Mia screamed and hollered with a smile on her face.

I glanced back to faintly see Kendall snapping a few pictures and then hurrying down to us and splashing me. Salt water clouded my eyes, but nothing was clearer than my future. No matter how many bumps are making their way in front of us, I know we'll fight and argue and blame the other, but she's mine, and I won't let her go. The voices in my head are quieter. They were since the moment I saw her walk down to me and vow her everlasting love to me and mine to her, Mia hugging my leg in the process.

Mia squealed again in my arms as Kendall fell down into the water, soaking her hair completely. I leaned down to grab her hand as Mia wiggled down to play in the water more. "You okay?" I laughed at her. Before I could brace myself, she leaped into my arms and took me underwater. I surfaced in time to see her smug smile, and Mia swam onto my stomach, trying to push me back under. "Hey." I stopped her.

"Ahhh!" Kendall shouted as she collapsed beside me. I looked over at her face as she wiped her eyes. "Mia!" she shouted again as she attacked her mother by hugging her.

Later that day, when we were back from dinner and Mia was in the next building over with her grandmother, probably sleeping by now, I sat on the bed while Kendall went into the bathroom getting ready for bed. When the door opened, I was too occupied with my thoughts, even when her hands gripped my shoulders, as I faced the window. Her lips met just below my ear. "Something bothering you?" she whispered in my ear, kissing my neck. I turned my head and placed one hand over hers. I shook my head. "This is my last outfit."

I looked down at her lacy lingerie that barely covered her body. "It's not much of an outfit." I pulled at the fabric. She grabbed my hand as I turned my body completely and shielded her beneath me. "You're so beautiful." I kissed her cheek as she blushed and laced our fingers together on one side of her head and looked over at them. I looked back down at her eyes as they stared up into mine.

"You're only saying that because I'm naked under you."

I tilted my head to the side, causing her to erupt in a fit of giggles. "That may be part of it." I grinned proudly.

"Shut up." She batted at my chest with her free hand.

"Excuse me, Mrs. Harlan?" I smirked while leaning down so we were nose to nose and her legs wrapped around my waist, her feet nudging my shorts down my legs so only my black briefs were hugging my hips.

"I said shut up and help me make more memories in New Zealand." She put on a terrible fake accent.

"That's insulting." I laughed.

She opened her mouth offended. "It's not that bad," she complained.

"No? Maybe we should teach them ours then?" I pressed my hips down against hers. She gasped with the sudden growing friction between our clammy bodies. I started to slide my hand down her side as she shivered under my touch. Finally, my palm rested on her hip, and I slapped the skin suddenly as she sucked in a deep breath and released it moments later. I grinned up at her. I shimmied down her body and lifted the see-through tank-top-like part of her lingerie and bunched it up at her breasts. I kissed above her belly button as he fingers tugged at the crème-colored sheets, her breathing heavy and uneven and panting like. I moved my lips down to her belly button and kissed it multiple times, my hands resting on her hip bones to hold her to me. I tugged her body so her legs hung off the bed and dangled while I sat on my knees in front of her.

My hands slid down to her knees as I pulled her down on to the floor to sit in my lap. "Micah." She kissed me. The kiss meant everything to us, how much we've been through. All the love and passion pushed out into that kiss, her hands cupping my face.

"Say it," I panted.

"I love you. I'm all yours, Micah. I love you so much."

I dipped my head and tipped her forward so her back was now against the white rug. The kiss continued once she was laid down beneath me, and all of our emotions poured into it, her arms wrapped around my back to pull me closer to her body. Then when I pulled back to gaze down at her and rip that damn fabric from her body, her hands slowly made their way down my chest and stomach to my scar. Her fingers traced the permanent mark where the bullet went in. "When I think about that day, I cry," she spoke softly like she was going to cry, and the movement of her fingers ceased. She looked up at me. "I want to spend eternity with you. I can never be without you."

"Same," I barely spoke as I stared at her lips and placed a single peck on them. I slid my hand to her chest and cupped her left breast.

"Micah, I've never asked you . . ." She gasped as I slid the fabric from covering her breast from me and my mouth was now on her soft skin, her back arching up to push forward into my mouth further. "What did you do when I told you I-I was pregnant?"

"What did I do?" I glanced up at her. She nodded. I shrugged. "I was freaked out?" I shrugged. "I don't know. I felt stupid that I wasn't able to puzzle everything together, the signs."

"I was scared you didn't want a baby then excited when you came home that day." She smiled at the memory she dug up. "Little Mia." She looked up at me. "She looks so much like you." I shook my head and looked back down at her naked chest as her tits moved up and down with each breath she took.

"She's beautiful. I don't feel like talking right now though." The pain was starting to really irritate me now so I pressed my erection against her harder to try and ease it. She giggled. "We'll talk later." I kissed her again.

This is paradise. Right now, it is quiet, but nothing will stay perfect; there will always be noise. Right now, though, it is silent. When we all get back and into our actual reality, new problems will occur and surface; the volume will rise. Getting through them is the only problem, not the problem itself, but Kendall is mine, and I'm not letting her go no matter how loud times get.

***

Being back to our small home feels good. It feels fresh, and I can tell this is where we are supposed to be, here in this moment, with my wife still upstairs and our daughter on my shoulders, messing with my hair as I finish up the pan of scrambled eggs. Kendall will yell at me for the mess on the counter from when Mia was insisting that she knew what she was doing in cracking eggs. Then she'll say how she got that from me because it is true actually.

This Johnny Cash song about stripes is stuck in my head, and I can't stop singing and humming it softly as I stand here and hear Kendall walking and pulling the chair out from the table and sitting down. I can feel her eyes on my back, so I switch which leg I put more of my weight onto. I turn my head briefly and catch her grinning while looking over at me and smirk. Mia lays her head on to my head as if it were a pillow and reminds me that I need a haircut. I hear Kendall giggle softly, which makes Mia's head snap up and twist and wiggle on my shoulders shouting, "Mommy!" I pick up the pan and saunter over to the small rounded table that she sits at.

I set both the pan of scrambled eggs and Mia on to the table, trying not to laugh, and Kendall scolds me while putting Mia into a chair of her own. I go back to grab plates for each of us, and Kendall makes Mia's plate once I hand it over to her. Meanwhile, I fill three glasses with orange juice.

I'm three years sober now, I don't even have glasses of wine anymore. It only turns up the volume. This isn't silence, though, and it never will be. The volume is simply turned down right now in this moment. I will always wonder what she is thinking about, what she is thinking about me, and what she is thinking about our future. When Mia is older, I guarantee the volume will rise every now and then, and I will only have to find the remote.

That volume is turned all the way down right now, though, because now I am only thinking of kissing this beautiful woman that I have the pleasure of calling my wife. Her kiss sends chills all through me still and turns the volume down more, as well as the lights, so she is the only other person in my life as well as our Mia. Her eyes give me solace and bliss that I never knew existed. I look to her eyes like my life depends on it, because it does.